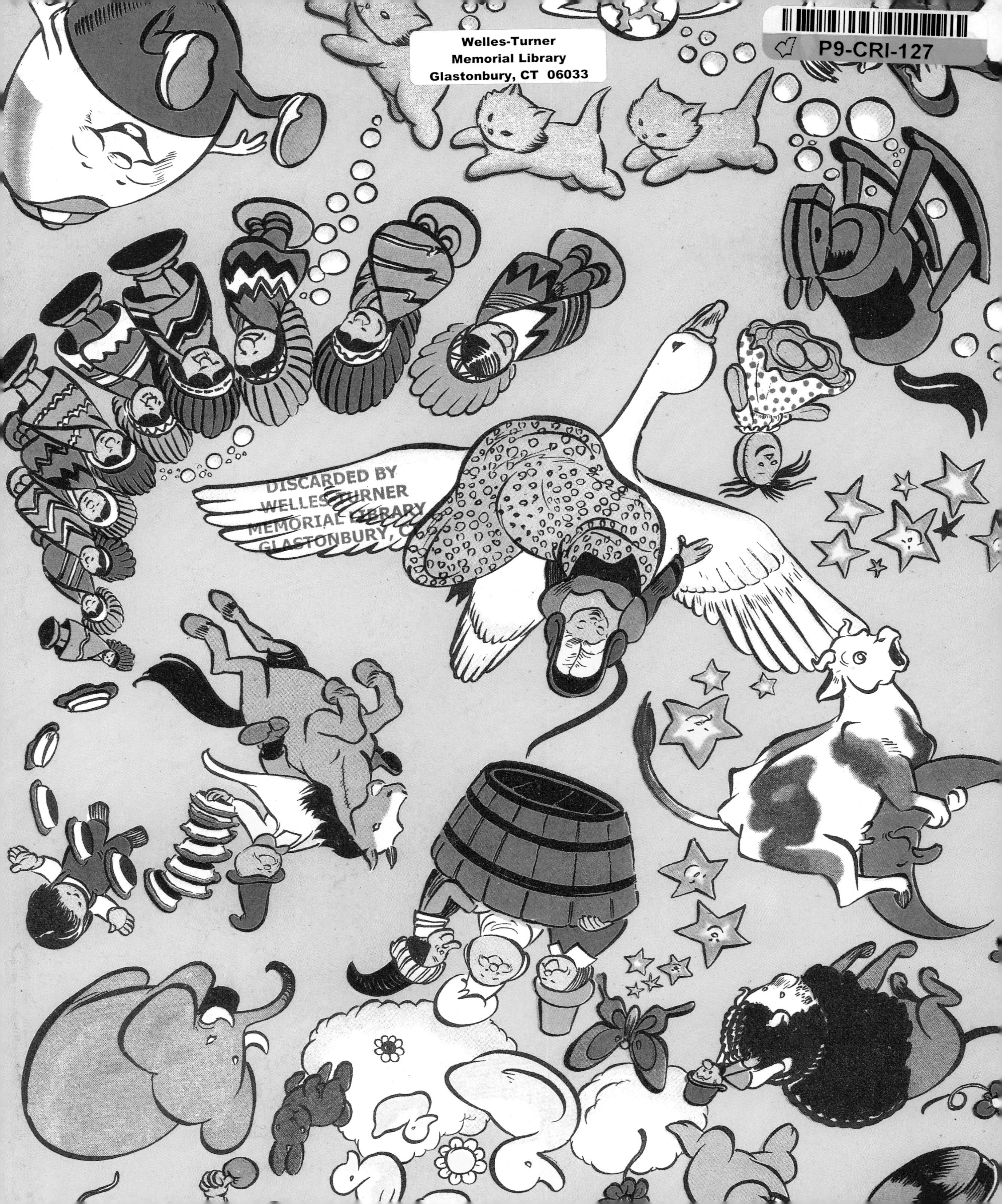

The Toon Treasury of Classic Children's Comics

A TOON BOOK

SELECTED AND EDITED BY

Art Spiegelman & Françoise Mouly

INTRODUCTION BY

JON SCIESZKA

ABRAMS COMICARTS, NEW YORK

Having already sacrificed our valuable comics collection to our kids, Nadja and Dash,
this book is for our eventual grandchildren

It took a village to raise this *Treasury* and send it off into the world; it was accomplished as a labor of love by a throng of laborers who shared our love for these comics. Although the editors accept responsibility for any errors of fact or judgment, we are especially grateful to the group of knowledgable historians, cartoonists, comics fans, and scholars who came to our aid. One of the greatest pleasures that came with this project was discussing (and sometimes debating) aesthetics and story choices with this amazing group:

THE TOON TREASURY BOARD OF ADVISORS

BILL ALGER
cartoonist

MICHAEL BARRIER
comics and animation historian
(michaelbarrier.com)

JOHN BENSON
comics historian

KIM DEITCH
cartoonist

CHRIS DUFFY
editor, *Nickelodeon* magazine

JEET HEER
journalist and comics historian

PAUL KARASIK
cartoonist

PAUL LEVITZ
president & publisher,
DC Comics

JAY LYNCH
cartoonist

SETH
cartoonist

JEFF SMITH
cartoonist

FRANK YOUNG
comics scholar and author, keeper of the John Stanley Blog (stanleystories.blogspot.com)

THE ONES WITHOUT WHOM NONE OF THIS WOULD HAVE COME TO PASS: While it was hard work for us to decide what to include and what to leave out, it easily could have remained a mere gleam in our eye had it not been for TOON Books' Julia Phillips, who found the collectors, researched the rights, and coordinated with everyone, gently coaxing but never cracking the whip; our equally cool designer, Jonathan Bennett, who managed to make this riot of old comics pages look like child's play; our editor, pal, and enabler at ABRAMS, Charlie Kochman, who patiently nursed this book into being with enthusiasm and grace.

MAJOR THANKS TO: The collectors of old paper who came to our aid, generously lending and scanning the rare comics that make up this anthology: Bill Alger, Steve Barghusen, Mike Barrier, John Benson, Glenn Bray, Chris Duffy, Harlan Ellison, Glenn Goggin, Paul Karasik, Mark Kausler, Jim Ludwig, Marc Newman at House of Comics (who was unbelievably helpful and never other than cheerful), Chuck Rozanski at Mile High Comics, Jeff Smith, Paul Tumey, Frank Young, and Vincent Zurzulo at Metropolis Comics.

All who helped us travel the winding road of rights and permissions: Charlie Kochman, Tammi Guthrie, and Tricia Kallett at ABRAMS; Victor Gorelick at Archie Comics Publications; Colin McLaughlin at Classic Media; Paul Levitz, Joel Press, and Thomas King at DC Comics; Lance Kreiter and Anita Nelson at Dark Horse; Jesse Post at Disney Publishing (to whom we owe an immense debt); Gary Groth at Fantagraphics; Steve Geppi at Gemstone; Carolyn Kelly for Kelly Studios; Dottie Roberson for the Ketcham estate; Denis Kitchen for the Kurtzman estate; Chris Duffy at Nickelodeon; Brian Palagallo at Paramount; Sherri Feldman at Random House; and Monte Wolverton for the Wolverton estate.

Our gang at ABRAMS: Eric Klopfer, Sofia Gutiérrez, Andrea Colvin, Neil Egan, and Ankur Ghosh.

And a special tip of the TOON lid to Leigh Stein, Dean Mullaney, Luca Boschi; to interns Matt Huynh, Saskia Leggett, Lauren Kaelin, Juliana Reiters, and Sarah Kim; and to those who helped us compile the further comics reading list: Janna Morishima, Katherine Dacey, Eva Volin, and Snow Wildsmith.

Editor: Charles Kochman
Editorial Assistant: Eric Klopfer
Designer: Jonathan Bennett
Production Managers: Anet Sirna-Bruder with Ankur Ghosh

Hand lettering for title page and chapter titles by Gary Hallgren

Library of Congress Cataloging-in-Publication Data

The Toon treasury of classic children's comics / edited by Art Spiegelman
and Françoise Mouly ; introduction by Jon Scieszka.
p. cm.
ISBN 978-0-8109-5730-5
1. Comic books, strips, etc. I. Spiegelman, Art. II. Mouly, Françoise.
PN6726.T66 2009
741.5'973—dc22

2009009830

Published in 2009 by Abrams ComicArts, an imprint of ABRAMS.

Printed and bound in the U.S.A.
10 9 8 7 6 5 4 3 2 1

Abrams ComicArts books are available at special discounts when purchased in quantity for premiums and promotions as well as fundraising or educational use. Special editions can also be created to specification. For details, contact specialmarkets@abramsbooks.com or the address below.

ABRAMS
THE ART OF BOOKS SINCE 1949
115 West 18th Street
New York, NY 10011
www.abramsbooks.com

Contents

Chapter 1
HEY, KIDS!

Chapter 2
FUNNY ANIMALS

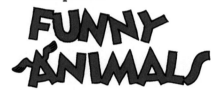

Chapter 3

Chapter 4

STORYTIME

Chapter 5
WEIRD and WACKY

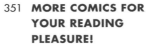

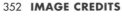

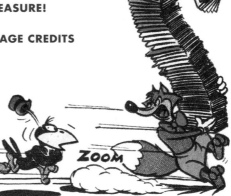

ZOOM

Introduction

Wow. "Treasury" is right. You have just entered the bank, the mint, the Ali Baba cave full of gold, silver, ruby, emerald, and diamond toons.

So now you don't have to moan about your mom throwing away your best comics anymore, because Uncle Art Spiegelman and Aunt Françoise Mouly have brought you a present. They have sifted through thousands of comic book stories and tales, and bundled together a gift of some of the best, weirdest, funniest, and most surreal.

This is not a collection of super hero comics. This is not a collection of sci-fi, western, or army comics. (Maybe later? When we're a little older? If we are good?) This is a collection of comic comics. The kind that just seemed to be around everywhere way back when. The kind you could pick up for ten cents, and get a few laughs but also stumble on some surprising tales.

I found plenty of my old, half-remembered comic pals in the *Treasury*: Little Lulu getting the last laugh as usual. Dennis the Menace from back when he really had some menace to him. Pogo. Uncle Wiggily. Fox and Crow. And Betty and Veronica in one of their earliest love/jealousy duels.

But I also found some new pals—Intellectual Amos? Nutsy Squirrel? How did I miss these guys? A squirrel who thinks he is an airplane, but is then convinced by a professor of logic that he is a motorboat? That's my kind of squirrel.

This *TOON Treasury* covers a great range of comic subjects and styles. The chapter headings explain a lot—from "Hey, Kids!" to "Funny Animals" to "Fantasyland" to "Storytime" to "Weird and Wacky."

Little babies discuss the adult world. Brave dogs save defenseless sheep. Prince Robin sets off with the magic dwarfs to fight the big-nosed Ogre. Tubby meets Death himself in the Ghost House. We shrink to the size of ants and take an action tour of the life of an anthill.

Then things get weird.

I always loved that about comics. That they could, and usually did, take a turn for the weird that wasn't anywhere to be found in school textbooks.

Why is there a guy in an old fashioned, long-legged, striped bathing suit who can take his head off of his shoulders? Why not? And why is his name Burp the Twerp? Because what else would it be?

Two talking frogs in straw boaters? Sure. Named Flip and Flop? Of course.

Frankenstein playing a tuba?

BAH! KID TALK! NO MAN IS POOR WHO CAN DO WHAT HE LIKES TO DO ONCE IN A WHILE!
AND I LIKE TO DIVE AROUND IN MY MONEY LIKE A PORPOISE!

From "Only a Poor Old Man," *Four Color Comics* no. 386, 1952

Captain Marvel enters a world where surrealism is the norm?

Heck, yeah. That's what comics can do.

My favorite stories in this *TOON Treasury* are, kind of unexpectedly, the Scrooge McDuck comics. I had almost forgotten about Scrooge, buried him under a preference for the hipper/weirder competition, wrote him off as a sappy Disney character. But the second I saw that duck with glasses and spats, shoveling his piles of money, I was eight years old again and right back in his world.

Scrooge McDuck. He's the guy who is always diving in his storehouse vault of money. He makes money. He saves money. He loves his money so much he swims around in it. He is the richest and cheapest duck in the world. What a great character. You know what his motivation is, and will always be. And you know he will always have trouble with his nephew Donald, and with Donald's nephews Huey, Dewey, and Louie.

Their adventure to the Land of Tralla La to escape the pressures of money is priceless. It's basically an illustration of the philosophy underpinning every and any monetary system.

And it's brought to you by a duck in a top hat and cane, wearing spectacles and spats, and (true to his more famous nephew Donald's style) no pants.

That is funny, with style.

This *TOON Treasury* is also history. You can see the beginnings of what is now called the Graphic Novel, the Wordless Book, Visual Narrative. You can see early illustrated meta-fiction, with characters talking about themselves, and to you, the Reader. You get Gerald McBoing Boing as a comic, and proto–Harvey Kurtzman *MAD* before there was *MAD*. A little secret extra value for you.

But the most essential gem in this *Treasury* is its great fun. Because isn't that the essence of comics? The reason we read comics?

No one I knew ever picked up *Archie* or *Lulu* or *Dennis the Menace* because it was Required Reading. We read comics because we wanted to see what was going to happen. We wanted to take that unexpected turn.

So dive in. Get reacquainted with some old comic friends. Get introduced to some new comic friends. Find your Scrooge McDuck. Swim around in this vault of toon treasures. Enjoy yourself.

And once you've had your fun, evolve. Learn to share. Pass the treasures on to the original audience these comics were made for—kids.

Thank you, Uncle Art and Aunt Françoise. You are the best. And our most favorite. Yes, we will be (mostly) good. Come back anytime. We love when you stop by with your comics.

Jon Scieszka
National Ambassador for Young People's Literature
Brooklyn, NY
March 2009

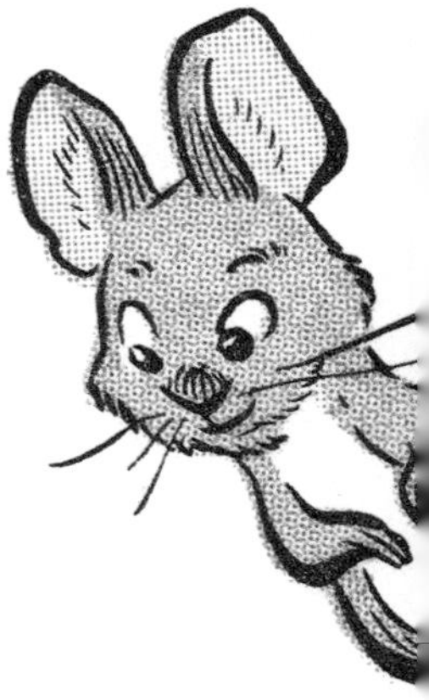

JON SCIESZKA is the author of several bestselling children's titles, including *The Stinky Cheese Man*, which won a Caldecott Honor medal, and *The True Story of the Three Little Pigs*. He is also the founder of Guys Read (guysread.com), a nonprofit literacy organization. In January 2008 Scieszka was appointed by the Librarian of Congress as the first ever National Ambassador for Young People's Literature.

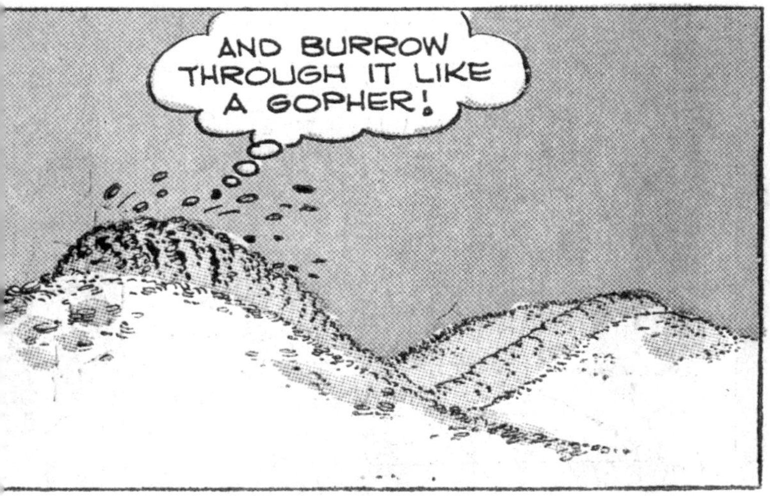
AND BURROW THROUGH IT LIKE A GOPHER!

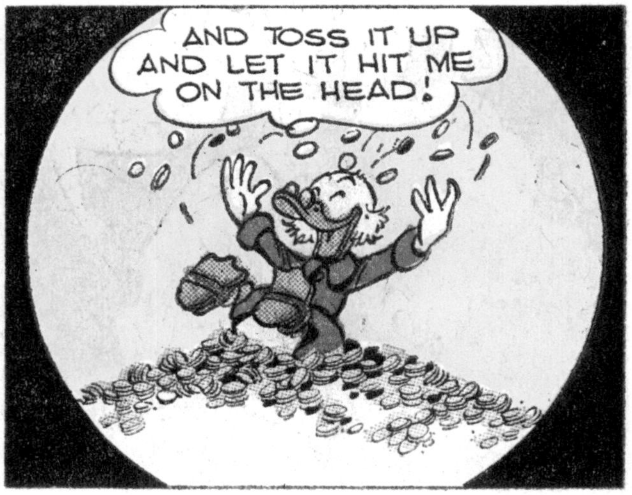
AND TOSS IT UP AND LET IT HIT ME ON THE HEAD!

Out of the Trash and into a Treasury

A WORD (AND SOME PICTURES) FOR GROWN-UPS

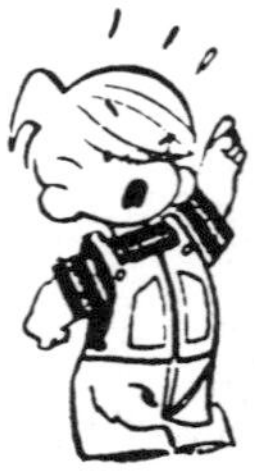

At last it's possible to test our idea that some of the best twentieth-century literature for kids appeared in lowly comic books that deserve an honored place next to the more traditional classics on every well-read child's bookshelf.

To gather the gems for this *TOON Treasury of Classic Children's Comics* we obsessively sifted through thousands of comic books published between the 1930s and the early 1960s, that golden time when comics first blossomed in the cracks of American culture and cost only ten cents. We plowed through piles of comic books the way a generation of kids once did. Like Carl Barks's Uncle Scrooge cavorting in his money bin, kids loved to dive around in them like porpoises, and burrow through them like gophers, and toss them up and let the comics hit them on the head. The adult world saw comics as junk culture—toxic, or at best, harmless. But today, in hipster clothing and Clark Kent glasses, the once disreputable comic book confidently strides into bookstores, museums, and universities cleverly disguised as the upwardly mobile "graphic novel." Librarians—no longer fearful that comics will blunt children's ability to appreciate more traditional kid books—are today among the greatest champions of the form, as they see young readers skip past the computer terminals to curl up with objects that look a lot like books.

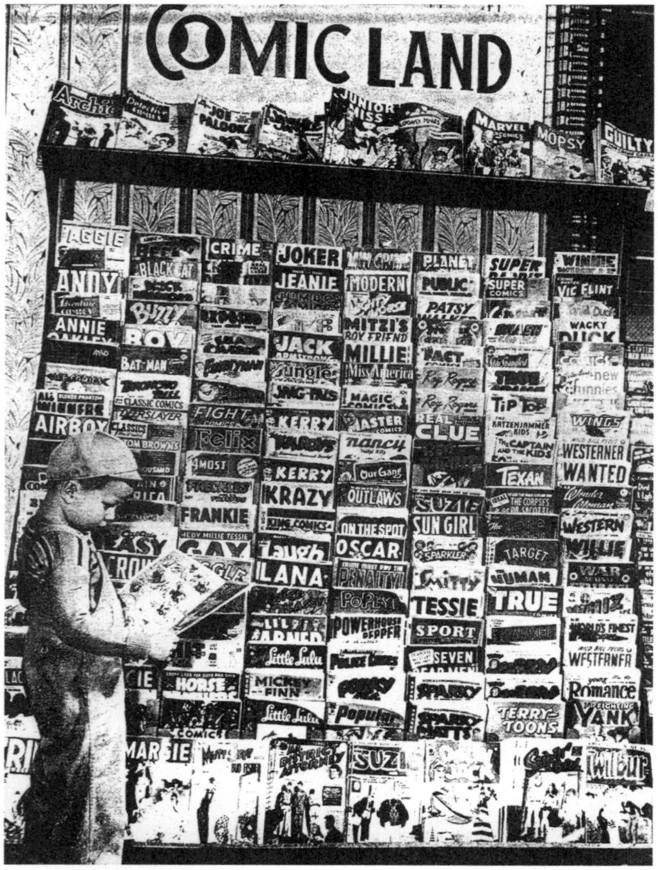
COMIC LAND
CRIME
JOKER
JEANIE
MODERN
PLANET
SUPER
ANDY
ANNIE
JACK
MILLIE
MITZI'S
KERRY
KRAZY
CLUE
TEXAN
WANTED
FRANKIE
OSCAR
SUN GIRL
LANA
TESSIE
TRUE
SPORT
WILLIE
Romance
YANK
TERRY-TOONS
SUZI
WILBUR
Newsstand, summer 1948

The first comic books were born in the mid-1930s. They gathered together popular newspaper comic strips in family-friendly collections that offered good value for a Depression-era dime. Reprint anthologies like *Famous Funnies* and *Popular Comics* achieved a fad-like appeal. Soon, having run out of existing comics to reprint at low page rates, publishers turned to pulp illustrators and writers, down-at-the-heels painters, failed comic strip artists, and even green teenagers to fill their magazines with cheap new material. Reflecting the medium's kinship to pulp fiction, genre anthologies like *Detective Comics* and *Western Picture Stories* began to sprout until, in 1938, two teenaged science-fiction fans from Cleveland who had been rejected by all the newspaper strip syndicates, found a home for their creation, Superman, in *Action Comics.* Superman introduced a new genre that came, for many, to define the whole medium. In truth, the super-hero fad crashed after World War II—comic-book-reading GIs, not caped crusaders, had won the war. Jungle, crime, romance, war, and horror genres now came to dominate the newsstands alongside the immensely popular "funny animal" comics that had started appearing in 1940 to appeal to the youngest readers and continued to flourish after the war.

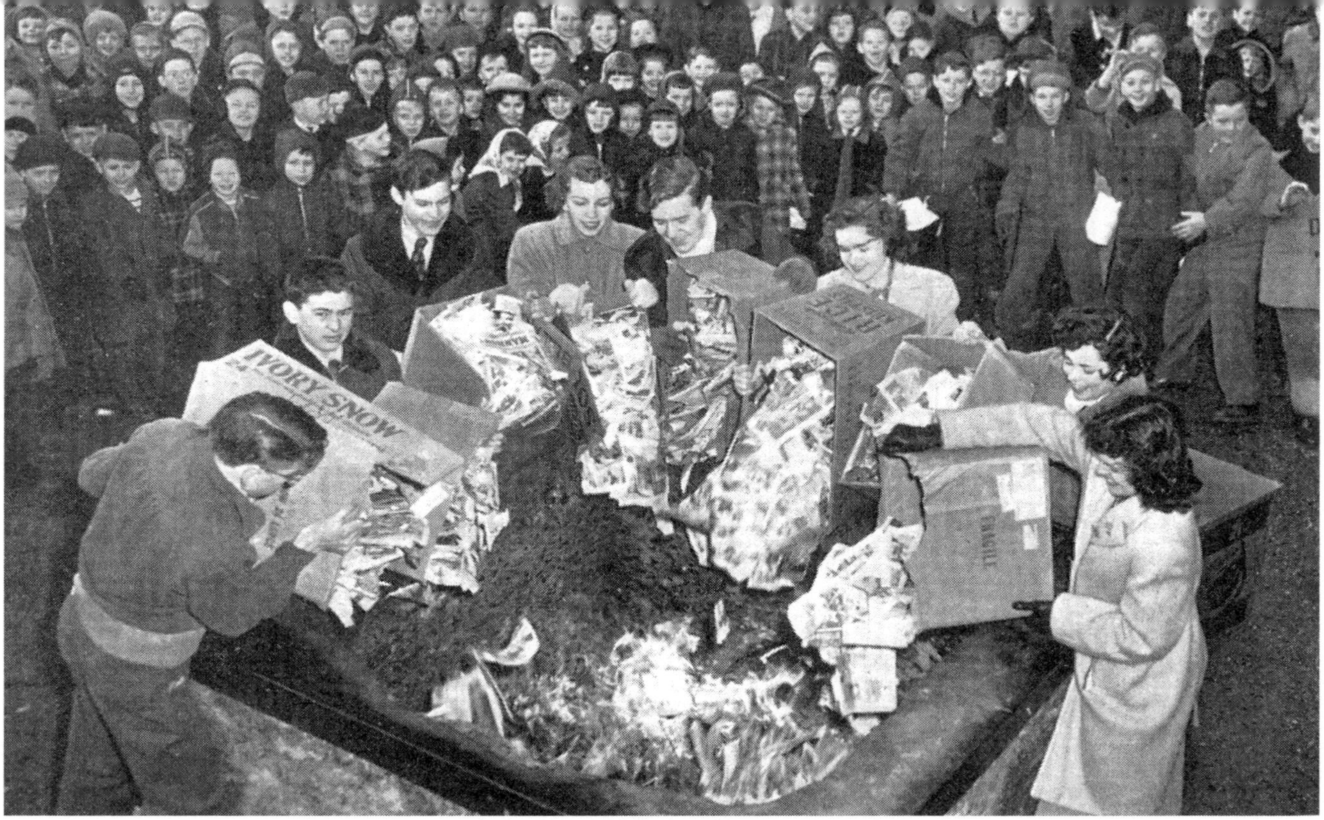
IVORY SNOW

Comic book burning, Binghamton, New York, 1949

Comic books were the first large-scale medium to appeal directly to kids as consumers a decade or more before rock and roll got grown-ups all shook up; while guardians of the culture could tolerate—if sometimes barely—the funny animal and humor titles featuring animated film stars like Donald Duck and Bugs Bunny, they became increasingly alarmed by the ever more lurid titles that competed for youngsters' dimes. Without even the fig leaf of a ratings system for guidance, comics came to be seen as the Grand Theft Auto of their day. In the years leading up to the 1954 Senate Hearings on Comic Books and Juvenile Delinquency that almost killed off the form, parents, teachers, and church groups had literally dumped comic books into giant bonfires. In 1953 there were over 650 regularly published titles with a combined monthly circulation of between 70 million and 100. By 1955 half the titles and many of the publishers had disappeared from the newsstands.

By the early 1960s comic books had become relatively marginal. Super heroes—gelded to live within the strict standards imposed by the Comics Code Authority that grew out of the Senate hearings—made a comeback, but it was the end of an era. The ten-cent price that had held for nearly three decades was raised to twelve cents. Television had come to dominate the landscape. Only anodyne adventure stories and comics for young children were left standing. Ironically, it was in the "kiddie" comics filled with talking ducks and mischievous tykes that one could still find the nuanced characters and memorable stories that helped nurture today's graphic novels.

One branch of the comic book family tree often obscures the other, and the kiddie comics are usually overlooked by comics fans in love with the darker reincarnations of the super hero that now fly into the world's multiplexes; but Carl Barks's acerbic duck adventures, John Stanley's character-driven tales of Little Lulu and Tubby, and the lyrical nonsense of Walt Kelly are at least as sophisticated as the Dark Knight and the X-Men—and a lot funnier. These comics had as direct an effect—arguably as strong as the influence of *MAD* and the horror comics—on many of the underground cartoonists of the 1960s who made comics come of age. The melancholy in many of today's more emotionally resonant graphic novels can be found right below the manic surface of John Stanley's work; Jeff Smith's Bone characters are clearly first cousin to Walt Kelly's Pogo; Uncle Scrooge's pince-nez seem to come from the same optician as Vladek Spiegelman's eyeglasses in *Maus.*

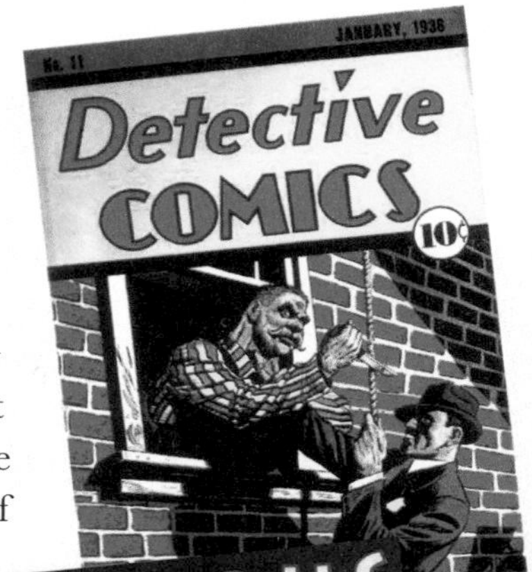
No. 11
JANUARY, 1938
Detective
COMICS
10¢

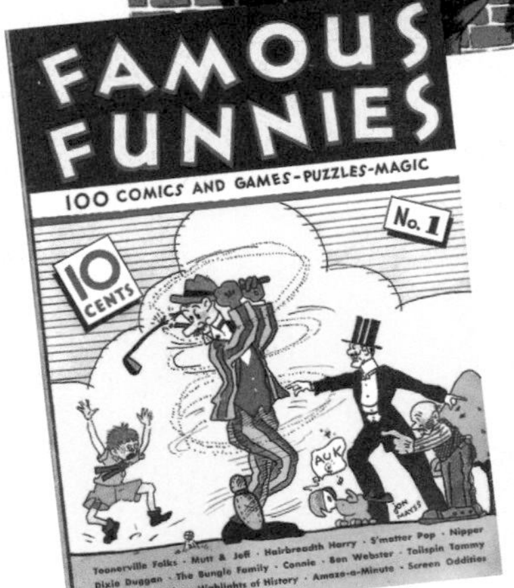
FAMOUS
FUNNIES
100 COMICS AND GAMES-PUZZLES-MAGIC
No. 1
10 CENTS

Still, we didn't put this *Treasury* together looking for works that may have influenced the course of comics history—this is hardly a book directed at historians, cartoonists, adult-comics fans, or scholars of the form, though some of the best of these were gratefully consulted every step of the way in our selection of this material. We set out to find great work that could be relished by kids of all ages.

The only trouble is there's no such thing as a "kid of all ages" . . . they're all at some *specific* stage of development while morphing quickly into another. Only grown-ups contain that "kid of all ages." As adults, you are invited to nostalgically revisit or discover all these stories with wide-eyed wonder. But we made this book for kids, selecting stories that can be read to very young children, then savored independently by kids mastering the secrets of reading—and then revisited often by them as they make the long march to adulthood when they contain their own "kid of all ages." We focused on comics for the younger set, steering clear of the highly charged sexual and horrific content that once got comics in such hot water. We avoided melodrama, concentrating instead on the funny end of the funnybook spectrum, a zone that of course includes the poignant, poetic, and revelatory as well as the silly. We rummaged through large piles of bland, condescending, and half-baked stuff—the predictable result of work made for low wages in a low-prestige field, often made anonymously and on tight deadlines—and ran into lots of work land-mined with the now painful negative ethnic, racial, and gender stereotypes that are part of our cultural heritage.

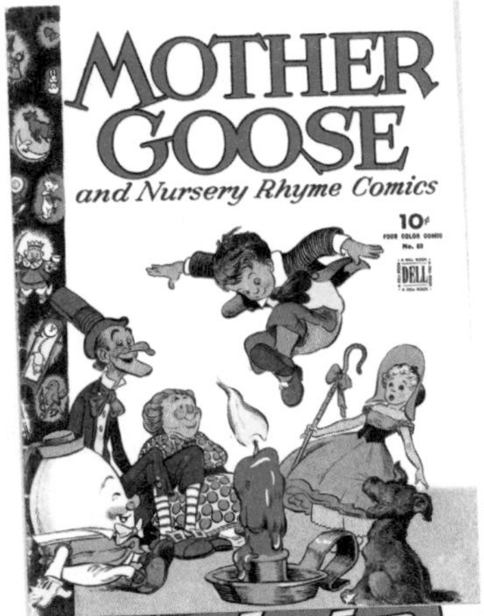
MOTHER GOOSE
and Nursery Rhyme Comics
10¢
DELL

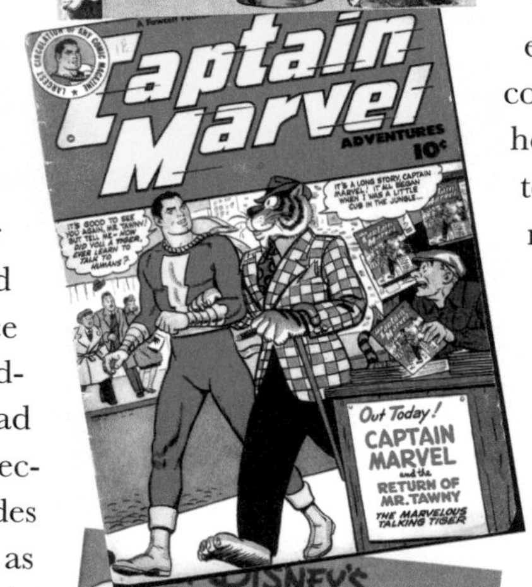
Captain Marvel
ADVENTURES
10¢
Out Today!
CAPTAIN MARVEL
and the
RETURN OF
MR. TAWNY
THE MARVELOUS TALKING TIGER

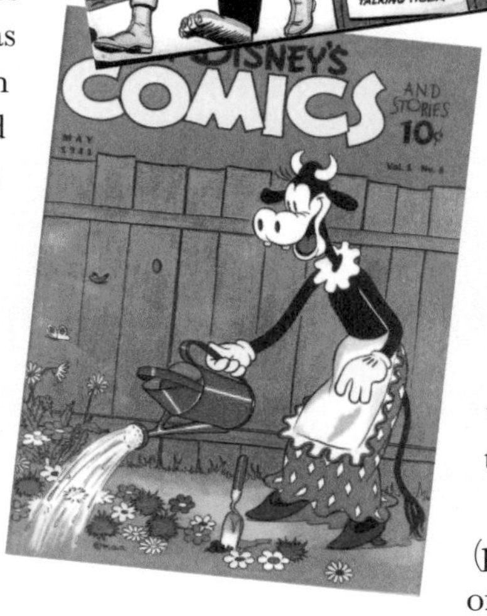
DISNEY'S
COMICS
AND STORIES
10¢
MAY

All the pieces here were chosen to stand the test of time and to reward re-reading (a seeming paradox when sifting through a medium as ephemeral as comics), and we found way more than could ever fit in one volume. Nevertheless, in studying the rich heritage, we kept returning to a small handful of great storytelling artists and finally ceded a large part of our treasury to four giants who tower over our corner of the comic book landscape: Sheldon Mayer, Walt Kelly, John Stanley, and Carl Barks. All were writers as well as illustrators and were able to express themselves fully in comics. Often we chose to offer more than one example of work by the other creators we selected as well, to give a better sense of the breadth and intensity of their achievement. Though designed for little kids, all our stories take on big themes, exploring the nature of the self and the other, love and death, revenge, greed, loyalty, and the demarcation of fantasy and reality. The common denominators for the stories we chose are a strong narrative thrust, a great sense of humor, and a distinctive authorial voice.

Cartooning was built into Sheldon Mayer's DNA, and his lifework is embedded in the DNA of American comic books. Barely past his own childhood when he began working as an editor on the very first comics, he recognized the potential of Superman when the crude submission first crossed his desk and he convinced his dubious bosses to give it a shot. His own first significant creation, *Scribbly*, was one of the earliest series drawn specifically for comic books, back when they still mimicked the format of the Sunday newspaper strips. Telling of a lower-middle-class New York teenager's passion to become a cartoonist, it is among the first overtly autobiographical comics ever made. In the 1939 sequence we selected (pages 61–67), the boy cartoonist's collision with school and authority echoes themes that harken back to Tom Sawyer.

Mayer's raffish J. Rufus Lion story (pages 285–91) carries the lowlife scent of vaudeville that permeated many of the early humor comics. It manages to smash the fourth wall to smithereens years before Harvey Kurtzman's *Hey Look!* feature (pages 284, 292, 332, and 345), and later *MAD*, atomized the smithereens, while painlessly introducing the notion of the unreliable narrator to

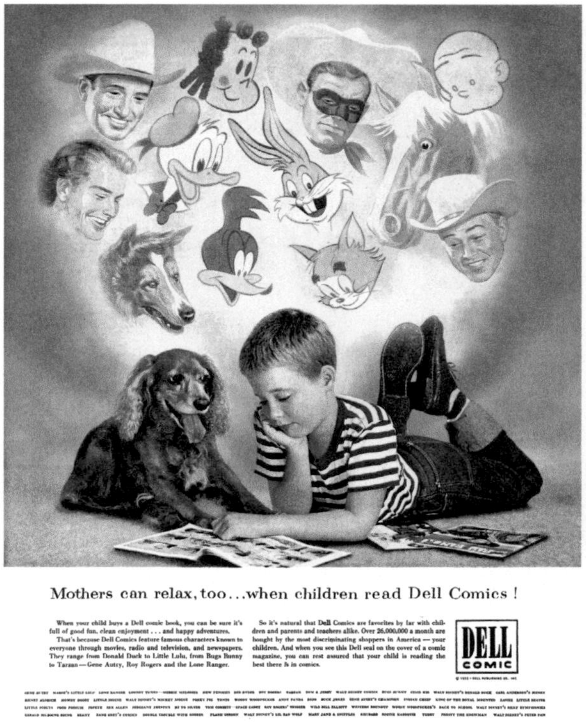
Mothers can relax, too...when children read Dell Comics !
DELL COMIC

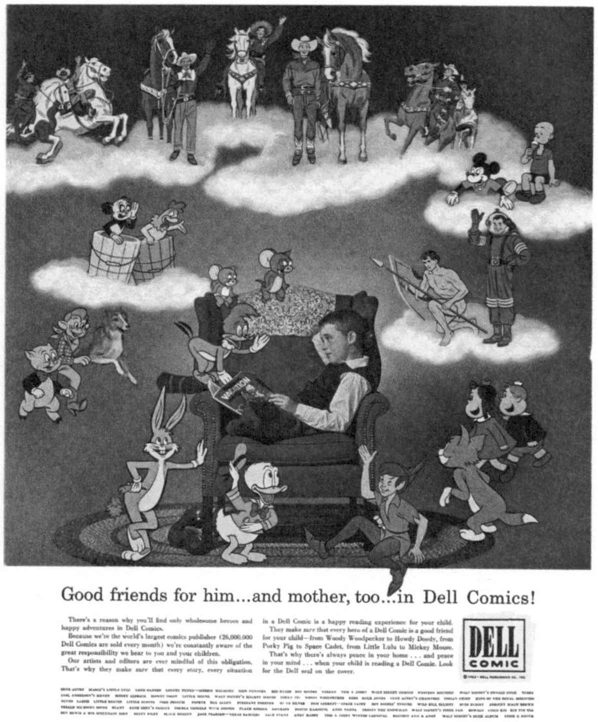
Good friends for him...and mother, too...in Dell Comics!
DELL COMIC

Dell Comics advertising, *Saturday Evening Post*, November 1, 1952 (left), and January 10, 1953 (right)

young readers. Mayer put aside his editor's visor to become a full-time cartoonist in 1948; his many funny animal comics that followed—best exemplified by his first Three Mouseketeers story on pages 115–20—still have the rhythms of vaudeville, but they now resonate with a sweetness, an engagement with character, and a sheer love of cartooning that shine through every panel. In most of the ninety-nine issues of *Sugar and Spike*, Mayer's definitive creation, parents exist with their heads lopped off by the tops of those panels. The endearing toddler sweethearts with a rug's-eye view of the world (conceived decades before TV's *Rugrats* was born) offer up stories about negotiating friendships and navigating the baffling adult world—themes explored further in many of the selections in our *Treasury*.

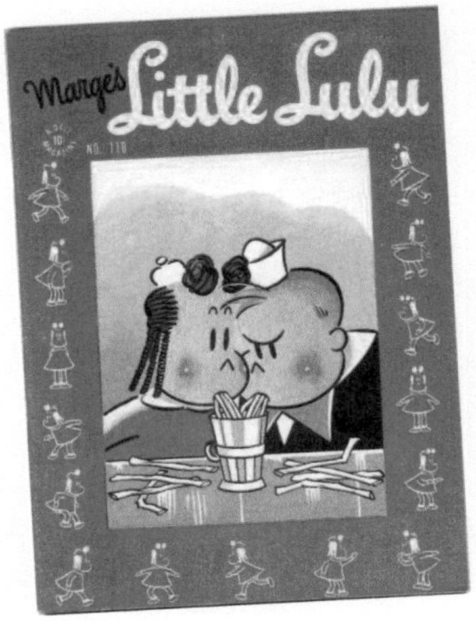
Marge's Little Lulu
NO. 118

This divide between adults and kids is bridged, for example, in Walt Kelly's original coming-of-age fairy tale, "Prince Robin and the Dwarfs" (pages 177–90). Young Prince Robin's dwarf pals take the true measure of the king's childish scoffing by shrinking him and his men down to kid size; the prince then displays his competence, defeating a giant-size ogre and teaching his father a lesson in tolerance. Kelly did some of the most sumptuous and charming comics for the very youngest readers in his adaptations of Mother Goose rhymes and fairy tales for several of Western Publishing's Dell comics titles in the 1940s and 1950s, stylistically looking back to the great children's book illustration of the late ninteenth and early twentieth centuries. The winsome quality that permeates his Hickory and Dickory (pages 87–94) was perfected at the Disney studios, where he had worked as an animator on features like *Snow White*, *Pinocchio*, and *Fantasia*. Kelly's rollicking and idiosyncratic *Pogo* was born in Dell's *Animal Comics* in 1942, and at the end of the decade matured into one of America's most highly regarded syndicated newspaper strips. In *Pogo*'s strip incarnation, Kelly added political and social commentary to the heady brew of virtuoso cartooning and whimsy that he'd already perfected in the comic books.

"Funny animal" comics are virtually synonymous with the kid comics genre, an outgrowth of the marketing of Mickey Mouse and other animated screen stars. Many of the comic book artists represented in this collection—like Walt Kelly, Dan Noonan, Woody Gelman, Dan Gordon, and others—were moonlighting or ex-animators glad of the relative autonomy that came with comic book work. Carl Barks, after spending his early years working as a logger, riveter, printer's assistant, mule driver, and cowboy, was hired by the Disney studios in his thirties, first as an animator and then as a story artist on Donald Duck cartoons. He left in 1942, launching into a thirty-year career as a freelancer, a self-described "duck man," the definitive artist and writer of Donald Duck comics for Western Publishing.

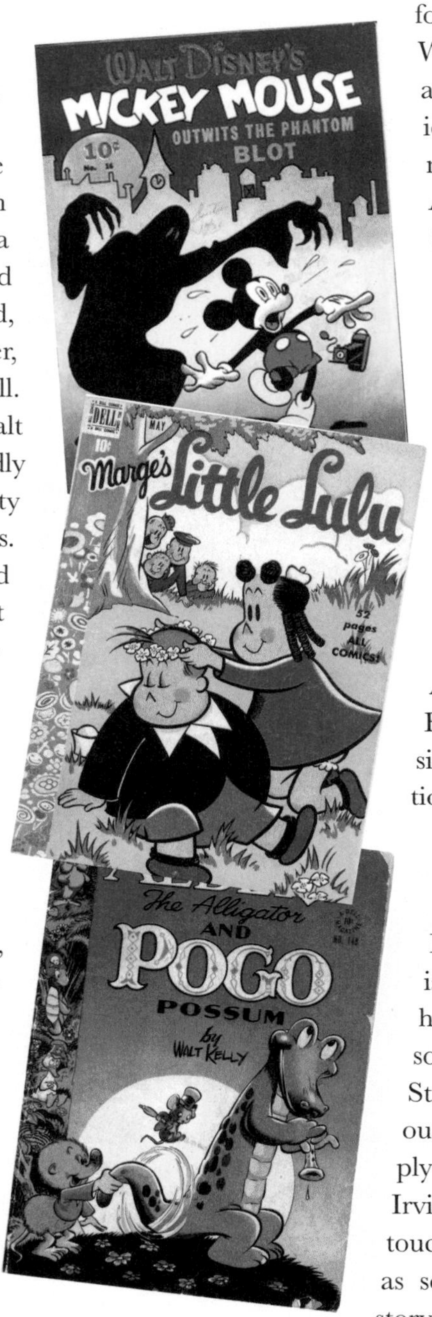
Walt Disney's
MICKEY MOUSE
OUTWITS THE PHANTOM BLOT
10¢
Marge's Little Lulu
52 pages ALL COMICS!
The Alligator AND
POGO
POSSUM
by Walt Kelly

In the course of a career that made him the most-read comic book artist in the world, Barks created Duckburg, a richly imagined world fully populated with archetypal characters he invented, like Uncle Scrooge, Gladstone Gander, Gyro Gearloose, and Magica De Spell. The Donald he inherited from Walt Disney was a choleric quacker, hardly the subtle and coherent personality Barks developed in his ten-page stories. As in our examples (pages 131–40 and 241–50), Donald is a well-intended but misguided parent, sometimes a buffoon, occasionally competent, though rarely as preternaturally level-headed as his nephews, Huey, Dewey, and Louie. In Barks's longer duck adventures, informed by the literature he'd absorbed since childhood—ranging from Jack London and Robert Louis Stevenson tales to cowboy pulps, historical tales, and mythology—the far-flung exotic stories are tautly written, scrupulously researched, and psychologically astute. The thrilling and often laugh-out-loud funny narratives are as rich as anything children's literature or cinema has ever offered. Drawn with precision, imbued with a crusty view of human (and duck) nature, his stories often reflect a flinty economic determinism, as in the astonishing "Tralla La" on pages 252–73. Though revered around the world, Barks's work still seems under-recognized in his home country, outside a wide circle of comics fans. That he worked anonymously under the broad Walt Disney corporate flag—and was known for most of his career only as "the good duck artist"—may have made it harder for many Americans to locate the singularity of his comics genius.

John Stanley, one of Barks's few equals as a comics storyteller, also produced most of his lifework for Dell comics under at least as large a shroud of anonymity. Over his years in the business he wrote comics scripts for many licensed characters, including Woody Woodpecker, Raggedy Ann, and Nancy, that displayed some of his idiosyncratic charms, but his most renowned work was a fifteen-year run of *Little Lulu* comics that began in 1945. Stanley transformed the licensed series of popular *Saturday Evening Post* gag cartoons by Marge Henderson Buell about a young hellion into a rich tapestry of comic stories about an uncannily convincing society of neighborhood kids. His competent and inquisitive little girl was more than just a tomboy: She was a ladylike proto-feminist, at least the equal of the boys who repeatedly try to keep her out of their "No Girls Allowed" club. Stanley's "Five Little Babies" story (pages 45–60) is a classic of escalating comedy and humiliation, a perfect prepubescent equivalent to James Thurber's epic battles of the sexes. Stanley's other Lulu story in our collection, "Two Foots Is Feet" (pages 79–83) shows off his relish for language and its absurdities—his verbal playfulness is as funny and sophisticated as his visual slapstick. Stanley wrote and visually planned out his Lulu stories, but most were simply rendered by journeyman cartoonist Irving Tripp, without the deftness of touch visible in Stanley's own drawing, as seen in the literally haunting Tubby story we selected: "The Guest in the Ghost Hotel" (pages 207–16). This dark and fantastical side of Stanley is also on view in his own later creation, Melvin Monster (pages 317–22), where he manages to build sympathetic comedy around something as genuinely horrific as child abuse in a mode that parallels Roald Dahl's contemporaneous children's stories.

Though Stanley's Lulu stories ran variations on a

few recurring themes, they are far from the carefully delineated sitcom world that Al Wiseman and Fred Toole elaborated from Hank Ketcham's *Dennis the Menace* newspaper feature (pages 29–37 and 75–78). The widely imitated *Dennis the Menace* comics offer the exuberant pleasures of a specific time and place; they seem to carry the smell of mid-century suburban American barbecues. Stanley's Lulu stories seem to be set in an earlier and less opulent small-town America that's far less specific in its details. The stories actually take place in a self-contained dreamscape that feels persuasively real, yet timelessly abstract.

It's no accident that so much of the material in our book was published by Western Publishing's line of Dell comics. In the first half of the twentieth century Western had played a significant role in democratizing (or "dumbing down," depending on which librarian you asked) children's literature with their low-priced, mass-produced Big Little Books and Little Golden Books as well as comics, mostly based on Disney's and other licensed properties. They exuded the monolithic mainstream wholesomeness of the entire Walt Disney enterprise. When the rest of the comics publishing industry was mowed down as a result of the 1954 Senate hearings, Helen Meyer, then Dell's vice president, offered testimony in the hearings, and seemed almost as disdainful of the rest of the comics industry as its most severe critics. Instead of running for cover under the Comic Code Authority's stamp of approval that allowed surviving publishers to limp toward the future, Dell—with the luxury of a strong distribution arm—unfurled a Dell Pledge to Parents on the back of each comic, that proudly stated:

A PLEDGE **DELL COMIC** **TO PARENTS**

The Dell Trademark is, and always has been, a positive guarantee that the comic magazine bearing it contains only clean and wholesome entertainment. The Dell code eliminates entirely, rather than regulates, objectionable material. That's why when your child buys a Dell Comic you can be sure it contains only good fun. "DELL COMICS ARE GOOD COMICS" *is our credo and constant goal.*

Don't miss FAIRY TALE PARADE
FAIRY TALE PARADE
10¢
FAIRY TALE PARADE IS A MAGAZINE WHICH BRINGS TO LIFE FOLK TALES AND STORIES OF MANY LANDS. IN ITS MANY ILLUSTRATIONS YOU WILL FIND THE SPRITES, ELVES, PIXIES TROLLS AND WITCHES OF PICTURE BOOK FAME.
On Sale Everywhere ..... 10¢

House ad, back cover of *Animal Comics* no. 4, August–September, 1943

Though this notion of wholesomeness did sometimes lead to treacly and dull Dell comics, it also managed to offer protection to some artists—like the ones we selected—to pursue their own visions unencumbered by the culture war that raged around them. It led us, as editors, to grapple with rather heady questions about the whole notion of childhood, our own psyches as ex-kids, and our own roles as parents. The idea of children pictured in the Middle Ages as miniature adults gave way in modern times to the idea of childhood as a zone of innocence to be protected. The Victorian idea of childhood, to vastly oversimplify, grew out of the need to allow the time and space necessary for our kids to learn to read and write rather than just hold a plow. This encouraged the kind of family values that led to the Dell Pledge on the one hand and the vision of comics as the defiler of youth on the other hand. The comic book exists in the no man's land between old-fashioned concepts of literacy and the more recent awareness of the need for a visual literacy; it exists somewhere between the Invention of Childhood and the End of Childhood—between the traditional and the transgressive.

As adults with that kid of all ages inside us, we can remember the thrill of tasting the forbidden horror comics and the wising up that came with *MAD*'s skepticism—we loved the irrational universe comics opened up for us, where men could fly and nutsy squirrels could insist they're really airplanes. But as parents we've desperately wanted to keep our kids safe on the ever-shrinking island of childhood, protected from the dangers of, say, Internet porn and the horrors of the nightly news, while still preparing them for the Real World. As evidenced in so many of our selected stories, adults can act very childishly, kids can be remarkably clear-eyed, and the battle between the rational and the irrational is more like a dance.

As editors, we ultimately leaned toward a traditional vision of childhood as a time of prelapsarian innocence and curiosity. We took our role as guardians seriously: Some of our favorite comics and cartoonists barely made the cut. We reluctantly excluded the ironic satire of Harvey Kurtzman's *MAD* that demands and encourages the kind of media savviness that marks the end of childhood, giving only a taste of his self-reflexive humor in the "Hey Look!" one-pagers that led to *MAD* Magazine (and eventually to the glories of *The Simpsons* and *The Daily Show*). We wrestled with the "teenage" genre invented and defined by Archie a few short years after the *concept* of teenagers was invented; we finally decided that the category became of most interest to kids whose hormonal changes were just about to kick in and instead opted for a *Little Archie* tale by Bob Bolling. We did an end run around the super-hero genre, nodding to the form with Supermouse, a funny animal variant, and a wacky Captain Marvel tale. C. C. Beck's *Captain Marvel*, with its emphasis on magic and cartoony humor, was not only the most popular, by far, of the first generation super-hero comics, it was the one most clearly directed at the youngest readers. And we sadly resisted the giddy and libidinous go-for-broke hilarity of Jack Cole's Plastic Man as somehow not age appropriate, though we did include a taste of his unique sensibility in the almost unknown Burp the Twerp pages. Acting *in loco parentis* we happily introduce some of the best of the unbridled "loco" wildness of comics as well as widely consensual classics. After all, the loving but somehow funny uncles, who might take junior out for an evening of poker and booze before tucking the kid in for the night, are part of the comics family. Milt Gross's doodly slapstick spritz (pages 293–99), Basil Wolverton's gleeful grotesquerie, Dick Briefer's gentle Frankenstein monster, and George Carlson's punch-drunk poetic nonsense so reminiscent of Carl Sandberg's Rootabaga Stories (pages 167–74) are all a proud part of our mix.

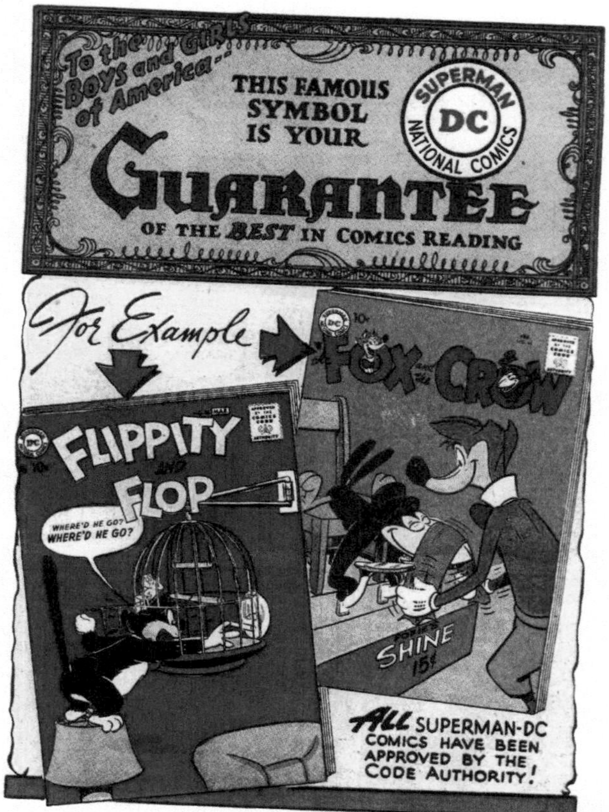
To the Boys and Girls of America--
THIS FAMOUS SYMBOL IS YOUR
SUPERMAN DC NATIONAL COMICS
GUARANTEE
OF THE BEST IN COMICS READING
For Example
FLIPPITY AND FLOP
WHERE'D HE GO? WHERE'D HE GO?
FOX AND CROW
SHINE 15¢
ALL SUPERMAN-DC COMICS HAVE BEEN APPROVED BY THE CODE AUTHORITY!

DC Comics house ad, *Sugar and Spike* no. 13, February 1958

In burrowing through our piles of comic books, we found that the gems in our treasury can take their place comfortably next to the justly lauded jewels on the more traditional picture book shelves. Books like Robert McCloskey's *Make Way for Ducklings*, Crockett Johnson's *Harold and the Purple Crayon*, William Steig's *Shrek*, Shel Silverstein's *The Giving Tree*, Maurice Sendak's *Where the Wild Things Are*, Dr. Seuss's *Cat in the Hat*, and P. D. Eastman's *Are You My Mother?* are all by cartoonists or comic book artist manqués who were working in tonier neighborhoods than the low-rent precincts of the comic book. In fact, the last story in our collection, "Gerald McBoing Boing," on pages 333–44, is P. D. Eastman's ingenious comic book adaptation of the Academy Award–winning animated film by Dr. Seuss. The ephemeral comics we selected from the 1930s to the 1960s are, of course, rooted in the time they were made, but they withstand the test of time very well. We invite you and the kids in your life to dive into this *Treasury*, toss these comics stories up in the air, and let them hit you on the head.

Art Spiegelman &
Françoise Mouly
Manhattan, NY
May 2009

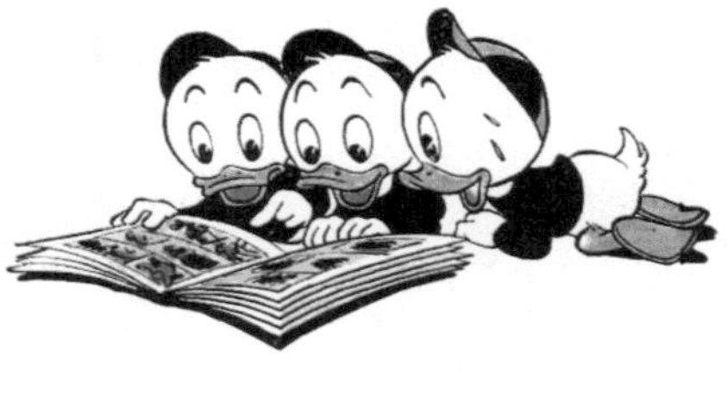

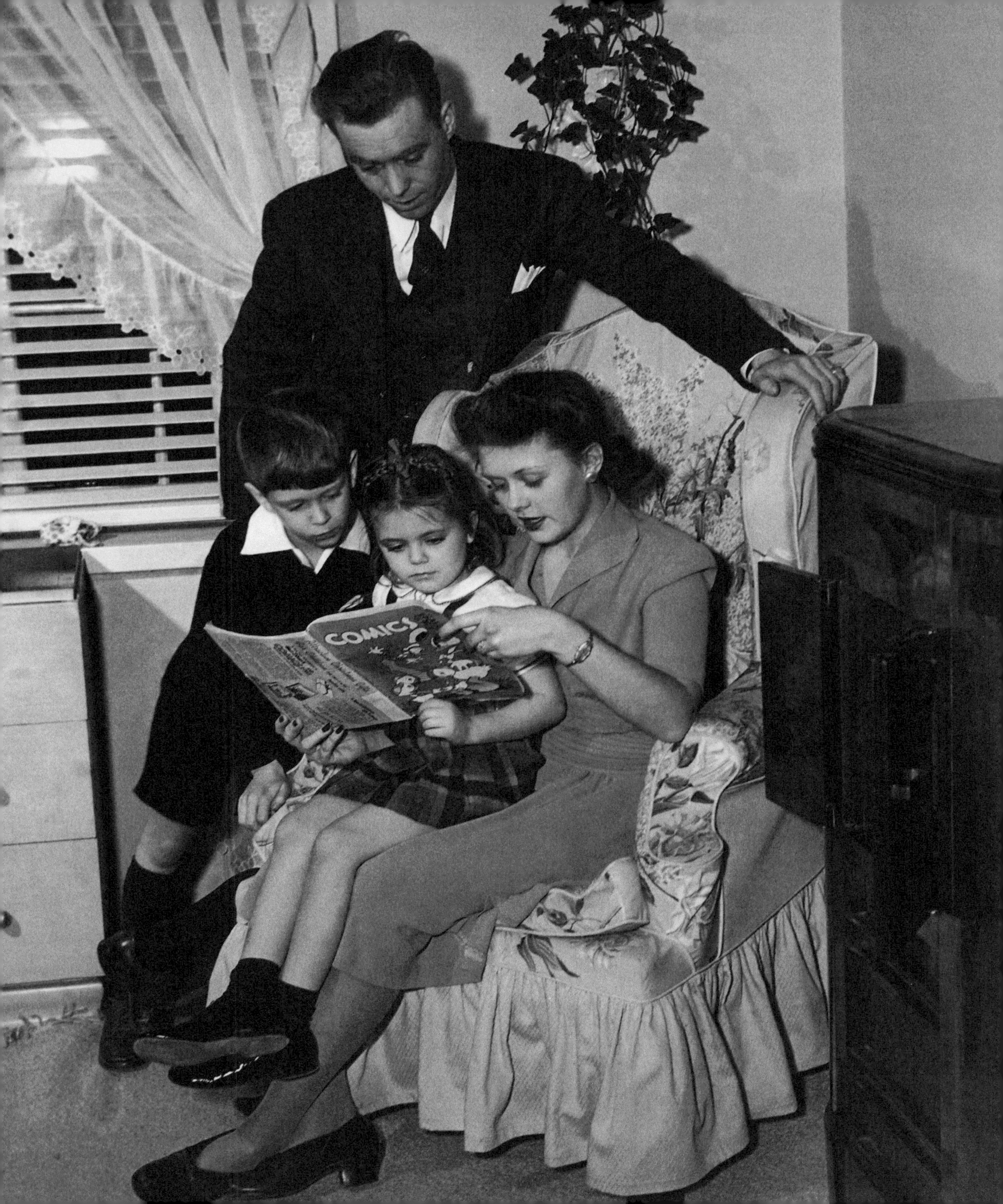
COMICS

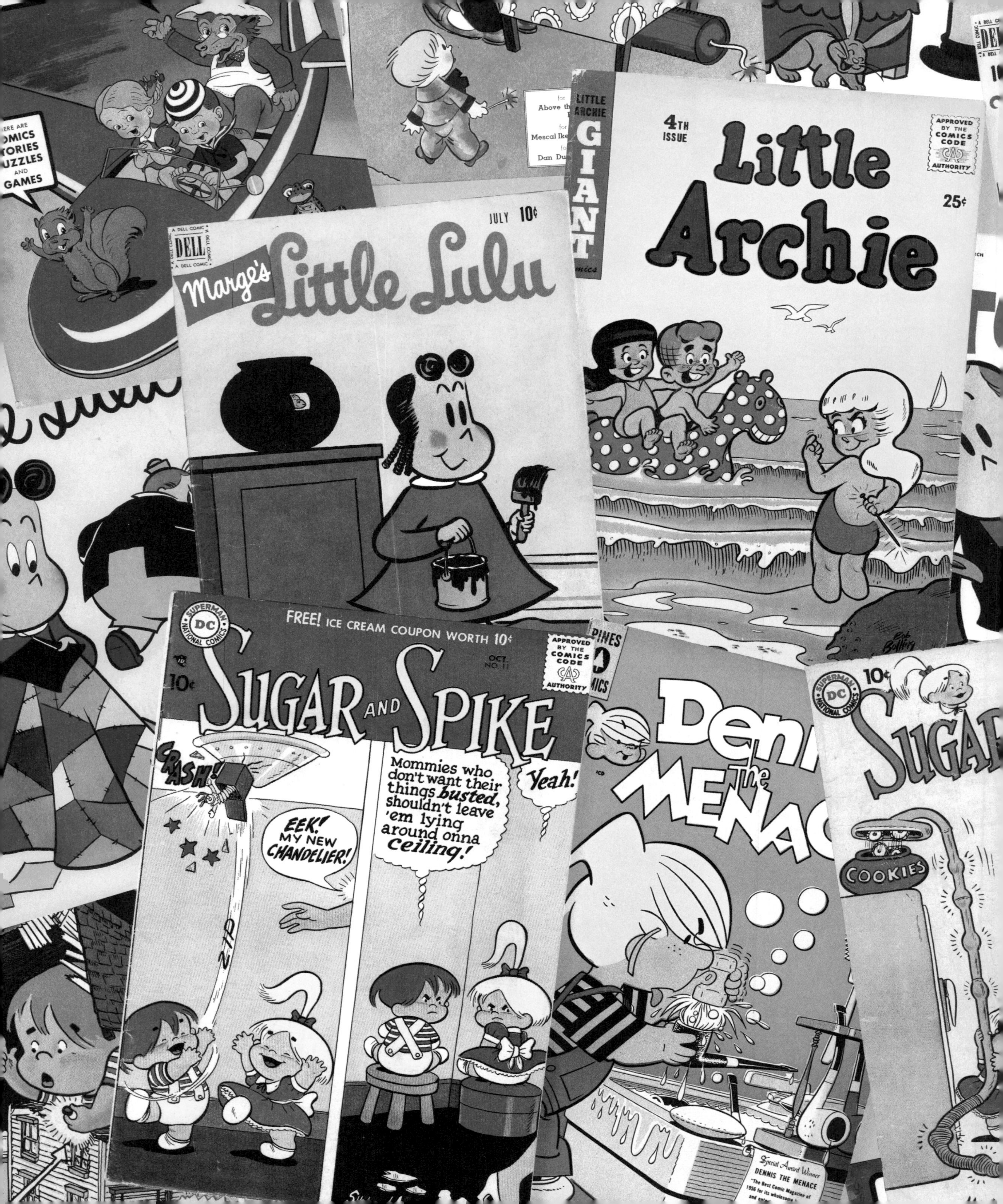

ERE ARE
OMICS
TORIES
UZZLES
AND
GAMES
A DELL COMIC
DELL
JULY 10¢
Marge's Little Lulu
LITTLE ARCHIE GIANT
4TH ISSUE
Little Archie
25¢
APPROVED BY THE COMICS CODE AUTHORITY
Bob Bolling
SUPERMAN DC NATIONAL COMICS
FREE! ICE CREAM COUPON WORTH 10¢
10¢
OCT. NO. 11
SUGAR AND SPIKE
APPROVED BY THE COMICS CODE AUTHORITY
CRASH!
EEK! MY NEW CHANDELIER!
Mommies who don't want their things busted, shouldn't leave 'em lying around onna ceiling!
Yeah!
ZIP
PINES
COMICS
Den
The
MENAC
Special Award Winner
DENNIS THE MENACE
10¢
SUGAR
COOKIES

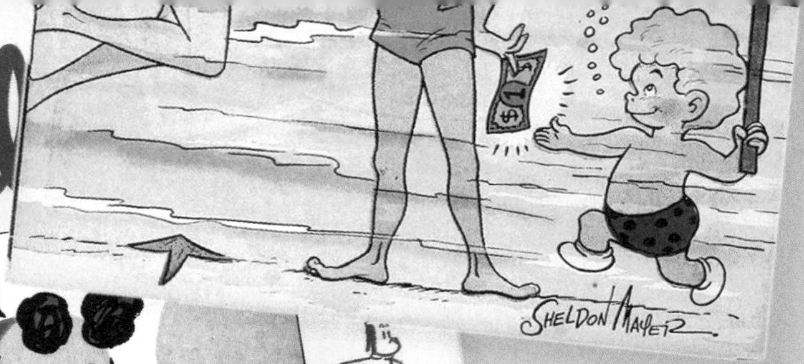
SHELDON MAYER

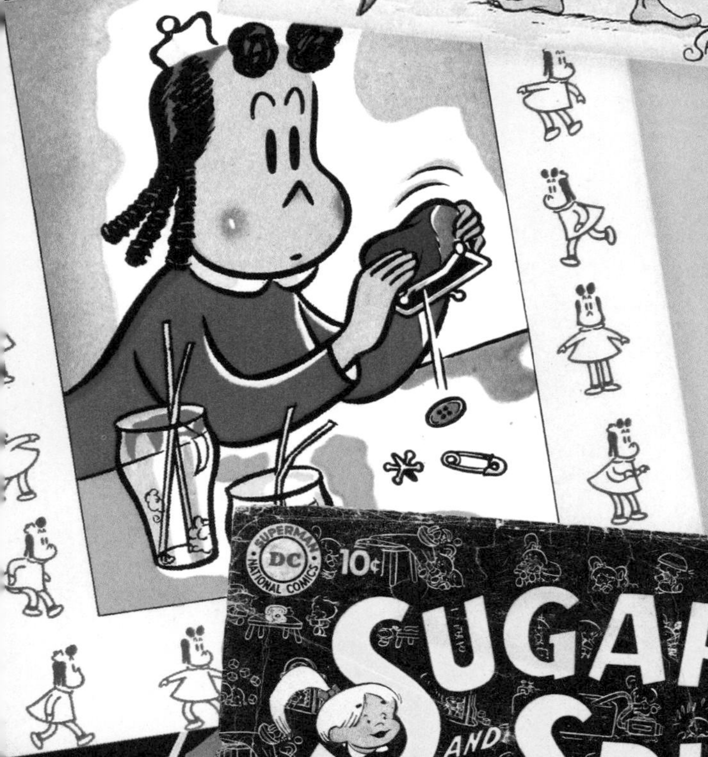

Chapter 1

HEY, KIDS!

For some reason, kids like reading about...kids!

So here they are, ranging from tykes to teens. Sheldon Mayer's beloved little toddlers, Sugar and Spike, live in a world of their own, one that parents can't understand. Mayer's Scribbly, one of the first characters ever created just for comic books, is a boy cartoonist loosely based on the artist's own life. A very young Betty and Veronica already battle with jealousy in *Little Archie.* Dennis the Menace finds a true friend. And the "war" between boys and girls is captured in all its glory in John Stanley's masterful Little Lulu story "Five Little Babies." In this chapter, kids try to figure out themselves, one another, and the world around them. Kids even try to figure out grown-ups—who often act much more childishly than their children.

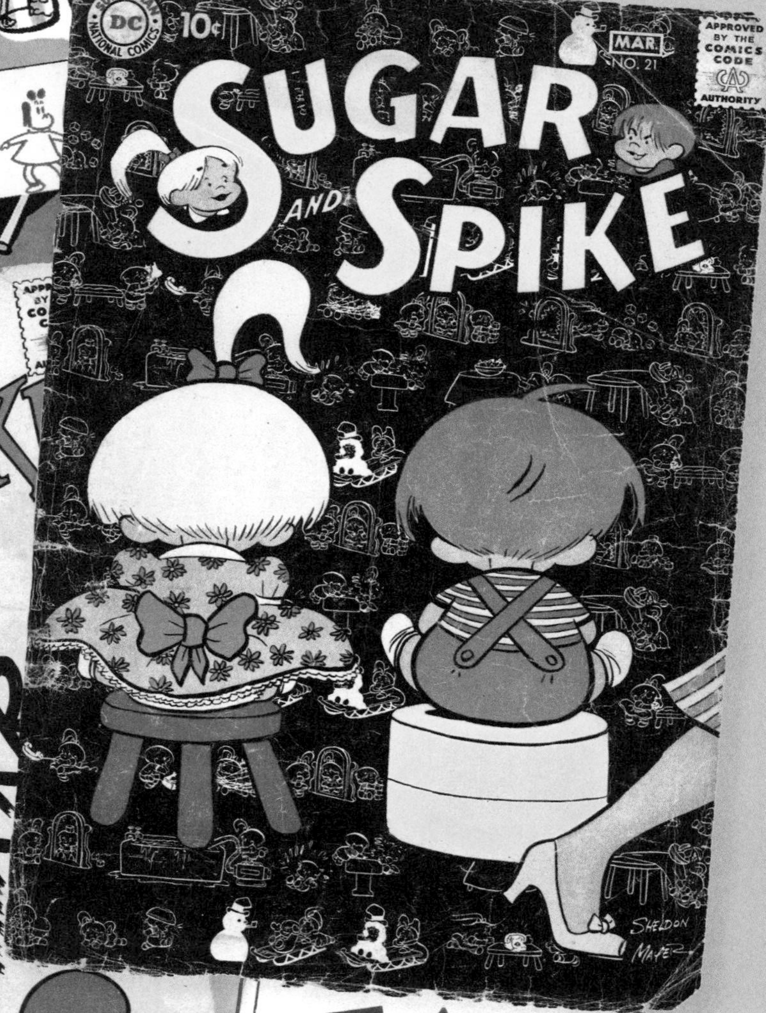
10¢
MAR.
NO. 21
APPROVED BY THE COMICS CODE AUTHORITY
SUGAR AND SPIKE
SHELDON MAYER

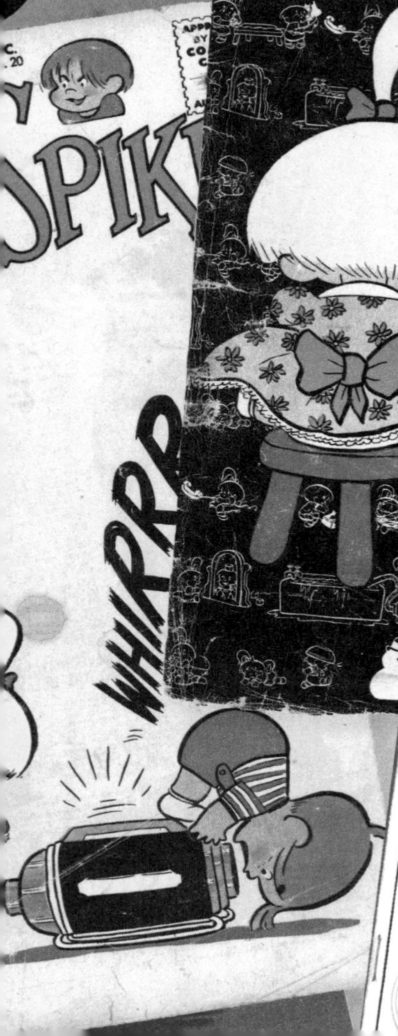

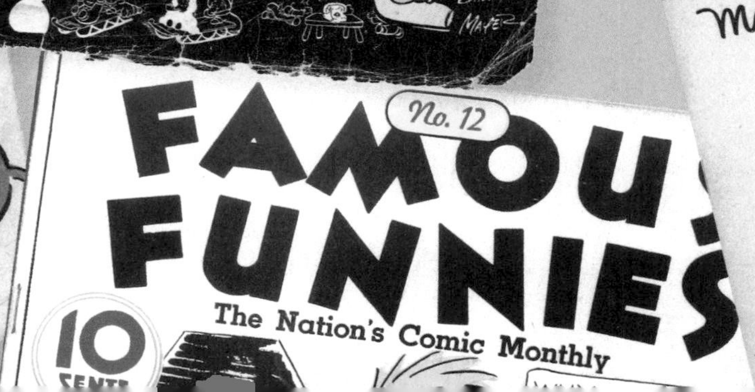
No. 12
FAMOUS FUNNIES
The Nation's Comic Monthly
10

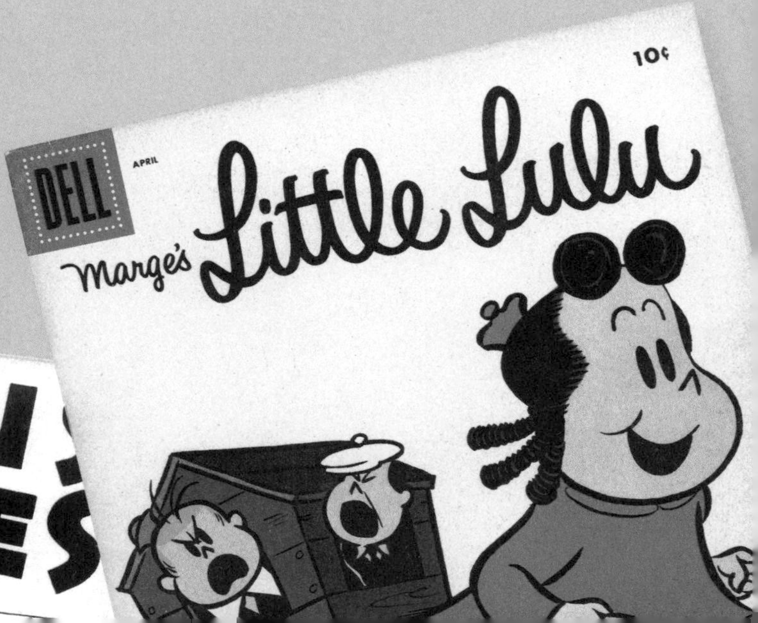
10¢
DELL
APRIL
Marge's Little Lulu

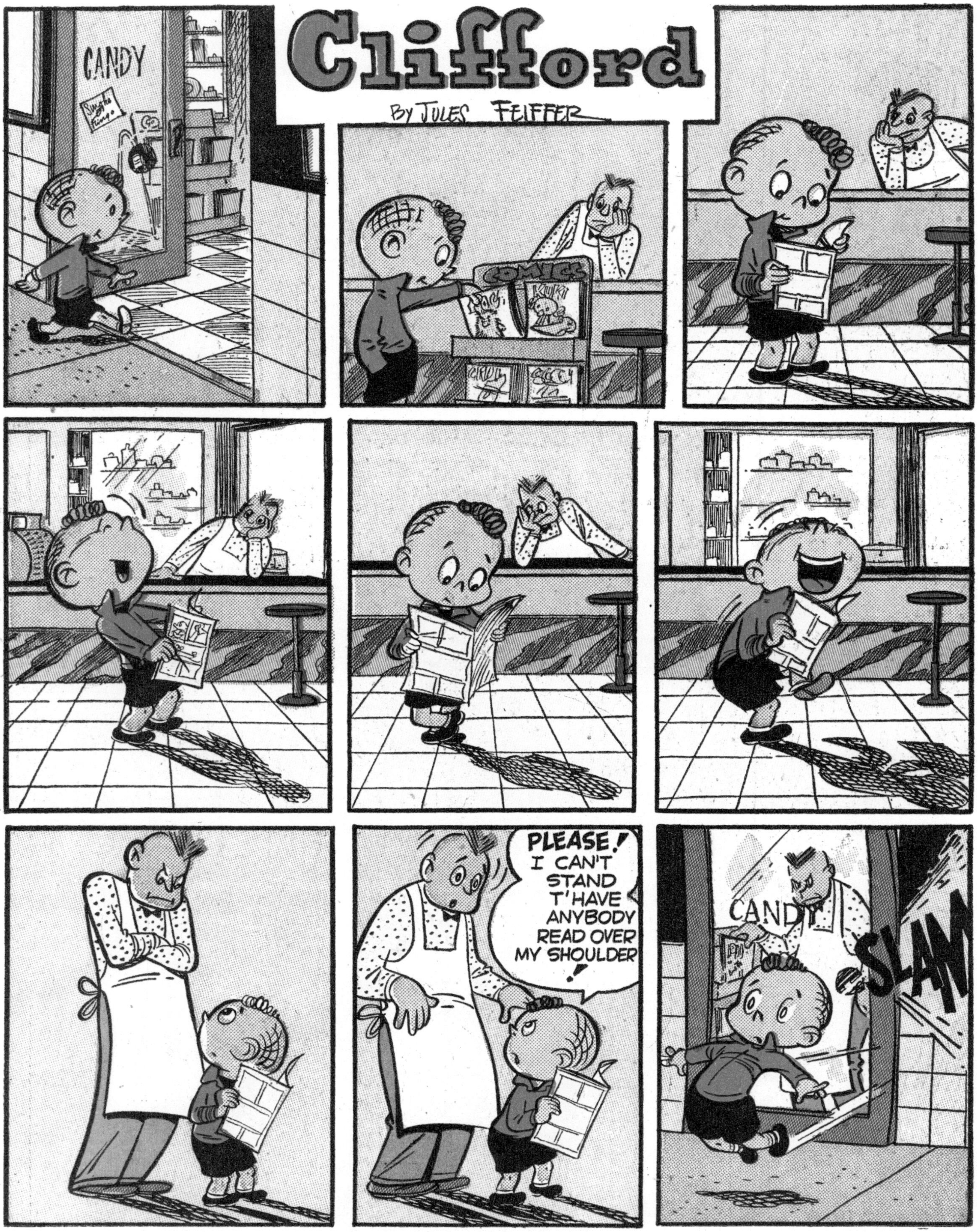
Clifford
BY JULES FEIFFER
CANDY
COMICS
KUKI
PLEASE! I CAN'T STAND T'HAVE ANYBODY READ OVER MY SHOULDER!
CANDY
SLAM

By Sheldon Mayer

ONCE UPON A TIME THERE WAS A CUTE LITTLE BABY BOY NAMED (OF ALL THINGS) *CECIL*--

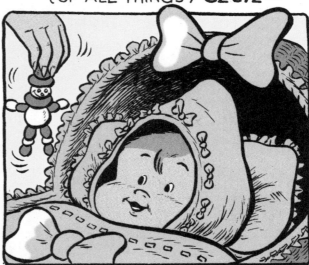

HOWEVER, AS THE MONTHS PASSED, HIS NAME SEEMED TO FIT HIM LESS AND LESS --

HIS MOTHER TRIED CALLING HIM...

MY LITTLE LAMBIE-PIE--

AH-- BUT HIS DADDY PREFERRED...

HEY-Y, THERE, *SPIKE!*

SOMETIMES IT CAME A LITTLE LOUDER...

SPI-IKE!

WHAT'S ALL THE *FUSS* ABOUT? A FELLA'S GOT TO LEARN TO HANDLE A HAMMER *SOME*-TIME!

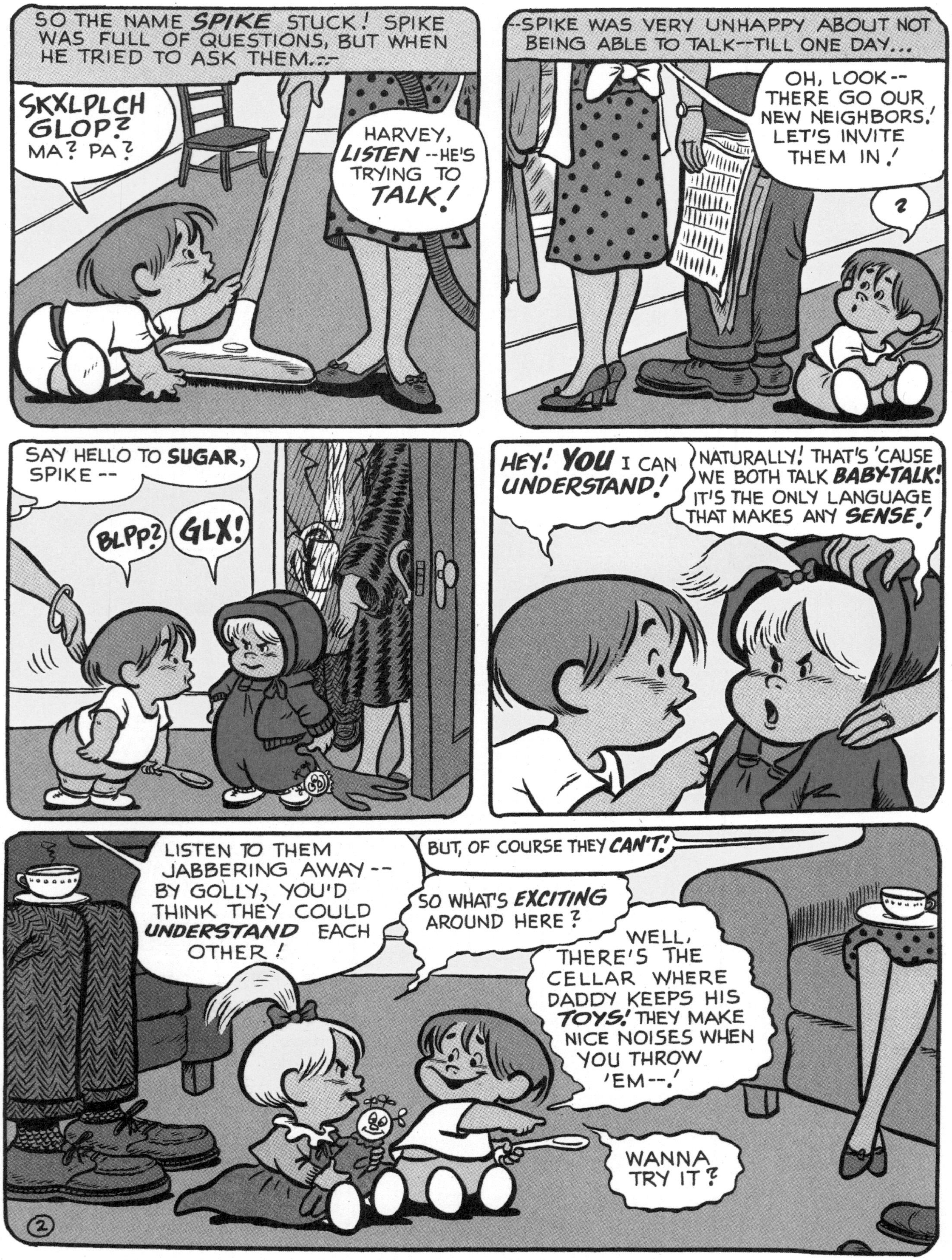
SO THE NAME SPIKE STUCK! SPIKE WAS FULL OF QUESTIONS, BUT WHEN HE TRIED TO ASK THEM.--
SKXLPLCH GLOP? MA? PA?
HARVEY, LISTEN --HE'S TRYING TO TALK!
--SPIKE WAS VERY UNHAPPY ABOUT NOT BEING ABLE TO TALK--TILL ONE DAY...
OH, LOOK-- THERE GO OUR NEW NEIGHBORS! LET'S INVITE THEM IN!
?
SAY HELLO TO SUGAR, SPIKE--
BLPP?
GLX!
HEY! YOU I CAN UNDERSTAND!
NATURALLY! THAT'S 'CAUSE WE BOTH TALK BABY-TALK! IT'S THE ONLY LANGUAGE THAT MAKES ANY SENSE!
LISTEN TO THEM JABBERING AWAY-- BY GOLLY, YOU'D THINK THEY COULD UNDERSTAND EACH OTHER!
BUT, OF COURSE THEY CAN'T!
SO WHAT'S EXCITING AROUND HERE?
WELL, THERE'S THE CELLAR WHERE DADDY KEEPS HIS TOYS! THEY MAKE NICE NOISES WHEN YOU THROW 'EM--!
WANNA TRY IT?
2

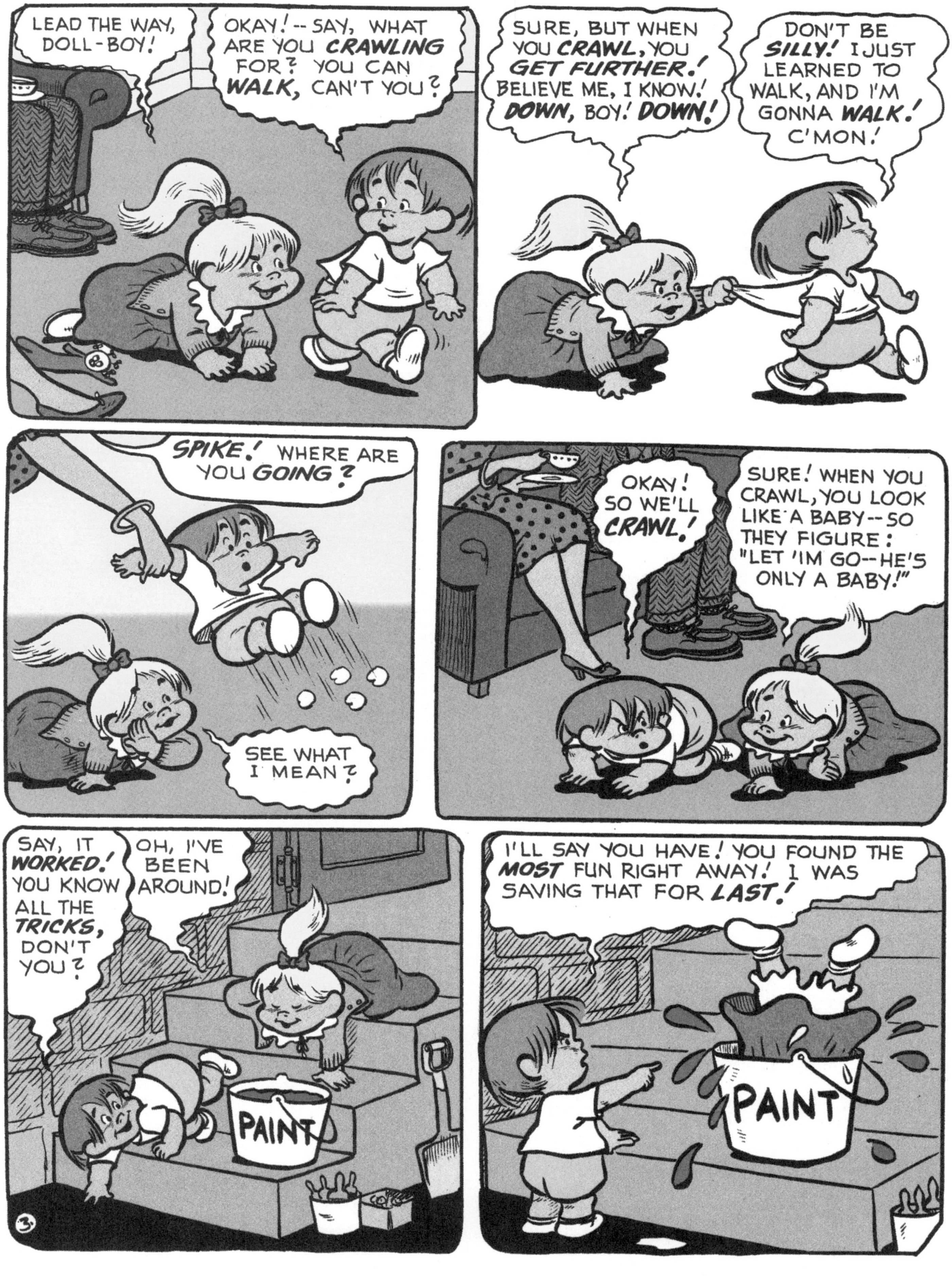
LEAD THE WAY, DOLL-BOY!
OKAY! -- SAY, WHAT ARE YOU CRAWLING FOR? YOU CAN WALK, CAN'T YOU?
SURE, BUT WHEN YOU CRAWL, YOU GET FURTHER! BELIEVE ME, I KNOW! DOWN, BOY! DOWN!
DON'T BE SILLY! I JUST LEARNED TO WALK, AND I'M GONNA WALK! C'MON!
SPIKE! WHERE ARE YOU GOING?
SEE WHAT I MEAN?
OKAY! SO WE'LL CRAWL!
SURE! WHEN YOU CRAWL, YOU LOOK LIKE A BABY -- SO THEY FIGURE: "LET 'IM GO -- HE'S ONLY A BABY!"
SAY, IT WORKED! YOU KNOW ALL THE TRICKS, DON'T YOU?
OH, I'VE BEEN AROUND!
PAINT
3
I'LL SAY YOU HAVE! YOU FOUND THE MOST FUN RIGHT AWAY! I WAS SAVING THAT FOR LAST!
PAINT

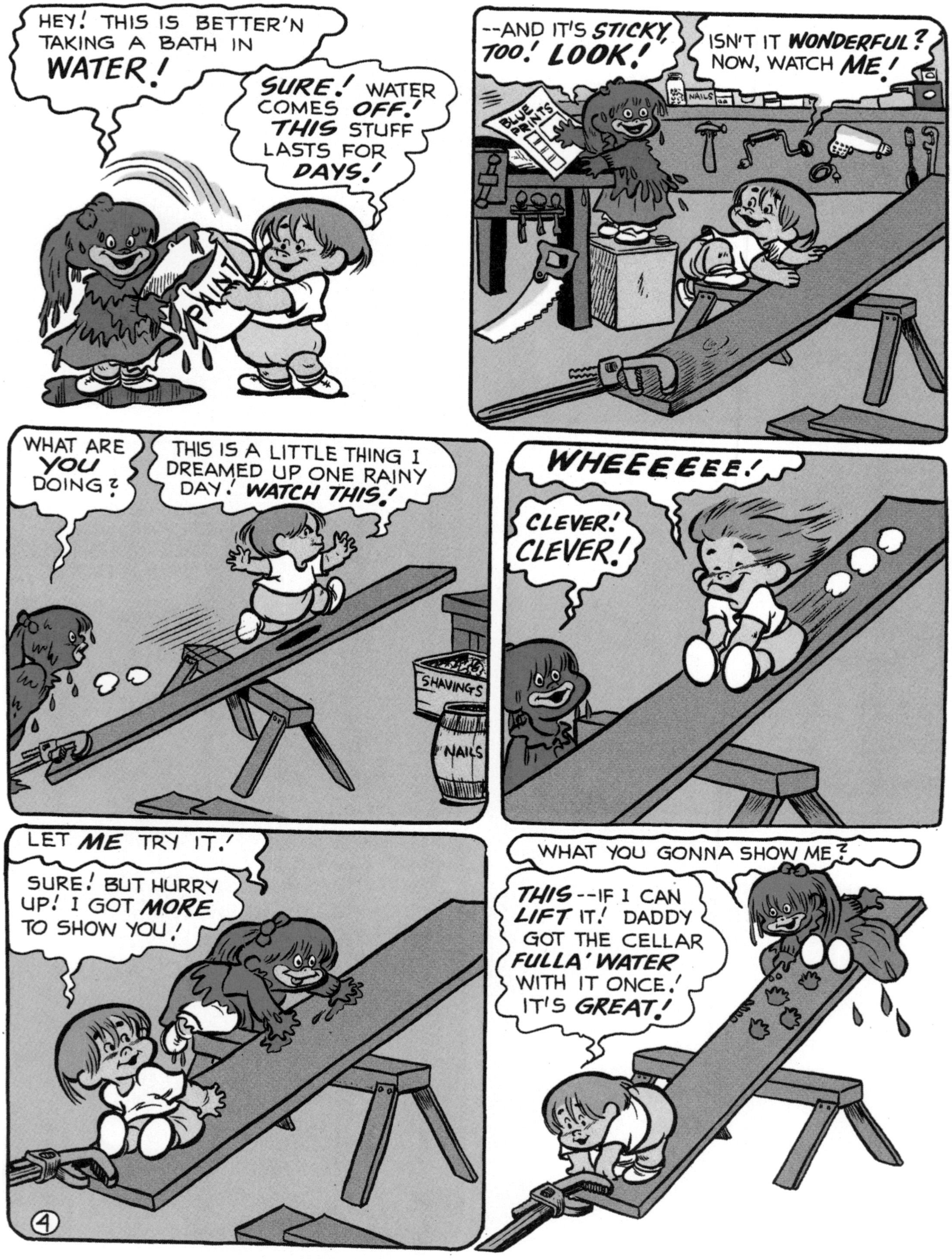
HEY! THIS IS BETTER'N TAKING A BATH IN WATER!
SURE! WATER COMES OFF! THIS STUFF LASTS FOR DAYS!
PAINT
--AND IT'S STICKY, TOO! LOOK!
ISN'T IT WONDERFUL? NOW, WATCH ME!
BLUE PRINTS
NAILS
WHAT ARE YOU DOING?
THIS IS A LITTLE THING I DREAMED UP ONE RAINY DAY! WATCH THIS!
SHAVINGS
NAILS
WHEEEEEEE!
CLEVER! CLEVER!
LET ME TRY IT!
SURE! BUT HURRY UP! I GOT MORE TO SHOW YOU!
WHAT YOU GONNA SHOW ME?
THIS--IF I CAN LIFT IT! DADDY GOT THE CELLAR FULLA' WATER WITH IT ONCE! IT'S GREAT!
4

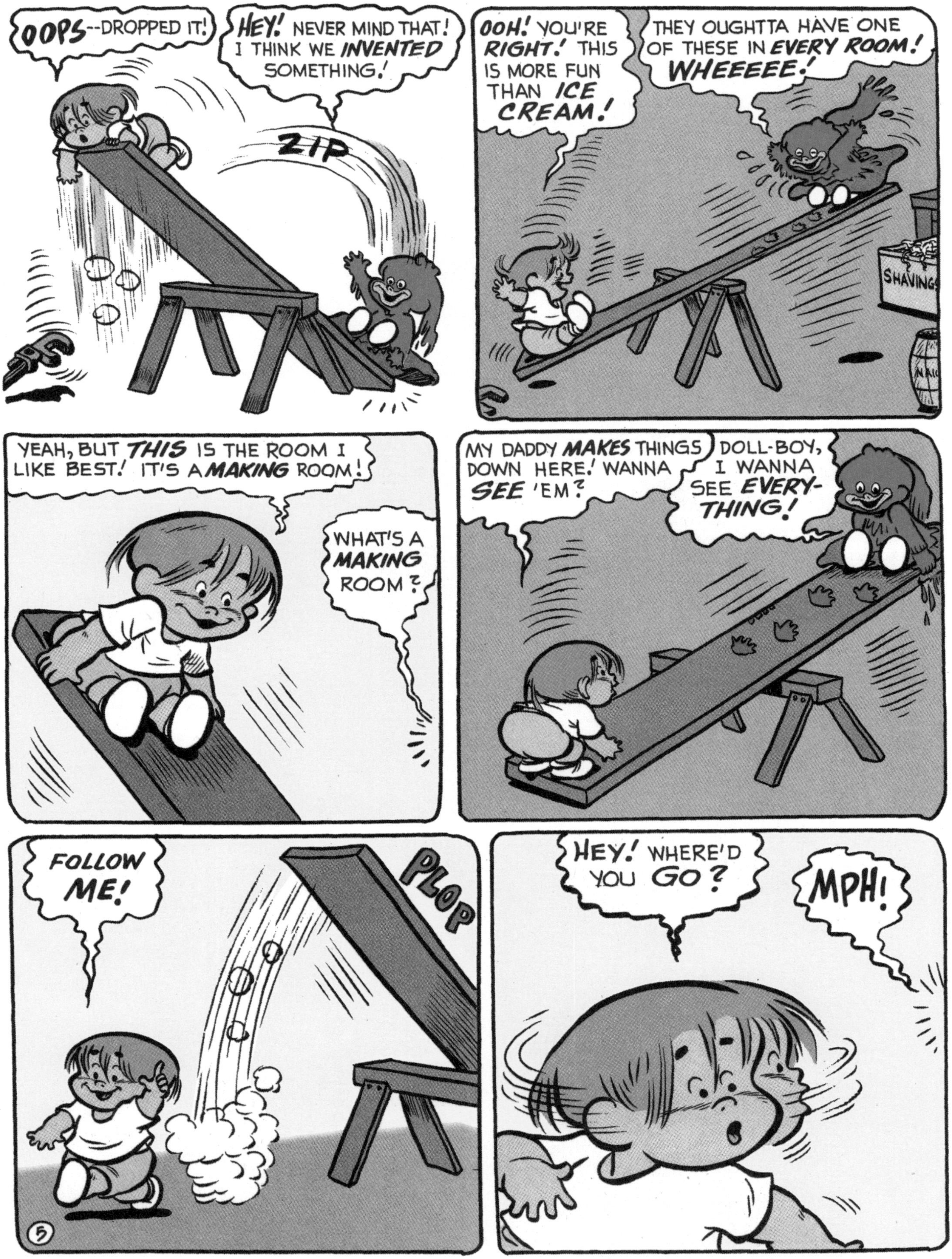
OOPS--DROPPED IT!
HEY! NEVER MIND THAT! I THINK WE INVENTED SOMETHING!
ZIP
OOH! YOU'RE RIGHT! THIS IS MORE FUN THAN ICE CREAM!
THEY OUGHTTA HAVE ONE OF THESE IN EVERY ROOM! WHEEEEE!
SHAVINGS
YEAH, BUT THIS IS THE ROOM I LIKE BEST! IT'S A MAKING ROOM!
WHAT'S A MAKING ROOM?
MY DADDY MAKES THINGS DOWN HERE! WANNA SEE 'EM?
DOLL-BOY, I WANNA SEE EVERYTHING!
FOLLOW ME!
PLOP
5
HEY! WHERE'D YOU GO?
MPH!

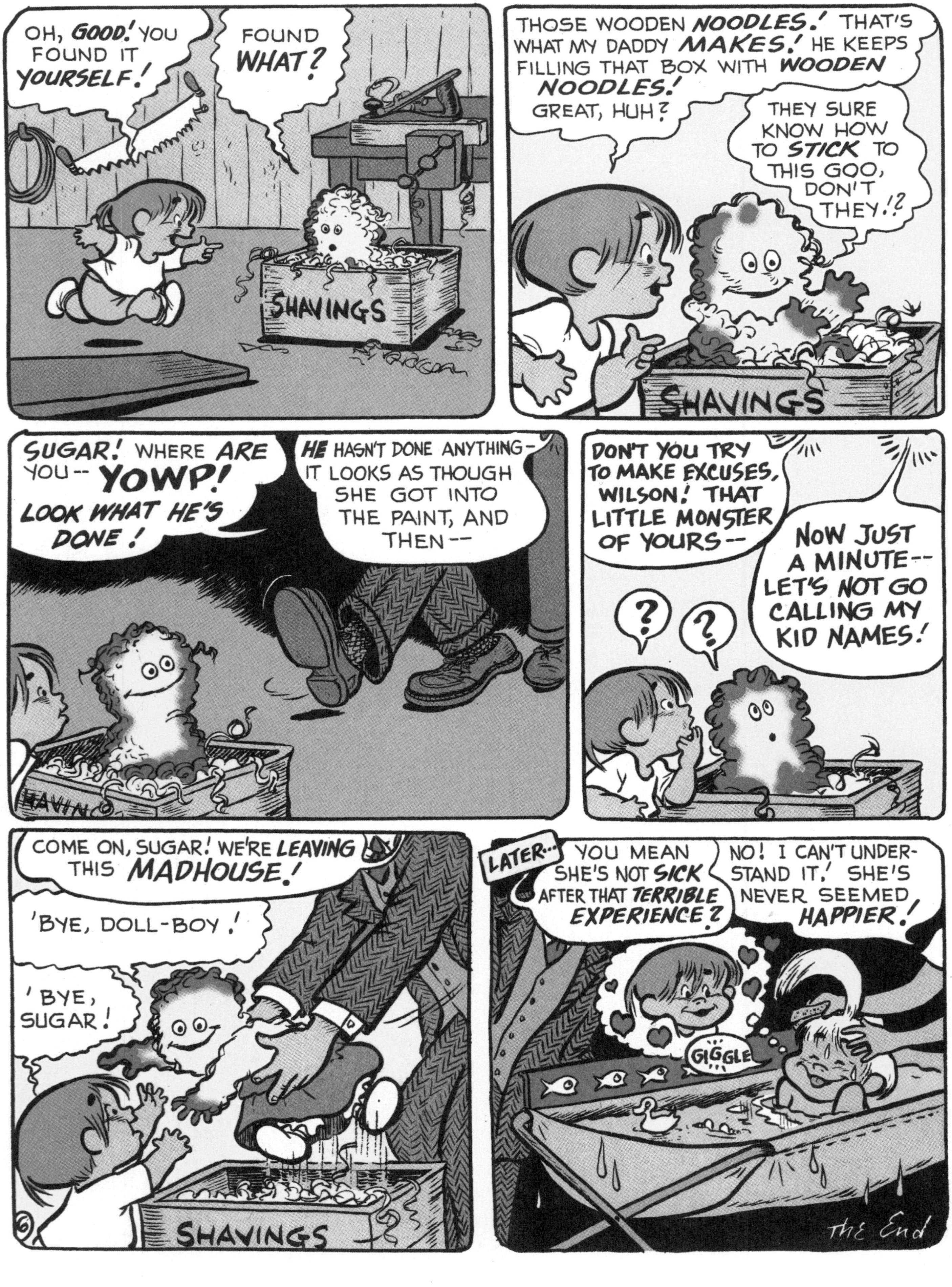
OH, GOOD! YOU FOUND IT YOURSELF!
FOUND WHAT?
SHAVINGS
THOSE WOODEN NOODLES! THAT'S WHAT MY DADDY MAKES! HE KEEPS FILLING THAT BOX WITH WOODEN NOODLES! GREAT, HUH?
THEY SURE KNOW HOW TO STICK TO THIS GOO, DON'T THEY!?
SHAVINGS
SUGAR! WHERE ARE YOU-- YOWP! LOOK WHAT HE'S DONE!
HE HASN'T DONE ANYTHING-- IT LOOKS AS THOUGH SHE GOT INTO THE PAINT, AND THEN--
DON'T YOU TRY TO MAKE EXCUSES, WILSON! THAT LITTLE MONSTER OF YOURS--
NOW JUST A MINUTE-- LET'S NOT GO CALLING MY KID NAMES!
?
?
COME ON, SUGAR! WE'RE LEAVING THIS MADHOUSE!
'BYE, DOLL-BOY!
'BYE, SUGAR!
6
SHAVINGS
LATER...
YOU MEAN SHE'S NOT SICK AFTER THAT TERRIBLE EXPERIENCE?
NO! I CAN'T UNDERSTAND IT! SHE'S NEVER SEEMED HAPPIER!
GIGGLE
THE End

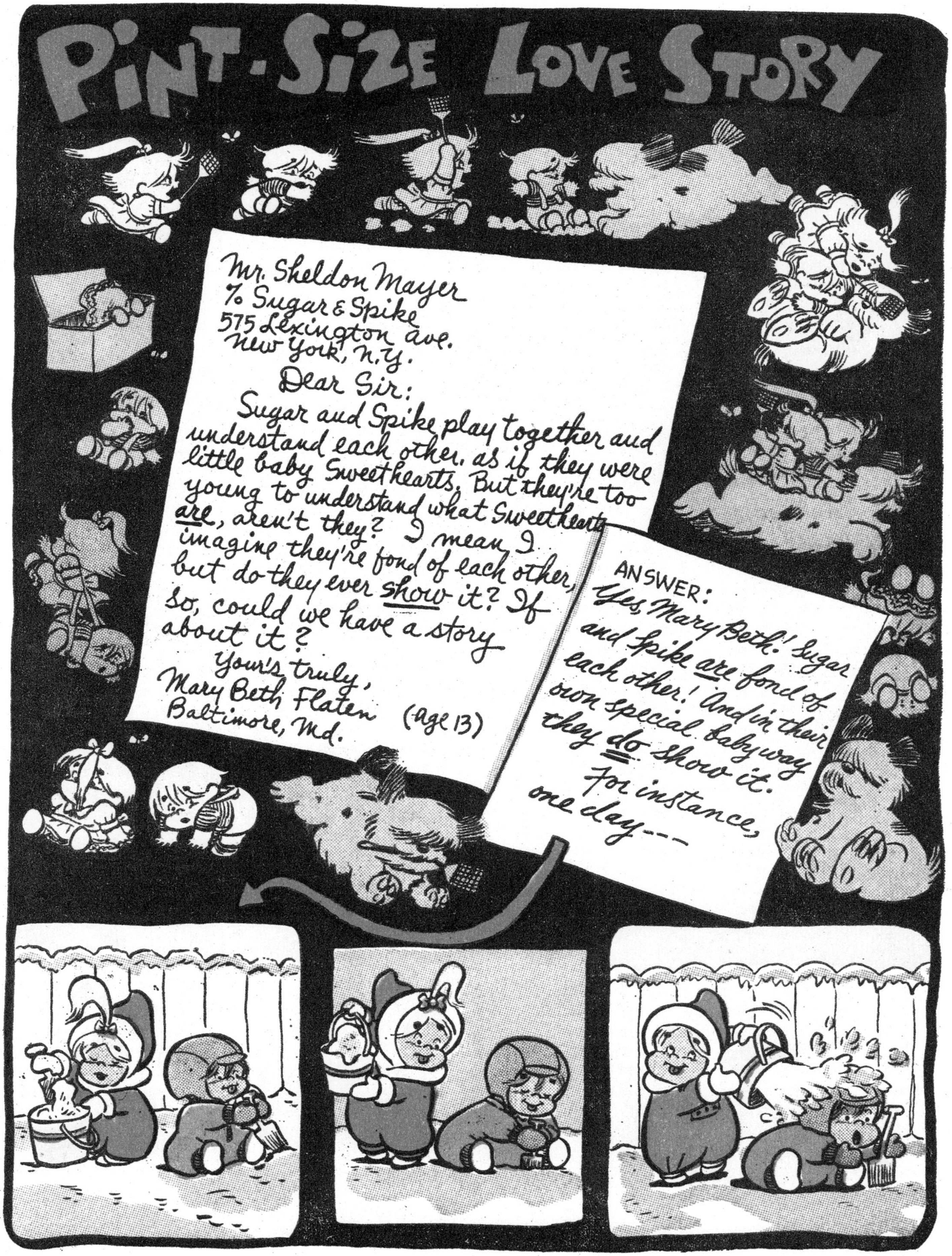
PINT-SIZE LOVE STORY
Mr. Sheldon Mayer
% Sugar & Spike
575 Lexington ave.
New York, N.Y.
Dear Sir:
Sugar and Spike play together and understand each other. as if they were little baby Sweethearts. But they're too young to understand what Sweethearts are, aren't they? I mean I imagine they're fond of each other, but do they ever show it? If so, could we have a story about it?
Your's truly,
Mary Beth Flaten (age 13)
Baltimore, Md.
ANSWER:
Yes, Mary Beth! Sugar and Spike are fond of each other! And in their own special baby way they do show it.
For instance, one day---

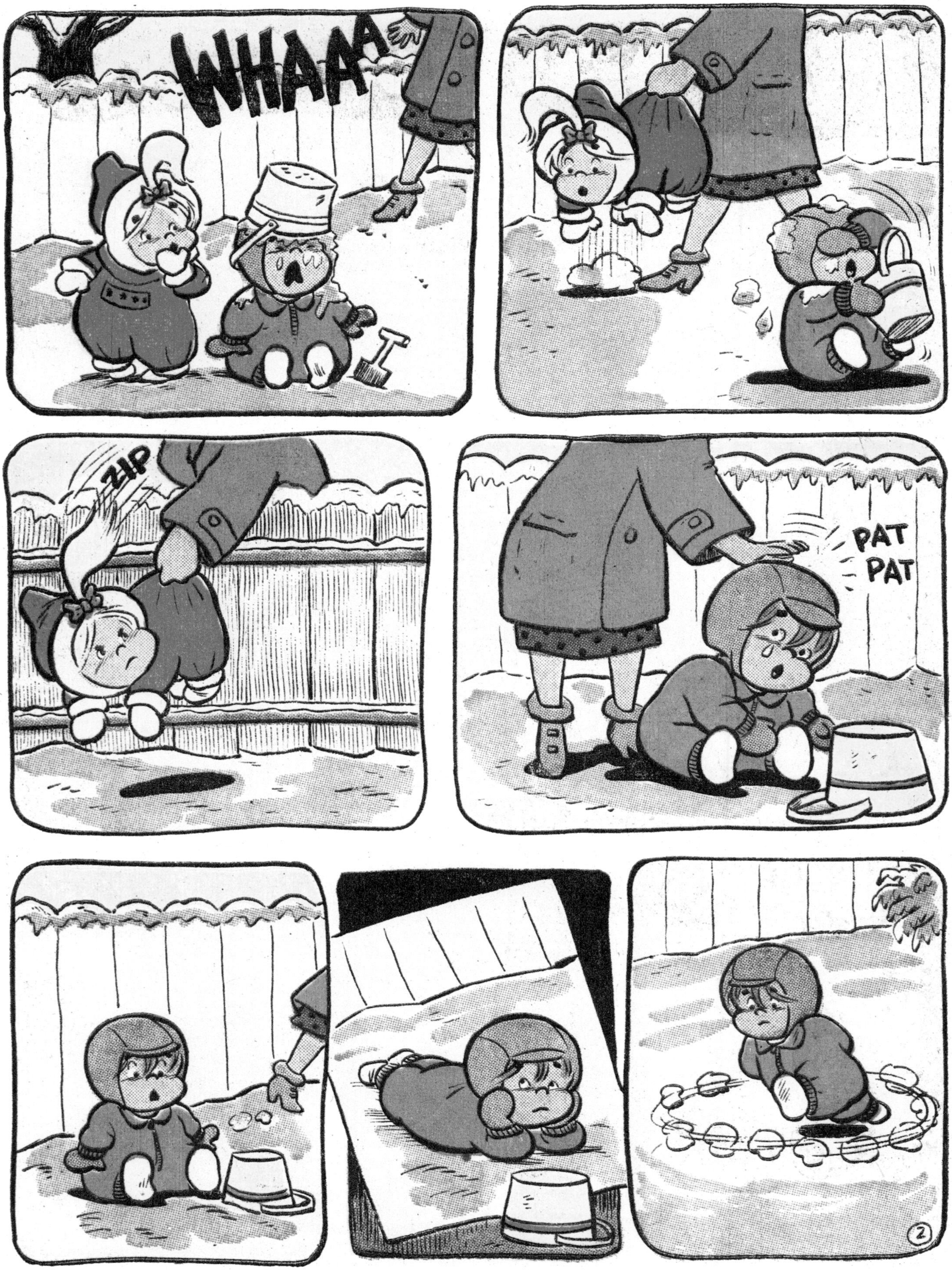
WHAAA
ZIP
PAT
PAT
2

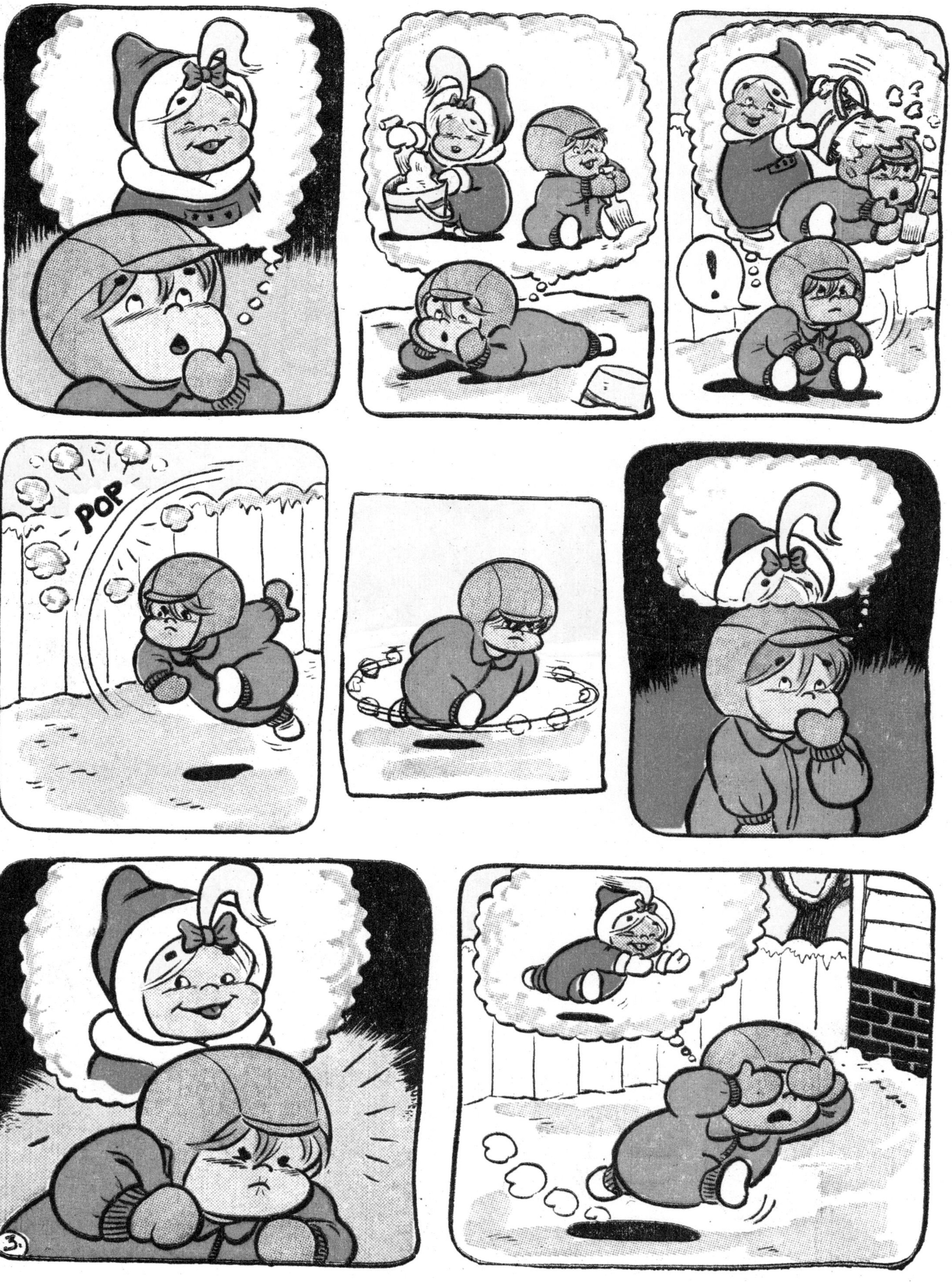
!
POP
3.

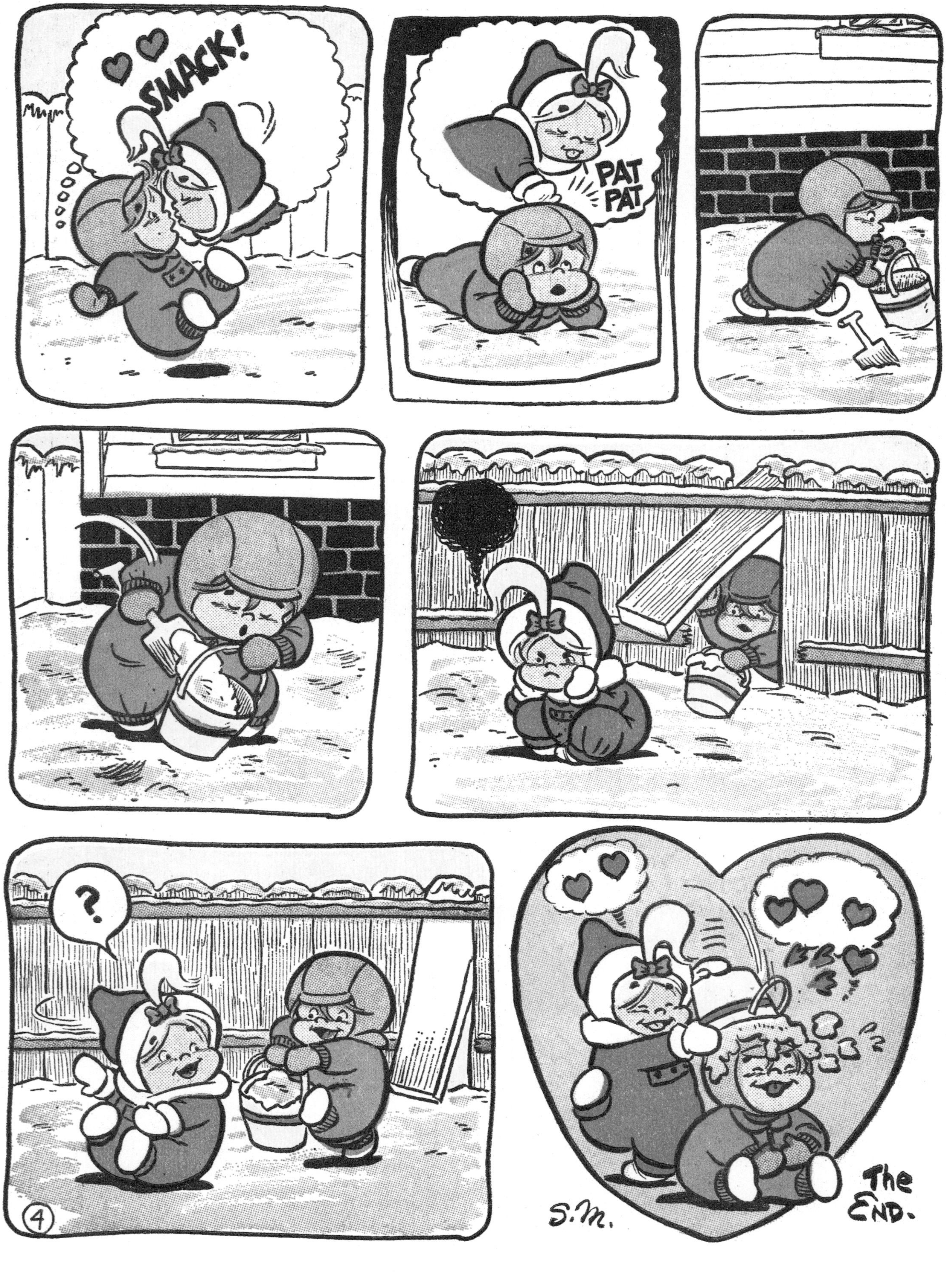
SMACK!
PAT PAT
?
4
S.M.
The END.

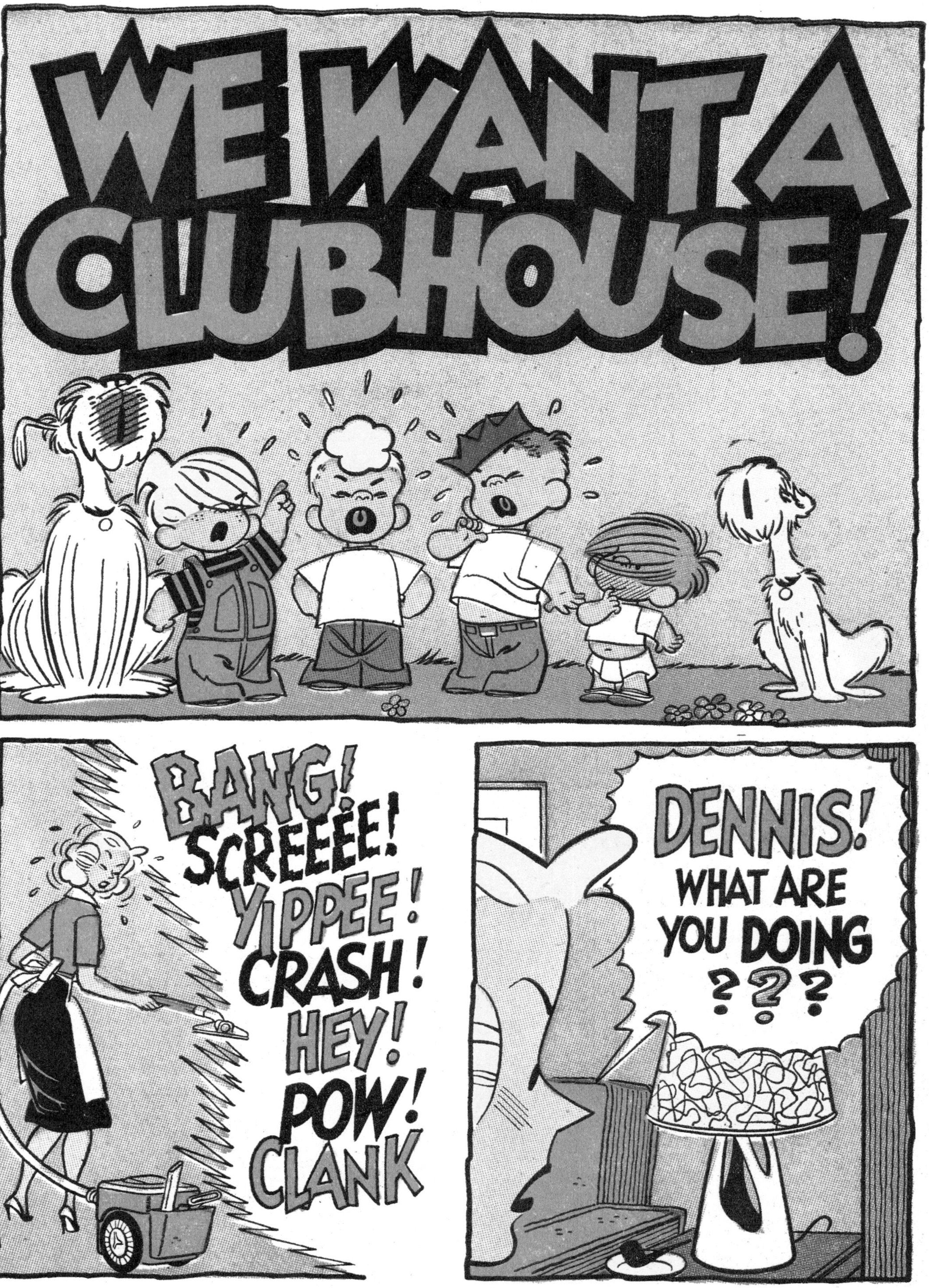
WE WANT A CLUBHOUSE!
BANG! SCREEEEE! YIPPEE! CRASH! HEY! POW! CLANK
DENNIS! WHAT ARE YOU DOING ???

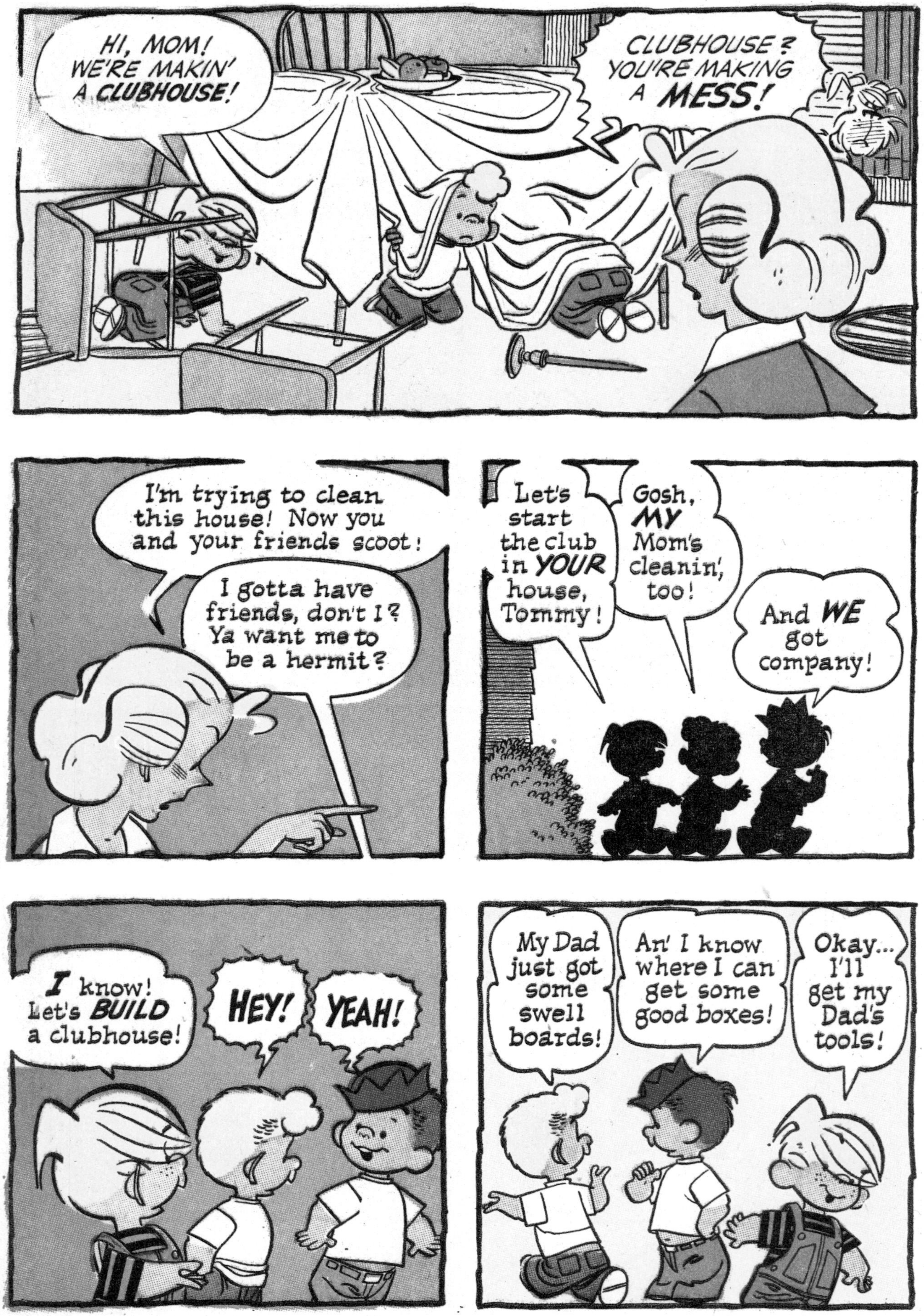
HI, MOM! WE'RE MAKIN' A CLUBHOUSE!
CLUBHOUSE? YOU'RE MAKING A MESS!
I'm trying to clean this house! Now you and your friends scoot!
I gotta have friends, don't I? Ya want me to be a hermit?
Let's start the club in YOUR house, Tommy!
Gosh, MY Mom's cleanin', too!
And WE got company!
I know! Let's BUILD a clubhouse!
HEY!
YEAH!
My Dad just got some swell boards!
An' I know where I can get some good boxes!
Okay... I'll get my Dad's tools!

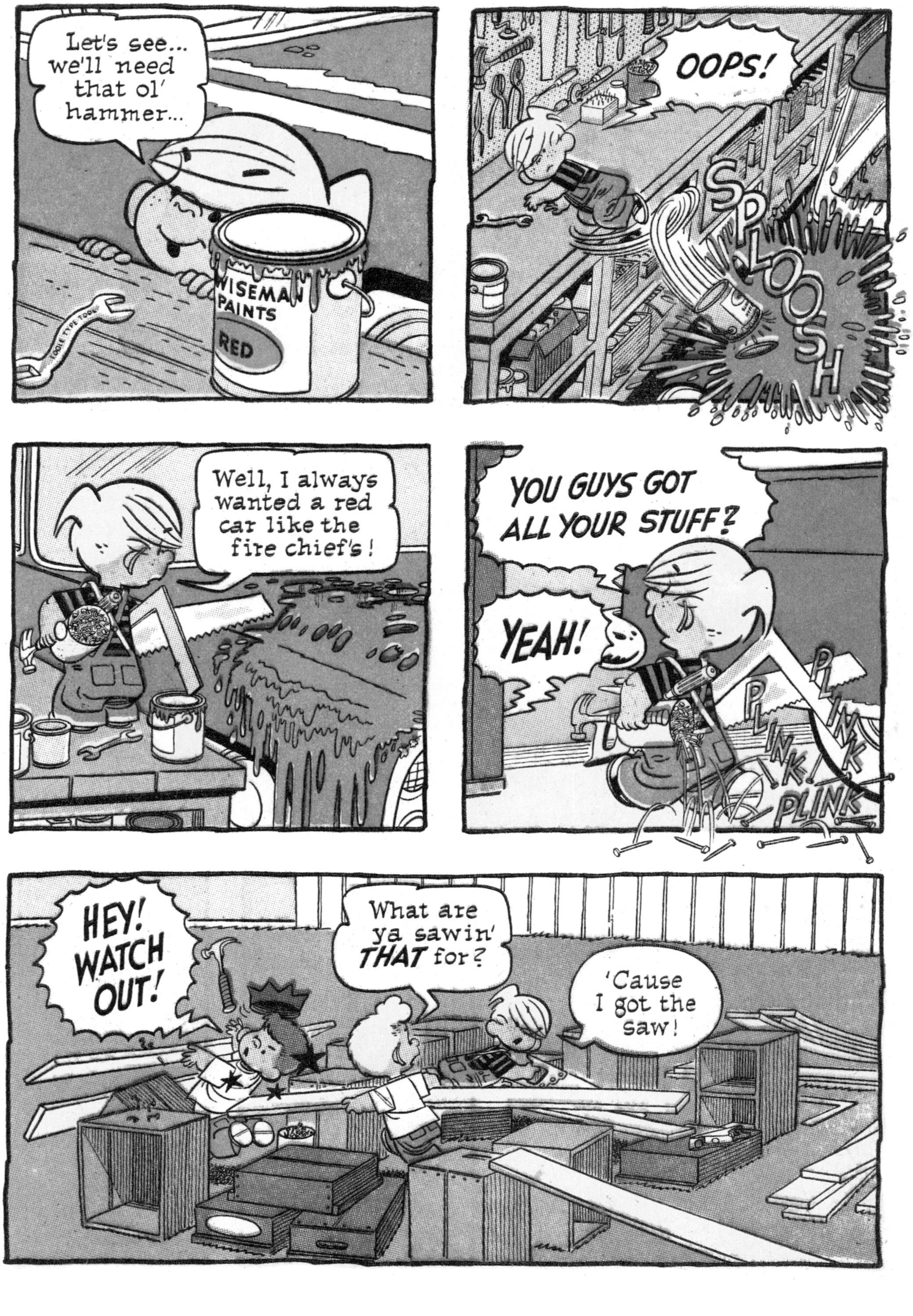
Let's see... we'll need that ol' hammer...
WISEMAN PAINTS RED
TOOLE TYPE TOOL
OOPS!
SPLOOSH
Well, I always wanted a red car like the fire chief's!
YOU GUYS GOT ALL YOUR STUFF?
YEAH!
PLINK
PLINK!
PLINK!
PLINK
HEY! WATCH OUT!
What are ya sawin' THAT for?
'Cause I got the saw!

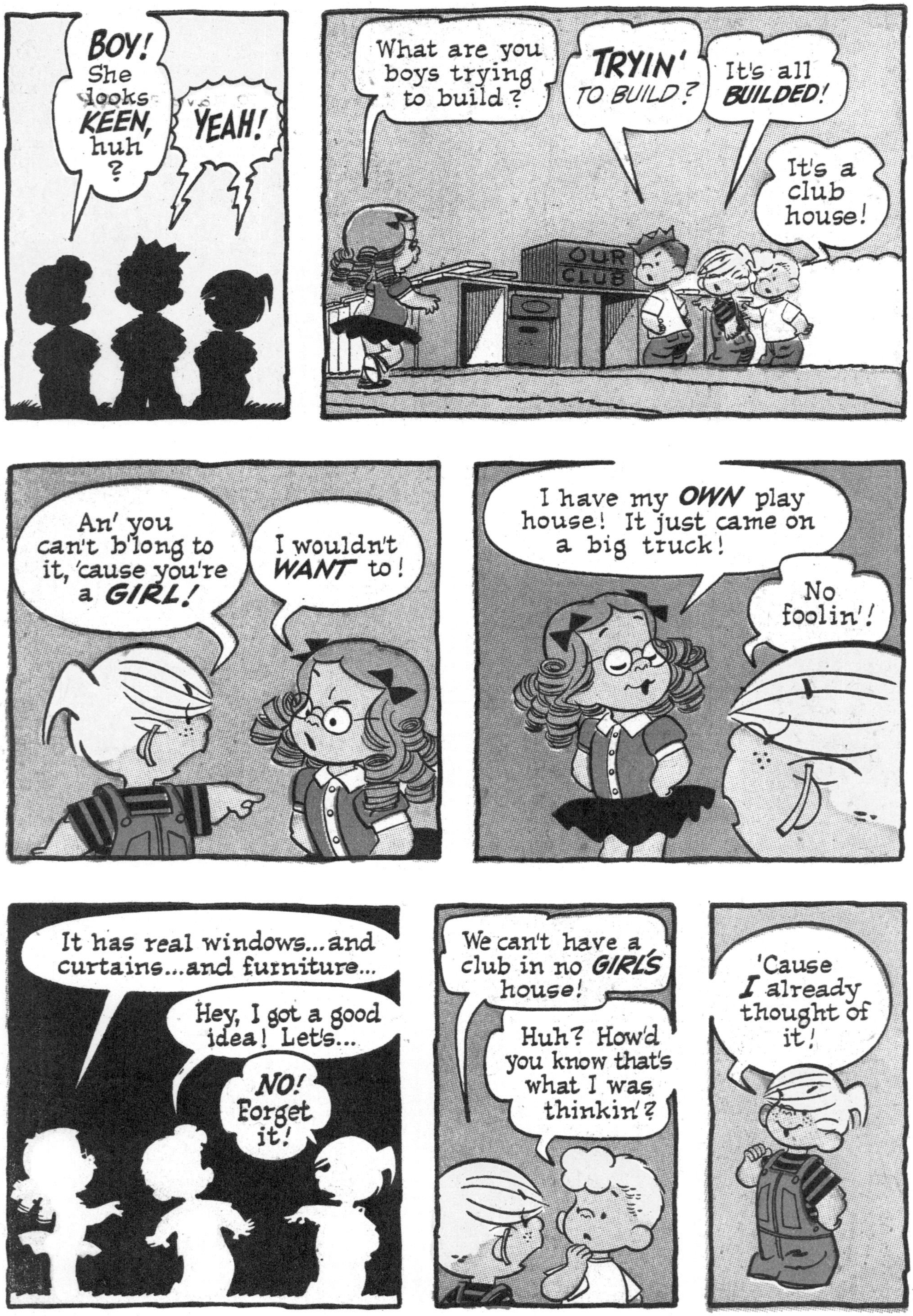
BOY! She looks KEEN, huh?
YEAH!
What are you boys trying to build?
TRYIN' TO BUILD?
It's all BUILDED!
It's a club house!
OUR CLUB
An' you can't b'long to it, 'cause you're a GIRL!
I wouldn't WANT to!
I have my OWN play house! It just came on a big truck!
No foolin'!
It has real windows...and curtains...and furniture...
Hey, I got a good idea! Let's...
NO! Forget it!
We can't have a club in no GIRL'S house!
Huh? How'd you know that's what I was thinkin'?
'Cause I already thought of it!

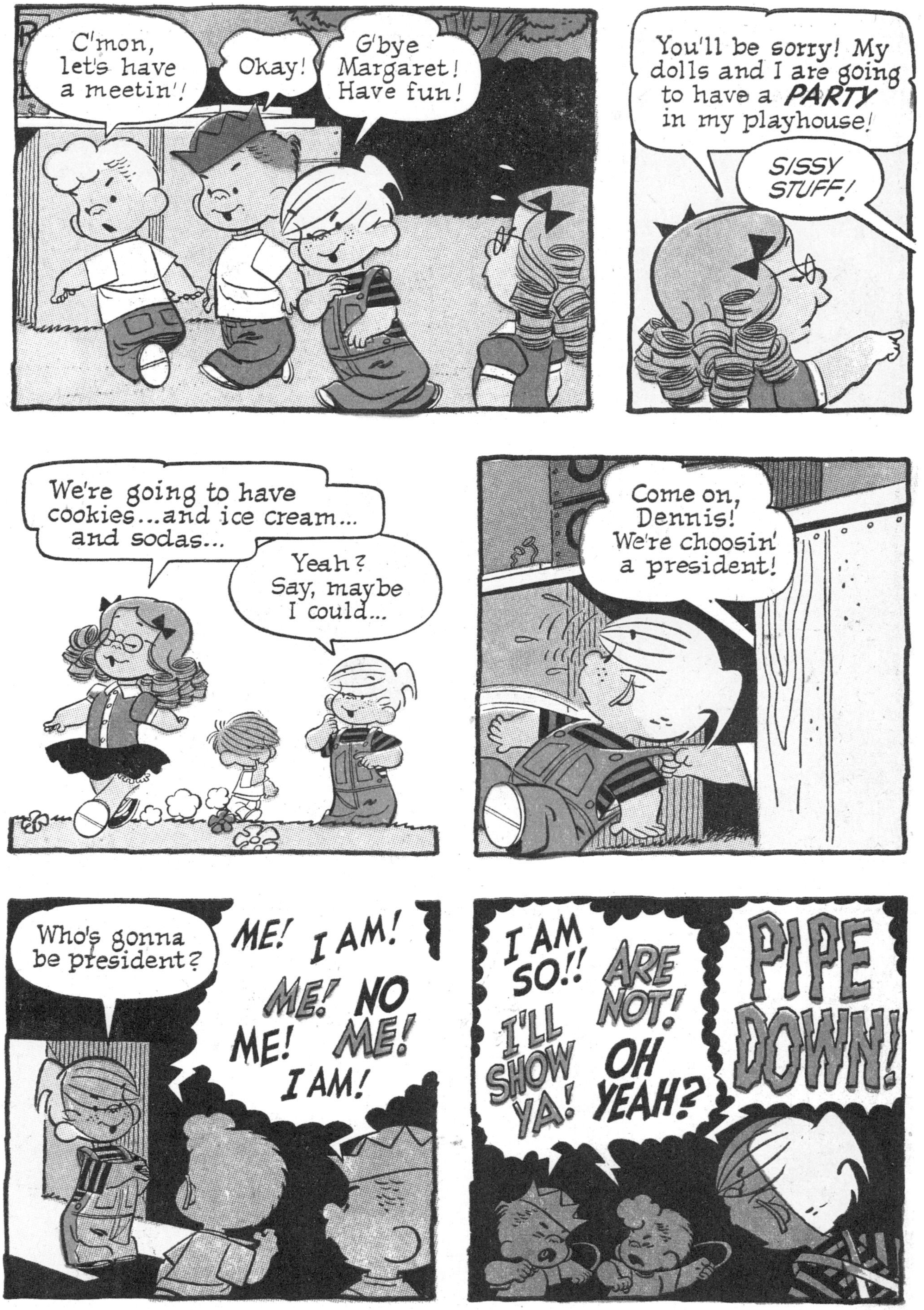
C'mon, let's have a meetin'!
Okay!
G'bye Margaret! Have fun!
You'll be sorry! My dolls and I are going to have a PARTY in my playhouse!
SISSY STUFF!
We're going to have cookies...and ice cream... and sodas...
Yeah? Say, maybe I could...
Come on, Dennis! We're choosin' a president!
Who's gonna be president?
ME! I AM!
ME! NO ME!
ME! I AM!
I AM SO!!
ARE NOT!
I'LL SHOW YA!
OH YEAH?
PIPE DOWN!

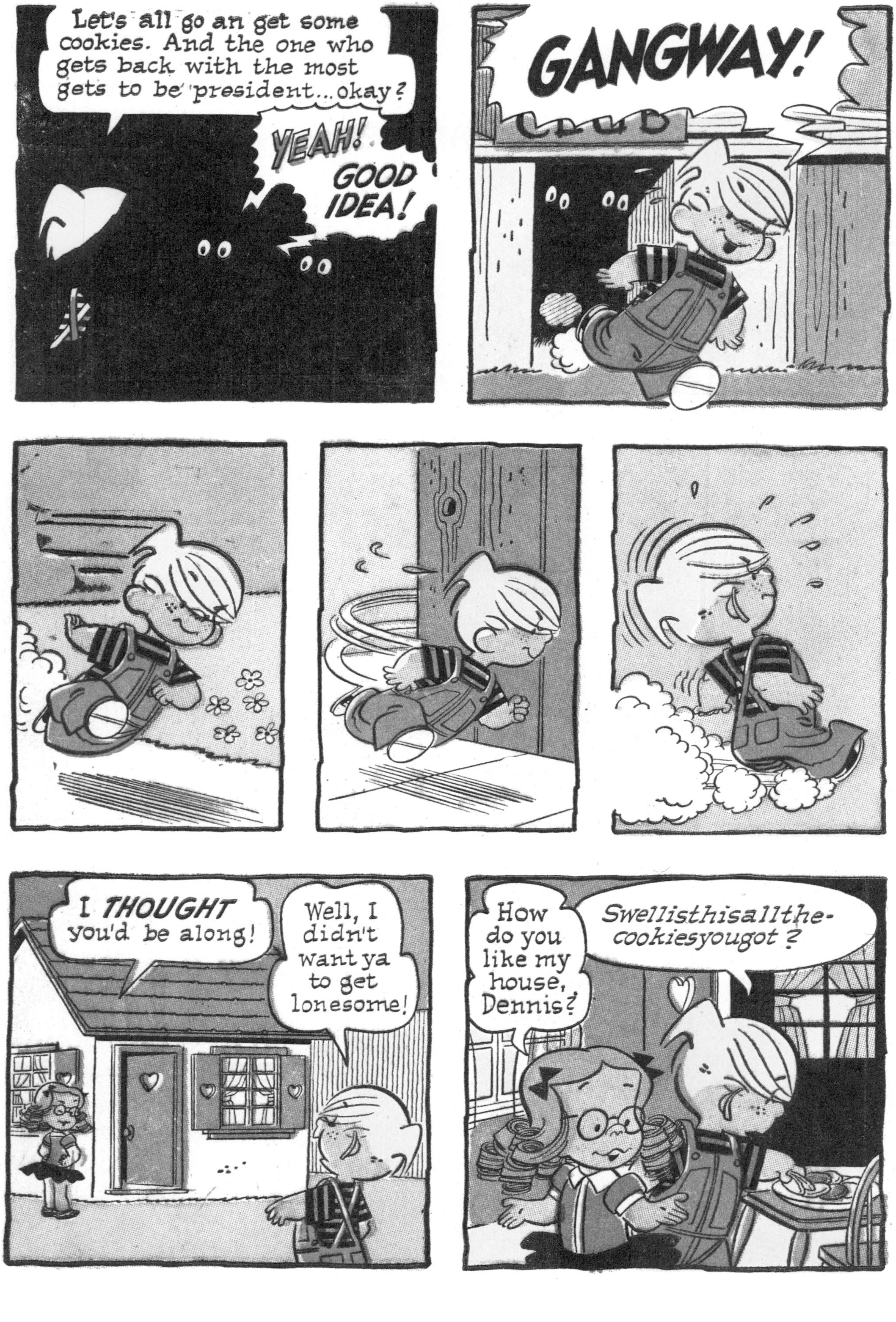
Let's all go an get some cookies. And the one who gets back with the most gets to be president...okay?
YEAH!
GOOD IDEA!
GANGWAY!
CLUB
I THOUGHT you'd be along!
Well, I didn't want ya to get lonesome!
How do you like my house, Dennis?
Swellisthisallthe-
cookiesyougot?

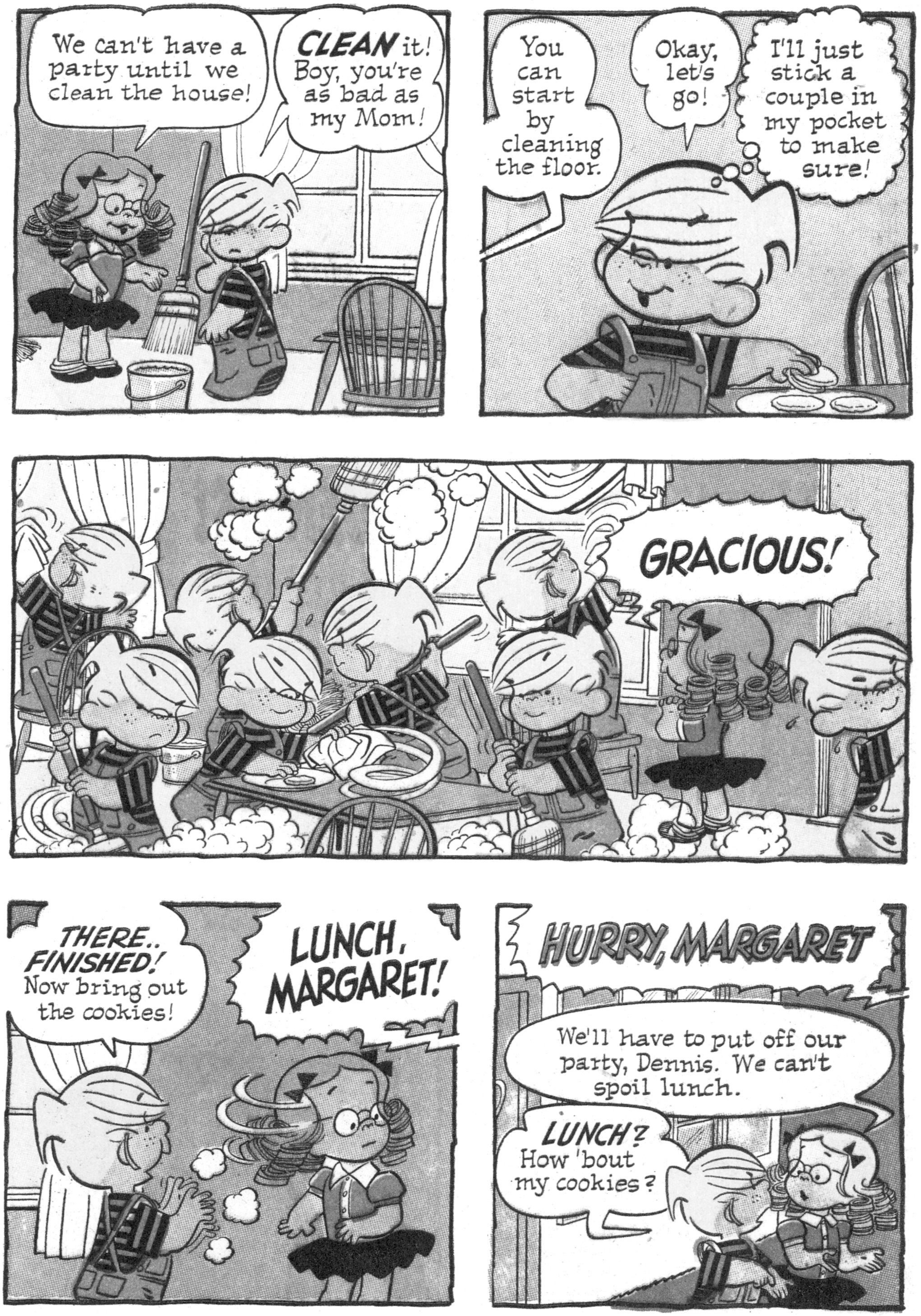
We can't have a party until we clean the house!
CLEAN it! Boy, you're as bad as my Mom!
You can start by cleaning the floor.
Okay, let's go!
I'll just stick a couple in my pocket to make sure!
GRACIOUS!
THERE.. FINISHED! Now bring out the cookies!
LUNCH, MARGARET!
HURRY, MARGARET
We'll have to put off our party, Dennis. We can't spoil lunch.
LUNCH? How 'bout my cookies?

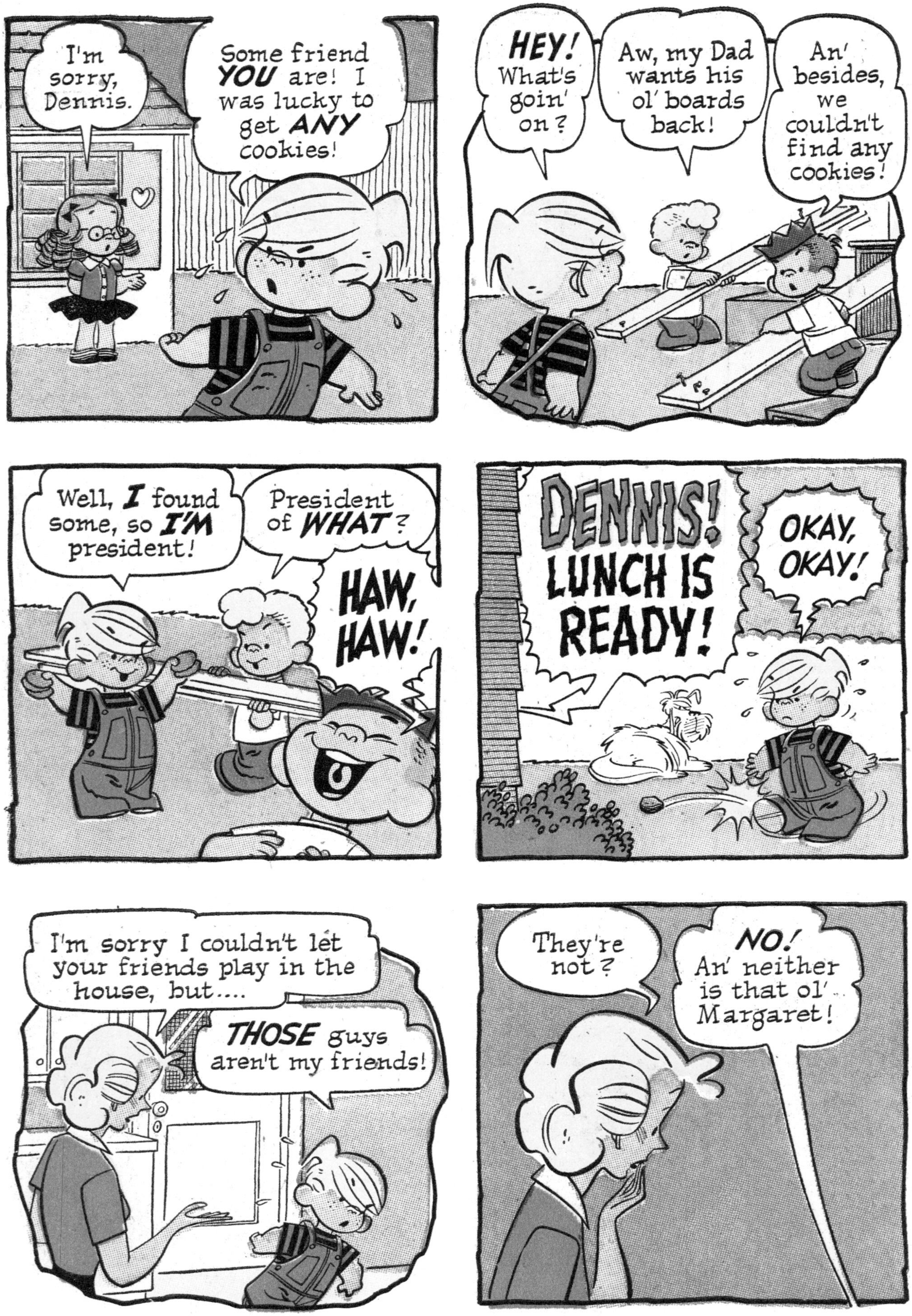
I'm sorry, Dennis.
Some friend YOU are! I was lucky to get ANY cookies!
HEY! What's goin' on?
Aw, my Dad wants his ol' boards back!
An' besides, we couldn't find any cookies!
Well, I found some, so I'M president!
President of WHAT?
HAW, HAW!
DENNIS! LUNCH IS READY!
OKAY, OKAY!
I'm sorry I couldn't let your friends play in the house, but....
THOSE guys aren't my friends!
They're not?
NO! An' neither is that ol' Margaret!

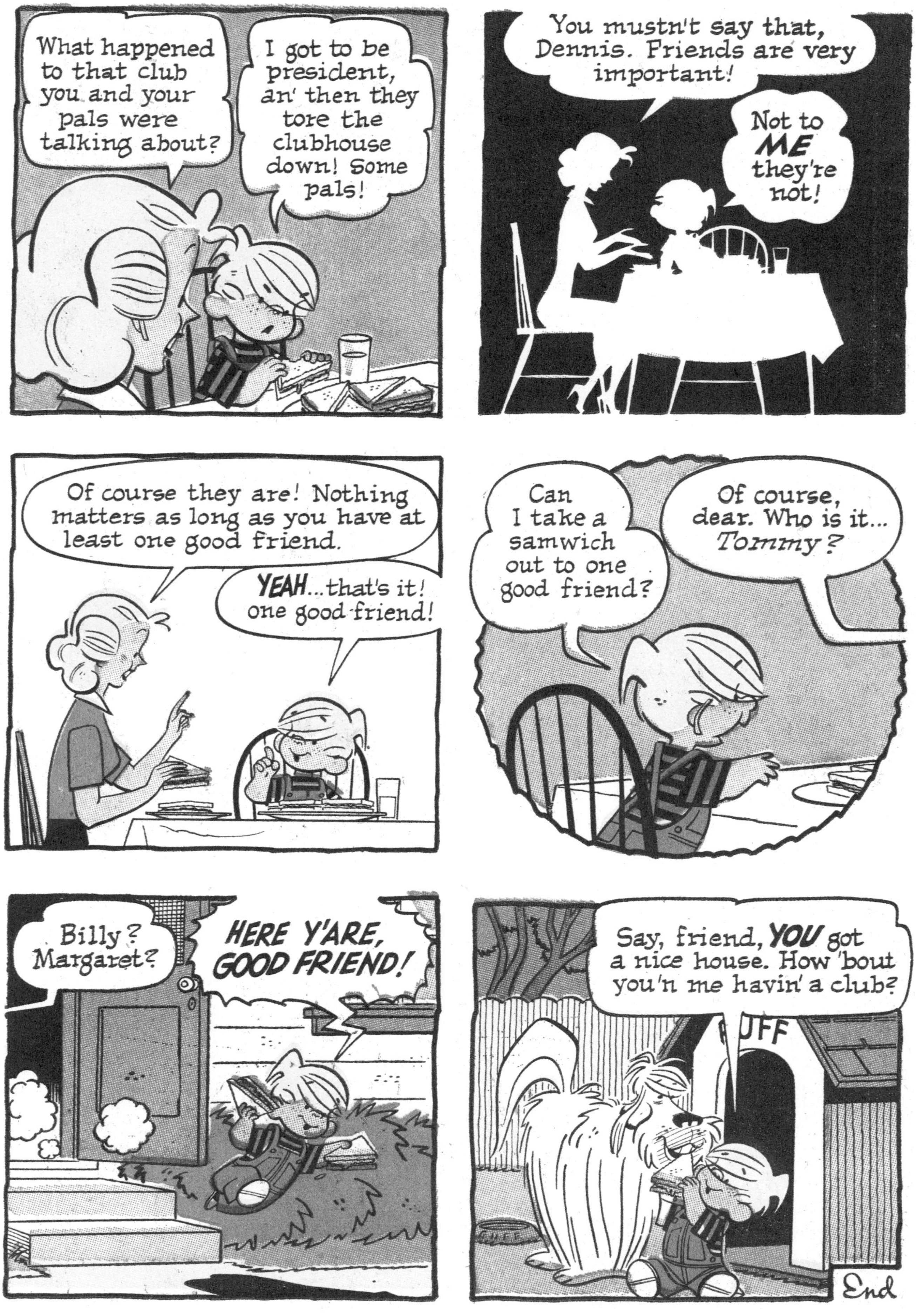
What happened to that club you and your pals were talking about?
I got to be president, an' then they tore the clubhouse down! Some pals!
You mustn't say that, Dennis. Friends are very important!
Not to ME they're not!
Of course they are! Nothing matters as long as you have at least one good friend.
YEAH...that's it! one good friend!
Can I take a samwich out to one good friend?
Of course, dear. Who is it... Tommy?
Billy? Margaret?
HERE Y'ARE, GOOD FRIEND!
Say, friend, YOU got a nice house. How 'bout you'n me havin' a club?
RUFF
End

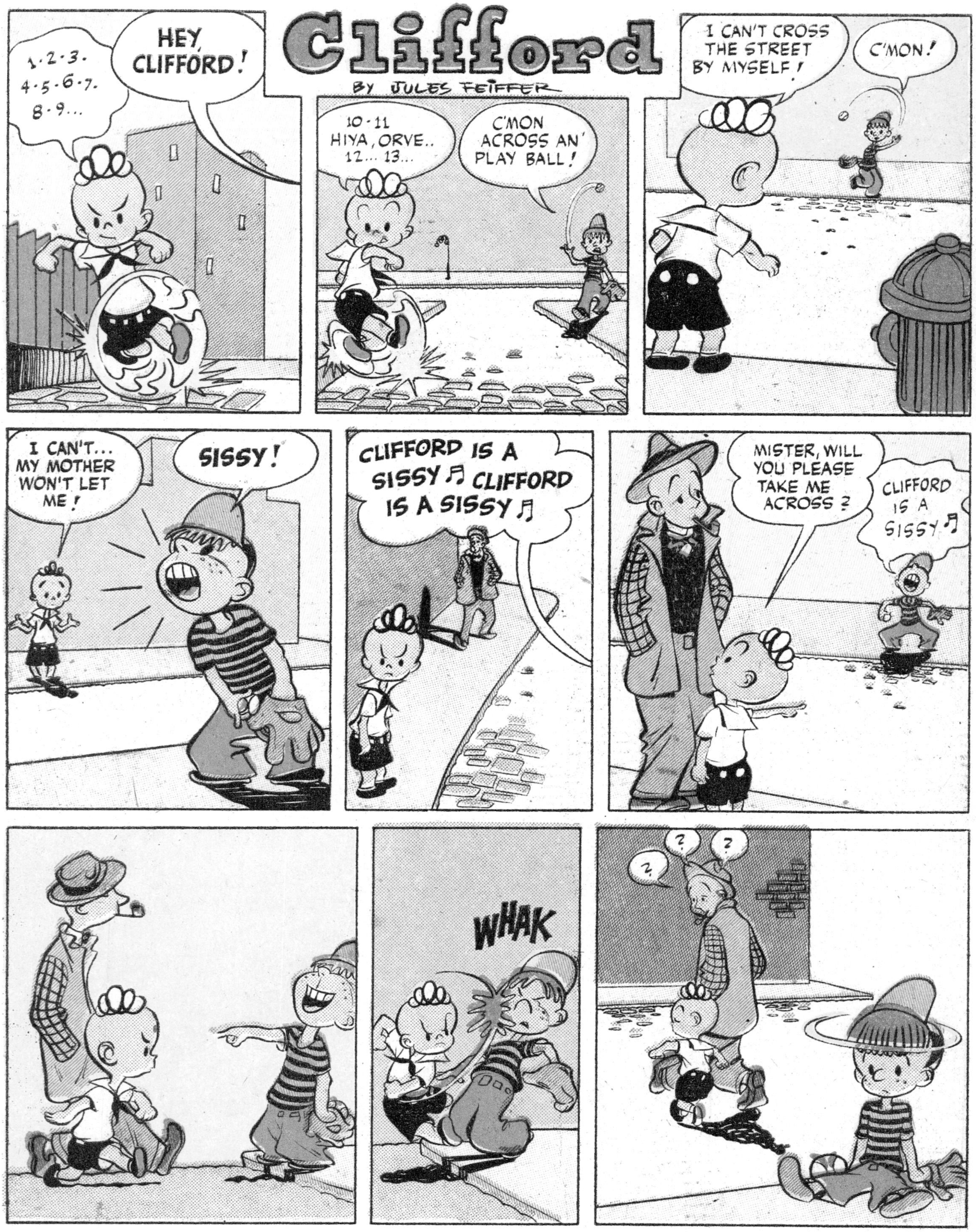
Clifford
BY JULES FEIFFER
1·2·3· 4·5·6·7· 8·9...
HEY, CLIFFORD!
10·11 HIYA, ORVE.. 12... 13...
C'MON ACROSS AN' PLAY BALL!
I CAN'T CROSS THE STREET BY MYSELF!
C'MON!
I CAN'T... MY MOTHER WON'T LET ME!
SISSY!
CLIFFORD IS A SISSY ♫ CLIFFORD IS A SISSY ♫
MISTER, WILL YOU PLEASE TAKE ME ACROSS ?
CLIFFORD IS A SISSY ♫
WHAK
?
?
?

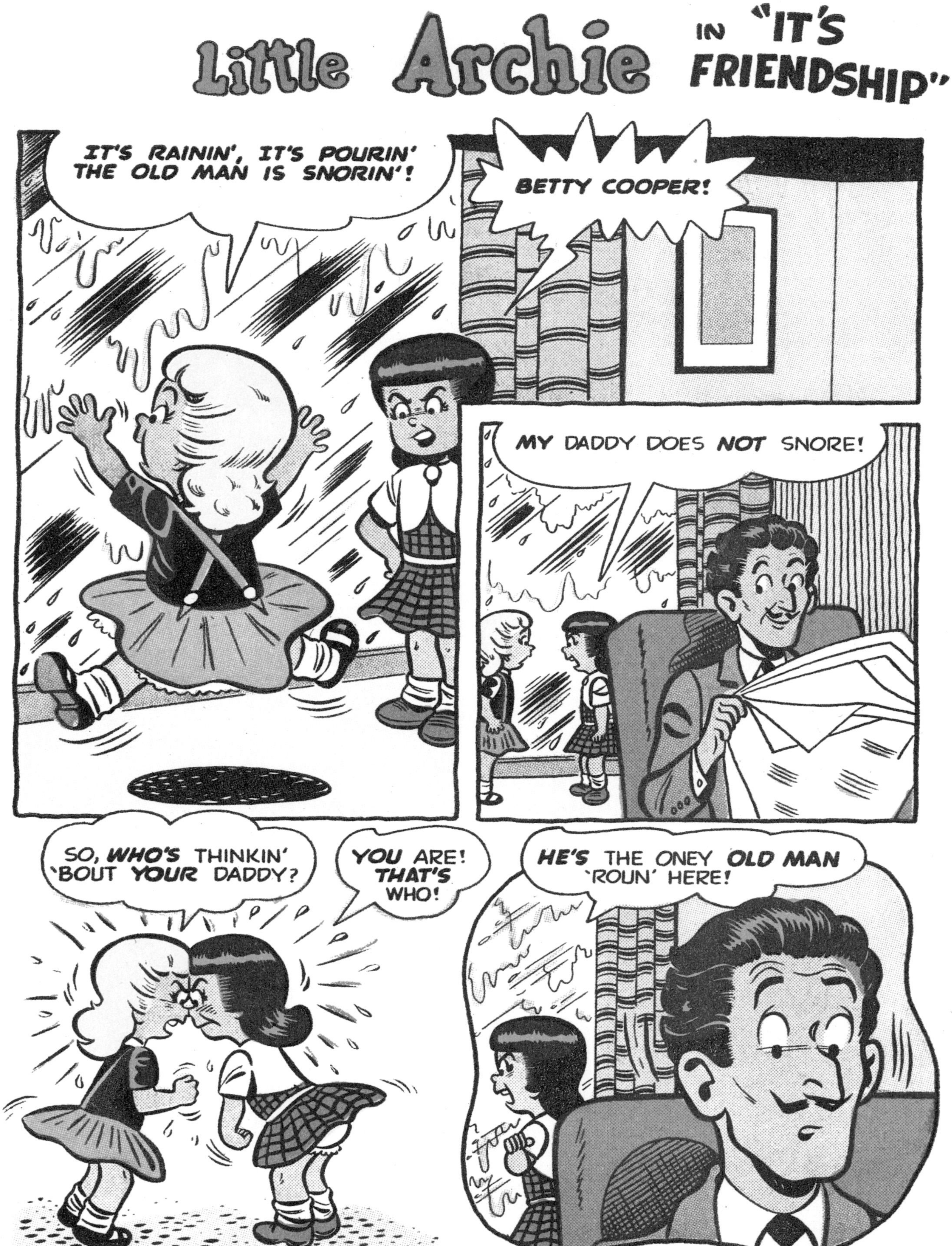
Little Archie IN "IT'S FRIENDSHIP"
IT'S RAININ', IT'S POURIN' THE OLD MAN IS SNORIN'!
BETTY COOPER!
MY DADDY DOES NOT SNORE!
SO, WHO'S THINKIN' 'BOUT YOUR DADDY?
YOU ARE! THAT'S WHO!
HE'S THE ONEY OLD MAN 'ROUN' HERE!

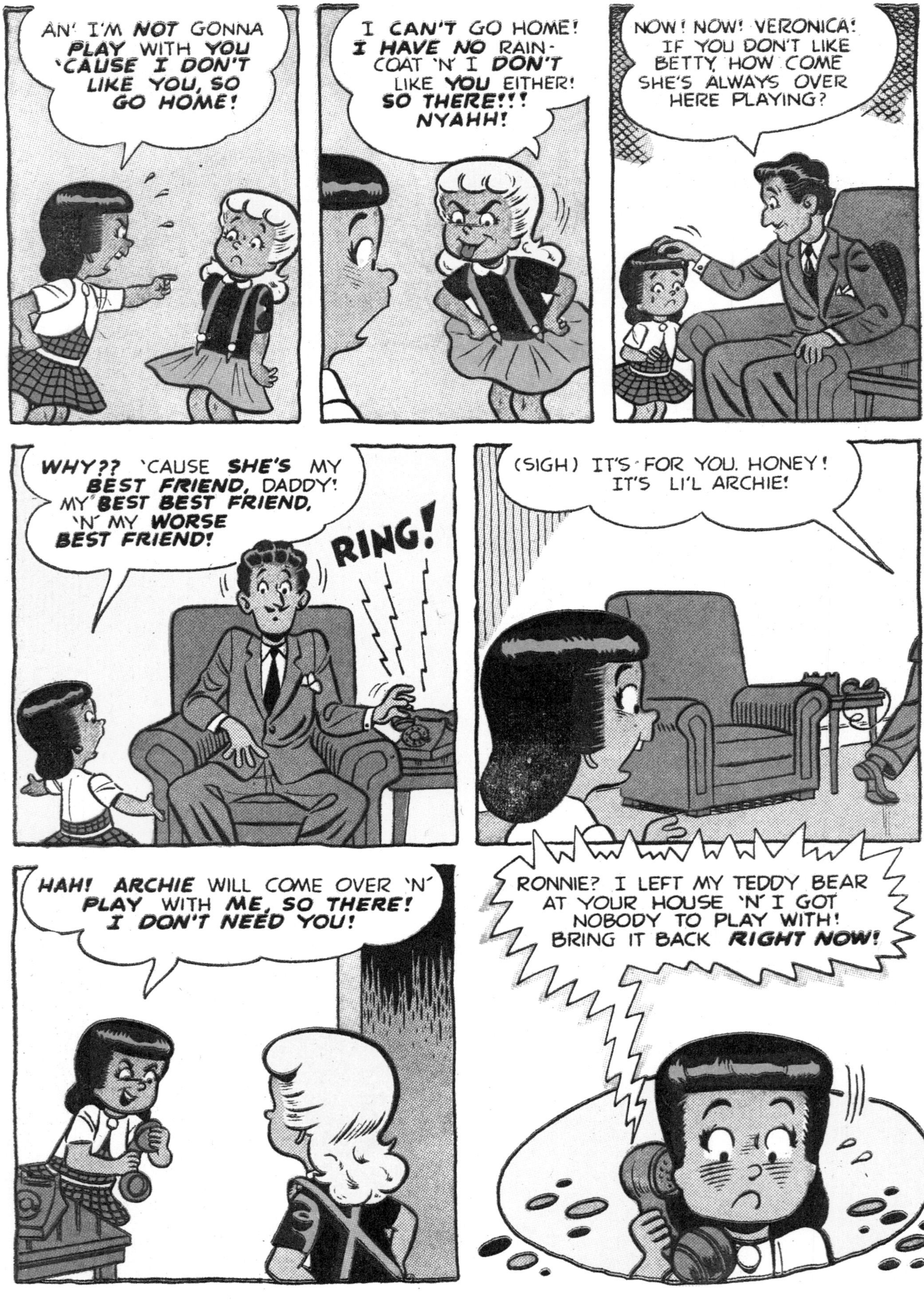
AN' I'M NOT GONNA PLAY WITH YOU 'CAUSE I DON'T LIKE YOU, SO GO HOME!
I CAN'T GO HOME! I HAVE NO RAIN-COAT 'N' I DON'T LIKE YOU EITHER! SO THERE!!! NYAHH!
NOW! NOW! VERONICA! IF YOU DON'T LIKE BETTY, HOW COME SHE'S ALWAYS OVER HERE PLAYING?
WHY?? 'CAUSE SHE'S MY BEST FRIEND, DADDY! MY BEST BEST FRIEND, 'N' MY WORSE BEST FRIEND!
RING!
(SIGH) IT'S FOR YOU, HONEY! IT'S LI'L ARCHIE!
HAH! ARCHIE WILL COME OVER 'N' PLAY WITH ME, SO THERE! I DON'T NEED YOU!
RONNIE? I LEFT MY TEDDY BEAR AT YOUR HOUSE 'N' I GOT NOBODY TO PLAY WITH! BRING IT BACK RIGHT NOW!

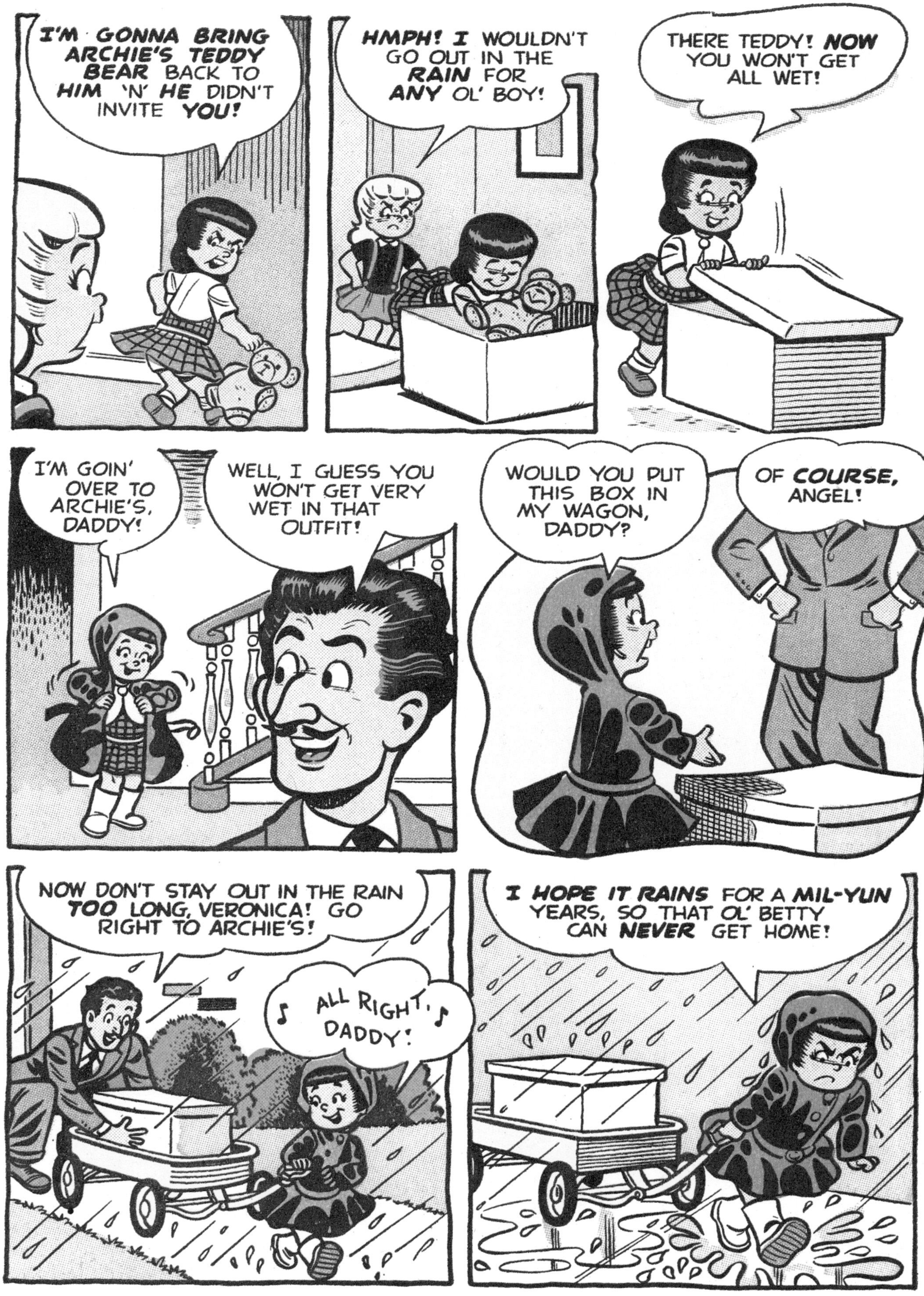
I'M GONNA BRING ARCHIE'S TEDDY BEAR BACK TO HIM 'N' HE DIDN'T INVITE YOU!
HMPH! I WOULDN'T GO OUT IN THE RAIN FOR ANY OL' BOY!
THERE TEDDY! NOW YOU WON'T GET ALL WET!
I'M GOIN' OVER TO ARCHIE'S, DADDY!
WELL, I GUESS YOU WON'T GET VERY WET IN THAT OUTFIT!
WOULD YOU PUT THIS BOX IN MY WAGON, DADDY?
OF COURSE, ANGEL!
NOW DON'T STAY OUT IN THE RAIN TOO LONG, VERONICA! GO RIGHT TO ARCHIE'S!
ALL RIGHT, DADDY!
I HOPE IT RAINS FOR A MIL-YUN YEARS, SO THAT OL' BETTY CAN NEVER GET HOME!

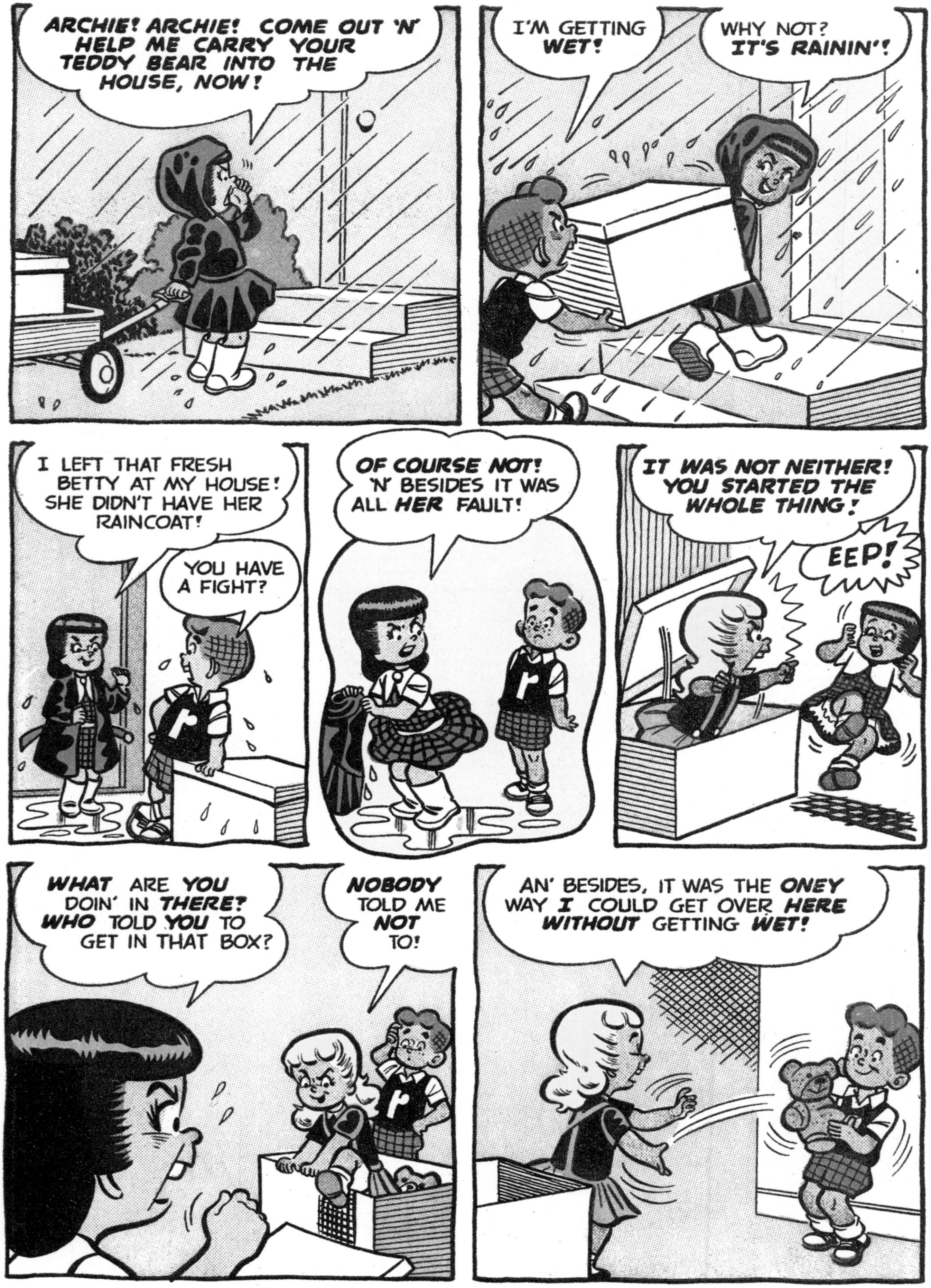
ARCHIE! ARCHIE! COME OUT 'N' HELP ME CARRY YOUR TEDDY BEAR INTO THE HOUSE, NOW!
I'M GETTING WET!
WHY NOT? IT'S RAININ'!
I LEFT THAT FRESH BETTY AT MY HOUSE! SHE DIDN'T HAVE HER RAINCOAT!
YOU HAVE A FIGHT?
OF COURSE NOT! 'N' BESIDES IT WAS ALL HER FAULT!
IT WAS NOT NEITHER! YOU STARTED THE WHOLE THING!
EEP!
WHAT ARE YOU DOIN' IN THERE? WHO TOLD YOU TO GET IN THAT BOX?
NOBODY TOLD ME NOT TO!
AN' BESIDES, IT WAS THE ONEY WAY I COULD GET OVER HERE WITHOUT GETTING WET!

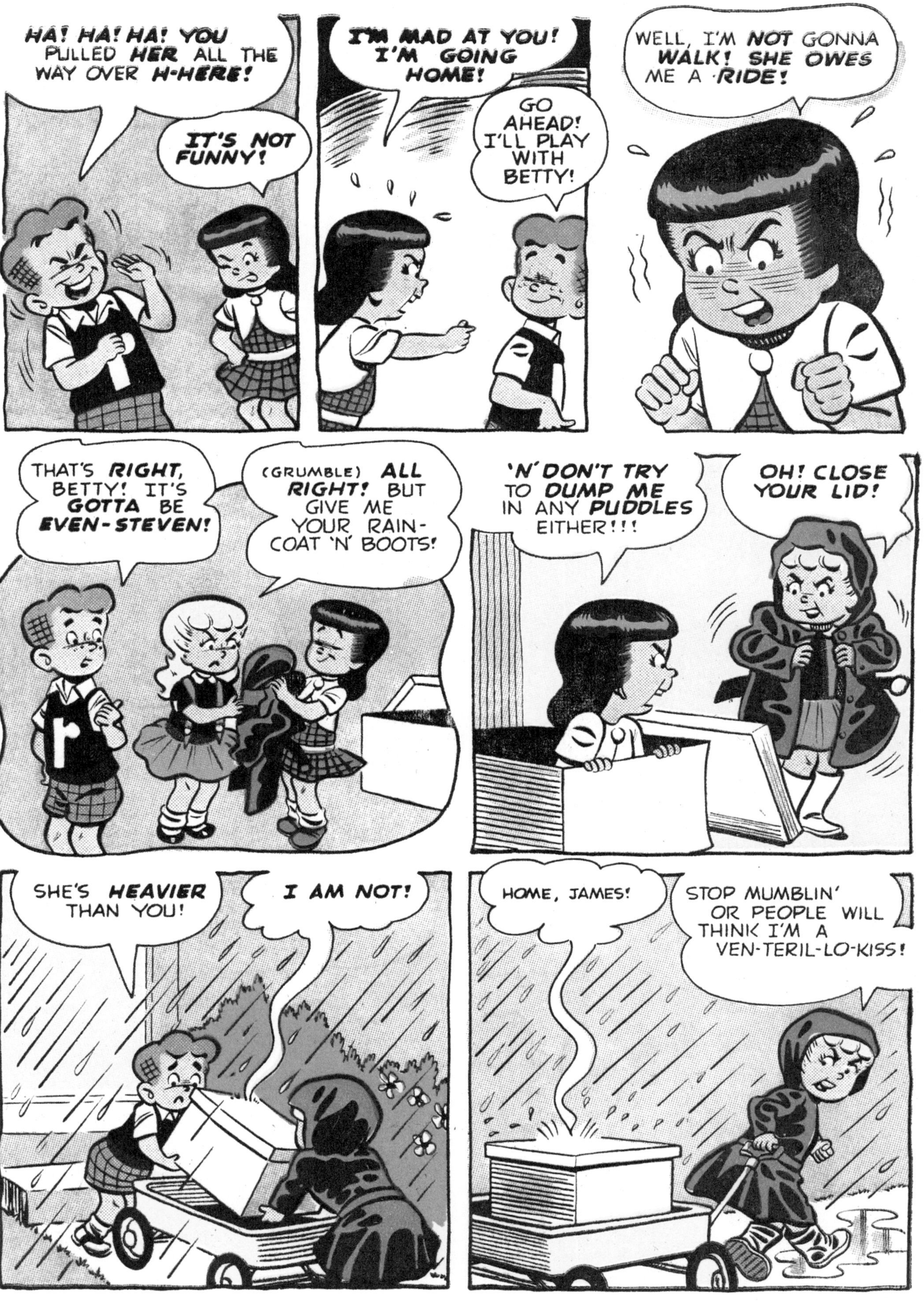
HA! HA! HA! YOU PULLED HER ALL THE WAY OVER H-HERE!
IT'S NOT FUNNY!
I'M MAD AT YOU! I'M GOING HOME!
GO AHEAD! I'LL PLAY WITH BETTY!
WELL, I'M NOT GONNA WALK! SHE OWES ME A RIDE!
THAT'S RIGHT, BETTY! IT'S GOTTA BE EVEN-STEVEN!
(GRUMBLE) ALL RIGHT! BUT GIVE ME YOUR RAIN-COAT 'N' BOOTS!
'N' DON'T TRY TO DUMP ME IN ANY PUDDLES EITHER!!!
OH! CLOSE YOUR LID!
SHE'S HEAVIER THAN YOU!
I AM NOT!
HOME, JAMES!
STOP MUMBLIN' OR PEOPLE WILL THINK I'M A VEN-TERIL-LO-KISS!

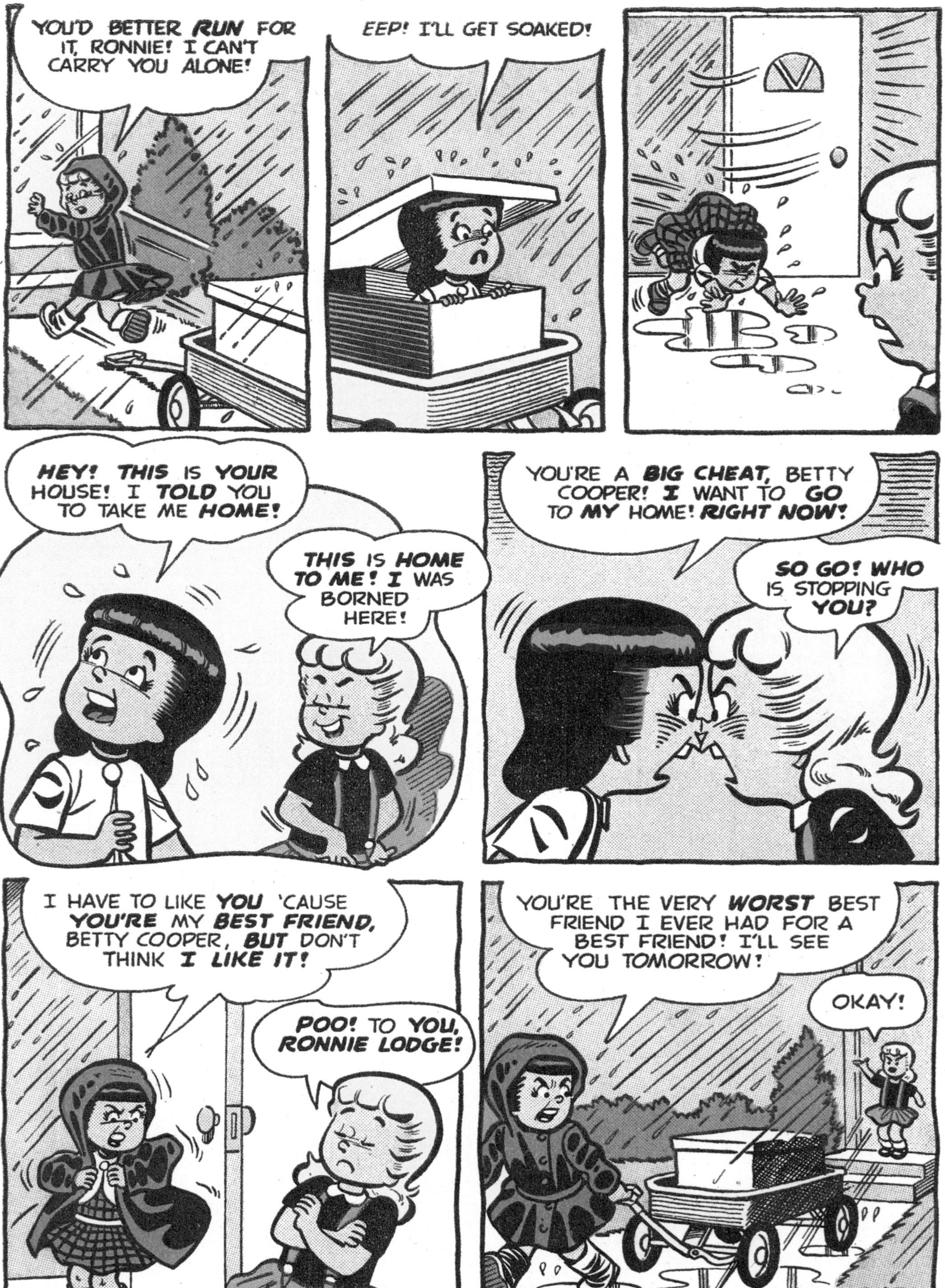
YOU'D BETTER RUN FOR IT, RONNIE! I CAN'T CARRY YOU ALONE!
EEP! I'LL GET SOAKED!
HEY! THIS IS YOUR HOUSE! I TOLD YOU TO TAKE ME HOME!
THIS IS HOME TO ME! I WAS BORNED HERE!
YOU'RE A BIG CHEAT, BETTY COOPER! I WANT TO GO TO MY HOME! RIGHT NOW!
SO GO! WHO IS STOPPING YOU?
I HAVE TO LIKE YOU 'CAUSE YOU'RE MY BEST FRIEND, BETTY COOPER, BUT DON'T THINK I LIKE IT!
POO! TO YOU, RONNIE LODGE!
YOU'RE THE VERY WORST BEST FRIEND I EVER HAD FOR A BEST FRIEND! I'LL SEE YOU TOMORROW!
OKAY!
THE END

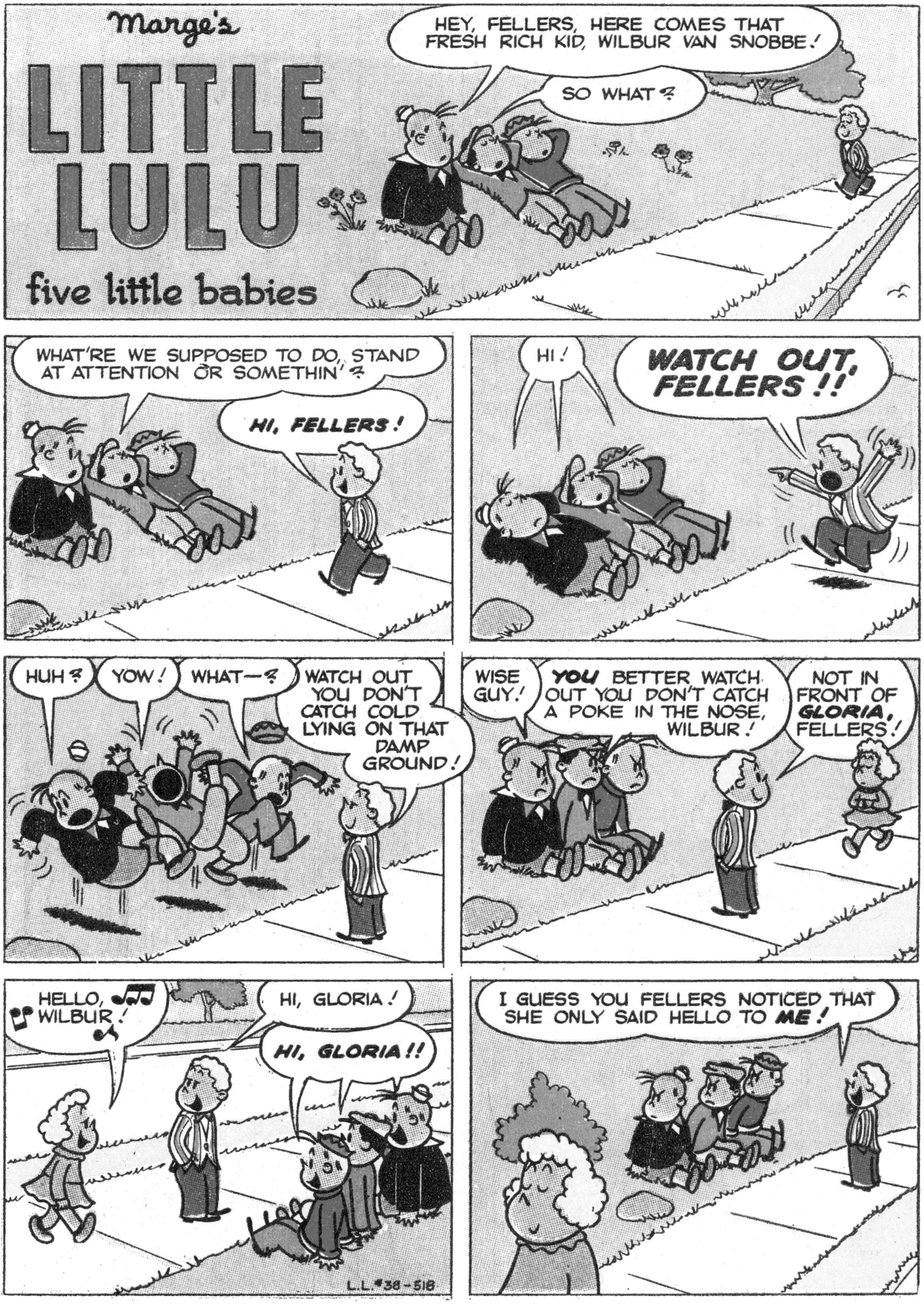
Marge's
LITTLE LULU
five little babies
HEY, FELLERS, HERE COMES THAT FRESH RICH KID, WILBUR VAN SNOBBE!
SO WHAT?
WHAT'RE WE SUPPOSED TO DO, STAND AT ATTENTION OR SOMETHIN'?
HI, FELLERS!
HI!
WATCH OUT, FELLERS!!
HUH?
YOW!
WHAT—?
WATCH OUT YOU DON'T CATCH COLD LYING ON THAT DAMP GROUND!
WISE GUY!
YOU BETTER WATCH OUT YOU DON'T CATCH A POKE IN THE NOSE, WILBUR!
NOT IN FRONT OF GLORIA, FELLERS!
HELLO, WILBUR!
HI, GLORIA!
HI, GLORIA!!
L.L. #38-518
I GUESS YOU FELLERS NOTICED THAT SHE ONLY SAID HELLO TO ME!

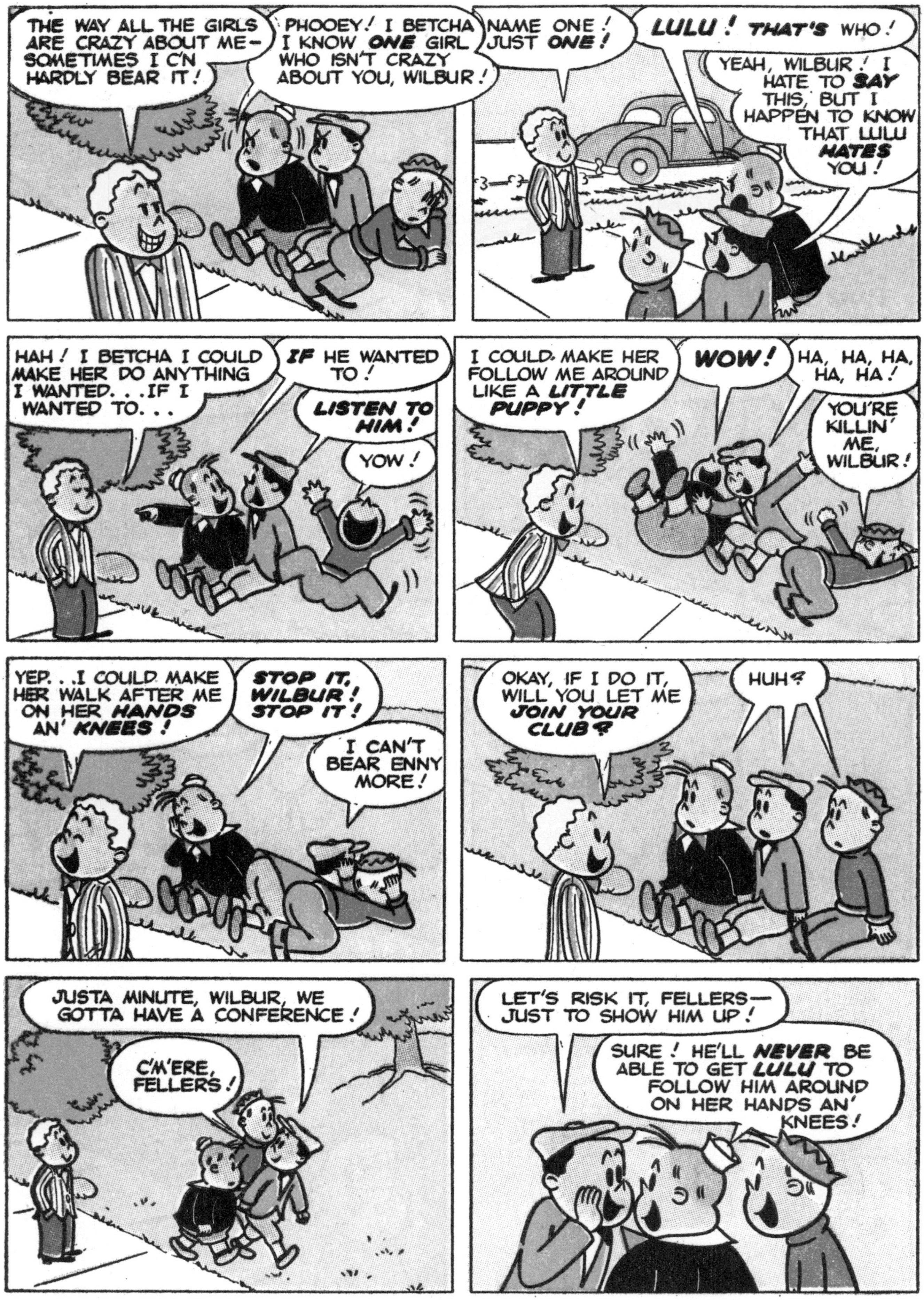
THE WAY ALL THE GIRLS ARE CRAZY ABOUT ME— SOMETIMES I C'N HARDLY BEAR IT!
PHOOEY! I BETCHA I KNOW ONE GIRL WHO ISN'T CRAZY ABOUT YOU, WILBUR!
NAME ONE! JUST ONE!
LULU! THAT'S WHO!
YEAH, WILBUR! I HATE TO SAY THIS, BUT I HAPPEN TO KNOW THAT LULU HATES YOU!
HAH! I BETCHA I COULD MAKE HER DO ANYTHING I WANTED. . .IF I WANTED TO. . .
IF HE WANTED TO!
LISTEN TO HIM!
YOW!
I COULD MAKE HER FOLLOW ME AROUND LIKE A LITTLE PUPPY!
WOW!
HA, HA, HA, HA, HA!
YOU'RE KILLIN' ME, WILBUR!
YEP. . .I COULD MAKE HER WALK AFTER ME ON HER HANDS AN' KNEES!
STOP IT, WILBUR! STOP IT!
I CAN'T BEAR ENNY MORE!
OKAY, IF I DO IT, WILL YOU LET ME JOIN YOUR CLUB?
HUH?
JUSTA MINUTE, WILBUR, WE GOTTA HAVE A CONFERENCE!
C'M'ERE, FELLERS!
LET'S RISK IT, FELLERS— JUST TO SHOW HIM UP!
SURE! HE'LL NEVER BE ABLE TO GET LULU TO FOLLOW HIM AROUND ON HER HANDS AN' KNEES!

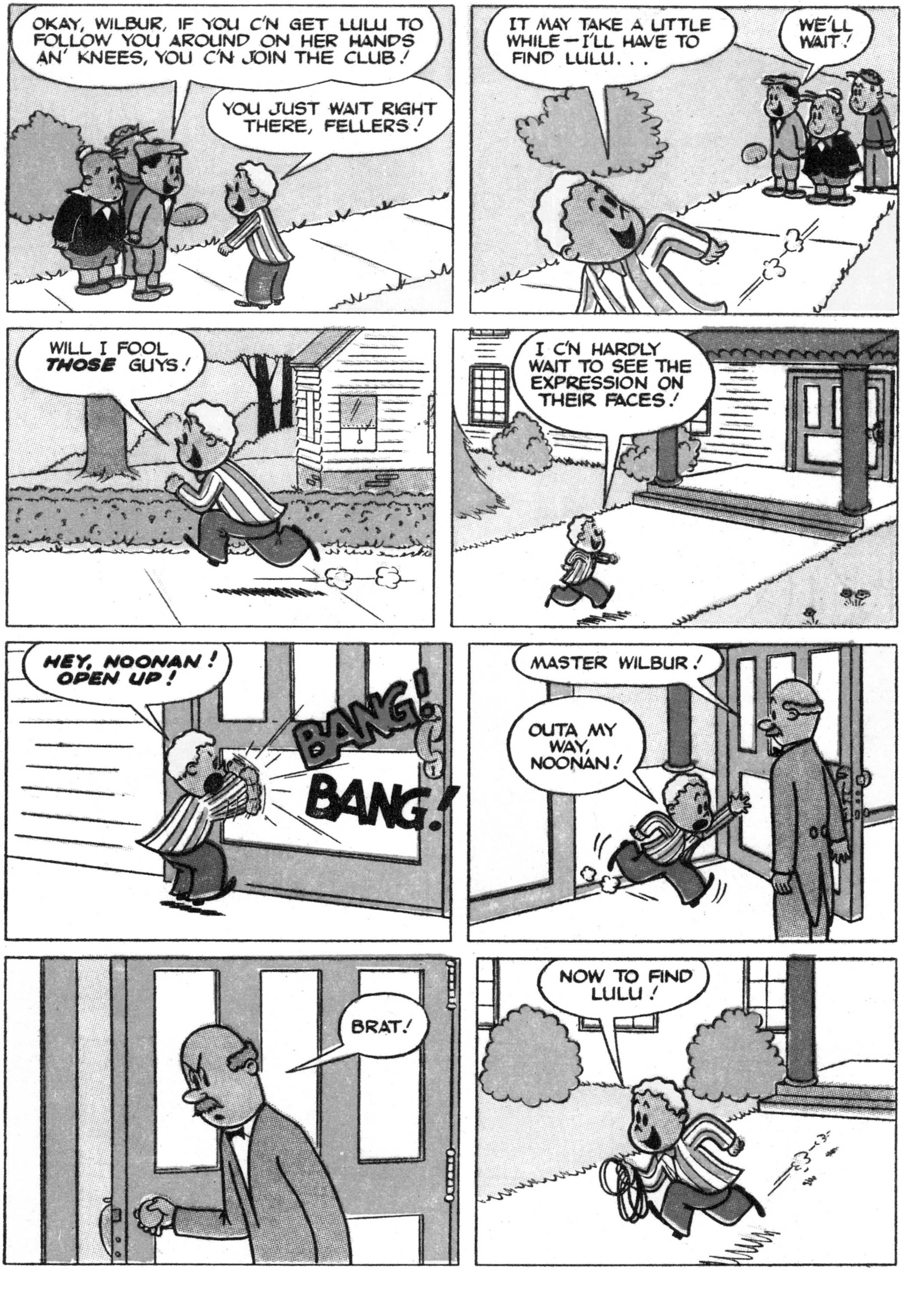
OKAY, WILBUR, IF YOU C'N GET LULU TO FOLLOW YOU AROUND ON HER HANDS AN' KNEES, YOU C'N JOIN THE CLUB!
YOU JUST WAIT RIGHT THERE, FELLERS!
IT MAY TAKE A LITTLE WHILE—I'LL HAVE TO FIND LULU. . .
WE'LL WAIT!
WILL I FOOL *THOSE* GUYS!
I C'N HARDLY WAIT TO SEE THE EXPRESSION ON THEIR FACES!
HEY, NOONAN! OPEN UP!
BANG!
BANG!
MASTER WILBUR!
OUTA MY WAY, NOONAN!
BRAT!
NOW TO FIND LULU!

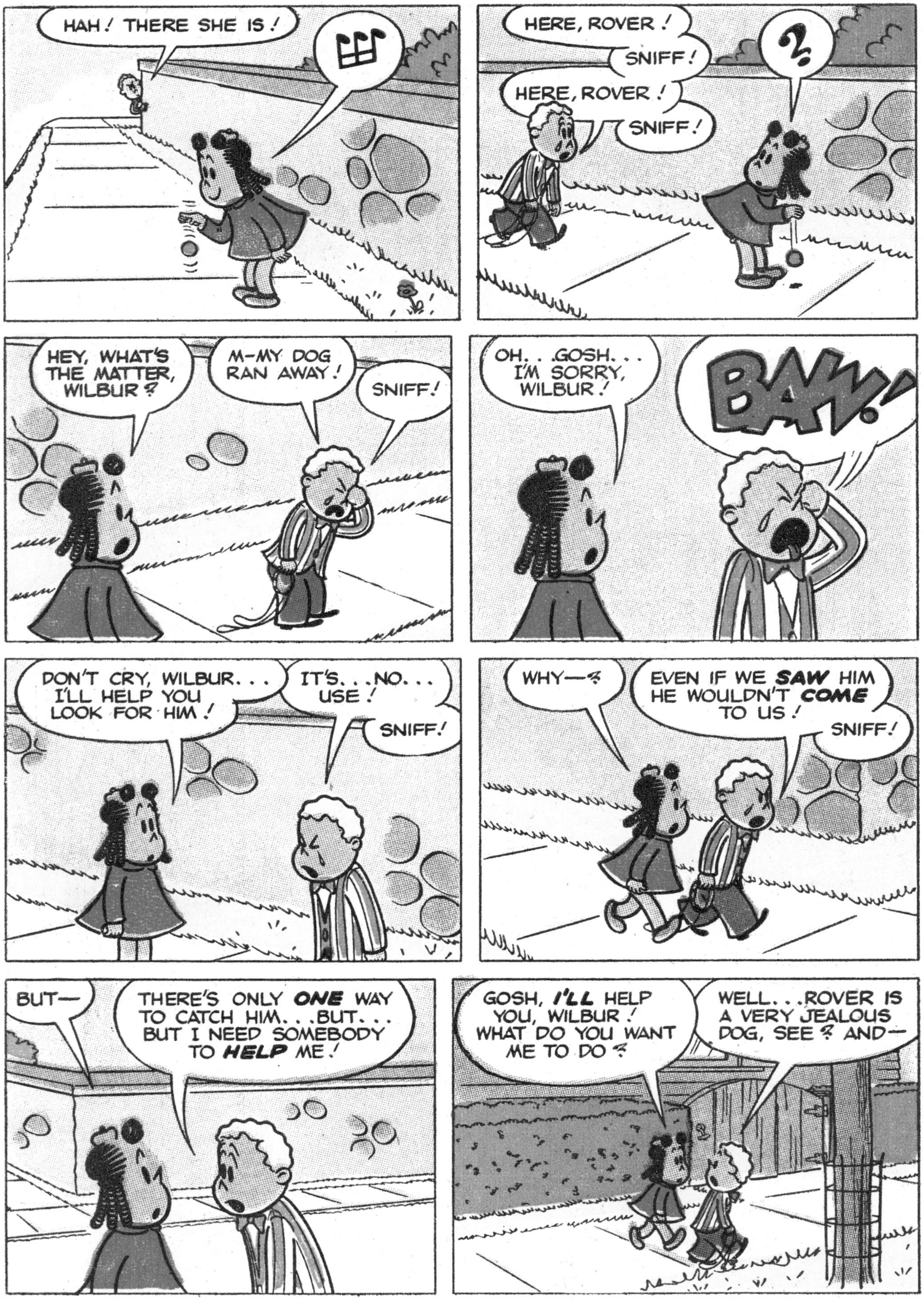
HAH! THERE SHE IS!
HERE, ROVER!
SNIFF!
HERE, ROVER!
SNIFF!
?
HEY, WHAT'S THE MATTER, WILBUR?
M-MY DOG RAN AWAY!
SNIFF!
OH. . .GOSH. . . I'M SORRY, WILBUR!
BAW!
DON'T CRY, WILBUR. . . I'LL HELP YOU LOOK FOR HIM!
IT'S. . .NO. . . USE!
SNIFF!
WHY—?
EVEN IF WE SAW HIM HE WOULDN'T COME TO US!
SNIFF!
BUT—
THERE'S ONLY ONE WAY TO CATCH HIM. . .BUT. . . BUT I NEED SOMEBODY TO HELP ME!
GOSH, I'LL HELP YOU, WILBUR! WHAT DO YOU WANT ME TO DO?
WELL. . .ROVER IS A VERY JEALOUS DOG, SEE? AND—

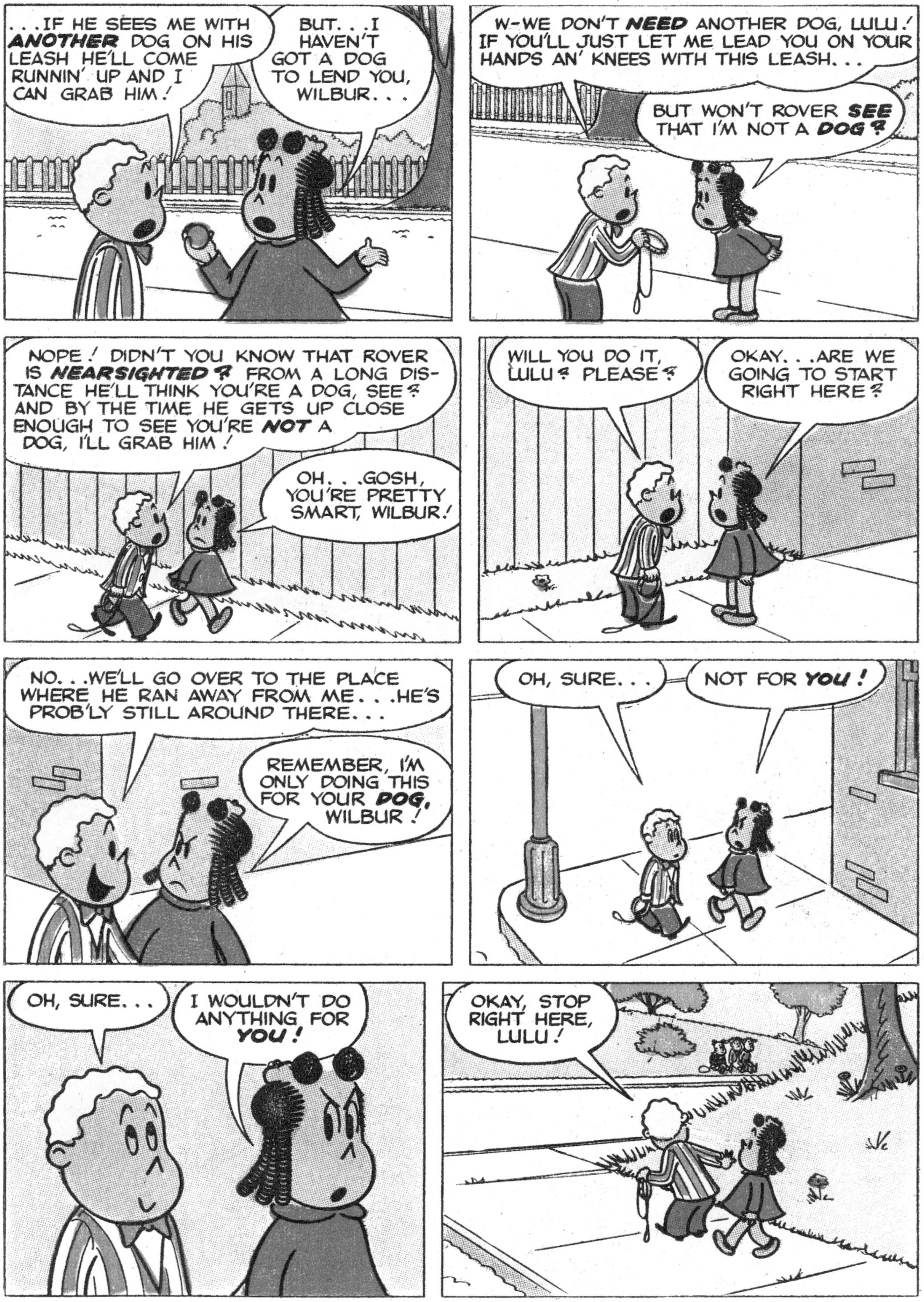
...IF HE SEES ME WITH ANOTHER DOG ON HIS LEASH HE'LL COME RUNNIN' UP AND I CAN GRAB HIM!
BUT...I HAVEN'T GOT A DOG TO LEND YOU, WILBUR...
W-WE DON'T NEED ANOTHER DOG, LULU! IF YOU'LL JUST LET ME LEAD YOU ON YOUR HANDS AN' KNEES WITH THIS LEASH...
BUT WON'T ROVER SEE THAT I'M NOT A DOG?
NOPE! DIDN'T YOU KNOW THAT ROVER IS NEARSIGHTED? FROM A LONG DISTANCE HE'LL THINK YOU'RE A DOG, SEE? AND BY THE TIME HE GETS UP CLOSE ENOUGH TO SEE YOU'RE NOT A DOG, I'LL GRAB HIM!
OH...GOSH, YOU'RE PRETTY SMART, WILBUR!
WILL YOU DO IT, LULU? PLEASE?
OKAY...ARE WE GOING TO START RIGHT HERE?
NO...WE'LL GO OVER TO THE PLACE WHERE HE RAN AWAY FROM ME...HE'S PROB'LY STILL AROUND THERE...
REMEMBER, I'M ONLY DOING THIS FOR YOUR DOG, WILBUR!
OH, SURE...
NOT FOR YOU!
OH, SURE...
I WOULDN'T DO ANYTHING FOR YOU!
OKAY, STOP RIGHT HERE, LULU!

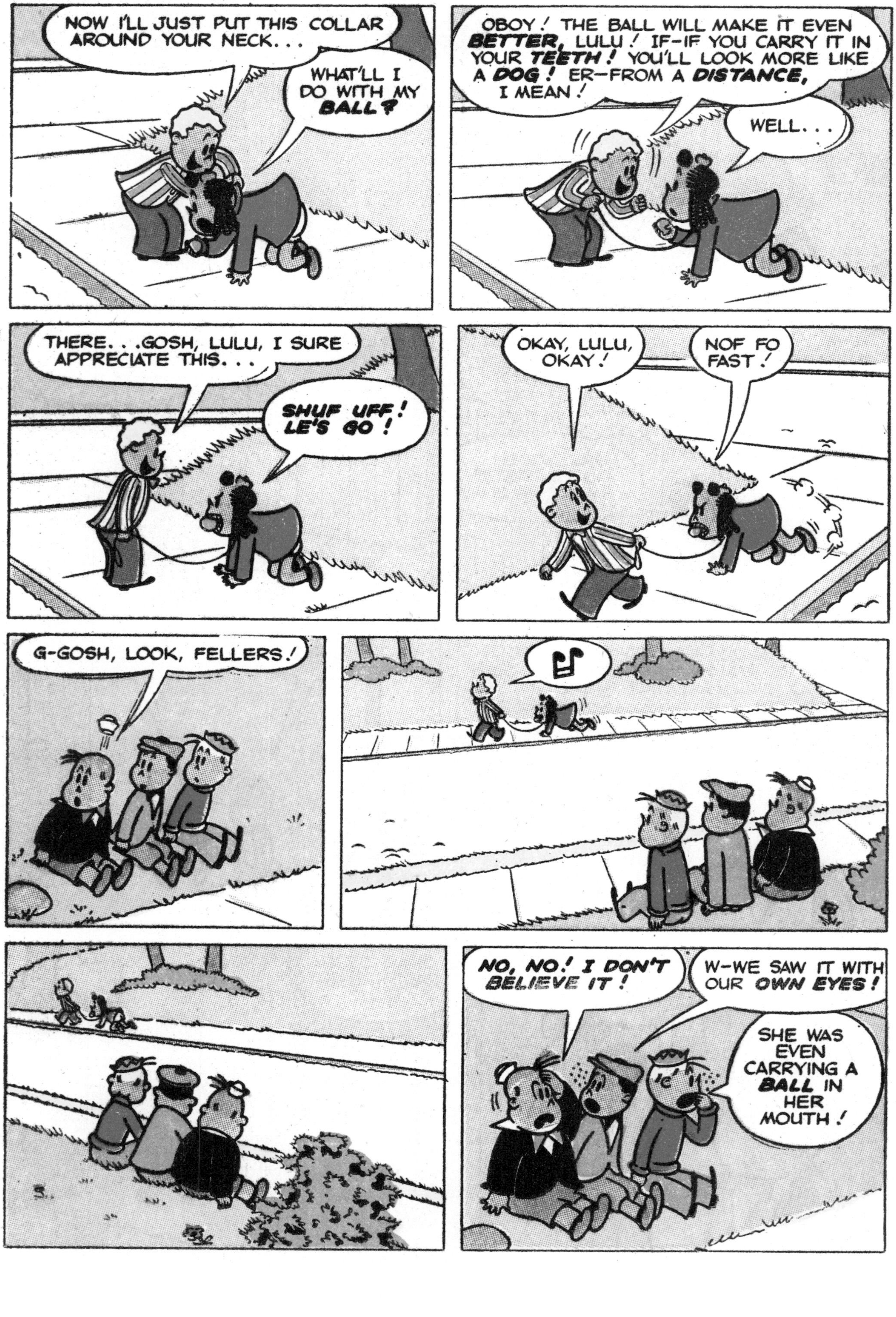
NOW I'LL JUST PUT THIS COLLAR AROUND YOUR NECK...
WHAT'LL I DO WITH MY BALL?
OBOY! THE BALL WILL MAKE IT EVEN BETTER, LULU! IF-IF YOU CARRY IT IN YOUR TEETH! YOU'LL LOOK MORE LIKE A DOG! ER—FROM A DISTANCE, I MEAN!
WELL...
THERE...GOSH, LULU, I SURE APPRECIATE THIS...
SHUF UFF! LE'S GO!
OKAY, LULU, OKAY!
NOF FO FAST!
G-GOSH, LOOK, FELLERS!
NO, NO! I DON'T BELIEVE IT!
W-WE SAW IT WITH OUR OWN EYES!
SHE WAS EVEN CARRYING A BALL IN HER MOUTH!

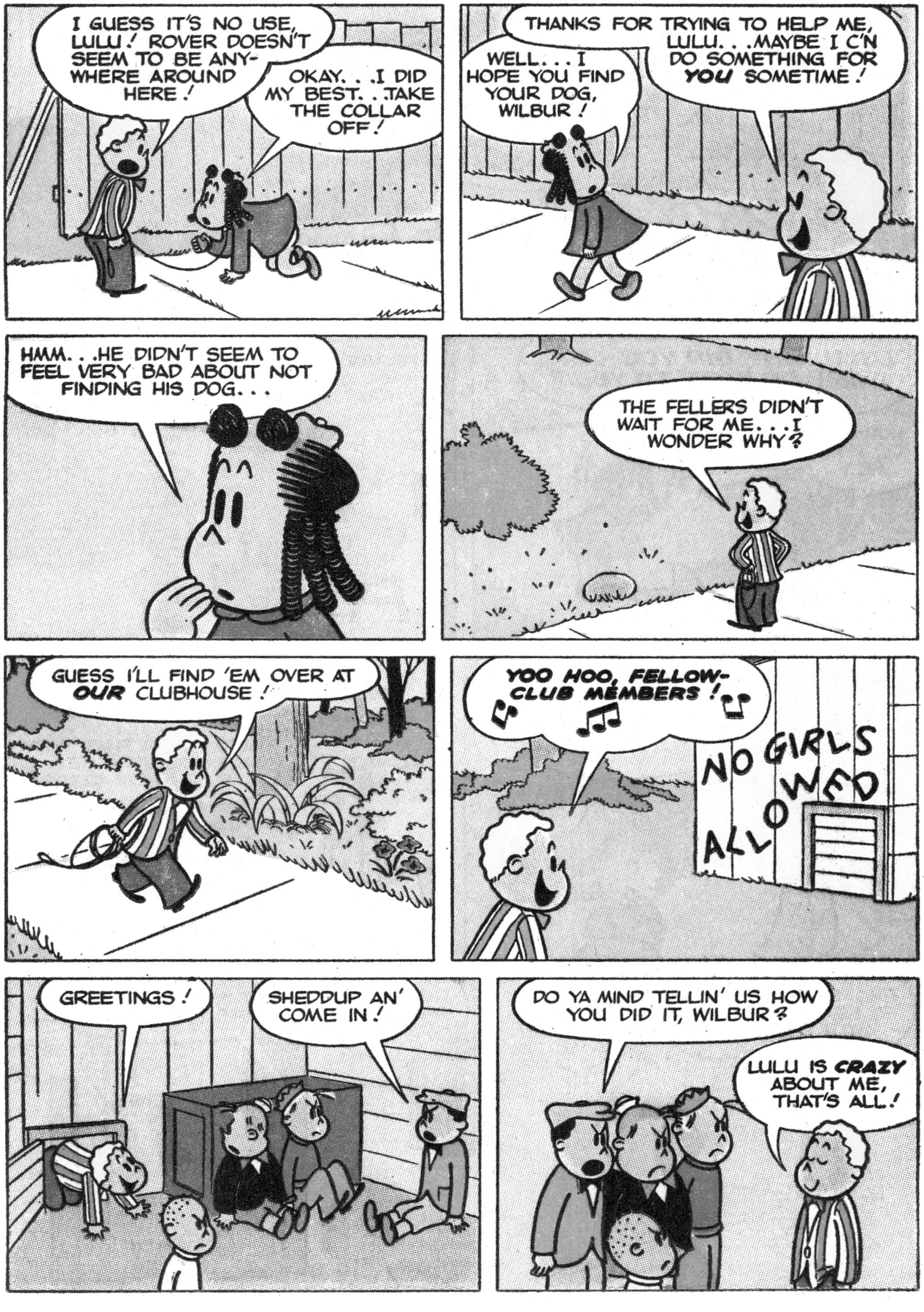
I GUESS IT'S NO USE, LULU! ROVER DOESN'T SEEM TO BE ANY-WHERE AROUND HERE!
OKAY. . .I DID MY BEST. . .TAKE THE COLLAR OFF!
THANKS FOR TRYING TO HELP ME, LULU. . .MAYBE I C'N DO SOMETHING FOR YOU SOMETIME!
WELL. . .I HOPE YOU FIND YOUR DOG, WILBUR!
HMM. . .HE DIDN'T SEEM TO FEEL VERY BAD ABOUT NOT FINDING HIS DOG. . .
THE FELLERS DIDN'T WAIT FOR ME. . .I WONDER WHY?
GUESS I'LL FIND 'EM OVER AT OUR CLUBHOUSE!
YOO HOO, FELLOW-CLUB MEMBERS!
NO GIRLS ALLOWED
GREETINGS!
SHEDDUP AN' COME IN!
DO YA MIND TELLIN' US HOW YOU DID IT, WILBUR?
LULU IS CRAZY ABOUT ME, THAT'S ALL!

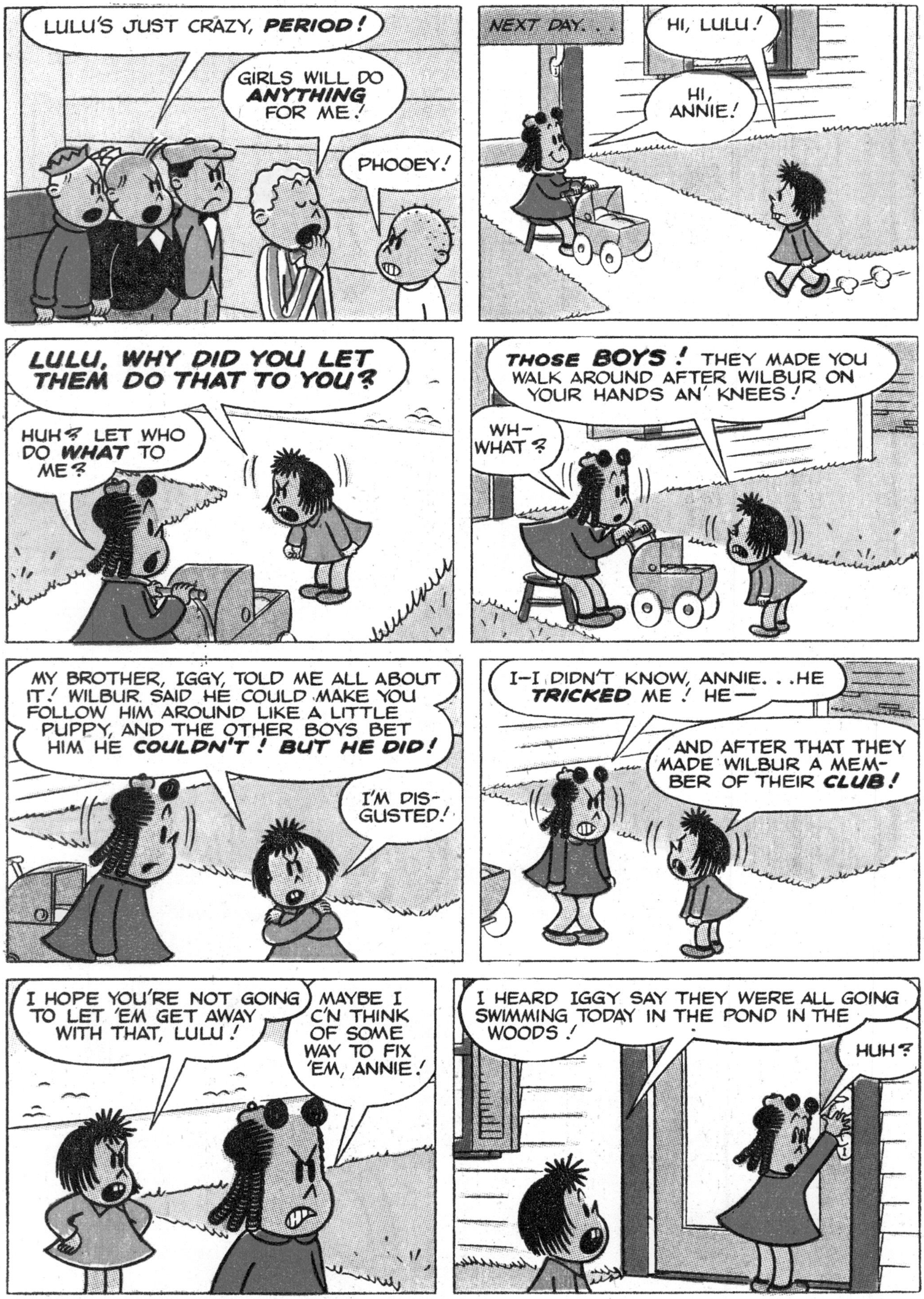
LULU'S JUST CRAZY, PERIOD!
GIRLS WILL DO ANYTHING FOR ME!
PHOOEY!
NEXT DAY. . .
HI, LULU!
HI, ANNIE!
LULU, WHY DID YOU LET THEM DO THAT TO YOU?
HUH? LET WHO DO WHAT TO ME?
THOSE BOYS! THEY MADE YOU WALK AROUND AFTER WILBUR ON YOUR HANDS AN' KNEES!
WH-WHAT?
MY BROTHER, IGGY, TOLD ME ALL ABOUT IT! WILBUR SAID HE COULD MAKE YOU FOLLOW HIM AROUND LIKE A LITTLE PUPPY, AND THE OTHER BOYS BET HIM HE COULDN'T! BUT HE DID!
I'M DISGUSTED!
I-I DIDN'T KNOW, ANNIE. . .HE TRICKED ME! HE—
AND AFTER THAT THEY MADE WILBUR A MEMBER OF THEIR CLUB!
I HOPE YOU'RE NOT GOING TO LET 'EM GET AWAY WITH THAT, LULU!
MAYBE I C'N THINK OF SOME WAY TO FIX 'EM, ANNIE!
I HEARD IGGY SAY THEY WERE ALL GOING SWIMMING TODAY IN THE POND IN THE WOODS!
HUH?

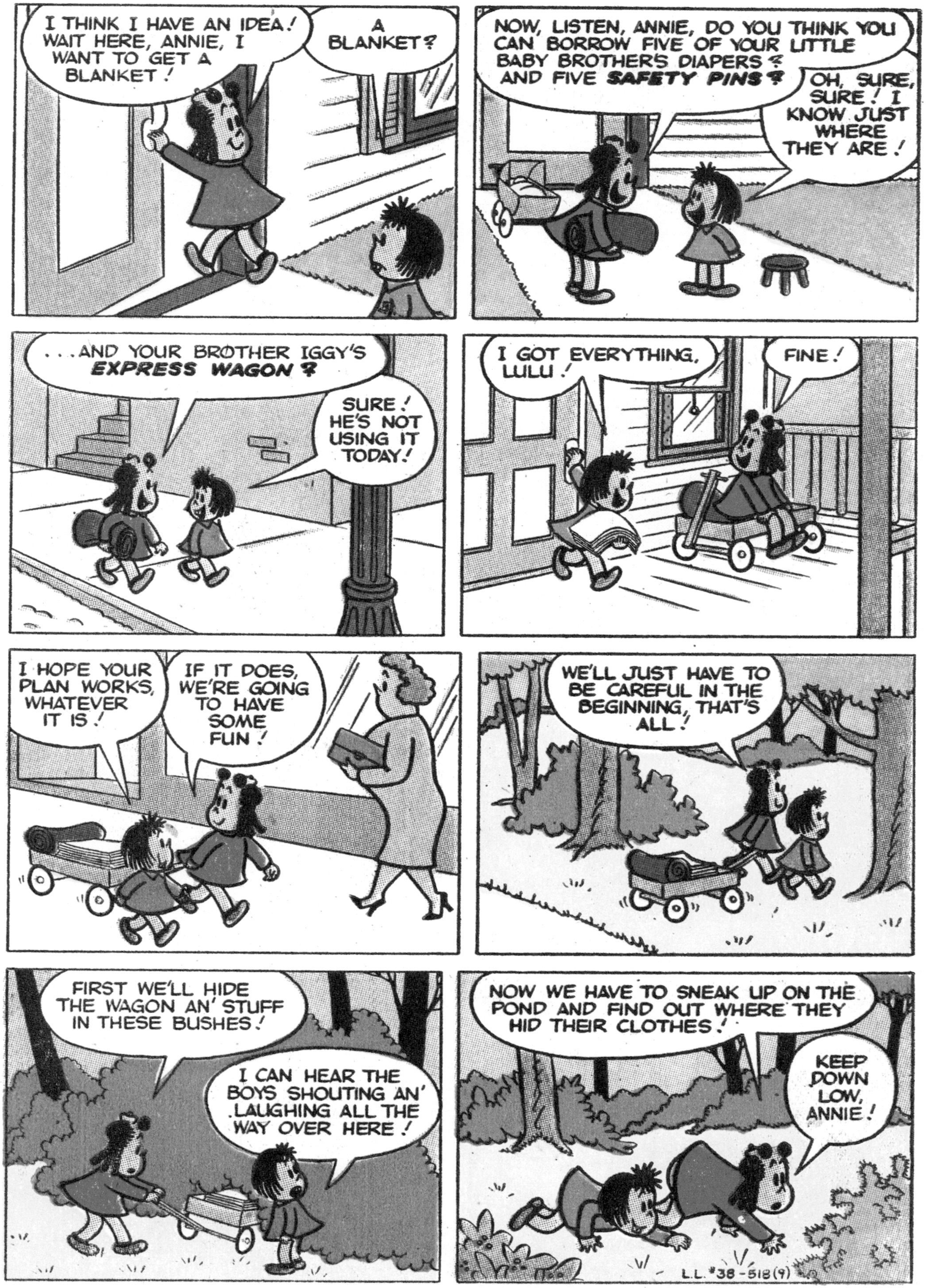
I THINK I HAVE AN IDEA! WAIT HERE, ANNIE, I WANT TO GET A BLANKET!
A BLANKET?
NOW, LISTEN, ANNIE, DO YOU THINK YOU CAN BORROW FIVE OF YOUR LITTLE BABY BROTHER'S DIAPERS? AND FIVE SAFETY PINS?
OH, SURE, SURE! I KNOW JUST WHERE THEY ARE!
...AND YOUR BROTHER IGGY'S EXPRESS WAGON?
SURE! HE'S NOT USING IT TODAY!
I GOT EVERYTHING, LULU!
FINE!
I HOPE YOUR PLAN WORKS, WHATEVER IT IS!
IF IT DOES, WE'RE GOING TO HAVE SOME FUN!
WE'LL JUST HAVE TO BE CAREFUL IN THE BEGINNING, THAT'S ALL!
FIRST WE'LL HIDE THE WAGON AN' STUFF IN THESE BUSHES!
I CAN HEAR THE BOYS SHOUTING AN' LAUGHING ALL THE WAY OVER HERE!
NOW WE HAVE TO SNEAK UP ON THE POND AND FIND OUT WHERE THEY HID THEIR CLOTHES!
KEEP DOWN LOW, ANNIE!
L.L. #38-518(9)

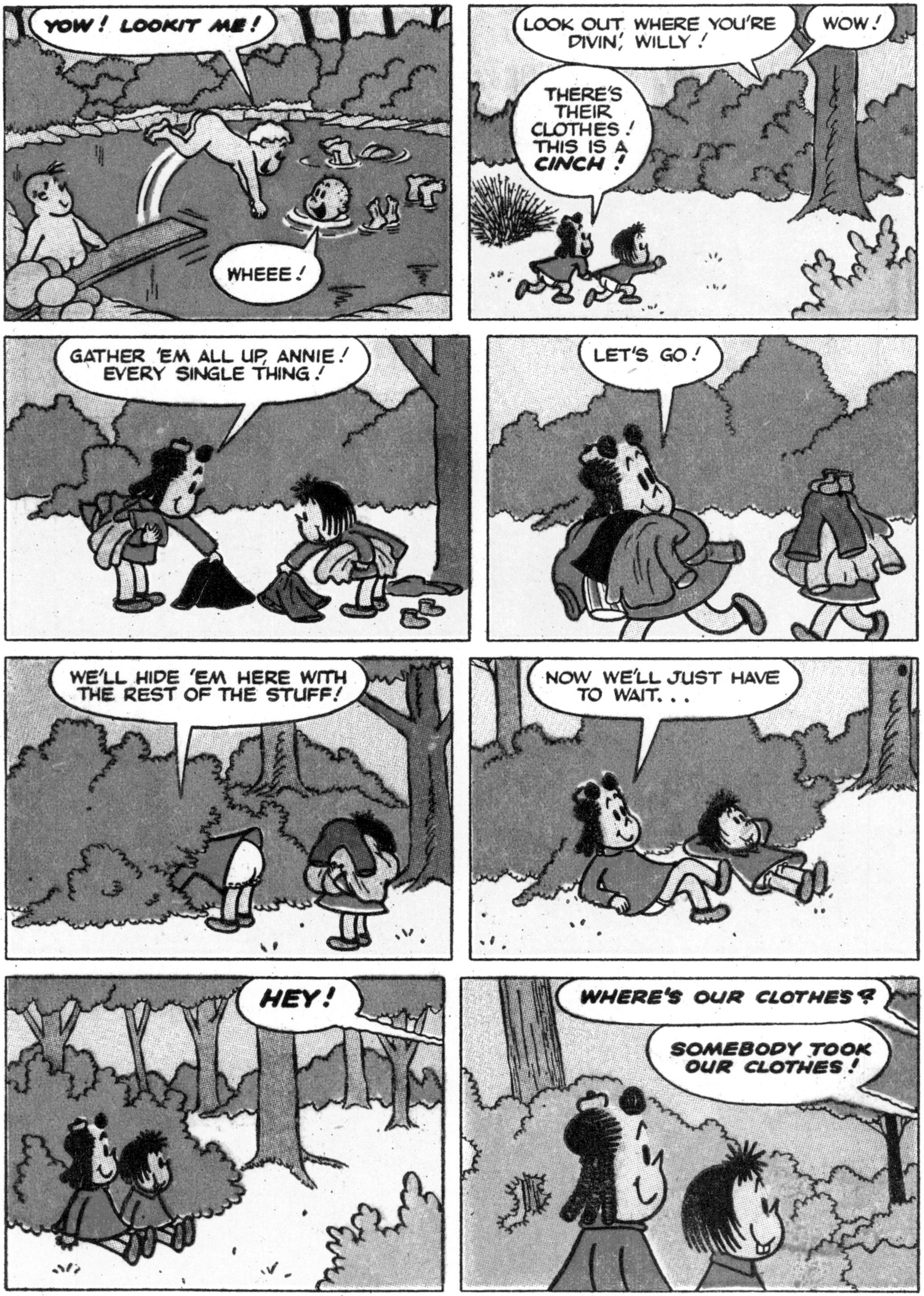
YOW! LOOKIT ME!
WHEEE!
LOOK OUT WHERE YOU'RE DIVIN', WILLY!
WOW!
THERE'S THEIR CLOTHES! THIS IS A CINCH!
GATHER 'EM ALL UP, ANNIE! EVERY SINGLE THING!
LET'S GO!
WE'LL HIDE 'EM HERE WITH THE REST OF THE STUFF!
NOW WE'LL JUST HAVE TO WAIT...
HEY!
WHERE'S OUR CLOTHES?
SOMEBODY TOOK OUR CLOTHES!

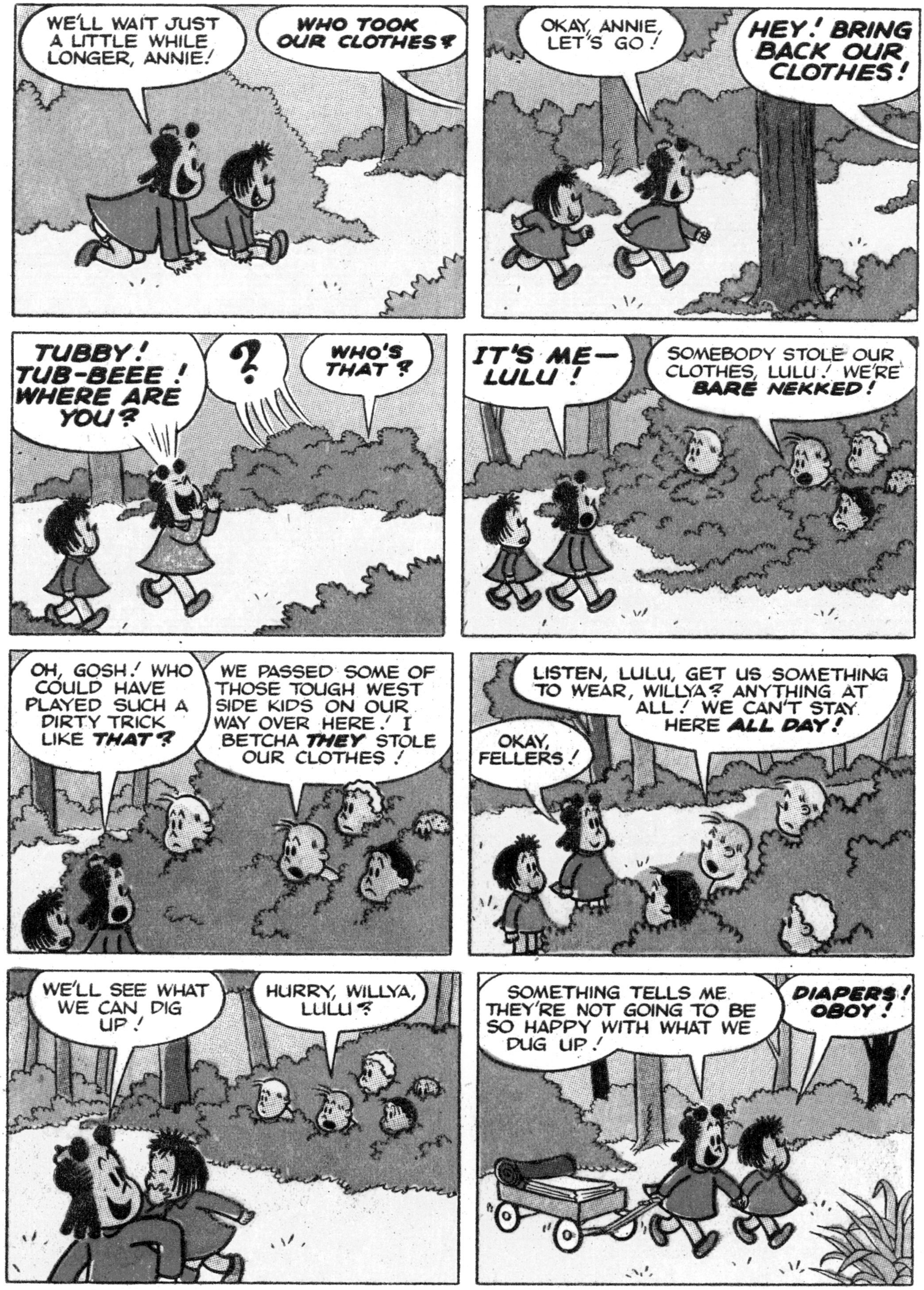
WE'LL WAIT JUST A LITTLE WHILE LONGER, ANNIE!
WHO TOOK OUR CLOTHES?
OKAY, ANNIE, LET'S GO!
HEY! BRING BACK OUR CLOTHES!
TUBBY! TUB-BEEE! WHERE ARE YOU?
?
WHO'S THAT?
IT'S ME— LULU!
SOMEBODY STOLE OUR CLOTHES, LULU! WE'RE BARE NEKKED!
OH, GOSH! WHO COULD HAVE PLAYED SUCH A DIRTY TRICK LIKE THAT?
WE PASSED SOME OF THOSE TOUGH WEST SIDE KIDS ON OUR WAY OVER HERE! I BETCHA THEY STOLE OUR CLOTHES!
LISTEN, LULU, GET US SOMETHING TO WEAR, WILLYA? ANYTHING AT ALL! WE CAN'T STAY HERE ALL DAY!
OKAY, FELLERS!
WE'LL SEE WHAT WE CAN DIG UP!
HURRY, WILLYA, LULU?
SOMETHING TELLS ME THEY'RE NOT GOING TO BE SO HAPPY WITH WHAT WE DUG UP!
DIAPERS! OBOY!

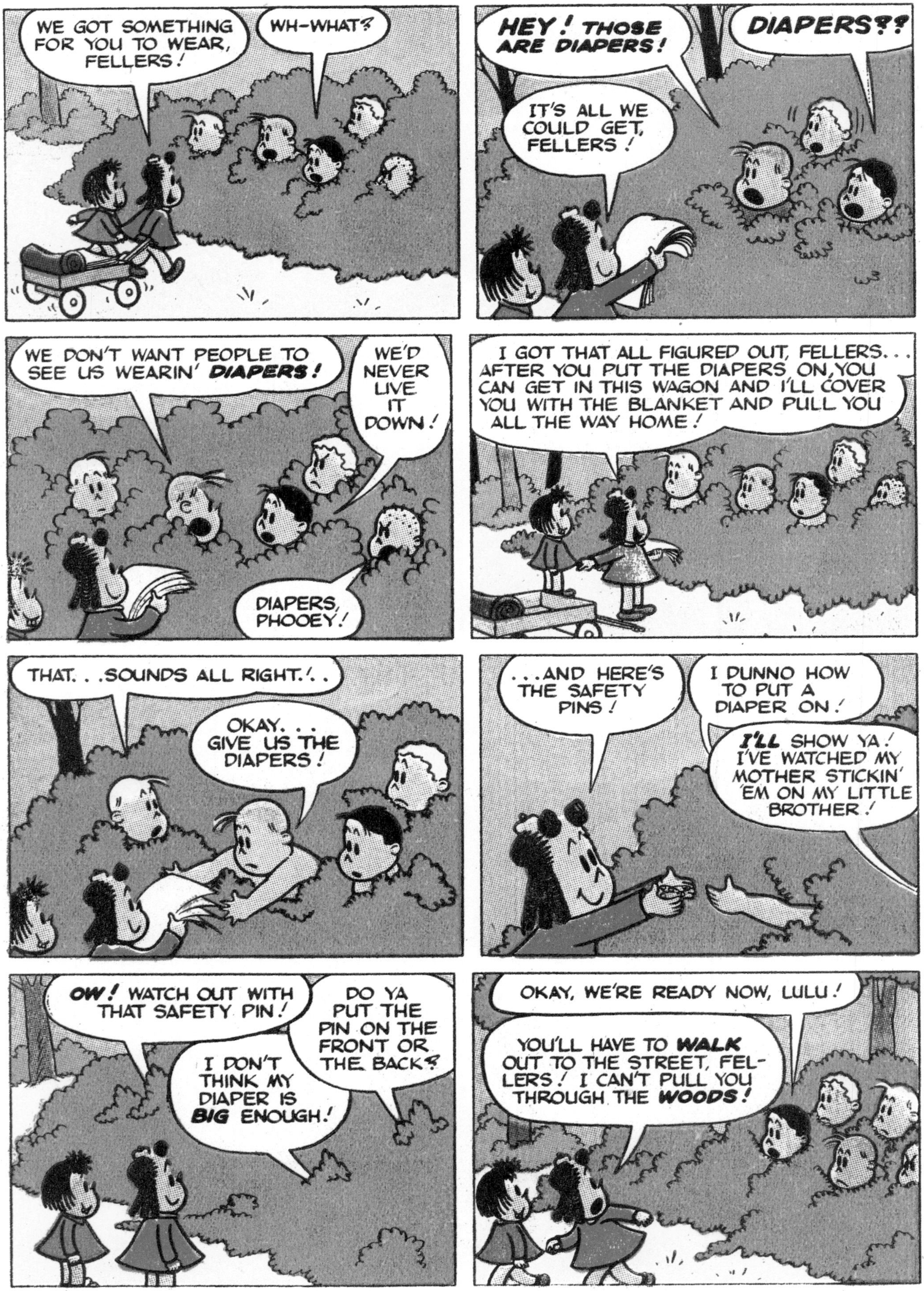
WE GOT SOMETHING FOR YOU TO WEAR, FELLERS!
WH-WHAT?
HEY! THOSE ARE DIAPERS!
DIAPERS??
IT'S ALL WE COULD GET, FELLERS!
WE DON'T WANT PEOPLE TO SEE US WEARIN' DIAPERS!
WE'D NEVER LIVE IT DOWN!
DIAPERS, PHOOEY!
I GOT THAT ALL FIGURED OUT, FELLERS... AFTER YOU PUT THE DIAPERS ON, YOU CAN GET IN THIS WAGON AND I'LL COVER YOU WITH THE BLANKET AND PULL YOU ALL THE WAY HOME!
THAT...SOUNDS ALL RIGHT!..
OKAY... GIVE US THE DIAPERS!
...AND HERE'S THE SAFETY PINS!
I DUNNO HOW TO PUT A DIAPER ON!
I'LL SHOW YA! I'VE WATCHED MY MOTHER STICKIN' 'EM ON MY LITTLE BROTHER!
OW! WATCH OUT WITH THAT SAFETY PIN!
DO YA PUT THE PIN ON THE FRONT OR THE BACK?
I DON'T THINK MY DIAPER IS BIG ENOUGH!
OKAY, WE'RE READY NOW, LULU!
YOU'LL HAVE TO WALK OUT TO THE STREET, FELLERS! I CAN'T PULL YOU THROUGH THE WOODS!

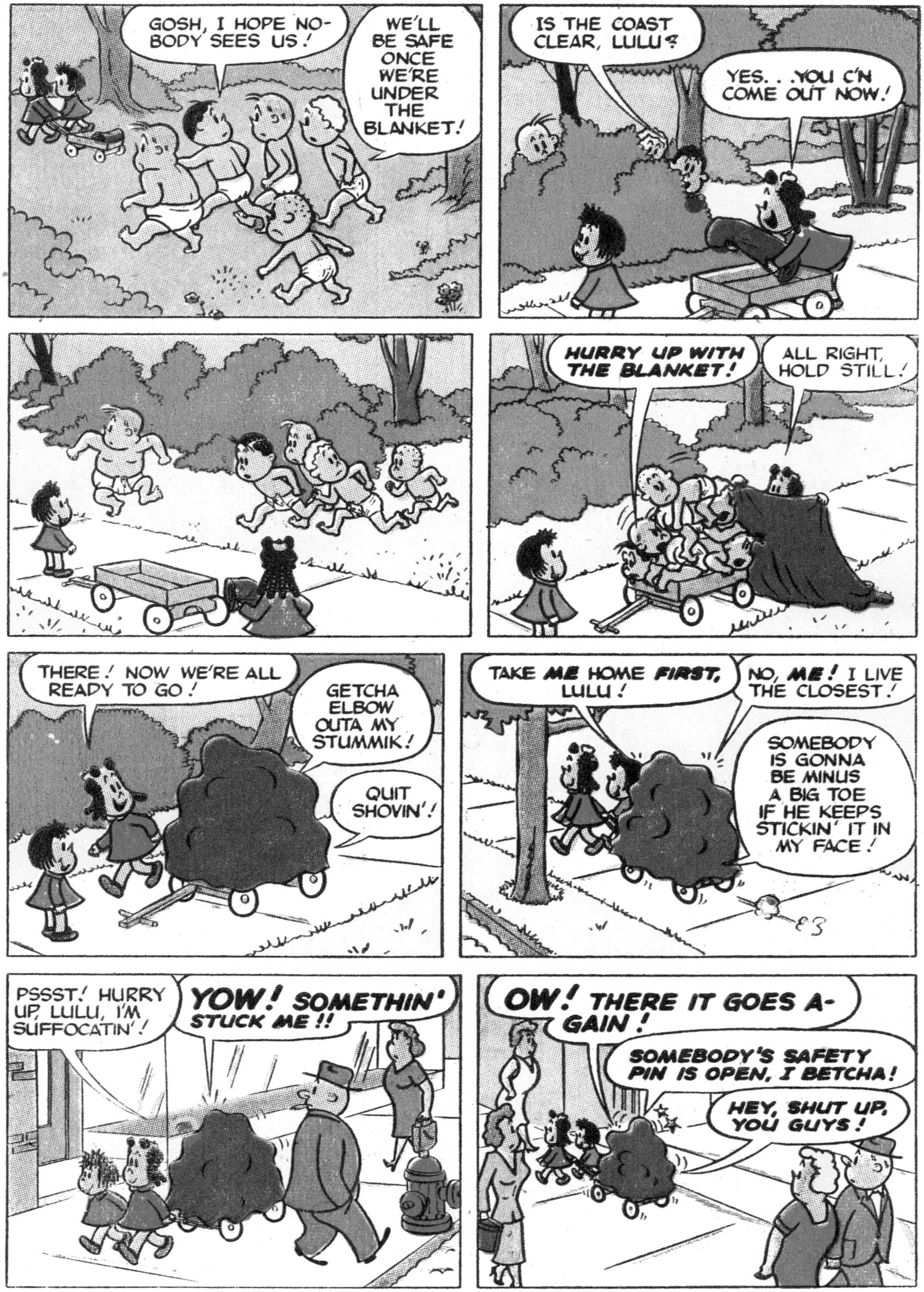
GOSH, I HOPE NOBODY SEES US!
WE'LL BE SAFE ONCE WE'RE UNDER THE BLANKET!
IS THE COAST CLEAR, LULU?
YES. . .YOU C'N COME OUT NOW!
HURRY UP WITH THE BLANKET!
ALL RIGHT, HOLD STILL!
THERE! NOW WE'RE ALL READY TO GO!
GETCHA ELBOW OUTA MY STUMMIK!
QUIT SHOVIN'!
TAKE ME HOME FIRST, LULU!
NO, ME! I LIVE THE CLOSEST!
SOMEBODY IS GONNA BE MINUS A BIG TOE IF HE KEEPS STICKIN' IT IN MY FACE!
PSSST! HURRY UP, LULU, I'M SUFFOCATIN'!
YOW! SOMETHIN' STUCK ME!!
OW! THERE IT GOES AGAIN!
SOMEBODY'S SAFETY PIN IS OPEN, I BETCHA!
HEY, SHUT UP, YOU GUYS!

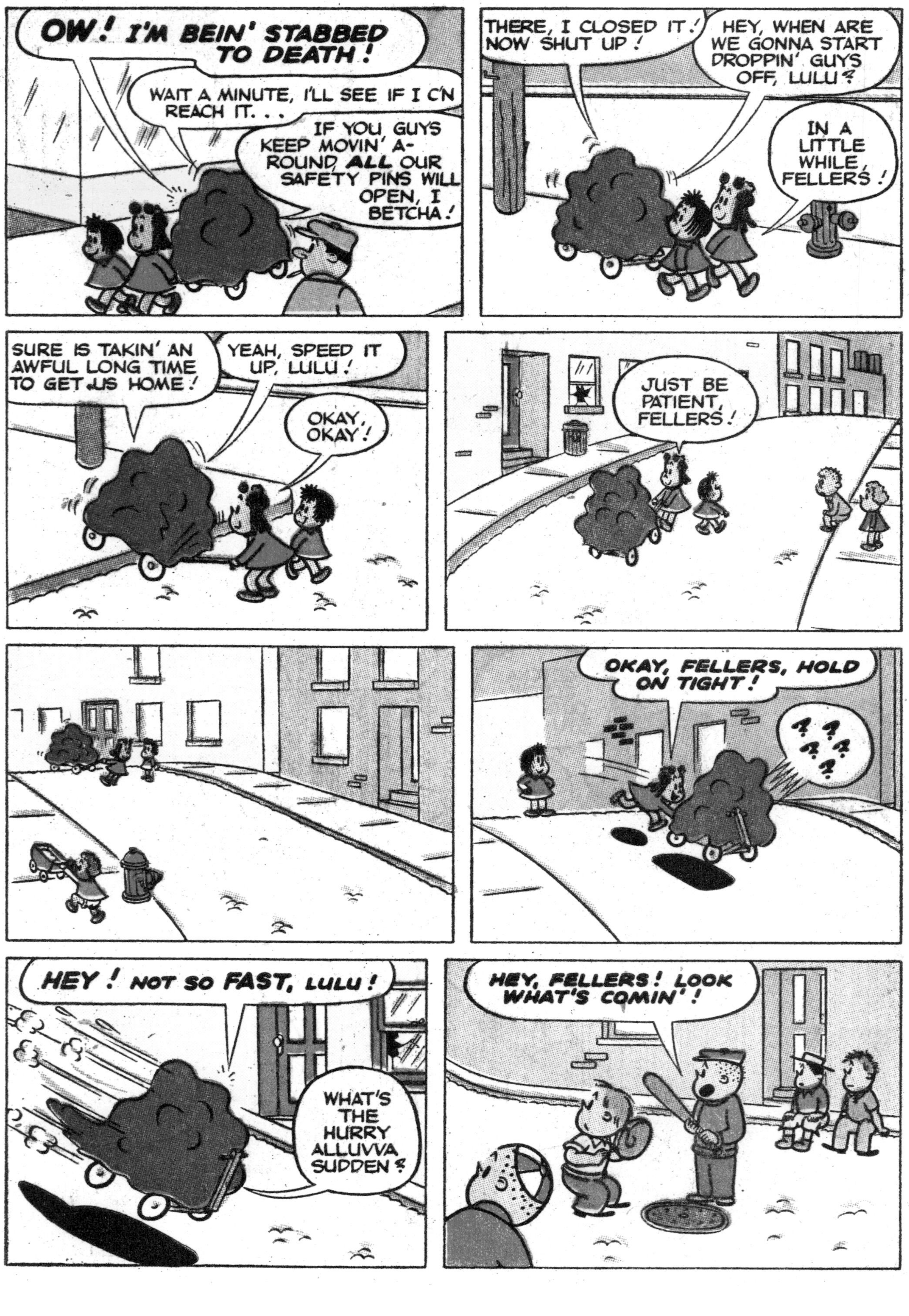
OW! I'M BEIN' STABBED TO DEATH!
WAIT A MINUTE, I'LL SEE IF I C'N REACH IT. . .
IF YOU GUYS KEEP MOVIN' A-ROUND ALL OUR SAFETY PINS WILL OPEN, I BETCHA!
THERE, I CLOSED IT! NOW SHUT UP!
HEY, WHEN ARE WE GONNA START DROPPIN' GUYS OFF, LULU?
IN A LITTLE WHILE, FELLERS!
SURE IS TAKIN' AN AWFUL LONG TIME TO GET US HOME!
YEAH, SPEED IT UP, LULU!
OKAY, OKAY!
JUST BE PATIENT, FELLERS!
OKAY, FELLERS, HOLD ON TIGHT!
?? ?? ?
HEY! NOT SO FAST, LULU!
WHAT'S THE HURRY ALLUVVA SUDDEN?
HEY, FELLERS! LOOK WHAT'S COMIN'!

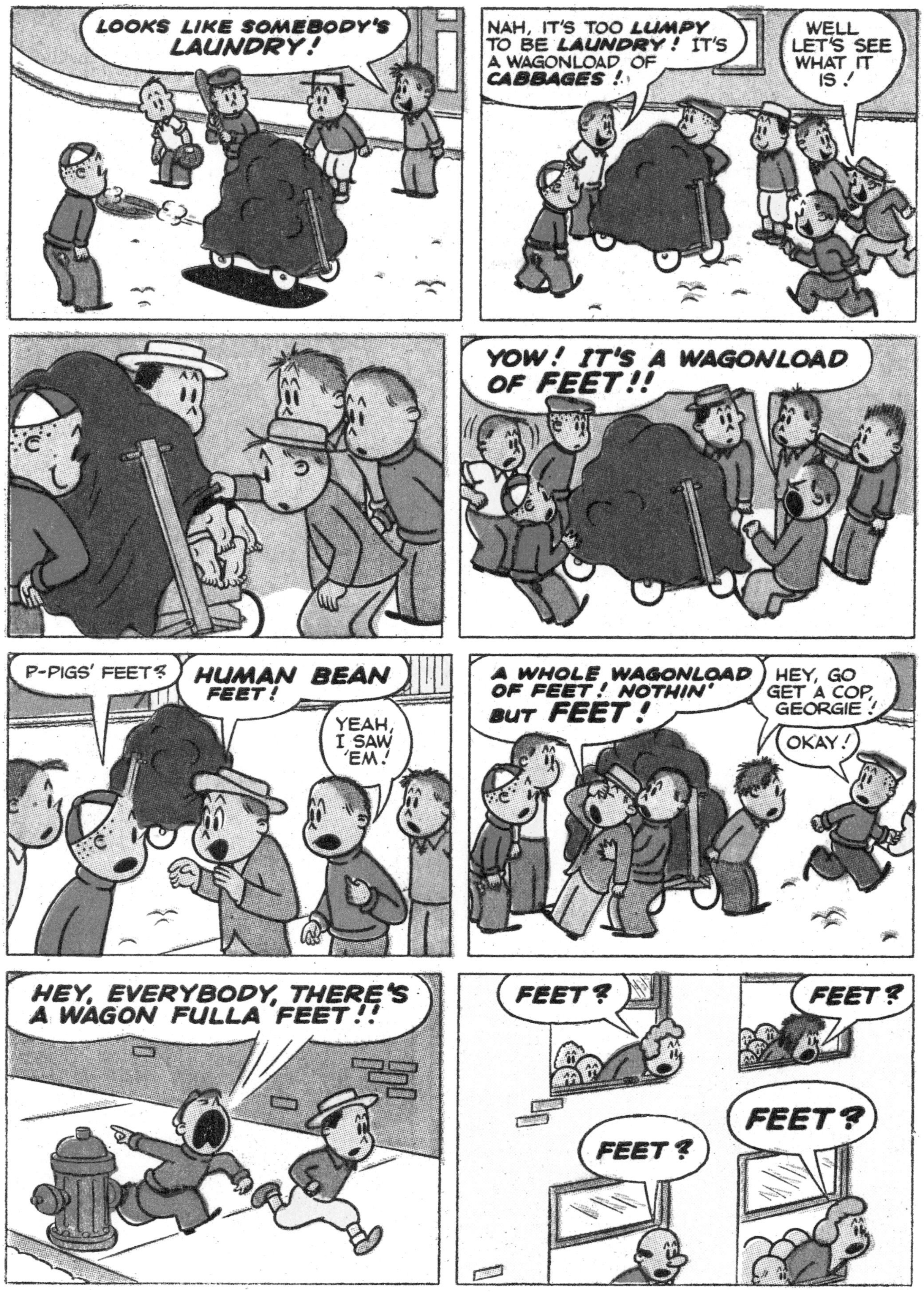
LOOKS LIKE SOMEBODY'S LAUNDRY!
NAH, IT'S TOO LUMPY TO BE LAUNDRY! IT'S A WAGONLOAD OF CABBAGES!
WELL LET'S SEE WHAT IT IS!
YOW! IT'S A WAGONLOAD OF FEET!!
P-PIGS' FEET?
HUMAN BEAN FEET!
YEAH, I SAW 'EM!
A WHOLE WAGONLOAD OF FEET! NOTHIN' BUT FEET!
HEY, GO GET A COP, GEORGIE!
OKAY!
HEY, EVERYBODY, THERE'S A WAGON FULLA FEET!!
FEET?
FEET?
FEET?
FEET?

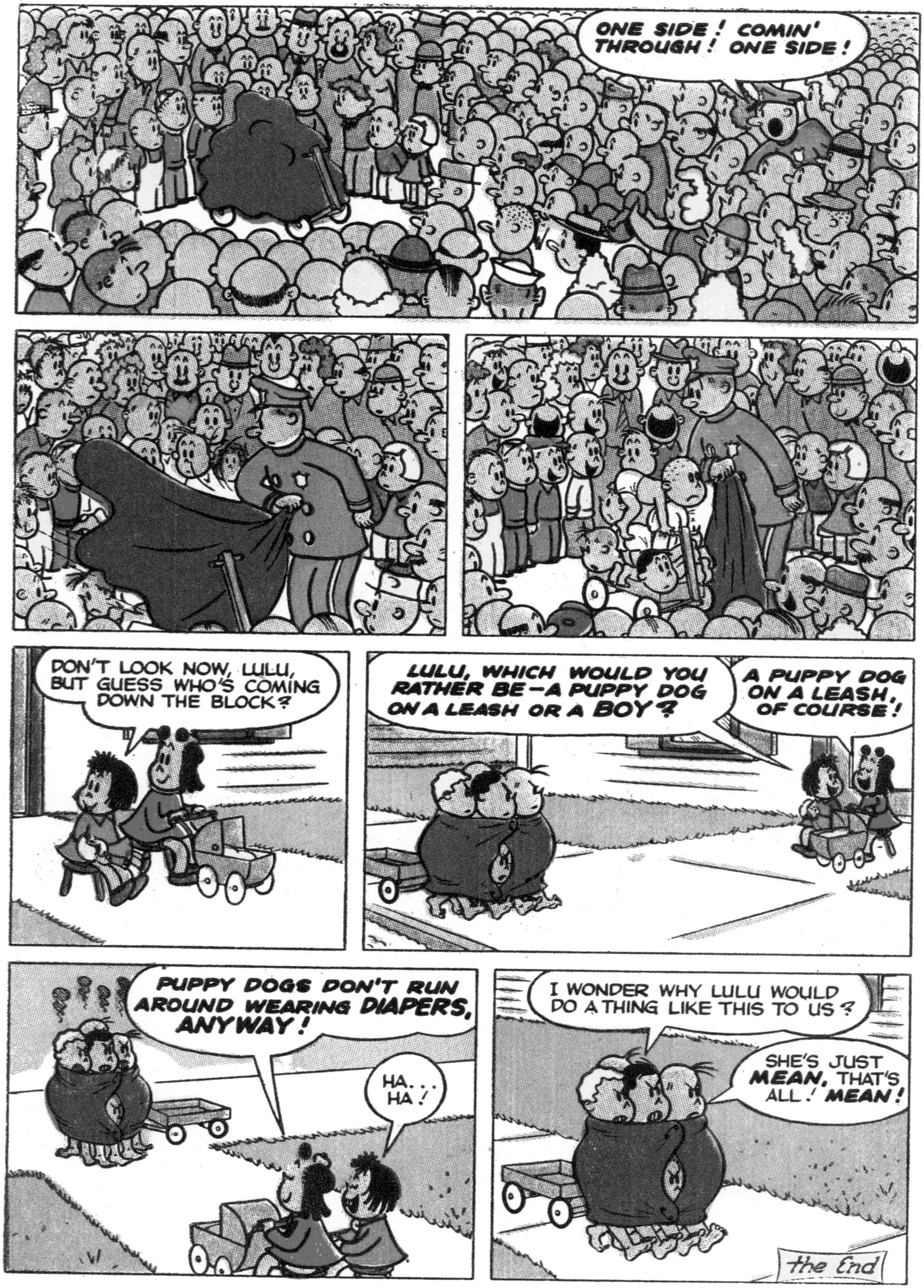
ONE SIDE! COMIN' THROUGH! ONE SIDE!
DON'T LOOK NOW, LULU, BUT GUESS WHO'S COMING DOWN THE BLOCK?
LULU, WHICH WOULD YOU RATHER BE—A PUPPY DOG ON A LEASH OR A BOY?
A PUPPY DOG ON A LEASH, OF COURSE!
PUPPY DOGS DON'T RUN AROUND WEARING DIAPERS, ANYWAY!
HA... HA!
I WONDER WHY LULU WOULD DO A THING LIKE THIS TO US?
SHE'S JUST MEAN, THAT'S ALL! MEAN!
the End

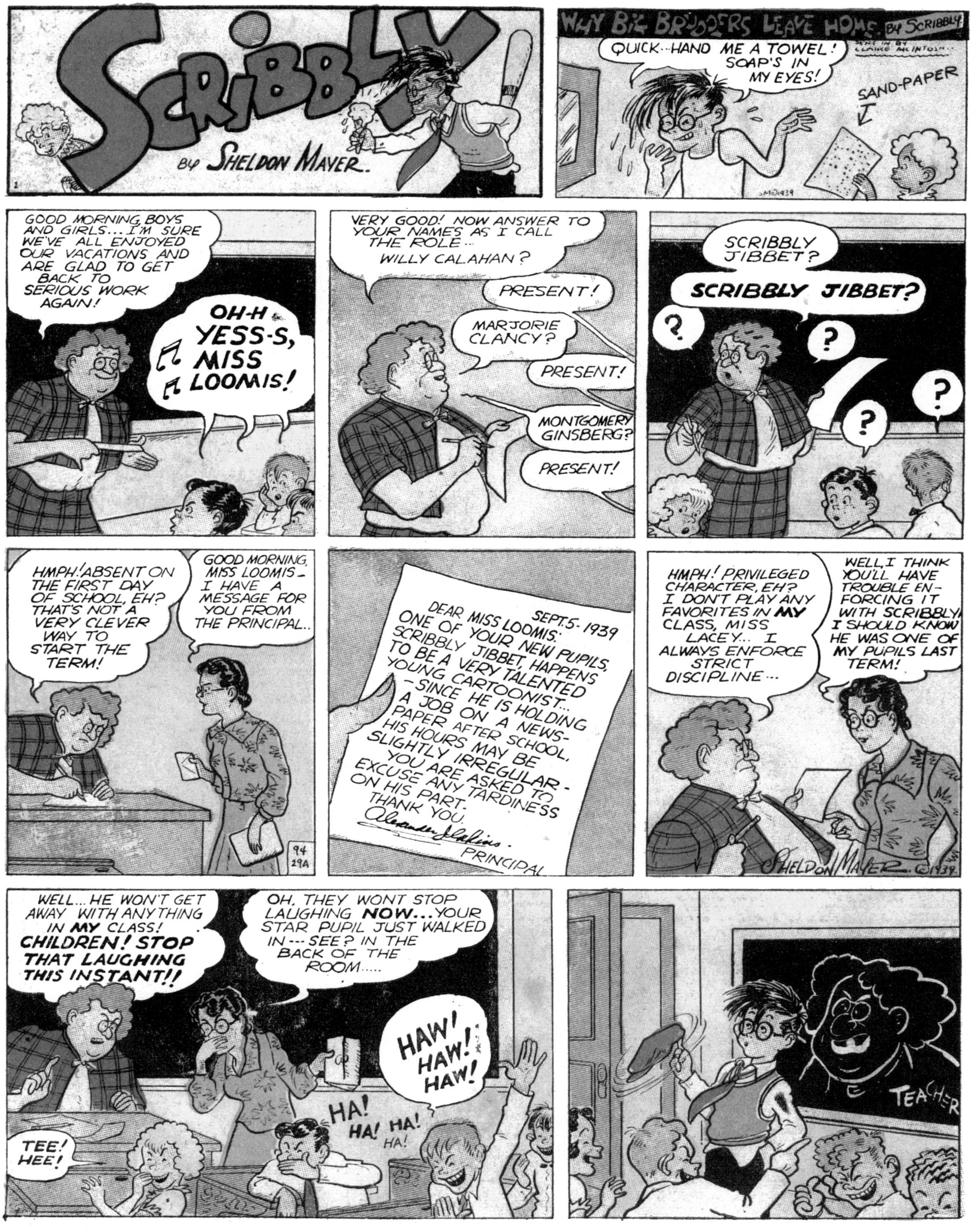
SCRIBBLY
BY SHELDON MAYER
WHY BIG BRUDDERS LEAVE HOME BY SCRIBBLY
QUICK... HAND ME A TOWEL! SOAP'S IN MY EYES!
SAND-PAPER
GOOD MORNING, BOYS AND GIRLS... I'M SURE WE'VE ALL ENJOYED OUR VACATIONS AND ARE GLAD TO GET BACK TO SERIOUS WORK AGAIN!
OH-H YESS-S, MISS LOOMIS!
VERY GOOD! NOW ANSWER TO YOUR NAMES AS I CALL THE ROLE... WILLY CALAHAN?
PRESENT!
MARJORIE CLANCY?
PRESENT!
MONTGOMERY GINSBERG?
PRESENT!
SCRIBBLY JIBBET?
SCRIBBLY JIBBET?
?
?
?
?
HMPH! ABSENT ON THE FIRST DAY OF SCHOOL, EH? THAT'S NOT A VERY CLEVER WAY TO START THE TERM!
GOOD MORNING, MISS LOOMIS - I HAVE A MESSAGE FOR YOU FROM THE PRINCIPAL...
SEPT. 5 - 1939
DEAR MISS LOOMIS: ONE OF YOUR NEW PUPILS, SCRIBBLY JIBBET, HAPPENS TO BE A VERY TALENTED YOUNG CARTOONIST... - SINCE HE IS HOLDING A JOB ON A NEWS-PAPER AFTER SCHOOL, HIS HOURS MAY BE SLIGHTLY IRREGULAR - YOU ARE ASKED TO EXCUSE ANY TARDINESS ON HIS PART - THANK YOU.
PRINCIPAL
HMPH! PRIVILEGED CHARACTER, EH? I DON'T PLAY ANY FAVORITES IN MY CLASS, MISS LACEY... I ALWAYS ENFORCE STRICT DISCIPLINE...
WELL, I THINK YOU'LL HAVE TROUBLE EN-FORCING IT WITH SCRIBBLY! I SHOULD KNOW HE WAS ONE OF MY PUPILS LAST TERM!
SHELDON MAYER © 1939
WELL... HE WON'T GET AWAY WITH ANYTHING IN MY CLASS! CHILDREN! STOP THAT LAUGHING THIS INSTANT!!
OH, THEY WONT STOP LAUGHING NOW... YOUR STAR PUPIL JUST WALKED IN --- SEE? IN THE BACK OF THE ROOM.....
HAW! HAW! HAW!
HA! HA! HA! HA!
TEE! HEE!
TEACHER

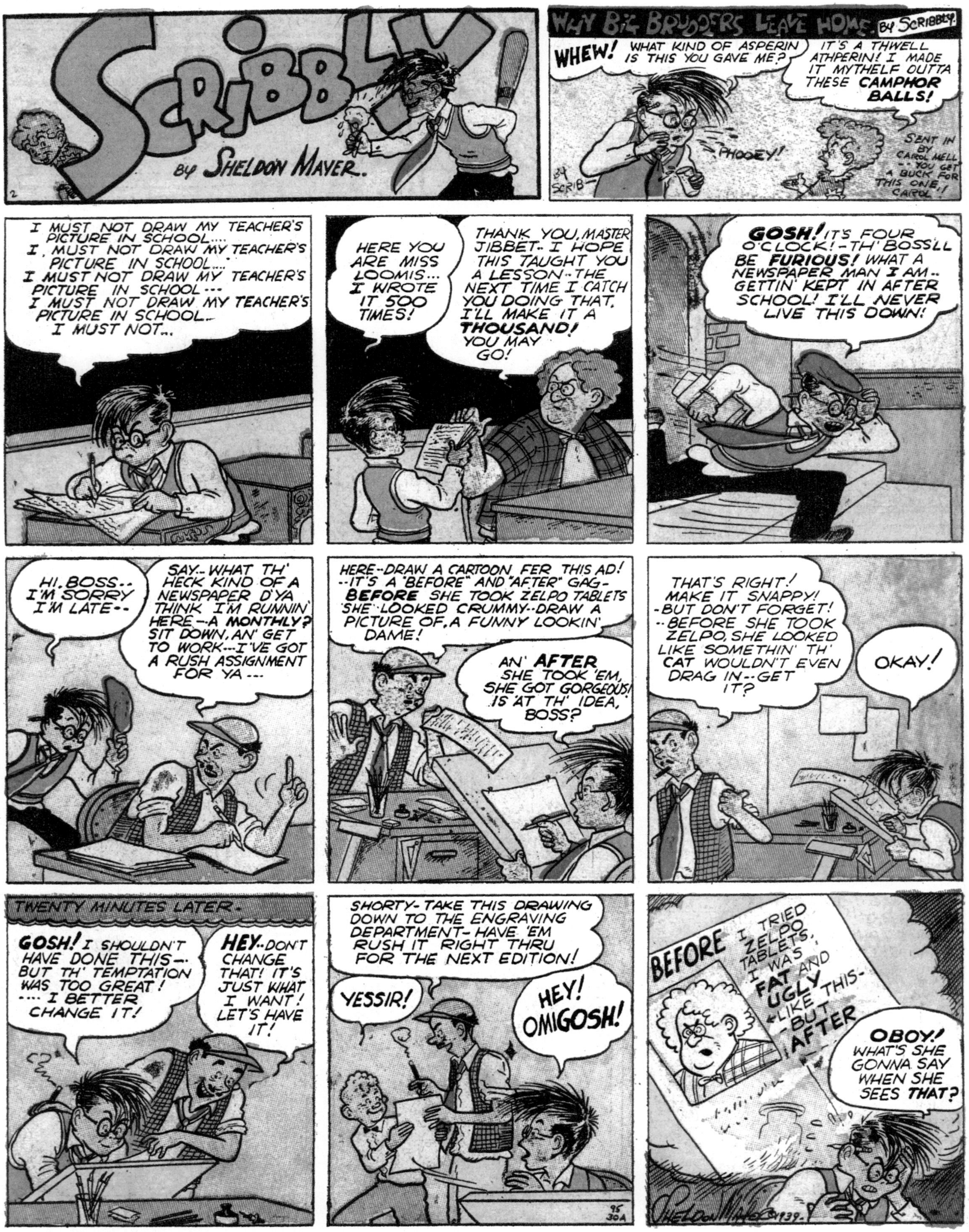
SCRIBBLY
BY SHELDON MAYER
WHY BIG BRUDDERS LEAVE HOME. BY SCRIBBLY
WHEW!
WHAT KIND OF ASPERIN IS THIS YOU GAVE ME?
IT'S A THWELL ATHPERIN! I MADE IT MYTHELF OUTTA THESE CAMPHOR BALLS!
PHOOEY!
SENT IN BY CAROL MELL -- YOU GET A BUCK FOR THIS ONE, CAROL!
I MUST NOT DRAW MY TEACHER'S PICTURE IN SCHOOL.... I MUST NOT DRAW MY TEACHER'S PICTURE IN SCHOOL.... I MUST NOT DRAW MY TEACHER'S PICTURE IN SCHOOL--- I MUST NOT DRAW MY TEACHER'S PICTURE IN SCHOOL-- I MUST NOT...
HERE YOU ARE MISS LOOMIS... I WROTE IT 500 TIMES!
THANK YOU, MASTER JIBBET-- I HOPE THIS TAUGHT YOU A LESSON--THE NEXT TIME I CATCH YOU DOING THAT, I'LL MAKE IT A THOUSAND! YOU MAY GO!
GOSH! IT'S FOUR O'CLOCK!--TH' BOSS'LL BE FURIOUS! WHAT A NEWSPAPER MAN I AM.. GETTIN' KEPT IN AFTER SCHOOL! I'LL NEVER LIVE THIS DOWN!
HI, BOSS-- I'M SORRY I'M LATE--
SAY--WHAT TH' HECK KIND OF A NEWSPAPER D'YA THINK I'M RUNNIN' HERE--A MONTHLY? SIT DOWN, AN' GET TO WORK---I'VE GOT A RUSH ASSIGNMENT FOR YA---
HERE--DRAW A CARTOON FER THIS AD! --IT'S A "BEFORE" AND "AFTER" GAG-- BEFORE SHE TOOK ZELPO TABLETS SHE LOOKED CRUMMY--DRAW A PICTURE OF A FUNNY LOOKIN' DAME!
AN' AFTER SHE TOOK 'EM, SHE GOT GORGEOUS! IS AT TH' IDEA, BOSS?
THAT'S RIGHT! MAKE IT SNAPPY! -BUT DON'T FORGET! --BEFORE SHE TOOK ZELPO, SHE LOOKED LIKE SOMETHIN' TH' CAT WOULDN'T EVEN DRAG IN--GET IT?
OKAY!
TWENTY MINUTES LATER-
GOSH! I SHOULDN'T HAVE DONE THIS-- BUT TH' TEMPTATION WAS TOO GREAT! ---- I BETTER CHANGE IT!
HEY..DON'T CHANGE THAT! IT'S JUST WHAT I WANT! LET'S HAVE IT!
SHORTY- TAKE THIS DRAWING DOWN TO THE ENGRAVING DEPARTMENT- HAVE 'EM RUSH IT RIGHT THRU FOR THE NEXT EDITION!
YESSIR!
HEY! OMIGOSH!
BEFORE I TRIED ZELPO TABLETS, I WAS FAT AND UGLY LIKE THIS- -BUT AFTER
OBOY! WHAT'S SHE GONNA SAY WHEN SHE SEES THAT?
SHELDON MAYER 1939.

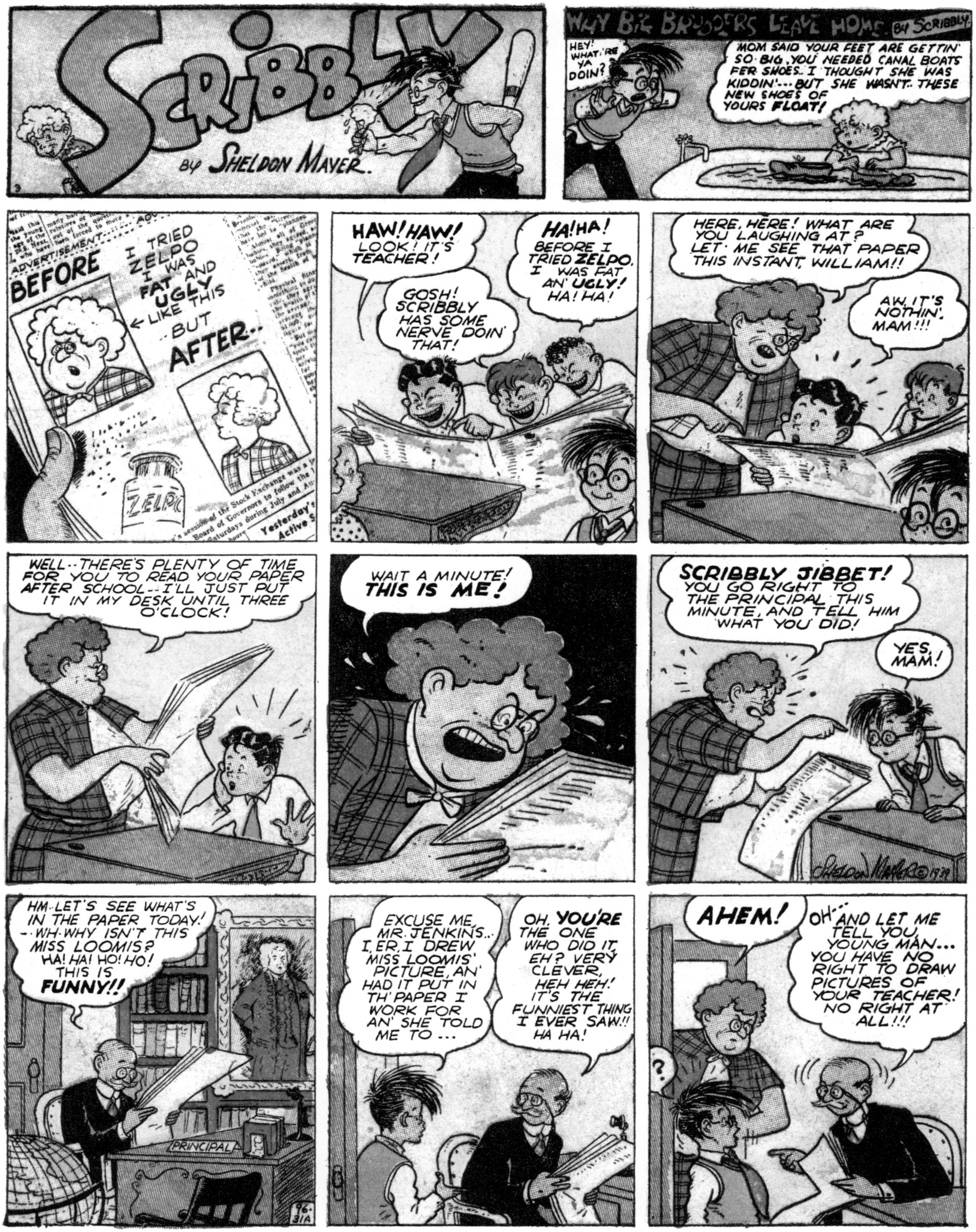
SCRIBBLY
BY SHELDON MAYER.
WHY BIG BRUDDERS LEAVE HOME. BY SCRIBBLY.
HEY! WHAT 'RE YA DOIN?
MOM SAID YOUR FEET ARE GETTIN' SO BIG, YOU NEEDED CANAL BOATS FER SHOES.. I THOUGHT SHE WAS KIDDIN'--- BUT SHE WASN'T.. THESE NEW SHOES OF YOURS FLOAT!
ADVERTISEMENT
BEFORE I TRIED ZELPO I WAS FAT AND UGLY ← LIKE THIS
BUT AFTER..
ZELPO
HAW! HAW! LOOK! IT'S TEACHER!
GOSH! SCRIBBLY HAS SOME NERVE DOIN' THAT!
HA! HA! BEFORE I TRIED ZELPO, I WAS FAT AN' UGLY! HA! HA!
HERE, HERE! WHAT ARE YOU LAUGHING AT? LET ME SEE THAT PAPER THIS INSTANT, WILLIAM!!
AW, IT'S NOTHIN', MAM!!!
WELL-- THERE'S PLENTY OF TIME FOR YOU TO READ YOUR PAPER AFTER SCHOOL-- I'LL JUST PUT IT IN MY DESK UNTIL THREE O'CLOCK!
WAIT A MINUTE! THIS IS ME!
SCRIBBLY JIBBET! YOU GO RIGHT TO THE PRINCIPAL THIS MINUTE, AND TELL HIM WHAT YOU DID!
YES, MAM!
SHELDON MAYER © 1939
HM. LET'S SEE WHAT'S IN THE PAPER TODAY! -- WH- WHY ISN'T THIS MISS LOOMIS? HA! HA! HO! HO! THIS IS FUNNY!!
PRINCIPAL
EXCUSE ME, MR. JENKINS... I, ER, I DREW MISS LOOMIS' PICTURE, AN' HAD IT PUT IN TH' PAPER I WORK FOR AN' SHE TOLD ME TO ...
OH, YOU'RE THE ONE WHO DID IT, EH? VERY CLEVER, HEH HEH! IT'S THE FUNNIEST THING I EVER SAW!! HA HA!
AHEM!
OH--- AND LET ME TELL YOU, YOUNG MAN... YOU HAVE NO RIGHT TO DRAW PICTURES OF YOUR TEACHER! NO RIGHT AT ALL!!!
?

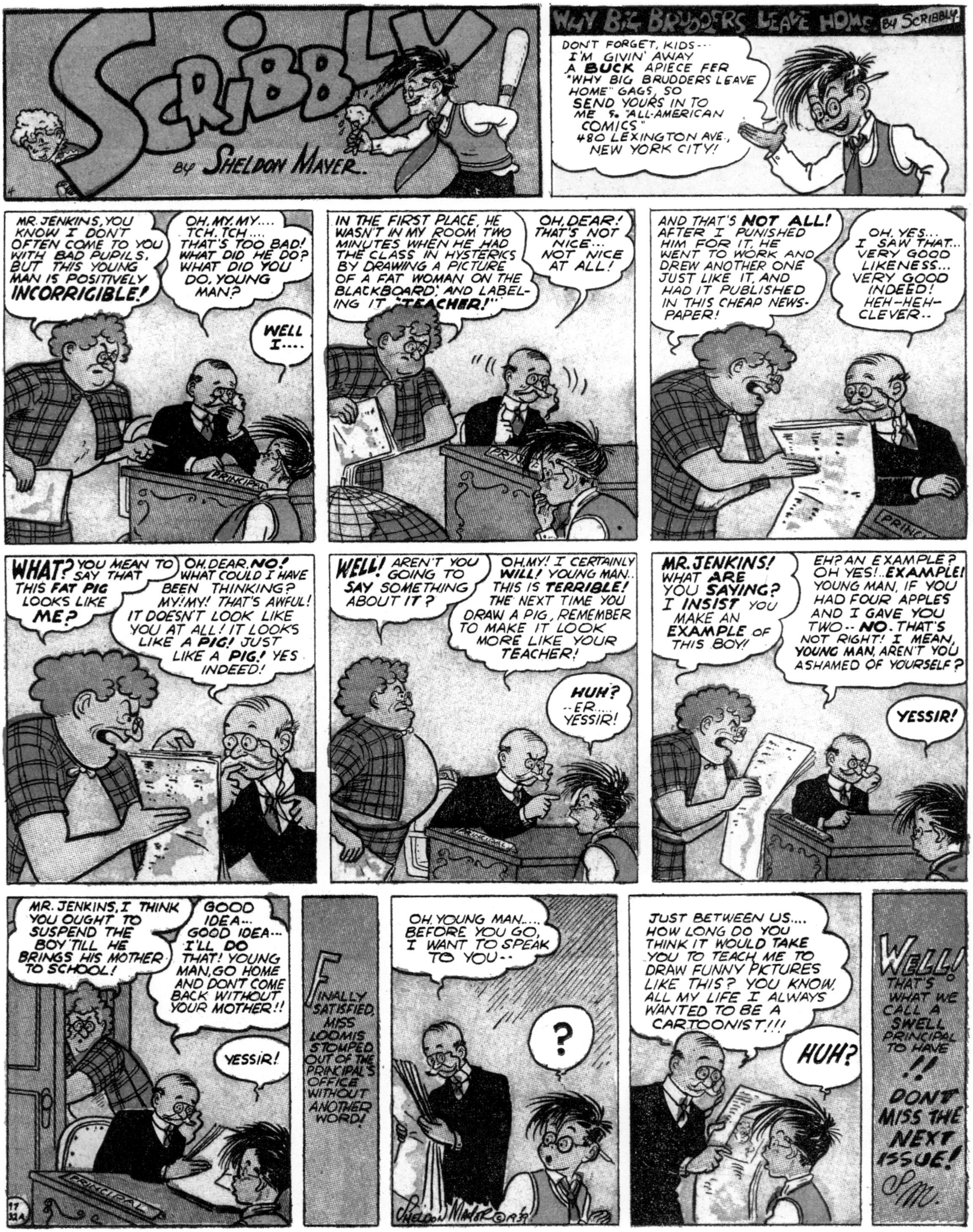
SCRIBBLY
BY SHELDON MAYER
WHY BIG BRUDDERS LEAVE HOME. BY SCRIBBLY
DON'T FORGET, KIDS--- I'M GIVIN' AWAY A BUCK APIECE FER "WHY BIG BRUDDERS LEAVE HOME" GAGS, SO SEND YOURS IN TO ME % "ALL-AMERICAN COMICS" 480 LEXINGTON AVE., NEW YORK CITY!
MR. JENKINS, YOU KNOW I DON'T OFTEN COME TO YOU WITH BAD PUPILS, BUT THIS YOUNG MAN IS POSITIVELY INCORRIGIBLE!
OH, MY, MY.... TCH, TCH.... THAT'S TOO BAD! WHAT DID HE DO? WHAT DID YOU DO, YOUNG MAN?
WELL I....
IN THE FIRST PLACE, HE WASN'T IN MY ROOM TWO MINUTES WHEN HE HAD THE CLASS IN HYSTERICS BY DRAWING A PICTURE OF A FAT WOMAN ON THE BLACKBOARD, AND LABELING IT "TEACHER!"
OH, DEAR! THAT'S NOT NICE... NOT NICE AT ALL!
AND THAT'S NOT ALL! AFTER I PUNISHED HIM FOR IT, HE WENT TO WORK AND DREW ANOTHER ONE JUST LIKE IT, AND HAD IT PUBLISHED IN THIS CHEAP NEWSPAPER!
OH, YES... I SAW THAT... VERY GOOD LIKENESS... VERY GOOD INDEED! HEH-HEH CLEVER--
WHAT? YOU MEAN TO SAY THAT THIS FAT PIG LOOKS LIKE ME?
OH, DEAR, NO! WHAT COULD I HAVE BEEN THINKING? MY! MY! THAT'S AWFUL! IT DOESN'T LOOK LIKE YOU AT ALL! IT LOOKS LIKE A PIG! JUST LIKE A PIG! YES INDEED!
WELL! AREN'T YOU GOING TO SAY SOMETHING ABOUT IT?
OH, MY! I CERTAINLY WILL! YOUNG MAN.. THIS IS TERRIBLE! THE NEXT TIME YOU DRAW A PIG, REMEMBER TO MAKE IT LOOK MORE LIKE YOUR TEACHER!
HUH? --ER..... YESSIR!
MR. JENKINS! WHAT ARE YOU SAYING? I INSIST YOU MAKE AN EXAMPLE OF THIS BOY!
EH? AN EXAMPLE? OH YES!..EXAMPLE! YOUNG MAN, IF YOU HAD FOUR APPLES AND I GAVE YOU TWO -- NO. THAT'S NOT RIGHT! I MEAN, YOUNG MAN, AREN'T YOU ASHAMED OF YOURSELF?
YESSIR!
MR. JENKINS, I THINK YOU OUGHT TO SUSPEND THE BOY 'TILL HE BRINGS HIS MOTHER TO SCHOOL!
GOOD IDEA... GOOD IDEA--- I'LL DO THAT! YOUNG MAN, GO HOME AND DON'T COME BACK WITHOUT YOUR MOTHER!!
YESSIR!
FINALLY SATISFIED, MISS LOOMIS STOMPED OUT OF THE PRINCIPAL'S OFFICE WITHOUT ANOTHER WORD!
OH, YOUNG MAN.... BEFORE YOU GO, I WANT TO SPEAK TO YOU--
?
JUST BETWEEN US.... HOW LONG DO YOU THINK IT WOULD TAKE YOU TO TEACH ME TO DRAW FUNNY PICTURES LIKE THIS? YOU KNOW, ALL MY LIFE I ALWAYS WANTED TO BE A CARTOONIST!!!
HUH?
WELL! THAT'S WHAT WE CALL A SWELL PRINCIPAL TO HAVE !! DON'T MISS THE NEXT ISSUE!
S.M.
SHELDON MAYER ©1939
PRINCIPAL

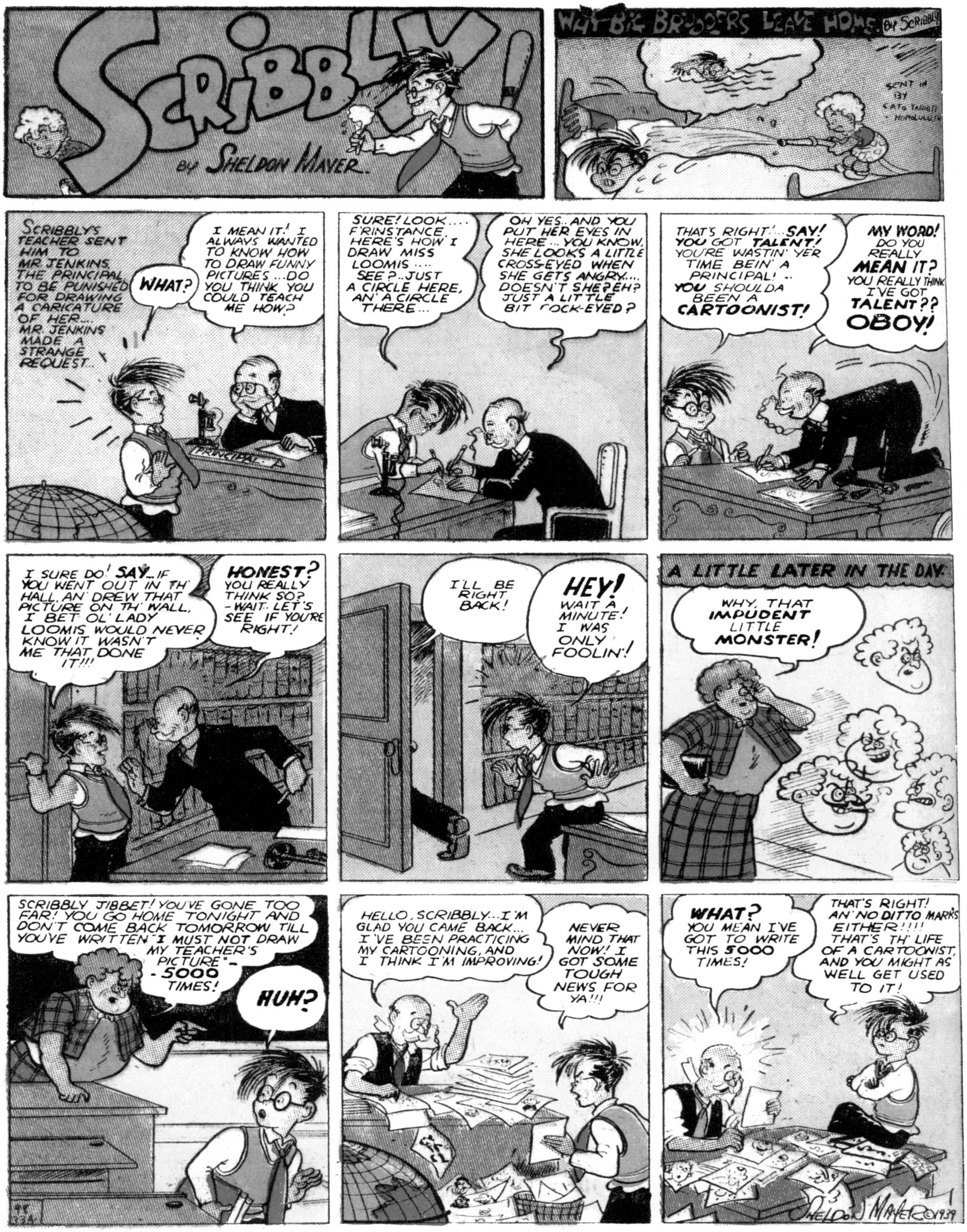
SCRIBBLY!
BY SHELDON MAYER
WHY BIG BRUDDERS LEAVE HOME. BY SCRIBBLY
SCRIBBLY'S TEACHER SENT HIM TO MR. JENKINS, THE PRINCIPAL, TO BE PUNISHED FOR DRAWING A CARICATURE OF HER.... MR. JENKINS MADE A STRANGE REQUEST...
I MEAN IT! I ALWAYS WANTED TO KNOW HOW TO DRAW FUNNY PICTURES ...DO YOU THINK YOU COULD TEACH ME HOW?
WHAT?
PRINCIPAL
SURE! LOOK.... F'RINSTANCE, HERE'S HOW I DRAW MISS LOOMIS .... SEE?..JUST A CIRCLE HERE, AN' A CIRCLE THERE...
OH YES..AND YOU PUT HER EYES IN HERE... YOU KNOW, SHE LOOKS A LITTLE CROSS-EYED WHEN SHE GETS ANGRY.... DOESN'T SHE? EH? JUST A LITTLE BIT COCK-EYED?
THAT'S RIGHT!...SAY! YOU GOT TALENT! YOU'RE WASTIN' YER TIME BEIN' A PRINCIPAL! .. YOU SHOULDA BEEN A CARTOONIST!
MY WORD! DO YOU REALLY MEAN IT? YOU REALLY THINK I'VE GOT TALENT?? OBOY!
I SURE DO! SAY...IF YOU WENT OUT IN TH' HALL, AN' DREW THAT PICTURE ON TH' WALL, I BET OL' LADY LOOMIS WOULD NEVER KNOW IT WASN'T ME THAT DONE IT!!!
HONEST? YOU REALLY THINK SO? -WAIT- LET'S SEE IF YOU'RE RIGHT!
I'LL BE RIGHT BACK!
HEY! WAIT A MINUTE! I WAS ONLY FOOLIN'!
A LITTLE LATER IN THE DAY.
WHY, THAT IMPUDENT LITTLE MONSTER!
SCRIBBLY JIBBET! YOU'VE GONE TOO FAR! YOU GO HOME TONIGHT AND DON'T COME BACK TOMORROW TILL YOU'VE WRITTEN "I MUST NOT DRAW MY TEACHER'S PICTURE" - 5000 TIMES!
HUH?
HELLO, SCRIBBLY...I'M GLAD YOU CAME BACK... I'VE BEEN PRACTICING MY CARTOONING, AND I THINK I'M IMPROVING!
NEVER MIND THAT NOW! I GOT SOME TOUGH NEWS FOR YA!!!
WHAT? YOU MEAN I'VE GOT TO WRITE THIS 5000 TIMES!
THAT'S RIGHT! AN' NO DITTO MARKS EITHER!!!! THAT'S TH' LIFE OF A CARTOONIST, AND YOU MIGHT AS WELL GET USED TO IT!
SHELDON MAYER ©1939

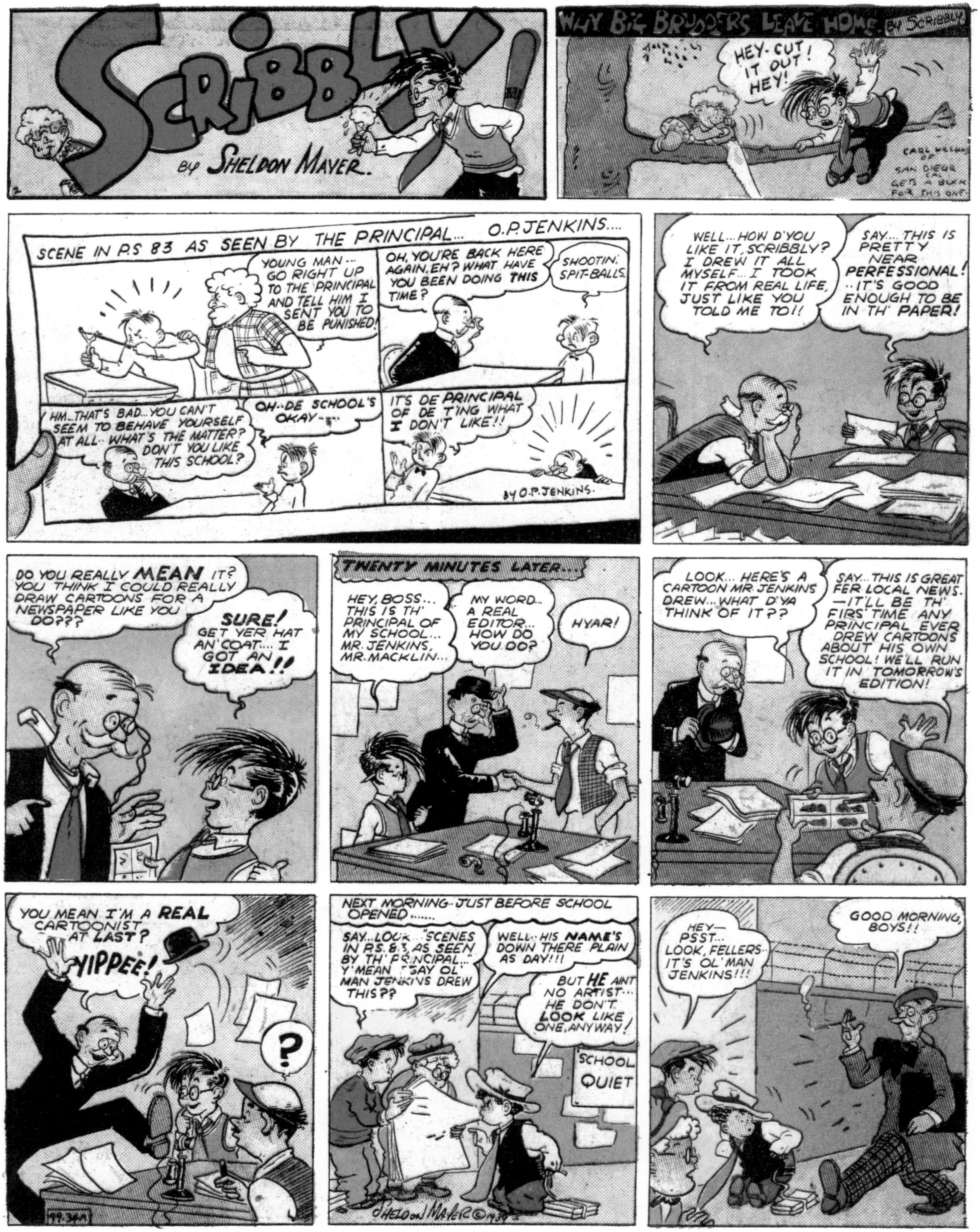
SCRIBBLY!
BY SHELDON MAYER.
WHY BIG BRUDDERS LEAVE HOME. BY SCRIBBLY
HEY-CUT IT OUT! HEY!
SCENE IN P.S 83 AS SEEN BY THE PRINCIPAL... O.P. JENKINS....
YOUNG MAN... GO RIGHT UP TO THE PRINCIPAL AND TELL HIM I SENT YOU TO BE PUNISHED!
OH, YOU'RE BACK HERE AGAIN, EH? WHAT HAVE YOU BEEN DOING THIS TIME?
SHOOTIN' SPIT-BALLS.
HM... THAT'S BAD... YOU CAN'T SEEM TO BEHAVE YOURSELF AT ALL.. WHAT'S THE MATTER? DON'T YOU LIKE THIS SCHOOL?
OH.. DE SCHOOL'S OKAY--
IT'S DE PRINCIPAL OF DE T'ING WHAT I DON'T LIKE!!
BY O.P. JENKINS.
WELL... HOW D'YOU LIKE IT, SCRIBBLY? I DREW IT ALL MYSELF... I TOOK IT FROM REAL LIFE, JUST LIKE YOU TOLD ME TO!!
SAY.... THIS IS PRETTY NEAR PERFESSIONAL! ..IT'S GOOD ENOUGH TO BE IN TH' PAPER!
DO YOU REALLY MEAN IT? YOU THINK I COULD REALLY DRAW CARTOONS FOR A NEWSPAPER LIKE YOU DO???
SURE! GET YER HAT AN' COAT.... I GOT AN IDEA!!
TWENTY MINUTES LATER...
HEY, BOSS... THIS IS TH' PRINCIPAL OF MY SCHOOL... MR. JENKINS, MR. MACKLIN...
MY WORD.. A REAL EDITOR... HOW DO YOU DO?
HYAR!
LOOK... HERE'S A CARTOON MR JENKINS DREW... WHAT D'YA THINK OF IT??
SAY... THIS IS GREAT FER LOCAL NEWS. —IT'LL BE TH' FIRS' TIME ANY PRINCIPAL EVER DREW CARTOONS ABOUT HIS OWN SCHOOL! WE'LL RUN IT IN TOMORROW'S EDITION!
YOU MEAN I'M A REAL CARTOONIST AT LAST?
YIPPEE!
?
NEXT MORNING.. JUST BEFORE SCHOOL OPENED.......
SAY...LOOK... "SCENES IN P.S. 83, AS SEEN BY TH' PRINCIPAL..." Y'MEAN SAY OL' MAN JENKINS DREW THIS??
WELL.. HIS NAME'S DOWN THERE PLAIN AS DAY!!!
BUT HE AINT NO ARTIST... HE DON'T LOOK LIKE ONE, ANYWAY!
SCHOOL
QUIET
SHELDON MAYER ©1939
HEY— PSST... LOOK, FELLERS.. IT'S OL' MAN JENKINS!!!
GOOD MORNING, BOYS!!

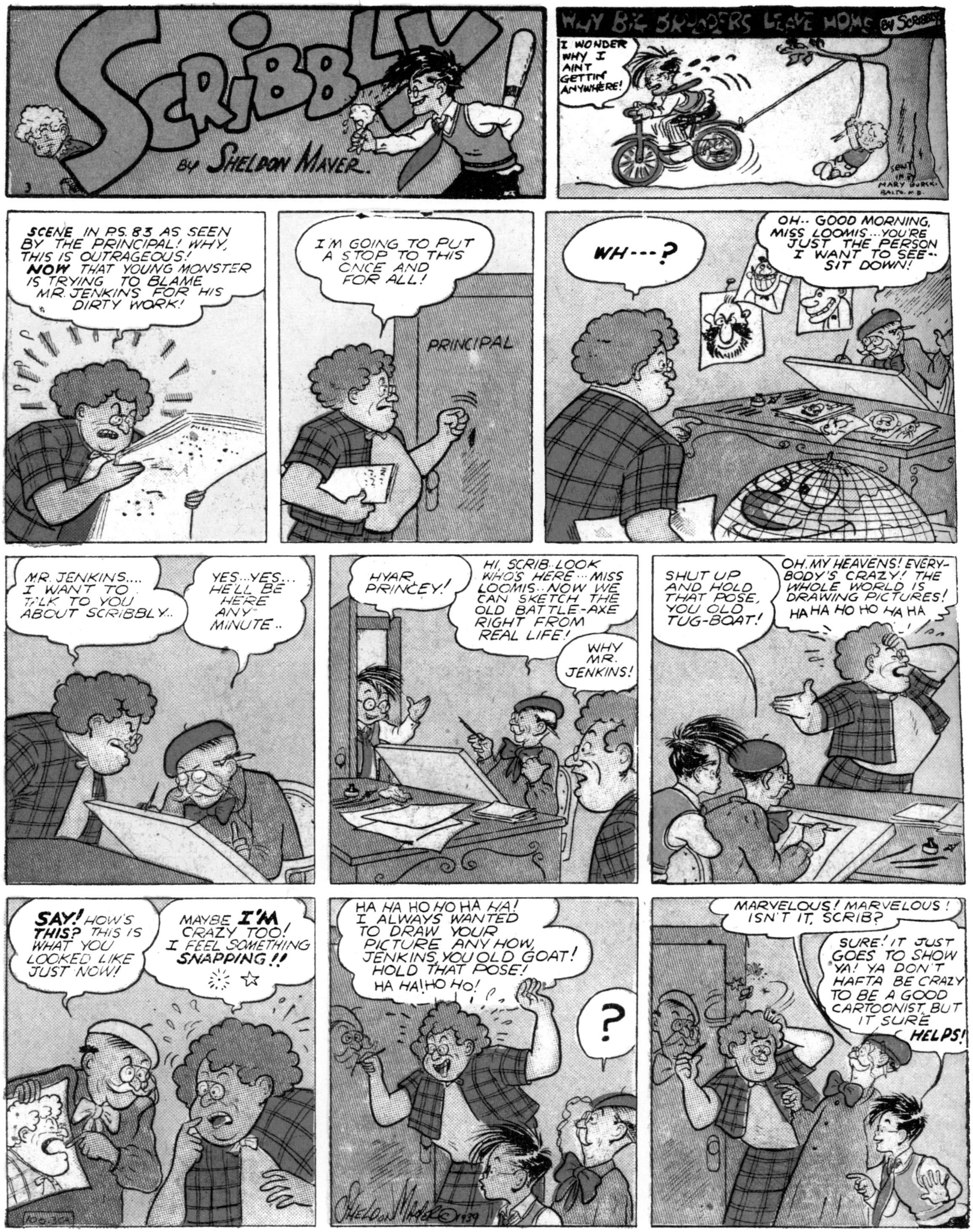
SCRIBBLY
BY SHELDON MAYER
WHY BIG BRUDDERS LEAVE HOME BY SCRIBBLY
I WONDER WHY I AINT GETTIN ANYWHERE!
SCENE IN P.S. 83 AS SEEN BY THE PRINCIPAL! WHY, THIS IS OUTRAGEOUS! NOW THAT YOUNG MONSTER IS TRYING TO BLAME MR. JENKINS FOR HIS DIRTY WORK!
I'M GOING TO PUT A STOP TO THIS ONCE AND FOR ALL!
PRINCIPAL
WH---?
OH.. GOOD MORNING, MISS LOOMIS... YOU'RE JUST THE PERSON I WANT TO SEE.. SIT DOWN!
MR. JENKINS.... I WANT TO TALK TO YOU ABOUT SCRIBBLY..
YES...YES... HE'LL BE HERE ANY MINUTE..
HYAR, PRINCEY!
HI, SCRIB..LOOK WHO'S HERE...MISS LOOMIS..NOW WE CAN SKETCH THE OLD BATTLE-AXE RIGHT FROM REAL LIFE!
WHY MR. JENKINS!
SHUT UP AND HOLD THAT POSE, YOU OLD TUG-BOAT!
OH, MY HEAVENS! EVERYBODY'S CRAZY! THE WHOLE WORLD IS DRAWING PICTURES! HA HA HO HO HA HA
SAY! HOW'S THIS? THIS IS WHAT YOU LOOKED LIKE JUST NOW!
MAYBE I'M CRAZY TOO! I FEEL SOMETHING SNAPPING!!
HA HA HO HO HA HA! I ALWAYS WANTED TO DRAW YOUR PICTURE ANY HOW, JENKINS, YOU OLD GOAT! HOLD THAT POSE! HA HA! HO HO!
?
SHELDON MAYER © 1939
MARVELOUS! MARVELOUS! ISN'T IT, SCRIB?
SURE! IT JUST GOES TO SHOW YA! YA DON'T HAFTA BE CRAZY TO BE A GOOD CARTOONIST, BUT IT SURE HELPS!

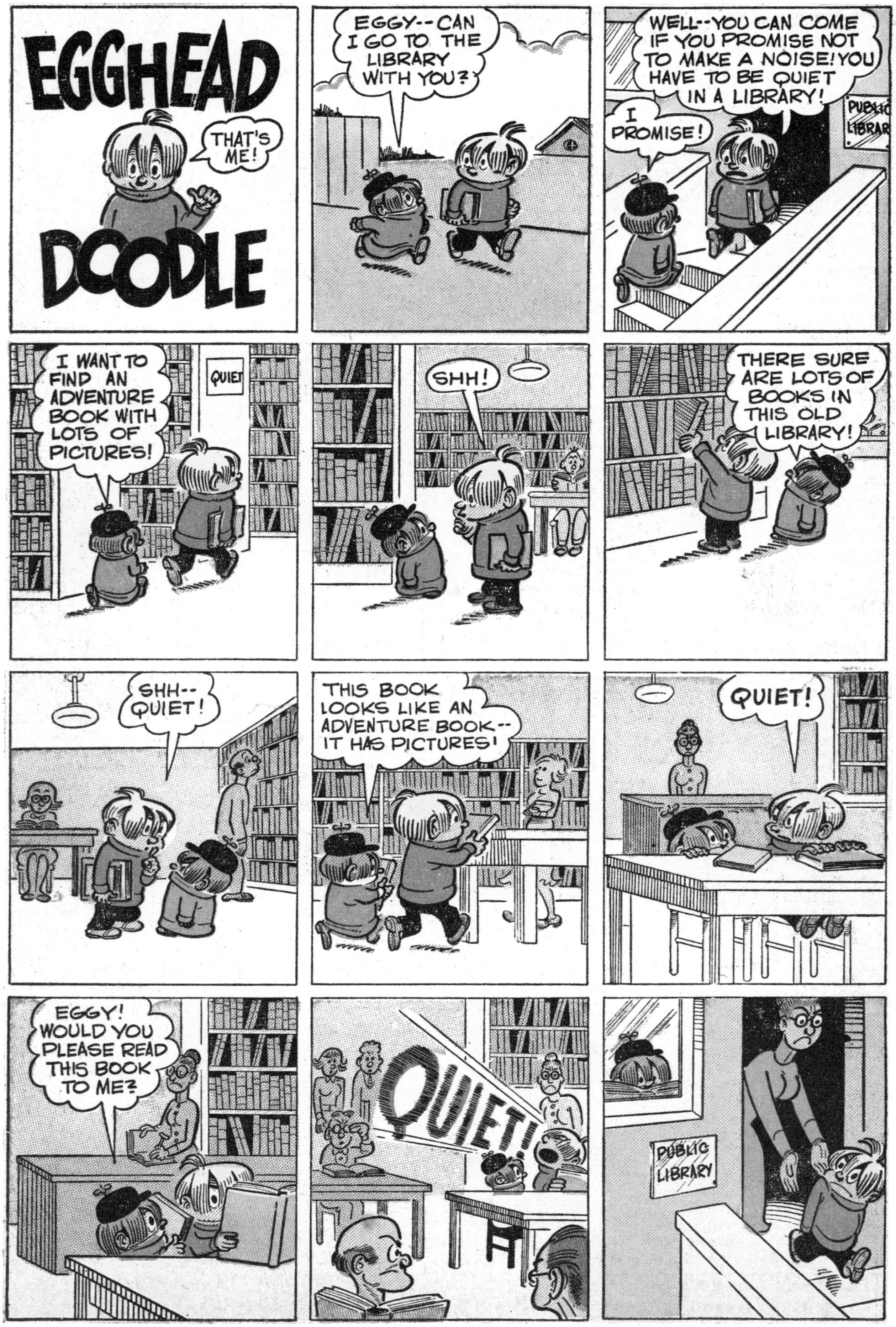
EGGHEAD DOODLE
THAT'S ME!
EGGY--CAN I GO TO THE LIBRARY WITH YOU?
WELL--YOU CAN COME IF YOU PROMISE NOT TO MAKE A NOISE! YOU HAVE TO BE QUIET IN A LIBRARY!
I PROMISE!
PUBLIC LIBRARY
I WANT TO FIND AN ADVENTURE BOOK WITH LOTS OF PICTURES!
QUIET
SHH!
THERE SURE ARE LOTS OF BOOKS IN THIS OLD LIBRARY!
SHH--QUIET!
THIS BOOK LOOKS LIKE AN ADVENTURE BOOK--IT HAS PICTURES!
QUIET!
EGGY! WOULD YOU PLEASE READ THIS BOOK TO ME?
QUIET!
PUBLIC LIBRARY

Intellectual AMOS

by André LeBlanc

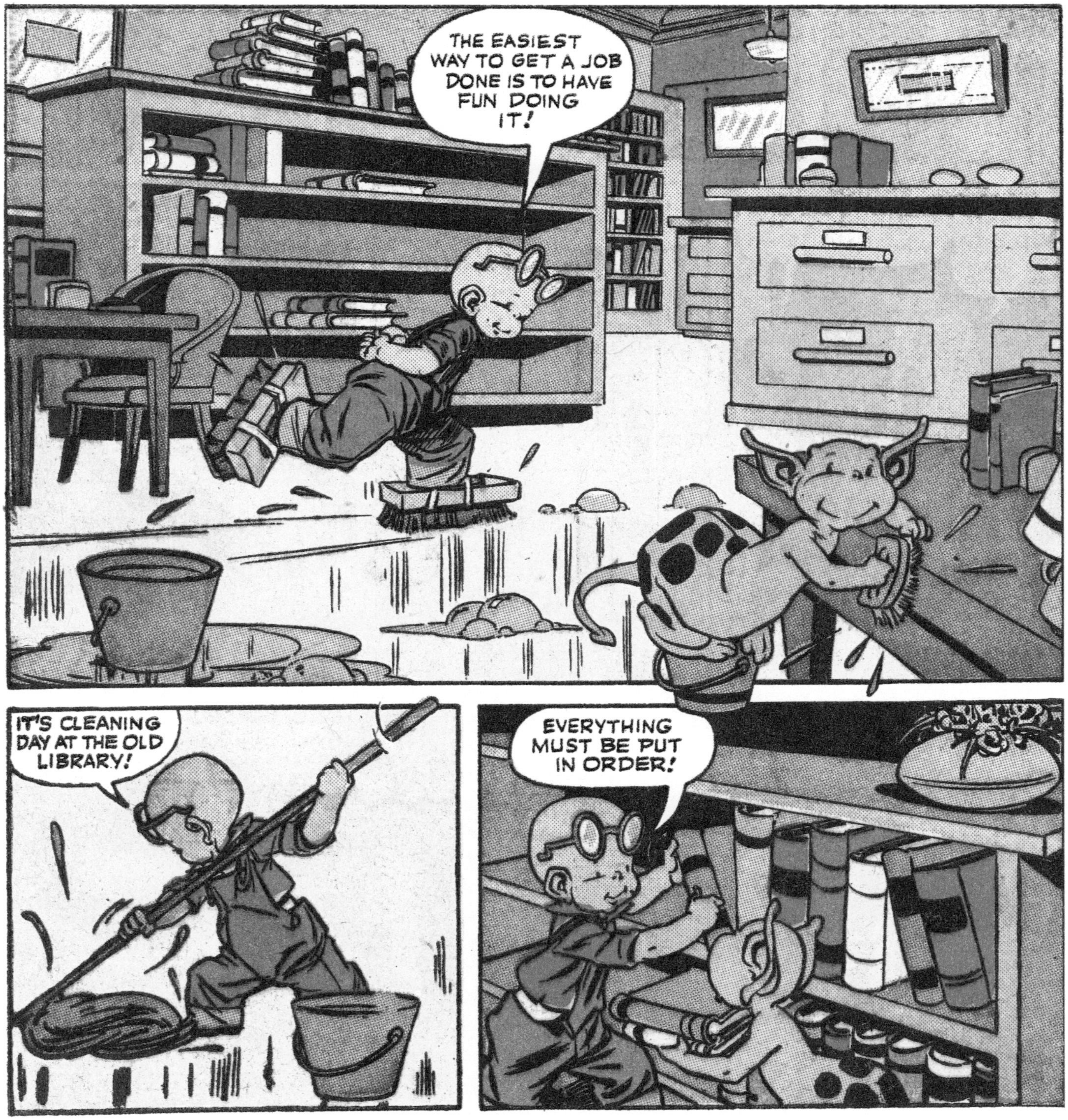
THE EASIEST WAY TO GET A JOB DONE IS TO HAVE FUN DOING IT!
IT'S CLEANING DAY AT THE OLD LIBRARY!
EVERYTHING MUST BE PUT IN ORDER!

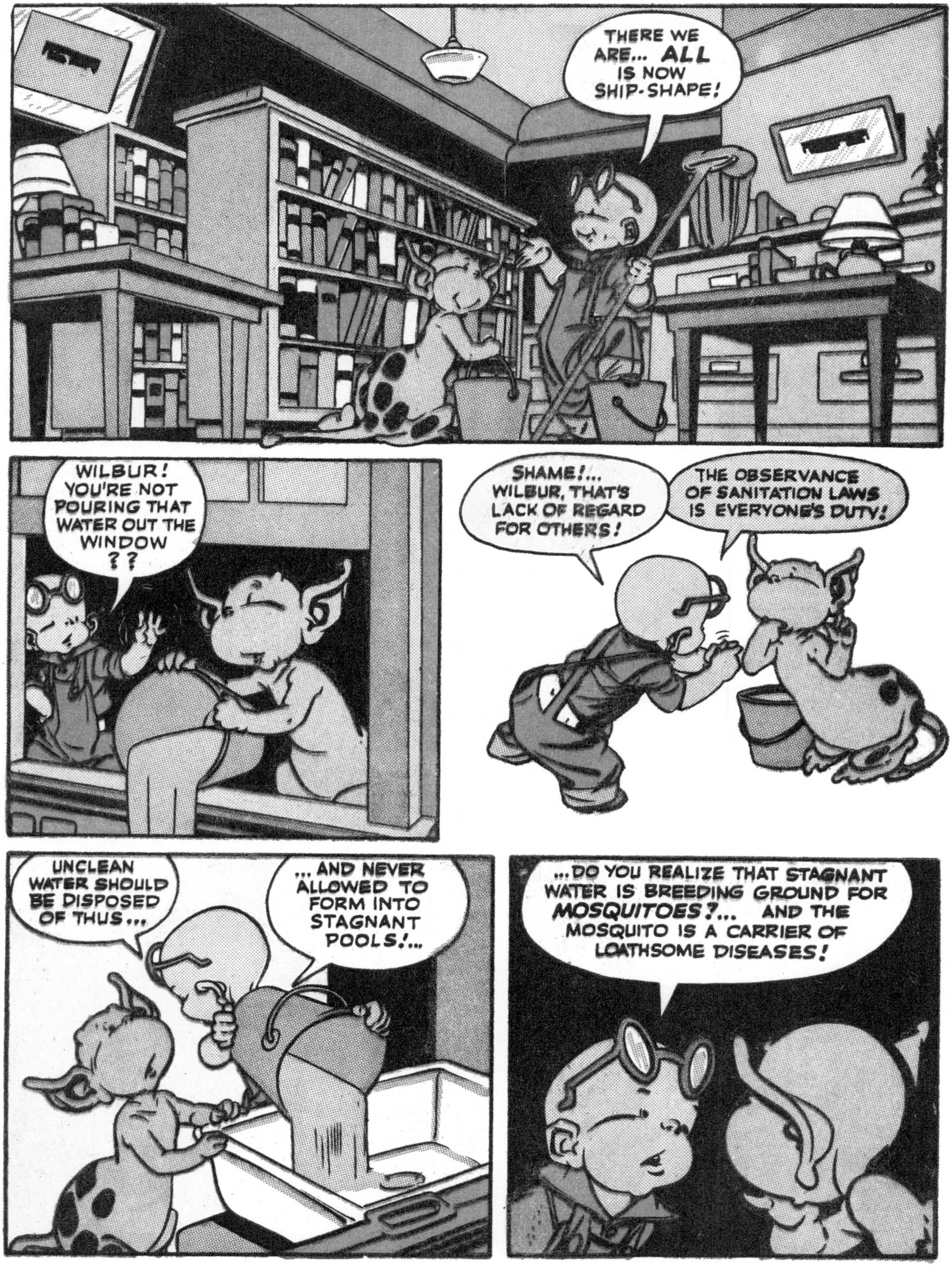
THERE WE ARE... ALL IS NOW SHIP-SHAPE!
WILBUR! YOU'RE NOT POURING THAT WATER OUT THE WINDOW ??
SHAME!... WILBUR, THAT'S LACK OF REGARD FOR OTHERS!
THE OBSERVANCE OF SANITATION LAWS IS EVERYONE'S DUTY!
UNCLEAN WATER SHOULD BE DISPOSED OF THUS...
...AND NEVER ALLOWED TO FORM INTO STAGNANT POOLS!...
...DO YOU REALIZE THAT STAGNANT WATER IS BREEDING GROUND FOR MOSQUITOES?... AND THE MOSQUITO IS A CARRIER OF LOATHSOME DISEASES!

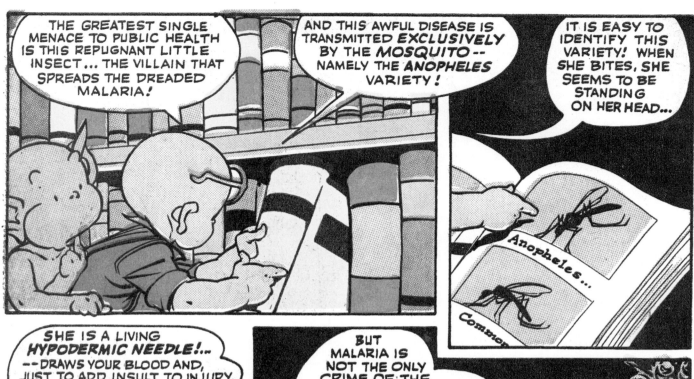

THE GREATEST SINGLE MENACE TO PUBLIC HEALTH IS THIS REPUGNANT LITTLE INSECT... THE VILLAIN THAT SPREADS THE DREADED MALARIA!

AND THIS AWFUL DISEASE IS TRANSMITTED *EXCLUSIVELY* BY THE *MOSQUITO* -- NAMELY THE *ANOPHELES* VARIETY!

IT IS EASY TO IDENTIFY THIS VARIETY! WHEN SHE BITES, SHE SEEMS TO BE STANDING ON HER HEAD...

SHE IS A LIVING *HYPODERMIC NEEDLE!*...-- DRAWS YOUR BLOOD AND, JUST TO ADD INSULT TO INJURY, -- MAY *INJECT* A VILE DISEASE INTO YOUR BLOOD STREAM!

BUT MALARIA IS NOT THE ONLY CRIME OF THE MOSQUITO! IT IS ALSO AGENT OF YELLOW FEVER, DENGUE, ELE- PHANTIASIS, AND OTHER HORRIBLE DISEASES!...

HO-HUM! AND SO TO BED... THEY EVEN SAY MALARIA WAS ONE OF THE FACTORS THAT WEAKENED THE ROMAN EMPIRE!

HEED WELL, WILBUR!... A MOSQUITO IS A *LITTLE* MITE, BUT IT CAN CAUSE GREAT DAMAGE!

GOOD NIGHT!

ZZZZZZ!

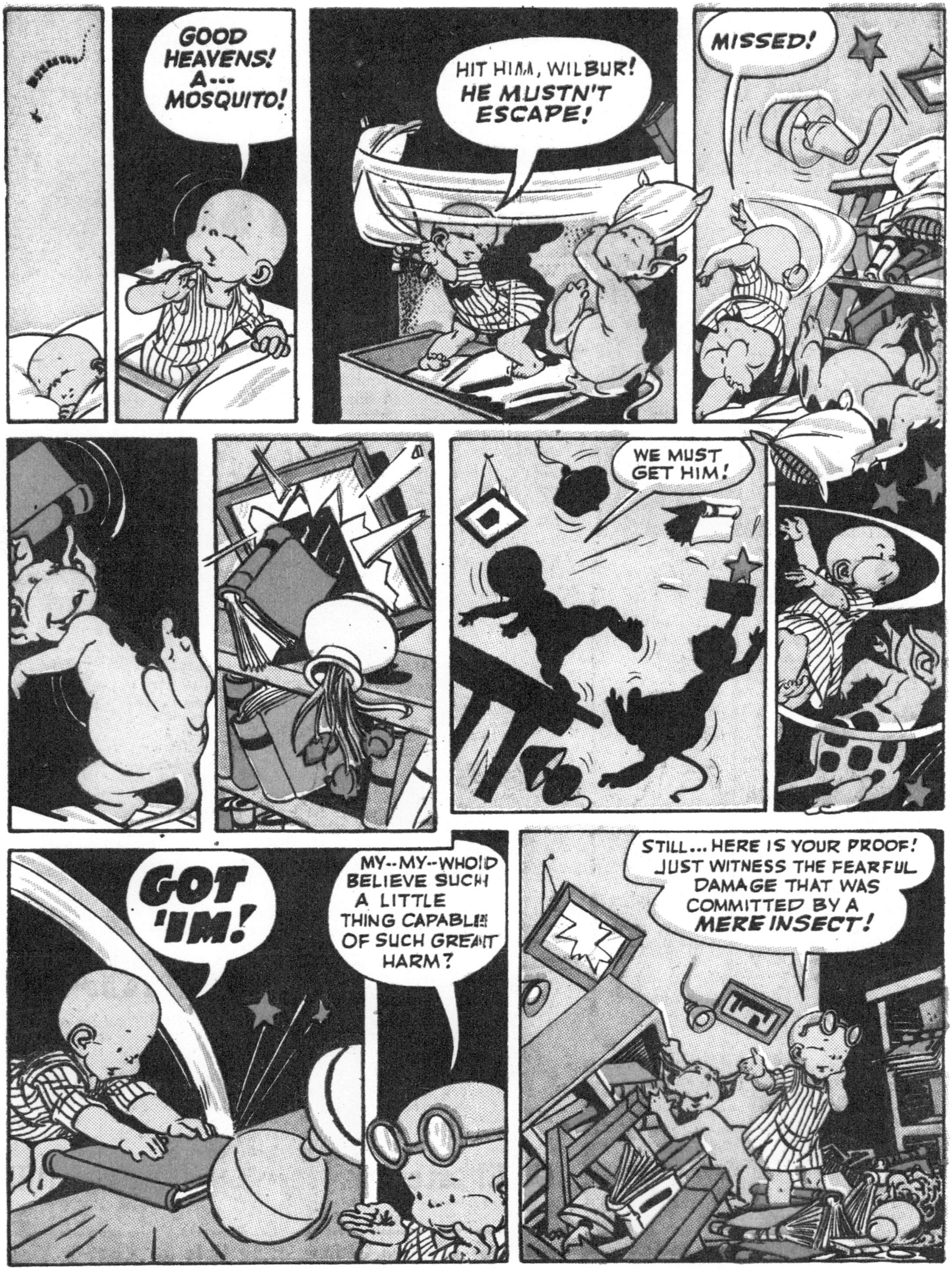
GOOD HEAVENS! A... MOSQUITO!
HIT HIM, WILBUR! HE MUSTN'T ESCAPE!
MISSED!
WE MUST GET HIM!
GOT 'IM!
MY--MY--WHO'D BELIEVE SUCH A LITTLE THING CAPABLE OF SUCH GREAT HARM?
STILL... HERE IS YOUR PROOF! JUST WITNESS THE FEARFUL DAMAGE THAT WAS COMMITTED BY A MERE INSECT!

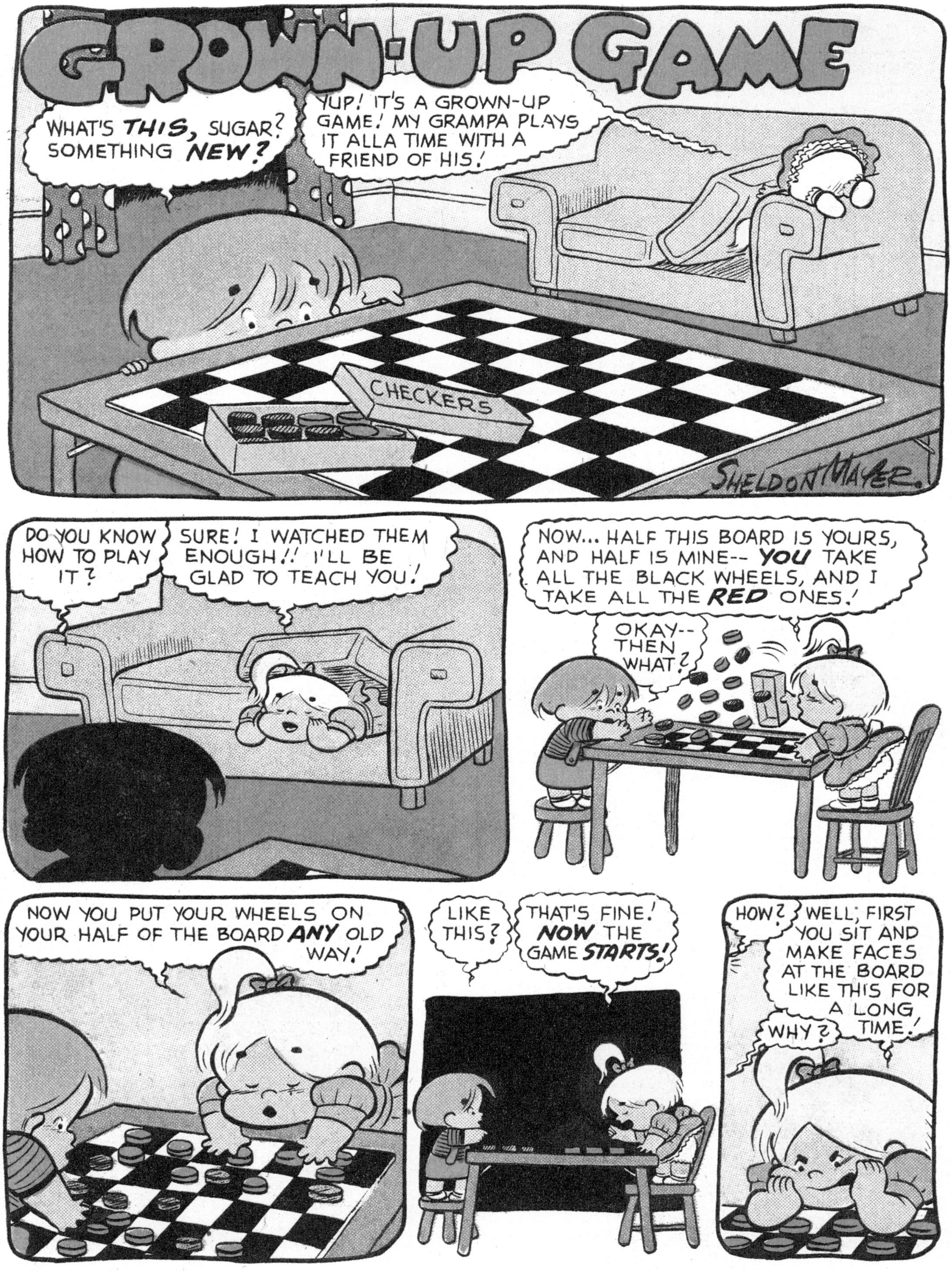
GROWN-UP GAME
WHAT'S THIS, SUGAR? SOMETHING NEW?
YUP! IT'S A GROWN-UP GAME! MY GRAMPA PLAYS IT ALLA TIME WITH A FRIEND OF HIS!
CHECKERS
SHELDON MAYER
DO YOU KNOW HOW TO PLAY IT?
SURE! I WATCHED THEM ENOUGH!! I'LL BE GLAD TO TEACH YOU!
NOW... HALF THIS BOARD IS YOURS, AND HALF IS MINE-- YOU TAKE ALL THE BLACK WHEELS, AND I TAKE ALL THE RED ONES!
OKAY-- THEN WHAT?
NOW YOU PUT YOUR WHEELS ON YOUR HALF OF THE BOARD ANY OLD WAY!
LIKE THIS?
THAT'S FINE! NOW THE GAME STARTS!
HOW?
WELL, FIRST YOU SIT AND MAKE FACES AT THE BOARD LIKE THIS FOR A LONG TIME!
WHY?

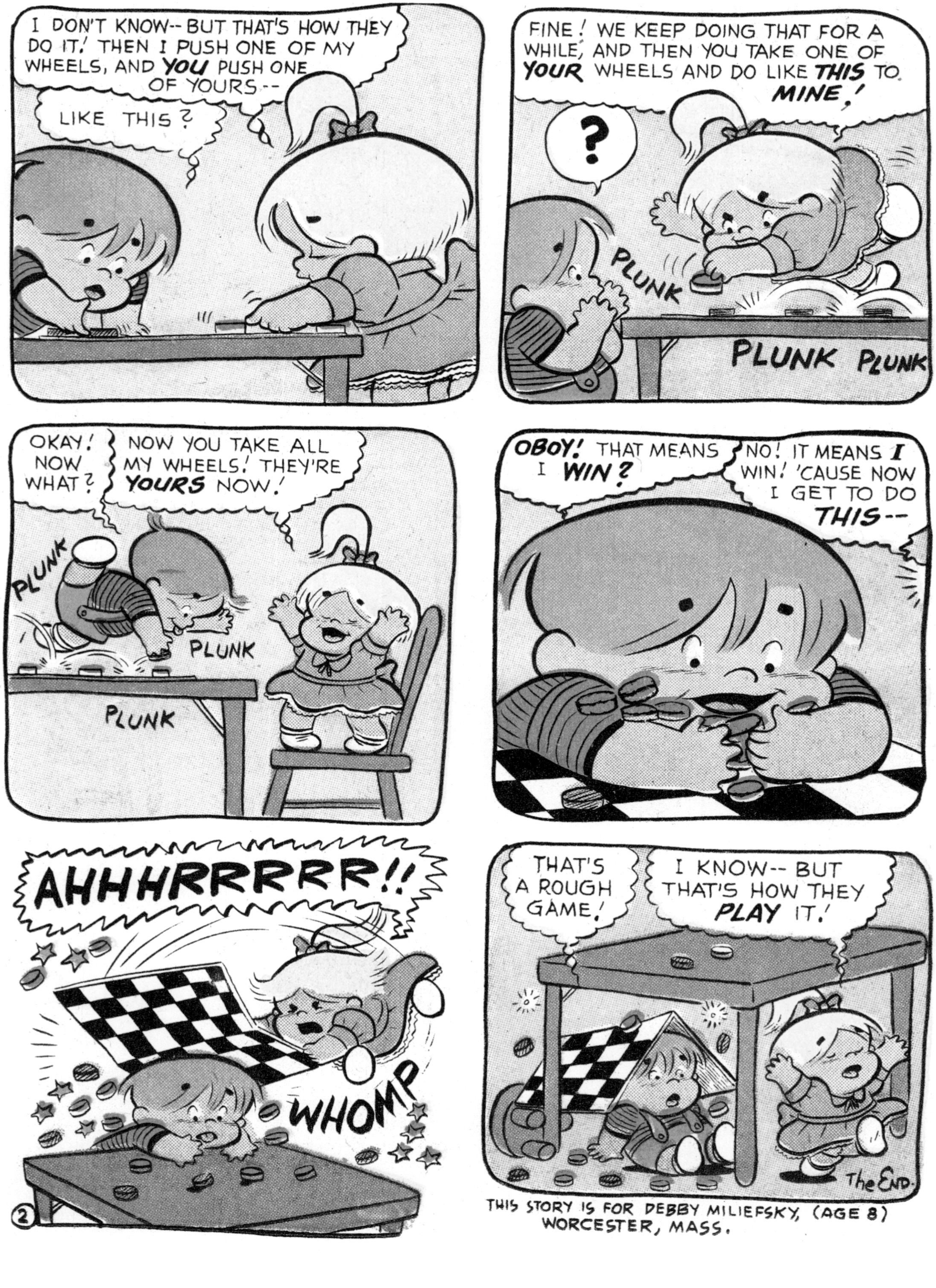
I DON'T KNOW-- BUT THAT'S HOW THEY DO IT! THEN I PUSH ONE OF MY WHEELS, AND YOU PUSH ONE OF YOURS--
LIKE THIS?
FINE! WE KEEP DOING THAT FOR A WHILE, AND THEN YOU TAKE ONE OF YOUR WHEELS AND DO LIKE THIS TO MINE!
?
PLUNK
PLUNK PLUNK
OKAY! NOW WHAT?
NOW YOU TAKE ALL MY WHEELS! THEY'RE YOURS NOW!
PLUNK
PLUNK
PLUNK
OBOY! THAT MEANS I WIN?
NO! IT MEANS I WIN! 'CAUSE NOW I GET TO DO THIS--
AHHHRRRRR!!
WHOMP
2
THAT'S A ROUGH GAME!
I KNOW-- BUT THAT'S HOW THEY PLAY IT!
The END
THIS STORY IS FOR DEBBY MILIEFSKY, (AGE 8) WORCESTER, MASS.

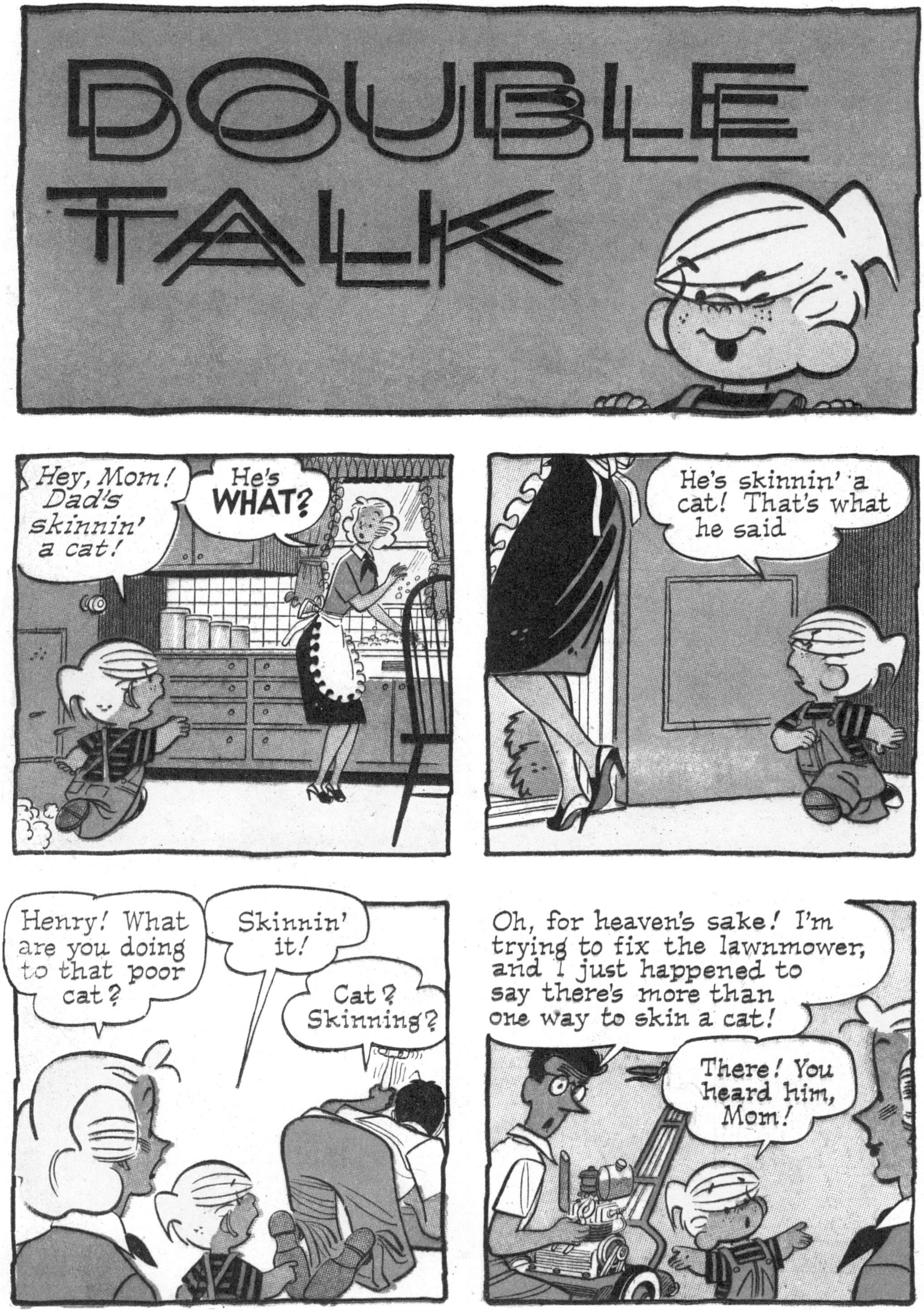
DOUBLE TALK
Hey, Mom! Dad's skinnin' a cat!
He's WHAT?
He's skinnin' a cat! That's what he said
Henry! What are you doing to that poor cat?
Skinnin' it!
Cat? Skinning?
Oh, for heaven's sake! I'm trying to fix the lawnmower, and I just happened to say there's more than one way to skin a cat!
There! You heard him, Mom!

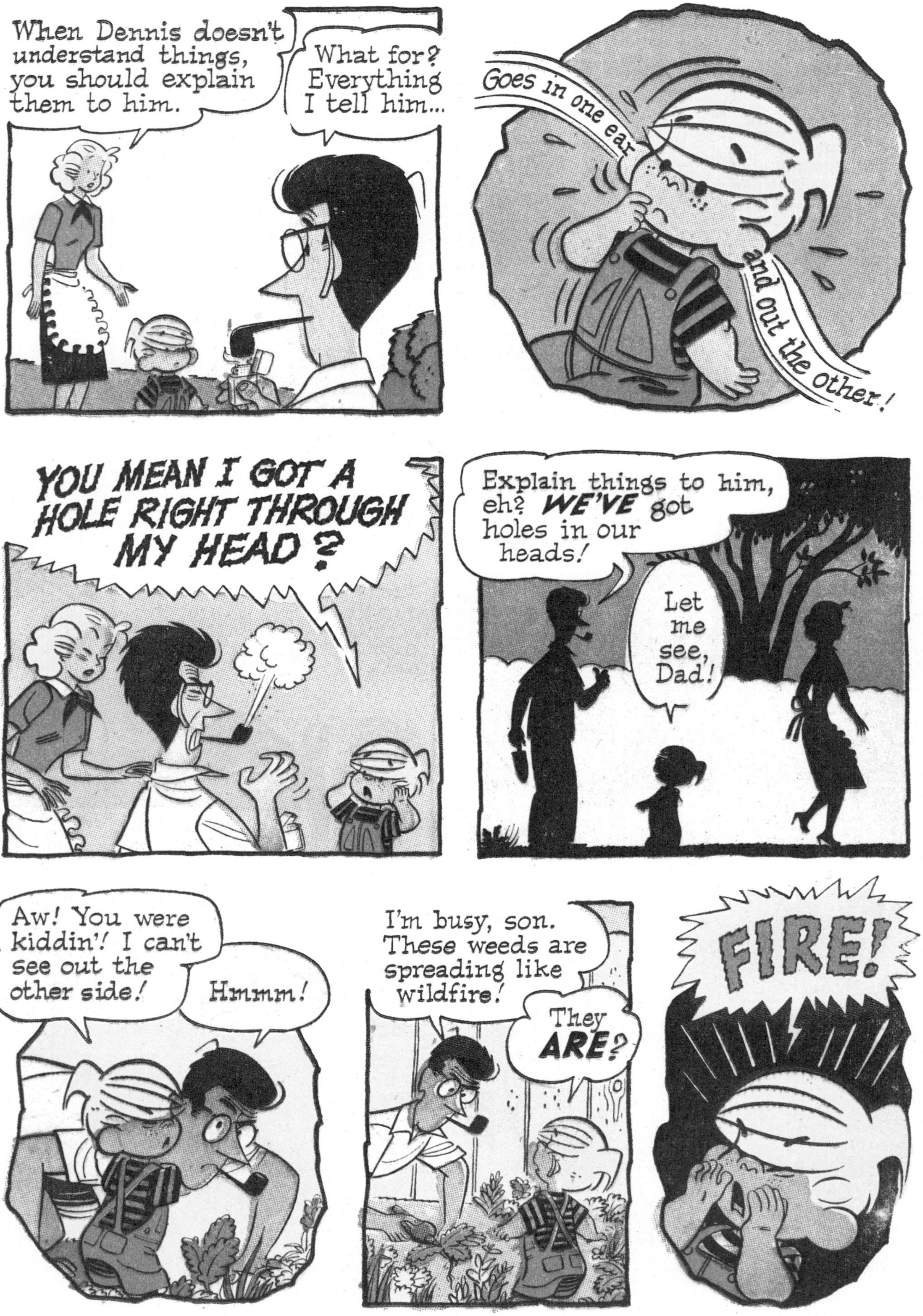
When Dennis doesn't understand things, you should explain them to him.
What for? Everything I tell him...
Goes in one ear
and out the other!
YOU MEAN I GOT A HOLE RIGHT THROUGH MY HEAD?
Explain things to him, eh? WE'VE got holes in our heads!
Let me see, Dad!
Aw! You were kiddin'! I can't see out the other side!
Hmmm!
I'm busy, son. These weeds are spreading like wildfire!
They ARE?
FIRE!

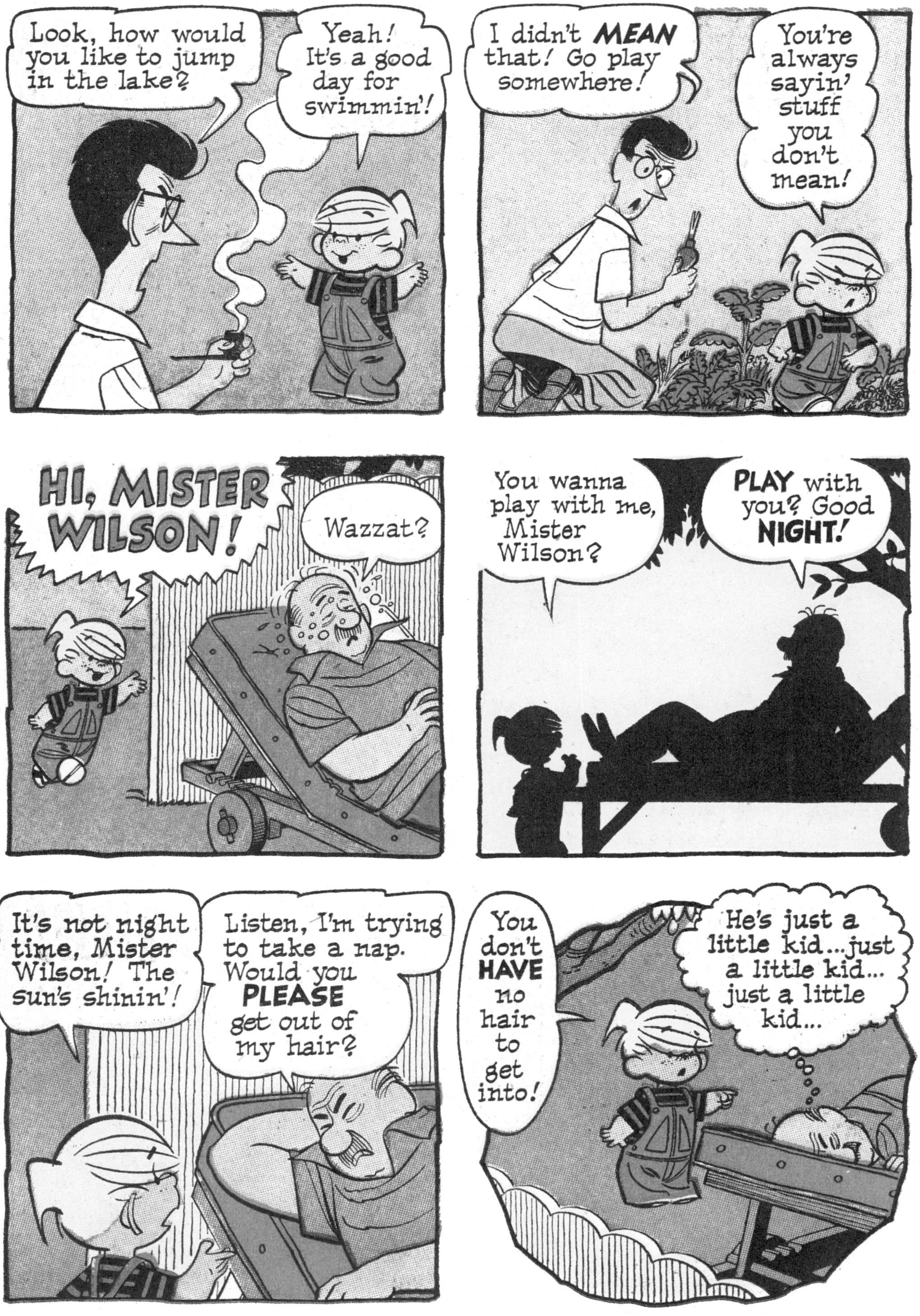
Look, how would you like to jump in the lake?
Yeah! It's a good day for swimmin'!
I didn't MEAN that! Go play somewhere!
You're always sayin' stuff you don't mean!
HI, MISTER WILSON!
Wazzat?
You wanna play with me, Mister Wilson?
PLAY with you? Good NIGHT!
It's not night time, Mister Wilson! The sun's shinin'!
Listen, I'm trying to take a nap. Would you PLEASE get out of my hair?
You don't HAVE no hair to get into!
He's just a little kid... just a little kid... just a little kid...

Lunch is ready, boys!
Okay! If you guys wanna talk silly, I can, too!
Hungry, Dennis?
Yeah! I could eat a gopher!
A gopher? Ug!
Were you over to the Wilsons, dear?
Yeah! but Mister Wilson was sleeping like a snorkle!
Like a WHAT?
Don't mind him, Henry. He's just...
But he said...
What's for dizzypalizzy?
Dizzypalizzy?
That's what I THOUGHT he said!
That means DESSERT!
What do you suppose makes him talk like that?
I dunno...he doesn't get it from ME!
END

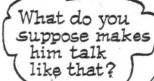

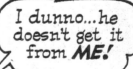

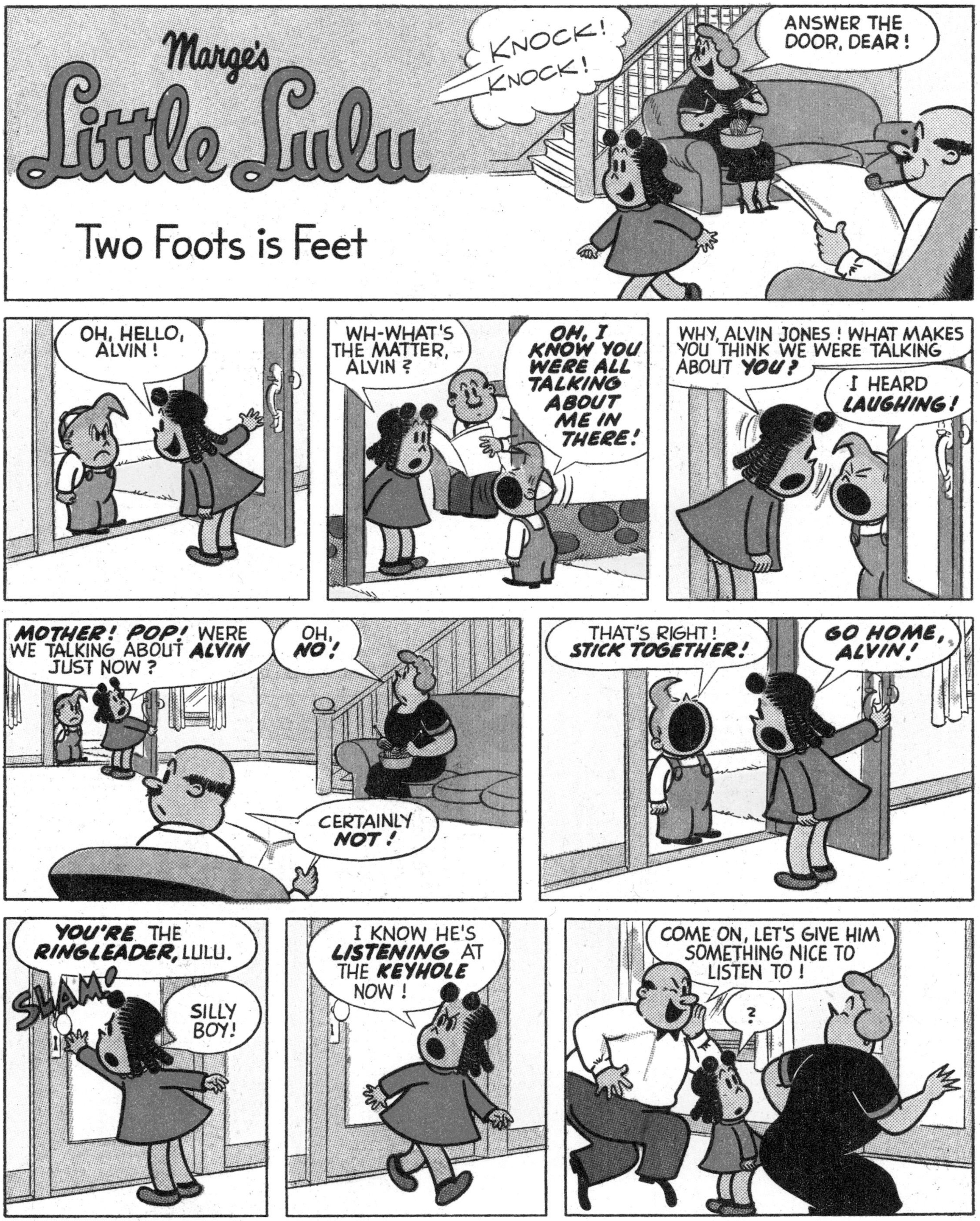
Marge's Little Lulu
Two Foots is Feet
KNOCK! KNOCK!
ANSWER THE DOOR, DEAR!
OH, HELLO, ALVIN!
WH-WHAT'S THE MATTER, ALVIN?
OH, I KNOW YOU WERE ALL TALKING ABOUT ME IN THERE!
WHY, ALVIN JONES! WHAT MAKES YOU THINK WE WERE TALKING ABOUT YOU?
I HEARD LAUGHING!
MOTHER! POP! WERE WE TALKING ABOUT ALVIN JUST NOW?
OH, NO!
CERTAINLY NOT!
THAT'S RIGHT! STICK TOGETHER!
GO HOME, ALVIN!
YOU'RE THE RINGLEADER, LULU.
SLAM!
SILLY BOY!
I KNOW HE'S LISTENING AT THE KEYHOLE NOW!
COME ON, LET'S GIVE HIM SOMETHING NICE TO LISTEN TO!
?

HEY, KIDS! LITTLE LULU "TWO FOOTS IS FEET" by JOHN STANLEY and IRVING TRIPP

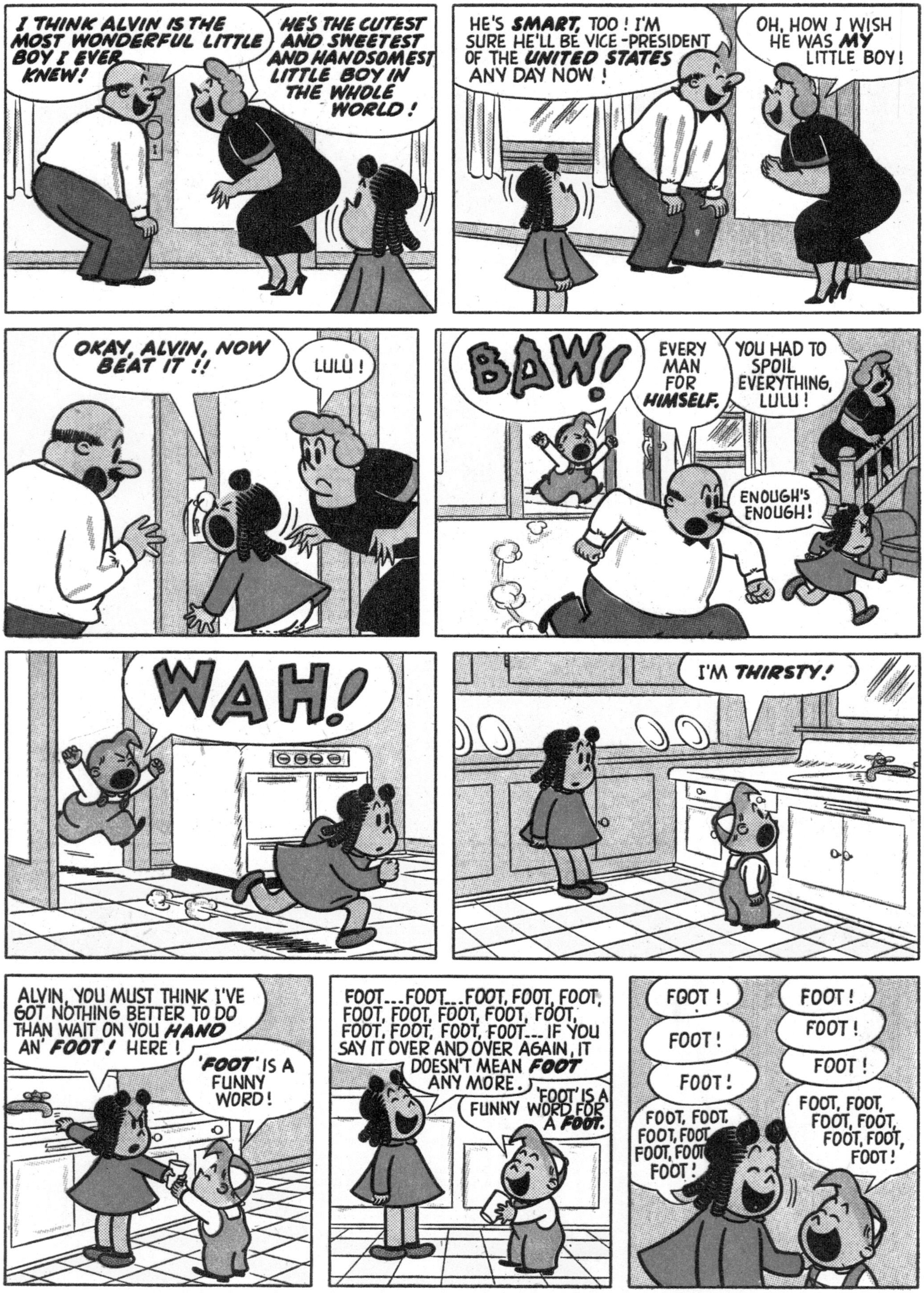
I THINK ALVIN IS THE MOST WONDERFUL LITTLE BOY I EVER KNEW!
HE'S THE CUTEST AND SWEETEST AND HANDSOMEST LITTLE BOY IN THE WHOLE WORLD!
HE'S SMART, TOO! I'M SURE HE'LL BE VICE-PRESIDENT OF THE UNITED STATES ANY DAY NOW!
OH, HOW I WISH HE WAS MY LITTLE BOY!
OKAY, ALVIN, NOW BEAT IT !!
LULU!
BAW!
EVERY MAN FOR HIMSELF.
YOU HAD TO SPOIL EVERYTHING, LULU!
ENOUGH'S ENOUGH!
WAH!
I'M THIRSTY!
ALVIN, YOU MUST THINK I'VE GOT NOTHING BETTER TO DO THAN WAIT ON YOU HAND AN' FOOT! HERE!
'FOOT' IS A FUNNY WORD!
FOOT...FOOT...FOOT, FOOT, FOOT, FOOT, FOOT, FOOT, FOOT, FOOT, FOOT, FOOT, FOOT, FOOT... IF YOU SAY IT OVER AND OVER AGAIN, IT DOESN'T MEAN FOOT ANY MORE.
'FOOT' IS A FUNNY WORD FOR A FOOT.
FOOT!
FOOT!
FOOT!
FOOT, FOOT, FOOT, FOOT, FOOT, FOOT, FOOT!
FOOT!
FOOT!
FOOT!
FOOT, FOOT, FOOT, FOOT, FOOT, FOOT, FOOT!

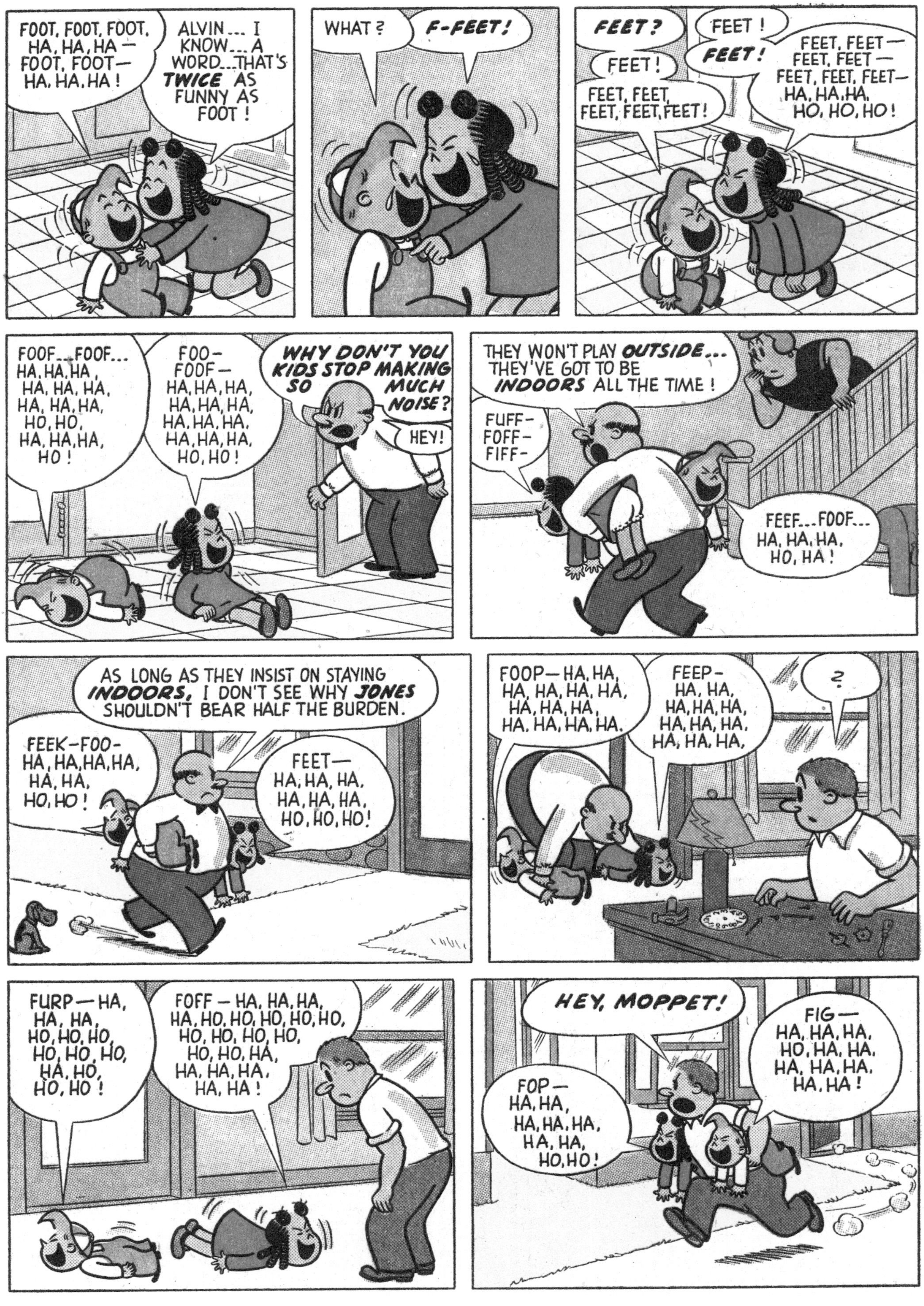
FOOT, FOOT, FOOT, HA, HA, HA— FOOT, FOOT— HA, HA, HA!
ALVIN... I KNOW... A WORD...THAT'S **TWICE** AS FUNNY AS FOOT!
WHAT?
F-FEET!
FEET?
FEET!
FEET!
FEET!
FEET, FEET, FEET, FEET, FEET!
FEET, FEET— FEET, FEET— FEET, FEET, FEET— HA, HA, HA, HO, HO, HO!
FOOF...FOOF... HA, HA, HA, HA, HA, HA, HA, HA, HA, HO, HO, HA, HA, HA, HO!
FOO- FOOF— HA, HA, HA, HA, HA, HA, HA, HA, HA, HA, HA, HA, HO, HO!
WHY DON'T YOU KIDS STOP MAKING SO MUCH NOISE?
HEY!
THEY WON'T PLAY **OUTSIDE**... THEY'VE GOT TO BE **INDOORS** ALL THE TIME!
FUFF- FOFF- FIFF-
FEEF...FOOF... HA, HA, HA, HO, HA!
AS LONG AS THEY INSIST ON STAYING **INDOORS**, I DON'T SEE WHY **JONES** SHOULDN'T BEAR HALF THE BURDEN.
FEEK-FOO- HA, HA, HA, HA, HA, HA, HO, HO!
FEET— HA, HA, HA, HA, HA, HA, HO, HO, HO!
FOOP—HA, HA, HA, HA, HA, HA, HA, HA, HA, HA, HA, HA, HA.
FEEP- HA, HA, HA, HA, HA, HA, HA, HA, HA, HA, HA,
?
FURP—HA, HA, HA, HO, HO, HO, HO, HO, HO, HA, HO, HO, HO!
FOFF—HA, HA, HA, HA, HO, HO, HO, HO, HO, HO, HO, HO, HO, HO, HO, HA, HA, HA, HA, HA, HA!
HEY, MOPPET!
FIG— HA, HA, HA, HO, HA, HA, HA, HA, HA, HA, HA!
FOP— HA, HA, HA, HA, HA, HA, HA, HO, HO!

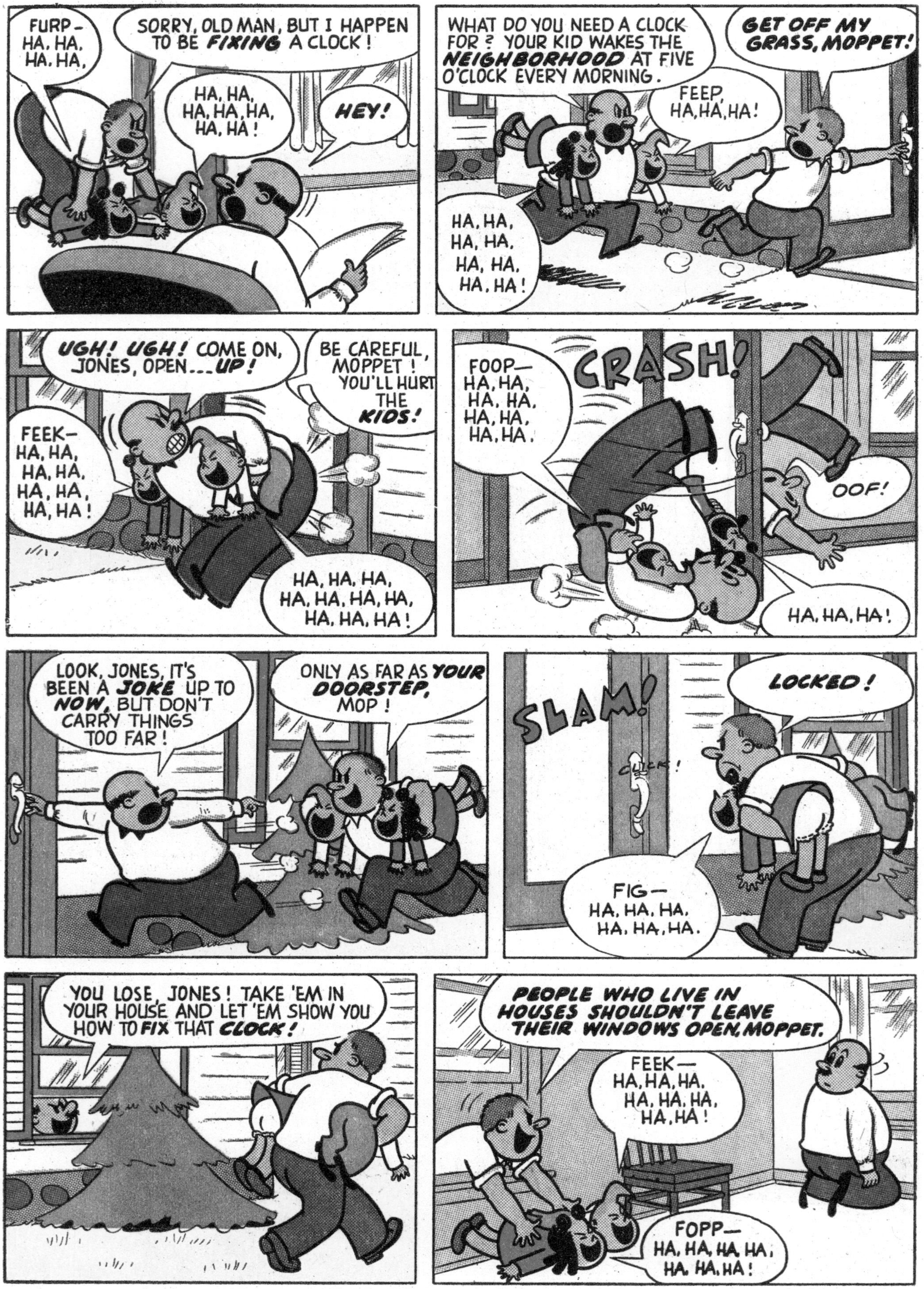
FURP- HA, HA, HA, HA,
SORRY, OLD MAN, BUT I HAPPEN TO BE FIXING A CLOCK!
HA, HA, HA, HA, HA, HA, HA!
HEY!
WHAT DO YOU NEED A CLOCK FOR? YOUR KID WAKES THE NEIGHBORHOOD AT FIVE O'CLOCK EVERY MORNING.
GET OFF MY GRASS, MOPPET!
FEEP, HA, HA, HA!
HA, HA, HA, HA, HA, HA, HA, HA!
UGH! UGH! COME ON, JONES, OPEN...UP!
BE CAREFUL, MOPPET! YOU'LL HURT THE KIDS!
FEEK- HA, HA, HA, HA, HA, HA, HA, HA!
HA, HA, HA, HA, HA, HA, HA, HA, HA, HA!
FOOP- HA, HA, HA, HA, HA, HA, HA, HA.
CRASH!
OOF!
HA, HA, HA!
LOOK, JONES, IT'S BEEN A JOKE UP TO NOW, BUT DON'T CARRY THINGS TOO FAR!
ONLY AS FAR AS YOUR DOORSTEP, MOP!
SLAM!
CLICK!
LOCKED!
FIG- HA, HA, HA, HA, HA, HA.
YOU LOSE, JONES! TAKE 'EM IN YOUR HOUSE AND LET 'EM SHOW YOU HOW TO FIX THAT CLOCK!
PEOPLE WHO LIVE IN HOUSES SHOULDN'T LEAVE THEIR WINDOWS OPEN, MOPPET.
FEEK- HA, HA, HA, HA, HA, HA, HA, HA!
FOPP- HA, HA, HA, HA, HA, HA, HA!

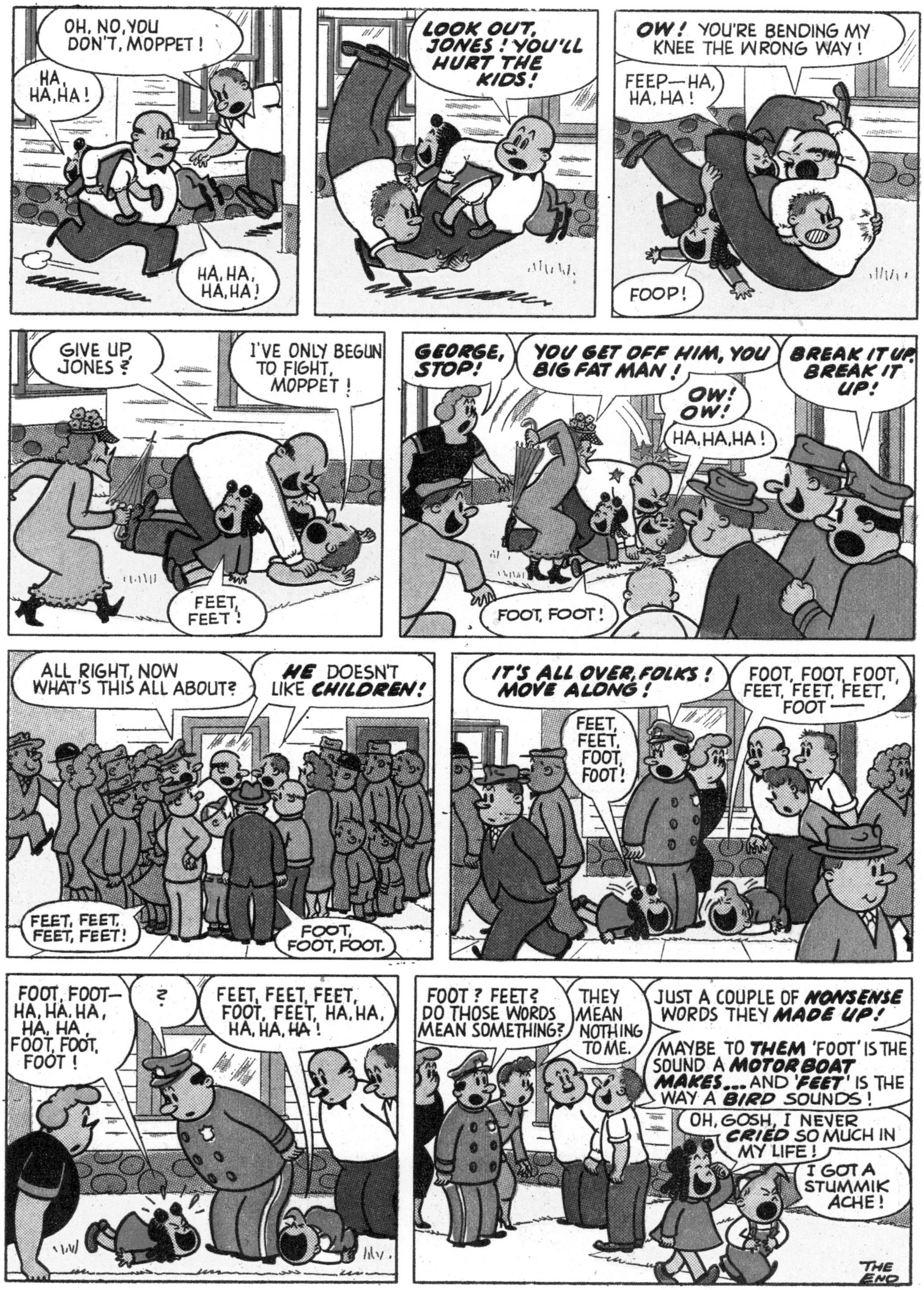
OH, NO, YOU DON'T, MOPPET!
HA, HA, HA!
HA, HA, HA, HA!
LOOK OUT, JONES! YOU'LL HURT THE KIDS!
OW! YOU'RE BENDING MY KNEE THE WRONG WAY!
FEEP—HA, HA, HA!
FOOP!
GIVE UP, JONES?
I'VE ONLY BEGUN TO FIGHT, MOPPET!
FEET, FEET!
GEORGE, STOP!
YOU GET OFF HIM, YOU BIG FAT MAN!
OW! OW!
HA, HA, HA!
BREAK IT UP. BREAK IT UP!
FOOT, FOOT!
ALL RIGHT, NOW WHAT'S THIS ALL ABOUT?
HE DOESN'T LIKE CHILDREN!
FEET, FEET, FEET, FEET!
FOOT, FOOT, FOOT.
IT'S ALL OVER, FOLKS! MOVE ALONG!
FOOT, FOOT, FOOT, FEET, FEET, FEET, FOOT —
FEET, FEET, FOOT, FOOT!
FOOT, FOOT— HA, HA, HA, HA, HA, FOOT, FOOT, FOOT!
?
FEET, FEET, FEET, FOOT, FEET, HA, HA, HA, HA, HA!
FOOT? FEET? DO THOSE WORDS MEAN SOMETHING?
THEY MEAN NOTHING TO ME.
JUST A COUPLE OF NONSENSE WORDS THEY MADE UP!
MAYBE TO THEM 'FOOT' IS THE SOUND A MOTORBOAT MAKES... AND 'FEET' IS THE WAY A BIRD SOUNDS!
OH, GOSH, I NEVER CRIED SO MUCH IN MY LIFE!
I GOT A STUMMIK ACHE!
THE END

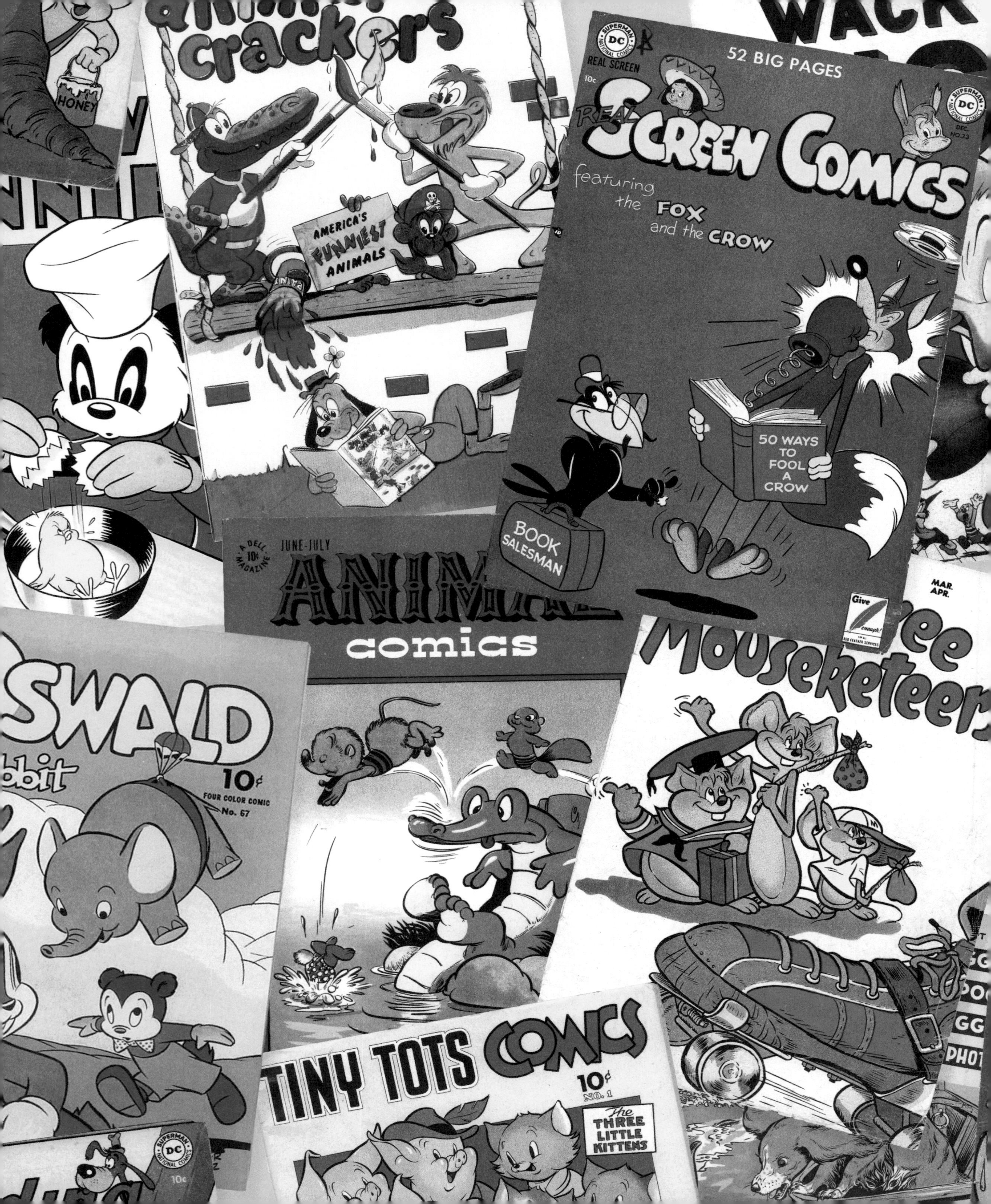

crackers
HONEY
AMERICA'S FUNNIEST ANIMALS
WACK
SUPERMAN DC NATIONAL COMICS
REAL SCREEN
10¢
52 BIG PAGES
REAL SCREEN COMICS
DEC. NO.33
featuring the FOX and the CROW
50 WAYS TO FOOL A CROW
BOOK SALESMAN
Give enough!
JUNE-JULY
A DELL 10¢ MAGAZINE
comics
MAR. APR.
Mouseketeers
SWALD
10¢
FOUR COLOR COMIC No. 67
TINY TOTS COMICS
10¢
NO. 1
The THREE LITTLE KITTENS

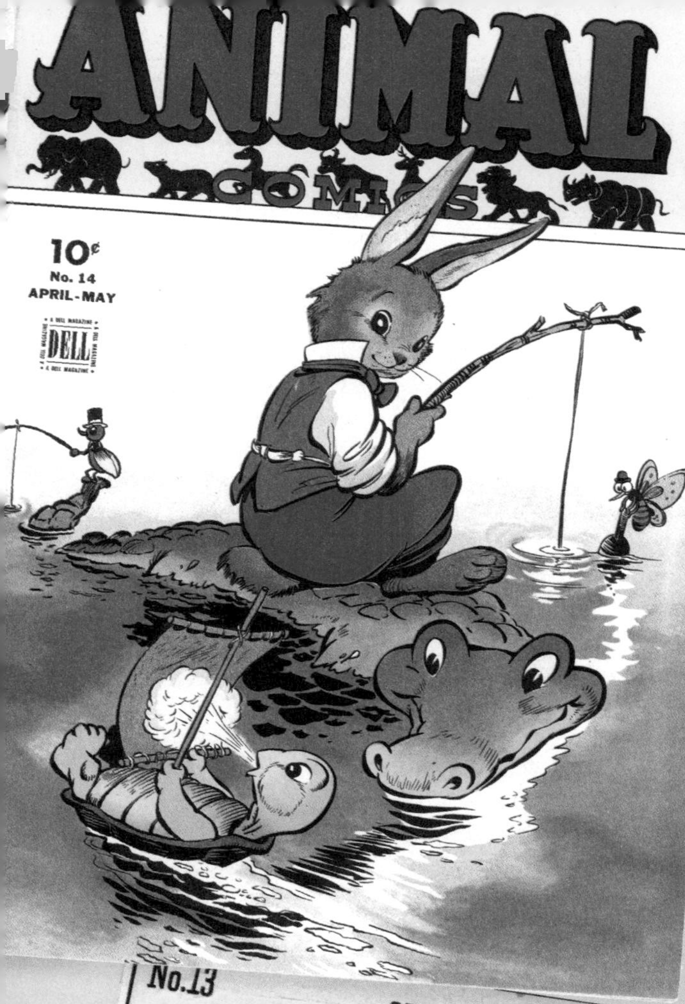
ANIMAL
COMICS
10¢
No. 14
APRIL-MAY
DELL

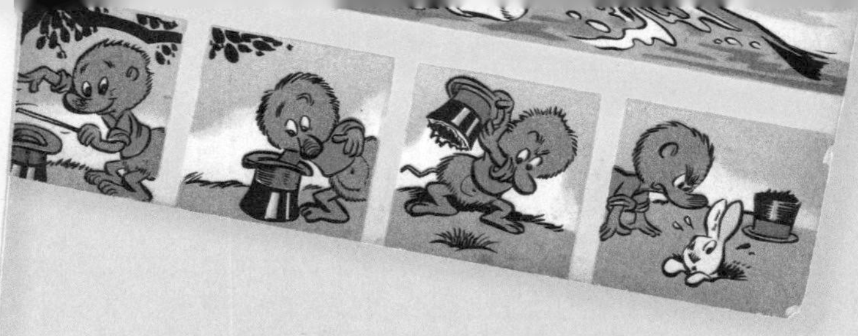

Chapter 2

FUNNY ANIMALS

Funny animals used to scamper all over the comic book racks.

Sometimes they leaped from animated cartoons onto the page, but changed considerably as they made the transition. In Carl Barks's classic stories, for example, Donald Duck becomes a character with many more sides than the hot-headed quacker he is on screen. Some of the animals, like Walt Kelly's swamp folks, act suspiciously like kids in furry suits, while others, like Jim Davis's Fox and Crow, are scheming adults with beaks or paws. Those "funny animal" comics did try to be funny, but they could still dig down into the nitty gritty of life-and-death struggles: hunting for food to survive in Dan Noonan's very serious Rover story, "Wolf Attack," or—in a more gentle tone—in John Stanley's *Jigger.*

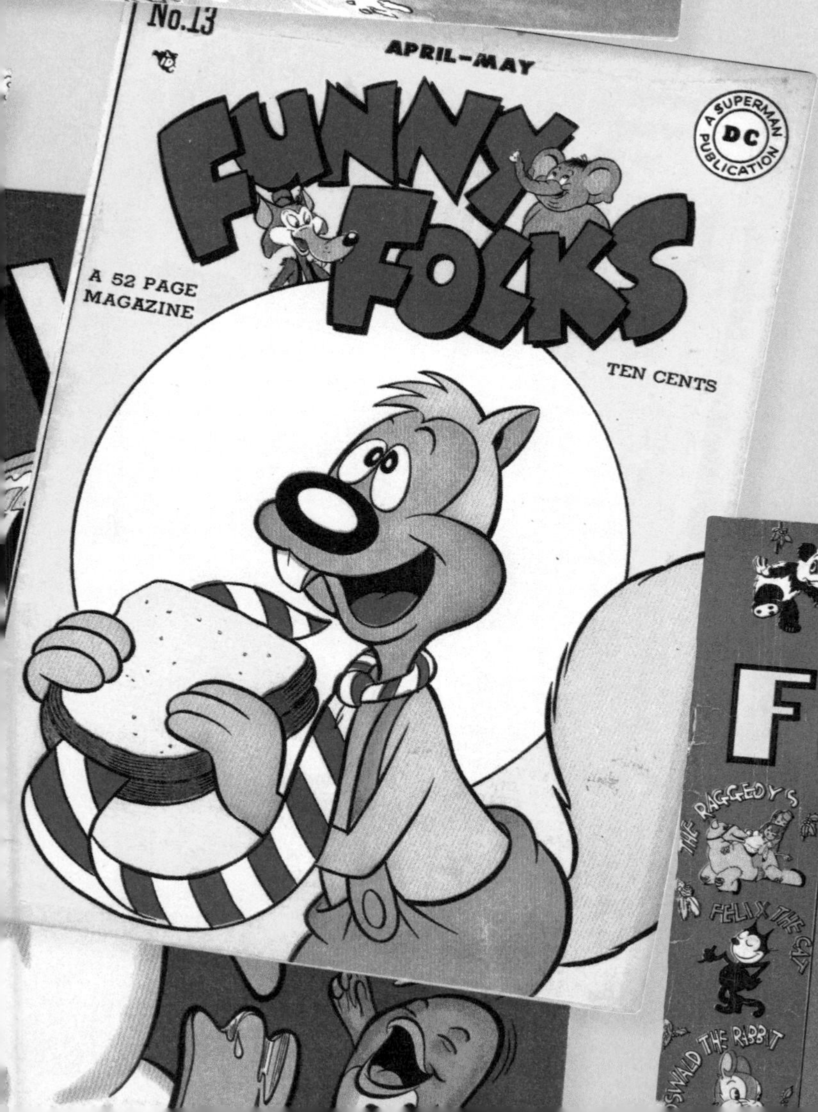
No.13
APRIL-MAY
FUNNY FOLKS
A SUPERMAN DC PUBLICATION
A 52 PAGE MAGAZINE
TEN CENTS

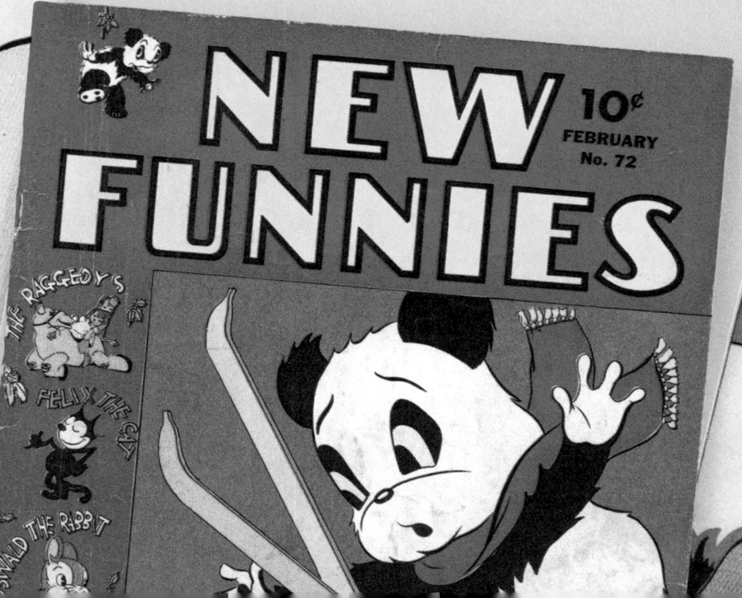
NEW FUNNIES
10¢
FEBRUARY
No. 72
THE RAGGEDY'S
FELIX THE CAT
SWALD THE RABBIT

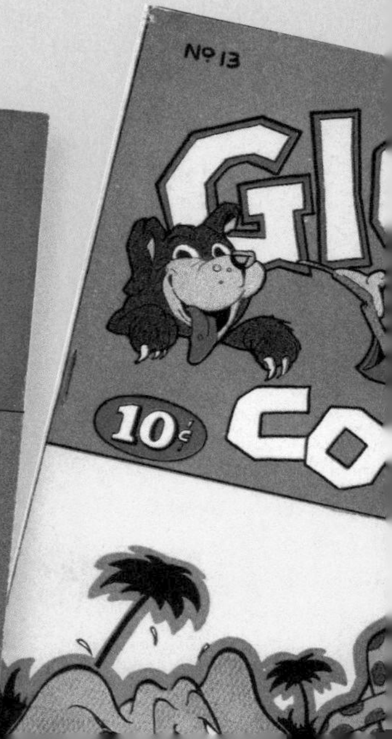
No 13
10¢

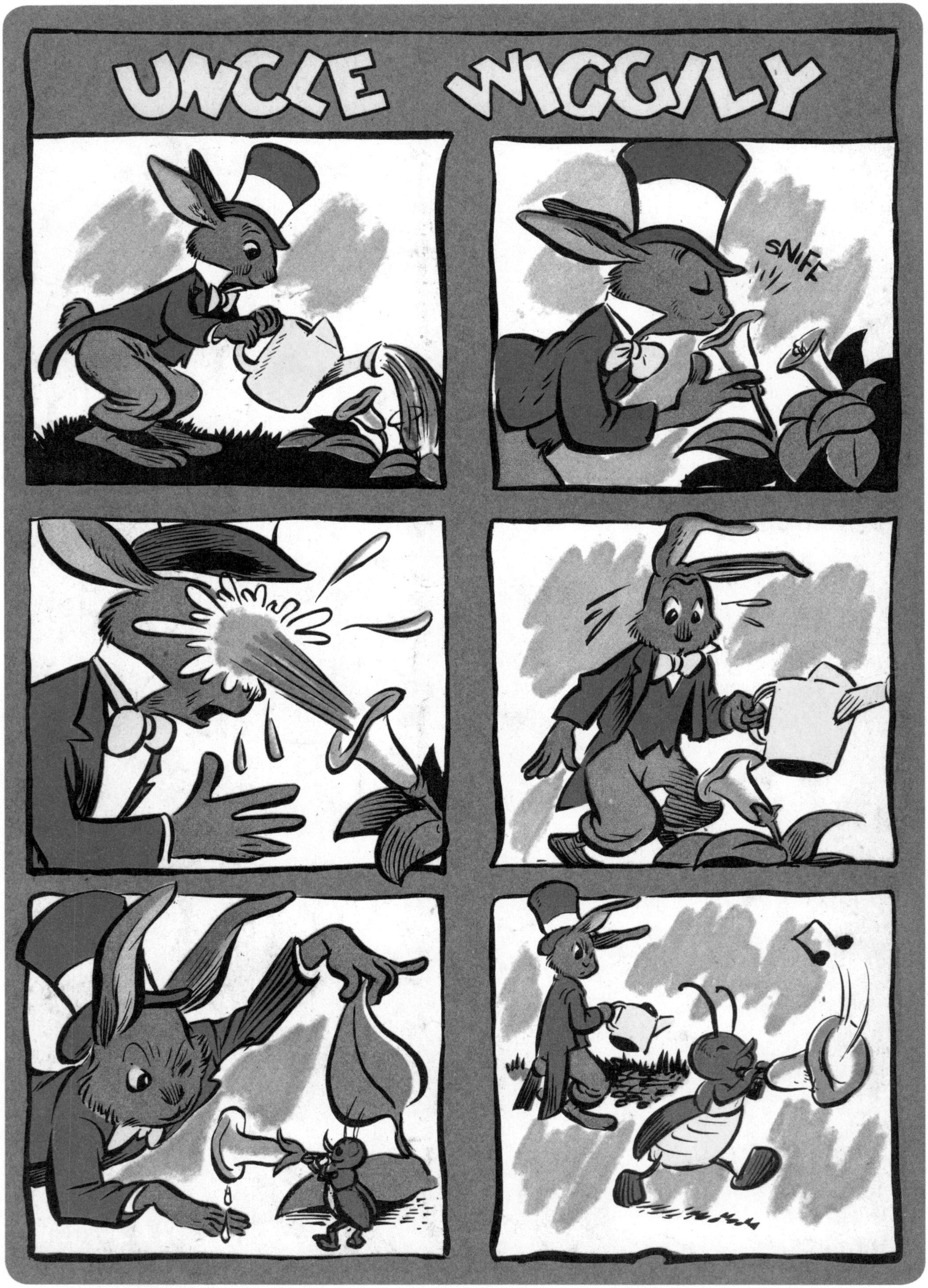
UNCLE WIGGILY
SNIFF

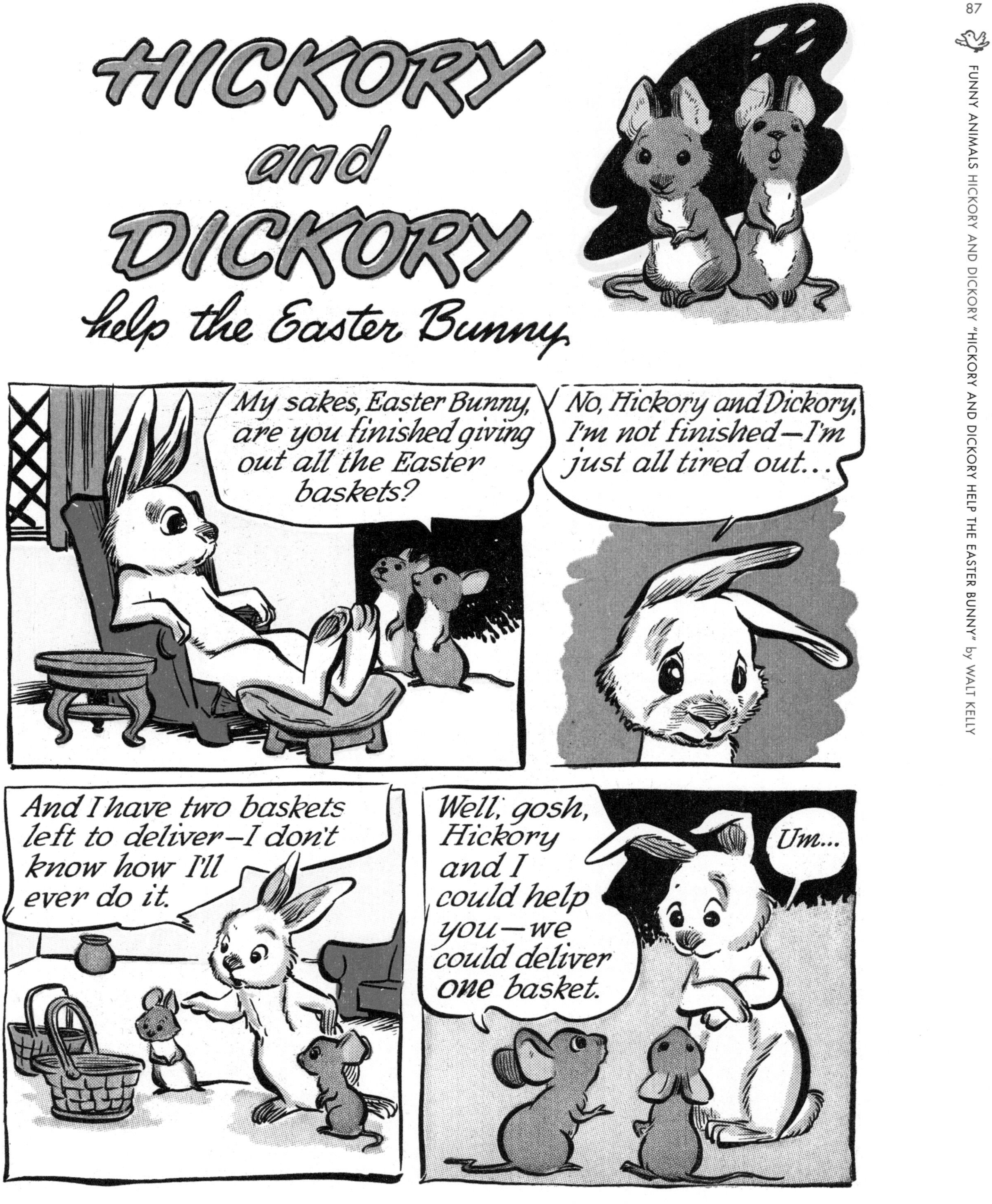
HICKORY and DICKORY
help the Easter Bunny
My sakes, Easter Bunny, are you finished giving out all the Easter baskets?
No, Hickory and Dickory, I'm not finished—I'm just all tired out...
And I have two baskets left to deliver—I don't know how I'll ever do it.
Well, gosh, Hickory and I could help you—we could deliver one basket.
Um...

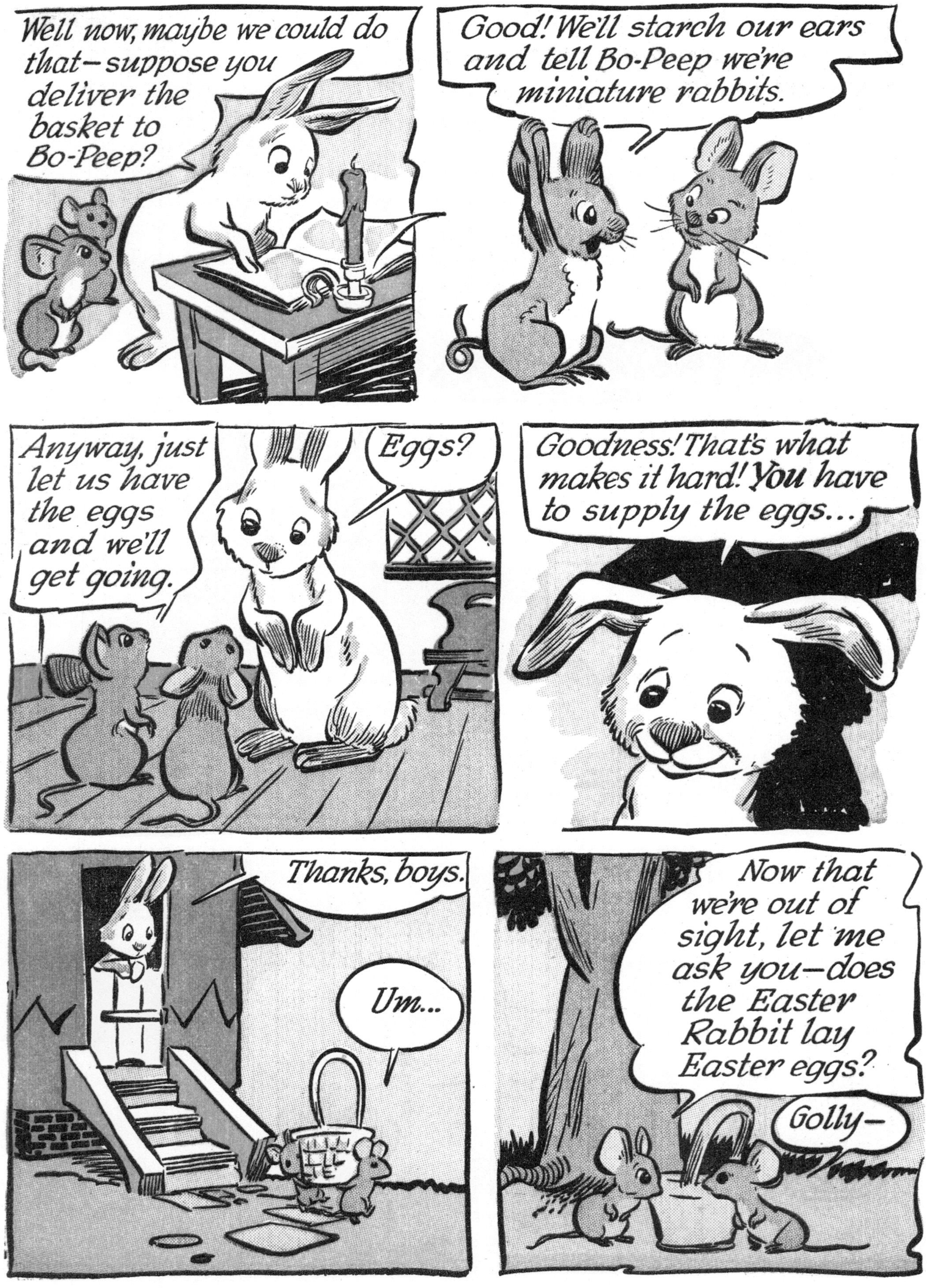
Well now, maybe we could do that–suppose you deliver the basket to Bo-Peep?
Good! We'll starch our ears and tell Bo-Peep we're miniature rabbits.
Anyway, just let us have the eggs and we'll get going.
Eggs?
Goodness! That's what makes it hard! You have to supply the eggs...
Thanks, boys.
Um...
Now that we're out of sight, let me ask you–does the Easter Rabbit lay Easter eggs?
Golly–

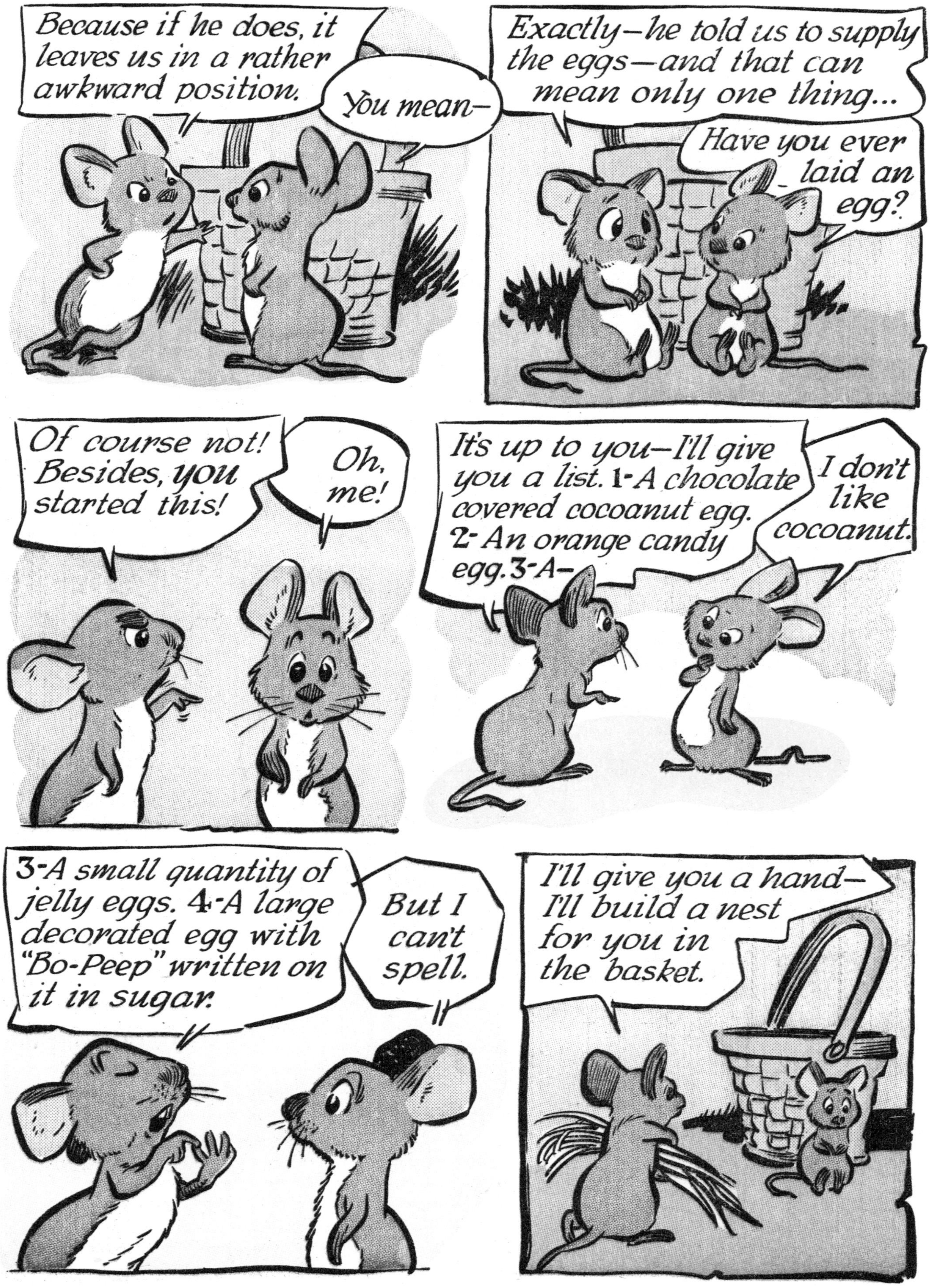
Because if he does, it leaves us in a rather awkward position.
You mean—
Exactly—he told us to supply the eggs—and that can mean only one thing...
Have you ever laid an egg?
Of course not! Besides, you started this!
Oh, me!
It's up to you—I'll give you a list. 1-A chocolate covered cocoanut egg. 2-An orange candy egg. 3-A—
I don't like cocoanut.
3-A small quantity of jelly eggs. 4-A large decorated egg with "Bo-Peep" written on it in sugar.
But I can't spell.
I'll give you a hand—I'll build a nest for you in the basket.

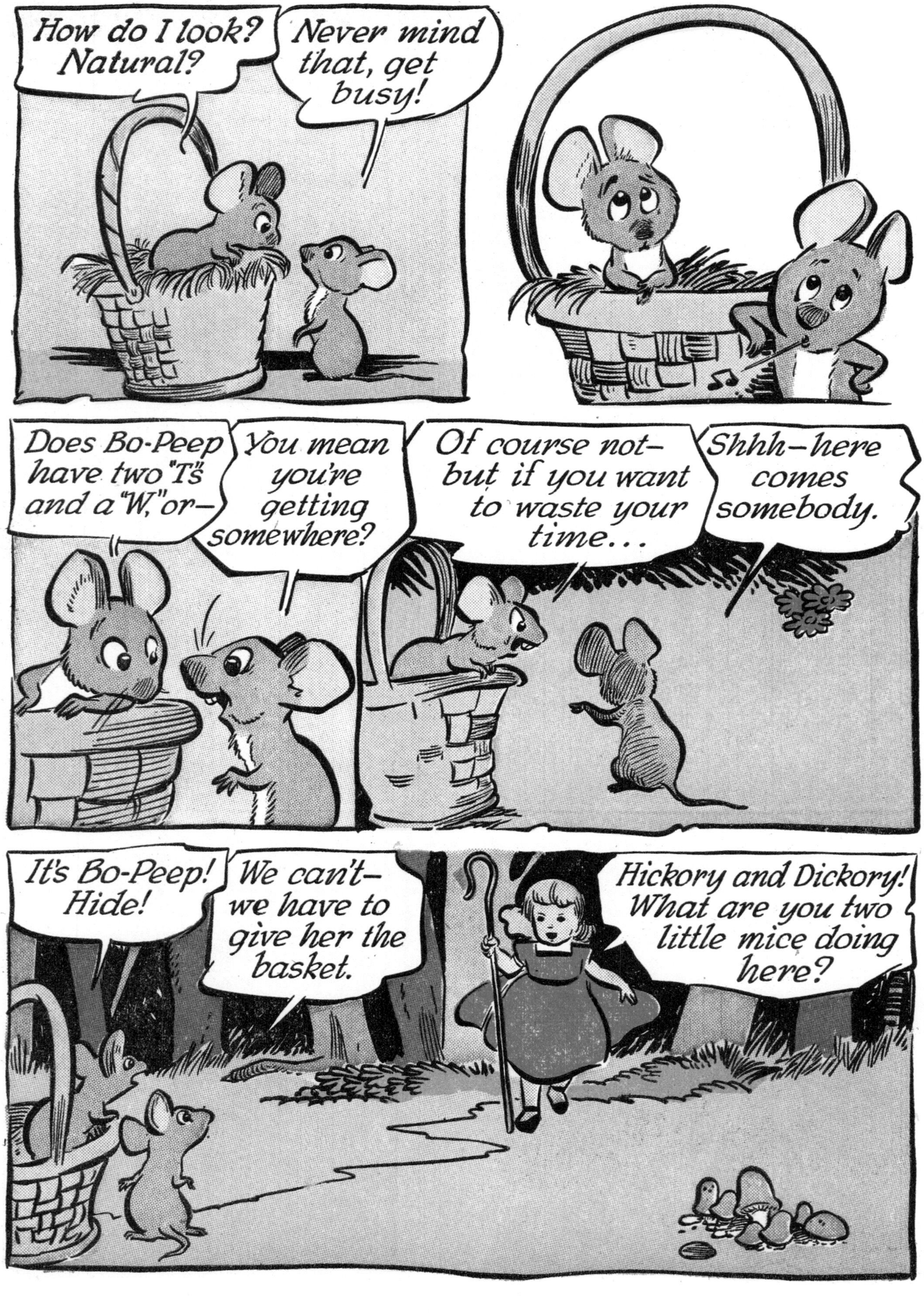
How do I look? Natural?
Never mind that, get busy!
Does Bo-Peep have two "T's" and a "W," or—
You mean you're getting somewhere?
Of course not—but if you want to waste your time...
Shhh—here comes somebody.
It's Bo-Peep! Hide!
We can't—we have to give her the basket.
Hickory and Dickory! What are you two little mice doing here?

We-uh-well— we-we-oh-um—

Isn't that my Easter basket?

Easter basket? Where?

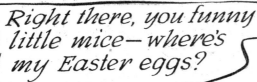

Right there, you funny little mice—where's my Easter eggs?

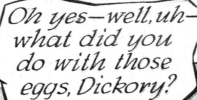

Oh yes—well, uh— what did you do with those eggs, Dickory?

What eggs? Oh, Easter eggs! Well, uh—

Hickory can explain everything, Miss Bo-Peep.

I can?

Yes—can you?

Why, yes—we all know what a fine character Dickory is—always willing to help...

Yes, indeed.

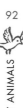

So Dickory has consented to be *your* Easter egg as a surprise gift!

What?

Wait!

How wonderful!

A beautiful gift–! I'll take you right home.

Hey!

Gosh!

That takes care of Bo-Peep– but how about Dickory?

People usually *eat* Easter eggs!

Maybe Bo-Peep will cover him with *chocolate* and–oh my, I must rescue him!

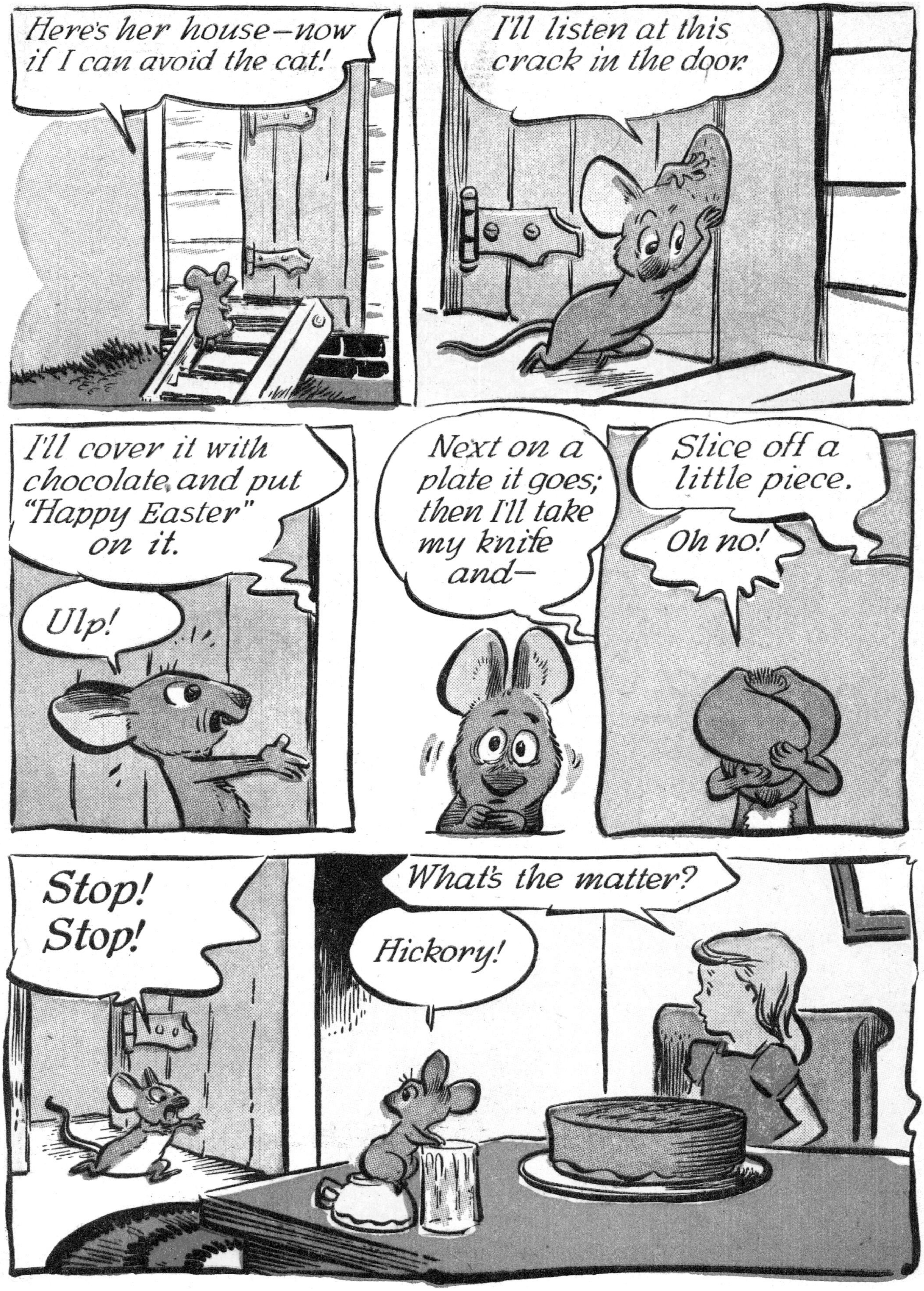
Here's her house—now if I can avoid the cat!
I'll listen at this crack in the door.
I'll cover it with chocolate and put "Happy Easter" on it.
Ulp!
Next on a plate it goes; then I'll take my knife and—
Slice off a little piece.
Oh no!
Stop! Stop!
What's the matter?
Hickory!

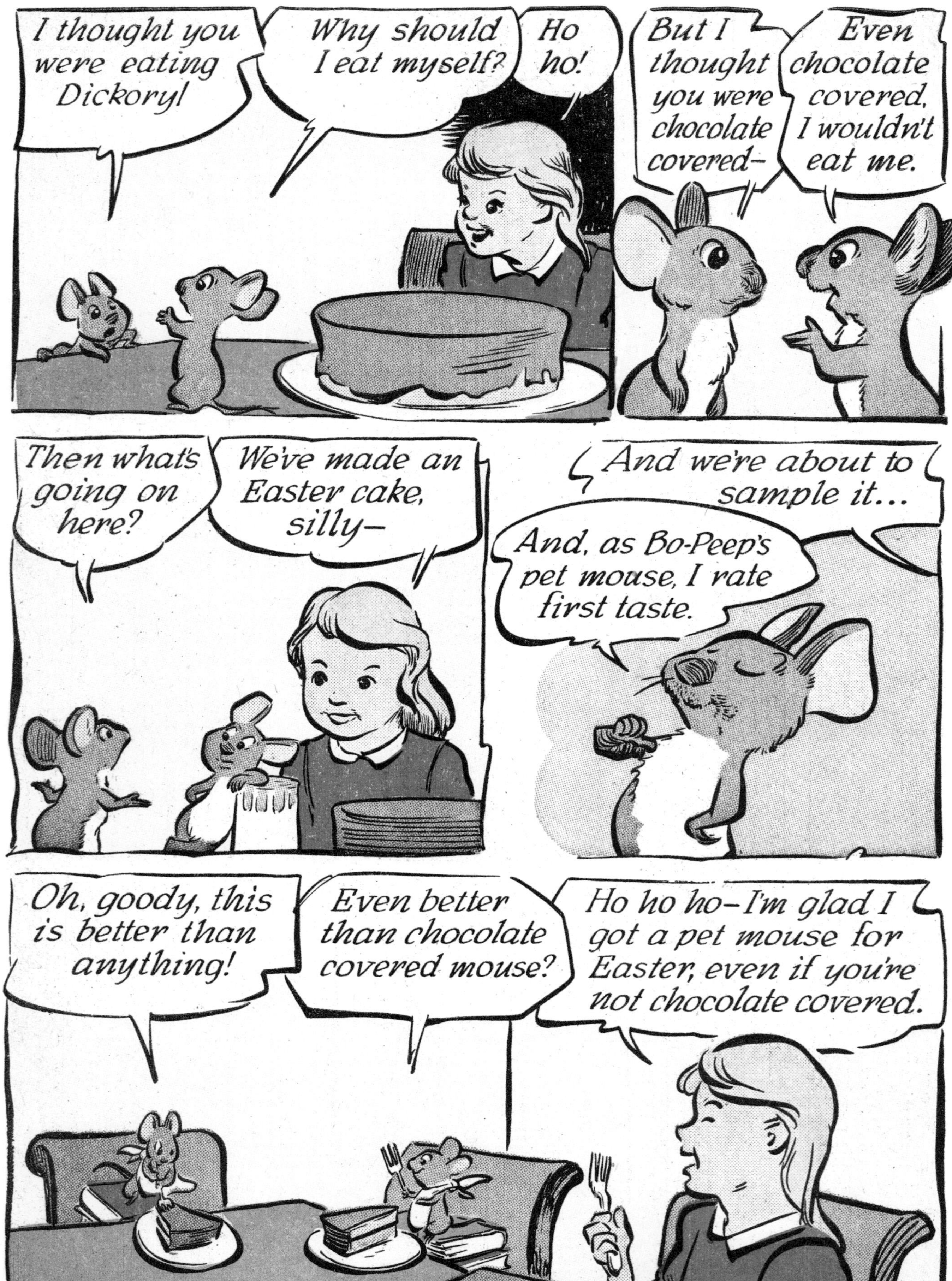
I thought you were eating Dickory!
Why should I eat myself?
Ho ho!
But I thought you were chocolate covered-
Even chocolate covered, I wouldn't eat me.
Then what's going on here?
We've made an Easter cake, silly-
And we're about to sample it...
And, as Bo-Peep's pet mouse, I rate first taste.
Oh, goody, this is better than anything!
Even better than chocolate covered mouse?
Ho ho ho-I'm glad I got a pet mouse for Easter, even if you're not chocolate covered.

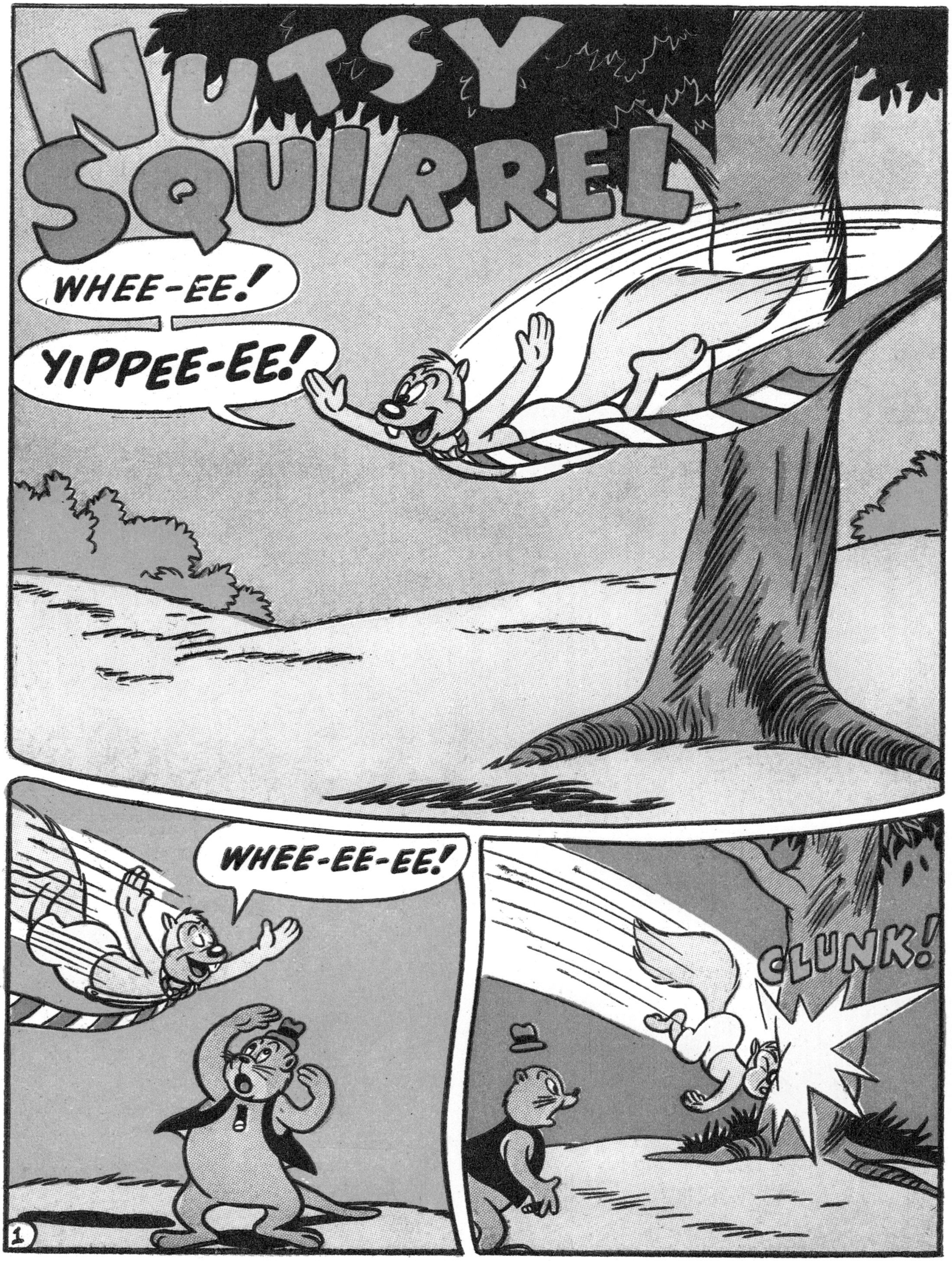
NUTSY SQUIRREL
WHEE-EE!
YIPPEE-EE!
WHEE-EE-EE!
CLUNK!
1

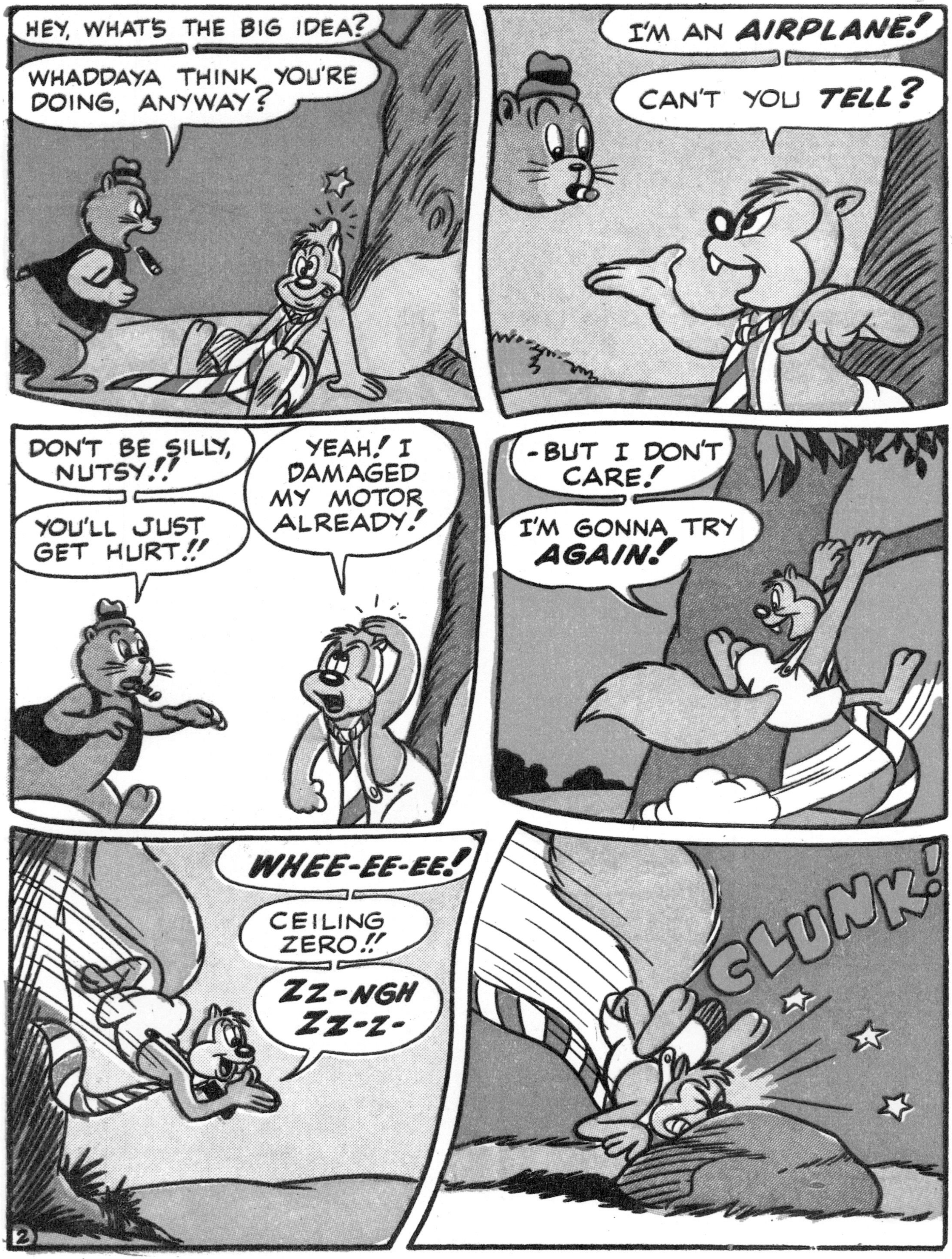
HEY, WHAT'S THE BIG IDEA?
WHADDAYA THINK YOU'RE DOING, ANYWAY?
I'M AN AIRPLANE!
CAN'T YOU TELL?
DON'T BE SILLY, NUTSY!!
YOU'LL JUST GET HURT!!
YEAH! I DAMAGED MY MOTOR ALREADY!
-BUT I DON'T CARE!
I'M GONNA TRY AGAIN!
WHEE-EE-EE!
CEILING ZERO!!
ZZ-NGH ZZ-Z-
CLUNK!
2

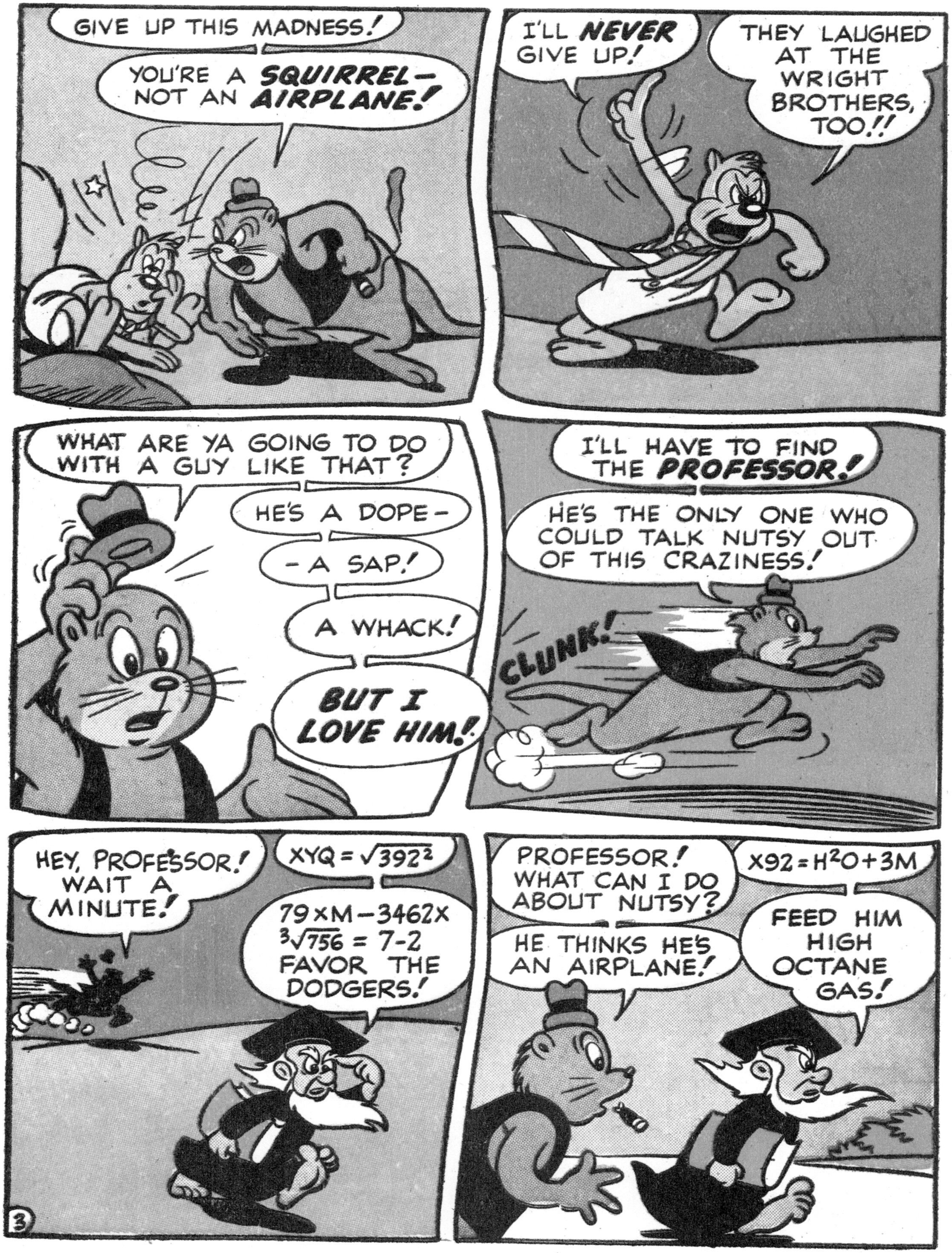
GIVE UP THIS MADNESS!
YOU'RE A SQUIRREL—NOT AN AIRPLANE!
I'LL NEVER GIVE UP!
THEY LAUGHED AT THE WRIGHT BROTHERS, TOO!!
WHAT ARE YA GOING TO DO WITH A GUY LIKE THAT?
HE'S A DOPE—
—A SAP!
A WHACK!
BUT I LOVE HIM!
I'LL HAVE TO FIND THE PROFESSOR!
HE'S THE ONLY ONE WHO COULD TALK NUTSY OUT OF THIS CRAZINESS!
CLUNK!
HEY, PROFESSOR! WAIT A MINUTE!
XYQ = √392²
79×M—3462X ∛756 = 7-2 FAVOR THE DODGERS!
PROFESSOR! WHAT CAN I DO ABOUT NUTSY?
X92 = H²O+3M
HE THINKS HE'S AN AIRPLANE!
FEED HIM HIGH OCTANE GAS!
3

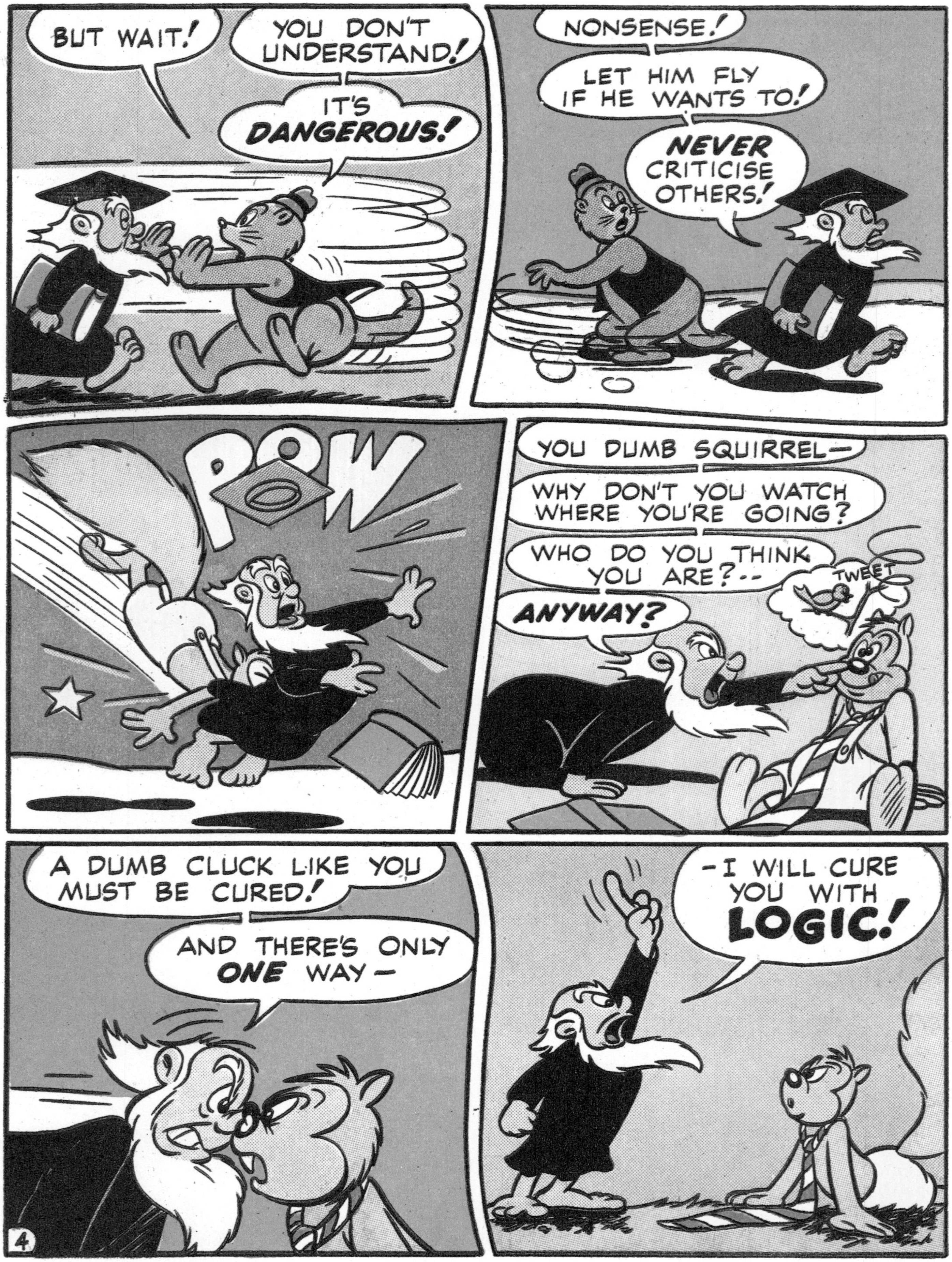
BUT WAIT!
YOU DON'T UNDERSTAND!
IT'S DANGEROUS!
NONSENSE!
LET HIM FLY IF HE WANTS TO!
NEVER CRITICISE OTHERS!
POW
YOU DUMB SQUIRREL—
WHY DON'T YOU WATCH WHERE YOU'RE GOING?
WHO DO YOU THINK YOU ARE?--
ANYWAY?
TWEET
A DUMB CLUCK LIKE YOU MUST BE CURED!
AND THERE'S ONLY ONE WAY—
—I WILL CURE YOU WITH LOGIC!
4

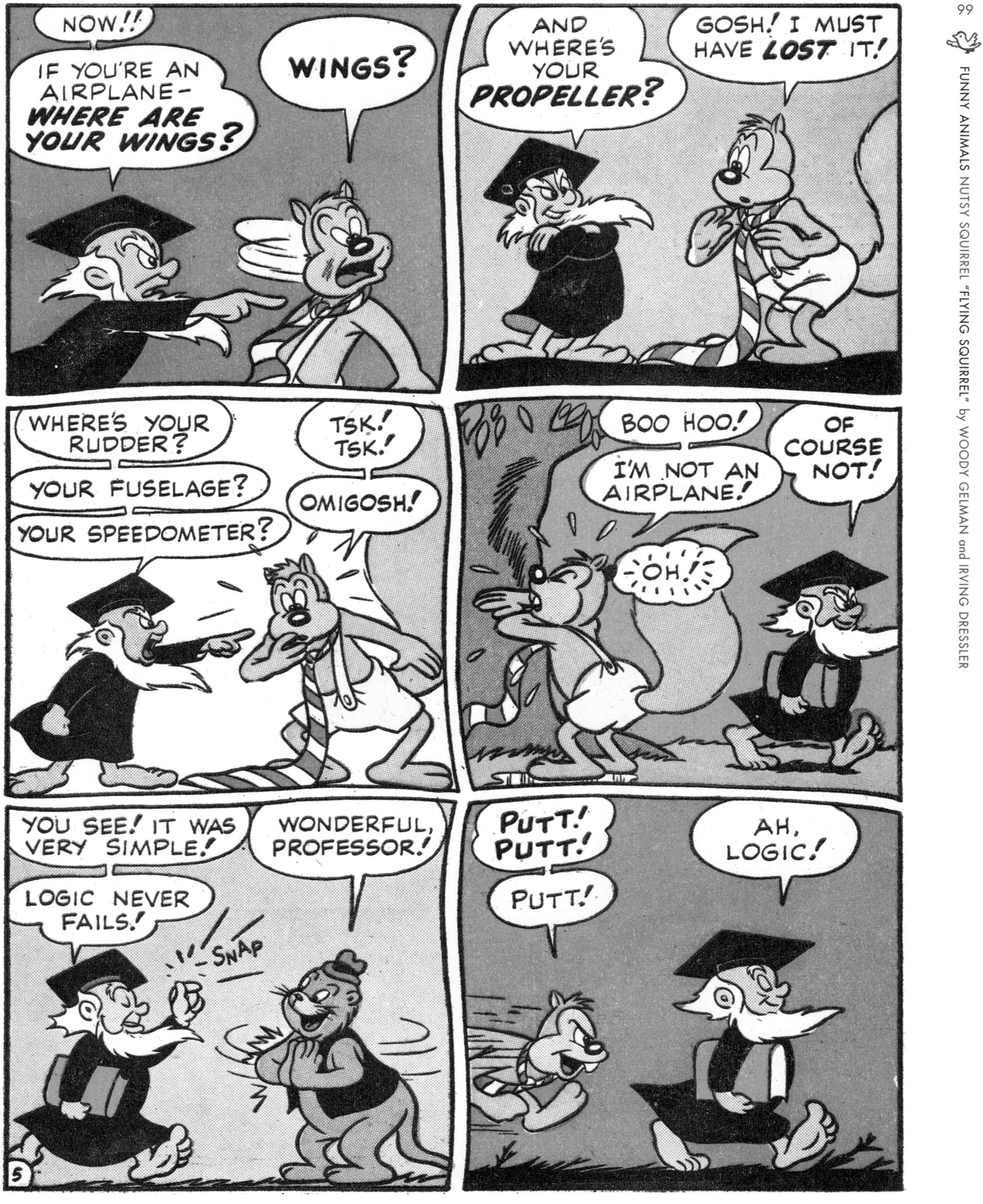
NOW!!
IF YOU'RE AN AIRPLANE- WHERE ARE YOUR WINGS?
WINGS?
AND WHERE'S YOUR PROPELLER?
GOSH! I MUST HAVE LOST IT!
WHERE'S YOUR RUDDER?
YOUR FUSELAGE?
YOUR SPEEDOMETER?
TSK! TSK!
OMIGOSH!
BOO HOO!
I'M NOT AN AIRPLANE!
OH!
OF COURSE NOT!
YOU SEE! IT WAS VERY SIMPLE!
LOGIC NEVER FAILS!
SNAP
WONDERFUL, PROFESSOR!
PUTT! PUTT!
PUTT!
AH, LOGIC!
5

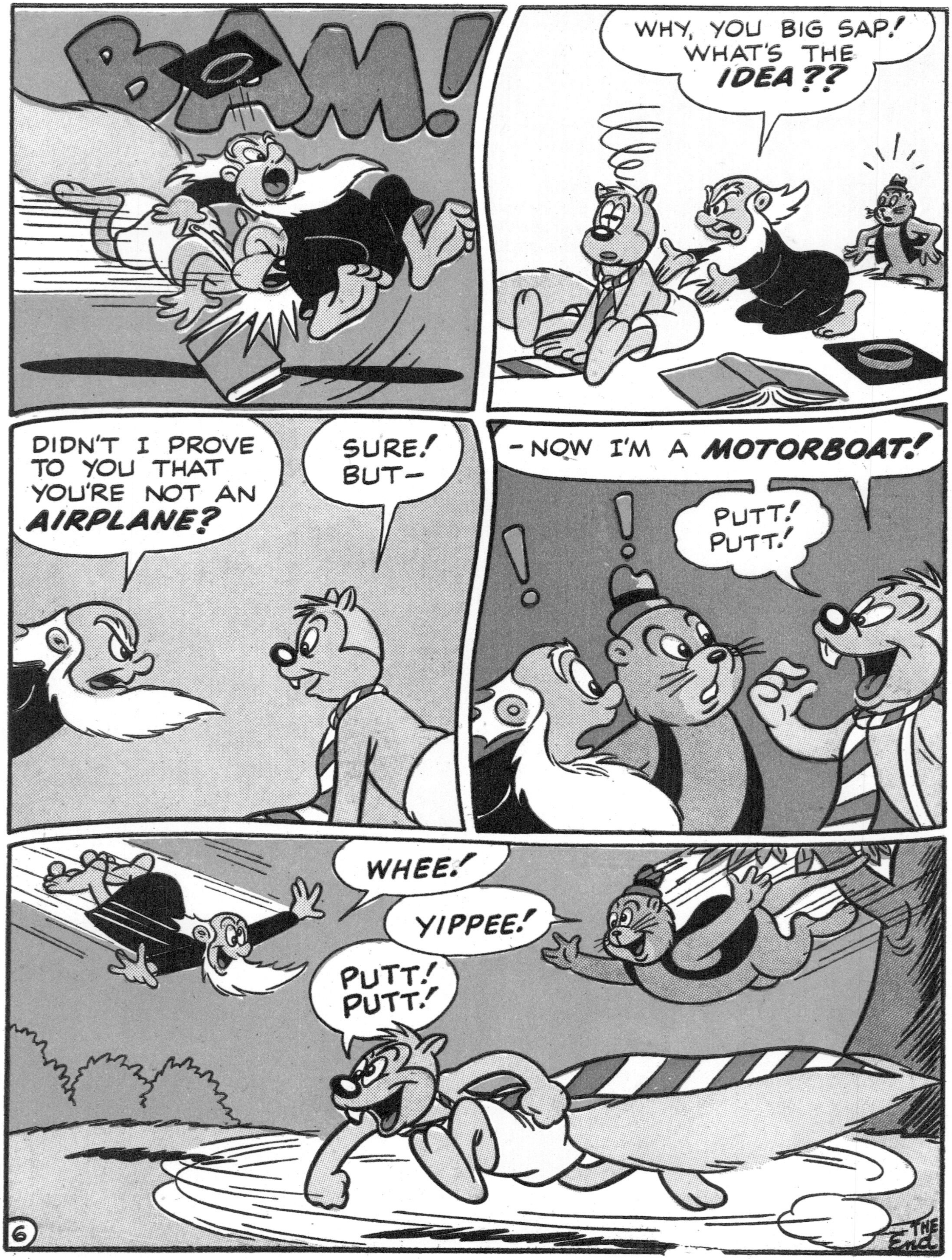
BAM!
WHY, YOU BIG SAP! WHAT'S THE IDEA??
DIDN'T I PROVE TO YOU THAT YOU'RE NOT AN AIRPLANE?
SURE! BUT—
—NOW I'M A MOTORBOAT!
PUTT! PUTT!
WHEE!
YIPPEE!
PUTT! PUTT!
6
THE End

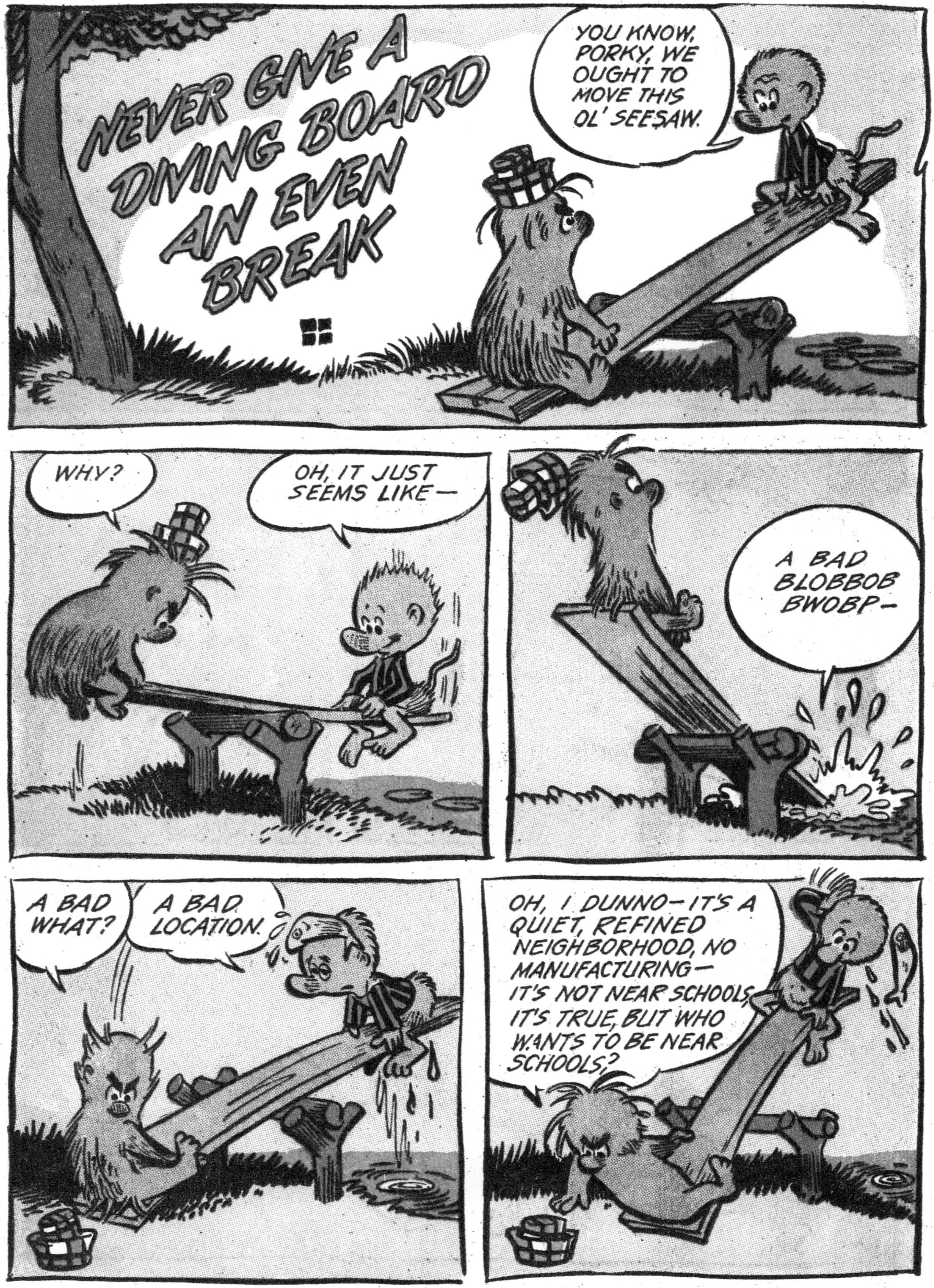
NEVER GIVE A DIVING BOARD AN EVEN BREAK
YOU KNOW, PORKY, WE OUGHT TO MOVE THIS OL' SEESAW.
WHY?
OH, IT JUST SEEMS LIKE—
A BAD BLOBBOB BWOBP—
A BAD WHAT?
A BAD LOCATION.
OH, I DUNNO—IT'S A QUIET, REFINED NEIGHBORHOOD, NO MANUFACTURING—IT'S NOT NEAR SCHOOLS, IT'S TRUE, BUT WHO WANTS TO BE NEAR SCHOOLS?

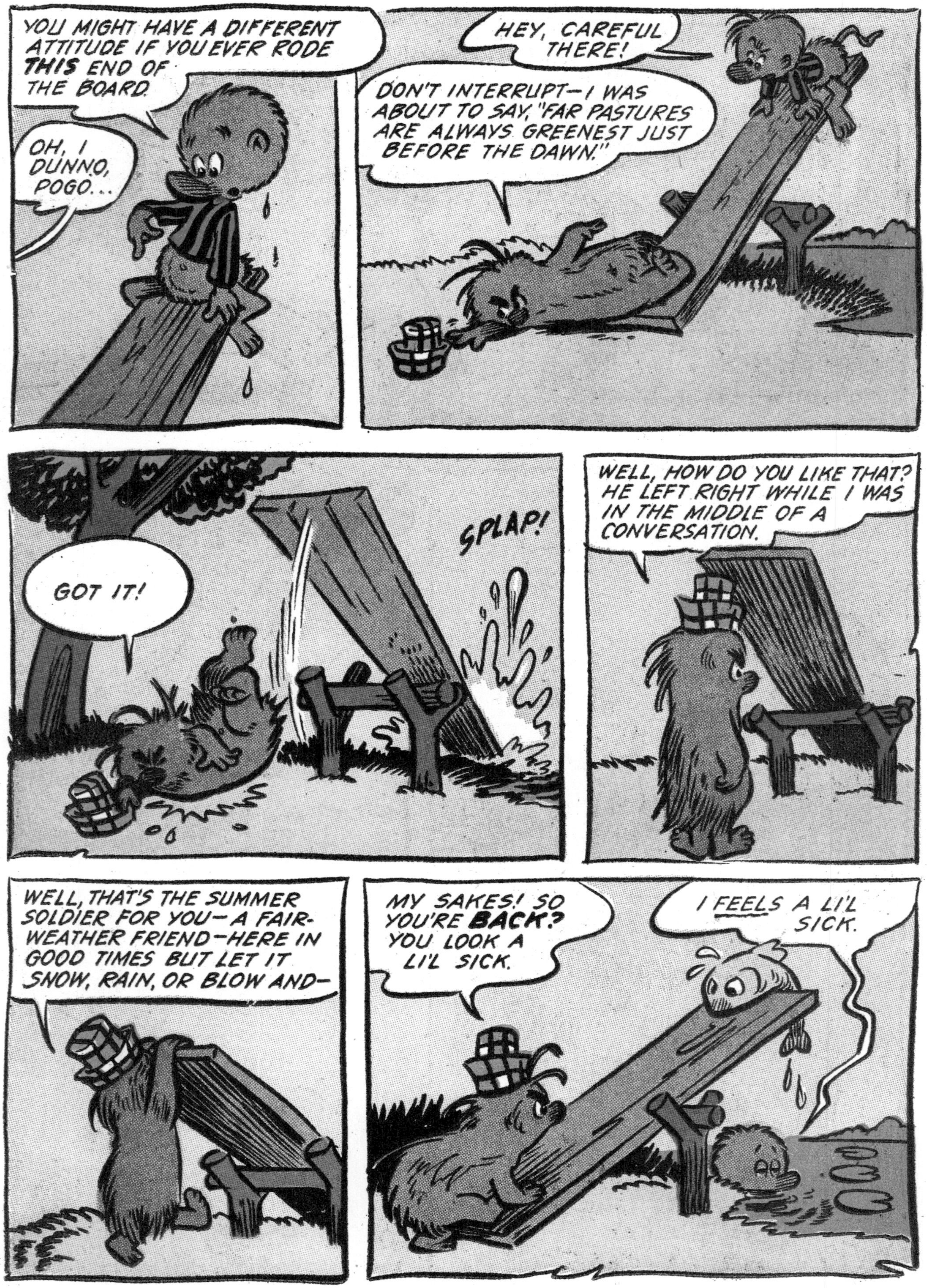
YOU MIGHT HAVE A DIFFERENT ATTITUDE IF YOU EVER RODE THIS END OF THE BOARD.
OH, I DUNNO, POGO...
HEY, CAREFUL THERE!
DON'T INTERRUPT—I WAS ABOUT TO SAY, "FAR PASTURES ARE ALWAYS GREENEST JUST BEFORE THE DAWN."
GOT IT!
SPLAP!
WELL, HOW DO YOU LIKE THAT? HE LEFT RIGHT WHILE I WAS IN THE MIDDLE OF A CONVERSATION.
WELL, THAT'S THE SUMMER SOLDIER FOR YOU—A FAIR-WEATHER FRIEND—HERE IN GOOD TIMES BUT LET IT SNOW, RAIN, OR BLOW AND—
MY SAKES! SO YOU'RE BACK? YOU LOOK A LI'L SICK.
I FEELS A LI'L SICK.

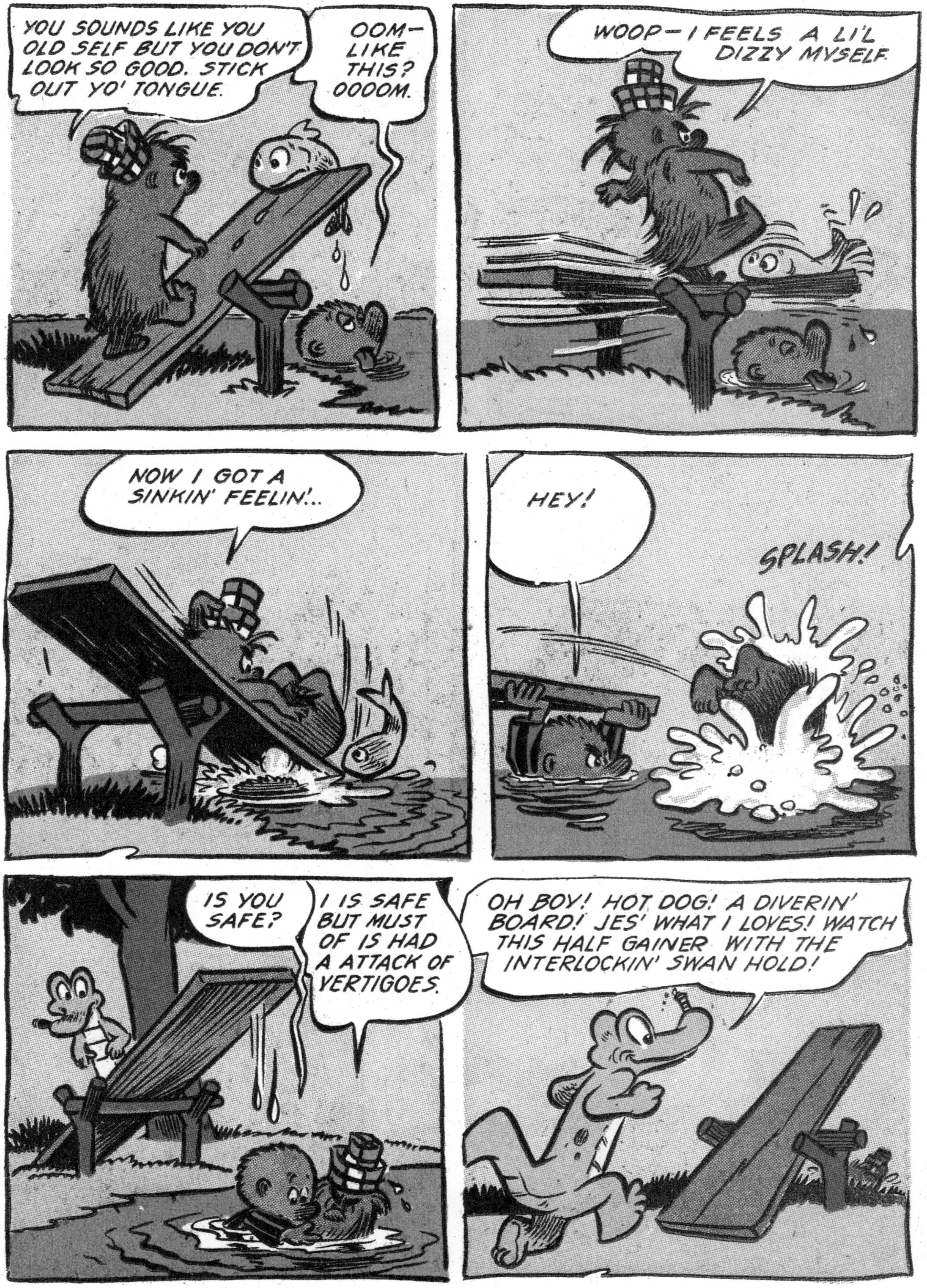
YOU SOUNDS LIKE YOU OLD SELF BUT YOU DON'T LOOK SO GOOD. STICK OUT YO' TONGUE.
OOM— LIKE THIS? OOOOM.
WOOP—I FEELS A LI'L DIZZY MYSELF.
NOW I GOT A SINKIN' FEELIN'...
HEY!
SPLASH!
IS YOU SAFE?
I IS SAFE BUT MUST OF IS HAD A ATTACK OF VERTIGOES.
OH BOY! HOT DOG! A DIVERIN' BOARD! JES' WHAT I LOVES! WATCH THIS HALF GAINER WITH THE INTERLOCKIN' SWAN HOLD!

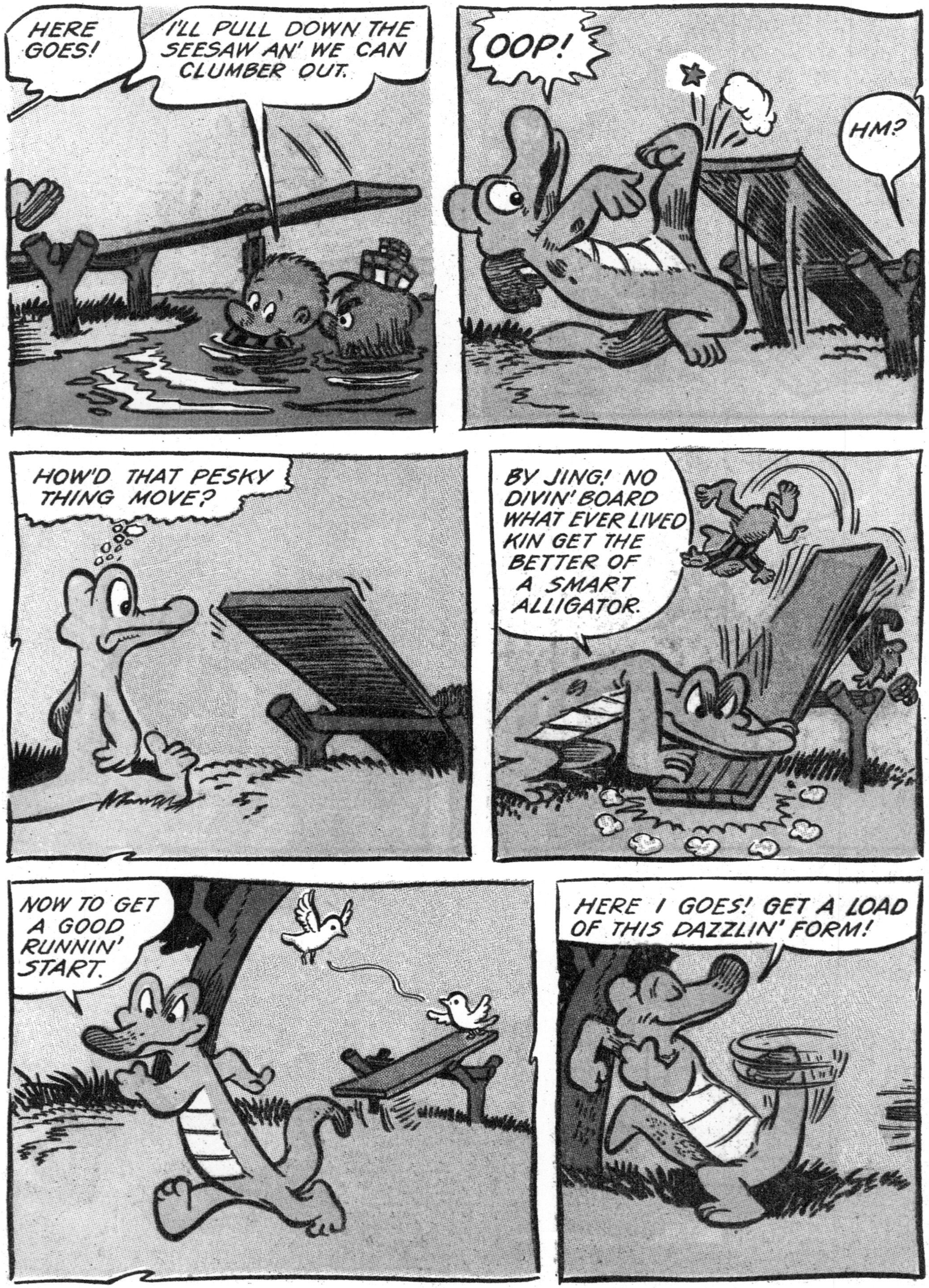
HERE GOES!
I'LL PULL DOWN THE SEESAW AN' WE CAN CLUMBER OUT.
OOP!
HM?
HOW'D THAT PESKY THING MOVE?
BY JING! NO DIVIN' BOARD WHAT EVER LIVED KIN GET THE BETTER OF A SMART ALLIGATOR.
NOW TO GET A GOOD RUNNIN' START.
HERE I GOES! GET A LOAD OF THIS DAZZLIN' FORM!

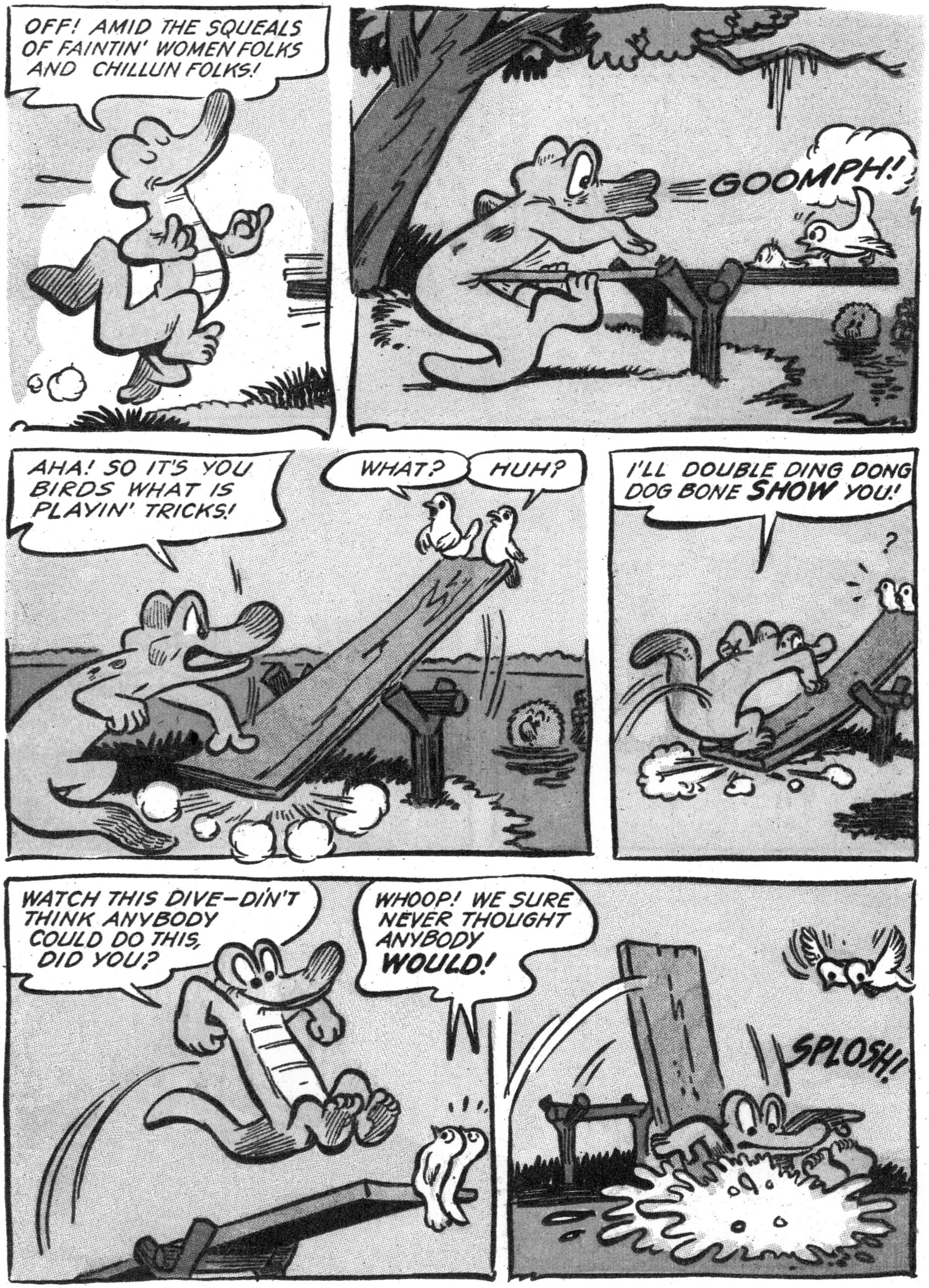
OFF! AMID THE SQUEALS OF FAINTIN' WOMEN FOLKS AND CHILLUN FOLKS!
GOOMPH!
AHA! SO IT'S YOU BIRDS WHAT IS PLAYIN' TRICKS!
WHAT?
HUH?
I'LL DOUBLE DING DONG DOG BONE SHOW YOU!
?
WATCH THIS DIVE—DIN'T THINK ANYBODY COULD DO THIS, DID YOU?
WHOOP! WE SURE NEVER THOUGHT ANYBODY WOULD!
SPLOSH!

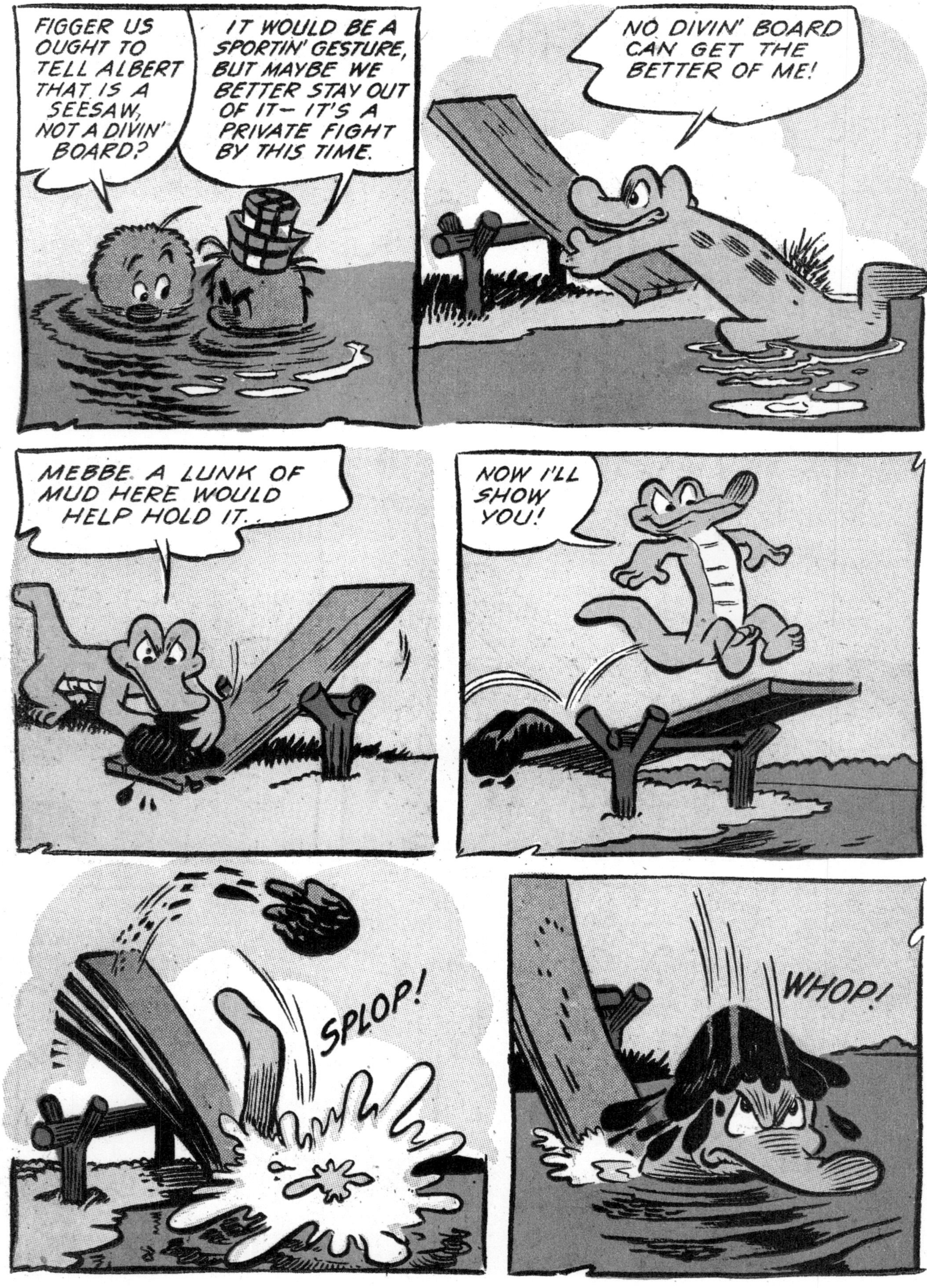
FIGGER US OUGHT TO TELL ALBERT THAT IS A SEESAW, NOT A DIVIN' BOARD?
IT WOULD BE A SPORTIN' GESTURE, BUT MAYBE WE BETTER STAY OUT OF IT— IT'S A PRIVATE FIGHT BY THIS TIME.
NO DIVIN' BOARD CAN GET THE BETTER OF ME!
MEBBE A LUNK OF MUD HERE WOULD HELP HOLD IT. . .
NOW I'LL SHOW YOU!
SPLOP!
WHOP!

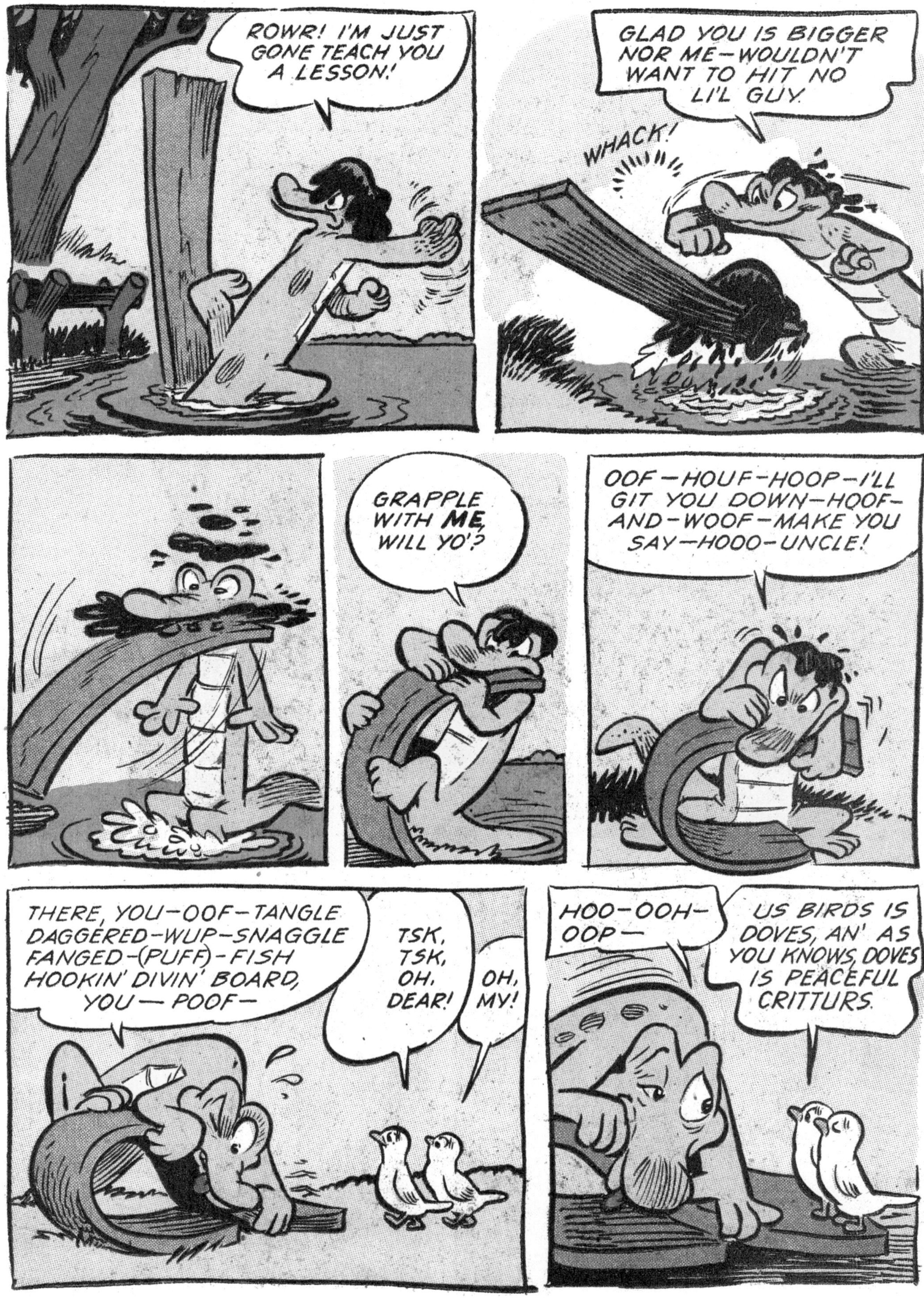
ROWR! I'M JUST GONE TEACH YOU A LESSON!
GLAD YOU IS BIGGER NOR ME—WOULDN'T WANT TO HIT NO LI'L GUY.
WHACK!
GRAPPLE WITH ME, WILL YO'?
OOF—HOUF—HOOP—I'LL GIT YOU DOWN—HOOF—AND—WOOF—MAKE YOU SAY—HOOO—UNCLE!
THERE, YOU—OOF—TANGLE DAGGERED—WUP—SNAGGLE FANGED—(PUFF)—FISH HOOKIN' DIVIN' BOARD, YOU — POOF—
TSK, TSK, OH. DEAR!
OH, MY!
HOO—OOH—OOP—
US BIRDS IS DOVES, AN' AS YOU KNOWS, DOVES IS PEACEFUL CRITTURS.

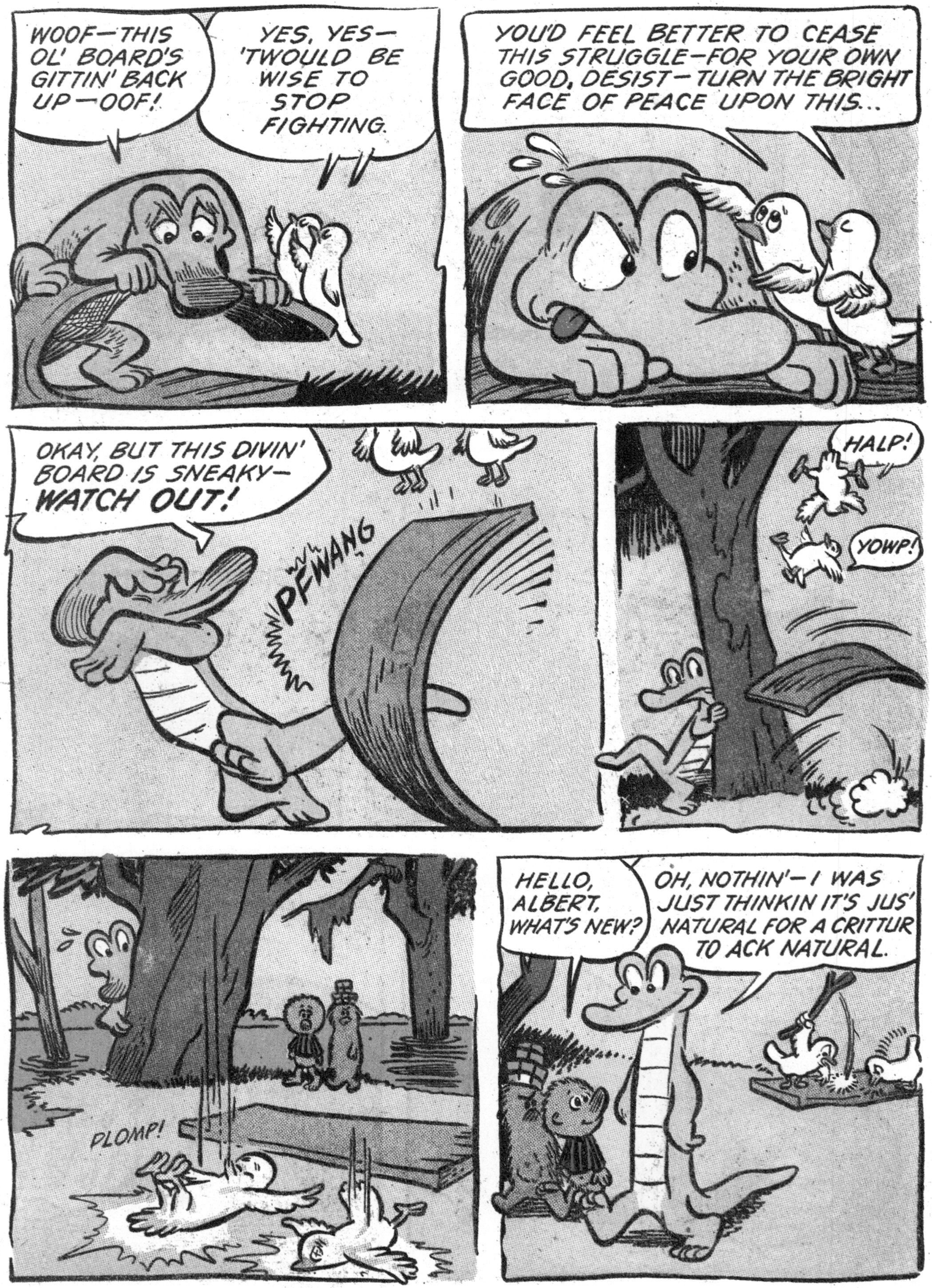
WOOF—THIS OL' BOARD'S GITTIN' BACK UP—OOF!
YES, YES— 'TWOULD BE WISE TO STOP FIGHTING.
YOU'D FEEL BETTER TO CEASE THIS STRUGGLE—FOR YOUR OWN GOOD, DESIST—TURN THE BRIGHT FACE OF PEACE UPON THIS...
OKAY, BUT THIS DIVIN' BOARD IS SNEAKY— WATCH OUT!
PFWANG
HALP!
YOWP!
PLOMP!
HELLO, ALBERT, WHAT'S NEW?
OH, NOTHIN'—I WAS JUST THINKIN IT'S JUS' NATURAL FOR A CRITTUR TO ACK NATURAL.

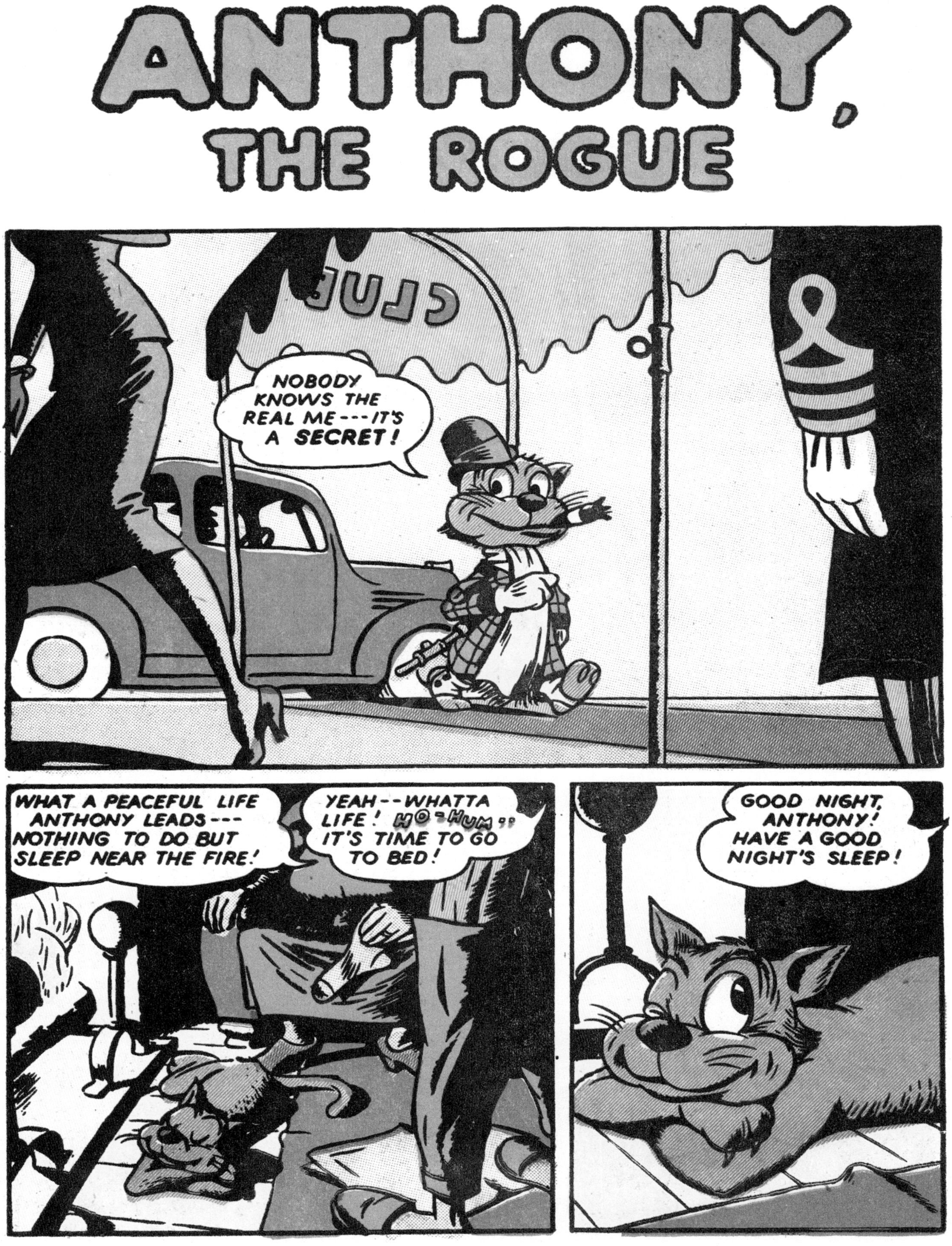
ANTHONY, THE ROGUE
CLUB
NOBODY KNOWS THE REAL ME---IT'S A SECRET!
WHAT A PEACEFUL LIFE ANTHONY LEADS--- NOTHING TO DO BUT SLEEP NEAR THE FIRE!
YEAH--WHATTA LIFE! HO-HUM.. IT'S TIME TO GO TO BED!
GOOD NIGHT, ANTHONY! HAVE A GOOD NIGHT'S SLEEP!

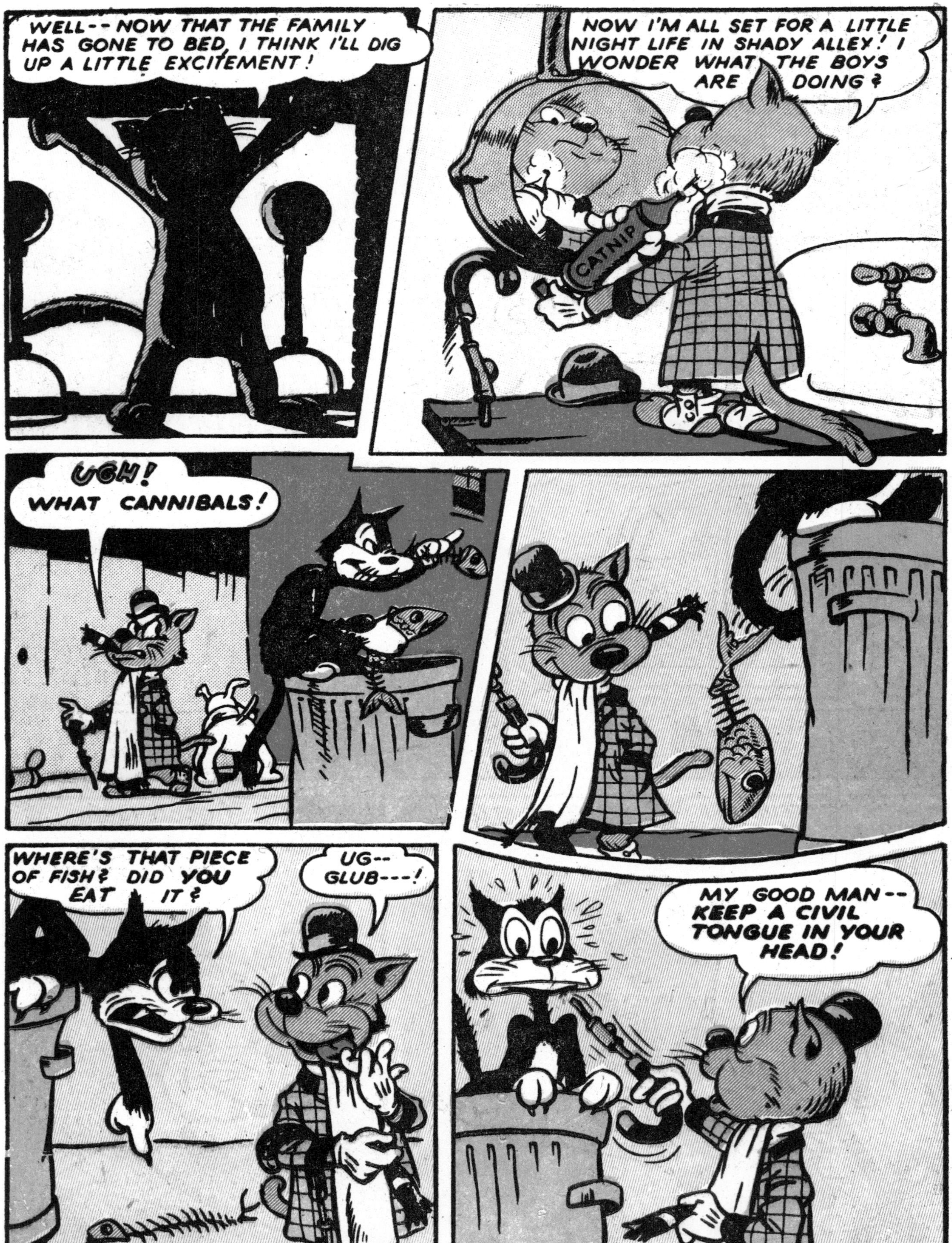
WELL-- NOW THAT THE FAMILY HAS GONE TO BED, I THINK I'LL DIG UP A LITTLE EXCITEMENT!
NOW I'M ALL SET FOR A LITTLE NIGHT LIFE IN SHADY ALLEY! I WONDER WHAT THE BOYS ARE DOING?
CATNIP
UGH! WHAT CANNIBALS!
WHERE'S THAT PIECE OF FISH? DID YOU EAT IT?
UG-- GLUB---!
MY GOOD MAN-- KEEP A CIVIL TONGUE IN YOUR HEAD!

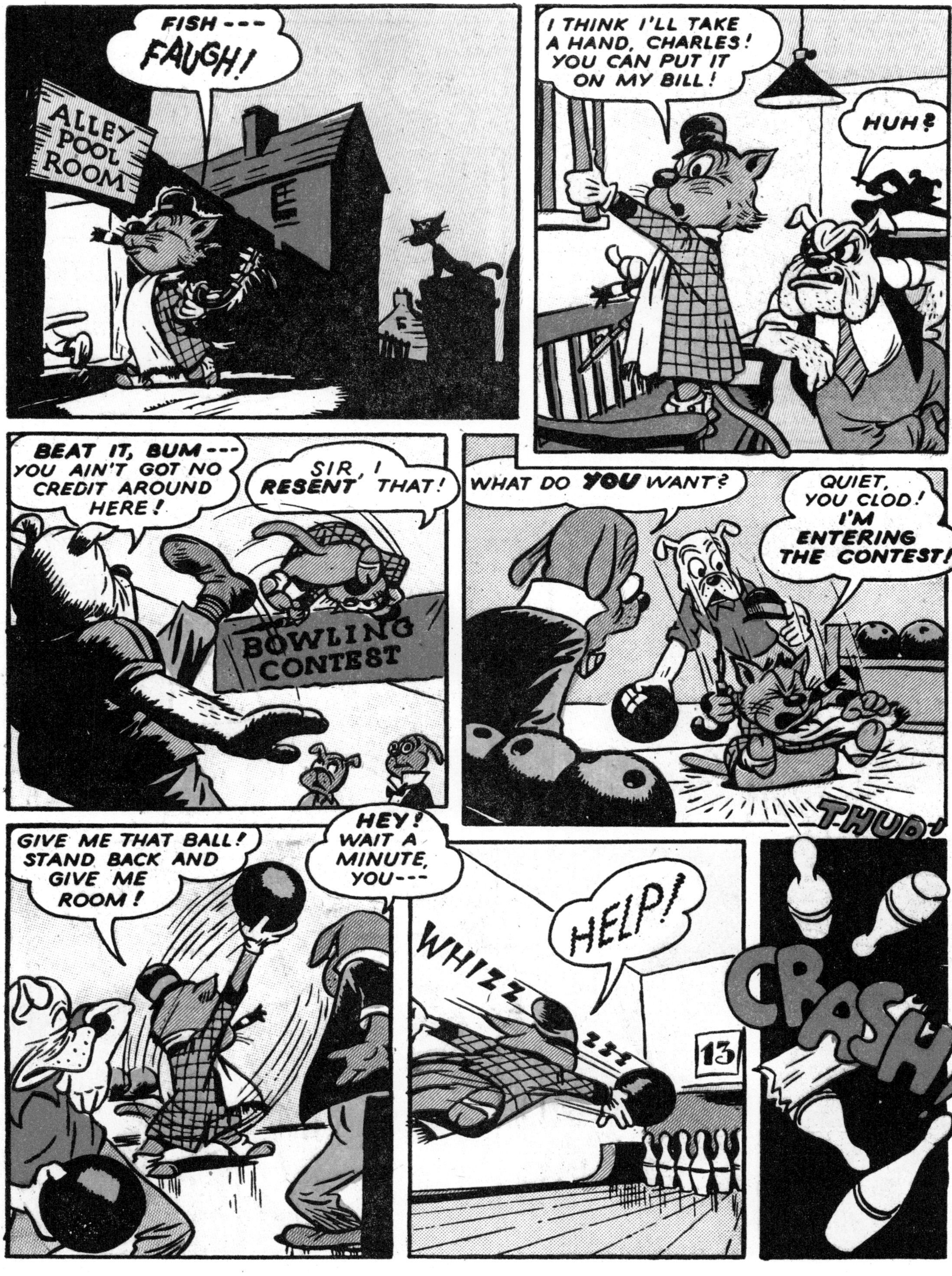
FISH --- FAUGH!
ALLEY POOL ROOM
I THINK I'LL TAKE A HAND, CHARLES! YOU CAN PUT IT ON MY BILL!
HUH?
BEAT IT, BUM --- YOU AIN'T GOT NO CREDIT AROUND HERE!
SIR, I RESENT THAT!
BOWLING CONTEST
WHAT DO YOU WANT?
QUIET, YOU CLOD! I'M ENTERING THE CONTEST!
THUD!
GIVE ME THAT BALL! STAND BACK AND GIVE ME ROOM!
HEY! WAIT A MINUTE, YOU---
HELP!
WHIZZZ
ZZZ
13
CRASH!

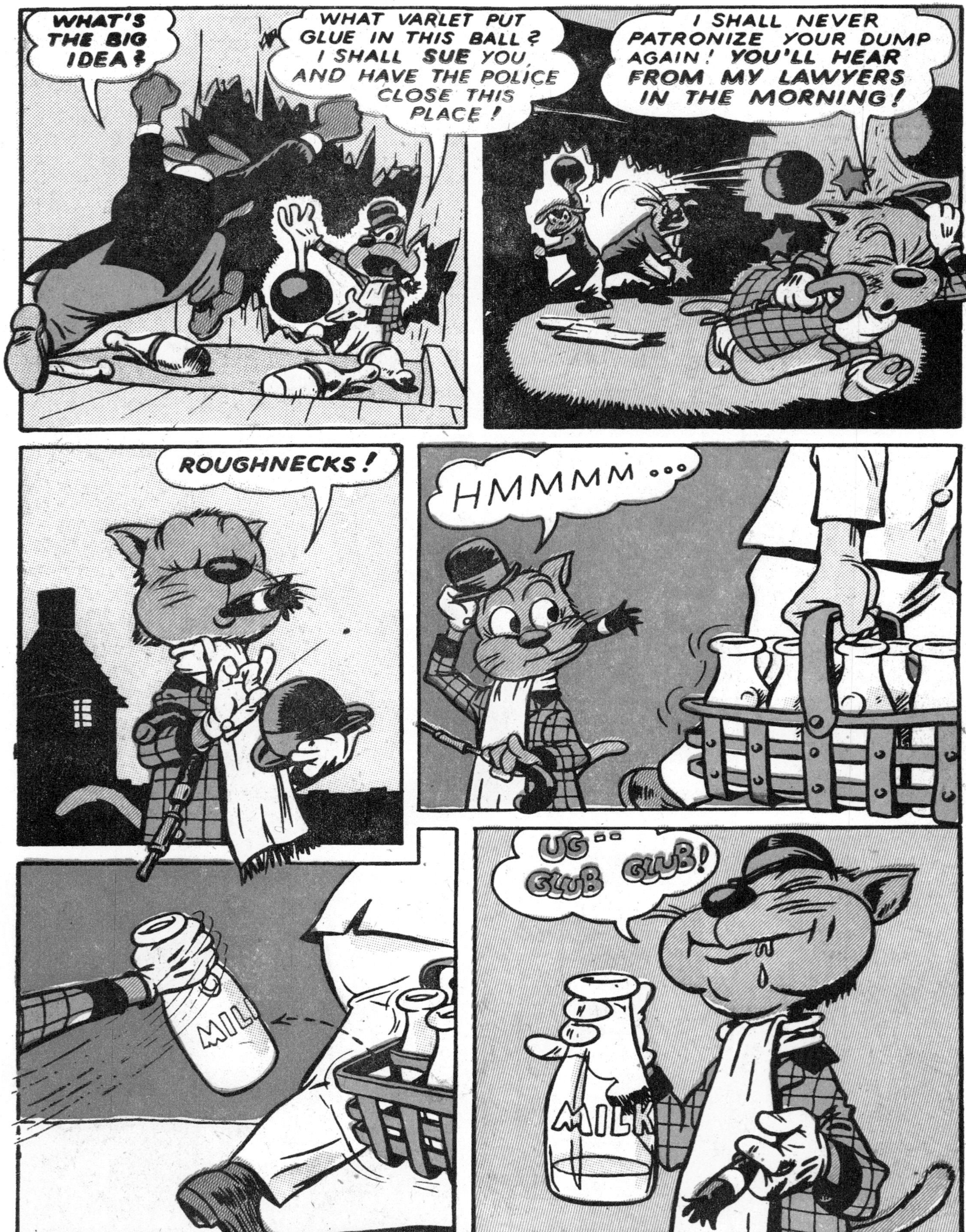
WHAT'S THE BIG IDEA?
WHAT VARLET PUT GLUE IN THIS BALL? I SHALL SUE YOU, AND HAVE THE POLICE CLOSE THIS PLACE!
I SHALL NEVER PATRONIZE YOUR DUMP AGAIN! YOU'LL HEAR FROM MY LAWYERS IN THE MORNING!
ROUGHNECKS!
HMMMM...
MILK
UG.. GLUB GLUB!
MILK

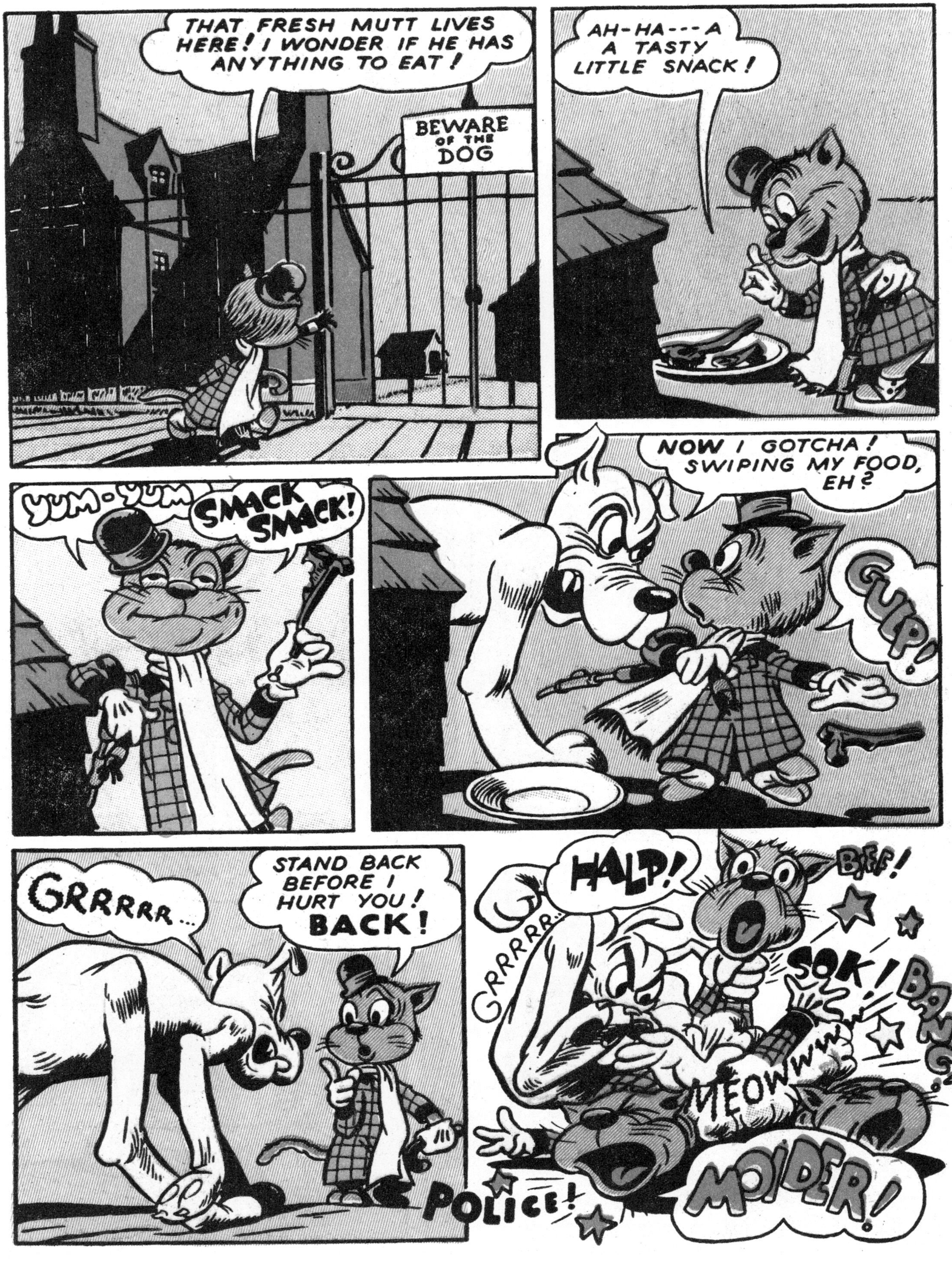
THAT FRESH MUTT LIVES HERE! I WONDER IF HE HAS ANYTHING TO EAT!
BEWARE OF THE DOG
AH-HA---A A TASTY LITTLE SNACK!
YUM-YUM
SMACK SMACK!
NOW I GOTCHA! SWIPING MY FOOD, EH?
GULP!
GRRRRRR...
STAND BACK BEFORE I HURT YOU! BACK!
HALP!
BIFF!
GRRRRRR
SOK!
BANG!
MEOWWWW
POLICE!
MOIDER!

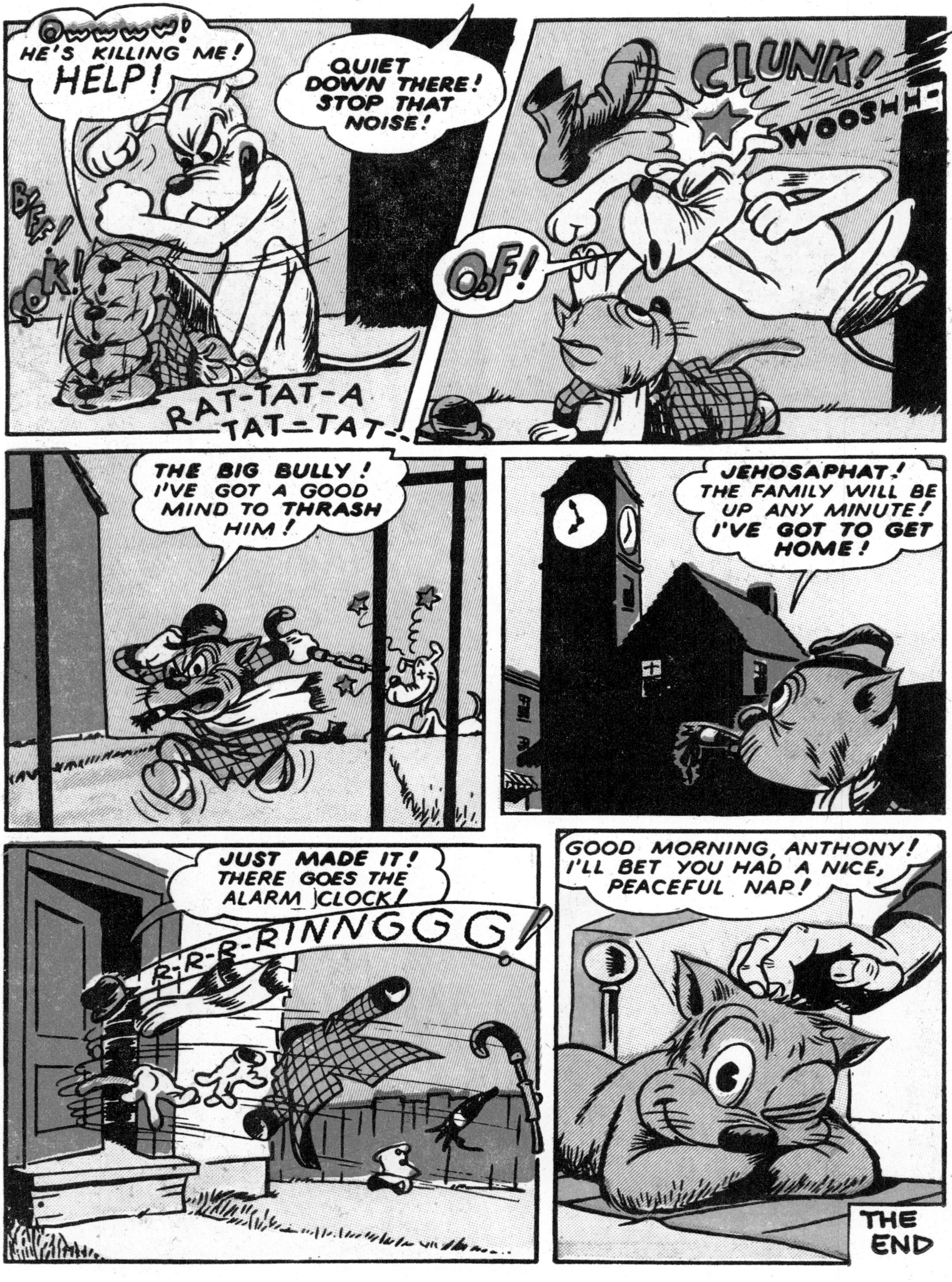
Owwwww! HE'S KILLING ME! HELP!
QUIET DOWN THERE! STOP THAT NOISE!
BIFF!
SOCK!
RAT-TAT-A TAT-TAT-
CLUNK!
WOOSHH
OOF!
THE BIG BULLY! I'VE GOT A GOOD MIND TO THRASH HIM!
JEHOSAPHAT! THE FAMILY WILL BE UP ANY MINUTE! I'VE GOT TO GET HOME!
JUST MADE IT! THERE GOES THE ALARM CLOCK!
R-R-R-RINNGGG!
GOOD MORNING, ANTHONY! I'LL BET YOU HAD A NICE, PEACEFUL NAP!
THE END

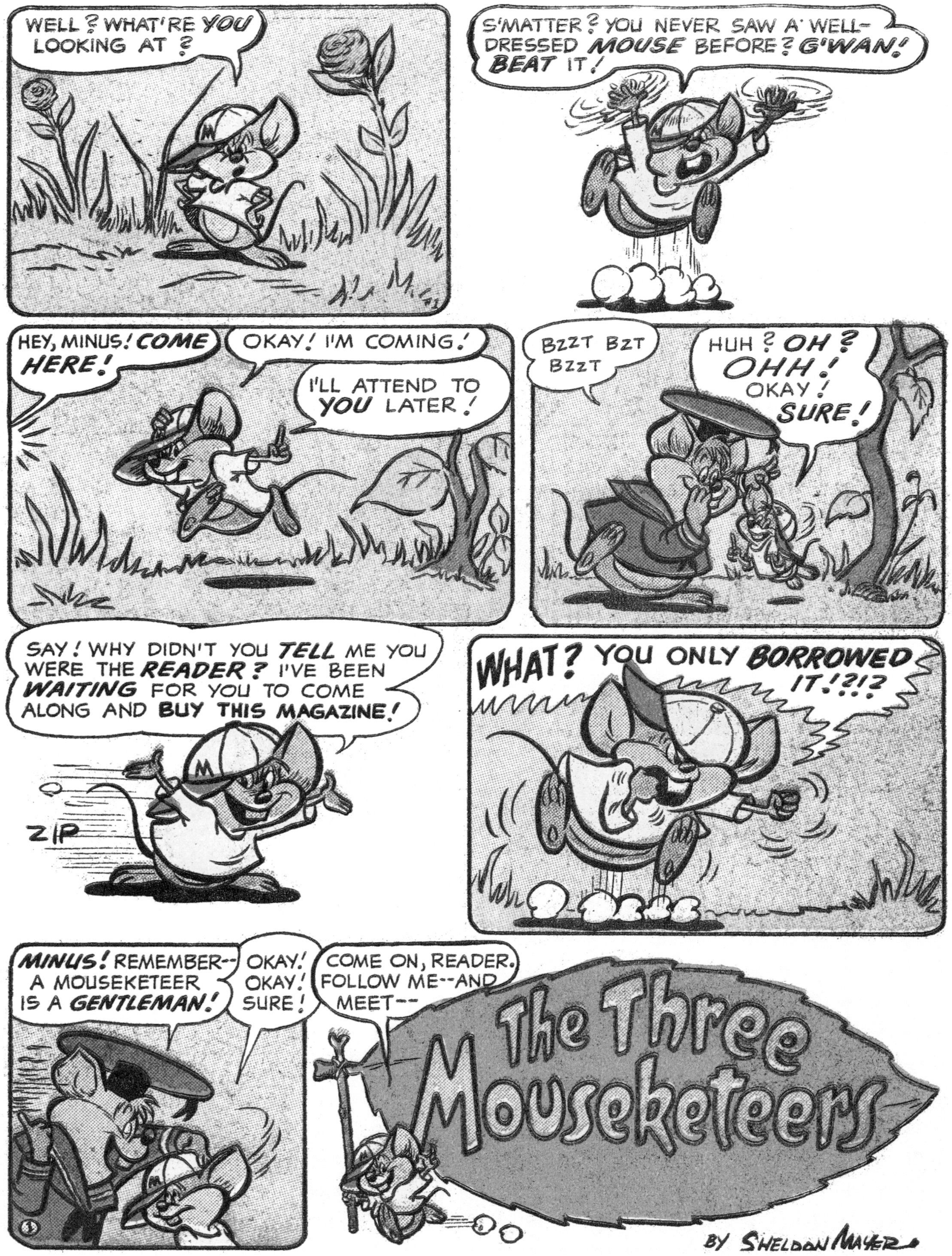
WELL? WHAT'RE YOU LOOKING AT?
S'MATTER? YOU NEVER SAW A' WELL-DRESSED MOUSE BEFORE? G'WAN! BEAT IT!
HEY, MINUS! COME HERE!
OKAY! I'M COMING!
I'LL ATTEND TO YOU LATER!
BZZT BZT BZZT
HUH? OH? OHH! OKAY! SURE!
SAY! WHY DIDN'T YOU TELL ME YOU WERE THE READER? I'VE BEEN WAITING FOR YOU TO COME ALONG AND BUY THIS MAGAZINE!
ZIP
WHAT? YOU ONLY BORROWED IT!?!?
MINUS! REMEMBER-- A MOUSEKETEER IS A GENTLEMAN!
OKAY! OKAY! SURE!
COME ON, READER. FOLLOW ME--AND MEET--
The Three Mouseketeers
BY SHELDON MAYER

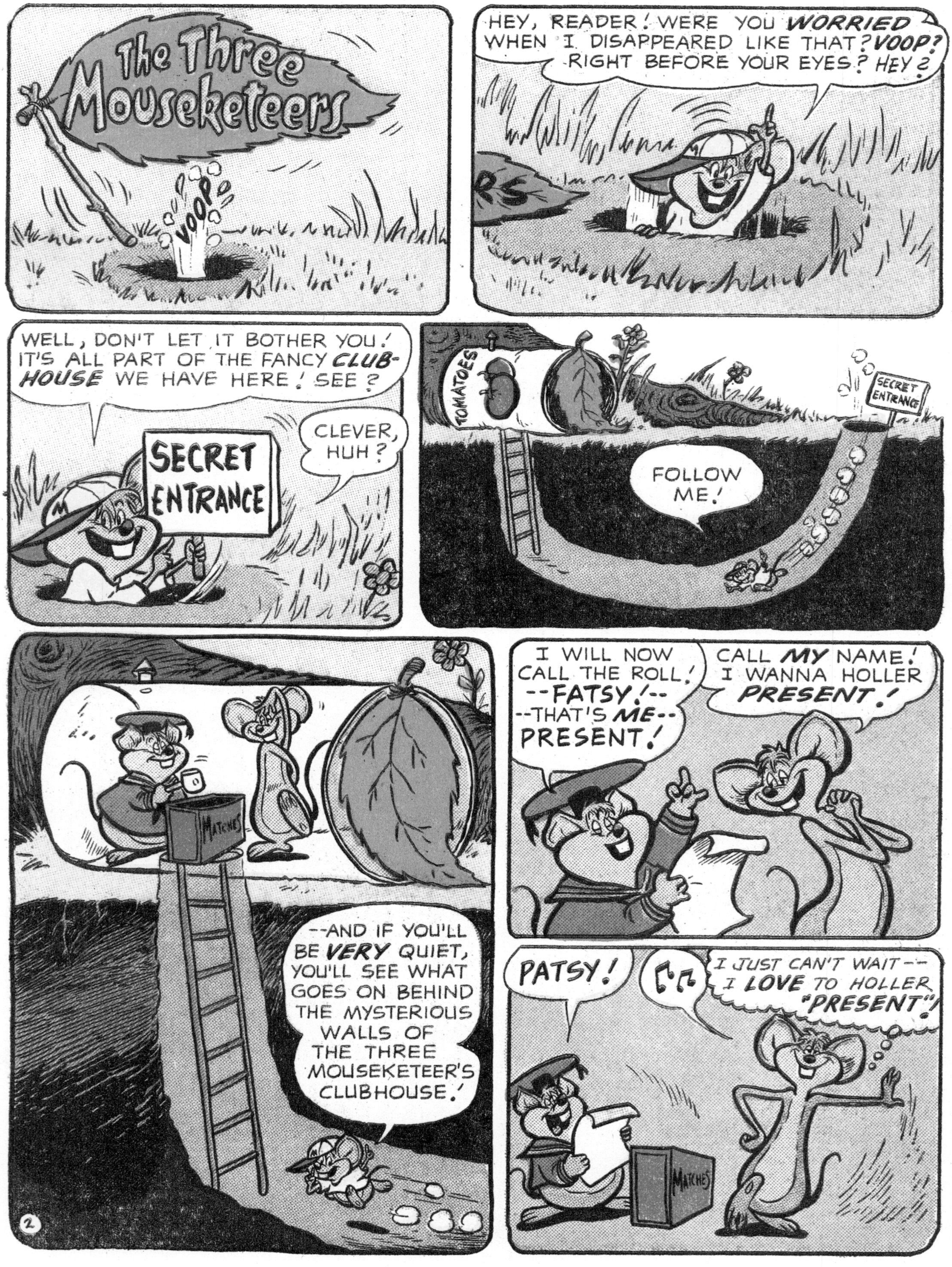
The Three Mouseketeers
VOOP
HEY, READER! WERE YOU WORRIED WHEN I DISAPPEARED LIKE THAT? VOOP? RIGHT BEFORE YOUR EYES? HEY?
WELL, DON'T LET IT BOTHER YOU! IT'S ALL PART OF THE FANCY CLUB-HOUSE WE HAVE HERE! SEE?
SECRET ENTRANCE
CLEVER, HUH?
TOMATOES
SECRET ENTRANCE
FOLLOW ME!
MATCHES
--AND IF YOU'LL BE VERY QUIET, YOU'LL SEE WHAT GOES ON BEHIND THE MYSTERIOUS WALLS OF THE THREE MOUSEKETEER'S CLUBHOUSE!
2
I WILL NOW CALL THE ROLL! --FATSY!-- --THAT'S ME-- PRESENT!
CALL MY NAME! I WANNA HOLLER PRESENT!
PATSY!
I JUST CAN'T WAIT-- I LOVE TO HOLLER "PRESENT"!
MATCHES

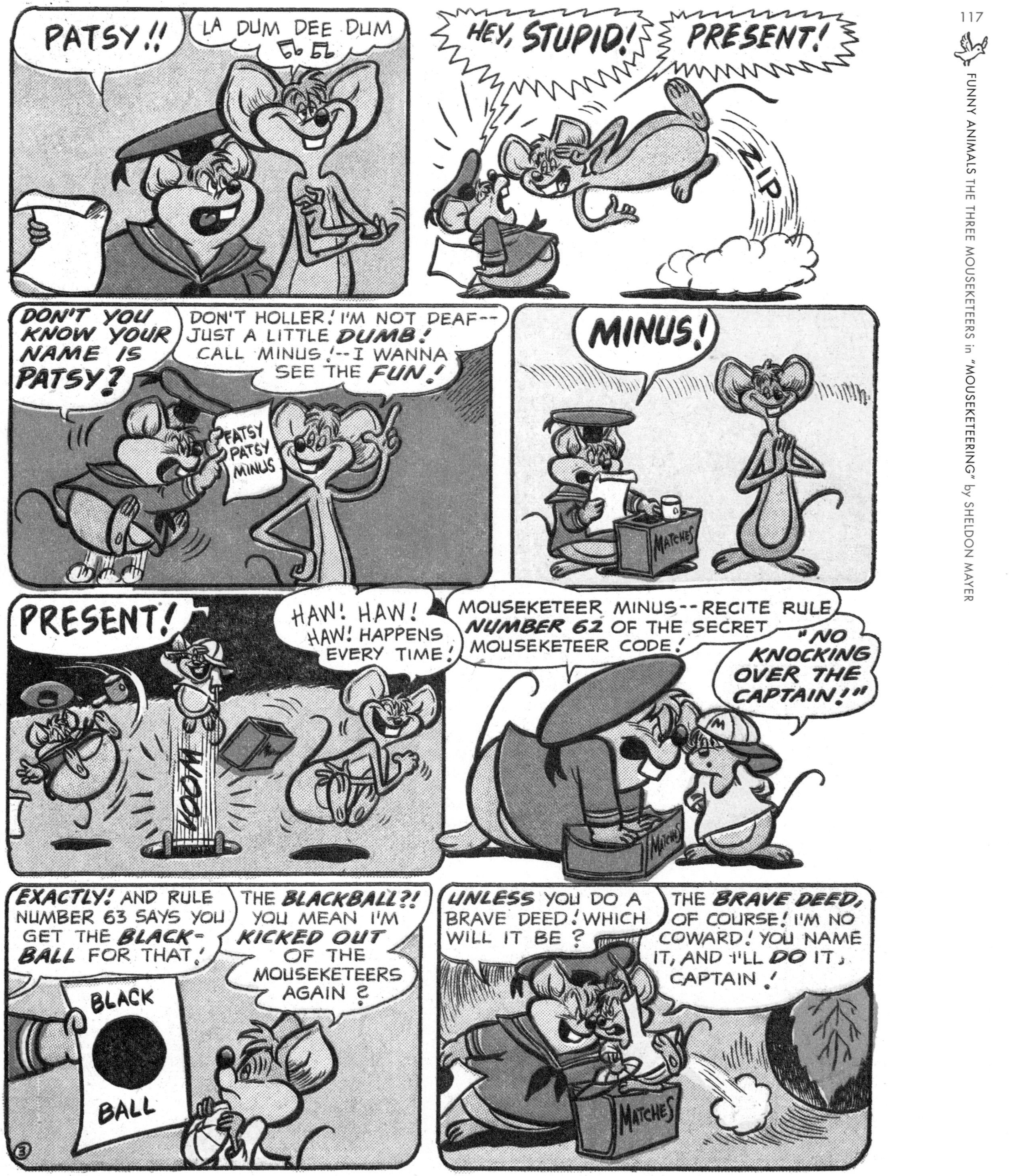
PATSY!!
LA DUM DEE DUM
HEY, STUPID!
PRESENT!
ZIP
DON'T YOU KNOW YOUR NAME IS PATSY?
DON'T HOLLER! I'M NOT DEAF-- JUST A LITTLE DUMB! CALL MINUS!--I WANNA SEE THE FUN!
FATSY
PATSY
MINUS
MINUS!
MATCHES
PRESENT!
HAW! HAW! HAW! HAPPENS EVERY TIME!
VOOM
MOUSEKETEER MINUS--RECITE RULE NUMBER 62 OF THE SECRET MOUSEKETEER CODE!
"NO KNOCKING OVER THE CAPTAIN!"
MATCHES
EXACTLY! AND RULE NUMBER 63 SAYS YOU GET THE BLACK-BALL FOR THAT!
THE BLACKBALL?! YOU MEAN I'M KICKED OUT OF THE MOUSEKETEERS AGAIN?
BLACK
BALL
UNLESS YOU DO A BRAVE DEED! WHICH WILL IT BE?
THE BRAVE DEED, OF COURSE! I'M NO COWARD! YOU NAME IT, AND I'LL DO IT, CAPTAIN!
MATCHES

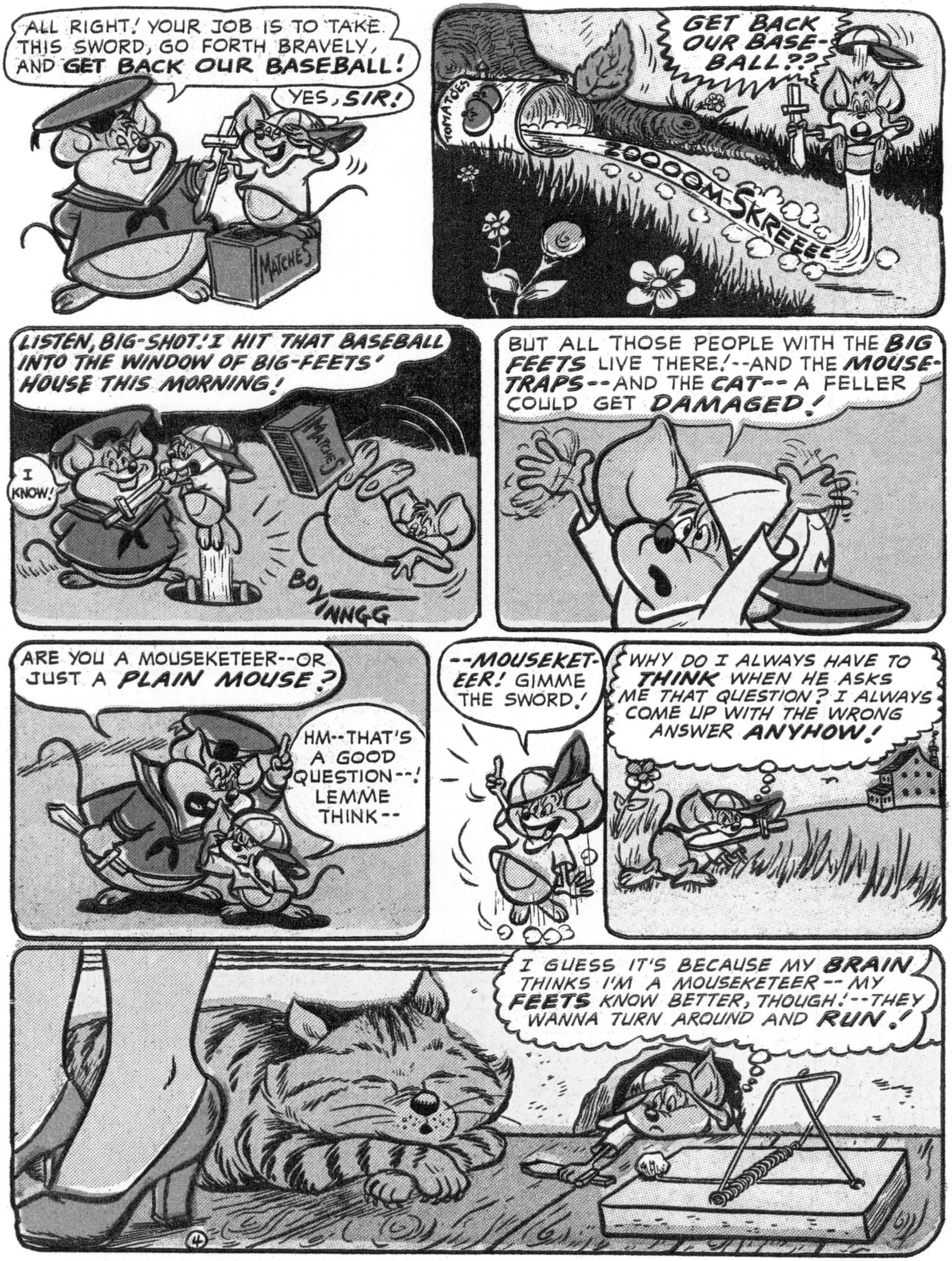
ALL RIGHT! YOUR JOB IS TO TAKE THIS SWORD, GO FORTH BRAVELY, AND GET BACK OUR BASEBALL!
YES, SIR!
MATCHES
GET BACK OUR BASE-BALL??
TOMATOES
ZOOOOM-SKREEEEE
LISTEN, BIG-SHOT! I HIT THAT BASEBALL INTO THE WINDOW OF BIG-FEETS' HOUSE THIS MORNING!
I KNOW!
MATCHES
BOYINNGG
BUT ALL THOSE PEOPLE WITH THE BIG FEETS LIVE THERE!--AND THE MOUSE-TRAPS--AND THE CAT--A FELLER COULD GET DAMAGED!
ARE YOU A MOUSEKETEER--OR JUST A PLAIN MOUSE?
HM--THAT'S A GOOD QUESTION--! LEMME THINK--
--MOUSEKET-EER! GIMME THE SWORD!
WHY DO I ALWAYS HAVE TO THINK WHEN HE ASKS ME THAT QUESTION? I ALWAYS COME UP WITH THE WRONG ANSWER ANYHOW!
I GUESS IT'S BECAUSE MY BRAIN THINKS I'M A MOUSEKETEER--MY FEETS KNOW BETTER, THOUGH!--THEY WANNA TURN AROUND AND RUN!
4

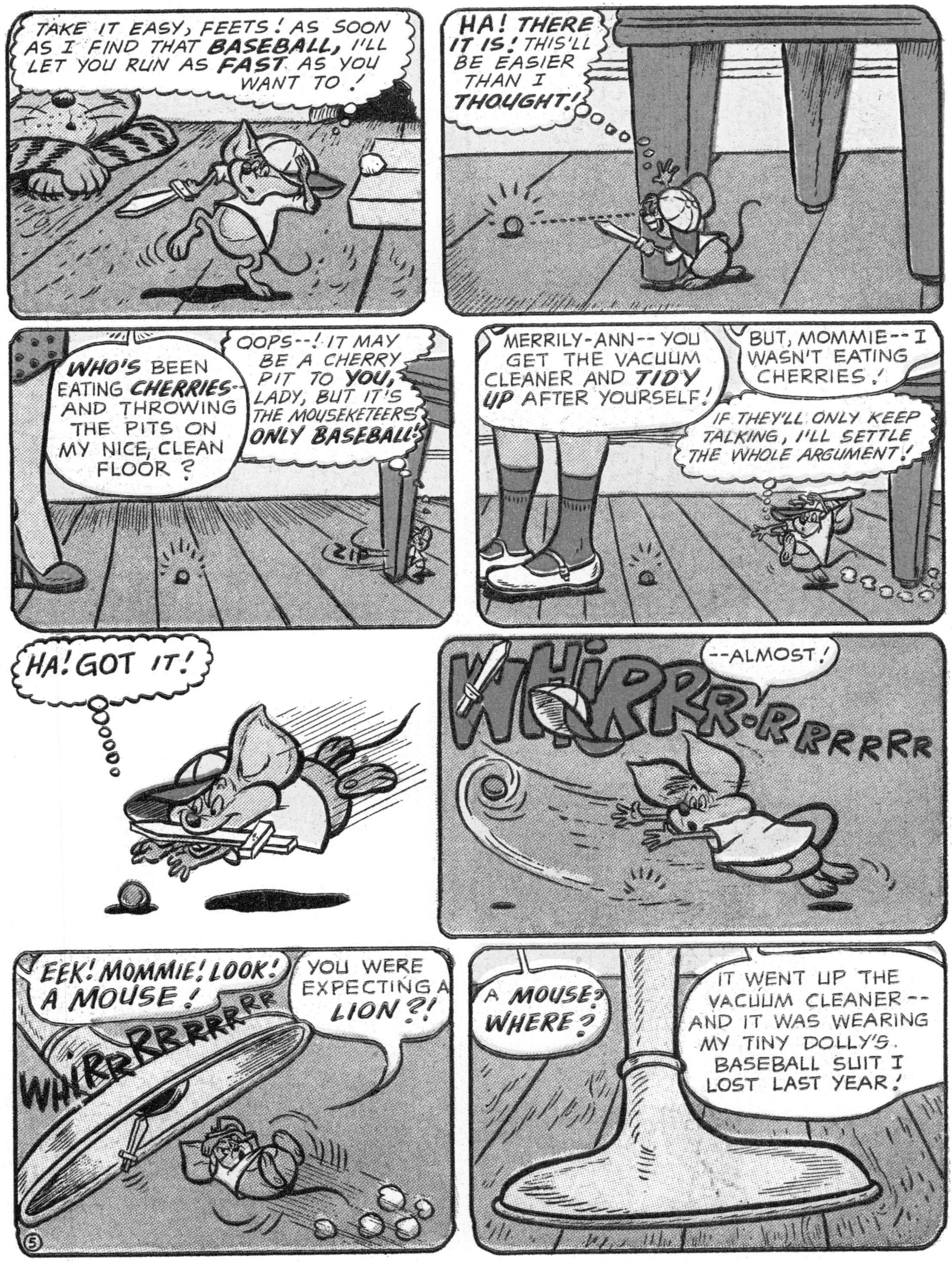
TAKE IT EASY, FEETS! AS SOON AS I FIND THAT BASEBALL, I'LL LET YOU RUN AS FAST AS YOU WANT TO!
HA! THERE IT IS! THIS'LL BE EASIER THAN I THOUGHT!
WHO'S BEEN EATING CHERRIES-- AND THROWING THE PITS ON MY NICE, CLEAN FLOOR?
OOPS--! IT MAY BE A CHERRY PIT TO YOU, LADY, BUT IT'S THE MOUSEKETEERS' ONLY BASEBALL!
ZIP
MERRILY-ANN-- YOU GET THE VACUUM CLEANER AND TIDY UP AFTER YOURSELF!
BUT, MOMMIE-- I WASN'T EATING CHERRIES!
IF THEY'LL ONLY KEEP TALKING, I'LL SETTLE THE WHOLE ARGUMENT!
HA! GOT IT!
--ALMOST!
WHIRRR-RRRRRRR
EEK! MOMMIE! LOOK! A MOUSE!
YOU WERE EXPECTING A LION?!
WHIRRRRRRRRRR
5
A MOUSE? WHERE?
IT WENT UP THE VACUUM CLEANER-- AND IT WAS WEARING MY TINY DOLLY'S BASEBALL SUIT I LOST LAST YEAR!

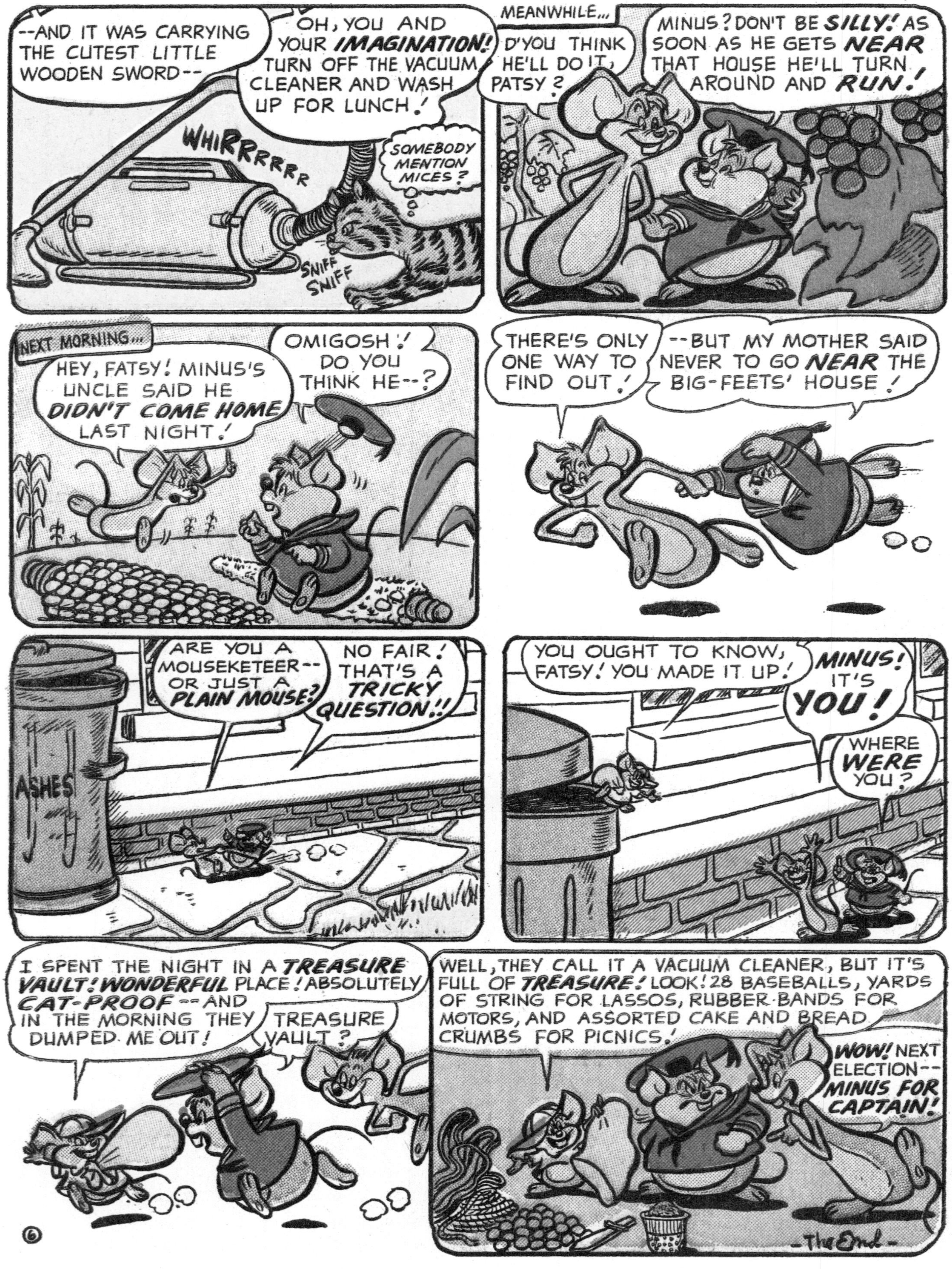
--AND IT WAS CARRYING THE CUTEST LITTLE WOODEN SWORD--
OH, YOU AND YOUR IMAGINATION! TURN OFF THE VACUUM CLEANER AND WASH UP FOR LUNCH!
WHIRRRRRRR
SOMEBODY MENTION MICES?
SNIFF SNIFF
MEANWHILE...
D'YOU THINK HE'LL DO IT, PATSY?
MINUS? DON'T BE SILLY! AS SOON AS HE GETS NEAR THAT HOUSE HE'LL TURN AROUND AND RUN!
NEXT MORNING...
HEY, FATSY! MINUS'S UNCLE SAID HE DIDN'T COME HOME LAST NIGHT!
OMIGOSH! DO YOU THINK HE--?
THERE'S ONLY ONE WAY TO FIND OUT!
--BUT MY MOTHER SAID NEVER TO GO NEAR THE BIG-FEETS' HOUSE!
ASHES
ARE YOU A MOUSEKETEER-- OR JUST A PLAIN MOUSE?
NO FAIR! THAT'S A TRICKY QUESTION!!
YOU OUGHT TO KNOW, FATSY! YOU MADE IT UP!
MINUS! IT'S YOU!
WHERE WERE YOU?
I SPENT THE NIGHT IN A TREASURE VAULT! WONDERFUL PLACE! ABSOLUTELY CAT-PROOF--AND IN THE MORNING THEY DUMPED ME OUT!
TREASURE VAULT?
WELL, THEY CALL IT A VACUUM CLEANER, BUT IT'S FULL OF TREASURE! LOOK! 28 BASEBALLS, YARDS OF STRING FOR LASSOS, RUBBER BANDS FOR MOTORS, AND ASSORTED CAKE AND BREAD CRUMBS FOR PICNICS!
WOW! NEXT ELECTION--MINUS FOR CAPTAIN!
6
-The End-

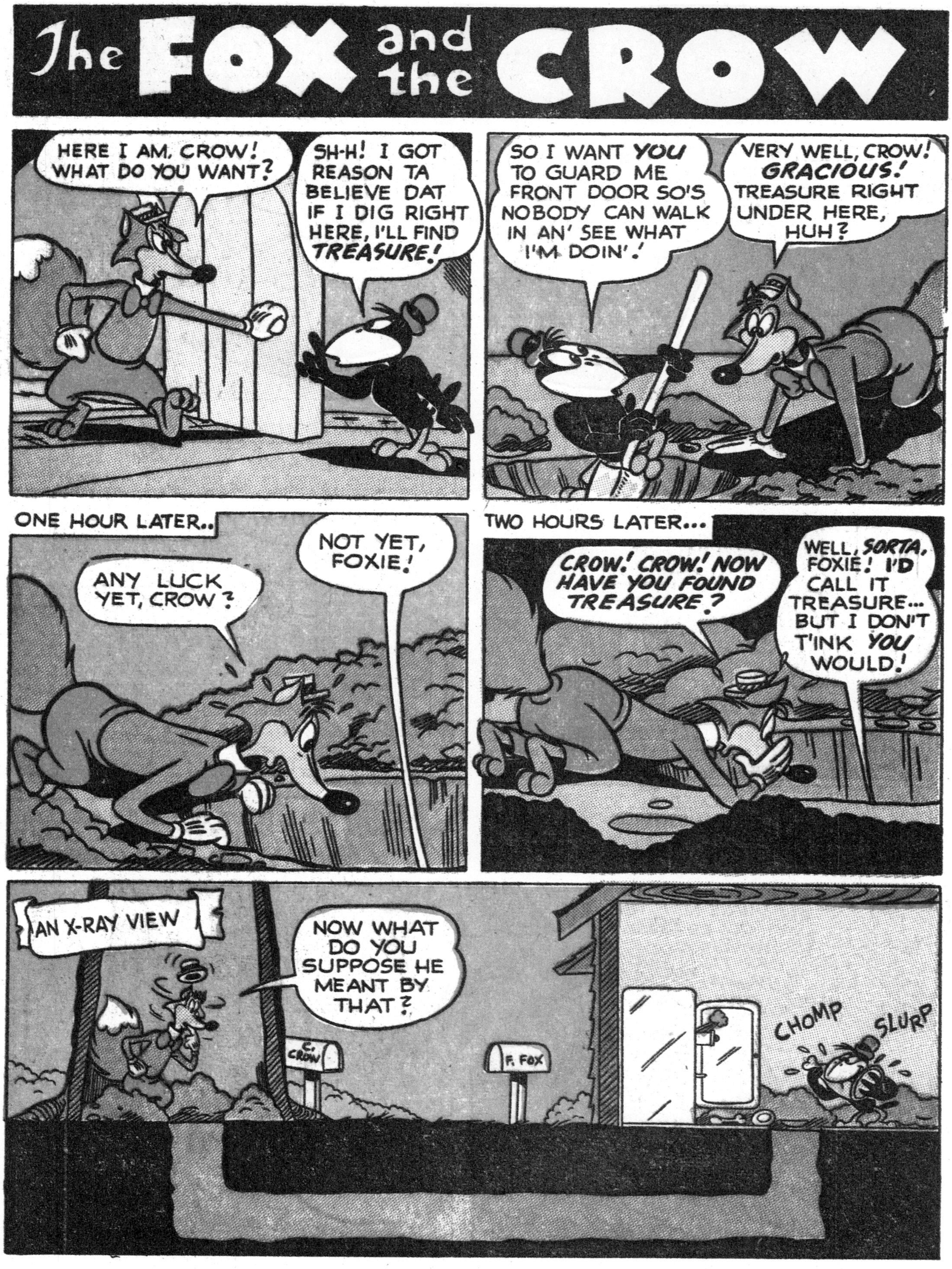
The FOX and the CROW
HERE I AM, CROW! WHAT DO YOU WANT?
SH-H! I GOT REASON TA BELIEVE DAT IF I DIG RIGHT HERE, I'LL FIND TREASURE!
SO I WANT YOU TO GUARD ME FRONT DOOR SO'S NOBODY CAN WALK IN AN' SEE WHAT I'M DOIN'!
VERY WELL, CROW! GRACIOUS! TREASURE RIGHT UNDER HERE, HUH?
ONE HOUR LATER..
ANY LUCK YET, CROW?
NOT YET, FOXIE!
TWO HOURS LATER...
CROW! CROW! NOW HAVE YOU FOUND TREASURE?
WELL, SORTA, FOXIE! I'D CALL IT TREASURE... BUT I DON'T T'INK YOU WOULD!
AN X-RAY VIEW
NOW WHAT DO YOU SUPPOSE HE MEANT BY THAT?
C. CROW
F. FOX
CHOMP
SLURP

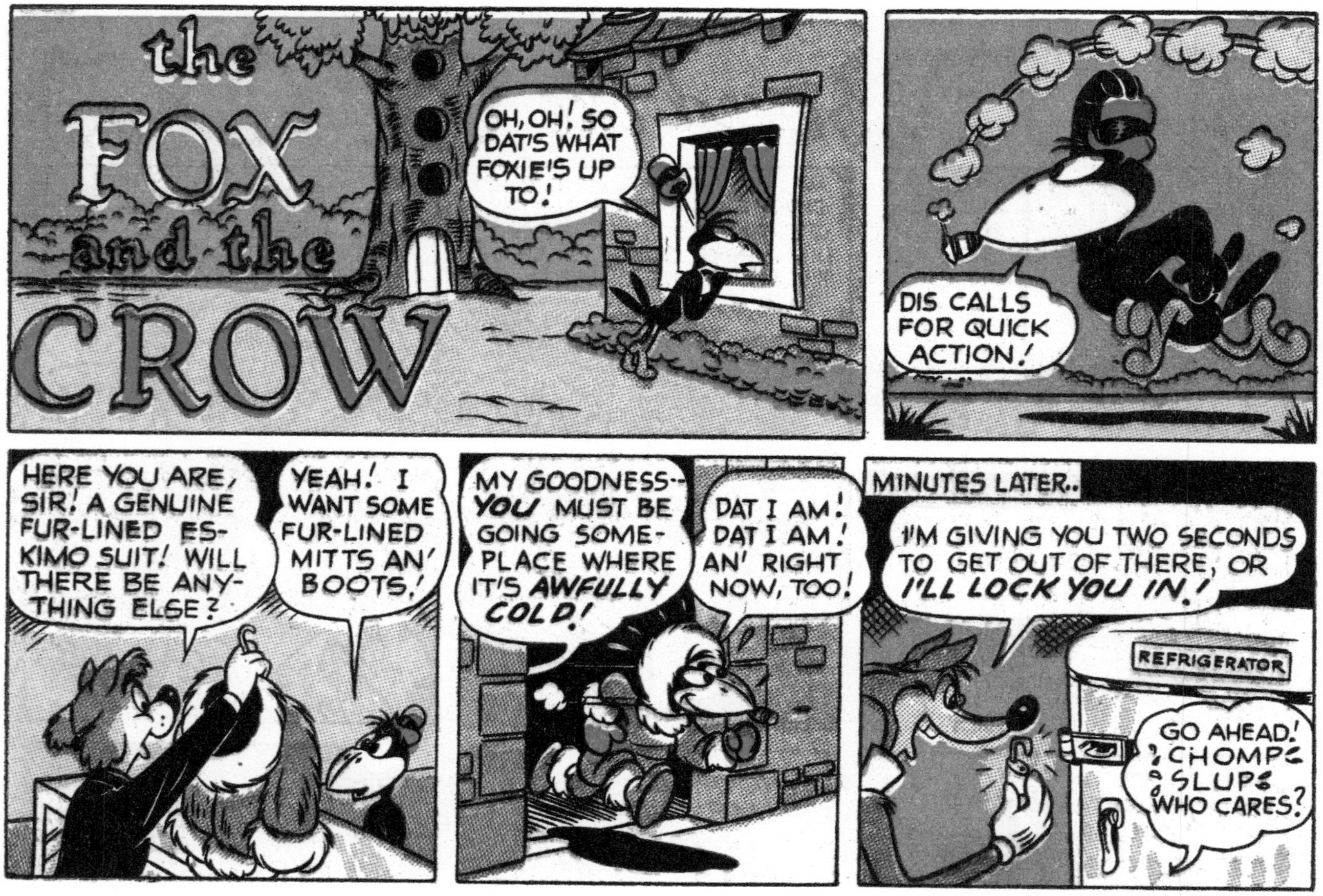
the FOX and the CROW
OH, OH! SO DAT'S WHAT FOXIE'S UP TO!
DIS CALLS FOR QUICK ACTION!
HERE YOU ARE, SIR! A GENUINE FUR-LINED ES-KIMO SUIT! WILL THERE BE ANY-THING ELSE?
YEAH! I WANT SOME FUR-LINED MITTS AN' BOOTS!
MY GOODNESS-- YOU MUST BE GOING SOME-PLACE WHERE IT'S AWFULLY COLD!
DAT I AM! DAT I AM! AN' RIGHT NOW, TOO!
MINUTES LATER..
I'M GIVING YOU TWO SECONDS TO GET OUT OF THERE, OR I'LL LOCK YOU IN!
REFRIGERATOR
GO AHEAD! CHOMP SLUP WHO CARES?

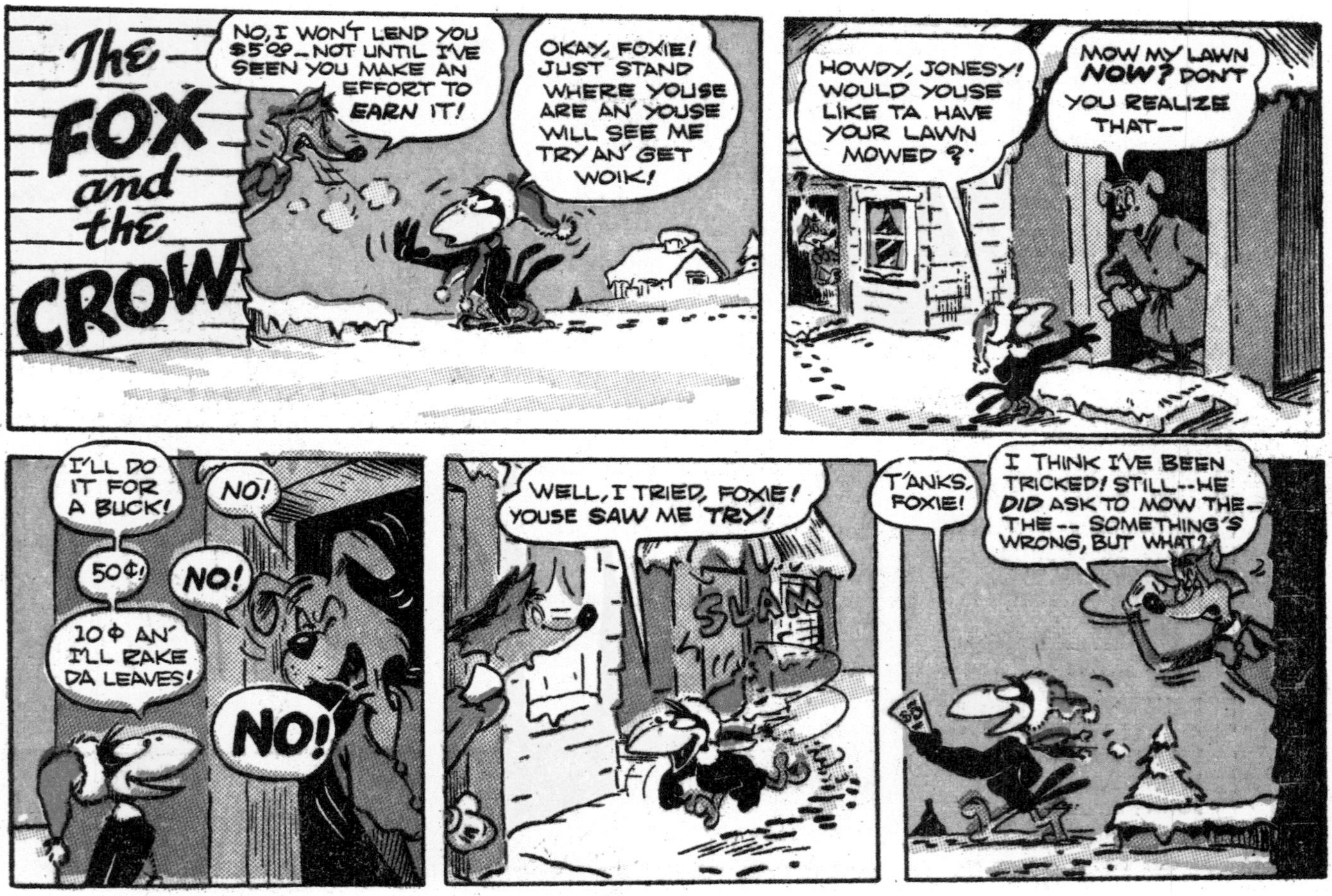
The FOX and the CROW
NO, I WON'T LEND YOU $5.00 -- NOT UNTIL I'VE SEEN YOU MAKE AN EFFORT TO EARN IT!
OKAY, FOXIE! JUST STAND WHERE YOUSE ARE AN' YOUSE WILL SEE ME TRY AN' GET WOIK!
HOWDY, JONESY! WOULD YOUSE LIKE TA HAVE YOUR LAWN MOWED?
MOW MY LAWN NOW? DON'T YOU REALIZE THAT--
I'LL DO IT FOR A BUCK!
NO!
50¢!
NO!
10¢ AN' I'LL RAKE DA LEAVES!
NO!
WELL, I TRIED, FOXIE! YOUSE SAW ME TRY!
SLAM
T'ANKS, FOXIE!
I THINK I'VE BEEN TRICKED! STILL--HE DID ASK TO MOW THE-- THE -- SOMETHING'S WRONG, BUT WHAT?

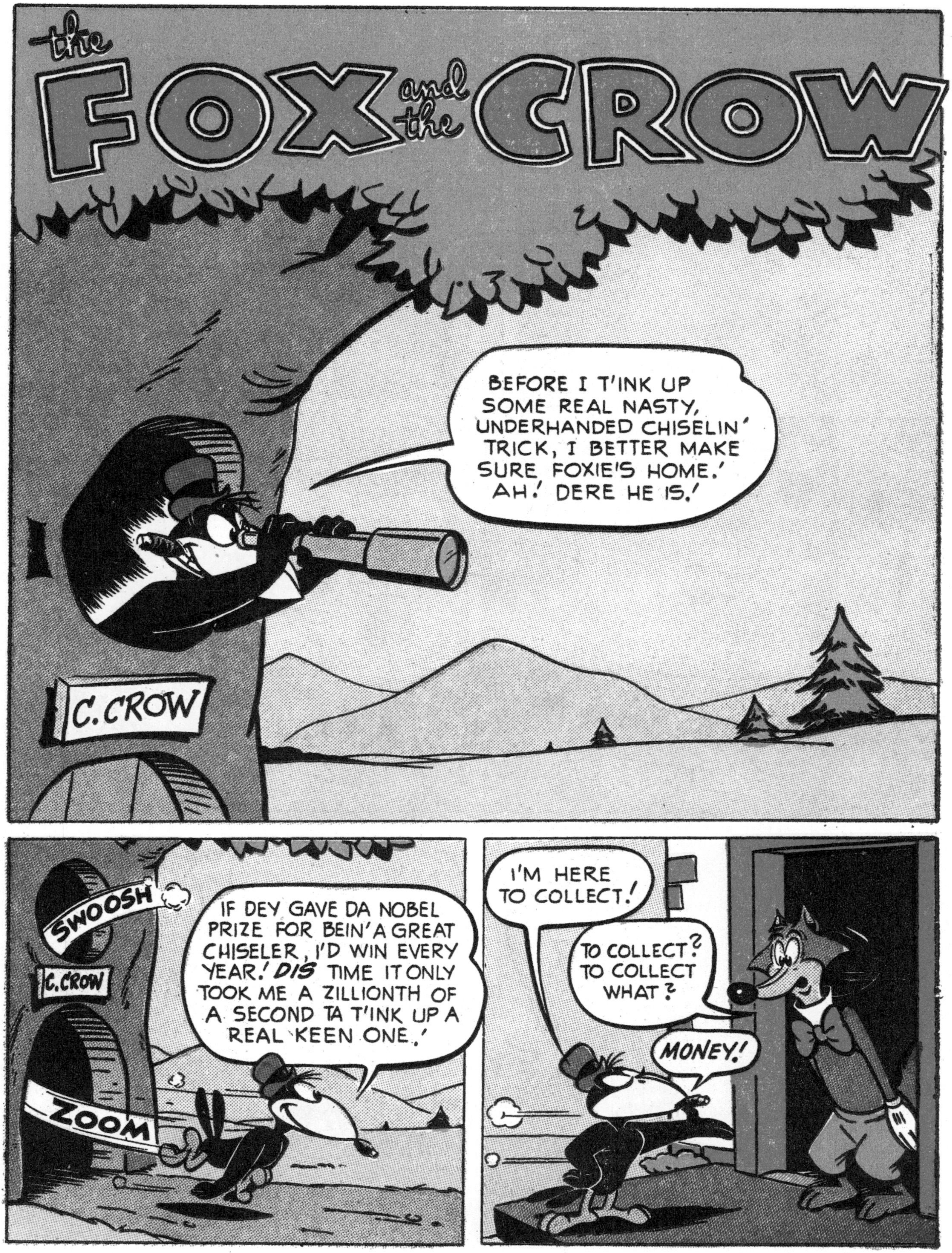
the FOX and the CROW
BEFORE I T'INK UP SOME REAL NASTY, UNDERHANDED CHISELIN' TRICK, I BETTER MAKE SURE FOXIE'S HOME.' AH.' DERE HE IS.'
C. CROW
SWOOSH
C. CROW
ZOOM
IF DEY GAVE DA NOBEL PRIZE FOR BEIN' A GREAT CHISELER, I'D WIN EVERY YEAR.' DIS TIME IT ONLY TOOK ME A ZILLIONTH OF A SECOND TA T'INK UP A REAL KEEN ONE.'
I'M HERE TO COLLECT.'
TO COLLECT? TO COLLECT WHAT?
MONEY.'

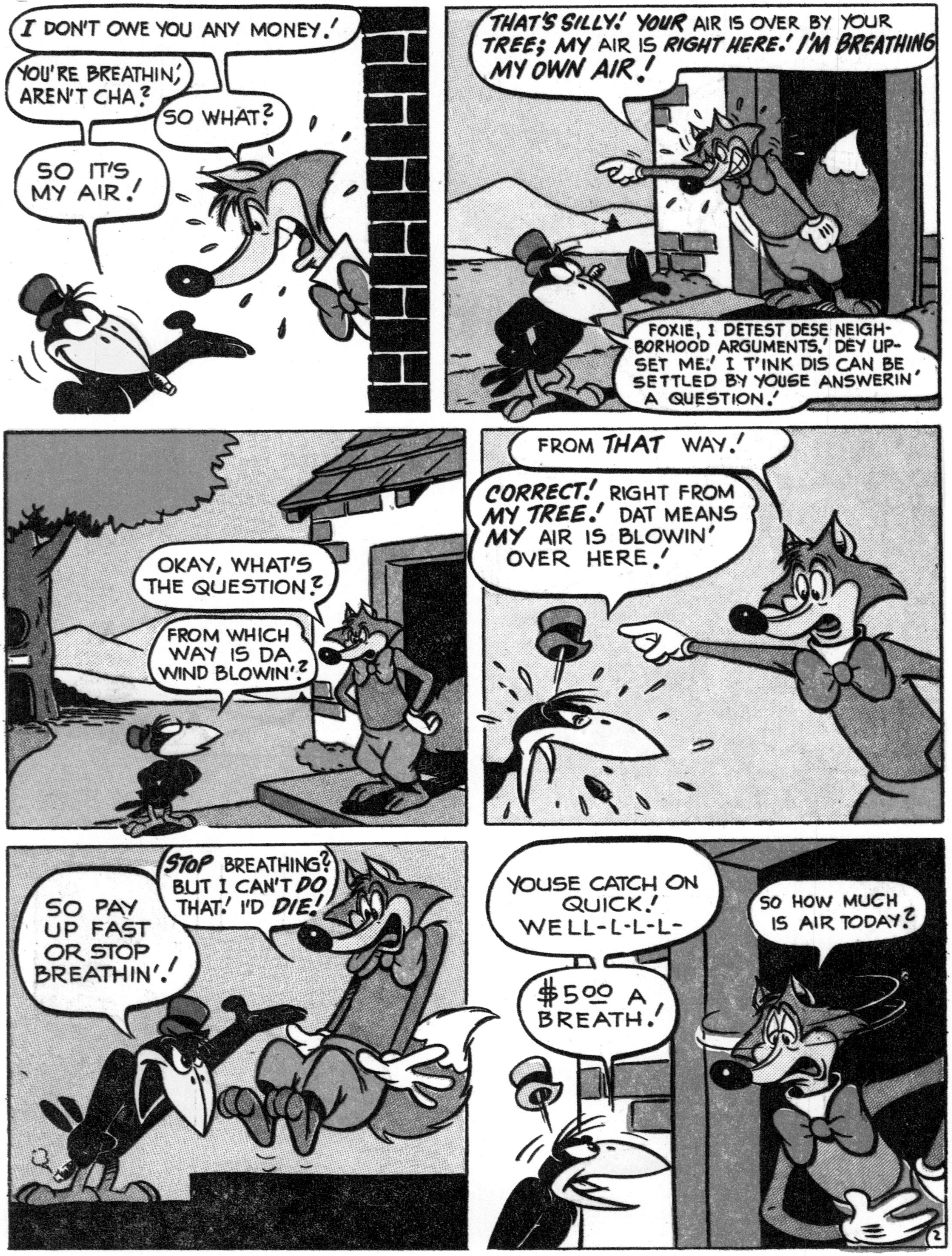
I DON'T OWE YOU ANY MONEY!
YOU'RE BREATHIN', AREN'T CHA?
SO WHAT?
SO IT'S MY AIR!
THAT'S SILLY! YOUR AIR IS OVER BY YOUR TREE; MY AIR IS RIGHT HERE! I'M BREATHING MY OWN AIR!
FOXIE, I DETEST DESE NEIGHBORHOOD ARGUMENTS! DEY UPSET ME! I T'INK DIS CAN BE SETTLED BY YOUSE ANSWERIN' A QUESTION!
OKAY, WHAT'S THE QUESTION?
FROM WHICH WAY IS DA WIND BLOWIN'?
FROM THAT WAY!
CORRECT! RIGHT FROM MY TREE! DAT MEANS MY AIR IS BLOWIN' OVER HERE!
SO PAY UP FAST OR STOP BREATHIN'!
STOP BREATHING? BUT I CAN'T DO THAT! I'D DIE!
YOUSE CATCH ON QUICK! WELL-L-L-L-
$5.00 A BREATH!
SO HOW MUCH IS AIR TODAY?
2

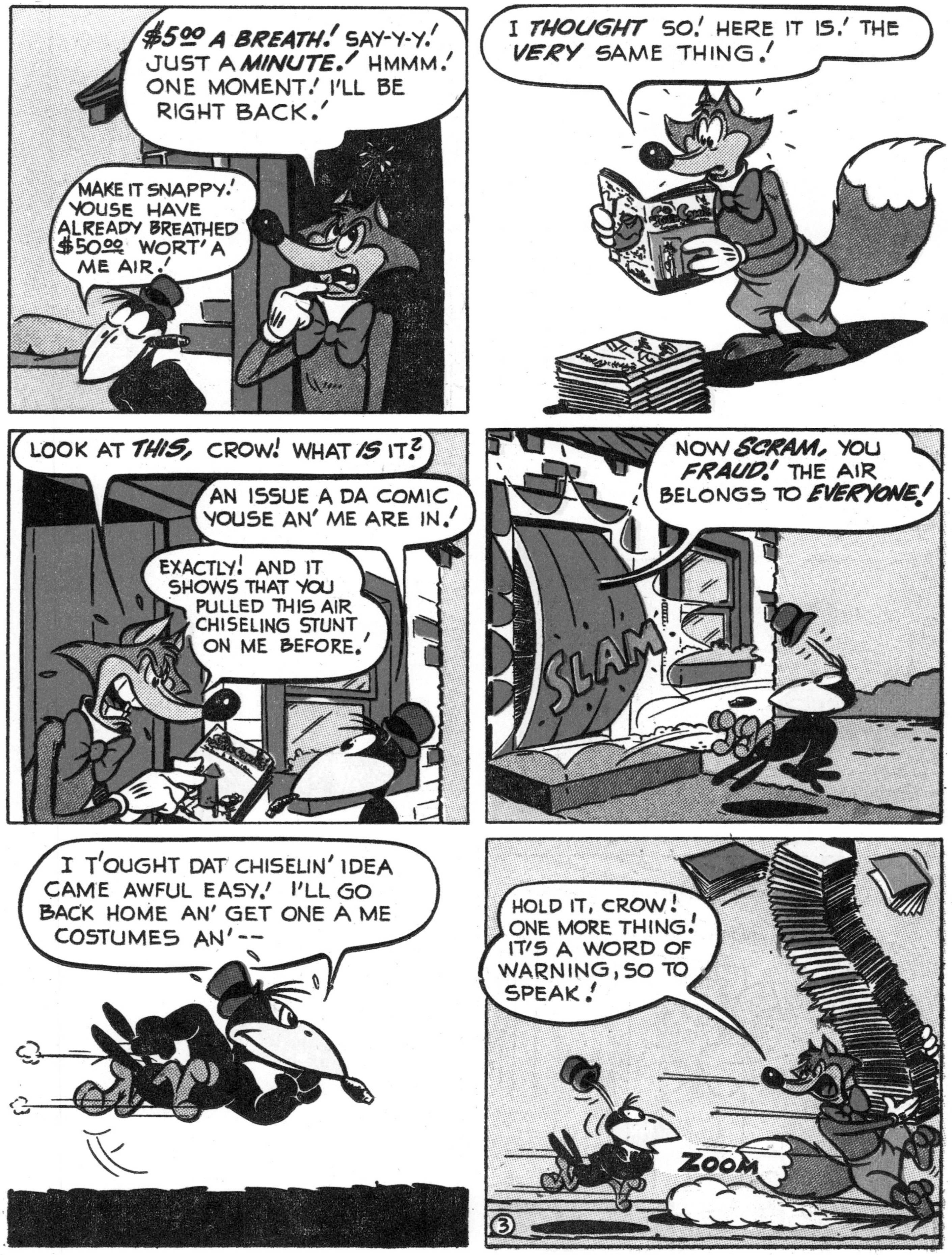
$5.00 A BREATH! SAY-Y-Y! JUST A MINUTE! HMMM! ONE MOMENT! I'LL BE RIGHT BACK!
MAKE IT SNAPPY! YOUSE HAVE ALREADY BREATHED $50.00 WORT' A ME AIR!
I THOUGHT SO! HERE IT IS! THE VERY SAME THING!
LOOK AT THIS, CROW! WHAT IS IT?
AN ISSUE A DA COMIC YOUSE AN' ME ARE IN!
EXACTLY! AND IT SHOWS THAT YOU PULLED THIS AIR CHISELING STUNT ON ME BEFORE!
NOW SCRAM, YOU FRAUD! THE AIR BELONGS TO EVERYONE!
SLAM
I T'OUGHT DAT CHISELIN' IDEA CAME AWFUL EASY! I'LL GO BACK HOME AN' GET ONE A ME COSTUMES AN'--
HOLD IT, CROW! ONE MORE THING! IT'S A WORD OF WARNING, SO TO SPEAK!
ZOOM
3

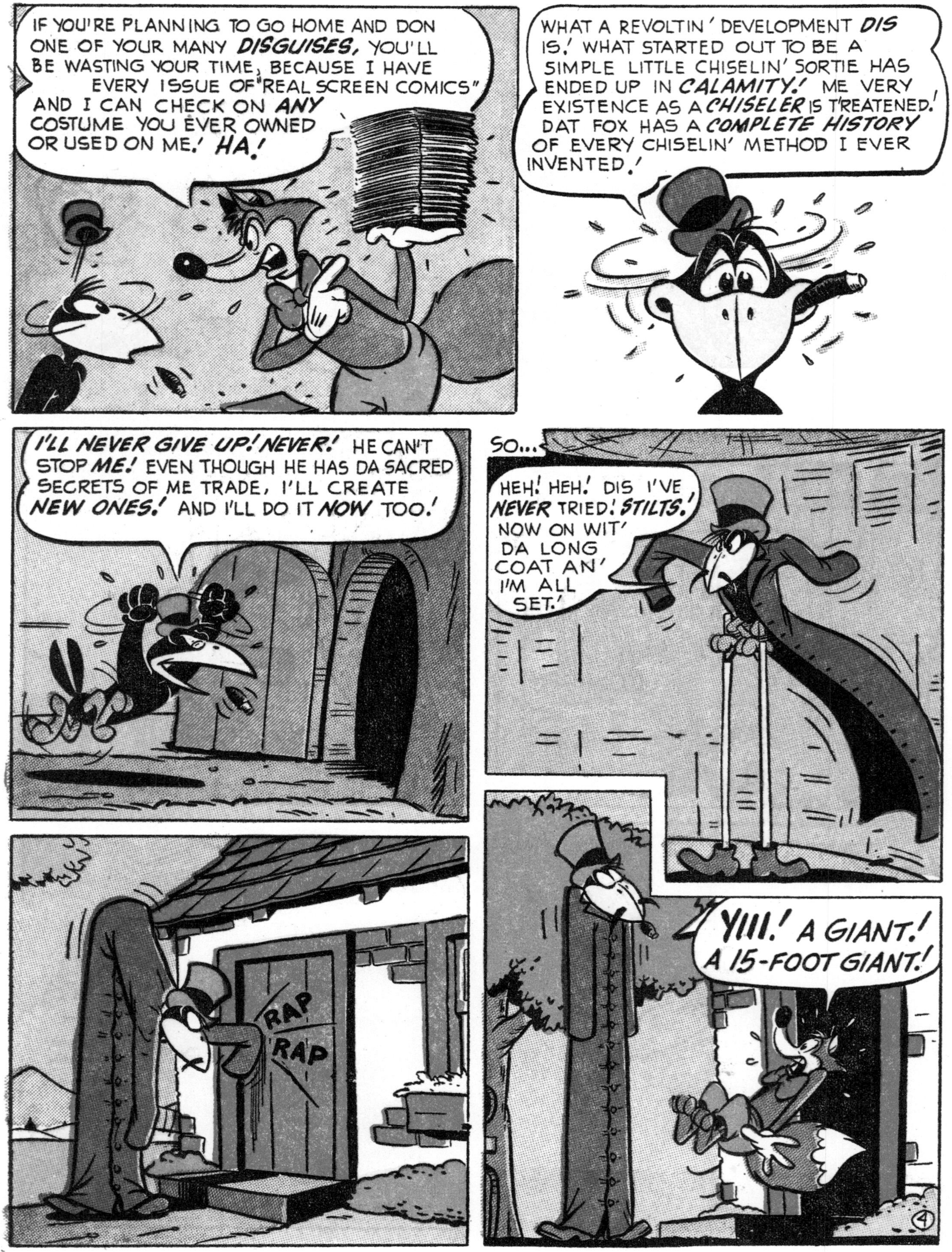
IF YOU'RE PLANNING TO GO HOME AND DON ONE OF YOUR MANY DISGUISES, YOU'LL BE WASTING YOUR TIME, BECAUSE I HAVE EVERY ISSUE OF "REAL SCREEN COMICS" AND I CAN CHECK ON ANY COSTUME YOU EVER OWNED OR USED ON ME! HA!
WHAT A REVOLTIN' DEVELOPMENT DIS IS! WHAT STARTED OUT TO BE A SIMPLE LITTLE CHISELIN' SORTIE HAS ENDED UP IN CALAMITY! ME VERY EXISTENCE AS A CHISELER IS T'REATENED! DAT FOX HAS A COMPLETE HISTORY OF EVERY CHISELIN' METHOD I EVER INVENTED!
I'LL NEVER GIVE UP! NEVER! HE CAN'T STOP ME! EVEN THOUGH HE HAS DA SACRED SECRETS OF ME TRADE, I'LL CREATE NEW ONES! AND I'LL DO IT NOW TOO!
SO...
HEH! HEH! DIS I'VE NEVER TRIED! STILTS! NOW ON WIT' DA LONG COAT AN' I'M ALL SET!
RAP
RAP
YIII! A GIANT! A 15-FOOT GIANT!
4

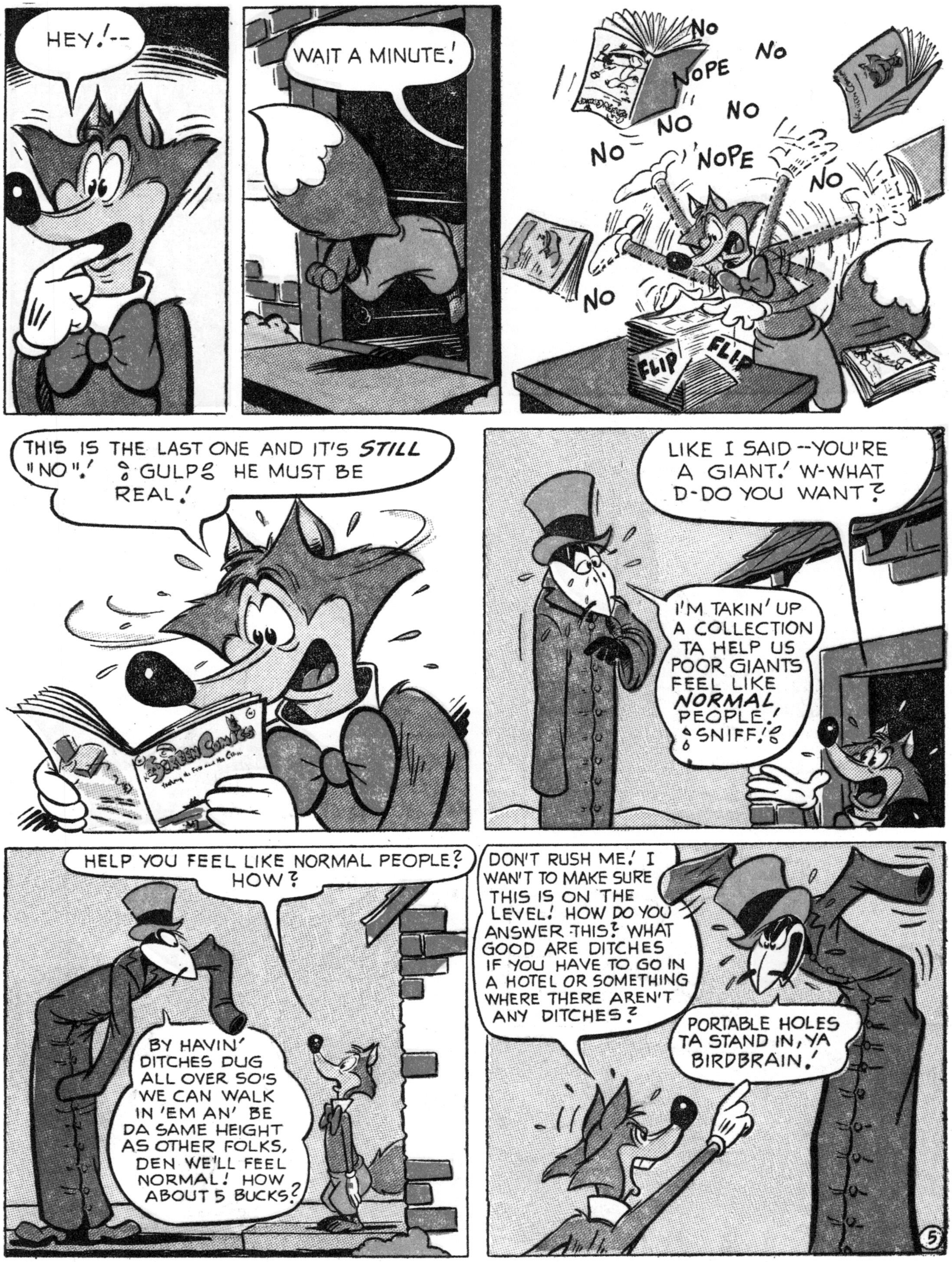
HEY!--
WAIT A MINUTE!
No
No
NOPE
NO
NO
NO
NOPE
NO
NO
FLIP
FLIP
THIS IS THE LAST ONE AND IT'S STILL "NO"! GULP HE MUST BE REAL!
LIKE I SAID--YOU'RE A GIANT! W-WHAT D-DO YOU WANT?
I'M TAKIN' UP A COLLECTION TA HELP US POOR GIANTS FEEL LIKE NORMAL PEOPLE! SNIFF!
HELP YOU FEEL LIKE NORMAL PEOPLE? HOW?
BY HAVIN' DITCHES DUG ALL OVER SO'S WE CAN WALK IN 'EM AN' BE DA SAME HEIGHT AS OTHER FOLKS, DEN WE'LL FEEL NORMAL! HOW ABOUT 5 BUCKS?
DON'T RUSH ME! I WAN'T TO MAKE SURE THIS IS ON THE LEVEL! HOW DO YOU ANSWER THIS? WHAT GOOD ARE DITCHES IF YOU HAVE TO GO IN A HOTEL OR SOMETHING WHERE THERE AREN'T ANY DITCHES?
PORTABLE HOLES TA STAND IN, YA BIRDBRAIN!
5

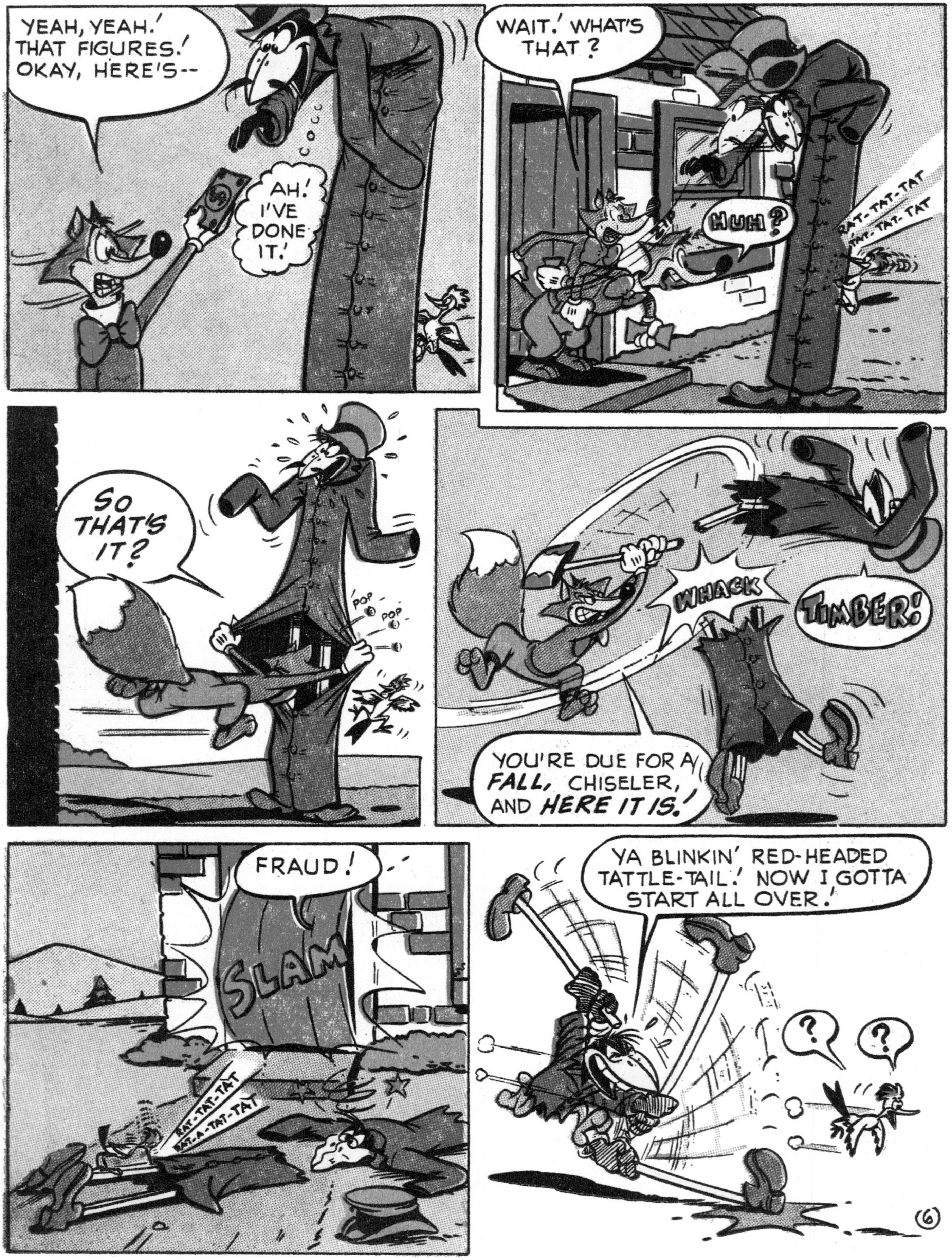
YEAH, YEAH.! THAT FIGURES.! OKAY, HERE'S--
AH.! I'VE DONE IT.!
WAIT.! WHAT'S THAT ?
HUH ?
RAT-TAT-TAT
SO THAT'S IT?
POP
POP
WHACK
TIMBER!
YOU'RE DUE FOR A FALL, CHISELER, AND HERE IT IS.!
FRAUD !
SLAM
RAT-TAT-TAT
RAT-A-TAT-TAT
YA BLINKIN' RED-HEADED TATTLE-TAIL.! NOW I GOTTA START ALL OVER.!
?
?
(6)

I *GOTTA* CHISEL DAT FOX *SOMEHOW!* IF I FAIL NOW, I'M *T'ROUGH!* WASHED UP! *FINISHED!*

T'INK T'INK T'INK T'INK

I *GOT* IT.' DA CLEVEREST UNDERHANDED CHISELIN' IDEA I'VE *EVER* HAD.' FOXIE'S WAITIN' FOR ME TA TAKE HIM, BUT I'M GONNA T'ROW HIM OFF GUARD.'

BACK AGAIN, EH? WELL, JUST REMEMBER, I *STILL* HAVE THIS COMPLETE FILE OF YOUR CHISELING ROUTINES, AND IF THIS IS ANOTHER --

HOLD IT, FOXIE! I JUS' DROPPED OVER TA ASK A QUESTION.'

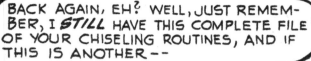

SEEIN' HOW YOUSE *GOT* DAT COMPLETE FILE OF ME CHISELIN' STUNTS, I WAS WONDERIN' IF YOUSE'D MIND LOOKIN' UP AN' TELLIN' ME HOW MUCH I GOT DA TIME I PULLED DA *"MY AIR"* GAG ON YOUSE.'

WHY, SURELY.' LET'S SEE! HERE IT IS RIGHT HERE.' $5,961.00 AND A BOILED HAM.'

I SEE! AN' HOW MUCH DA TIME I PRETENDED TA BE A ORPHAN?

ORPHAN! ORPHAN! OH, YES! $391 AND 1 BOTTLE OF MILK!

AN' DATIME I WAS DA GIANT ANT.

ANT? OH, YES! $6000 EVEN.'

WELL, DAT SETTLES IT.'

SETTLES WHAT?

AS LONG AS ME CHISELIN' CAREER IS OVER, AN' I OWE YOUSE SO MUCH DOUGH, DA BES' T'ING FOR ME TA DO IS MOVE AWAY SO YOUSE CAN'T COLLECT NUTTIN' FROM ME.'

7

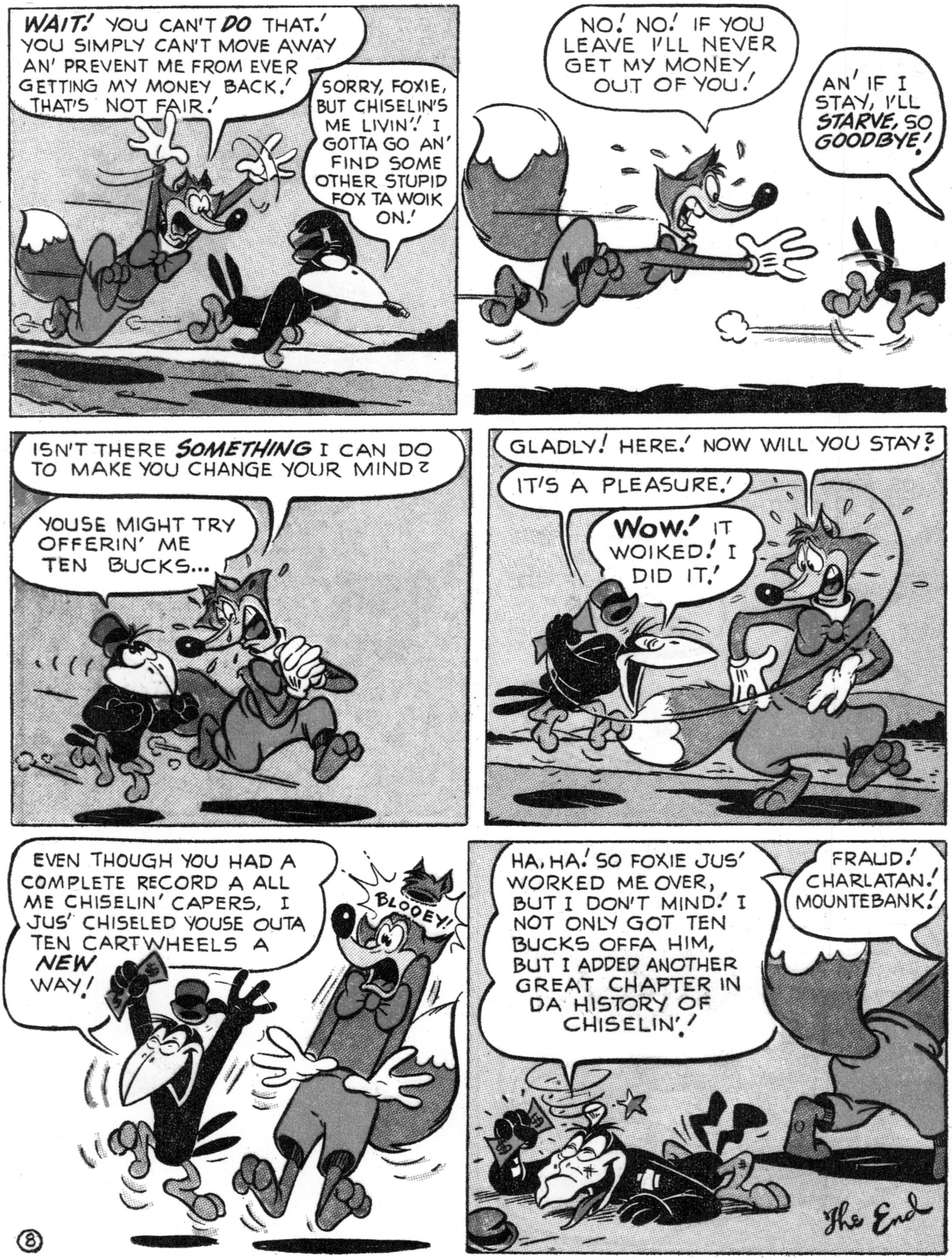
WAIT! YOU CAN'T DO THAT! YOU SIMPLY CAN'T MOVE AWAY AN' PREVENT ME FROM EVER GETTING MY MONEY BACK! THAT'S NOT FAIR!
SORRY, FOXIE, BUT CHISELIN'S ME LIVIN'! I GOTTA GO AN' FIND SOME OTHER STUPID FOX TA WOIK ON!
NO! NO! IF YOU LEAVE I'LL NEVER GET MY MONEY OUT OF YOU!
AN' IF I STAY, I'LL STARVE, SO GOODBYE!
ISN'T THERE SOMETHING I CAN DO TO MAKE YOU CHANGE YOUR MIND?
YOUSE MIGHT TRY OFFERIN' ME TEN BUCKS...
GLADLY! HERE! NOW WILL YOU STAY?
IT'S A PLEASURE!
WOW! IT WOIKED! I DID IT!
EVEN THOUGH YOU HAD A COMPLETE RECORD A ALL ME CHISELIN' CAPERS, I JUS' CHISELED YOUSE OUTA TEN CARTWHEELS A NEW WAY!
BLOOEY!
HA, HA! SO FOXIE JUS' WORKED ME OVER, BUT I DON'T MIND! I NOT ONLY GOT TEN BUCKS OFFA HIM, BUT I ADDED ANOTHER GREAT CHAPTER IN DA HISTORY OF CHISELIN'!
FRAUD! CHARLATAN! MOUNTEBANK!
The End
8

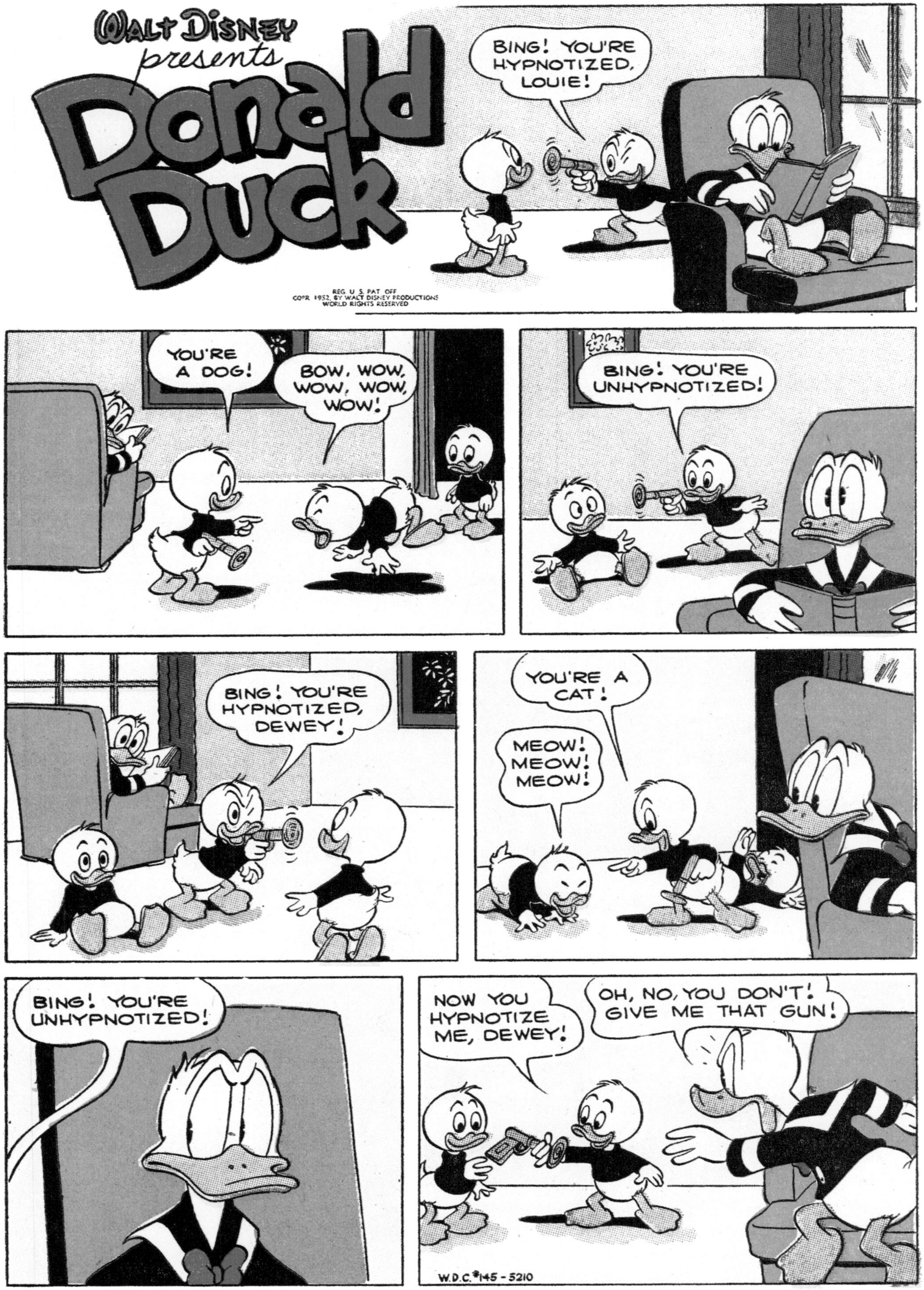
WALT DISNEY presents Donald Duck
REG. U.S. PAT. OFF.
COPR. 1952, BY WALT DISNEY PRODUCTIONS
WORLD RIGHTS RESERVED
BING! YOU'RE HYPNOTIZED, LOUIE!
YOU'RE A DOG!
BOW, WOW, WOW, WOW, WOW!
BING! YOU'RE UNHYPNOTIZED!
BING! YOU'RE HYPNOTIZED, DEWEY!
YOU'RE A CAT!
MEOW! MEOW! MEOW!
BING! YOU'RE UNHYPNOTIZED!
NOW YOU HYPNOTIZE ME, DEWEY!
OH, NO, YOU DON'T! GIVE ME THAT GUN!
W.D.C. #145 - 5210

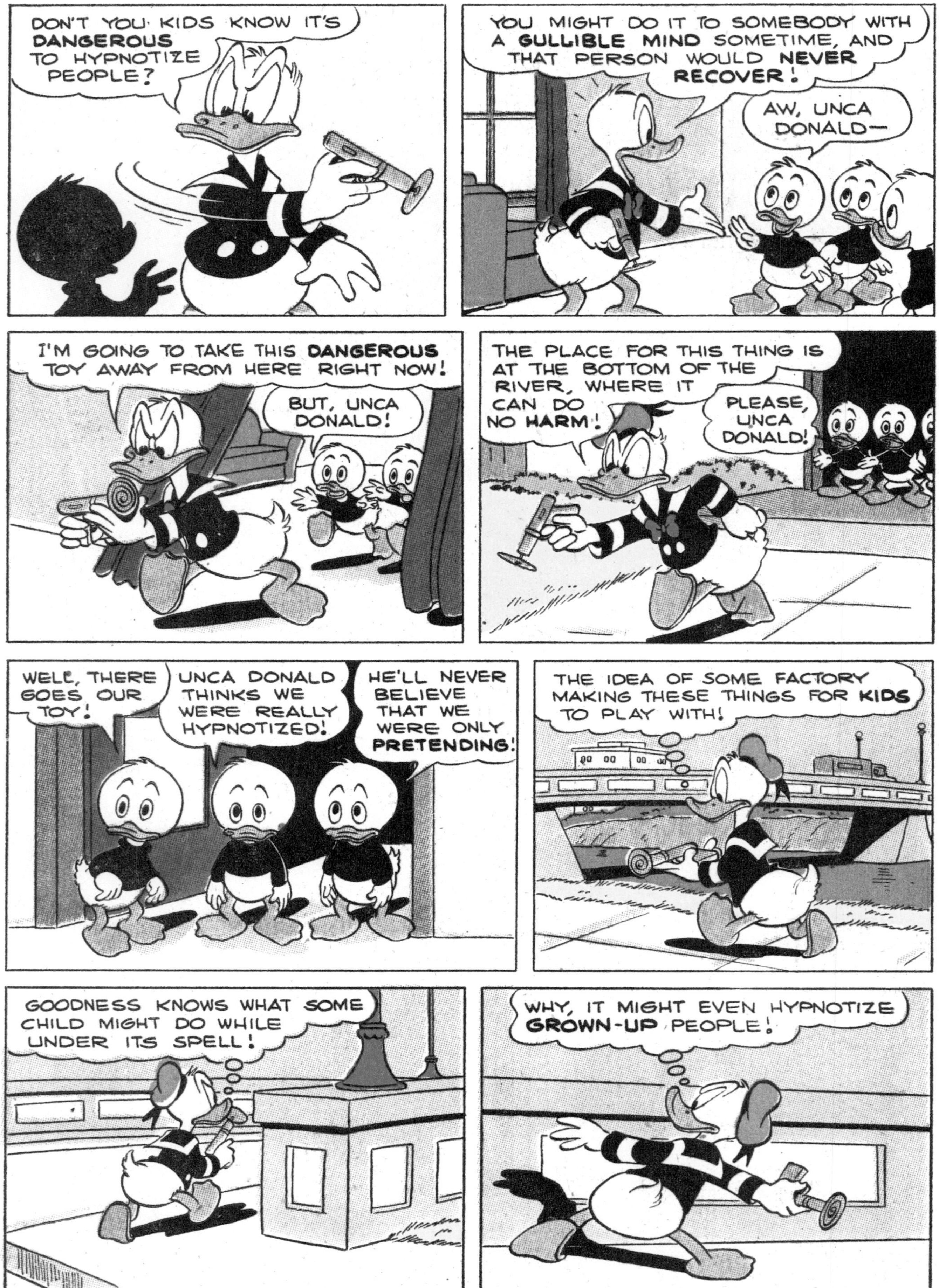
DON'T YOU KIDS KNOW IT'S DANGEROUS TO HYPNOTIZE PEOPLE?
YOU MIGHT DO IT TO SOMEBODY WITH A GULLIBLE MIND SOMETIME, AND THAT PERSON WOULD NEVER RECOVER!
AW, UNCA DONALD—
I'M GOING TO TAKE THIS DANGEROUS TOY AWAY FROM HERE RIGHT NOW!
BUT, UNCA DONALD!
THE PLACE FOR THIS THING IS AT THE BOTTOM OF THE RIVER, WHERE IT CAN DO NO HARM!
PLEASE, UNCA DONALD!
WELL, THERE GOES OUR TOY!
UNCA DONALD THINKS WE WERE REALLY HYPNOTIZED!
HE'LL NEVER BELIEVE THAT WE WERE ONLY PRETENDING!
THE IDEA OF SOME FACTORY MAKING THESE THINGS FOR KIDS TO PLAY WITH!
GOODNESS KNOWS WHAT SOME CHILD MIGHT DO WHILE UNDER ITS SPELL!
WHY, IT MIGHT EVEN HYPNOTIZE GROWN-UP PEOPLE!

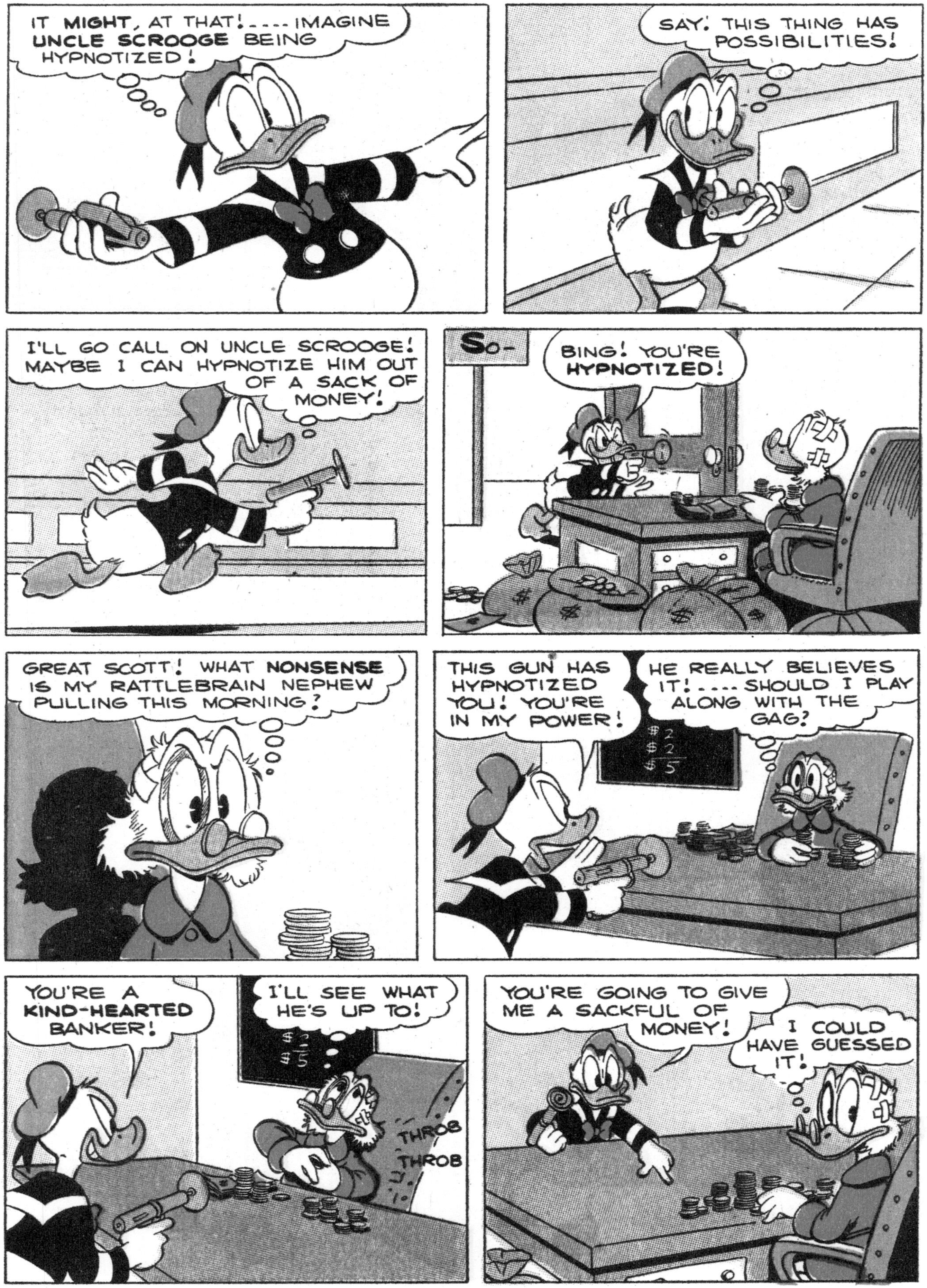
IT MIGHT, AT THAT!....IMAGINE UNCLE SCROOGE BEING HYPNOTIZED!
SAY! THIS THING HAS POSSIBILITIES!
I'LL GO CALL ON UNCLE SCROOGE! MAYBE I CAN HYPNOTIZE HIM OUT OF A SACK OF MONEY!
SO-
BING! YOU'RE HYPNOTIZED!
GREAT SCOTT! WHAT NONSENSE IS MY RATTLEBRAIN NEPHEW PULLING THIS MORNING?
THIS GUN HAS HYPNOTIZED YOU! YOU'RE IN MY POWER!
HE REALLY BELIEVES IT!....SHOULD I PLAY ALONG WITH THE GAG?
YOU'RE A KIND-HEARTED BANKER!
I'LL SEE WHAT HE'S UP TO!
THROB
THROB
YOU'RE GOING TO GIVE ME A SACKFUL OF MONEY!
I COULD HAVE GUESSED IT!

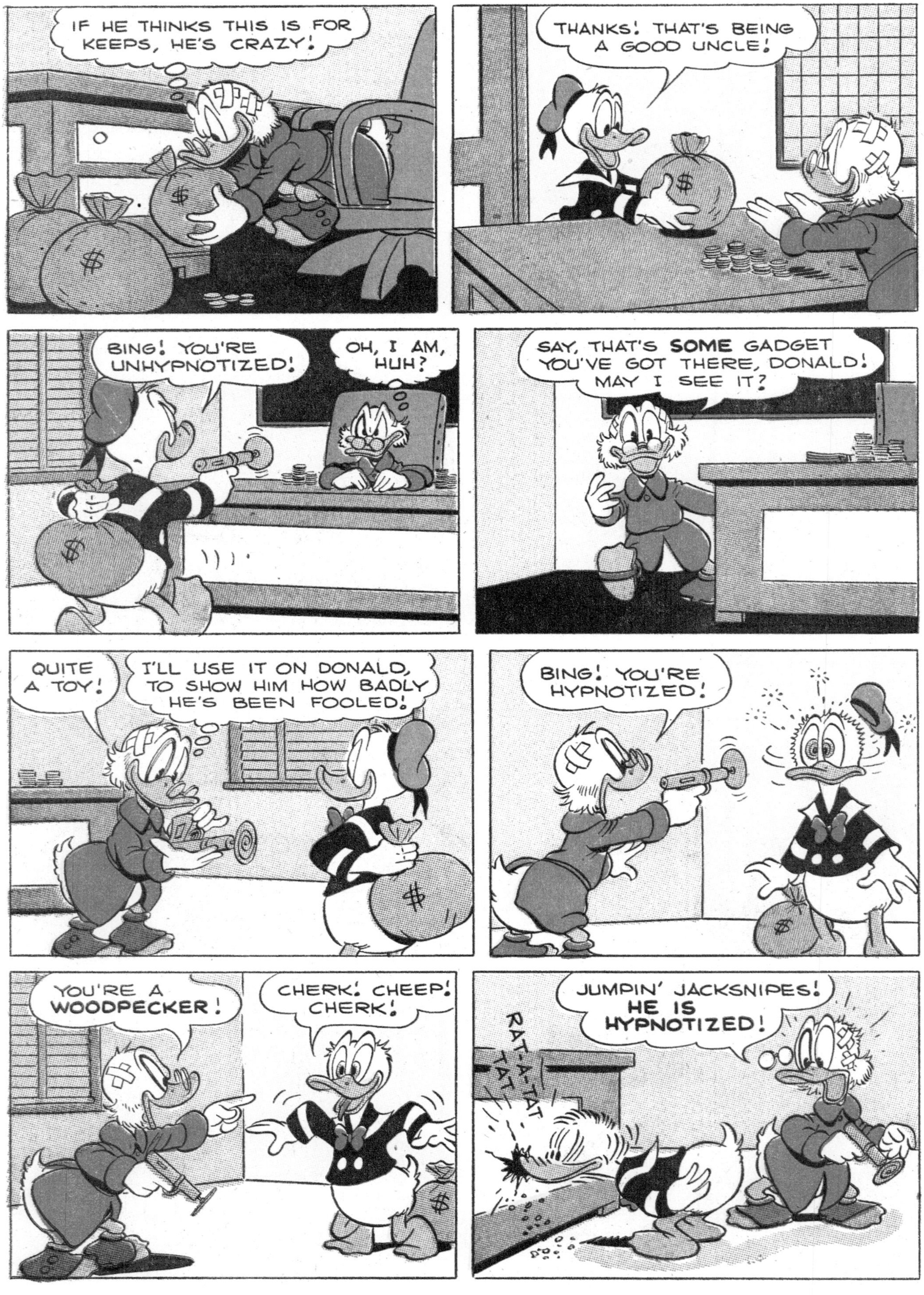
IF HE THINKS THIS IS FOR KEEPS, HE'S CRAZY!
THANKS! THAT'S BEING A GOOD UNCLE!
BING! YOU'RE UNHYPNOTIZED!
OH, I AM, HUH?
SAY, THAT'S **SOME** GADGET YOU'VE GOT THERE, DONALD! MAY I SEE IT?
QUITE A TOY!
I'LL USE IT ON DONALD, TO SHOW HIM HOW BADLY HE'S BEEN FOOLED!
BING! YOU'RE HYPNOTIZED!
YOU'RE A **WOODPECKER**!
CHERK! CHEEP! CHERK!
JUMPIN' JACKSNIPES! **HE IS HYPNOTIZED**!
RAT-A-TAT-TAT

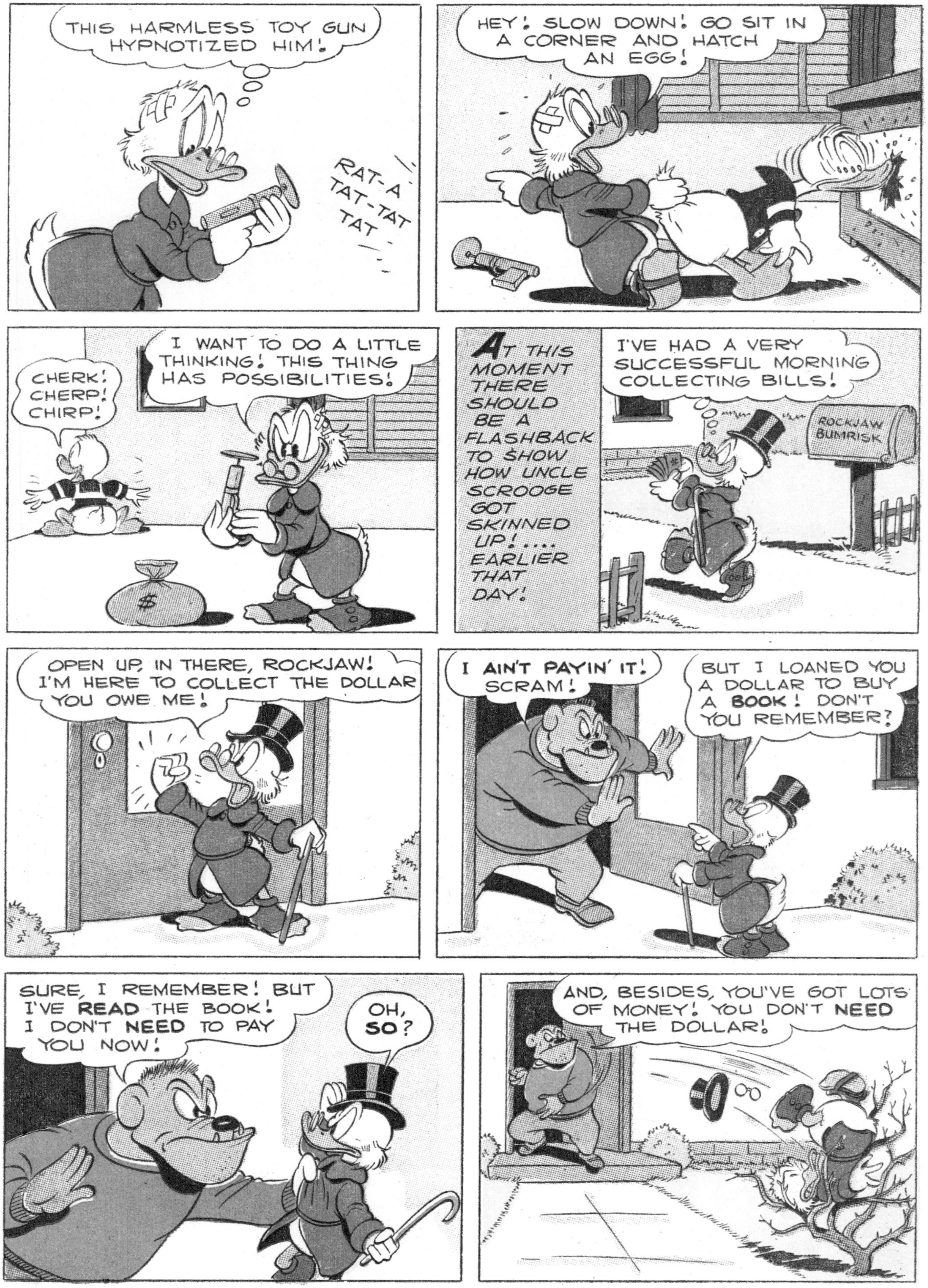
THIS HARMLESS TOY GUN HYPNOTIZED HIM!
RAT-A TAT-TAT TAT
HEY! SLOW DOWN! GO SIT IN A CORNER AND HATCH AN EGG!
CHERK! CHERP! CHIRP!
I WANT TO DO A LITTLE THINKING! THIS THING HAS POSSIBILITIES!
$
AT THIS MOMENT THERE SHOULD BE A FLASHBACK TO SHOW HOW UNCLE SCROOGE GOT SKINNED UP!.... EARLIER THAT DAY!
I'VE HAD A VERY SUCCESSFUL MORNING COLLECTING BILLS!
ROCKJAW BUMRISK
OPEN UP, IN THERE, ROCKJAW! I'M HERE TO COLLECT THE DOLLAR YOU OWE ME!
I AIN'T PAYIN' IT! SCRAM!
BUT I LOANED YOU A DOLLAR TO BUY A BOOK! DON'T YOU REMEMBER?
SURE, I REMEMBER! BUT I'VE READ THE BOOK! I DON'T NEED TO PAY YOU NOW!
OH, SO?
AND, BESIDES, YOU'VE GOT LOTS OF MONEY! YOU DON'T NEED THE DOLLAR!

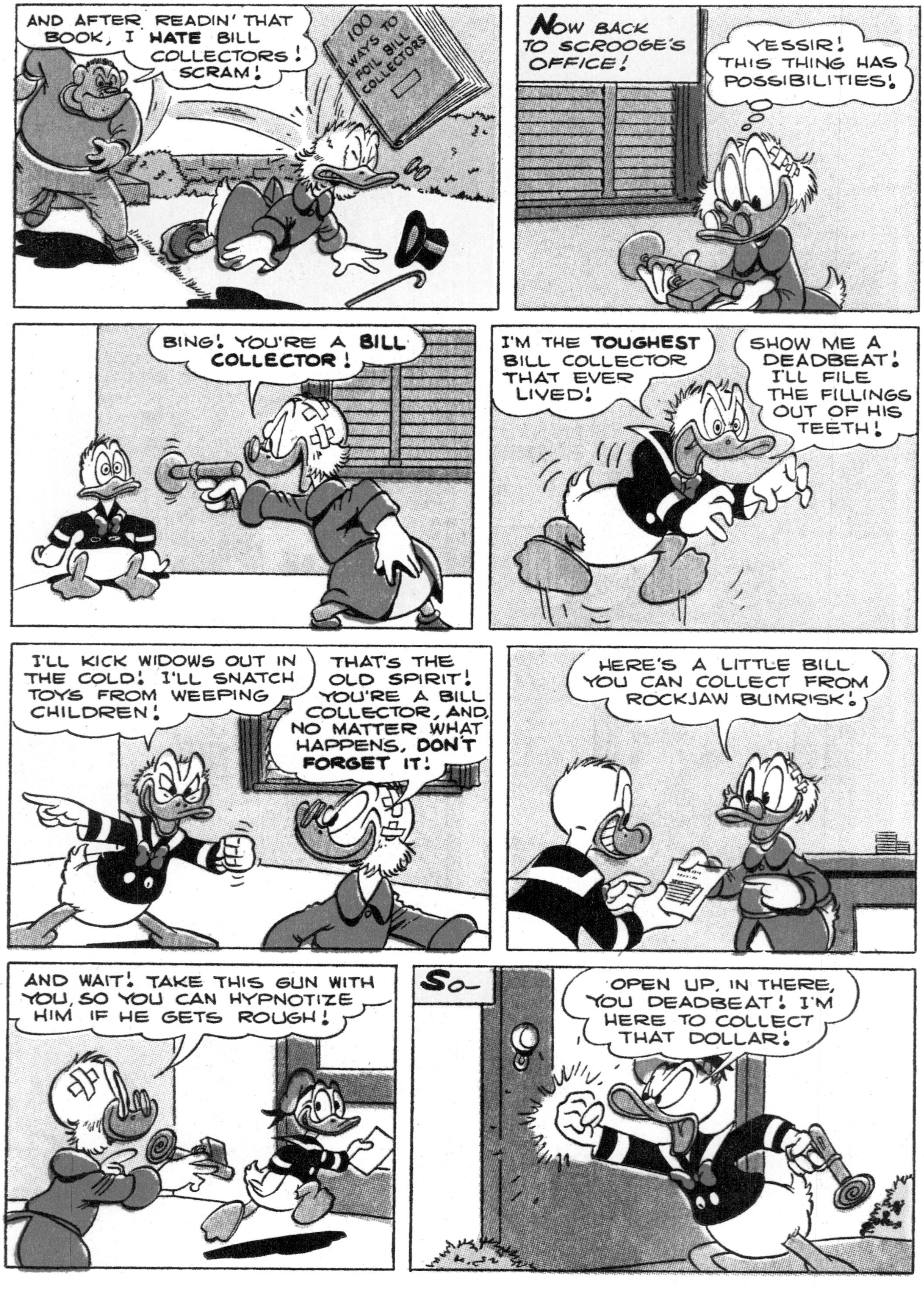
AND AFTER READIN' THAT BOOK, I HATE BILL COLLECTORS! SCRAM!
100 WAYS TO FOIL BILL COLLECTORS
NOW BACK TO SCROOGE'S OFFICE!
YESSIR! THIS THING HAS POSSIBILITIES!
BING! YOU'RE A BILL COLLECTOR!
I'M THE TOUGHEST BILL COLLECTOR THAT EVER LIVED!
SHOW ME A DEADBEAT! I'LL FILE THE FILLINGS OUT OF HIS TEETH!
I'LL KICK WIDOWS OUT IN THE COLD! I'LL SNATCH TOYS FROM WEEPING CHILDREN!
THAT'S THE OLD SPIRIT! YOU'RE A BILL COLLECTOR, AND, NO MATTER WHAT HAPPENS, DON'T FORGET IT!
HERE'S A LITTLE BILL YOU CAN COLLECT FROM ROCKJAW BUMRISK!
AND WAIT! TAKE THIS GUN WITH YOU, SO YOU CAN HYPNOTIZE HIM IF HE GETS ROUGH!
SO—
OPEN UP, IN THERE, YOU DEADBEAT! I'M HERE TO COLLECT THAT DOLLAR!

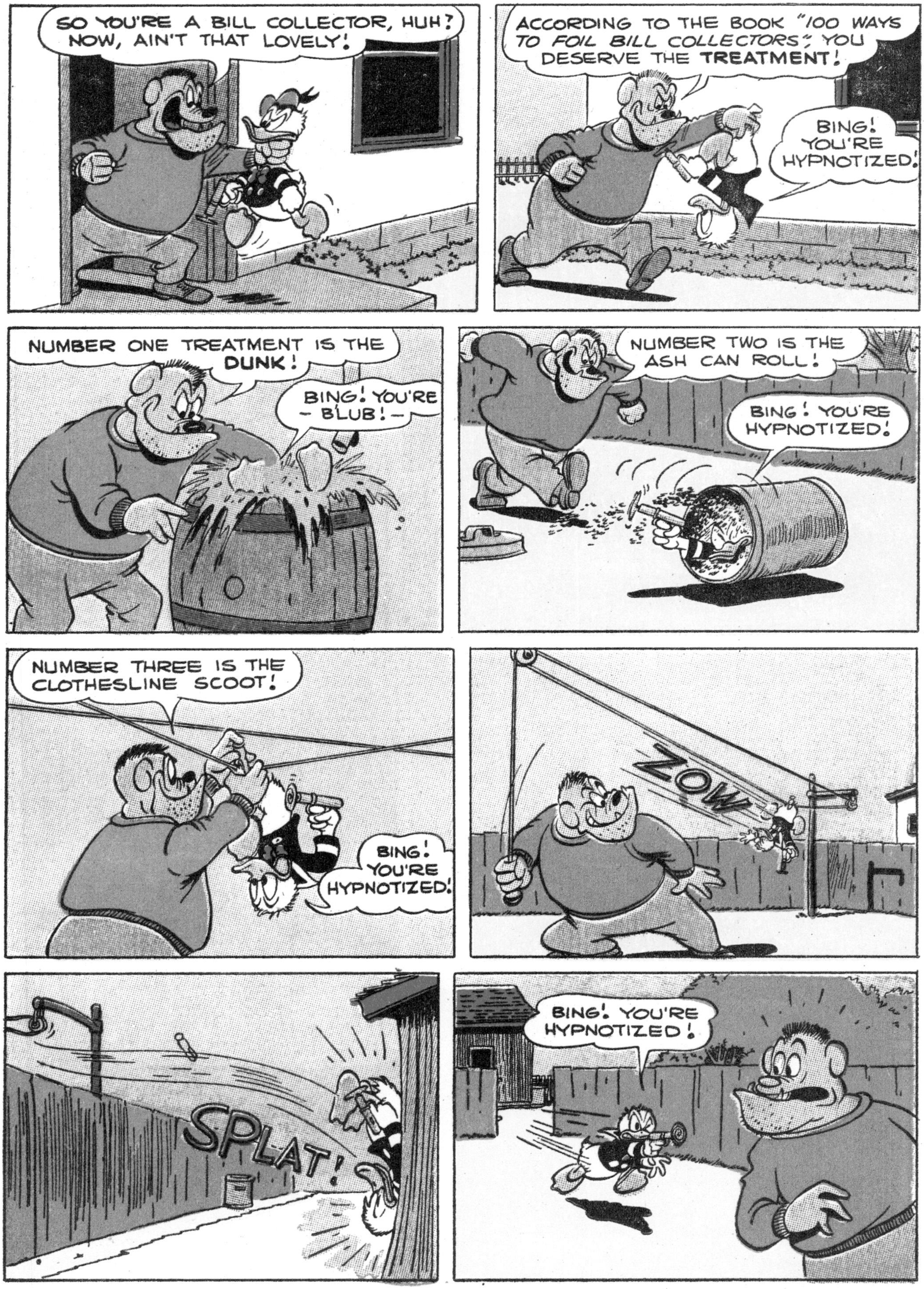
SO YOU'RE A BILL COLLECTOR, HUH? NOW, AIN'T THAT LOVELY!
ACCORDING TO THE BOOK "100 WAYS TO FOIL BILL COLLECTORS," YOU DESERVE THE TREATMENT!
BING! YOU'RE HYPNOTIZED!
NUMBER ONE TREATMENT IS THE DUNK!
BING! YOU'RE – BLUB! –
NUMBER TWO IS THE ASH CAN ROLL!
BING! YOU'RE HYPNOTIZED!
NUMBER THREE IS THE CLOTHESLINE SCOOT!
BING! YOU'RE HYPNOTIZED!
ZOW
SPLAT!
BING! YOU'RE HYPNOTIZED!

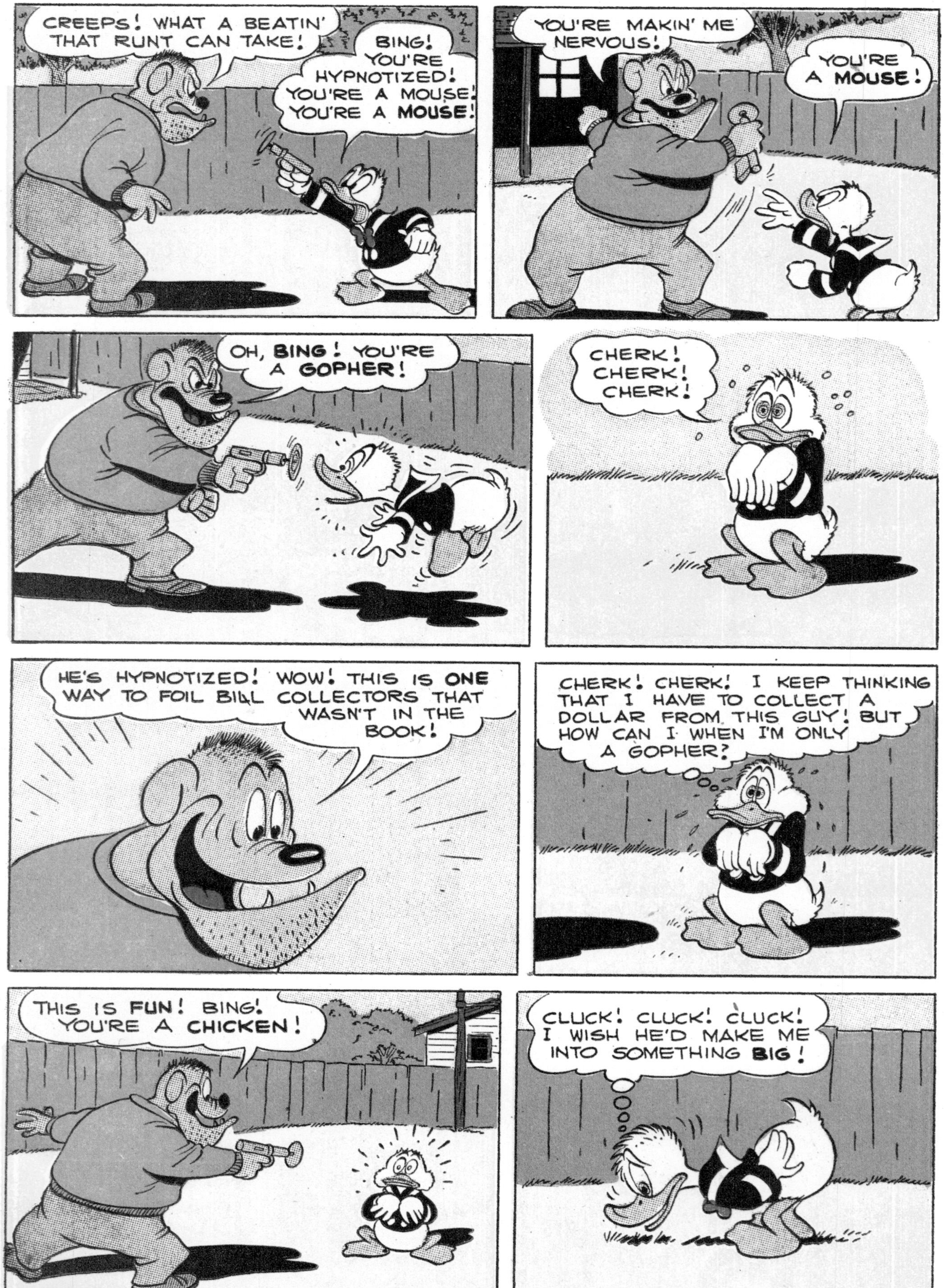
CREEPS! WHAT A BEATIN' THAT RUNT CAN TAKE!
BING! YOU'RE HYPNOTIZED! YOU'RE A MOUSE! YOU'RE A MOUSE!
YOU'RE MAKIN' ME NERVOUS!
YOU'RE A MOUSE!
OH, BING! YOU'RE A GOPHER!
CHERK! CHERK! CHERK!
HE'S HYPNOTIZED! WOW! THIS IS ONE WAY TO FOIL BILL COLLECTORS THAT WASN'T IN THE BOOK!
CHERK! CHERK! I KEEP THINKING THAT I HAVE TO COLLECT A DOLLAR FROM THIS GUY! BUT HOW CAN I WHEN I'M ONLY A GOPHER?
THIS IS FUN! BING! YOU'RE A CHICKEN!
CLUCK! CLUCK! CLUCK! I WISH HE'D MAKE ME INTO SOMETHING BIG!

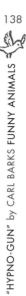

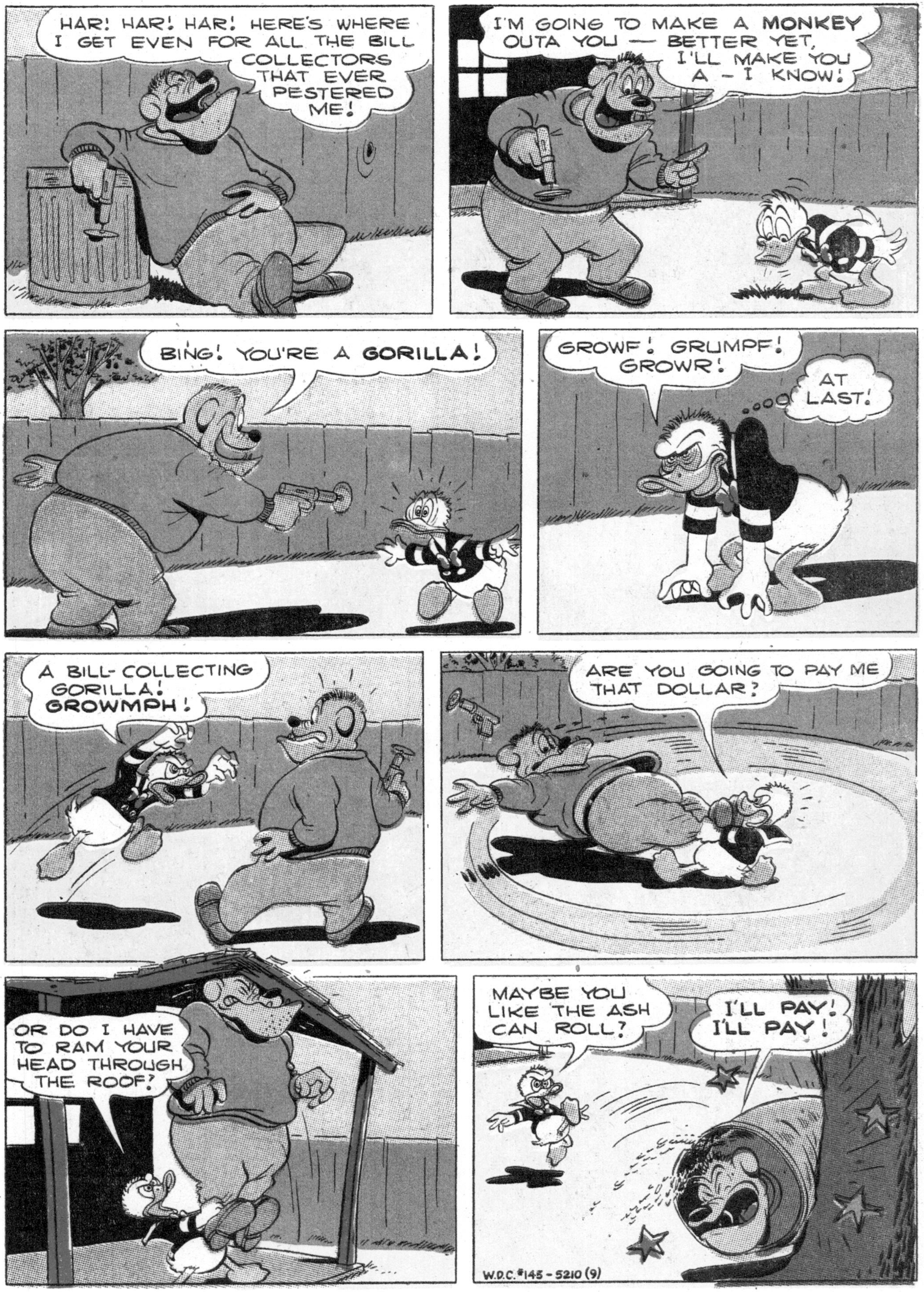
HAR! HAR! HAR! HERE'S WHERE I GET EVEN FOR ALL THE BILL COLLECTORS THAT EVER PESTERED ME!
I'M GOING TO MAKE A MONKEY OUTA YOU — BETTER YET, I'LL MAKE YOU A – I KNOW!
BING! YOU'RE A GORILLA!
GROWF! GRUMPF! GROWR!
AT LAST!
A BILL-COLLECTING GORILLA! GROWMPH!
ARE YOU GOING TO PAY ME THAT DOLLAR?
OR DO I HAVE TO RAM YOUR HEAD THROUGH THE ROOF?
MAYBE YOU LIKE THE ASH CAN ROLL?
I'LL PAY! I'LL PAY!
W.D.C. #145-5210 (9)

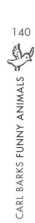

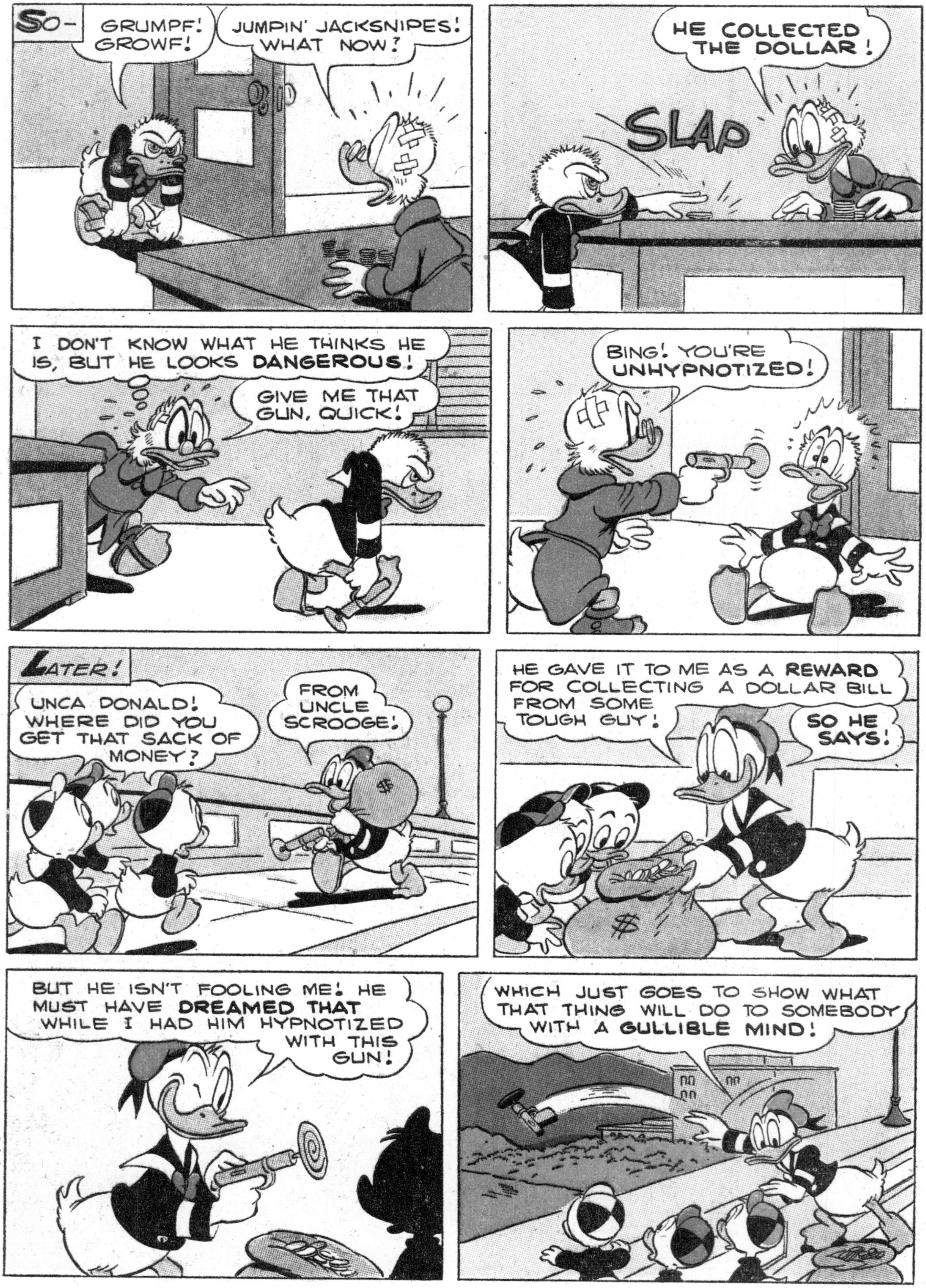
SO-
GRUMPF! GROWF!
JUMPIN' JACKSNIPES! WHAT NOW?
HE COLLECTED THE DOLLAR!
SLAP
I DON'T KNOW WHAT HE THINKS HE IS, BUT HE LOOKS DANGEROUS!
GIVE ME THAT GUN, QUICK!
BING! YOU'RE UNHYPNOTIZED!
LATER!
UNCA DONALD! WHERE DID YOU GET THAT SACK OF MONEY?
FROM UNCLE SCROOGE!
HE GAVE IT TO ME AS A REWARD FOR COLLECTING A DOLLAR BILL FROM SOME TOUGH GUY!
SO HE SAYS!
BUT HE ISN'T FOOLING ME! HE MUST HAVE DREAMED THAT WHILE I HAD HIM HYPNOTIZED WITH THIS GUN!
WHICH JUST GOES TO SHOW WHAT THAT THING WILL DO TO SOMEBODY WITH A GULLIBLE MIND!

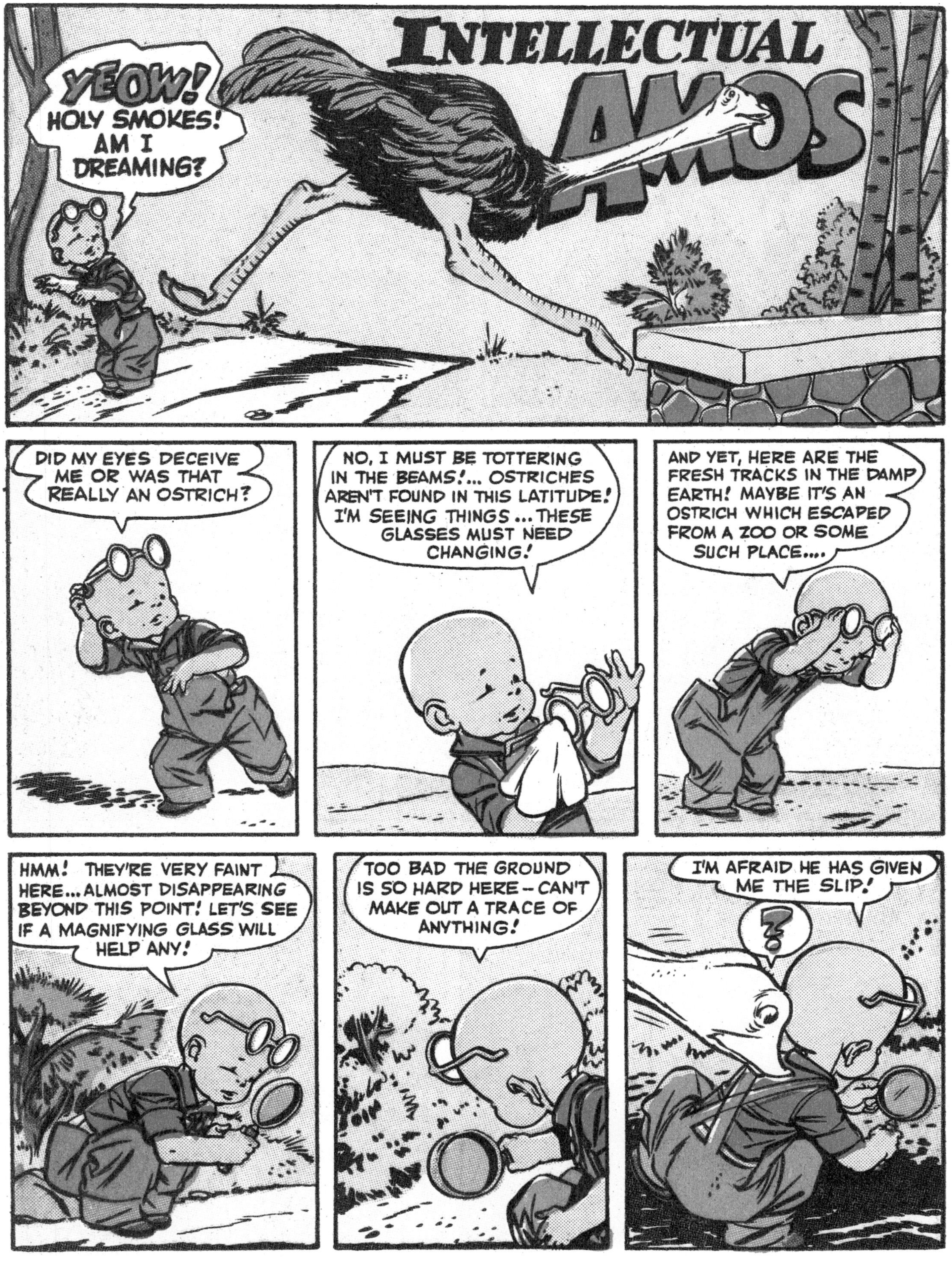
INTELLECTUAL AMOS
YEOW! HOLY SMOKES! AM I DREAMING?
DID MY EYES DECEIVE ME OR WAS THAT REALLY AN OSTRICH?
NO, I MUST BE TOTTERING IN THE BEAMS!... OSTRICHES AREN'T FOUND IN THIS LATITUDE! I'M SEEING THINGS ... THESE GLASSES MUST NEED CHANGING!
AND YET, HERE ARE THE FRESH TRACKS IN THE DAMP EARTH! MAYBE IT'S AN OSTRICH WHICH ESCAPED FROM A ZOO OR SOME SUCH PLACE....
HMM! THEY'RE VERY FAINT HERE... ALMOST DISAPPEARING BEYOND THIS POINT! LET'S SEE IF A MAGNIFYING GLASS WILL HELP ANY!
TOO BAD THE GROUND IS SO HARD HERE -- CAN'T MAKE OUT A TRACE OF ANYTHING!
I'M AFRAID HE HAS GIVEN ME THE SLIP!
?

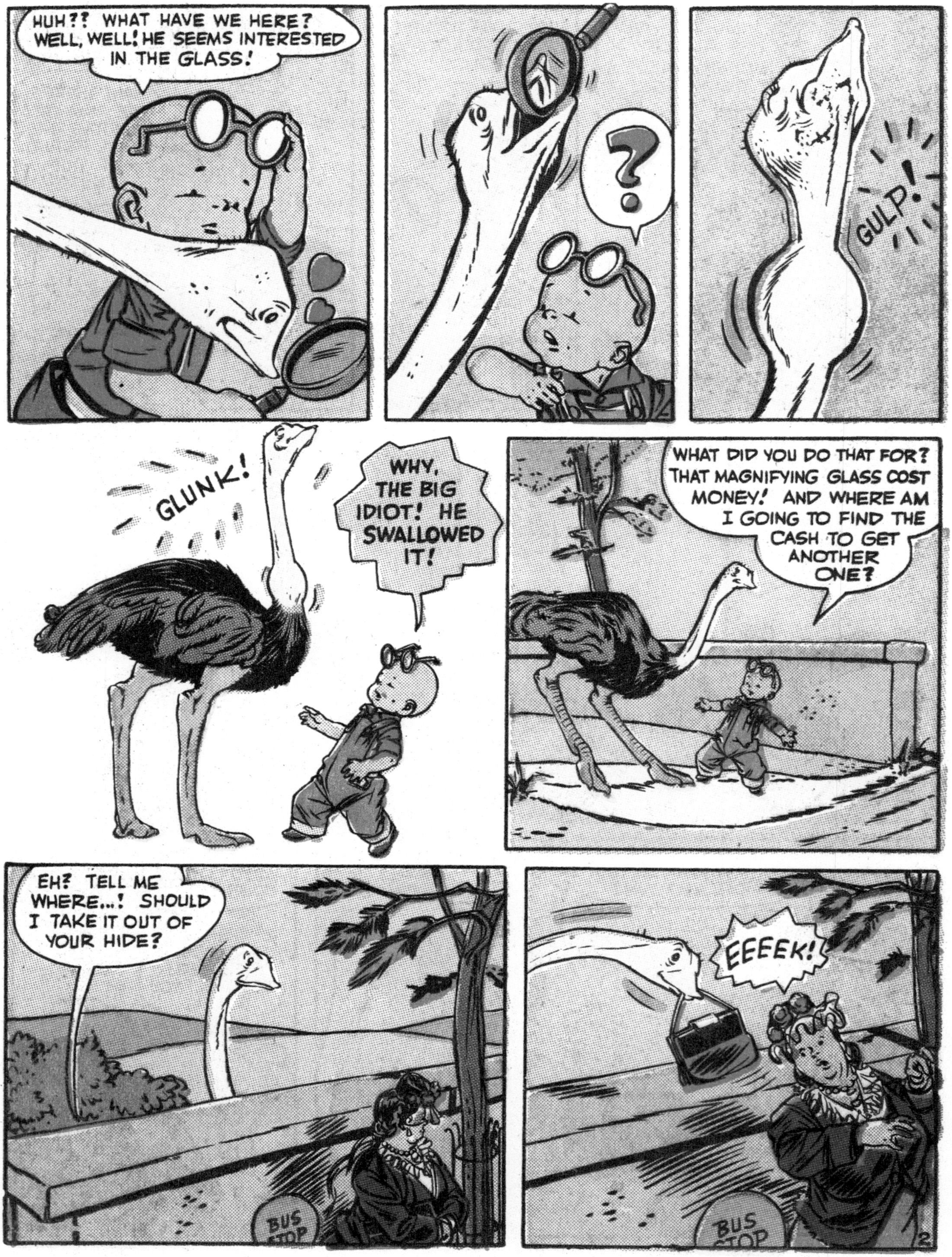
HUH?? WHAT HAVE WE HERE? WELL, WELL! HE SEEMS INTERESTED IN THE GLASS!
?
GULP!
GLUNK!
WHY, THE BIG IDIOT! HE SWALLOWED IT!
WHAT DID YOU DO THAT FOR? THAT MAGNIFYING GLASS COST MONEY! AND WHERE AM I GOING TO FIND THE CASH TO GET ANOTHER ONE?
EH? TELL ME WHERE...! SHOULD I TAKE IT OUT OF YOUR HIDE?
BUS STOP
EEEEK!
BUS STOP
2

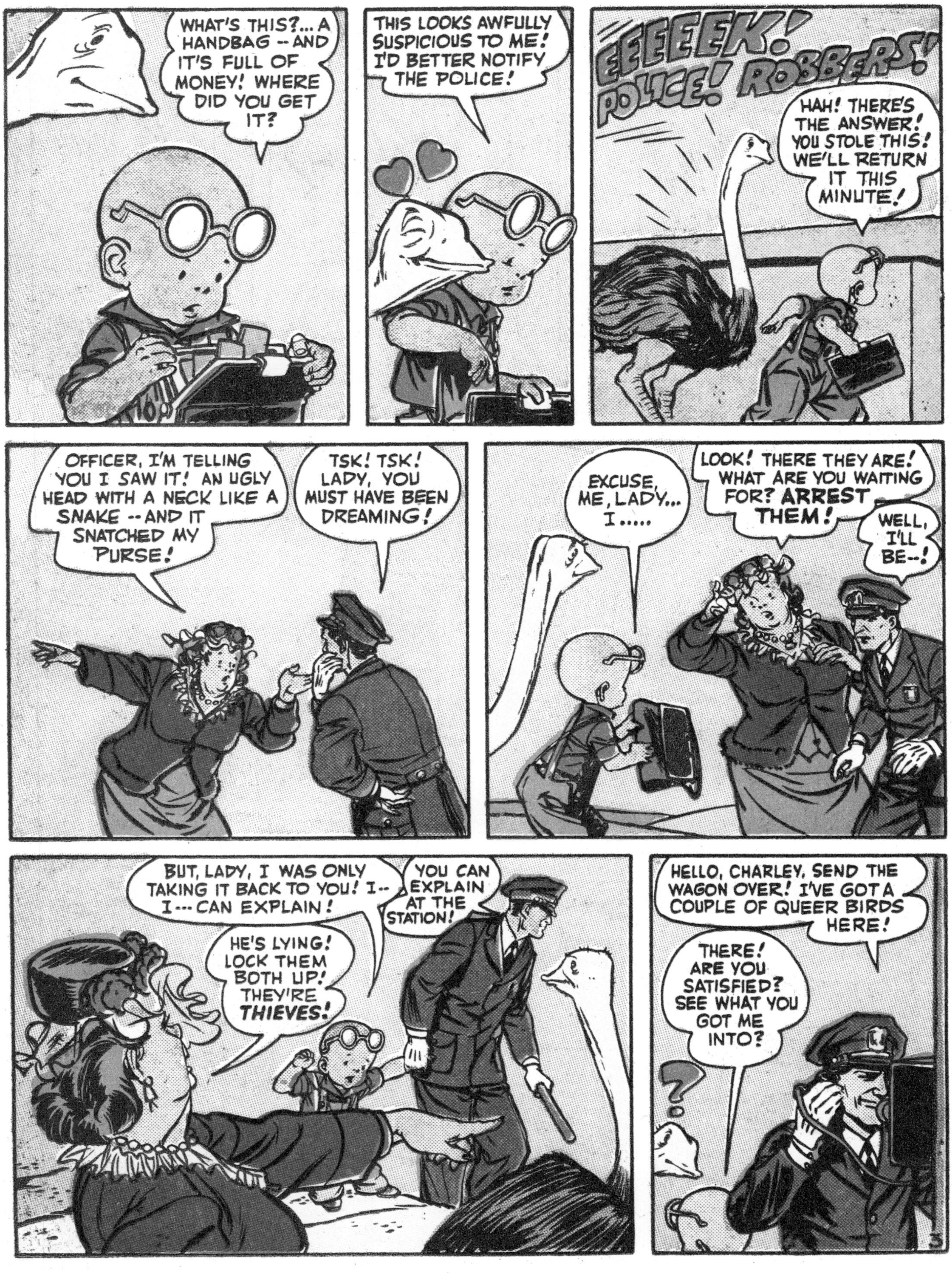
WHAT'S THIS?... A HANDBAG -- AND IT'S FULL OF MONEY! WHERE DID YOU GET IT?
THIS LOOKS AWFULLY SUSPICIOUS TO ME! I'D BETTER NOTIFY THE POLICE!
EEEEEK! POLICE! ROBBERS!
HAH! THERE'S THE ANSWER! YOU STOLE THIS! WE'LL RETURN IT THIS MINUTE!
OFFICER, I'M TELLING YOU I SAW IT! AN UGLY HEAD WITH A NECK LIKE A SNAKE -- AND IT SNATCHED MY PURSE!
TSK! TSK! LADY, YOU MUST HAVE BEEN DREAMING!
EXCUSE, ME, LADY... I.....
LOOK! THERE THEY ARE! WHAT ARE YOU WAITING FOR? ARREST THEM!
WELL, I'LL BE--!
BUT, LADY, I WAS ONLY TAKING IT BACK TO YOU! I-- I--- CAN EXPLAIN!
YOU CAN EXPLAIN AT THE STATION!
HE'S LYING! LOCK THEM BOTH UP! THEY'RE THIEVES!
HELLO, CHARLEY, SEND THE WAGON OVER! I'VE GOT A COUPLE OF QUEER BIRDS HERE!
THERE! ARE YOU SATISFIED? SEE WHAT YOU GOT ME INTO?
?
3

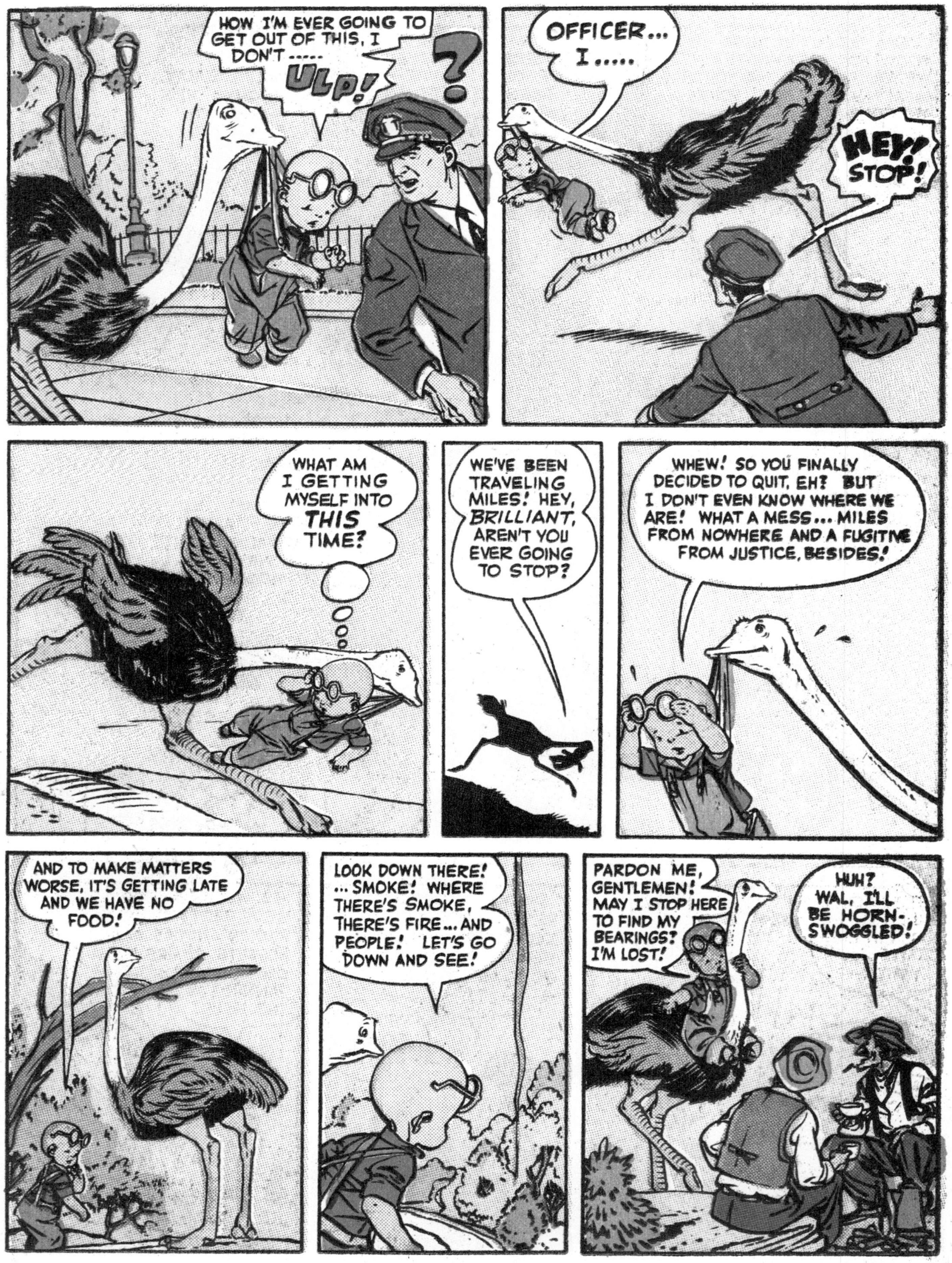
HOW I'M EVER GOING TO GET OUT OF THIS, I DON'T......
ULP!
?
OFFICER... I.....
HEY! STOP!
WHAT AM I GETTING MYSELF INTO THIS TIME?
WE'VE BEEN TRAVELING MILES! HEY, BRILLIANT, AREN'T YOU EVER GOING TO STOP?
WHEW! SO YOU FINALLY DECIDED TO QUIT, EH? BUT I DON'T EVEN KNOW WHERE WE ARE! WHAT A MESS... MILES FROM NOWHERE AND A FUGITIVE FROM JUSTICE, BESIDES!
AND TO MAKE MATTERS WORSE, IT'S GETTING LATE AND WE HAVE NO FOOD!
LOOK DOWN THERE! ...SMOKE! WHERE THERE'S SMOKE, THERE'S FIRE... AND PEOPLE! LET'S GO DOWN AND SEE!
PARDON ME, GENTLEMEN! MAY I STOP HERE TO FIND MY BEARINGS? I'M LOST!
HUH? WAL, I'LL BE HORN-SWOGGLED!

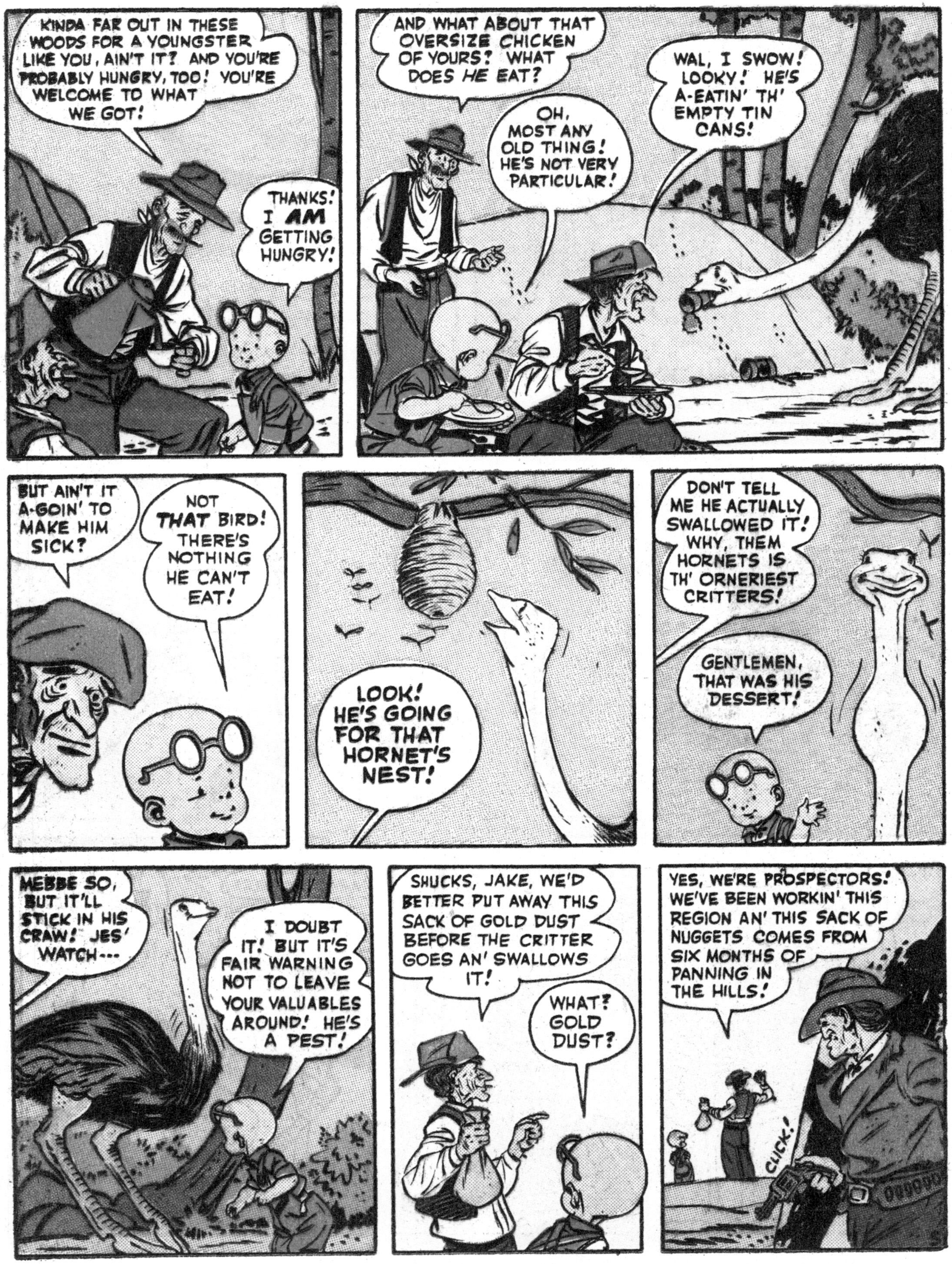
KINDA FAR OUT IN THESE WOODS FOR A YOUNGSTER LIKE YOU, AIN'T IT? AND YOU'RE PROBABLY HUNGRY, TOO! YOU'RE WELCOME TO WHAT WE GOT!
THANKS! I AM GETTING HUNGRY!
AND WHAT ABOUT THAT OVERSIZE CHICKEN OF YOURS? WHAT DOES HE EAT?
OH, MOST ANY OLD THING! HE'S NOT VERY PARTICULAR!
WAL, I SWOW! LOOKY! HE'S A-EATIN' TH' EMPTY TIN CANS!
BUT AIN'T IT A-GOIN' TO MAKE HIM SICK?
NOT THAT BIRD! THERE'S NOTHING HE CAN'T EAT!
LOOK! HE'S GOING FOR THAT HORNET'S NEST!
DON'T TELL ME HE ACTUALLY SWALLOWED IT! WHY, THEM HORNETS IS TH' ORNERIEST CRITTERS!
GENTLEMEN, THAT WAS HIS DESSERT!
MEBBE SO, BUT IT'LL STICK IN HIS CRAW! JES' WATCH...
I DOUBT IT! BUT IT'S FAIR WARNING NOT TO LEAVE YOUR VALUABLES AROUND! HE'S A PEST!
SHUCKS, JAKE, WE'D BETTER PUT AWAY THIS SACK OF GOLD DUST BEFORE THE CRITTER GOES AN' SWALLOWS IT!
WHAT? GOLD DUST?
YES, WE'RE PROSPECTORS! WE'VE BEEN WORKIN' THIS REGION AN' THIS SACK OF NUGGETS COMES FROM SIX MONTHS OF PANNING IN THE HILLS!
CLICK!

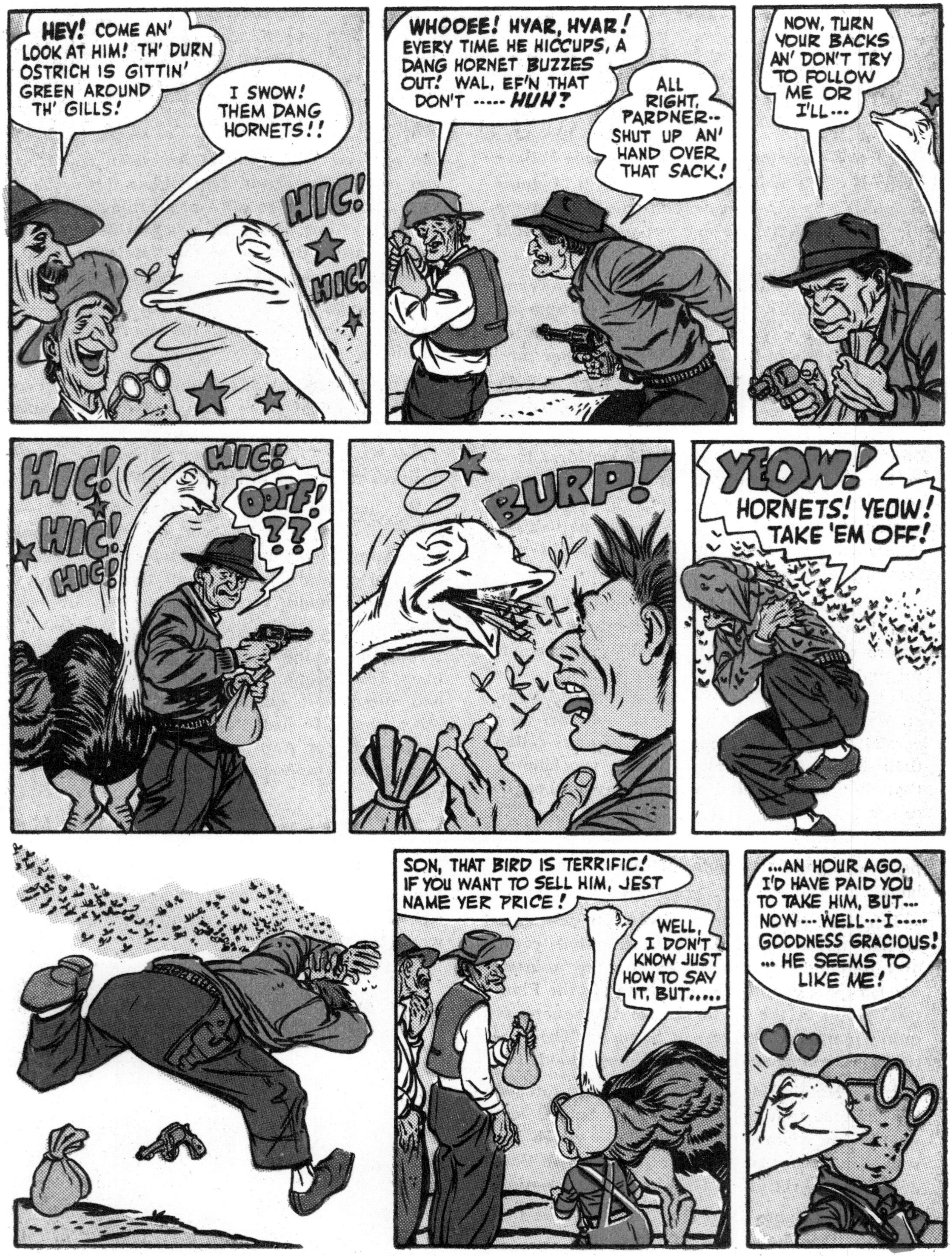
HEY! COME AN' LOOK AT HIM! TH' DURN OSTRICH IS GITTIN' GREEN AROUND TH' GILLS!
I SWOW! THEM DANG HORNETS!!
HIC!
HIC!
WHOOEE! HYAR, HYAR! EVERY TIME HE HICCUPS, A DANG HORNET BUZZES OUT! WAL, EF'N THAT DON'T ----- HUH?
ALL RIGHT, PARDNER-- SHUT UP AN' HAND OVER THAT SACK!
NOW, TURN YOUR BACKS AN' DON'T TRY TO FOLLOW ME OR I'LL...
HIC!
HIC!
HIC!
HIC!
OOPF! ??
BURP!
YEOW!
HORNETS! YEOW! TAKE 'EM OFF!
SON, THAT BIRD IS TERRIFIC! IF YOU WANT TO SELL HIM, JEST NAME YER PRICE!
WELL, I DON'T KNOW JUST HOW TO SAY IT, BUT.....
...AN HOUR AGO, I'D HAVE PAID YOU TO TAKE HIM, BUT... NOW --- WELL --- I ----- GOODNESS GRACIOUS! ... HE SEEMS TO LIKE ME!

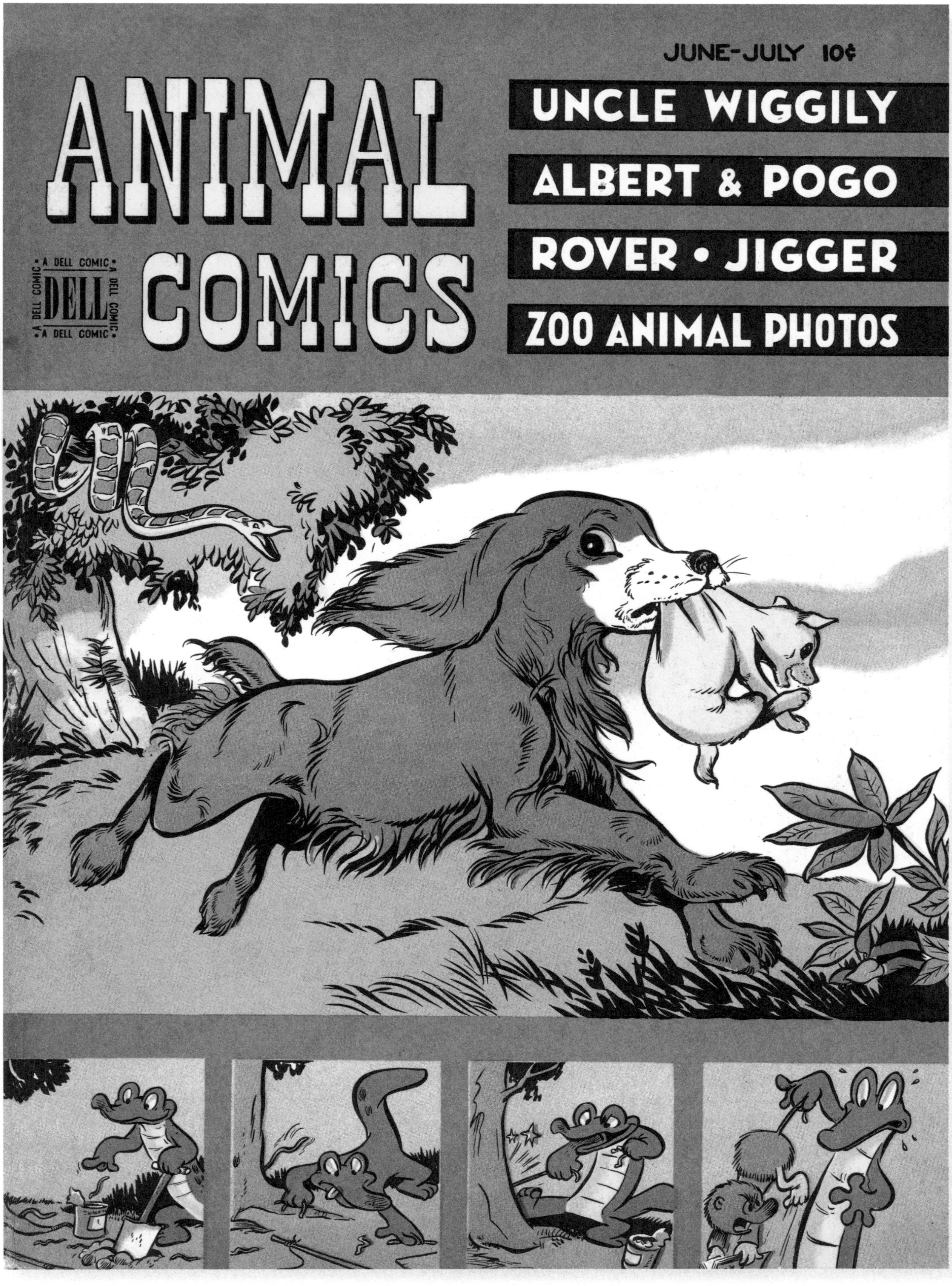
JUNE-JULY 10¢
ANIMAL COMICS
A DELL COMIC
DELL
UNCLE WIGGILY
ALBERT & POGO
ROVER • JIGGER
ZOO ANIMAL PHOTOS

FUNNY ANIMALS ANIMAL COMICS COVER by DAN NOONAN and WALT KELLY

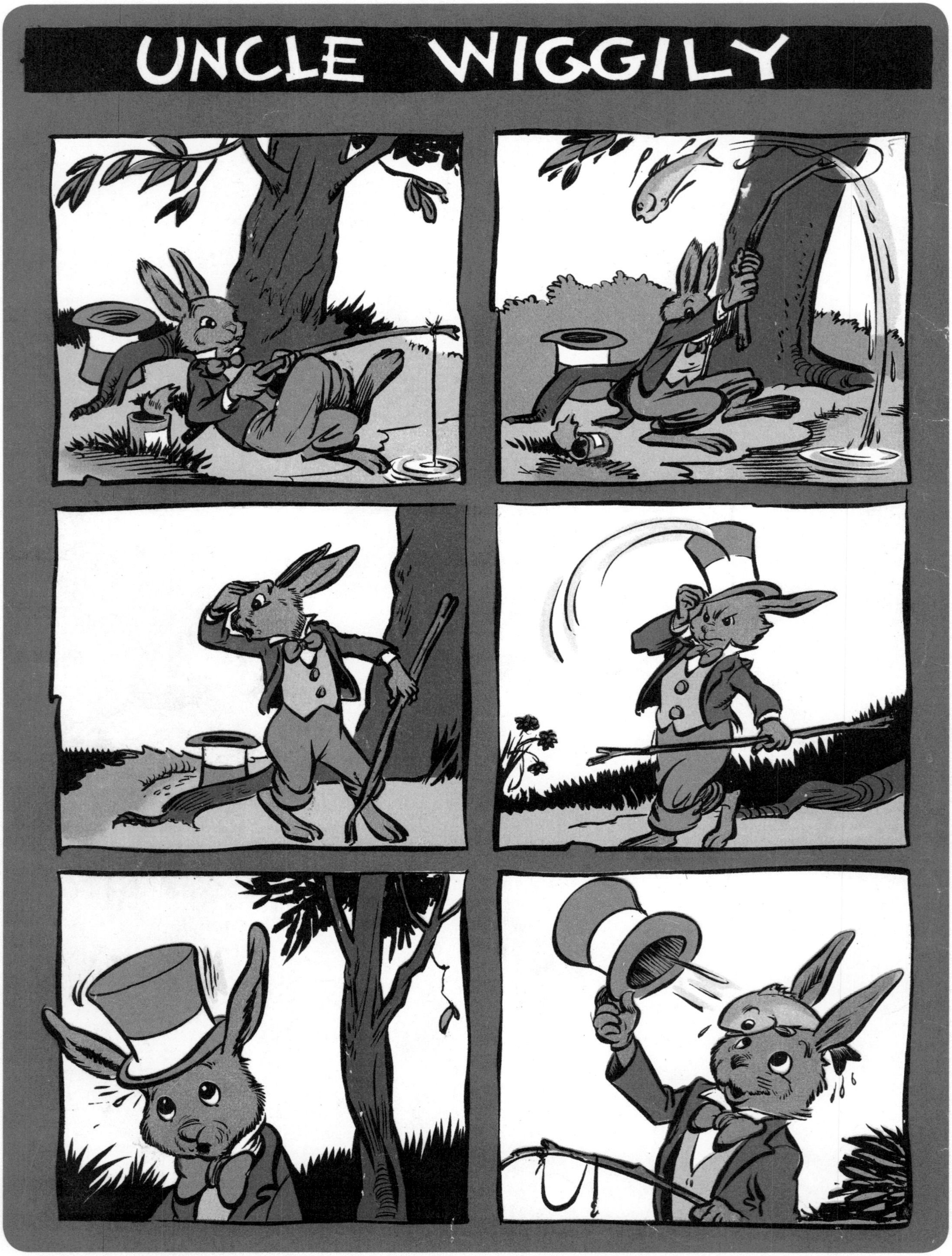
UNCLE WIGGILY

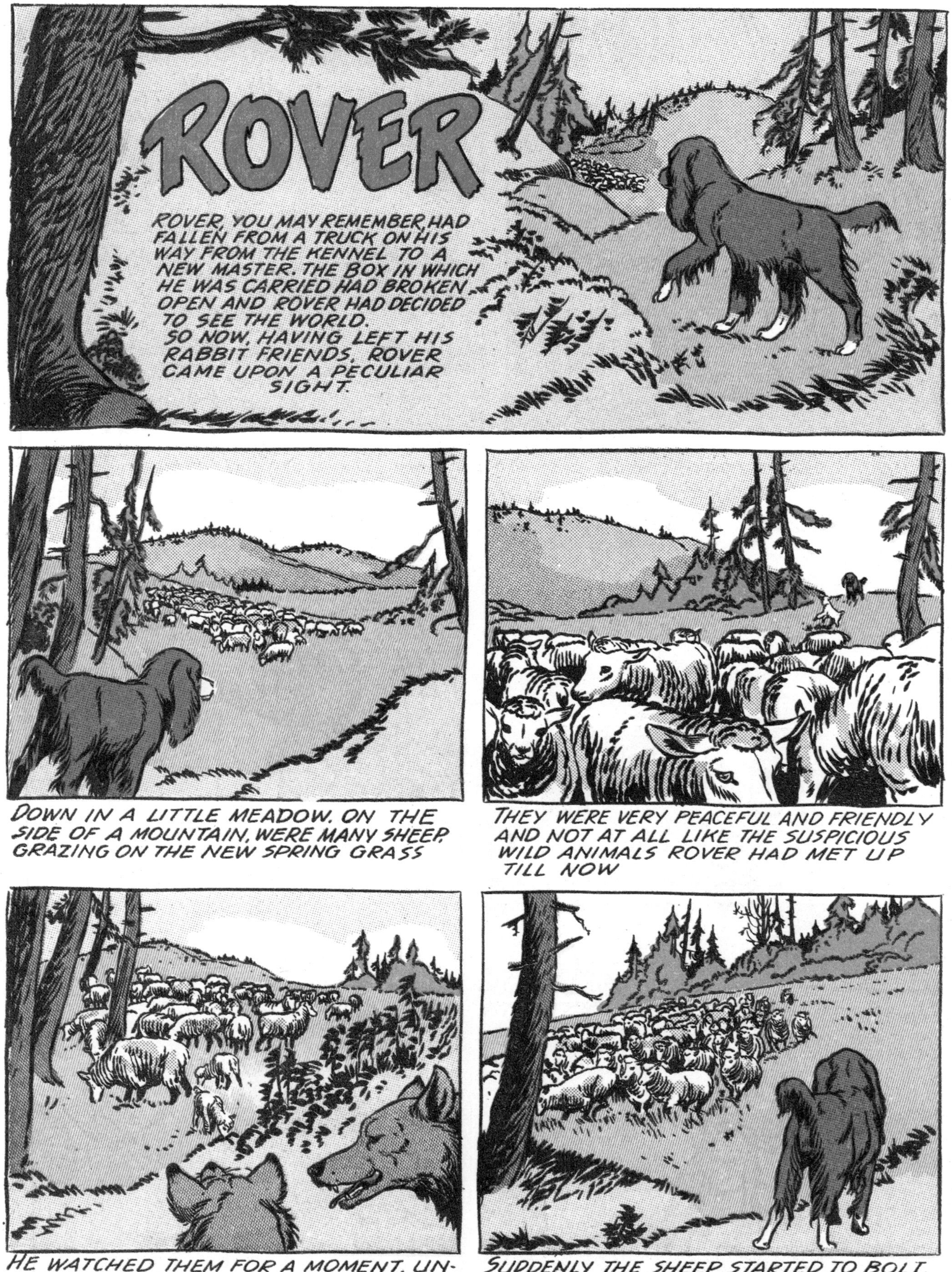
ROVER
ROVER, YOU MAY REMEMBER, HAD FALLEN FROM A TRUCK ON HIS WAY FROM THE KENNEL TO A NEW MASTER. THE BOX IN WHICH HE WAS CARRIED HAD BROKEN OPEN AND ROVER HAD DECIDED TO SEE THE WORLD.
SO NOW, HAVING LEFT HIS RABBIT FRIENDS, ROVER CAME UPON A PECULIAR SIGHT.
DOWN IN A LITTLE MEADOW, ON THE SIDE OF A MOUNTAIN, WERE MANY SHEEP, GRAZING ON THE NEW SPRING GRASS
THEY WERE VERY PEACEFUL AND FRIENDLY AND NOT AT ALL LIKE THE SUSPICIOUS WILD ANIMALS ROVER HAD MET UP TILL NOW
HE WATCHED THEM FOR A MOMENT, UNAWARE THAT ON THE OTHER SIDE OF THE MEADOW TWO YOUNG TIMBER WOLVES WERE WATCHING THE SHEEP, TOO.
SUDDENLY THE SHEEP STARTED TO BOLT. BEFORE ROVER'S EYES THEY CHANGED FROM QUIET CONTENTED CREATURES INTO A BAAING MASS.

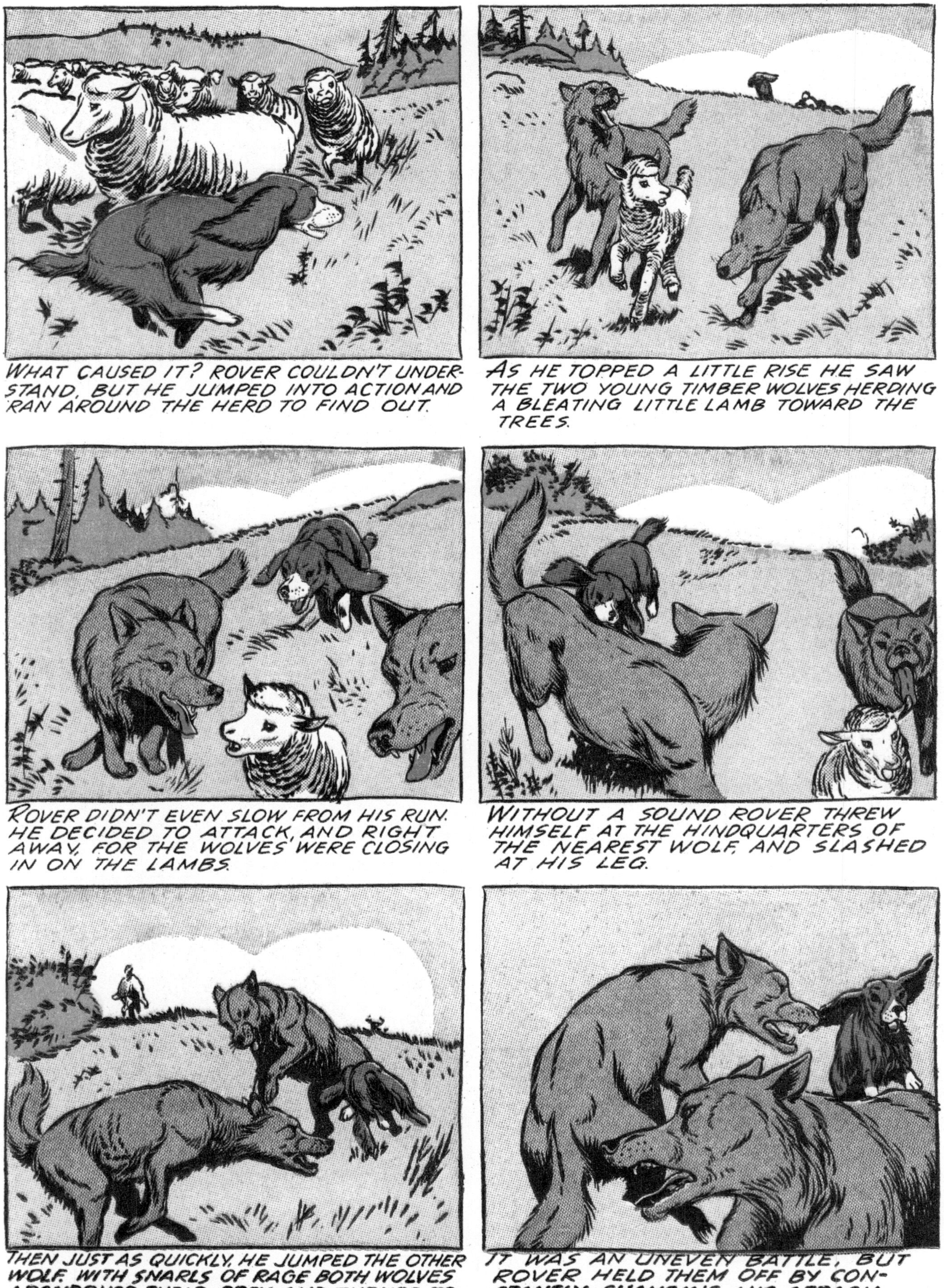
WHAT CAUSED IT? ROVER COULDN'T UNDERSTAND, BUT HE JUMPED INTO ACTION AND RAN AROUND THE HERD TO FIND OUT.
AS HE TOPPED A LITTLE RISE HE SAW THE TWO YOUNG TIMBER WOLVES HERDING A BLEATING LITTLE LAMB TOWARD THE TREES.
ROVER DIDN'T EVEN SLOW FROM HIS RUN. HE DECIDED TO ATTACK, AND RIGHT AWAY, FOR THE WOLVES WERE CLOSING IN ON THE LAMBS.
WITHOUT A SOUND ROVER THREW HIMSELF AT THE HINDQUARTERS OF THE NEAREST WOLF, AND SLASHED AT HIS LEG.
THEN JUST AS QUICKLY, HE JUMPED THE OTHER WOLF. WITH SNARLS OF RAGE BOTH WOLVES ABANDONED THEIR PREY AND TURNED TO DEAL WITH THEIR ATTACKER
IT WAS AN UNEVEN BATTLE, BUT ROVER HELD THEM OFF BY CONSTANTLY CHANGING HIS ATTACK FROM ONE TO THE OTHER.

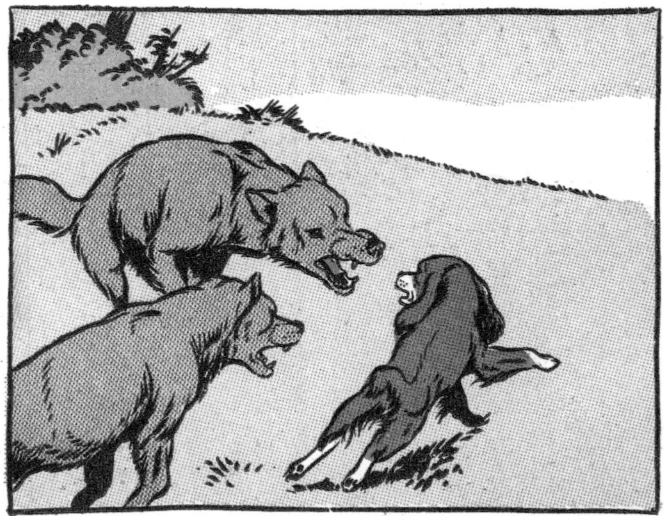

BUT IT WAS A LOSING STRUGGLE, FOR THE LITTLE SPANIEL WAS BEING FORCED TO GIVE GROUND AT EVERY LUNGE.

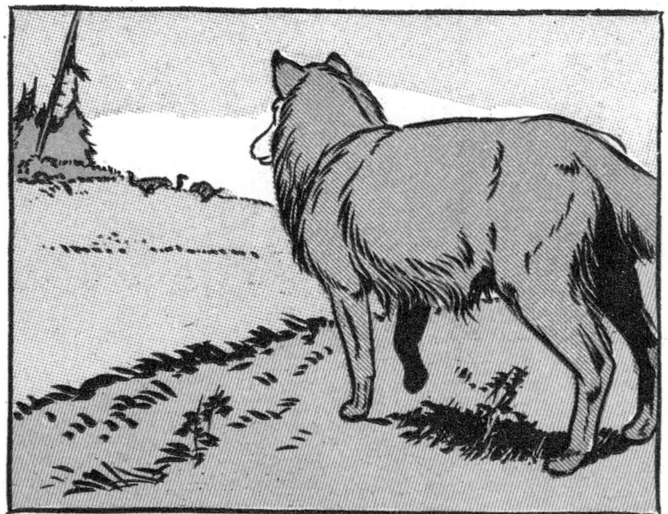

IT LOOKED VERY HOPELESS—WHEN SUDDENLY OUT ONTO THE MEADOW CAME "SHEP," THE SHEEP DOG, WHO HAD HEARD THE BATTLE.

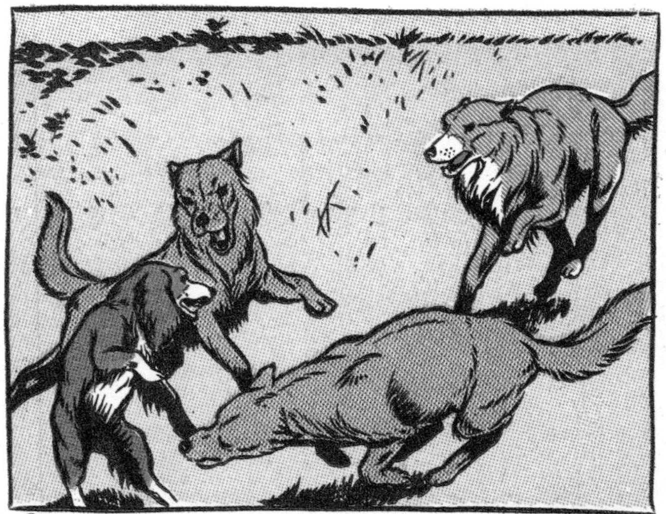

SHEP WASTED NO TIME, FOR FIGHTING WOLVES WAS SOMETHING SHEP HAD LEARNED FROM PUPPYHOOD, AND HE JOINED THE FIGHT IMMEDIATELY.

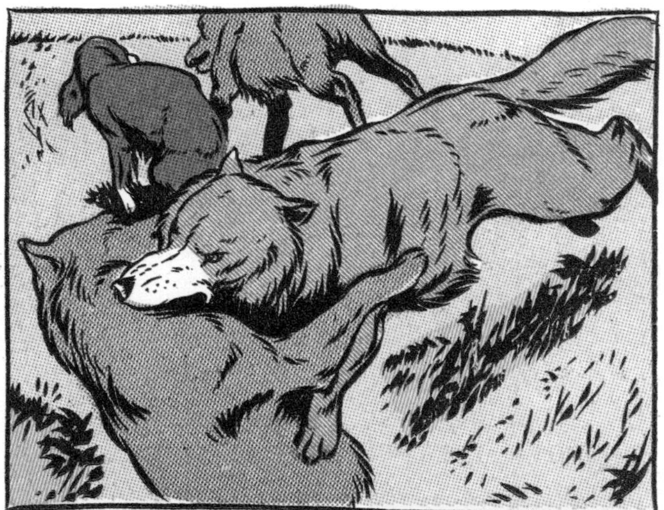

WITH A RUSH THE HEAVY SHEEP DOG THREW HIMSELF AT THE FIRST WOLF— AND BEFORE THAT PIRATE KNEW IT, SHEP HAD HIM...

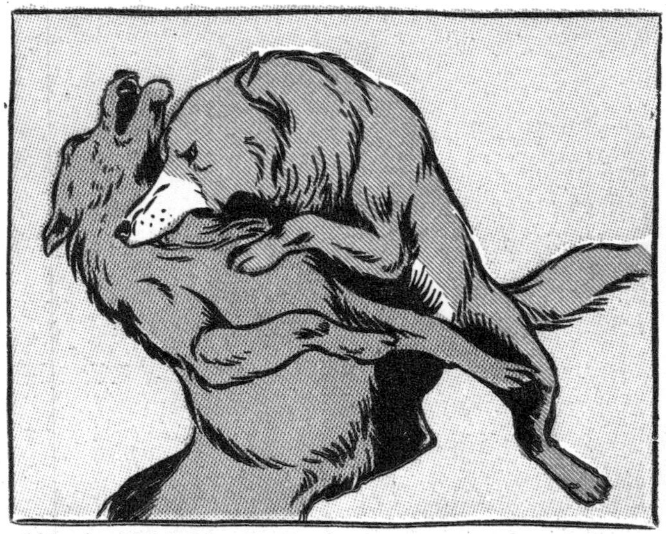

IN A DEATH GRIP THAT DIDN'T TAKE VERY LONG.

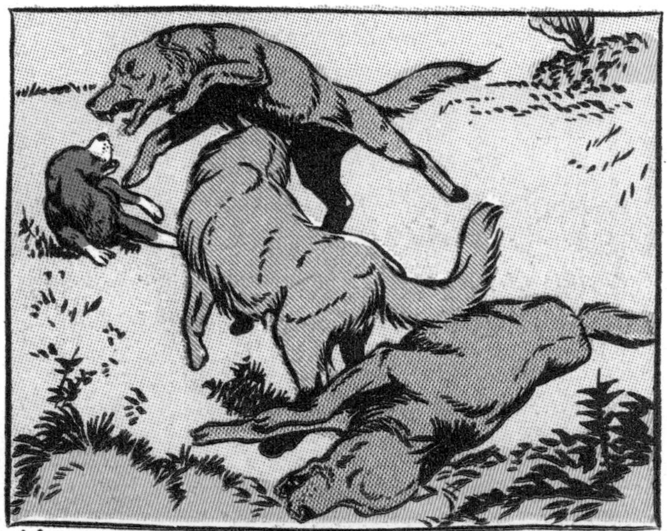

HARDLY PAUSING TO LOOK AT HIS DEAD FOE, SHEP WHEELED FOR THE OTHER, FOR ROVER WAS DOWN!

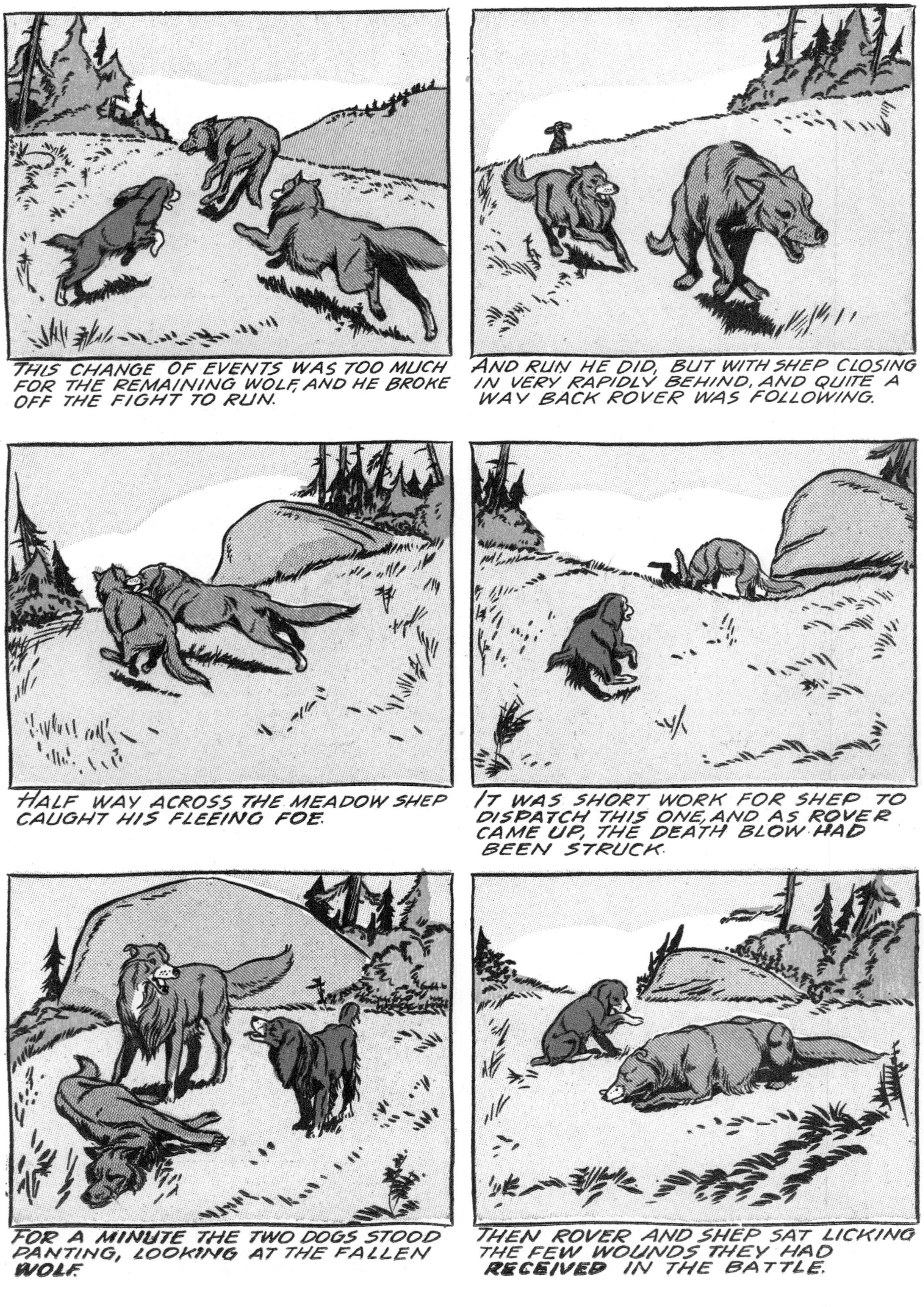
THIS CHANGE OF EVENTS WAS TOO MUCH FOR THE REMAINING WOLF, AND HE BROKE OFF THE FIGHT TO RUN.
AND RUN HE DID, BUT WITH SHEP CLOSING IN VERY RAPIDLY BEHIND, AND QUITE A WAY BACK ROVER WAS FOLLOWING.
HALF WAY ACROSS THE MEADOW SHEP CAUGHT HIS FLEEING FOE.
IT WAS SHORT WORK FOR SHEP TO DISPATCH THIS ONE, AND AS ROVER CAME UP, THE DEATH BLOW HAD BEEN STRUCK.
FOR A MINUTE THE TWO DOGS STOOD PANTING, LOOKING AT THE FALLEN WOLF.
THEN ROVER AND SHEP SAT LICKING THE FEW WOUNDS THEY HAD RECEIVED IN THE BATTLE.

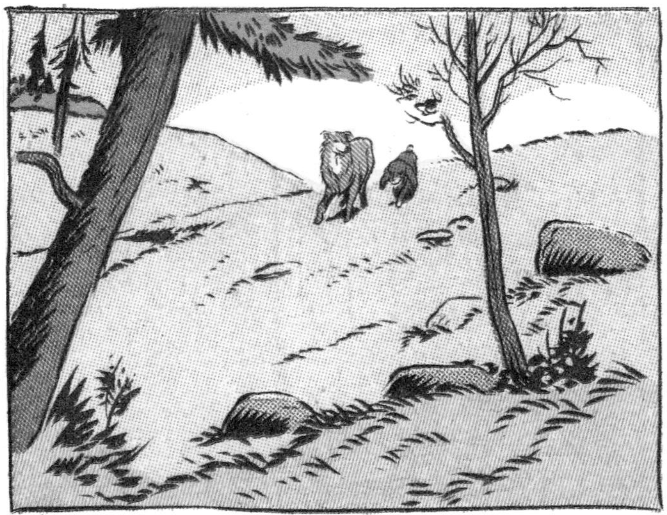

"YOU COME ALONG WITH ME," SAID ROVER'S NEW FRIEND, "MY MASTER FEEDS ME NOW, AND YOU MUST BE HUNGRY, TOO."

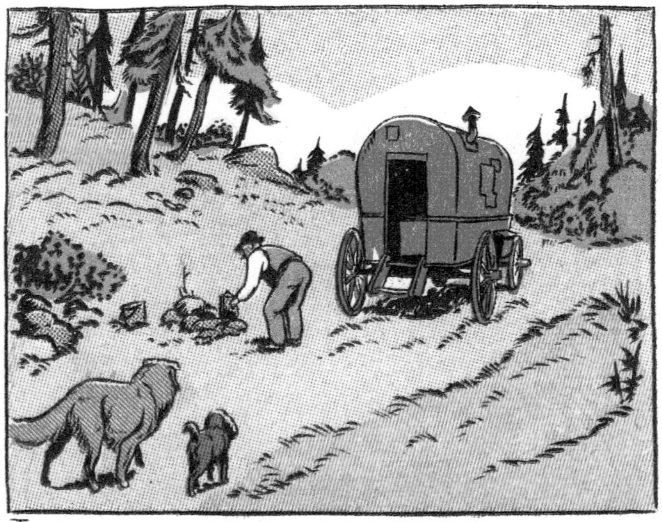

THE TWO DOGS CAME DOWN A LITTLE RAVINE AND THERE WAS THE SHEEPHERDER'S LITTLE WAGON AND THE SHEEPHERDER HIMSELF PREPARING SUPPER.

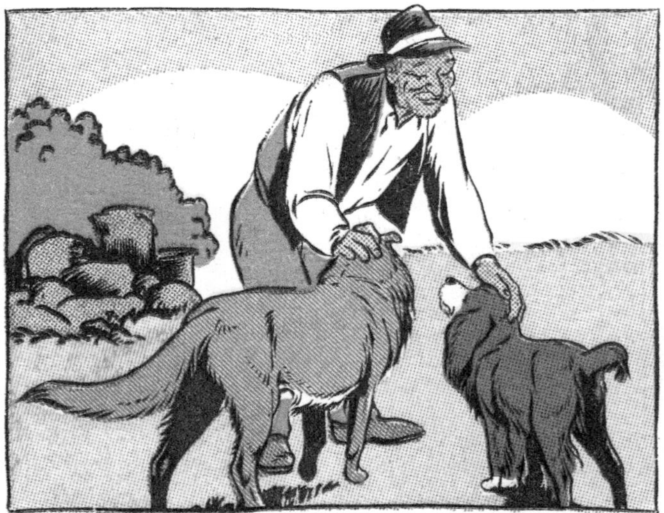

"WELL, WELL," CHUCKLED THE OLD MAN, WHEN HE SAW ROVER, "SHEP, I SEE YOU GOT YOURSELF A PAL, HAVEN'T YOU?"

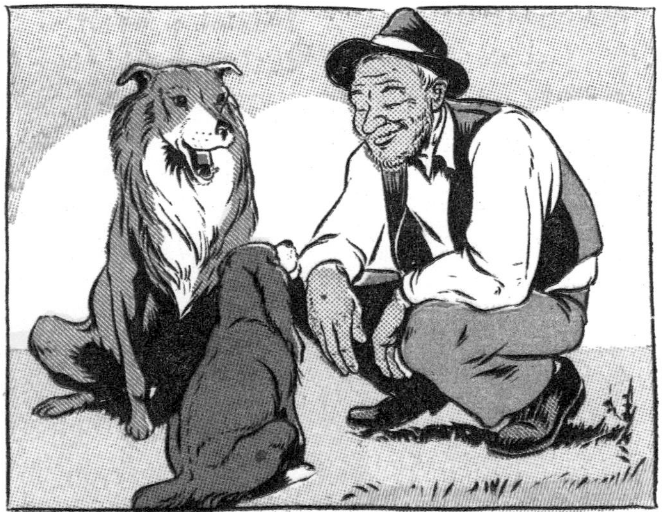

"AND I SEE YOU BOYS BEEN FIGHTING SOMETHING—WOLVES, I BET!" THE OLD SHEEPHERDER BENT DOWN TO PAT BOTH DOGS.

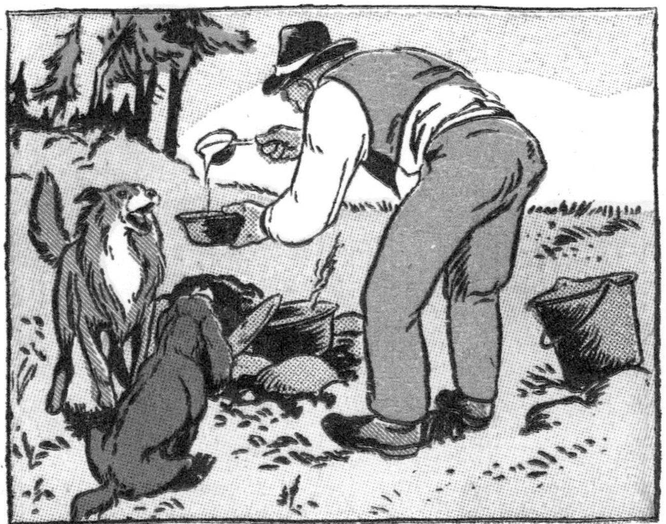

"WELL, I GUESS YOU BOYS EARNED YOUR SUPPER TONIGHT." HE LADLED OUT TWO BOWLS OF RICH STEW FROM THE POT ON THE FIRE.

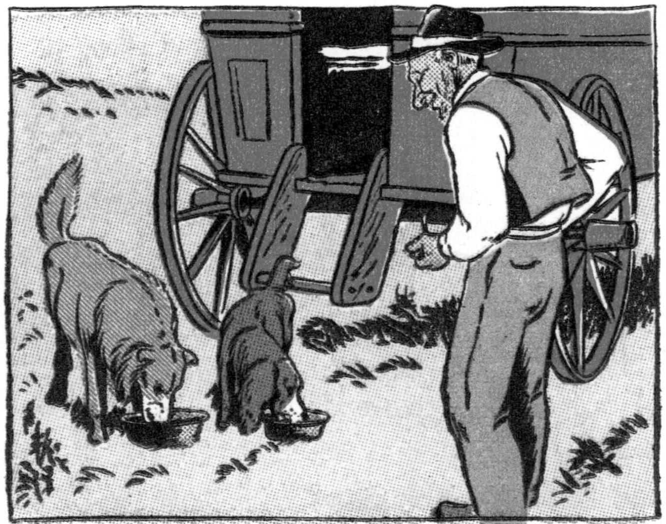

AND AS HE WATCHED THE TWO FRIENDS EAT, HE CHUCKLED TO HIMSELF. "DOGS ARE GREAT PEOPLE," HE OBSERVED.

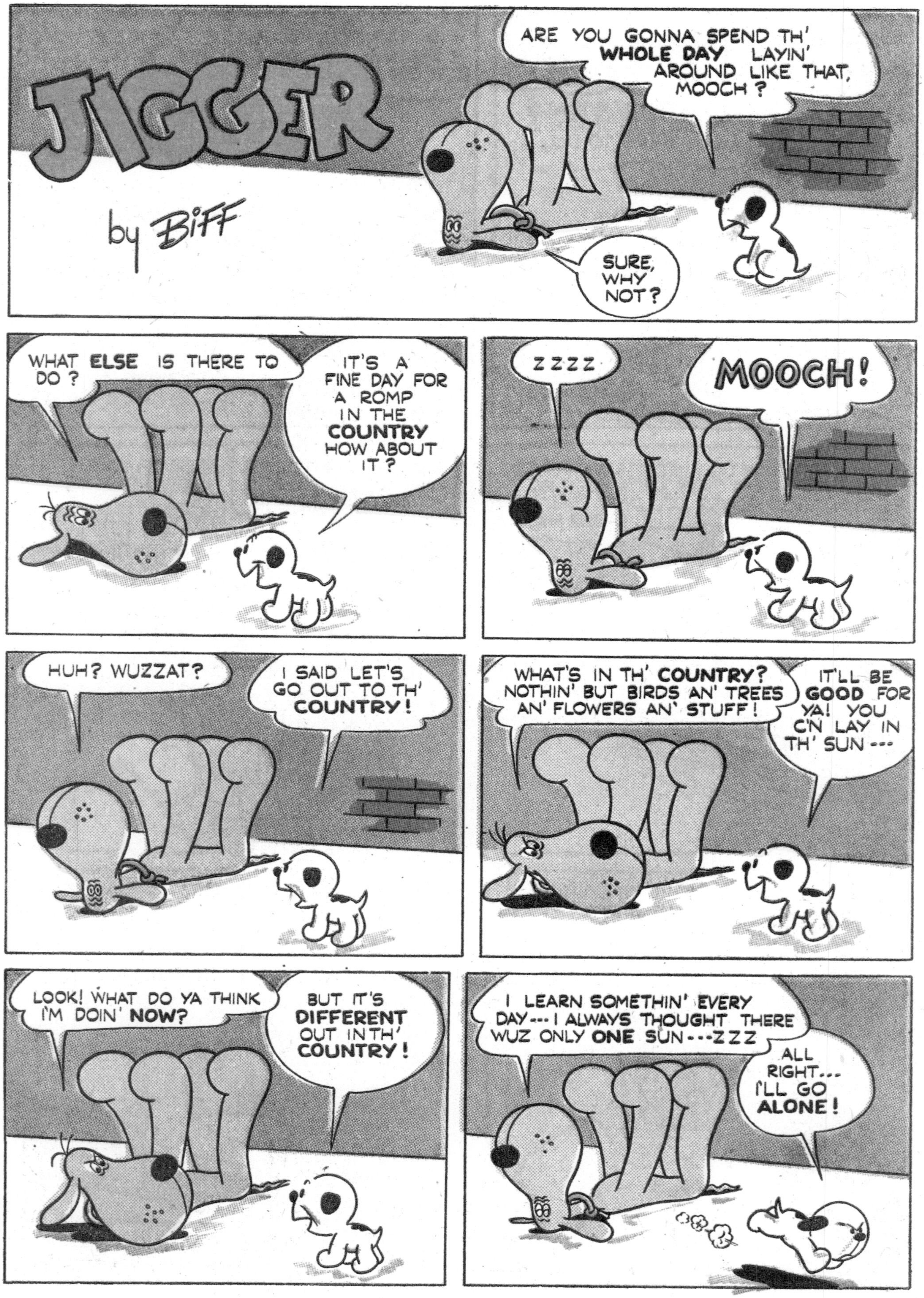
JIGGER
by BIFF
ARE YOU GONNA SPEND TH' WHOLE DAY LAYIN' AROUND LIKE THAT, MOOCH?
SURE, WHY NOT?
WHAT ELSE IS THERE TO DO?
IT'S A FINE DAY FOR A ROMP IN THE COUNTRY HOW ABOUT IT?
ZZZZ
MOOCH!
HUH? WUZZAT?
I SAID LET'S GO OUT TO TH' COUNTRY!
WHAT'S IN TH' COUNTRY? NOTHIN' BUT BIRDS AN' TREES AN' FLOWERS AN' STUFF!
IT'LL BE GOOD FOR YA! YOU C'N LAY IN TH' SUN---
LOOK! WHAT DO YA THINK I'M DOIN' NOW?
BUT IT'S DIFFERENT OUT IN TH' COUNTRY!
I LEARN SOMETHIN' EVERY DAY--- I ALWAYS THOUGHT THERE WUZ ONLY ONE SUN---ZZZ
ALL RIGHT... I'LL GO ALONE!

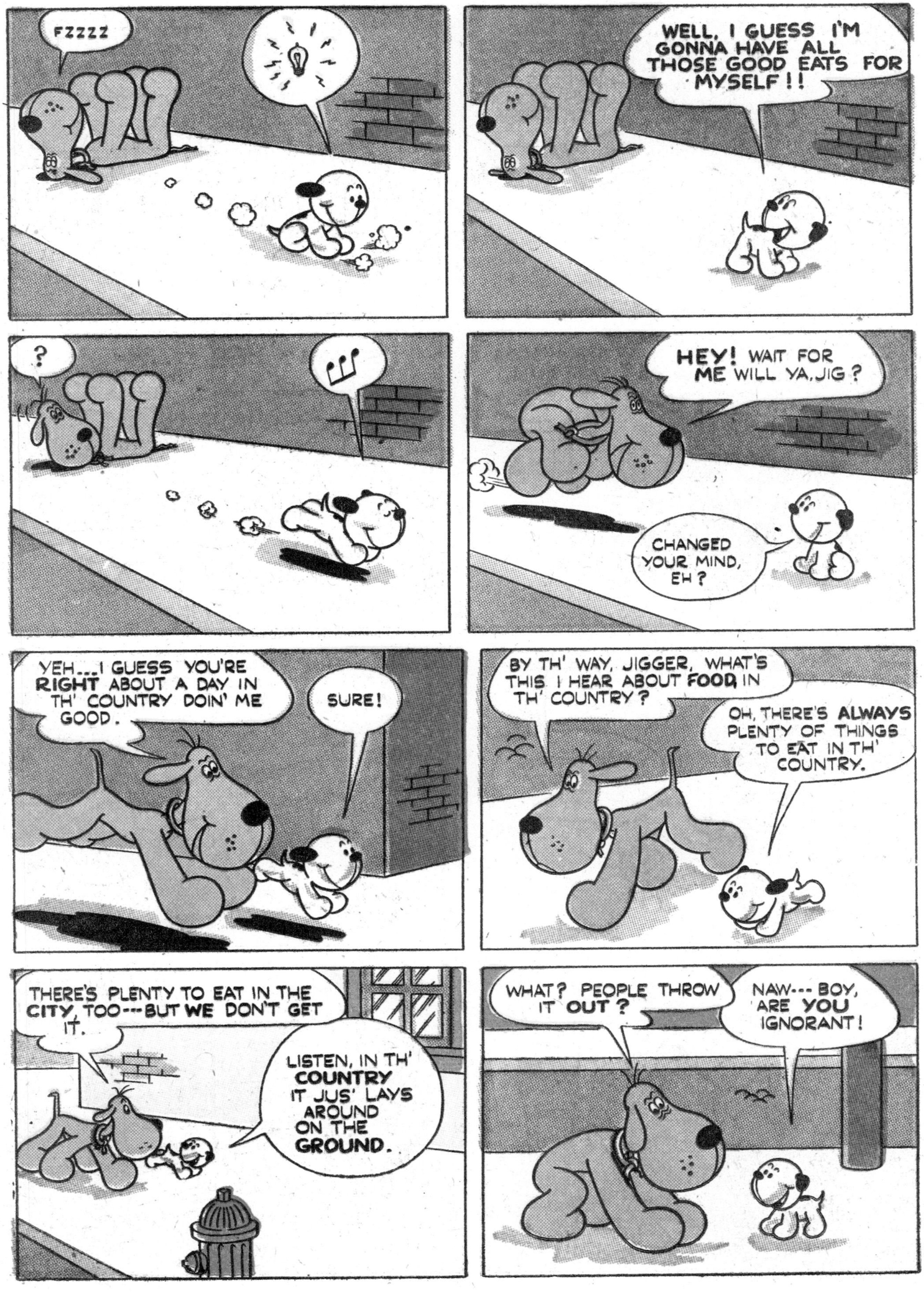
FZZZZ
WELL, I GUESS I'M GONNA HAVE ALL THOSE GOOD EATS FOR MYSELF!!
?
HEY! WAIT FOR ME WILL YA, JIG?
CHANGED YOUR MIND, EH?
YEH...I GUESS YOU'RE RIGHT ABOUT A DAY IN TH' COUNTRY DOIN' ME GOOD.
SURE!
BY TH' WAY, JIGGER, WHAT'S THIS I HEAR ABOUT FOOD IN TH' COUNTRY?
OH, THERE'S ALWAYS PLENTY OF THINGS TO EAT IN TH' COUNTRY.
THERE'S PLENTY TO EAT IN THE CITY, TOO---BUT WE DON'T GET IT.
LISTEN, IN TH' COUNTRY IT JUS' LAYS AROUND ON THE GROUND.
WHAT? PEOPLE THROW IT OUT?
NAW--- BOY, ARE YOU IGNORANT!

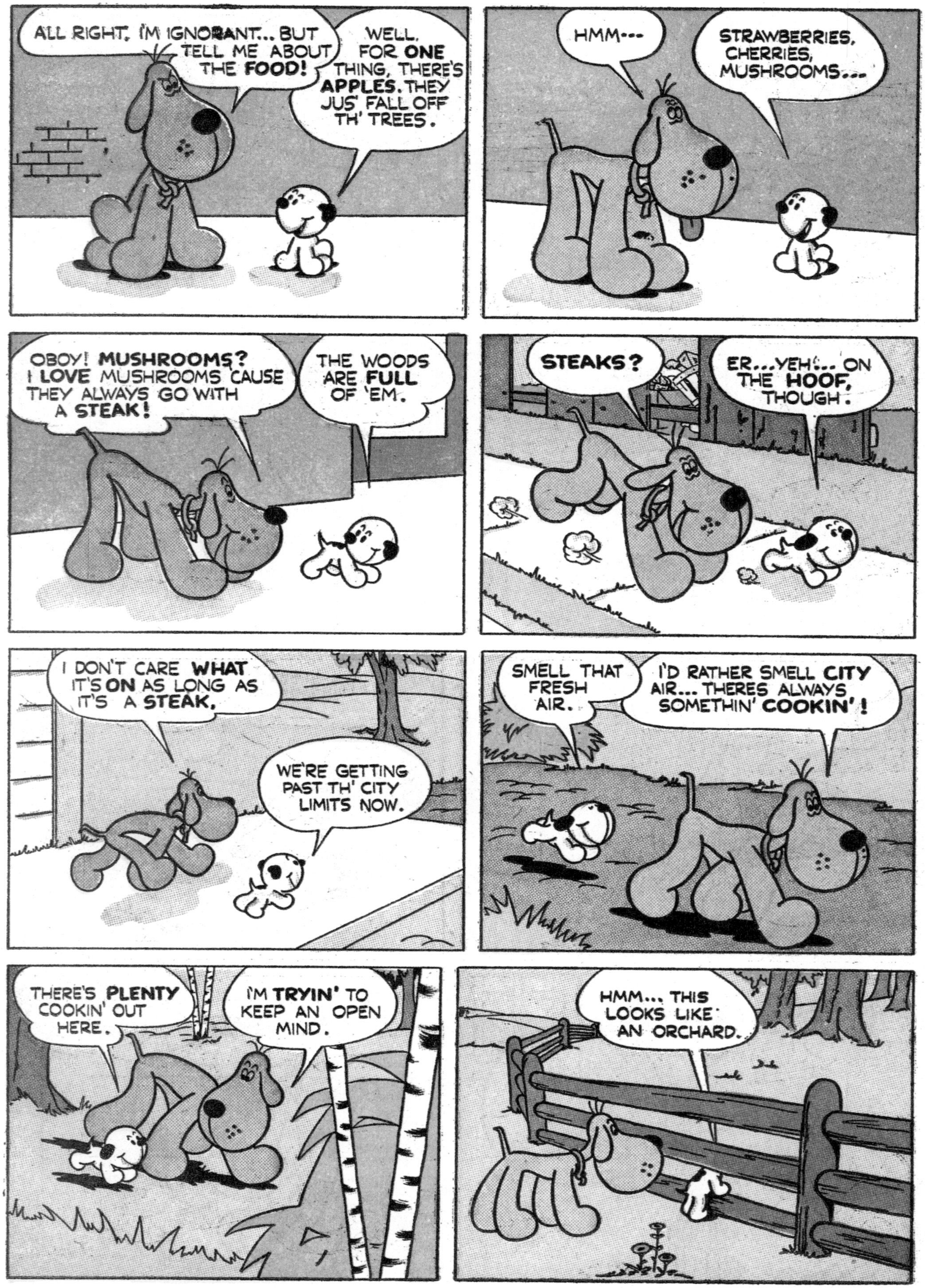
ALL RIGHT, I'M IGNORANT... BUT TELL ME ABOUT THE FOOD!
WELL, FOR ONE THING, THERE'S APPLES. THEY JUS' FALL OFF TH' TREES.
HMM...
STRAWBERRIES, CHERRIES, MUSHROOMS...
OBOY! MUSHROOMS? I LOVE MUSHROOMS CAUSE THEY ALWAYS GO WITH A STEAK!
THE WOODS ARE FULL OF 'EM.
STEAKS?
ER...YEH!... ON THE HOOF, THOUGH.
I DON'T CARE WHAT IT'S ON AS LONG AS IT'S A STEAK.
WE'RE GETTING PAST TH' CITY LIMITS NOW.
SMELL THAT FRESH AIR.
I'D RATHER SMELL CITY AIR... THERES ALWAYS SOMETHIN' COOKIN'!
THERE'S PLENTY COOKIN' OUT HERE.
I'M TRYIN' TO KEEP AN OPEN MIND.
HMM... THIS LOOKS LIKE AN ORCHARD.

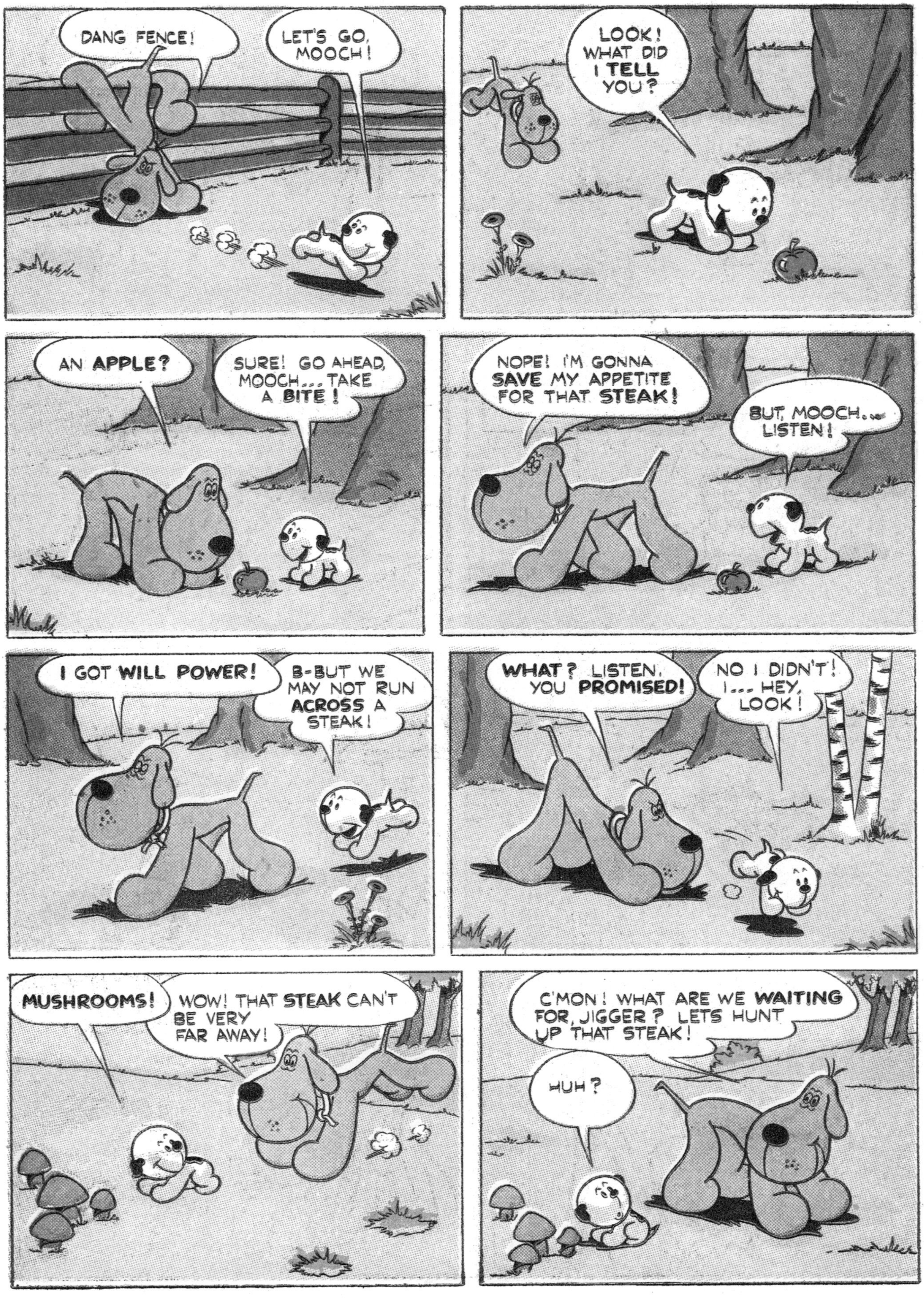
DANG FENCE!
LET'S GO, MOOCH!
LOOK! WHAT DID I TELL YOU?
AN APPLE?
SURE! GO AHEAD, MOOCH... TAKE A BITE!
NOPE! I'M GONNA SAVE MY APPETITE FOR THAT STEAK!
BUT, MOOCH... LISTEN!
I GOT WILL POWER!
B-BUT WE MAY NOT RUN ACROSS A STEAK!
WHAT? LISTEN, YOU PROMISED!
NO I DIDN'T! I... HEY, LOOK!
MUSHROOMS!
WOW! THAT STEAK CAN'T BE VERY FAR AWAY!
C'MON! WHAT ARE WE WAITING FOR, JIGGER? LETS HUNT UP THAT STEAK!
HUH?

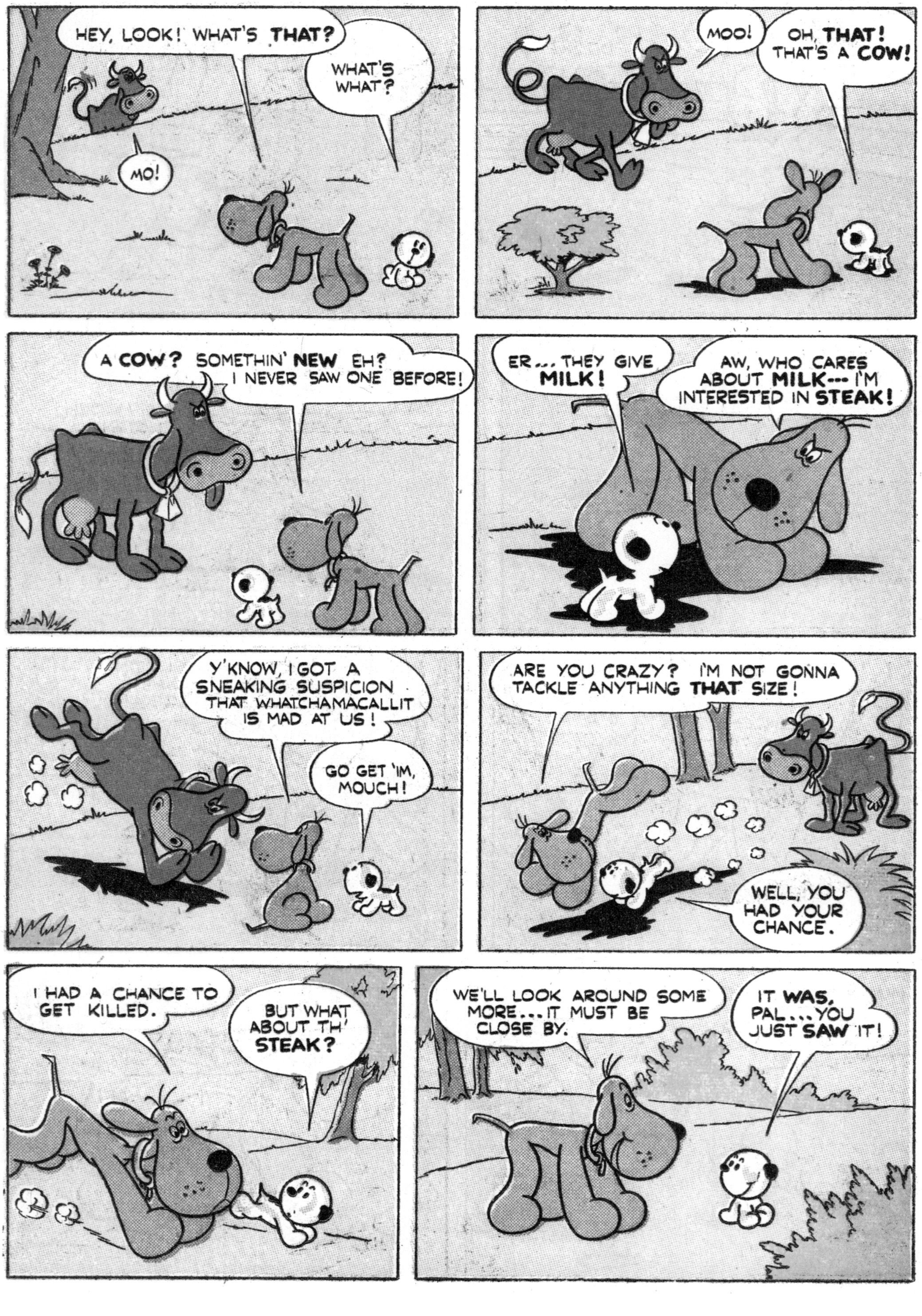
HEY, LOOK! WHAT'S THAT?
WHAT'S WHAT?
MO!
MOO!
OH, THAT! THAT'S A COW!
A COW? SOMETHIN' NEW EH? I NEVER SAW ONE BEFORE!
ER... THEY GIVE MILK!
AW, WHO CARES ABOUT MILK--- I'M INTERESTED IN STEAK!
Y'KNOW, I GOT A SNEAKING SUSPICION THAT WHATCHAMACALLIT IS MAD AT US!
GO GET 'IM, MOUCH!
ARE YOU CRAZY? I'M NOT GONNA TACKLE ANYTHING THAT SIZE!
WELL, YOU HAD YOUR CHANCE.
I HAD A CHANCE TO GET KILLED.
BUT WHAT ABOUT TH' STEAK?
WE'LL LOOK AROUND SOME MORE... IT MUST BE CLOSE BY.
IT WAS, PAL... YOU JUST SAW IT!

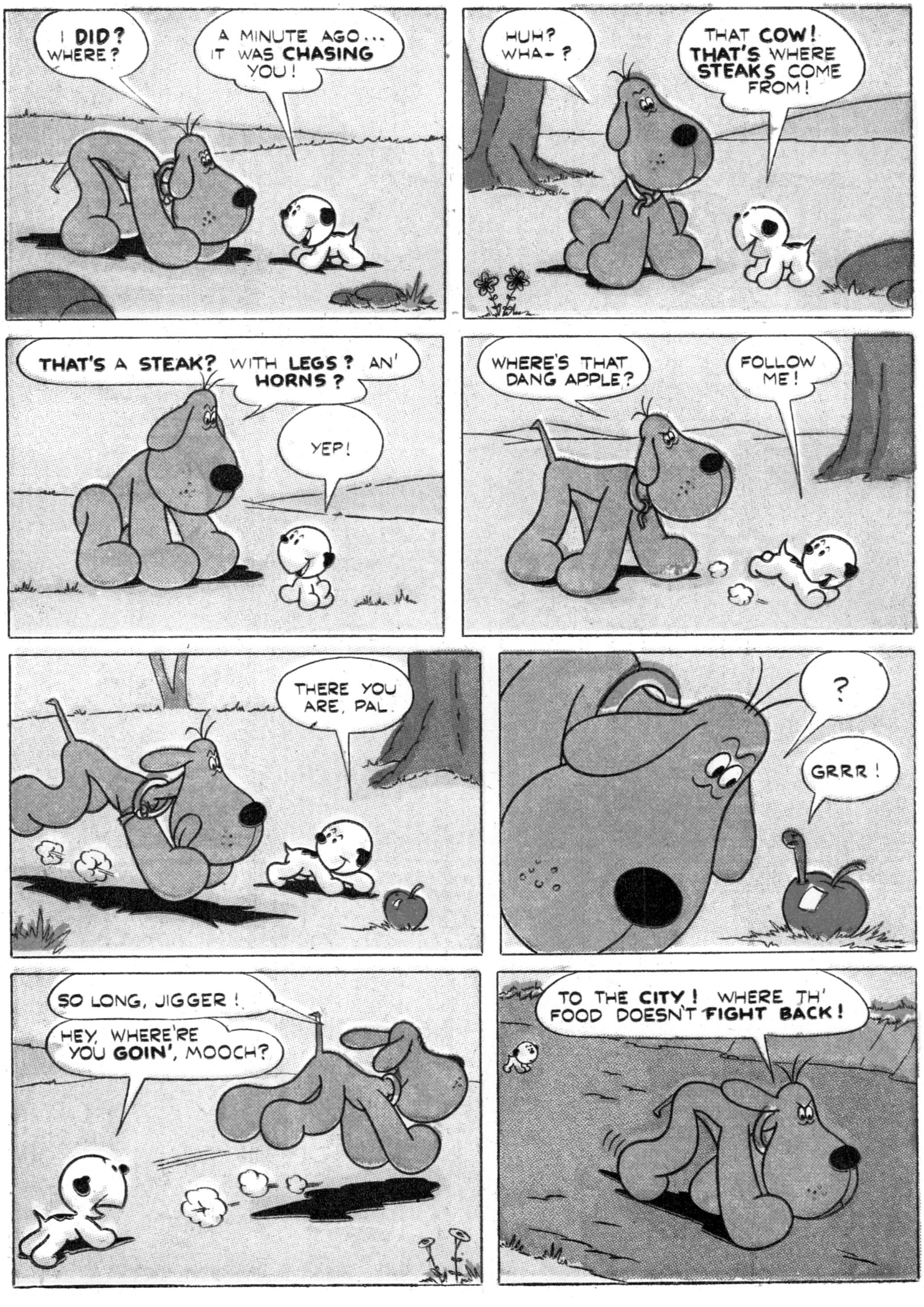
I DID? WHERE?
A MINUTE AGO... IT WAS CHASING YOU!
HUH? WHA-?
THAT COW! THAT'S WHERE STEAKS COME FROM!
THAT'S A STEAK? WITH LEGS? AN' HORNS?
YEP!
WHERE'S THAT DANG APPLE?
FOLLOW ME!
THERE YOU ARE, PAL.
?
GRRR!
SO LONG, JIGGER!
HEY, WHERE'RE YOU GOIN', MOOCH?
TO THE CITY! WHERE TH' FOOD DOESN'T FIGHT BACK!

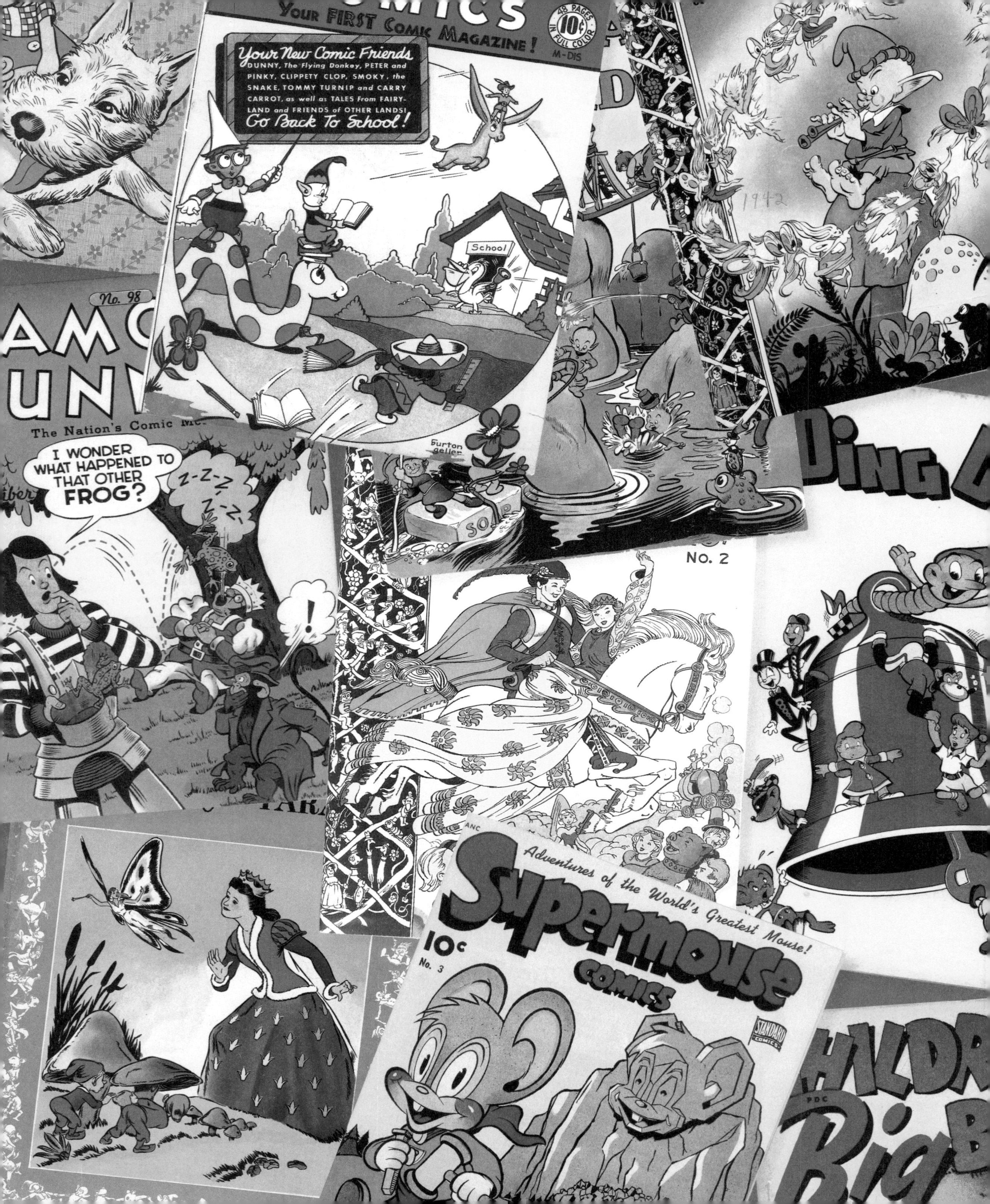

YOUR FIRST COMIC MAGAZINE!
48 PAGES IN FULL COLOR 10¢
M-DIS
Your New Comic Friends
DUNNY, The Flying Donkey, PETER and PINKY, CLIPPETY CLOP, SMOKY, the SNAKE, TOMMY TURNIP and CARRY CARROT, as well as TALES From FAIRY-LAND and FRIENDS of OTHER LANDS!
Go Back To School!
School
Burton geller
No. 98
The Nation's Comic
I WONDER WHAT HAPPENED TO THAT OTHER FROG?
Z-Z-Z
Z-Z
!
1942
NO. 2
ANC
Adventures of the World's Greatest Mouse!
Supermouse
COMICS
10¢
No. 3
STANDARD COMICS
PDC

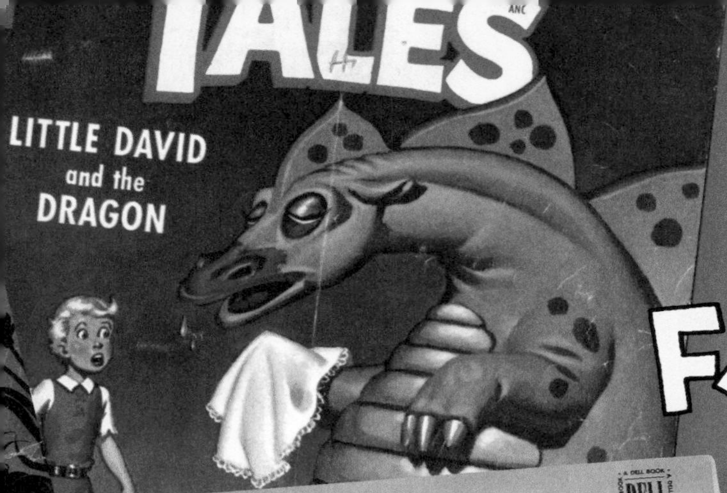
TALES
LITTLE DAVID
and the
DRAGON

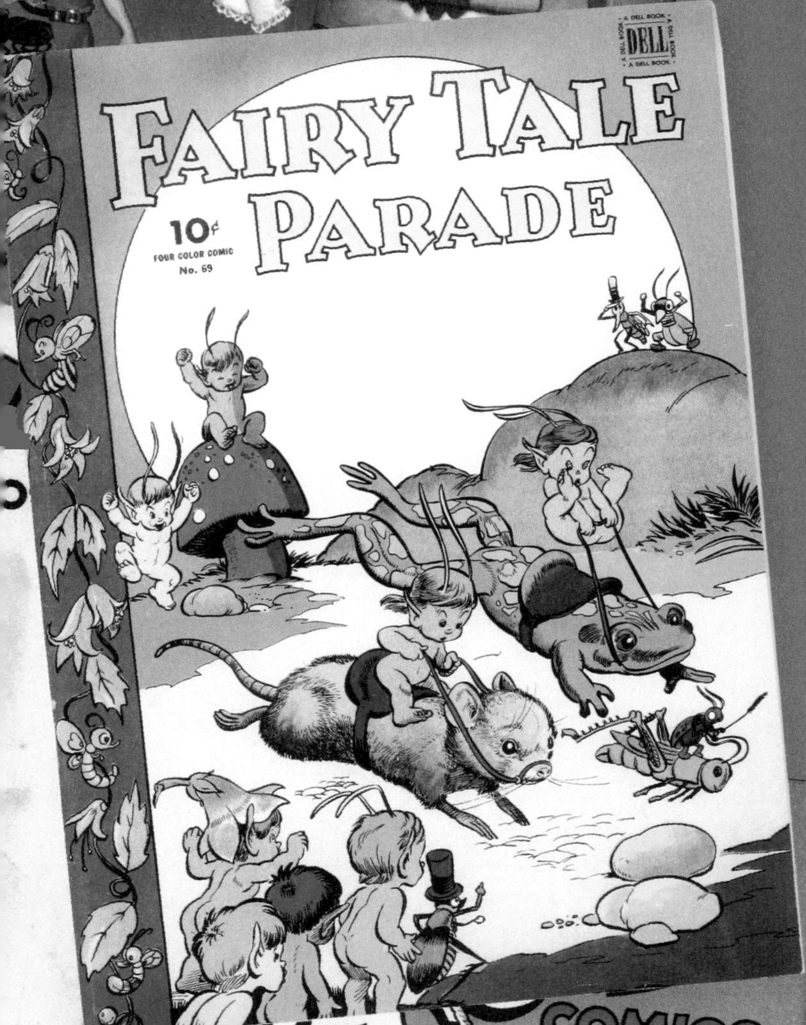
DELL
FAIRY TALE
PARADE
10¢
FOUR COLOR COMIC
No. 69

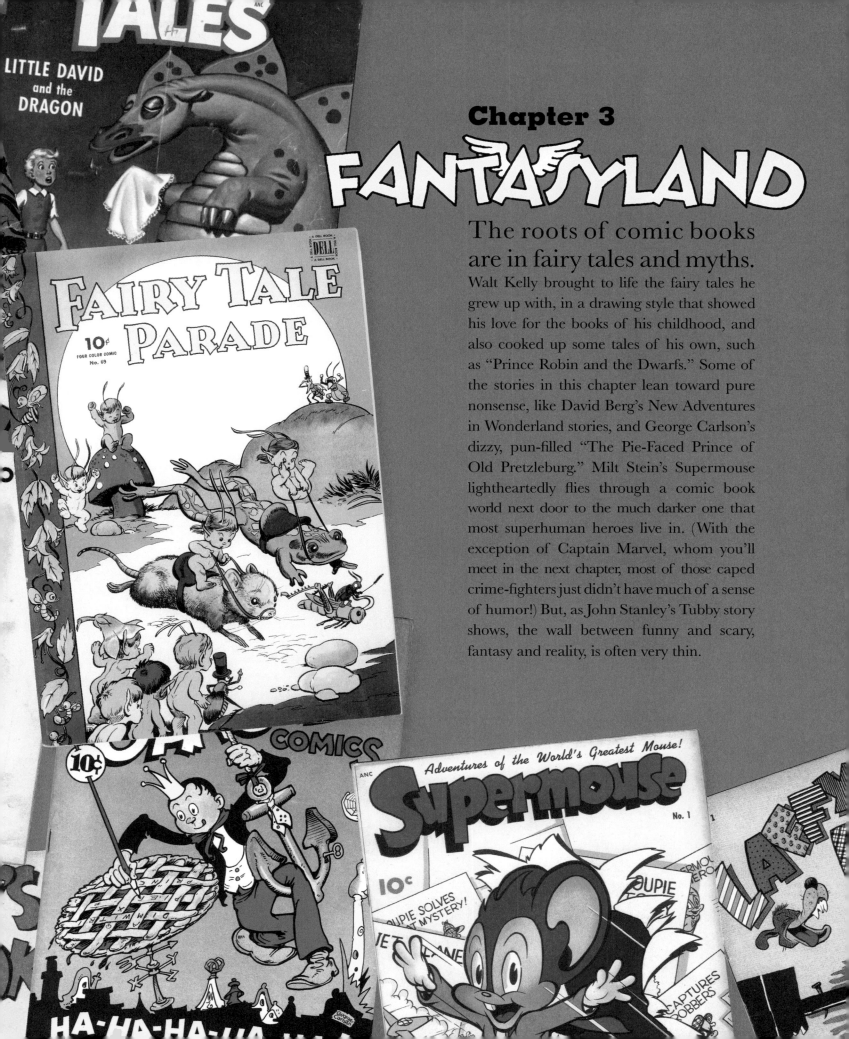

Chapter 3

FANTASYLAND

The roots of comic books are in fairy tales and myths.

Walt Kelly brought to life the fairy tales he grew up with, in a drawing style that showed his love for the books of his childhood, and also cooked up some tales of his own, such as "Prince Robin and the Dwarfs." Some of the stories in this chapter lean toward pure nonsense, like David Berg's New Adventures in Wonderland stories, and George Carlson's dizzy, pun-filled "The Pie-Faced Prince of Old Pretzleburg." Milt Stein's Supermouse lightheartedly flies through a comic book world next door to the much darker one that most superhuman heroes live in. (With the exception of Captain Marvel, whom you'll meet in the next chapter, most of those caped crime-fighters just didn't have much of a sense of humor!) But, as John Stanley's Tubby story shows, the wall between funny and scary, fantasy and reality, is often very thin.

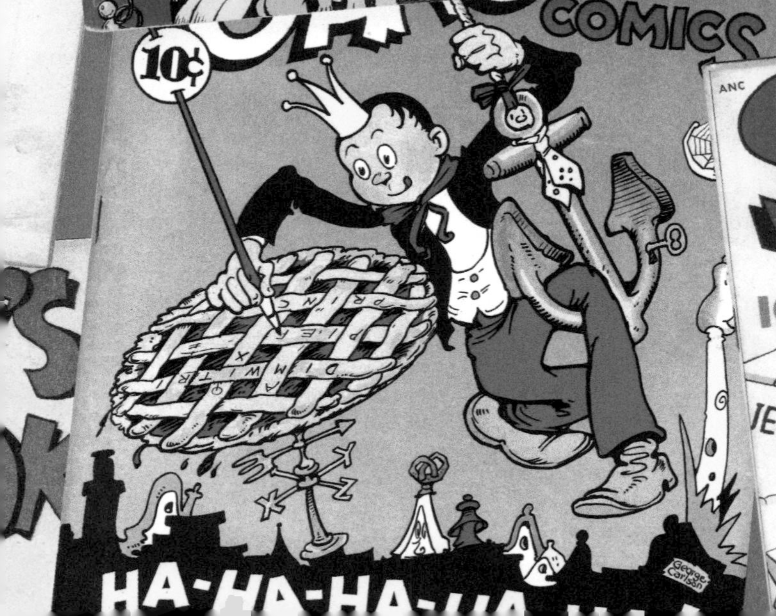
COMICS
10¢
HA-HA-HA-HA

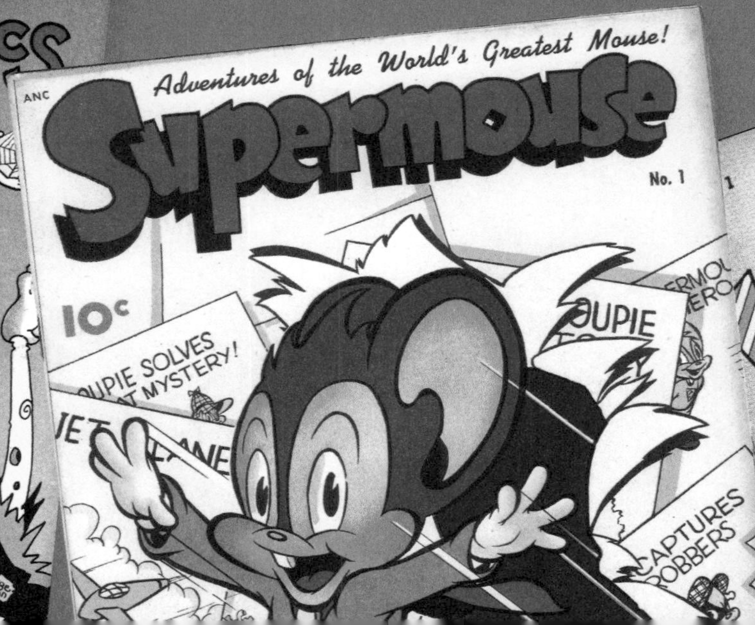
Adventures of the World's Greatest Mouse!
Supermouse
No. 1
10¢
PUPIE SOLVES
MYSTERY!
CAPTURES
ROBBERS

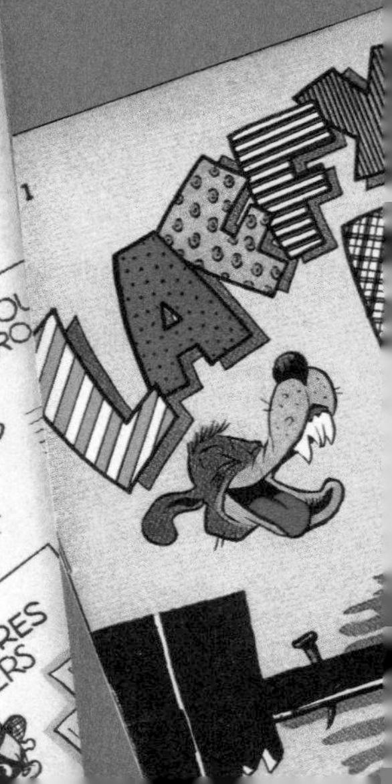

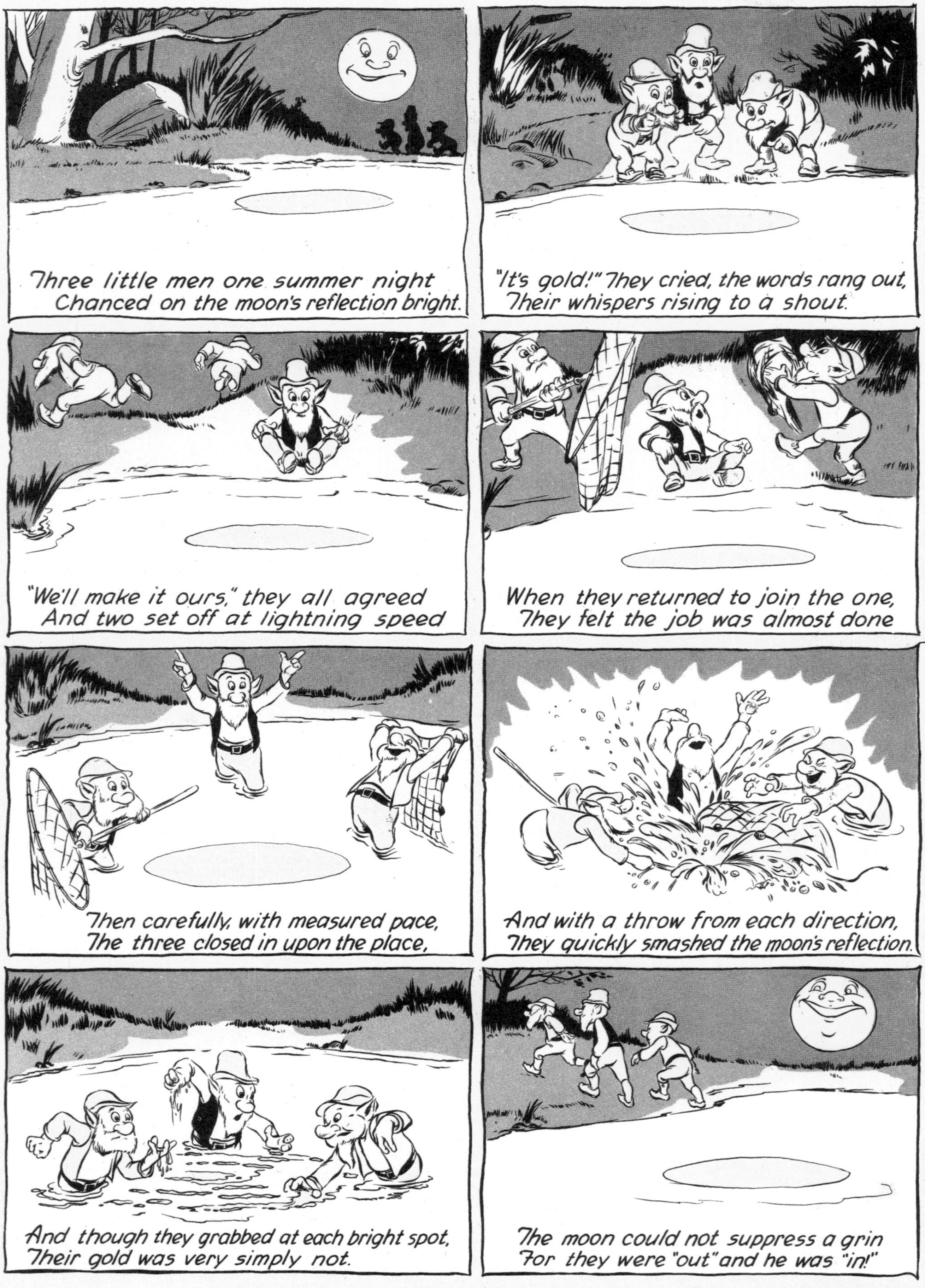
Three little men one summer night
Chanced on the moon's reflection bright.
"It's gold!" They cried, the words rang out,
Their whispers rising to a shout.
"We'll make it ours," they all agreed
And two set off at lightning speed
When they returned to join the one,
They felt the job was almost done
Then carefully, with measured pace,
The three closed in upon the place,
And with a throw from each direction,
They quickly smashed the moon's reflection.
And though they grabbed at each bright spot,
Their gold was very simply not.
The moon could not suppress a grin
For they were "out" and he was "in!"

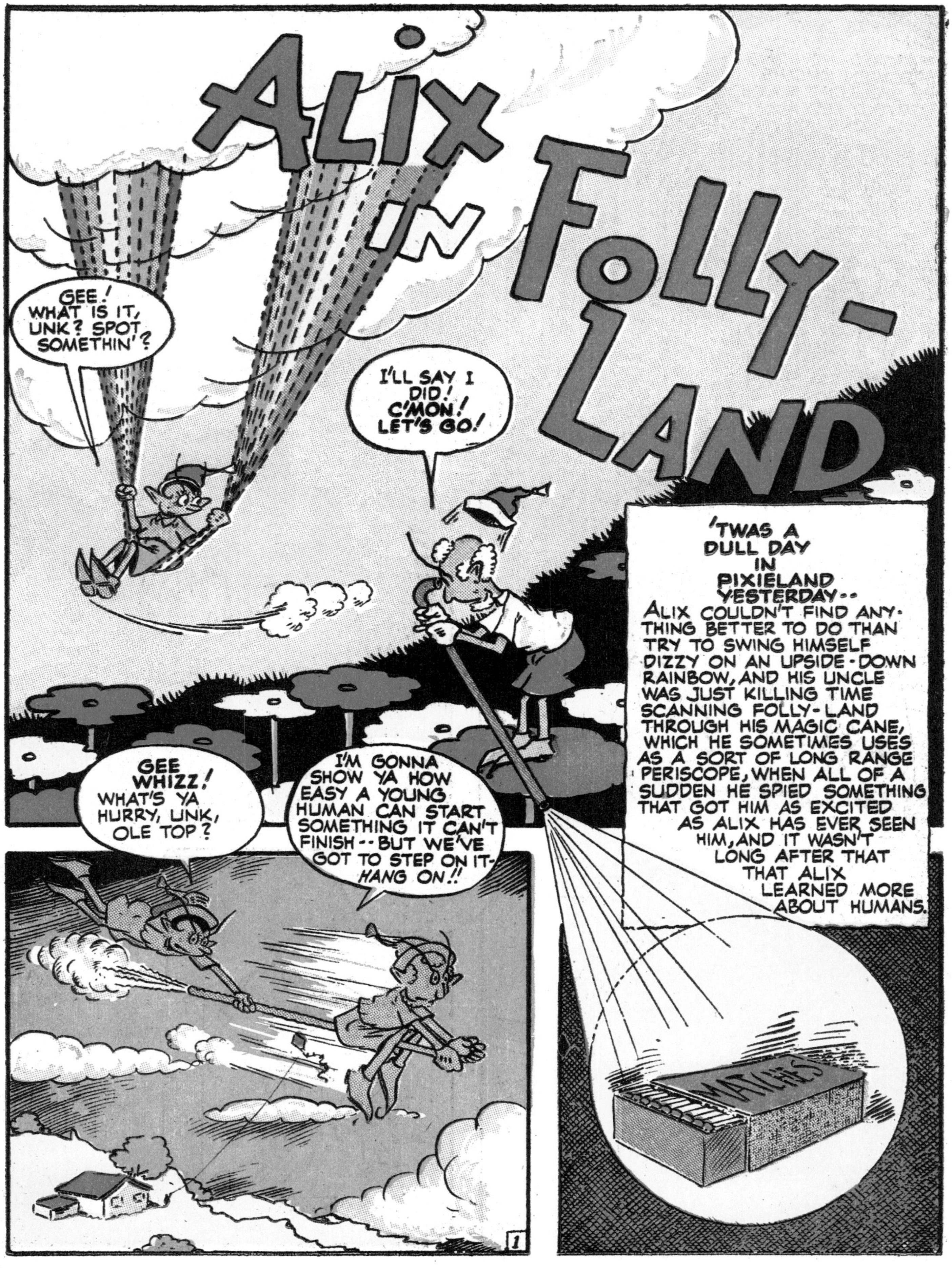
ALIX IN FOLLY-LAND
GEE! WHAT IS IT, UNK? SPOT SOMETHIN'?
I'LL SAY I DID! C'MON! LET'S GO!
'TWAS A DULL DAY IN PIXIELAND YESTERDAY.. ALIX COULDN'T FIND ANYTHING BETTER TO DO THAN TRY TO SWING HIMSELF DIZZY ON AN UPSIDE-DOWN RAINBOW, AND HIS UNCLE WAS JUST KILLING TIME SCANNING FOLLY-LAND THROUGH HIS MAGIC CANE, WHICH HE SOMETIMES USES AS A SORT OF LONG RANGE PERISCOPE, WHEN ALL OF A SUDDEN HE SPIED SOMETHING THAT GOT HIM AS EXCITED AS ALIX HAS EVER SEEN HIM, AND IT WASN'T LONG AFTER THAT THAT ALIX LEARNED MORE ABOUT HUMANS.
GEE WHIZZ! WHAT'S YA HURRY, UNK, OLE TOP?
I'M GONNA SHOW YA HOW EASY A YOUNG HUMAN CAN START SOMETHING IT CAN'T FINISH--BUT WE'VE GOT TO STEP ON IT- HANG ON!!
MATCHES
1

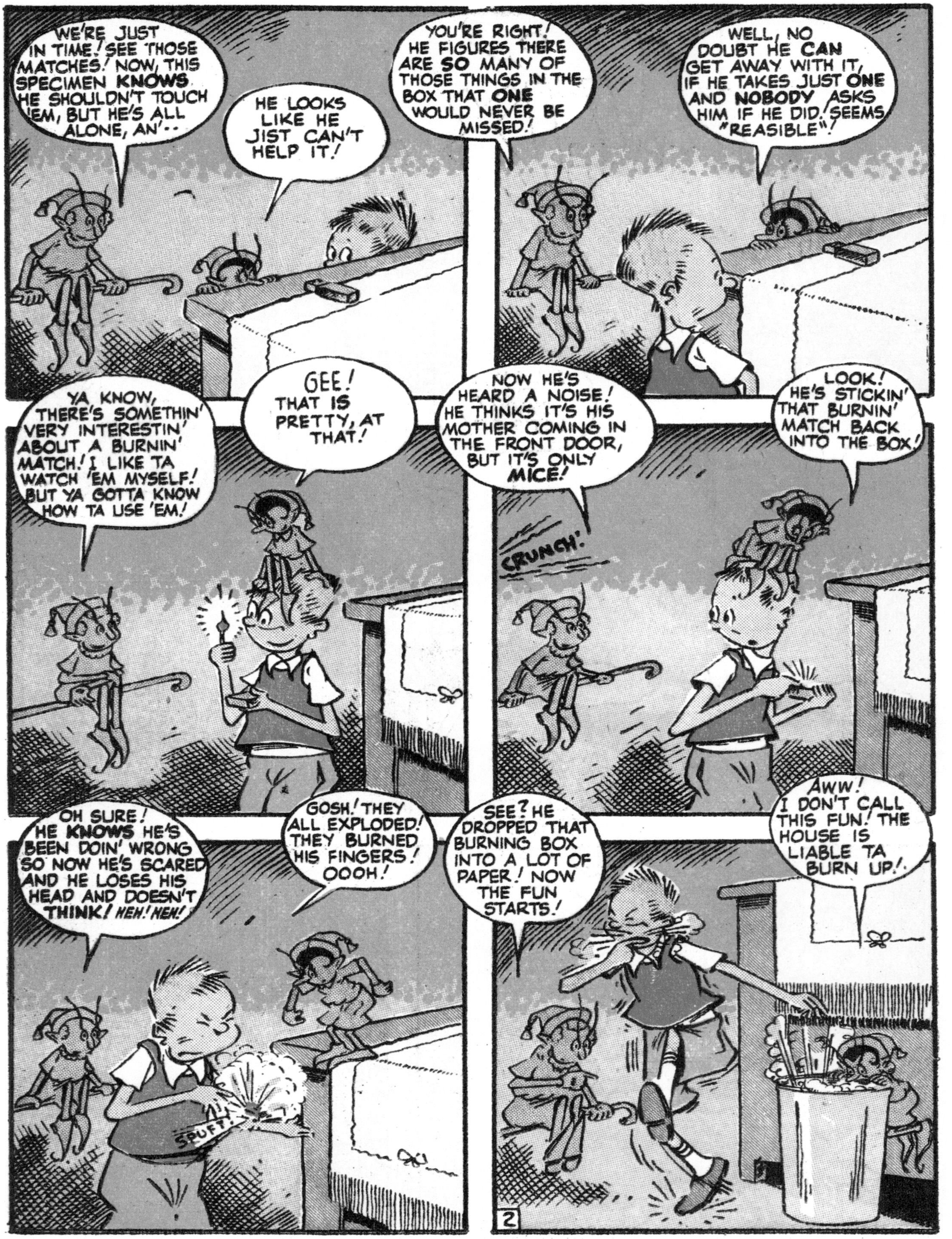
WE'RE JUST IN TIME! SEE THOSE MATCHES! NOW, THIS SPECIMEN KNOWS HE SHOULDN'T TOUCH 'EM, BUT HE'S ALL ALONE, AN'--
HE LOOKS LIKE HE JIST CAN'T HELP IT!
YOU'RE RIGHT! HE FIGURES THERE ARE SO MANY OF THOSE THINGS IN THE BOX THAT ONE WOULD NEVER BE MISSED!
WELL, NO DOUBT HE CAN GET AWAY WITH IT, IF HE TAKES JUST ONE AND NOBODY ASKS HIM IF HE DID! SEEMS "REASIBLE"!
YA KNOW, THERE'S SOMETHIN' VERY INTERESTIN' ABOUT A BURNIN' MATCH! I LIKE TA WATCH 'EM MYSELF! BUT YA GOTTA KNOW HOW TA USE 'EM!
GEE! THAT IS PRETTY, AT THAT!
NOW HE'S HEARD A NOISE! HE THINKS IT'S HIS MOTHER COMING IN THE FRONT DOOR, BUT IT'S ONLY MICE!
CRUNCH!
LOOK! HE'S STICKIN' THAT BURNIN' MATCH BACK INTO THE BOX!
OH SURE! HE KNOWS HE'S BEEN DOIN' WRONG SO NOW HE'S SCARED AND HE LOSES HIS HEAD AND DOESN'T THINK! HEH! HEH!
GOSH! THEY ALL EXPLODED! THEY BURNED HIS FINGERS! OOOH!
SPUFT
SEE? HE DROPPED THAT BURNING BOX INTO A LOT OF PAPER! NOW THE FUN STARTS!
AWW! I DON'T CALL THIS FUN! THE HOUSE IS LIABLE TA BURN UP!
2

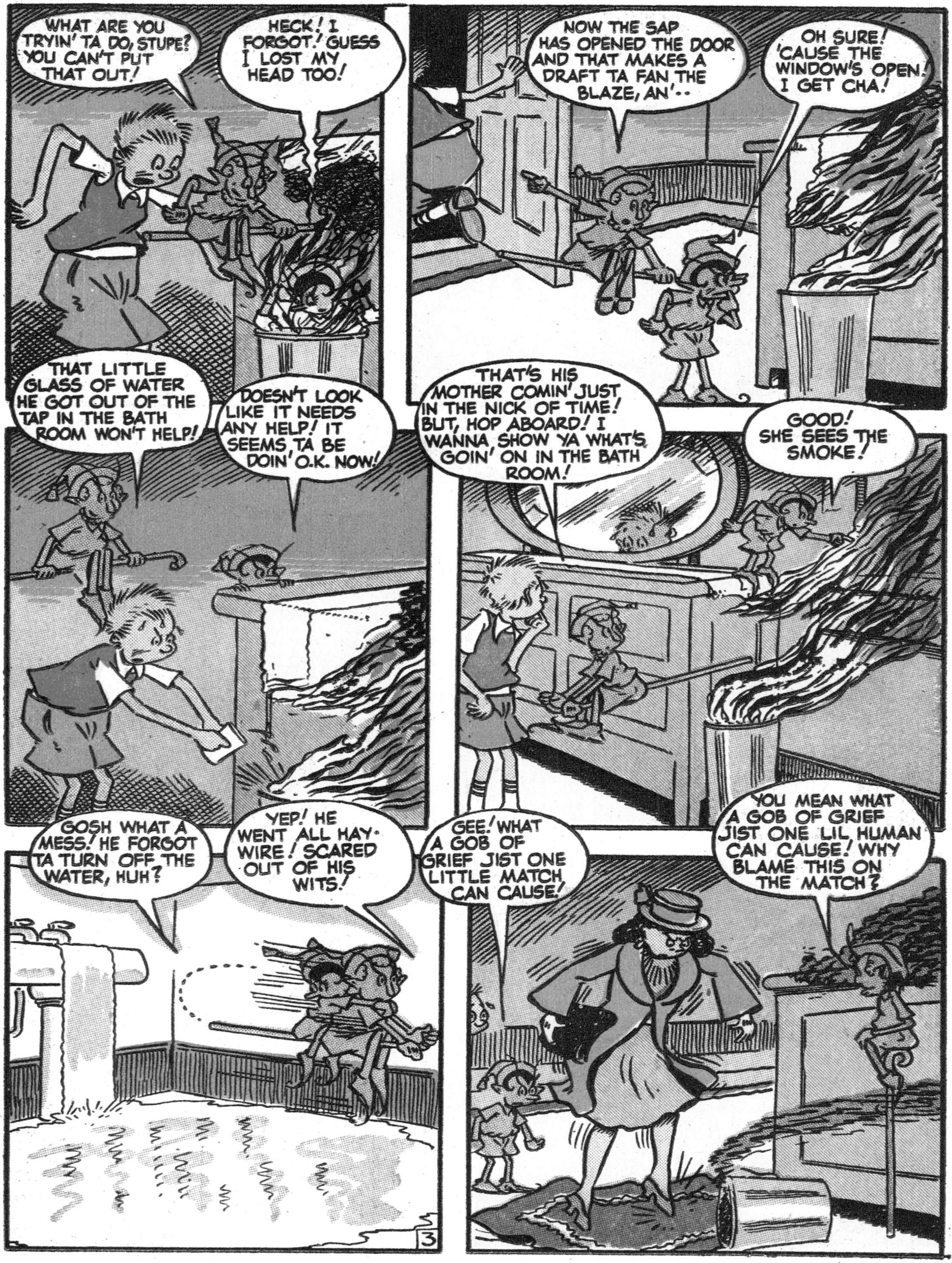
WHAT ARE YOU TRYIN' TA DO, STUPE? YOU CAN'T PUT THAT OUT!
HECK! I FORGOT! GUESS I LOST MY HEAD TOO!
NOW THE SAP HAS OPENED THE DOOR AND THAT MAKES A DRAFT TA FAN THE BLAZE, AN'..
OH SURE! 'CAUSE THE WINDOW'S OPEN! I GET CHA!
THAT LITTLE GLASS OF WATER HE GOT OUT OF THE TAP IN THE BATH ROOM WON'T HELP!
DOESN'T LOOK LIKE IT NEEDS ANY HELP! IT SEEMS TA BE DOIN' O.K. NOW!
THAT'S HIS MOTHER COMIN' JUST IN THE NICK OF TIME! BUT, HOP ABOARD! I WANNA SHOW YA WHAT'S GOIN' ON IN THE BATH ROOM!
GOOD! SHE SEES THE SMOKE!
GOSH WHAT A MESS! HE FORGOT TA TURN OFF THE WATER, HUH?
YEP! HE WENT ALL HAY-WIRE! SCARED OUT OF HIS WITS!
3
GEE! WHAT A GOB OF GRIEF JIST ONE LITTLE MATCH CAN CAUSE!
YOU MEAN WHAT A GOB OF GRIEF JIST ONE LIL HUMAN CAN CAUSE! WHY BLAME THIS ON THE MATCH?

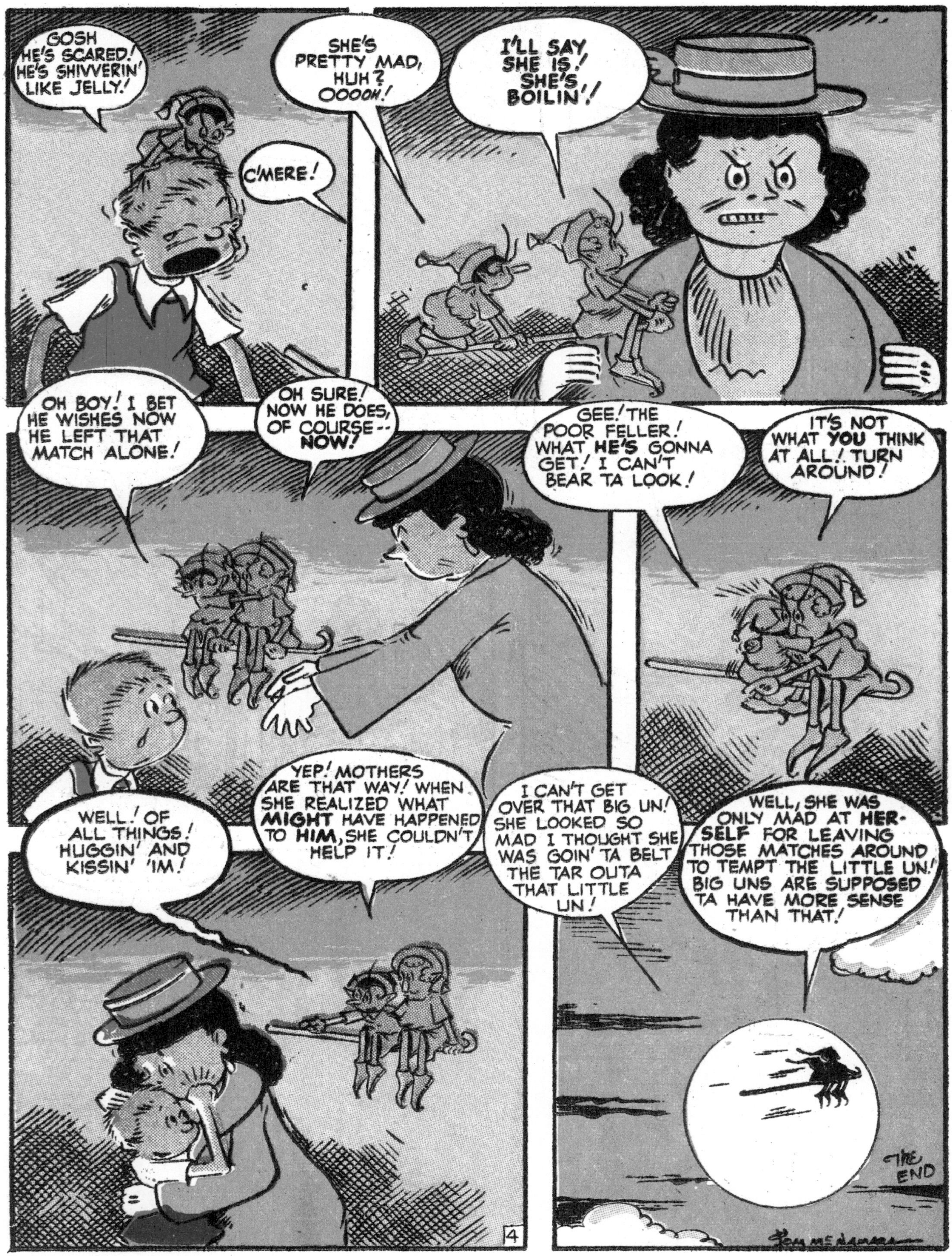
GOSH HE'S SCARED! HE'S SHIVVERIN' LIKE JELLY!
C'MERE!
SHE'S PRETTY MAD, HUH? OOOOH!
I'LL SAY SHE IS! SHE'S BOILIN'!
OH BOY! I BET HE WISHES NOW HE LEFT THAT MATCH ALONE!
OH SURE! NOW HE DOES, OF COURSE-- NOW!
GEE! THE POOR FELLER! WHAT HE'S GONNA GET! I CAN'T BEAR TA LOOK!
IT'S NOT WHAT YOU THINK AT ALL! TURN AROUND!
WELL! OF ALL THINGS! HUGGIN' AND KISSIN' 'IM!
YEP! MOTHERS ARE THAT WAY! WHEN SHE REALIZED WHAT MIGHT HAVE HAPPENED TO HIM, SHE COULDN'T HELP IT!
4
I CAN'T GET OVER THAT BIG UN! SHE LOOKED SO MAD I THOUGHT SHE WAS GOIN' TA BELT THE TAR OUTA THAT LITTLE UN!
WELL, SHE WAS ONLY MAD AT HER-SELF FOR LEAVING THOSE MATCHES AROUND TO TEMPT THE LITTLE UN! BIG UNS ARE SUPPOSED TA HAVE MORE SENSE THAN THAT!
THE END
TOM McNAMARA

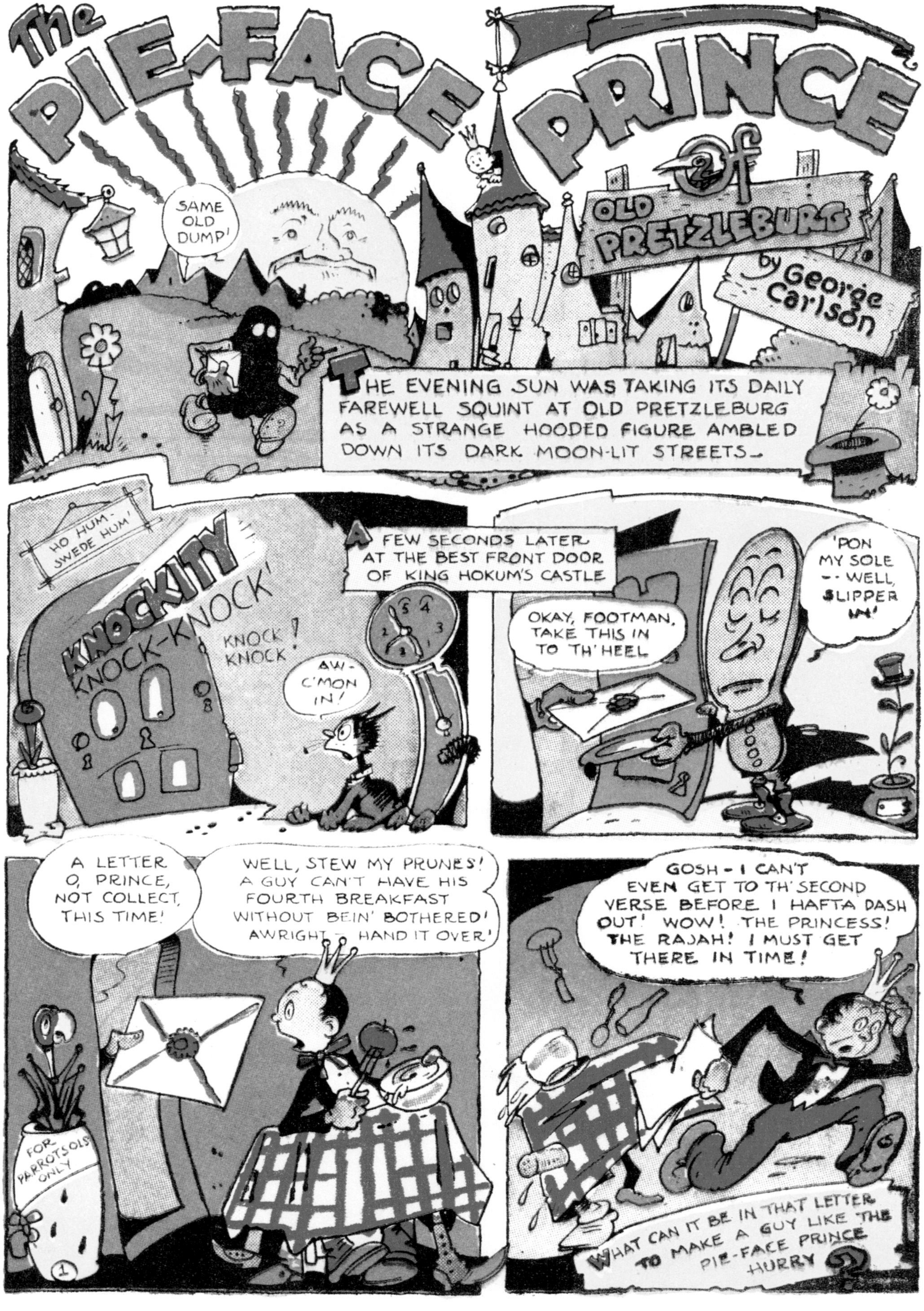
The PIE-FACE PRINCE of OLD PRETZLEBURG
by George Carlson
SAME OLD DUMP!
THE EVENING SUN WAS TAKING ITS DAILY FAREWELL SQUINT AT OLD PRETZLEBURG AS A STRANGE HOODED FIGURE AMBLED DOWN ITS DARK MOON-LIT STREETS_
HO HUM-SWEDE HUM!
A FEW SECONDS LATER AT THE BEST FRONT DOOR OF KING HOKUM'S CASTLE
KNOCKITY KNOCK-KNOCK-KNOCK!
KNOCK! KNOCK
AW-C'MON IN!
OKAY, FOOTMAN, TAKE THIS IN TO TH' HEEL
'PON MY SOLE -- WELL, SLIPPER IN!
A LETTER O, PRINCE, NOT COLLECT, THIS TIME!
WELL, STEW MY PRUNES! A GUY CAN'T HAVE HIS FOURTH BREAKFAST WITHOUT BEIN' BOTHERED! AWRIGHT - HAND IT OVER!
FOR PARROTSOLS ONLY
GOSH - I CAN'T EVEN GET TO TH' SECOND VERSE BEFORE I HAFTA DASH OUT! WOW! THE PRINCESS! THE RAJAH! I MUST GET THERE IN TIME!
WHAT CAN IT BE IN THAT LETTER TO MAKE A GUY LIKE THE PIE-FACE PRINCE HURRY?

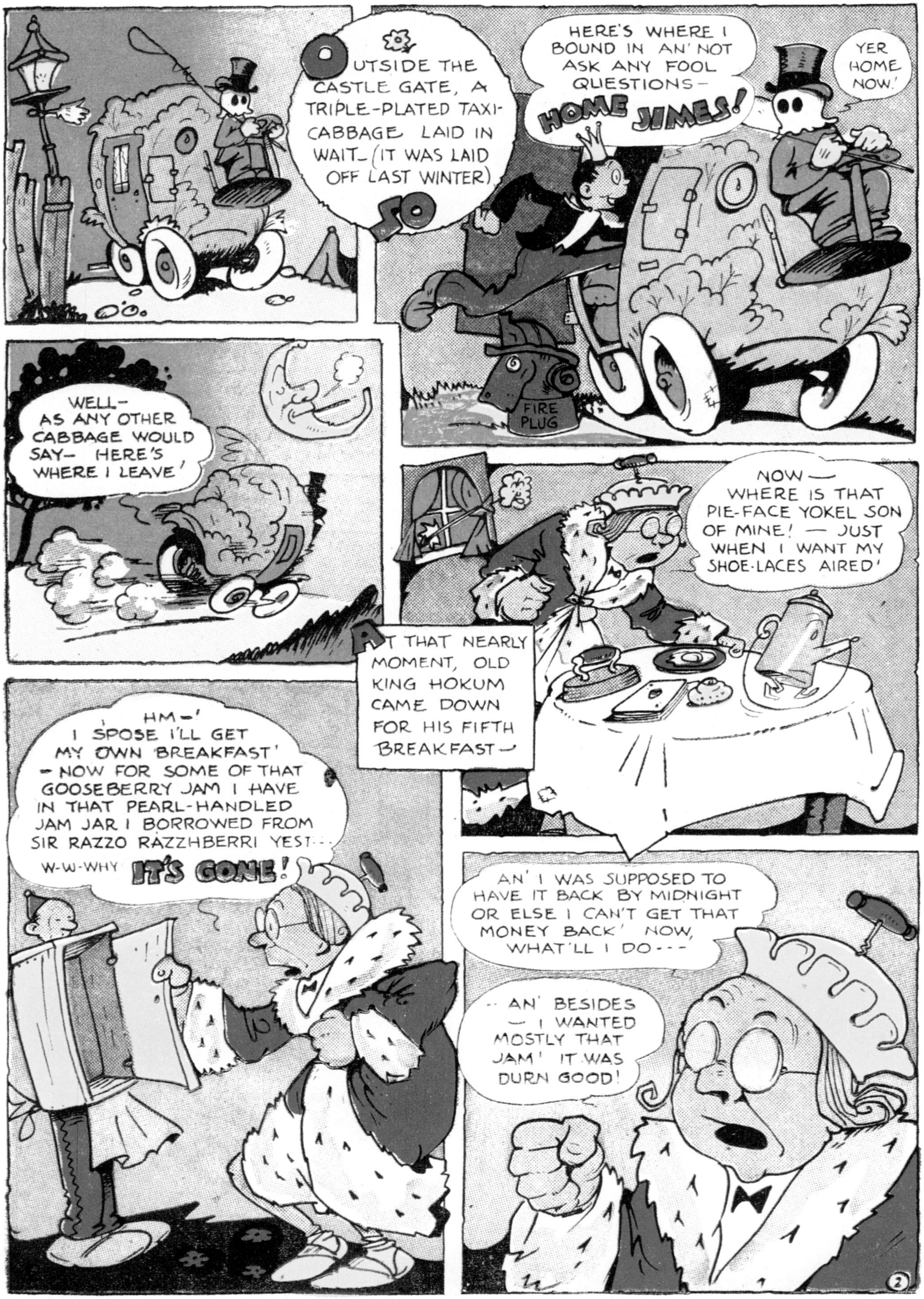
OUTSIDE THE CASTLE GATE, A TRIPLE-PLATED TAXI-CABBAGE LAID IN WAIT_ (IT WAS LAID OFF LAST WINTER) SO
HERE'S WHERE I BOUND IN AN' NOT ASK ANY FOOL QUESTIONS-
HOME JIMES!
YER HOME NOW!
FIRE PLUG
WELL- AS ANY OTHER CABBAGE WOULD SAY- HERE'S WHERE I LEAVE!
NOW — WHERE IS THAT PIE-FACE YOKEL SON OF MINE! — JUST WHEN I WANT MY SHOE-LACES AIRED!
AT THAT NEARLY MOMENT, OLD KING HOKUM CAME DOWN FOR HIS FIFTH BREAKFAST —
HM-! I SPOSE I'LL GET MY OWN BREAKFAST! - NOW FOR SOME OF THAT GOOSEBERRY JAM I HAVE IN THAT PEARL-HANDLED JAM JAR I BORROWED FROM SIR RAZZO RAZZHBERRI YEST--
W-W-WHY IT'S GONE!
AN' I WAS SUPPOSED TO HAVE IT BACK BY MIDNIGHT OR ELSE I CAN'T GET THAT MONEY BACK! NOW, WHAT'LL I DO---
-- AN' BESIDES — I WANTED MOSTLY THAT JAM! IT WAS DURN GOOD!
2

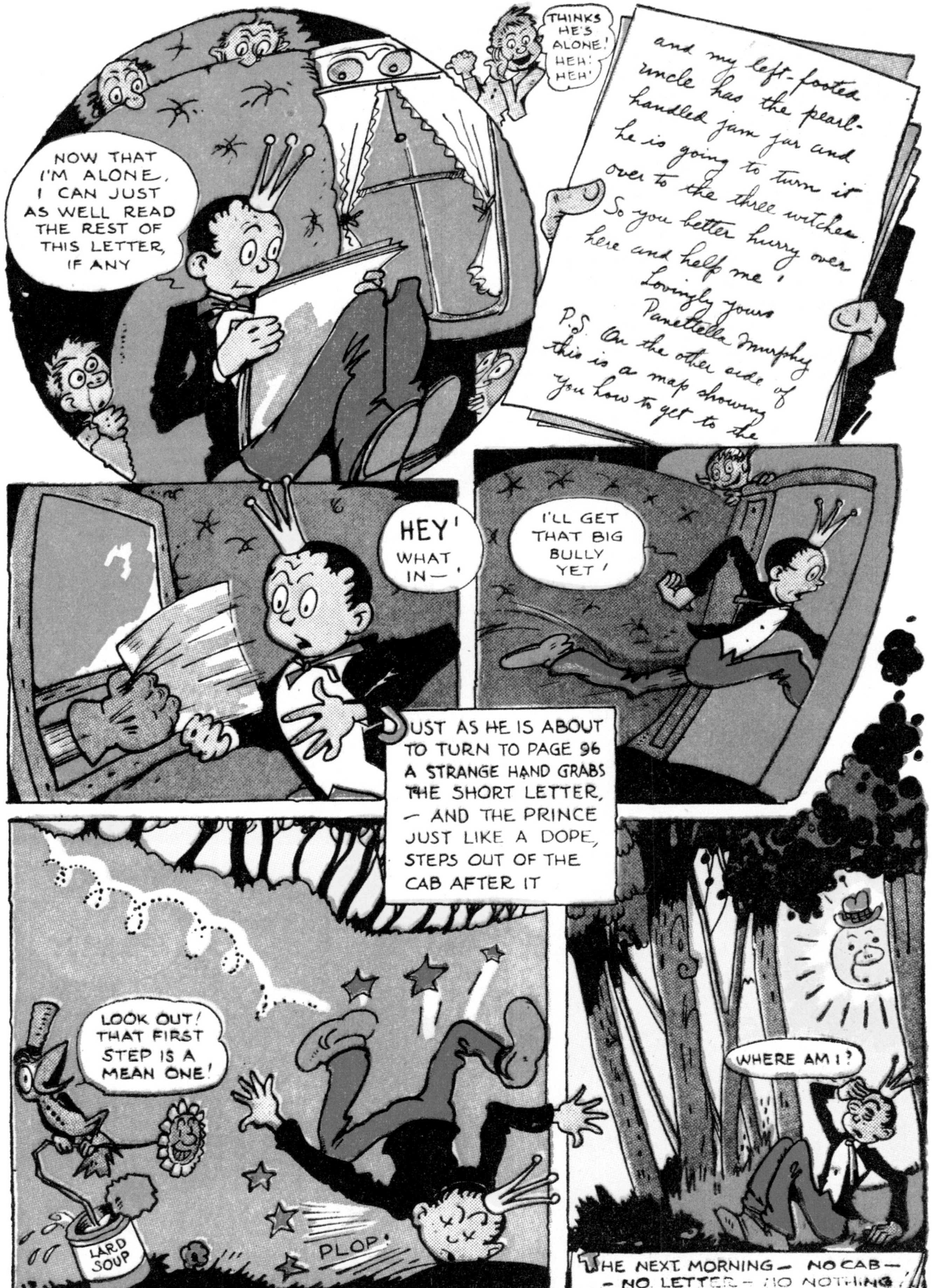
THINKS HE'S ALONE! HEH! HEH!
NOW THAT I'M ALONE, I CAN JUST AS WELL READ THE REST OF THIS LETTER, IF ANY
and my left-footed uncle has the pearl-handled jam jar and he is going to turn it over to the three witches. So you better hurry over here and help me!
Lovingly yours
Panettella Murphy
P.S. On the other side of this is a map showing you how to get to the
HEY! WHAT IN—!
I'LL GET THAT BIG BULLY YET!
JUST AS HE IS ABOUT TO TURN TO PAGE 96 A STRANGE HAND GRABS THE SHORT LETTER, — AND THE PRINCE JUST LIKE A DOPE, STEPS OUT OF THE CAB AFTER IT
LOOK OUT! THAT FIRST STEP IS A MEAN ONE!
LARD SOUP
PLOP!
WHERE AM I?
THE NEXT MORNING— NO CAB— —NO LETTER— NO NOTHING!

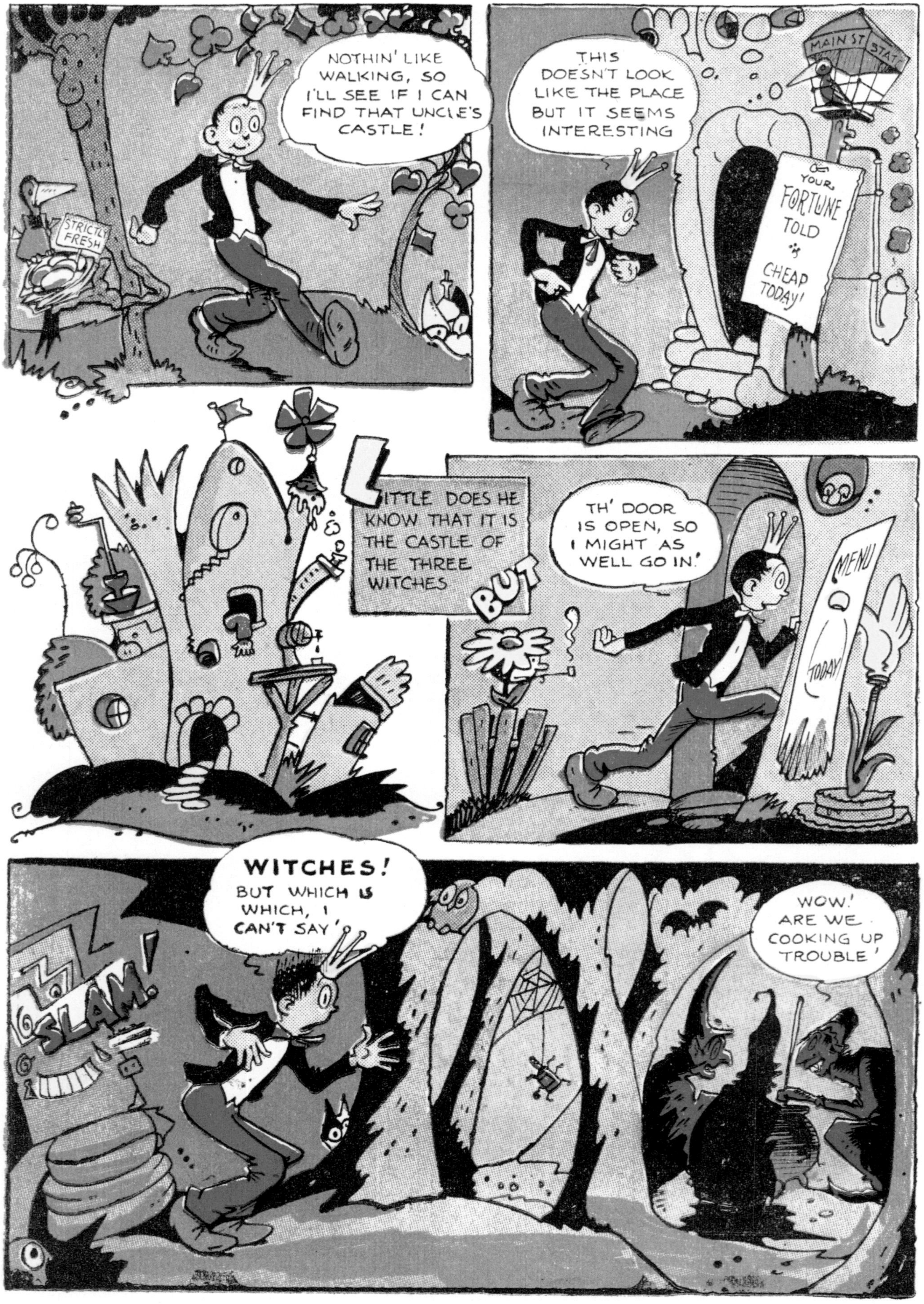
NOTHIN' LIKE WALKING, SO I'LL SEE IF I CAN FIND THAT UNCLE'S CASTLE!
STRICTLY FRESH
THIS DOESN'T LOOK LIKE THE PLACE BUT IT SEEMS INTERESTING
MAIN ST STAT
YOUR FORTUNE TOLD CHEAP TODAY!
LITTLE DOES HE KNOW THAT IT IS THE CASTLE OF THE THREE WITCHES
BUT
TH' DOOR IS OPEN, SO I MIGHT AS WELL GO IN!
MENU
TODAY!
WITCHES! BUT WHICH IS WHICH, I CAN'T SAY!
SLAM!
WOW! ARE WE COOKING UP TROUBLE!

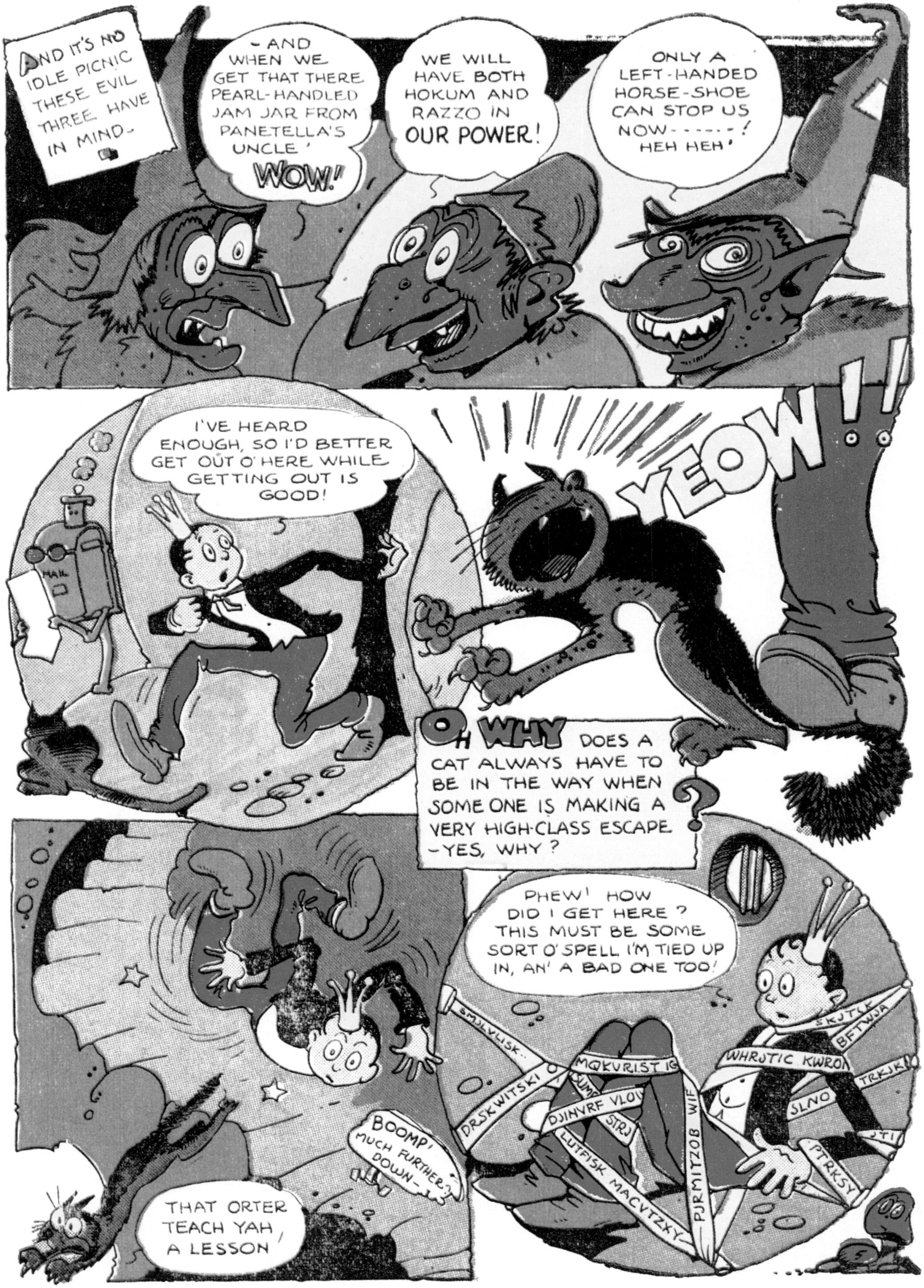
AND IT'S NO IDLE PICNIC THESE EVIL THREE HAVE IN MIND-
-AND WHEN WE GET THAT THERE PEARL-HANDLED JAM JAR FROM PANETELLA'S UNCLE! WOW!
WE WILL HAVE BOTH HOKUM AND RAZZO IN OUR POWER!
ONLY A LEFT-HANDED HORSE-SHOE CAN STOP US NOW------! HEH HEH!
I'VE HEARD ENOUGH, SO I'D BETTER GET OUT O' HERE WHILE GETTING OUT IS GOOD!
MAIL
YEOW!!!
OH WHY DOES A CAT ALWAYS HAVE TO BE IN THE WAY WHEN SOME ONE IS MAKING A VERY HIGH-CLASS ESCAPE -YES, WHY?
BOOMP! MUCH FURTHER DOWN-
THAT ORTER TEACH YAH A LESSON!
PHEW! HOW DID I GET HERE? THIS MUST BE SOME SORT O' SPELL I'M TIED UP IN, AN' A BAD ONE TOO!

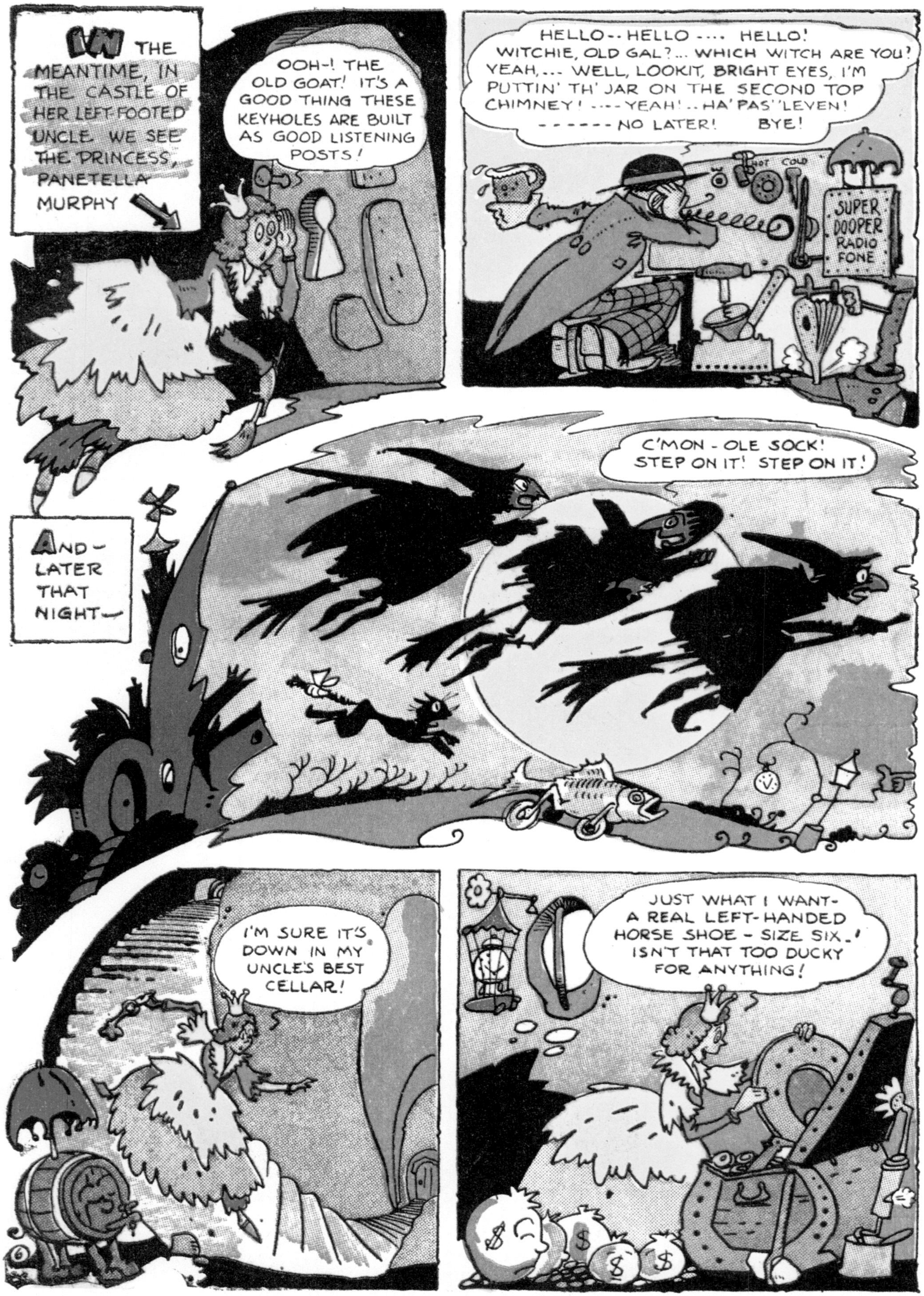
IN THE MEANTIME, IN THE CASTLE OF HER LEFT-FOOTED UNCLE WE SEE THE PRINCESS, PANETELLA MURPHY
OOH-! THE OLD GOAT! IT'S A GOOD THING THESE KEYHOLES ARE BUILT AS GOOD LISTENING POSTS!
HELLO-- HELLO ---- HELLO! WITCHIE, OLD GAL?... WHICH WITCH ARE YOU? YEAH,--- WELL, LOOKIT, BRIGHT EYES, I'M PUTTIN' TH' JAR ON THE SECOND TOP CHIMNEY! ----YEAH!--HA'PAS''LEVEN! ------ NO LATER! BYE!
HOT COLD
SUPER DOOPER RADIO FONE
AND-LATER THAT NIGHT—
C'MON - OLE SOCK! STEP ON IT! STEP ON IT!
I'M SURE IT'S DOWN IN MY UNCLE'S BEST CELLAR!
JUST WHAT I WANT- A REAL LEFT-HANDED HORSE SHOE - SIZE SIX! ISN'T THAT TOO DUCKY FOR ANYTHING!

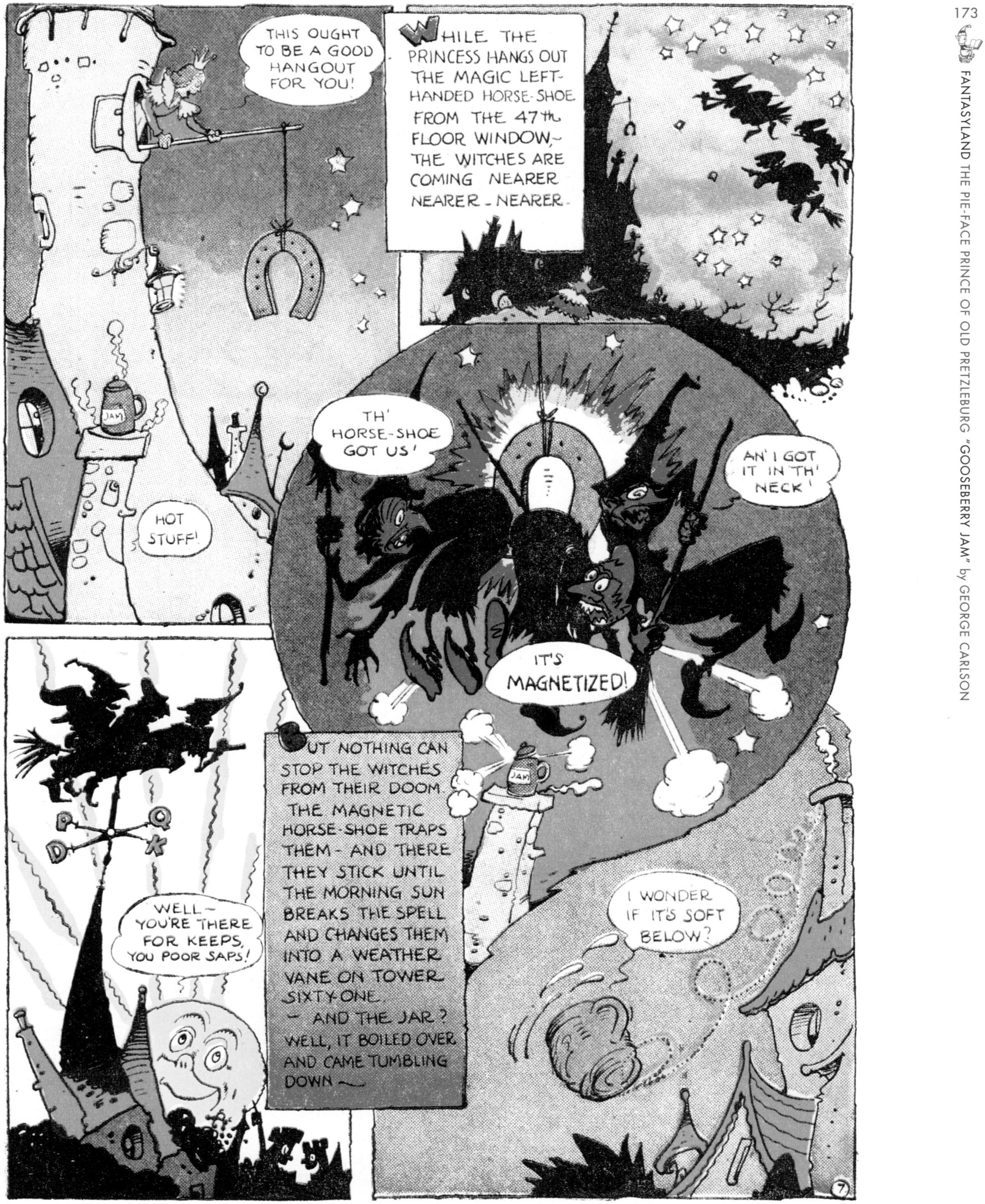
THIS OUGHT TO BE A GOOD HANGOUT FOR YOU!
WHILE THE PRINCESS HANGS OUT THE MAGIC LEFT-HANDED HORSE-SHOE FROM THE 47th FLOOR WINDOW,– THE WITCHES ARE COMING NEARER NEARER – NEARER –
JAM
HOT STUFF!
TH' HORSE-SHOE GOT US!
AN' I GOT IT IN TH' NECK!
IT'S MAGNETIZED!
BUT NOTHING CAN STOP THE WITCHES FROM THEIR DOOM. THE MAGNETIC HORSE-SHOE TRAPS THEM – AND THERE THEY STICK UNTIL THE MORNING SUN BREAKS THE SPELL AND CHANGES THEM INTO A WEATHER VANE ON TOWER SIXTY-ONE. – AND THE JAR? WELL, IT BOILED OVER AND CAME TUMBLING DOWN –
WELL – YOU'RE THERE FOR KEEPS, YOU POOR SAPS!
I WONDER IF IT'S SOFT BELOW?
7

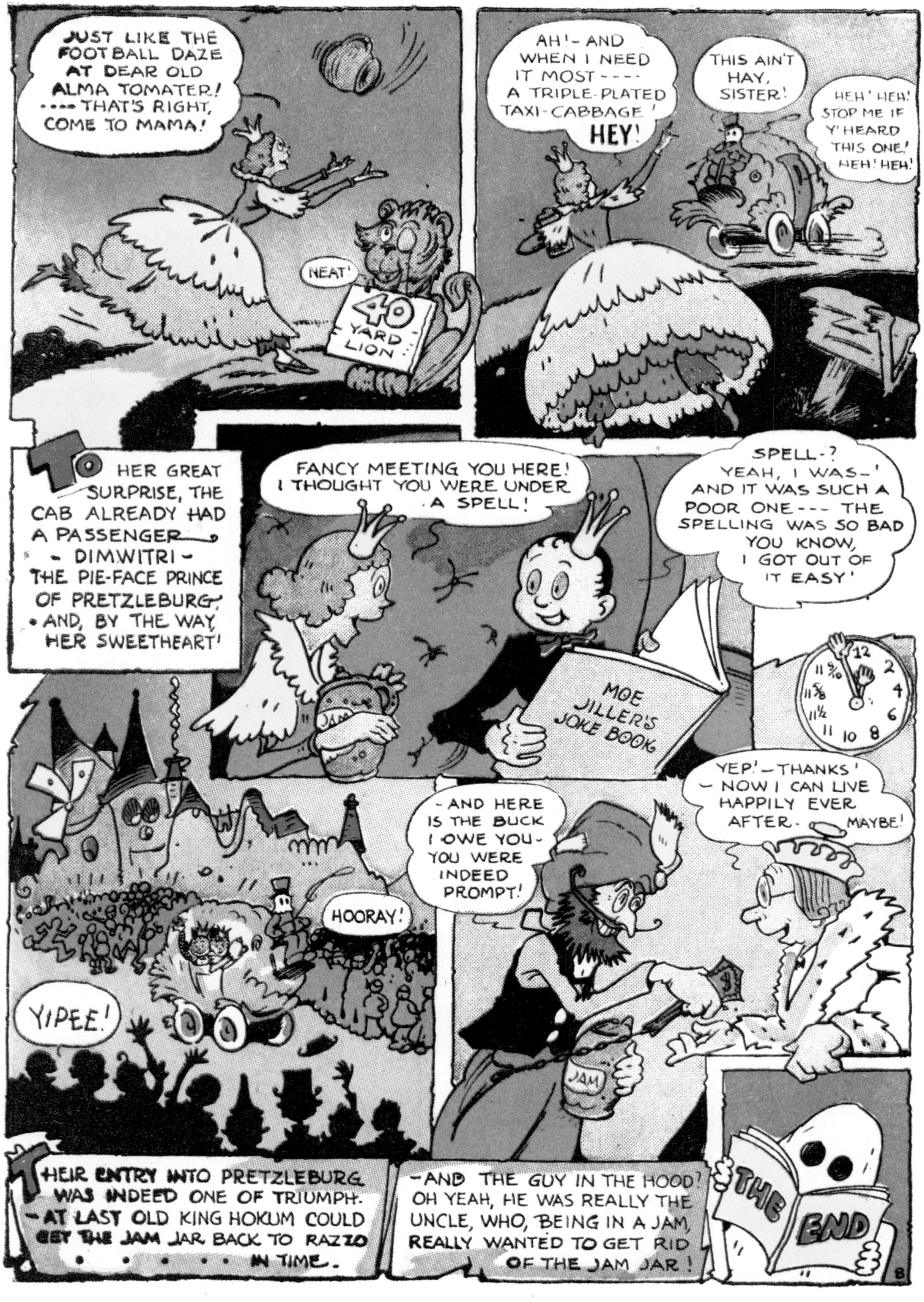
JUST LIKE THE FOOTBALL DAZE AT DEAR OLD ALMA TOMATER! ---- THAT'S RIGHT, COME TO MAMA!
NEAT!
40 YARD LION
AH!- AND WHEN I NEED IT MOST ---- A TRIPLE-PLATED TAXI-CABBAGE!
HEY!
THIS AIN'T HAY, SISTER!
HEH! HEH! STOP ME IF Y' HEARD THIS ONE! HEH! HEH!
TO HER GREAT SURPRISE, THE CAB ALREADY HAD A PASSENGER - DIMWITRI - THE PIE-FACE PRINCE OF PRETZLEBURG - AND, BY THE WAY, HER SWEETHEART!
FANCY MEETING YOU HERE! I THOUGHT YOU WERE UNDER A SPELL!
SPELL-? YEAH, I WAS-' AND IT WAS SUCH A POOR ONE--- THE SPELLING WAS SO BAD YOU KNOW, I GOT OUT OF IT EASY!
JAM
MOE JILLER'S JOKE BOOK
HOORAY!
YIPEE!
- AND HERE IS THE BUCK I OWE YOU - YOU WERE INDEED PROMPT!
YEP! - THANKS! - NOW I CAN LIVE HAPPILY EVER AFTER - MAYBE!
JAM
THEIR ENTRY INTO PRETZLEBURG WAS INDEED ONE OF TRIUMPH. - AT LAST OLD KING HOKUM COULD GET THE JAM JAR BACK TO RAZZO . . . . . . IN TIME.
- AND THE GUY IN THE HOOD? OH YEAH, HE WAS REALLY THE UNCLE, WHO, BEING IN A JAM, REALLY WANTED TO GET RID OF THE JAM JAR!
THE END
8

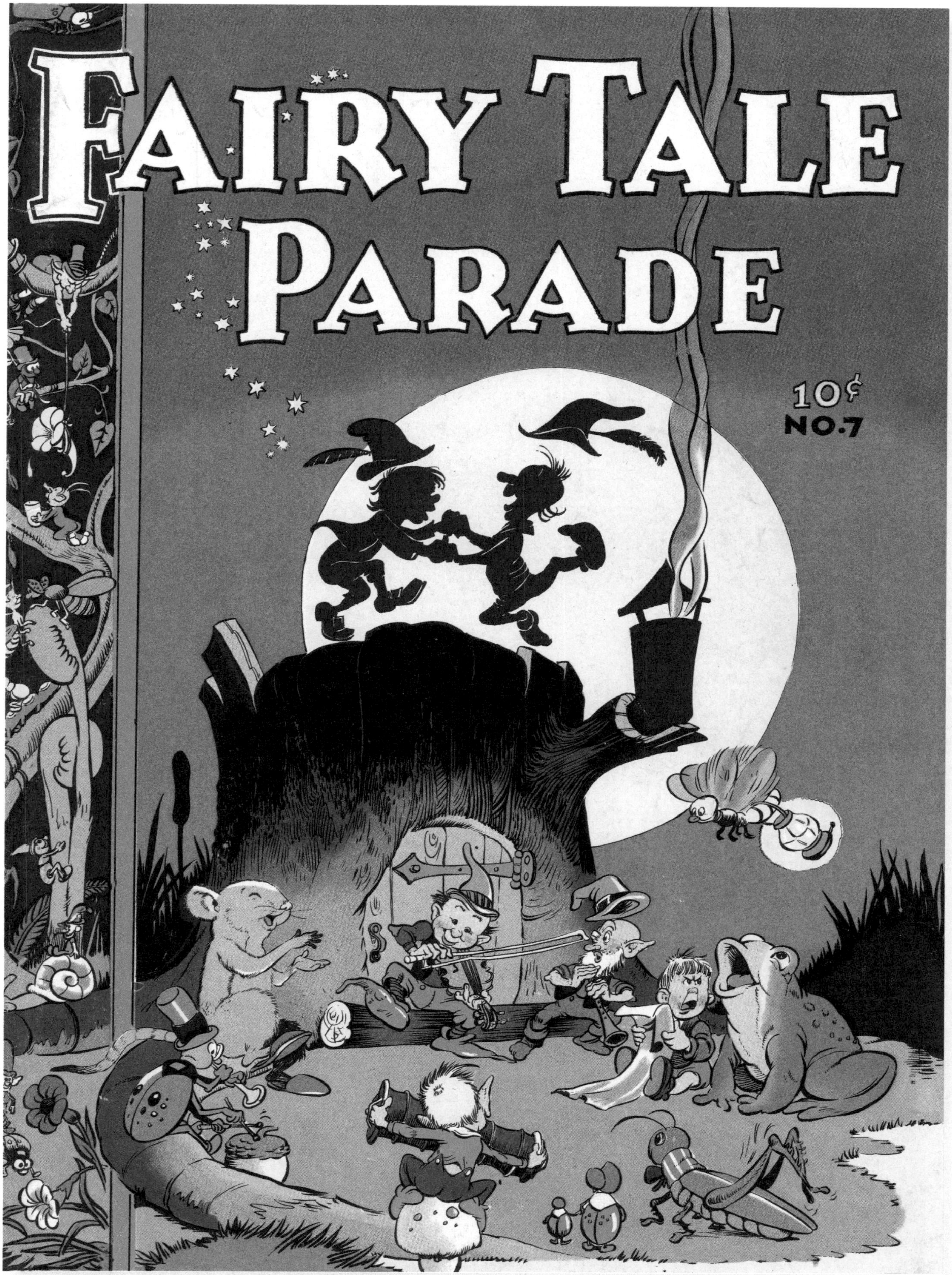
FAIRY TALE PARADE
10¢
NO. 7

FANTASYLAND FAIRY TALE PARADE COVER by WALT KELLY

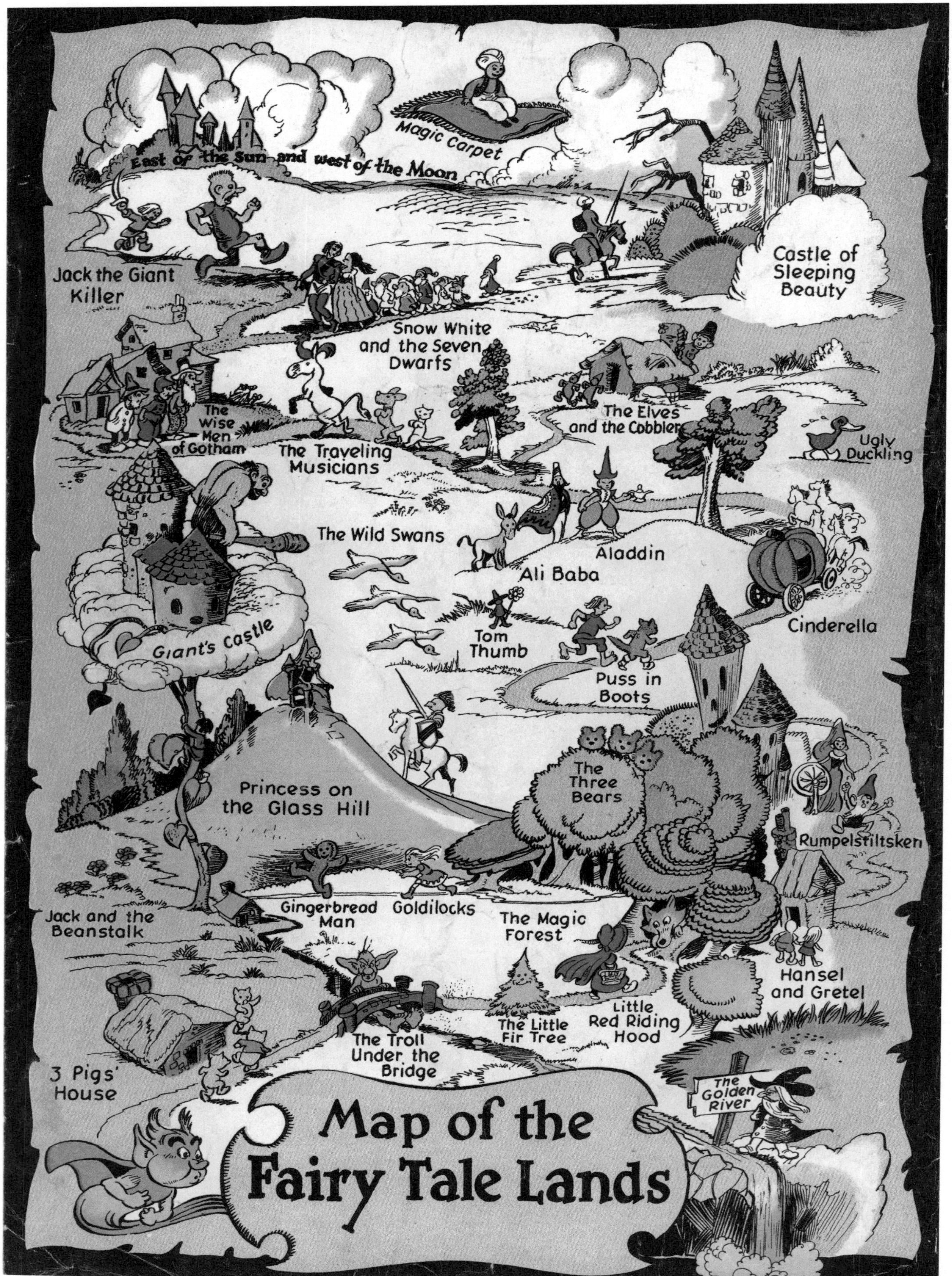
Magic Carpet
East of the Sun and west of the Moon
Jack the Giant Killer
Castle of Sleeping Beauty
Snow White and the Seven Dwarfs
The Wise Men of Gotham
The Traveling Musicians
The Elves and the Cobbler
Ugly Duckling
The Wild Swans
Aladdin
Ali Baba
Cinderella
Giant's Castle
Tom Thumb
Puss in Boots
The Three Bears
Princess on the Glass Hill
Rumpelstiltskin
Jack and the Beanstalk
Gingerbread Man
Goldilocks
The Magic Forest
Hansel and Gretel
The Little Fir Tree
Little Red Riding Hood
The Troll Under the Bridge
3 Pigs' House
The Golden River
Map of the Fairy Tale Lands

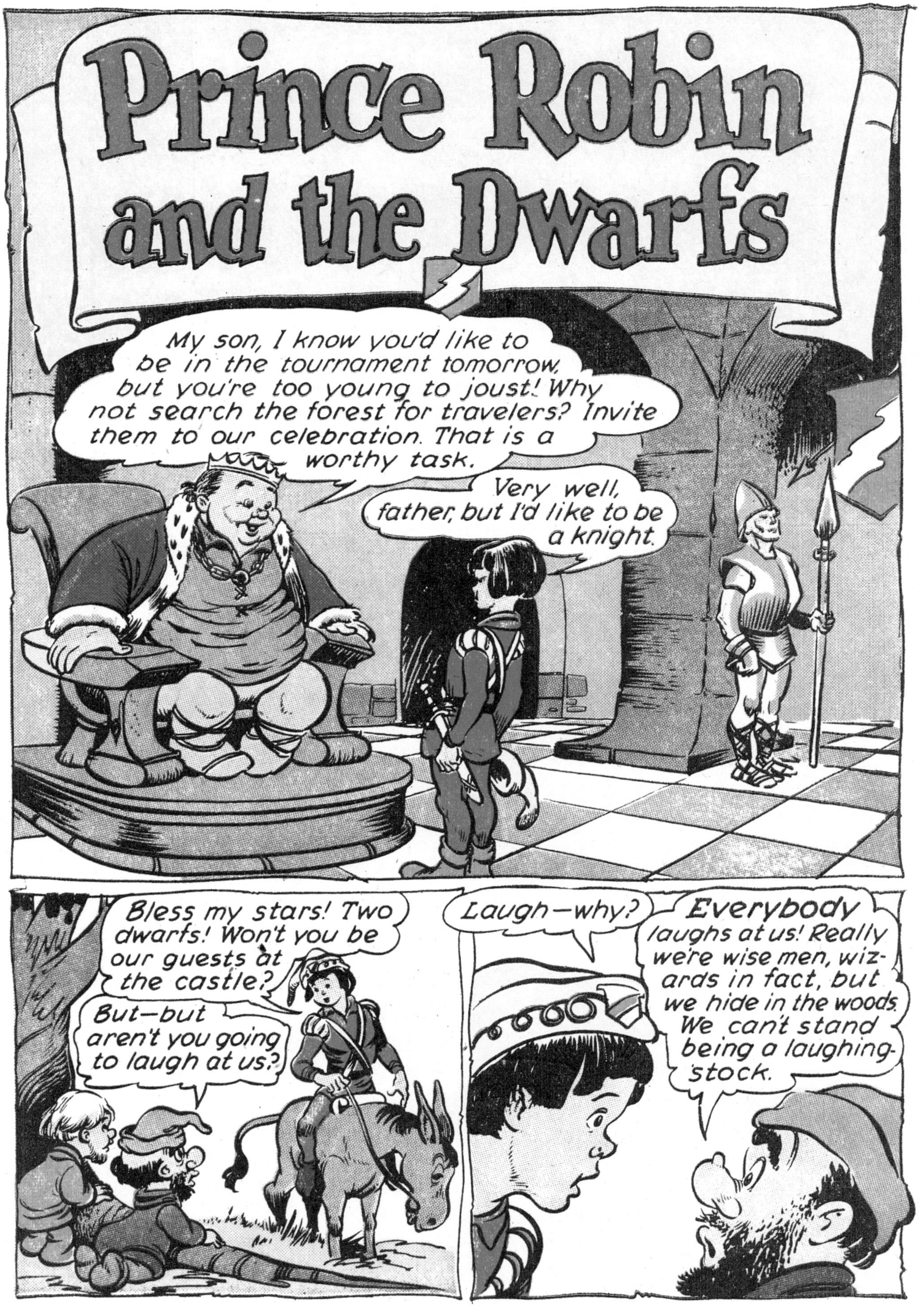
Prince Robin and the Dwarfs
My son, I know you'd like to be in the tournament tomorrow, but you're too young to joust! Why not search the forest for travelers? Invite them to our celebration. That is a worthy task.
Very well, father, but I'd like to be a knight.
Bless my stars! Two dwarfs! Won't you be our guests at the castle?
But—but aren't you going to laugh at us?
Laugh—why?
Everybody laughs at us! Really we're wise men, wizards in fact, but we hide in the woods. We can't stand being a laughing-stock.

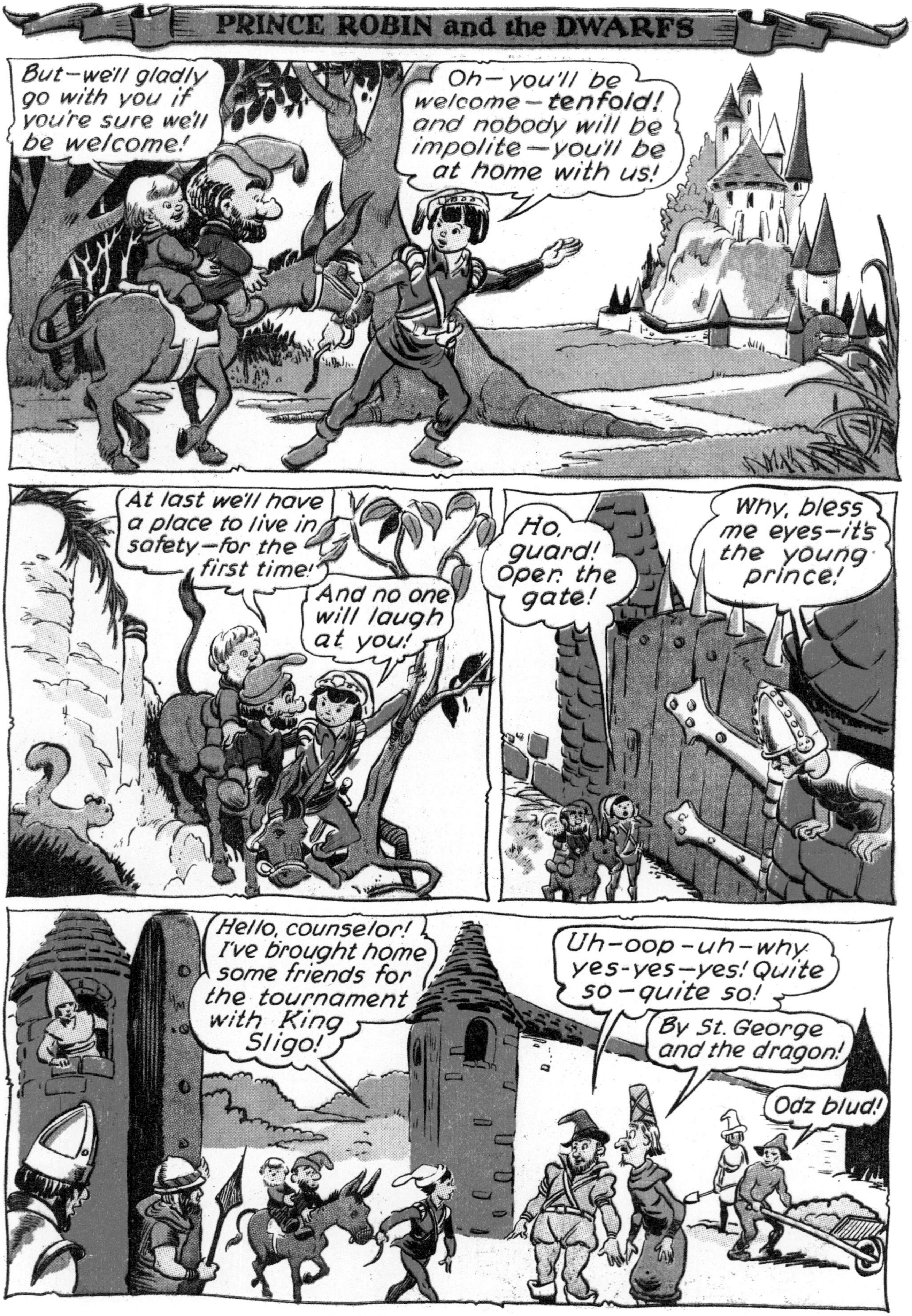
PRINCE ROBIN and the DWARFS
But—we'll gladly go with you if you're sure we'll be welcome!
Oh—you'll be welcome—tenfold! and nobody will be impolite—you'll be at home with us!
At last we'll have a place to live in safety—for the first time!
And no one will laugh at you!
Ho, guard! Open the gate!
Why, bless me eyes—it's the young prince!
Hello, counselor! I've brought home some friends for the tournament with King Sligo!
Uh-oop-uh-why yes-yes—yes! Quite so—quite so!
By St. George and the dragon!
Odz blud!

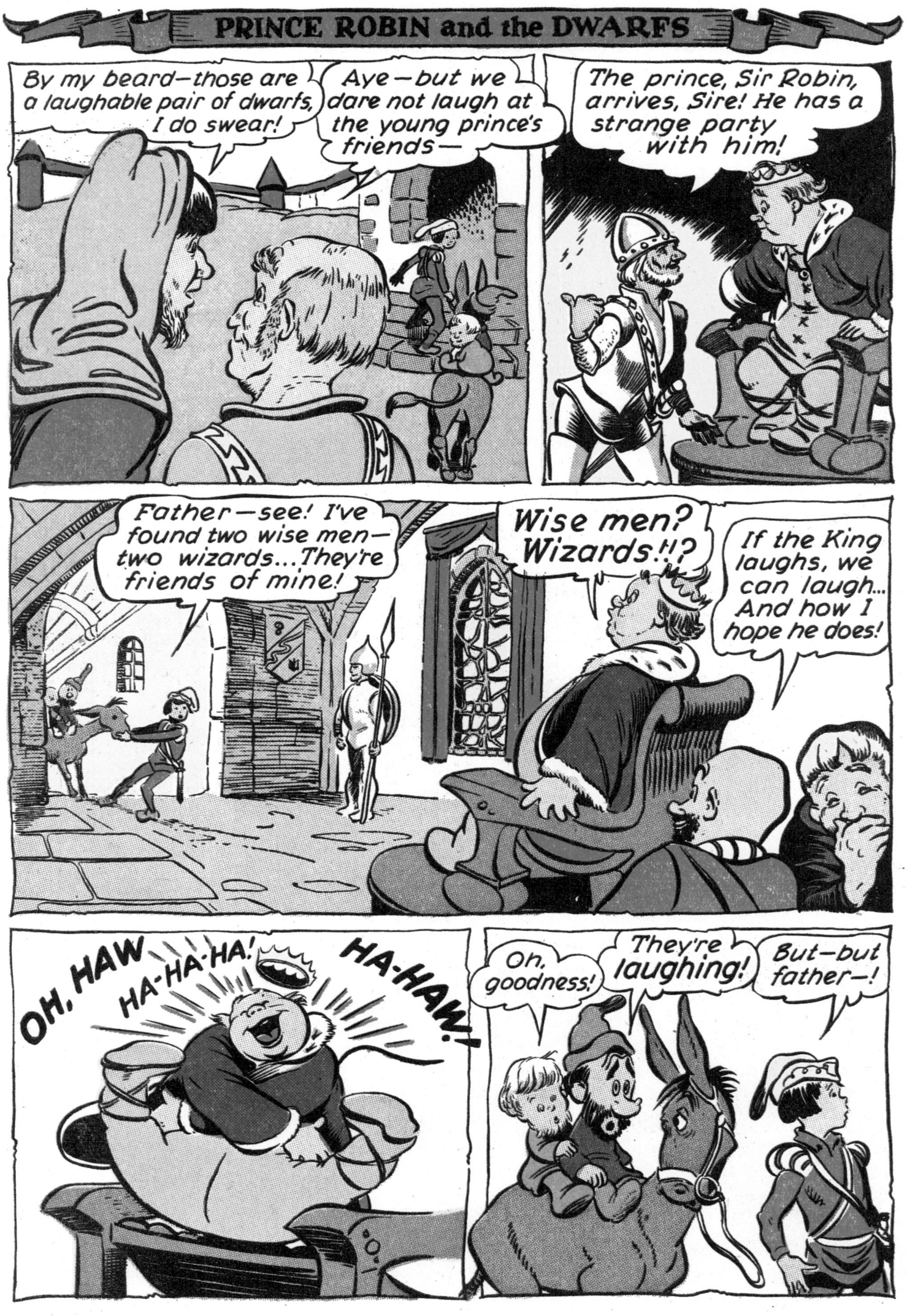
PRINCE ROBIN and the DWARFS
By my beard—those are a laughable pair of dwarfs, I do swear!
Aye—but we dare not laugh at the young prince's friends—
The prince, Sir Robin, arrives, Sire! He has a strange party with him!
Father—see! I've found two wise men—two wizards...They're friends of mine!
Wise men? Wizards!!?
If the King laughs, we can laugh... And how I hope he does!
OH, HAW
HA-HA-HA!
HA-HAW!
Oh, goodness!
They're laughing!
But—but father—!

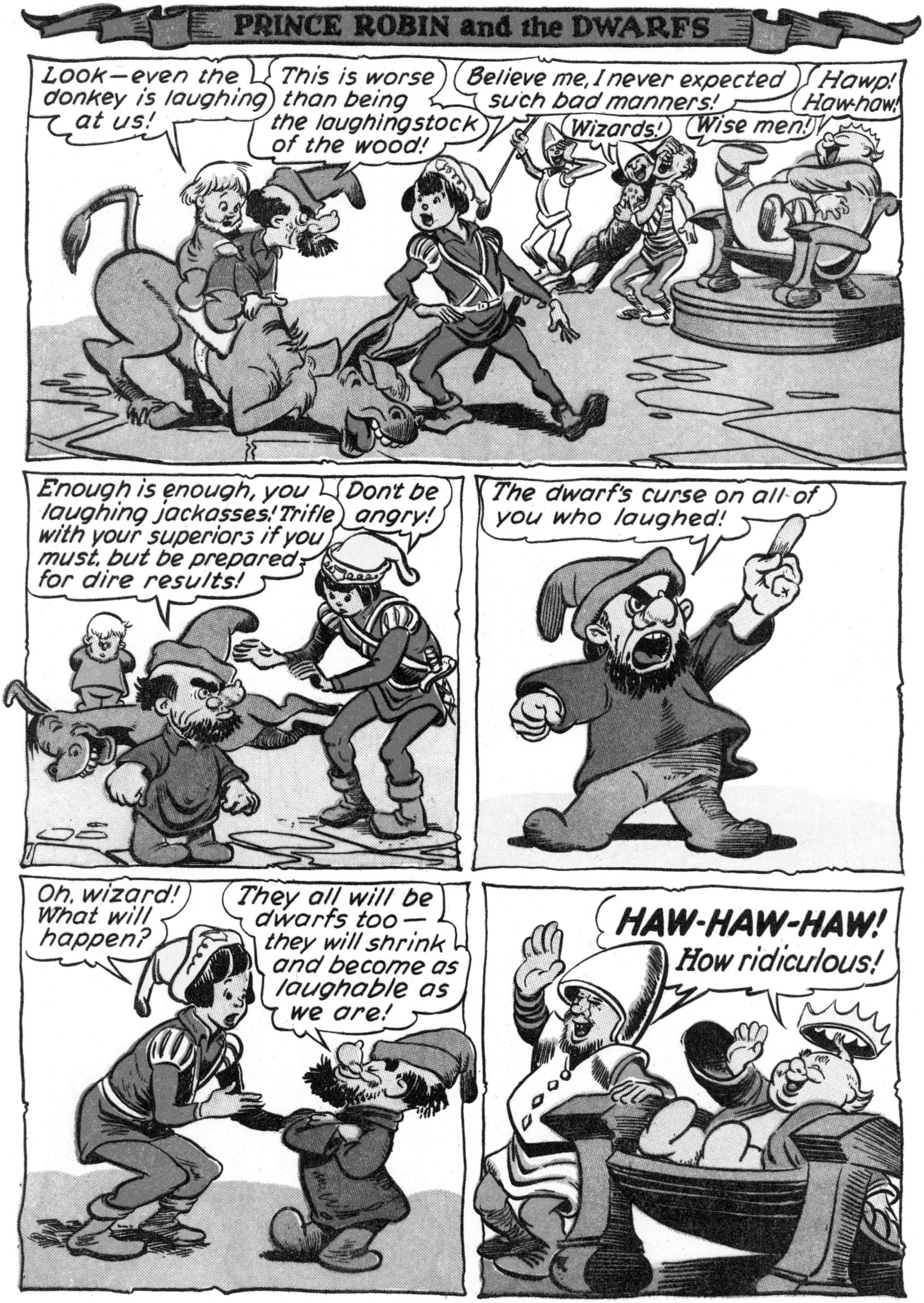
PRINCE ROBIN and the DWARFS
Look—even the donkey is laughing at us!
This is worse than being the laughingstock of the wood!
Believe me, I never expected such bad manners!
Wizards!
Wise men!
Hawp! Haw-haw!
Enough is enough, you laughing jackasses! Trifle with your superiors if you must, but be prepared for dire results!
Don't be angry!
The dwarf's curse on all of you who laughed!
Oh, wizard! What will happen?
They all will be dwarfs too—they will shrink and become as laughable as we are!
HAW-HAW-HAW! How ridiculous!

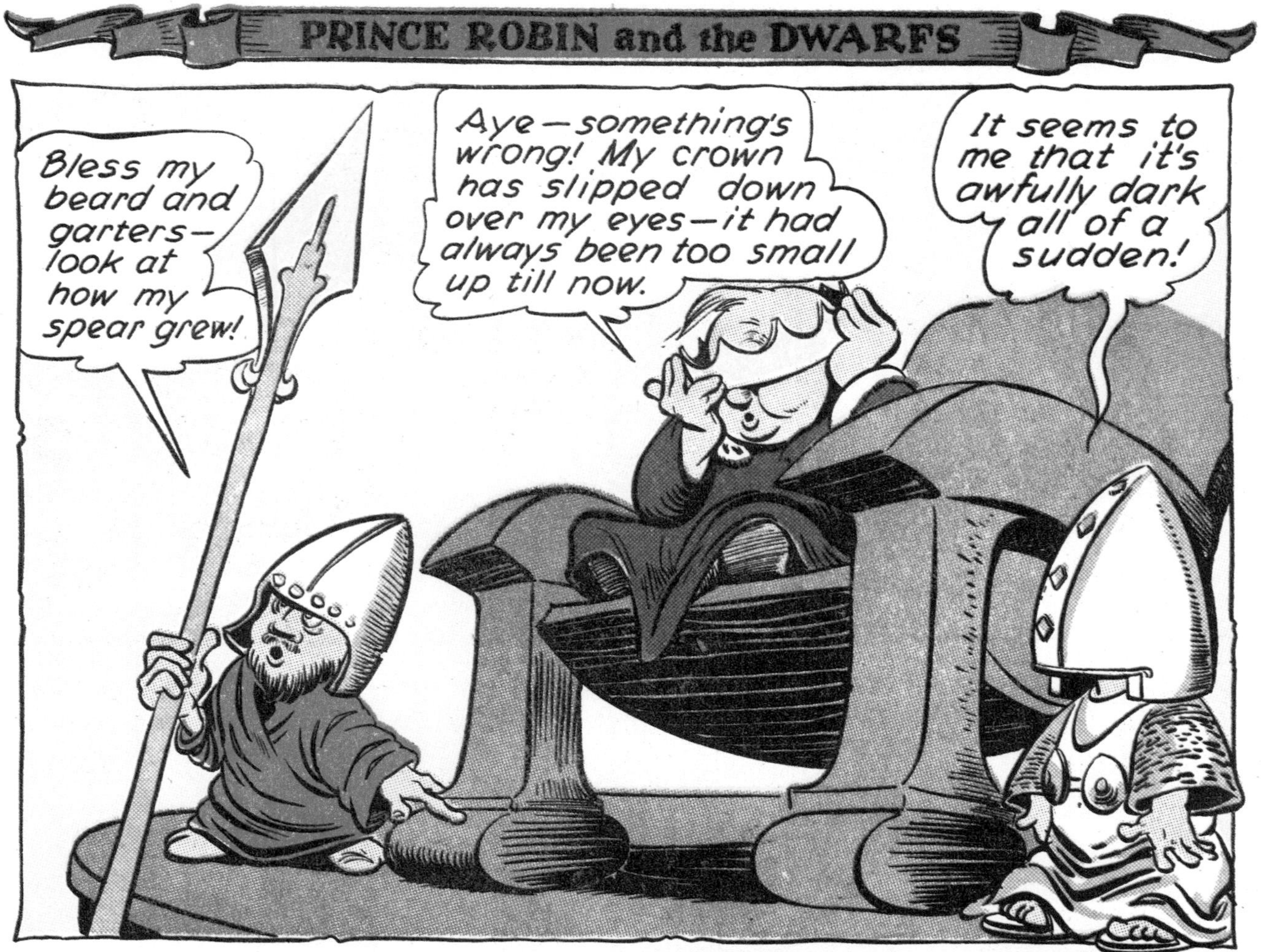
PRINCE ROBIN and the DWARFS
Bless my beard and garters—look at how my spear grew!
Aye—something's wrong! My crown has slipped down over my eyes—it had always been too small up till now.
It seems to me that it's awfully dark all of a sudden!

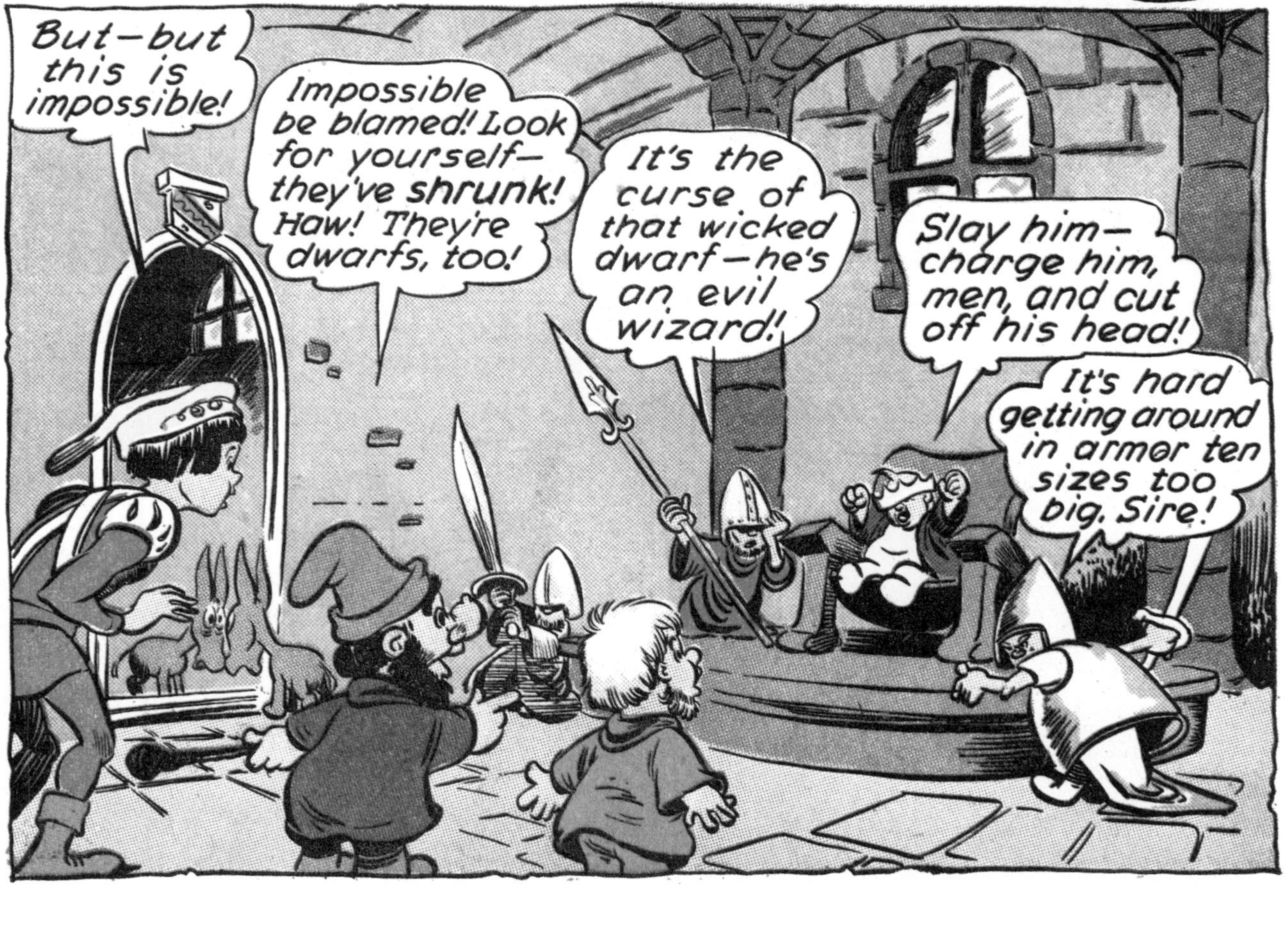
But—but this is impossible!
Impossible be blamed! Look for yourself—they've shrunk! Haw! They're dwarfs, too!
It's the curse of that wicked dwarf—he's an evil wizard!
Slay him—charge him, men, and cut off his head!
It's hard getting around in armor ten sizes too big, Sire!

PRINCE ROBIN and the DWARFS

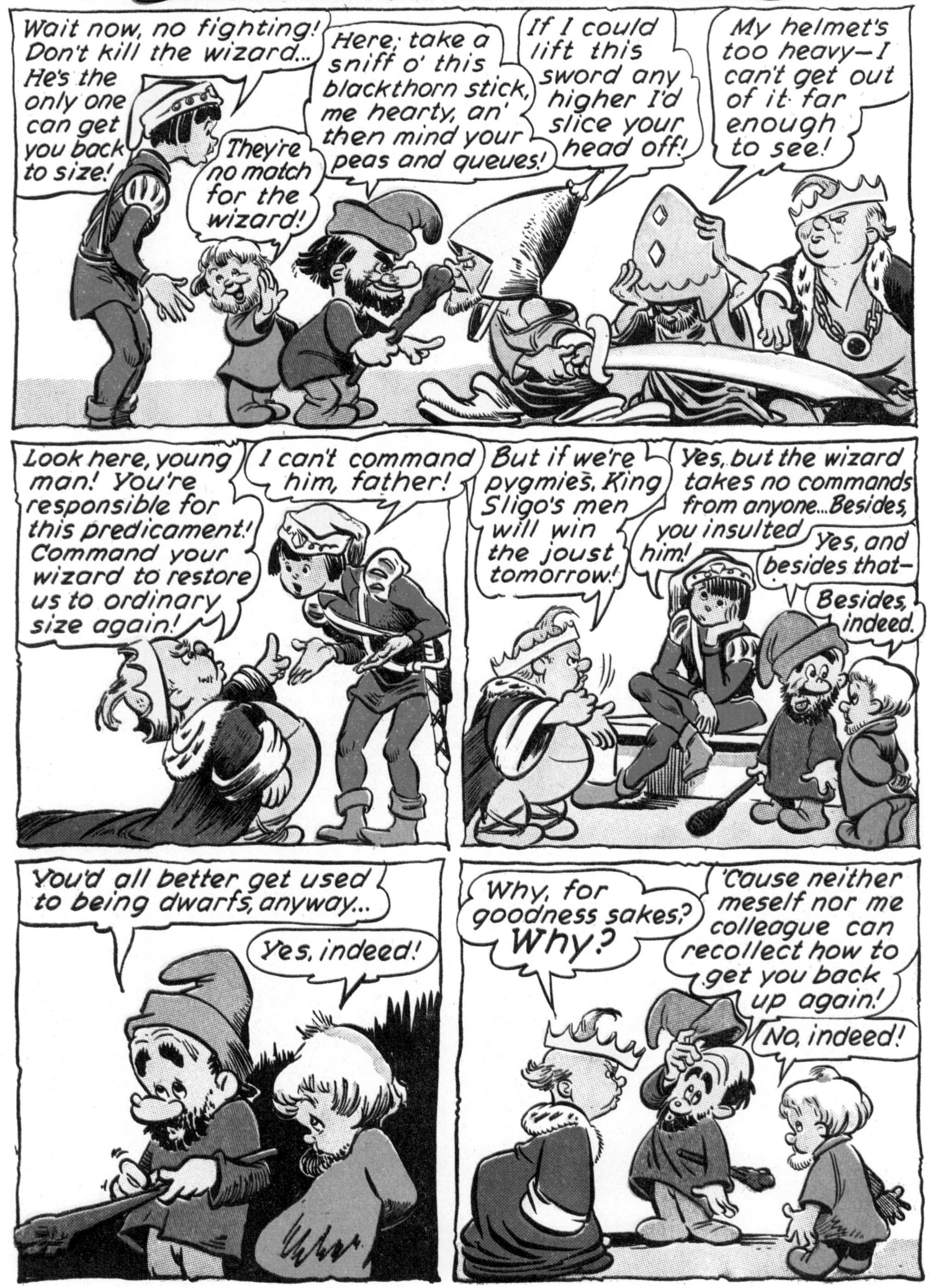
Wait now, no fighting! Don't kill the wizard... He's the only one can get you back to size!
They're no match for the wizard!
Here; take a sniff o' this blackthorn stick, me hearty, an' then mind your peas and queues!
If I could lift this sword any higher I'd slice your head off!
My helmet's too heavy—I can't get out of it far enough to see!
Look here, young man! You're responsible for this predicament! Command your wizard to restore us to ordinary size again!
I can't command him, father!
But if we're pygmies, King Sligo's men will win the joust tomorrow!
Yes, but the wizard takes no commands from anyone... Besides, you insulted him!
Yes, and besides that-
Besides, indeed.
You'd all better get used to being dwarfs, anyway...
Yes, indeed!
Why, for goodness sakes? Why?
'Cause neither meself nor me colleague can recollect how to get you back up again!
No, indeed!

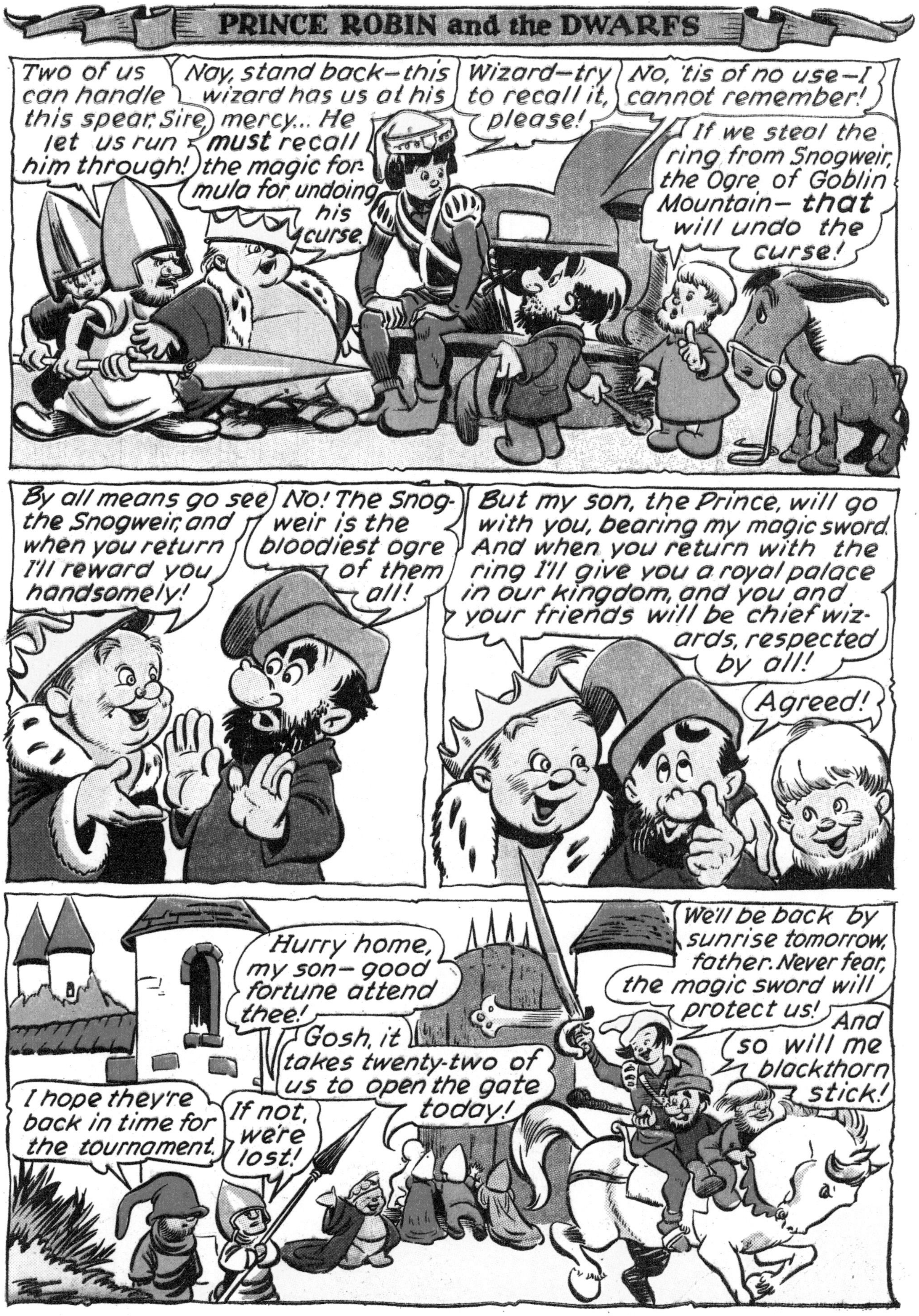
PRINCE ROBIN and the DWARFS
Two of us can handle this spear, Sire, let us run him through!
Nay, stand back—this wizard has us at his mercy... He must recall the magic formula for undoing his curse.
Wizard—try to recall it, please!
No, 'tis of no use—I cannot remember!
If we steal the ring from Snogweir, the Ogre of Goblin Mountain— that will undo the curse!
By all means go see the Snogweir, and when you return I'll reward you handsomely!
No! The Snogweir is the bloodiest ogre of them all!
But my son, the Prince, will go with you, bearing my magic sword. And when you return with the ring I'll give you a royal palace in our kingdom, and you and your friends will be chief wizards, respected by all!
Agreed!
Hurry home, my son— good fortune attend thee!
We'll be back by sunrise tomorrow, father. Never fear, the magic sword will protect us!
And so will me blackthorn stick!
Gosh, it takes twenty-two of us to open the gate today!
I hope they're back in time for the tournament.
If not, we're lost!

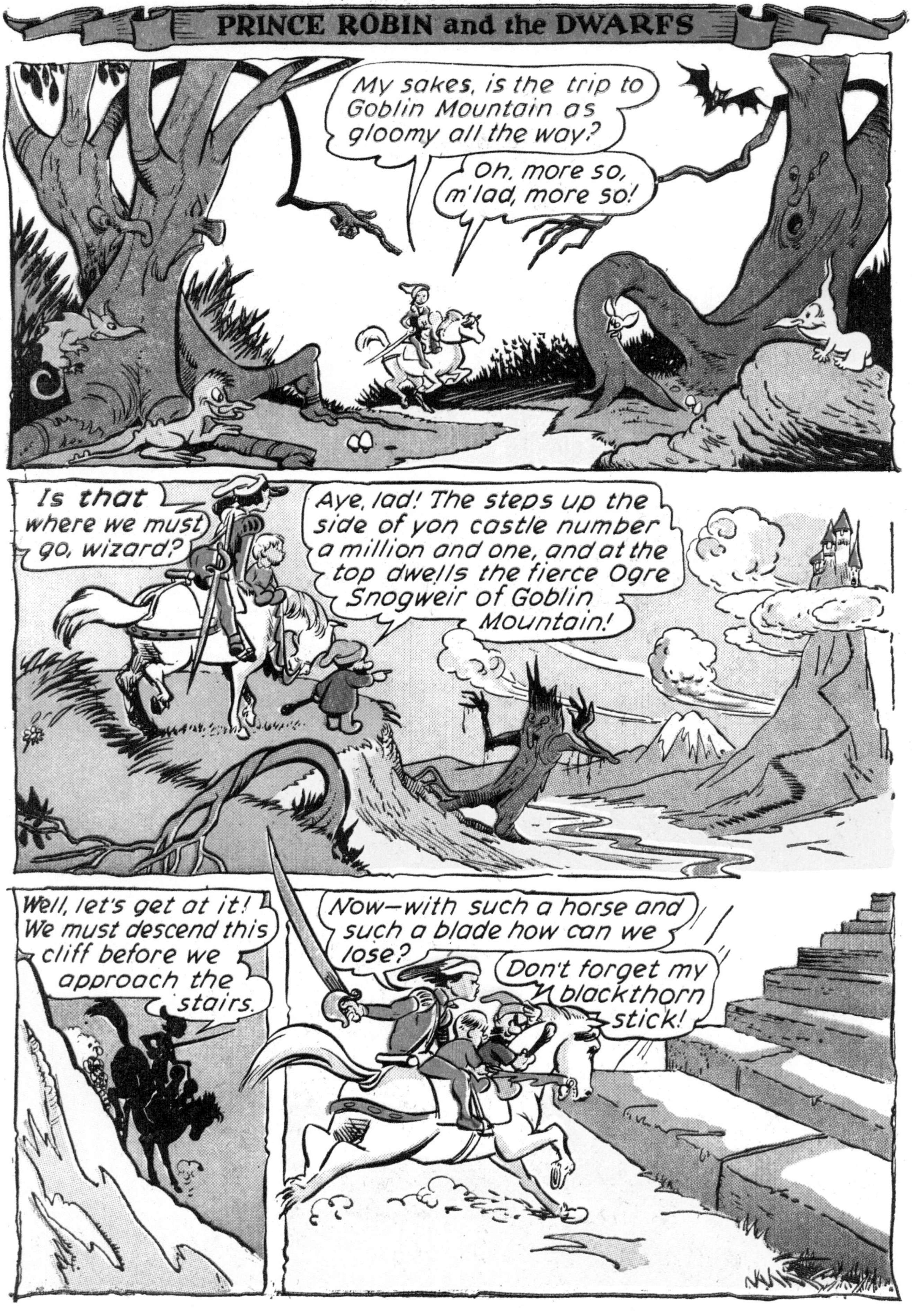
PRINCE ROBIN and the DWARFS
My sakes, is the trip to Goblin Mountain as gloomy all the way?
Oh, more so, m'lad, more so!
Is that where we must go, wizard?
Aye, lad! The steps up the side of yon castle number a million and one, and at the top dwells the fierce Ogre Snogweir of Goblin Mountain!
Well, let's get at it! We must descend this cliff before we approach the stairs.
Now—with such a horse and such a blade how can we lose?
Don't forget my blackthorn stick!

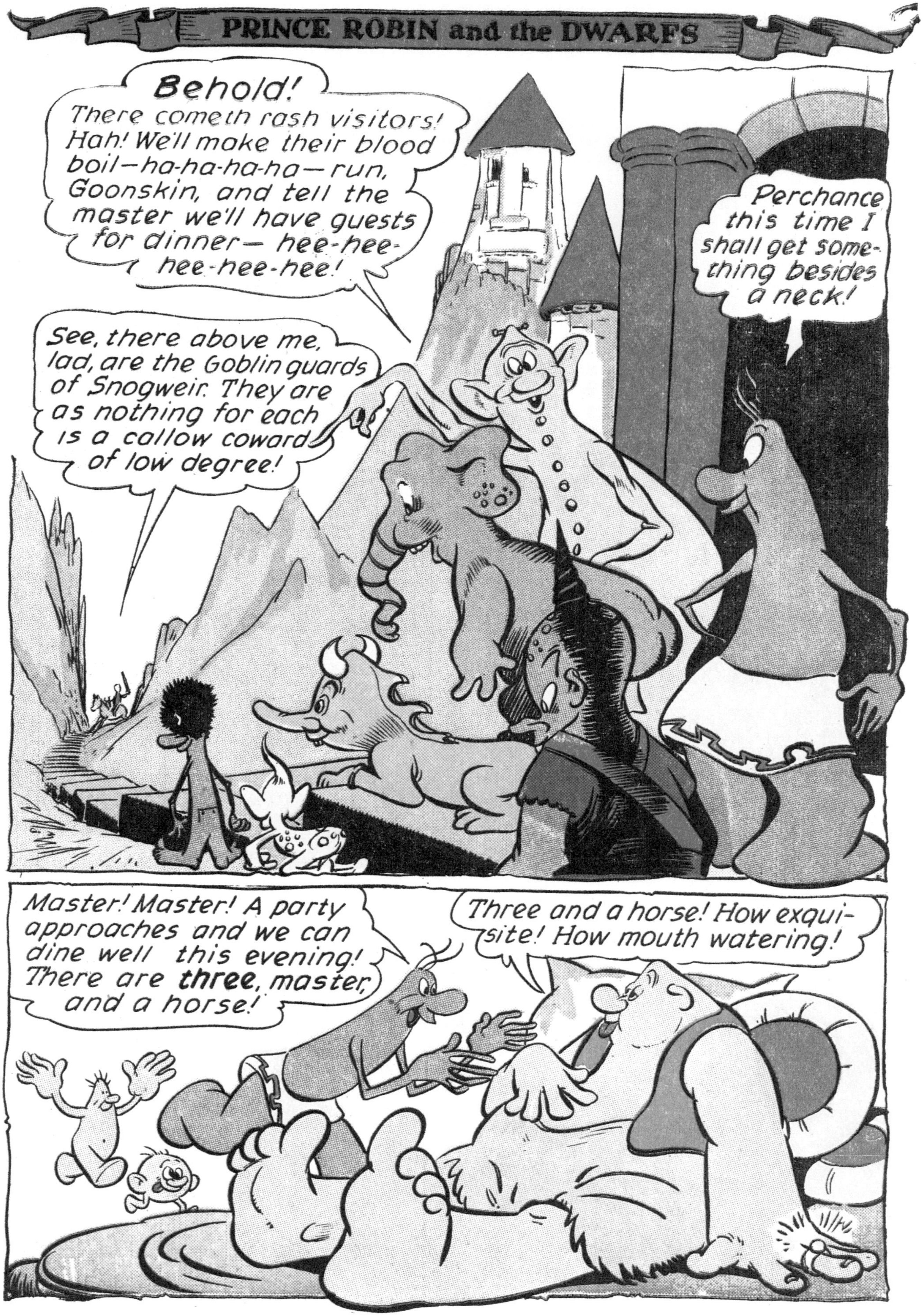
PRINCE ROBIN and the DWARFS
Behold! There cometh rash visitors! Hah! We'll make their blood boil—ha-ha-ha-ha—run, Goonskin, and tell the master we'll have guests for dinner— hee-hee-hee-hee-hee!
Perchance this time I shall get something besides a neck!
See, there above me, lad, are the Goblin guards of Snogweir. They are as nothing for each is a callow coward of low degree!
Master! Master! A party approaches and we can dine well this evening! There are three, master, and a horse!
Three and a horse! How exquisite! How mouth watering!

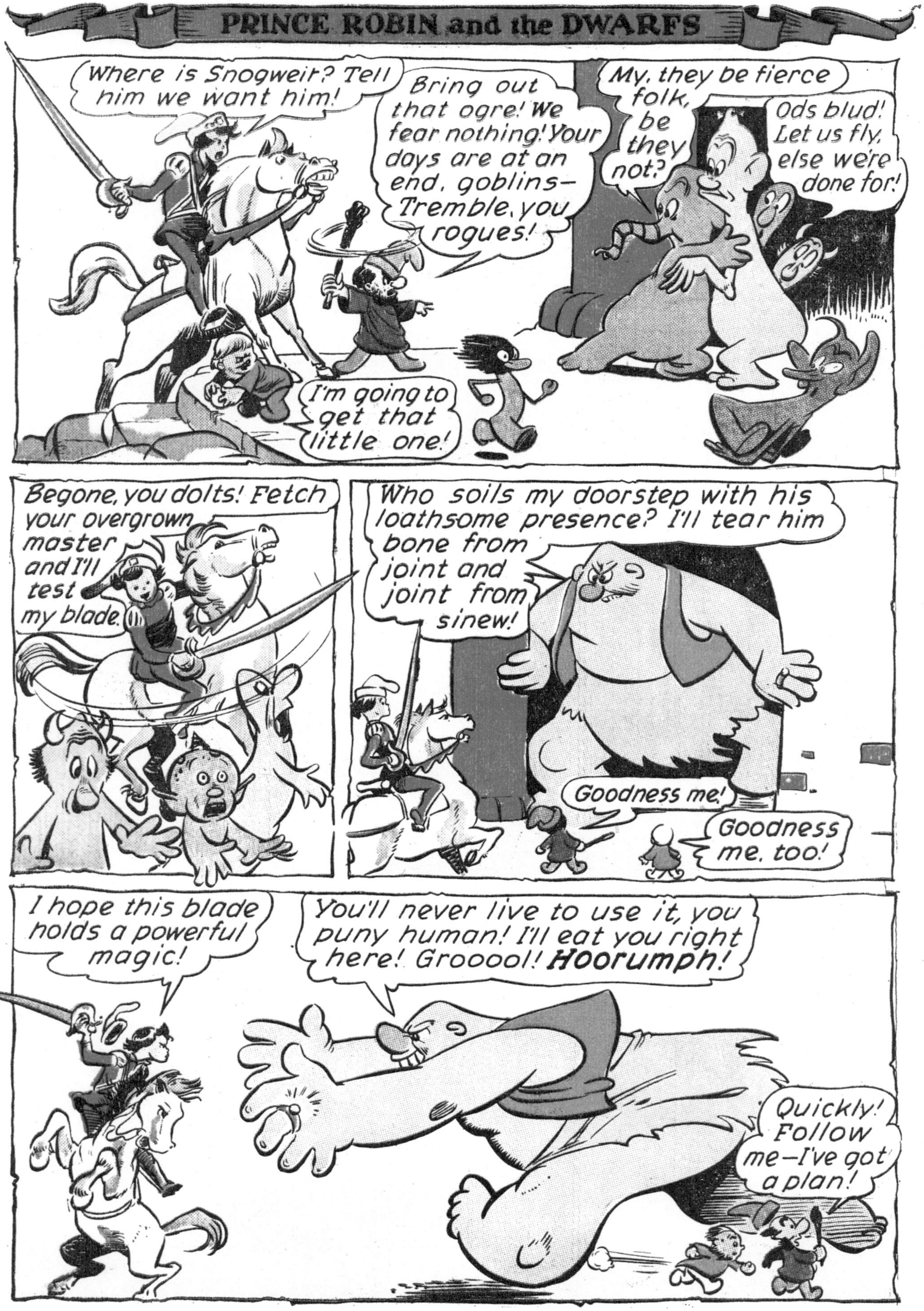
PRINCE ROBIN and the DWARFS
Where is Snogweir? Tell him we want him!
Bring out that ogre! We fear nothing! Your days are at an end, goblins— Tremble, you rogues!
I'm going to get that little one!
My, they be fierce folk, be they not?
Ods blud! Let us fly, else we're done for!
Begone, you dolts! Fetch your overgrown master and I'll test my blade.
Who soils my doorstep with his loathsome presence? I'll tear him bone from joint and joint from sinew!
Goodness me!
Goodness me, too!
I hope this blade holds a powerful magic!
You'll never live to use it, you puny human! I'll eat you right here! Grooool! HOORUMPH!
Quickly! Follow me—I've got a plan!

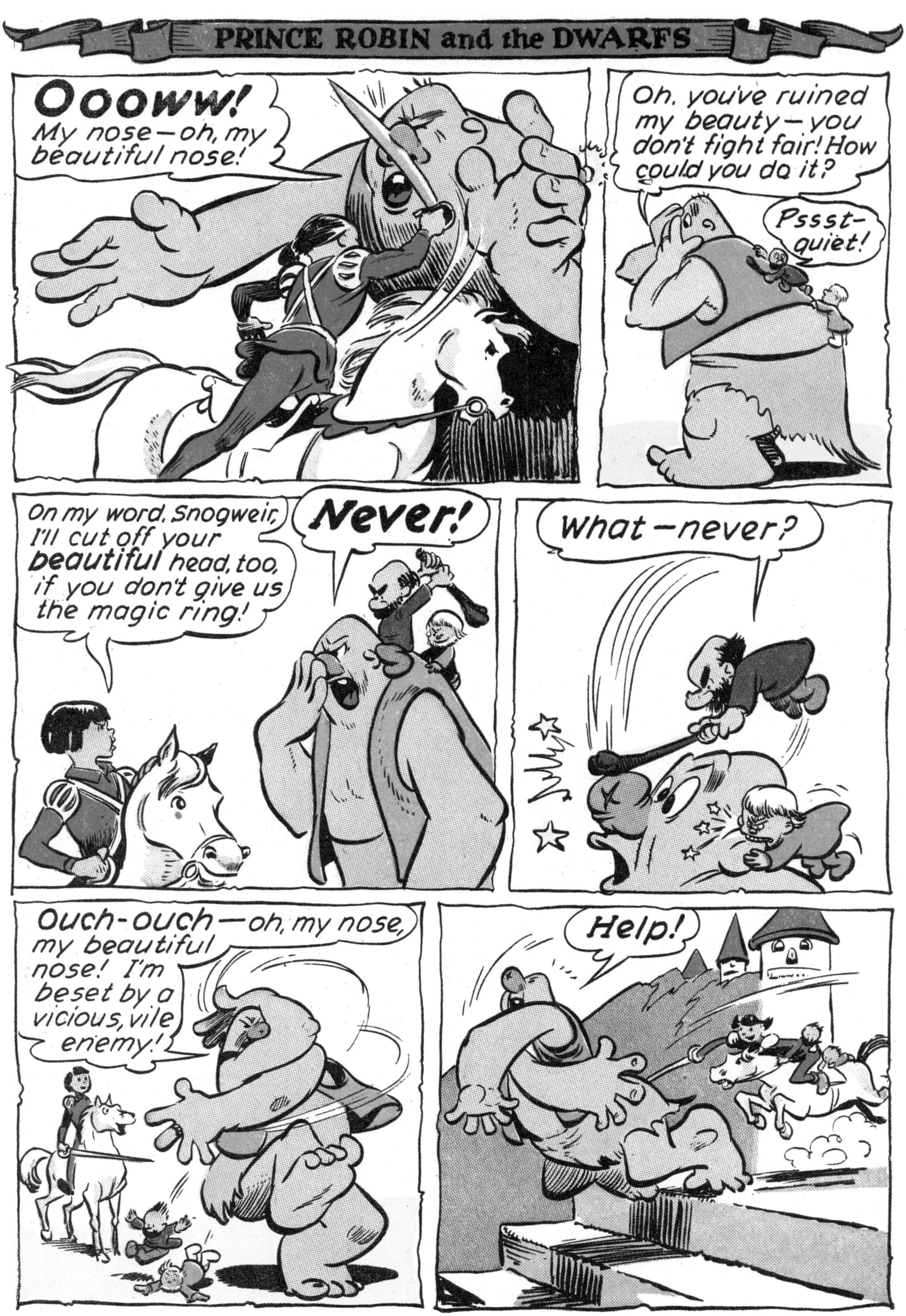
PRINCE ROBIN and the DWARFS
Oooww! My nose—oh, my beautiful nose!
Oh, you've ruined my beauty—you don't fight fair! How could you do it?
Pssst-quiet!
On my word, Snogweir, I'll cut off your beautiful head, too, if you don't give us the magic ring!
Never!
What—never?
Ouch-ouch—oh, my nose, my beautiful nose! I'm beset by a vicious, vile enemy!
Help!

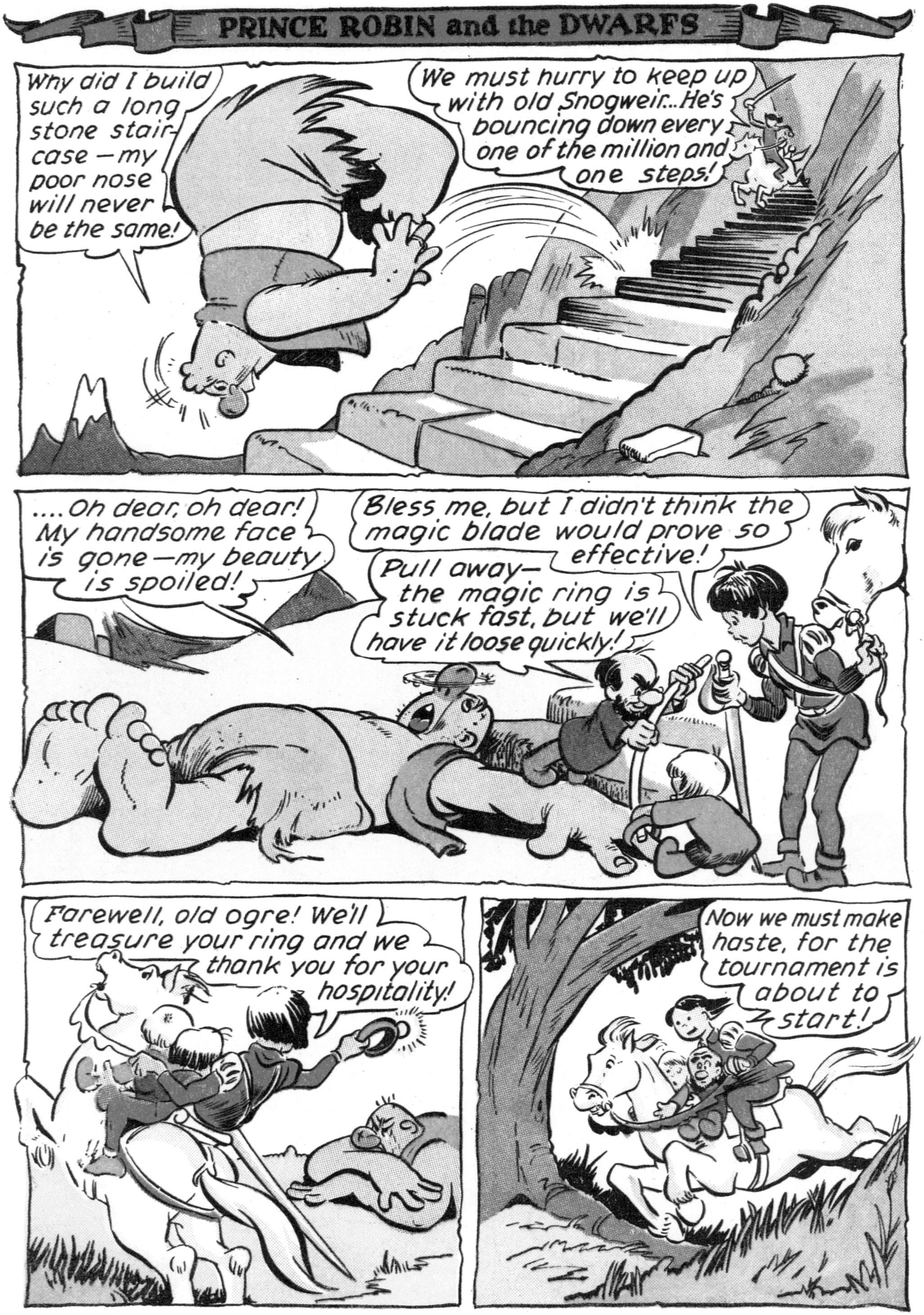
PRINCE ROBIN and the DWARFS
Why did I build such a long stone stair-case—my poor nose will never be the same!
We must hurry to keep up with old Snogweir...He's bouncing down every one of the million and one steps!
....Oh dear, oh dear! My handsome face is gone—my beauty is spoiled!
Bless me, but I didn't think the magic blade would prove so effective!
Pull away—the magic ring is stuck fast, but we'll have it loose quickly!
Farewell, old ogre! We'll treasure your ring and we thank you for your hospitality!
Now we must make haste, for the tournament is about to start!

PRINCE ROBIN and the DWARFS
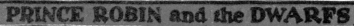

Meanwhile King Sligo has arrived for the tournament.

Hold, men, something's wrong here! Some dwarfs approach...If they have harmed my great friend King Shamos, I'll wipe out every last one of them!

Halt, you little rogue! What have you done with my friend King Shamos?

Look hard, Sligo... King Shamos stands before you!

Blood on the moon! 'Tis Shamos himself! I'd know that fat face anywhere!

Aye, I've been bewitched, but only for a little while.

Stop laughing—we'll be back to normal size as soon as Prince Robin returns.

Hoo-hoo-haw-haw-haw!

And here he comes now—also the two wizards... And by St. George's beard, he has the ring! Praises be!

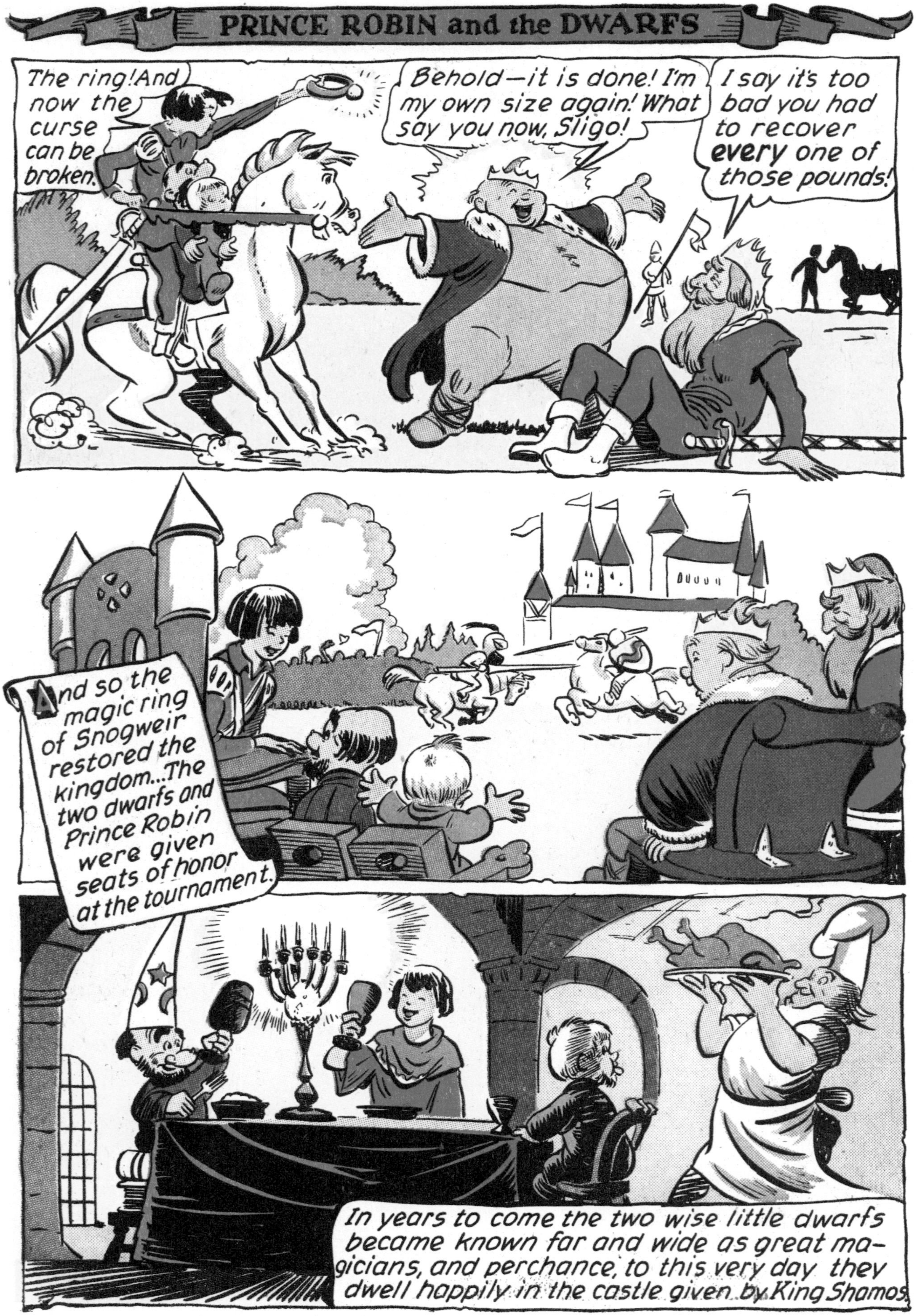
PRINCE ROBIN and the DWARFS
The ring! And now the curse can be broken.
Behold—it is done! I'm my own size again! What say you now, Sligo!
I say it's too bad you had to recover **every** one of those pounds!
And so the magic ring of Snogweir restored the kingdom...The two dwarfs and Prince Robin were given seats of honor at the tournament.
In years to come the two wise little dwarfs became known far and wide as great magicians, and perchance, to this very day they dwell happily in the castle given by King Shamos

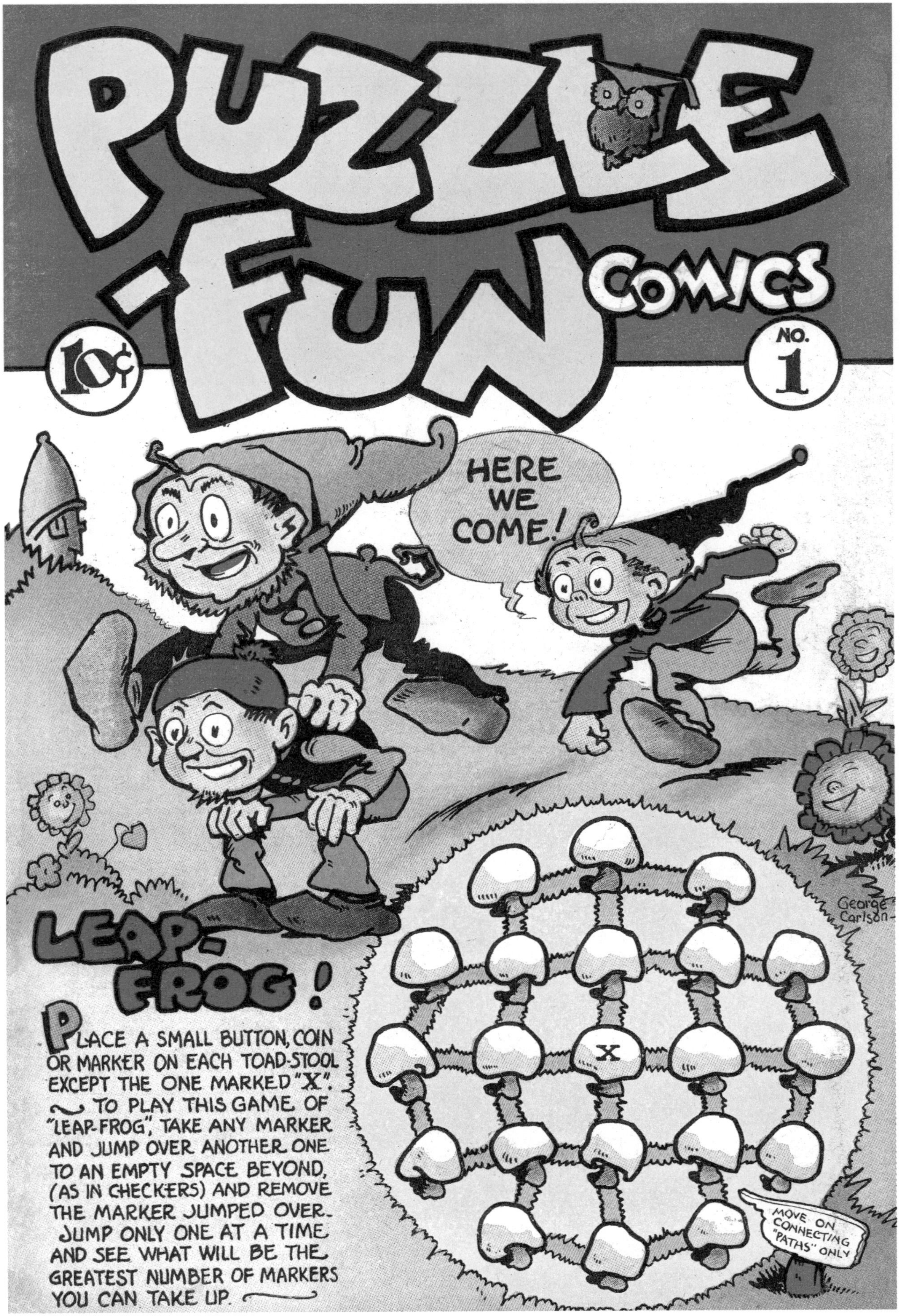
PUZZLE-FUN COMICS
10¢
NO. 1
HERE WE COME!
George Carlson
LEAP-FROG!
PLACE A SMALL BUTTON, COIN OR MARKER ON EACH TOAD-STOOL EXCEPT THE ONE MARKED "X". ~ TO PLAY THIS GAME OF "LEAP-FROG", TAKE ANY MARKER AND JUMP OVER ANOTHER ONE TO AN EMPTY SPACE BEYOND, (AS IN CHECKERS) AND REMOVE THE MARKER JUMPED OVER. JUMP ONLY ONE AT A TIME AND SEE WHAT WILL BE THE GREATEST NUMBER OF MARKERS YOU CAN TAKE UP.
X
MOVE ON CONNECTING "PATHS" ONLY

FANTASYLAND PUZZLE FUN COVER by GEORGE CARLSON

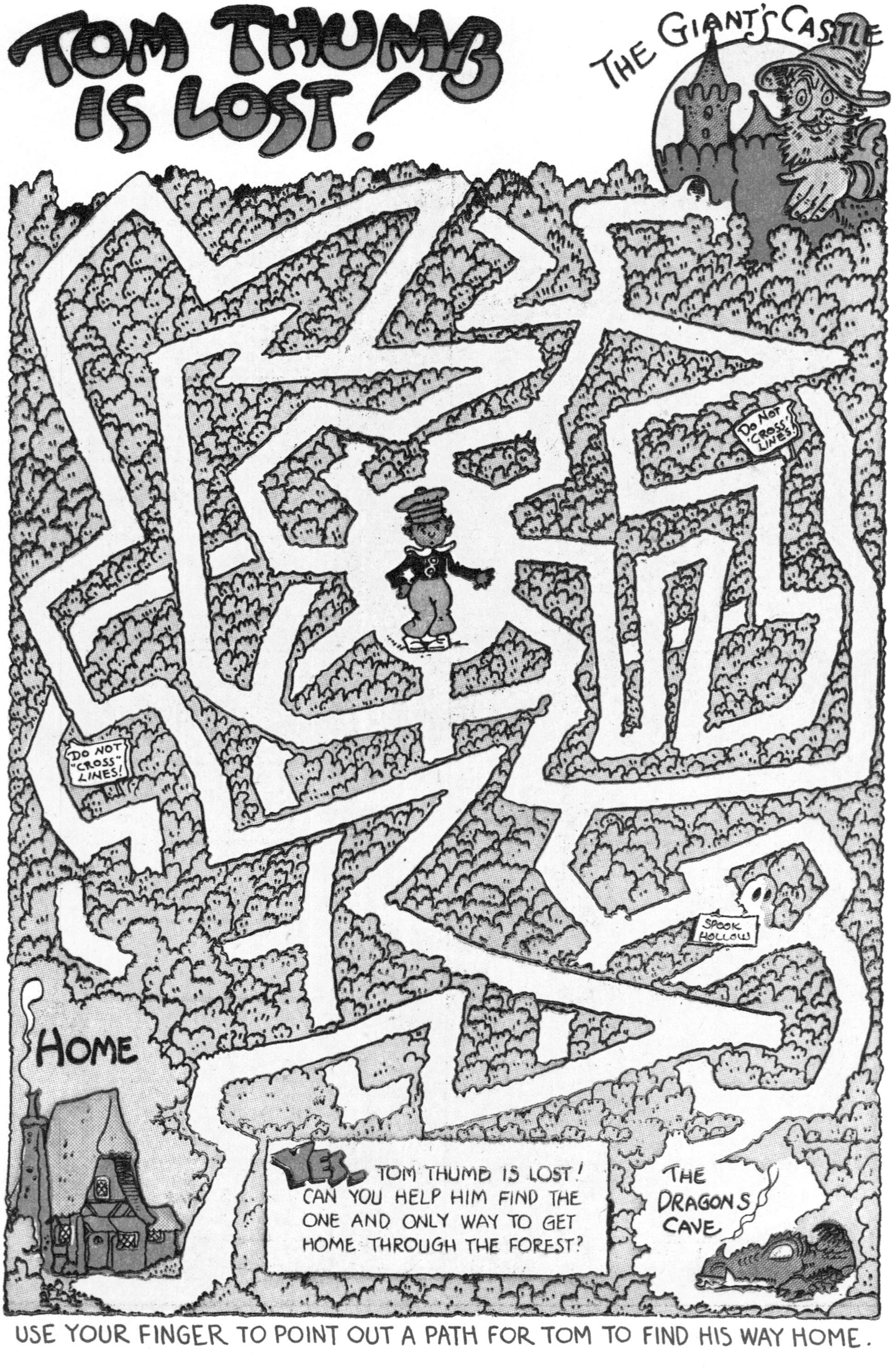
TOM THUMB IS LOST!
THE GIANT'S CASTLE
DO NOT 'CROSS' LINES!
DO NOT "CROSS" LINES!
SPOOK HOLLOW
HOME
YES, TOM THUMB IS LOST! CAN YOU HELP HIM FIND THE ONE AND ONLY WAY TO GET HOME THROUGH THE FOREST?
THE DRAGONS CAVE

USE YOUR FINGER TO POINT OUT A PATH FOR TOM TO FIND HIS WAY HOME.

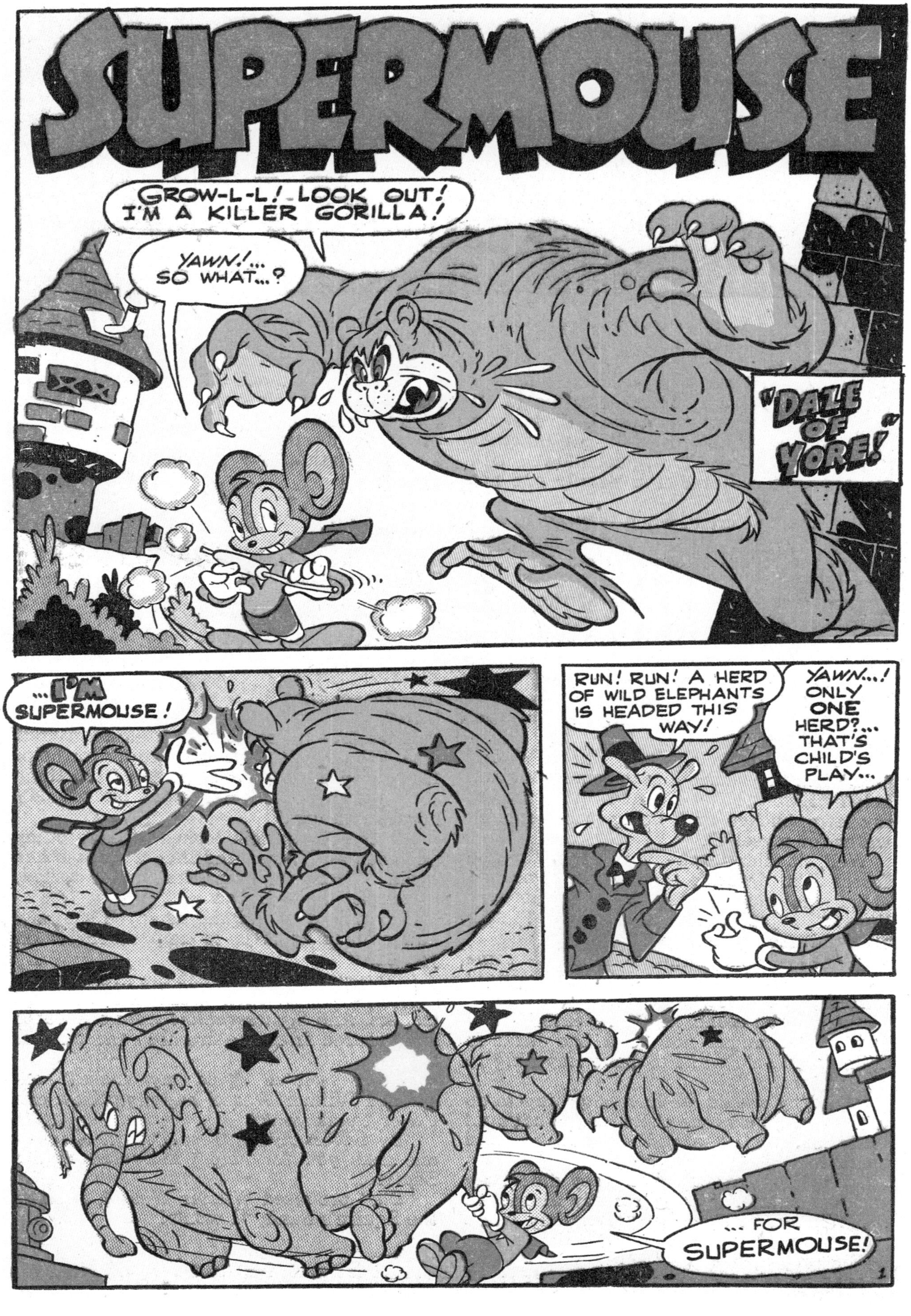
SUPERMOUSE
GROW-L-L! LOOK OUT! I'M A KILLER GORILLA!
YAWN!... SO WHAT...?
"DAZE OF YORE!"
...I'M SUPERMOUSE!
RUN! RUN! A HERD OF WILD ELEPHANTS IS HEADED THIS WAY!
YAWN...! ONLY ONE HERD?... THAT'S CHILD'S PLAY...
... FOR SUPERMOUSE!
1

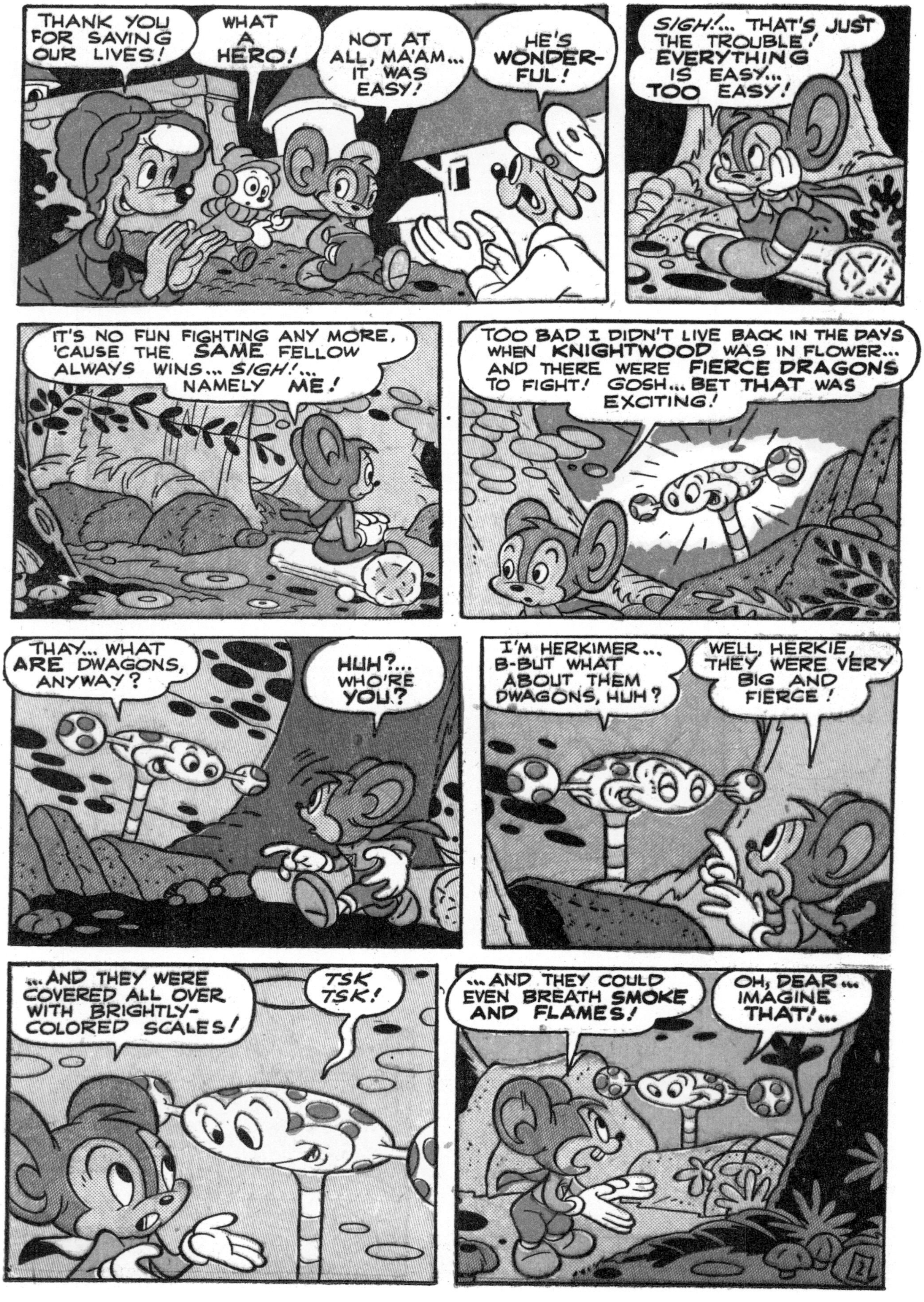
THANK YOU FOR SAVING OUR LIVES!
WHAT A HERO!
NOT AT ALL, MA'AM... IT WAS EASY!
HE'S WONDERFUL!
SIGH!... THAT'S JUST THE TROUBLE! EVERYTHING IS EASY... TOO EASY!
IT'S NO FUN FIGHTING ANY MORE, 'CAUSE THE SAME FELLOW ALWAYS WINS... SIGH!... NAMELY ME!
TOO BAD I DIDN'T LIVE BACK IN THE DAYS WHEN KNIGHTWOOD WAS IN FLOWER... AND THERE WERE FIERCE DRAGONS TO FIGHT! GOSH... BET THAT WAS EXCITING!
THAY... WHAT ARE DWAGONS, ANYWAY?
HUH?... WHO'RE YOU?
I'M HERKIMER... B-BUT WHAT ABOUT THEM DWAGONS, HUH?
WELL, HERKIE, THEY WERE VERY BIG AND FIERCE!
...AND THEY WERE COVERED ALL OVER WITH BRIGHTLY-COLORED SCALES!
TSK TSK!
...AND THEY COULD EVEN BREATH SMOKE AND FLAMES!
OH, DEAR... IMAGINE THAT!...
2

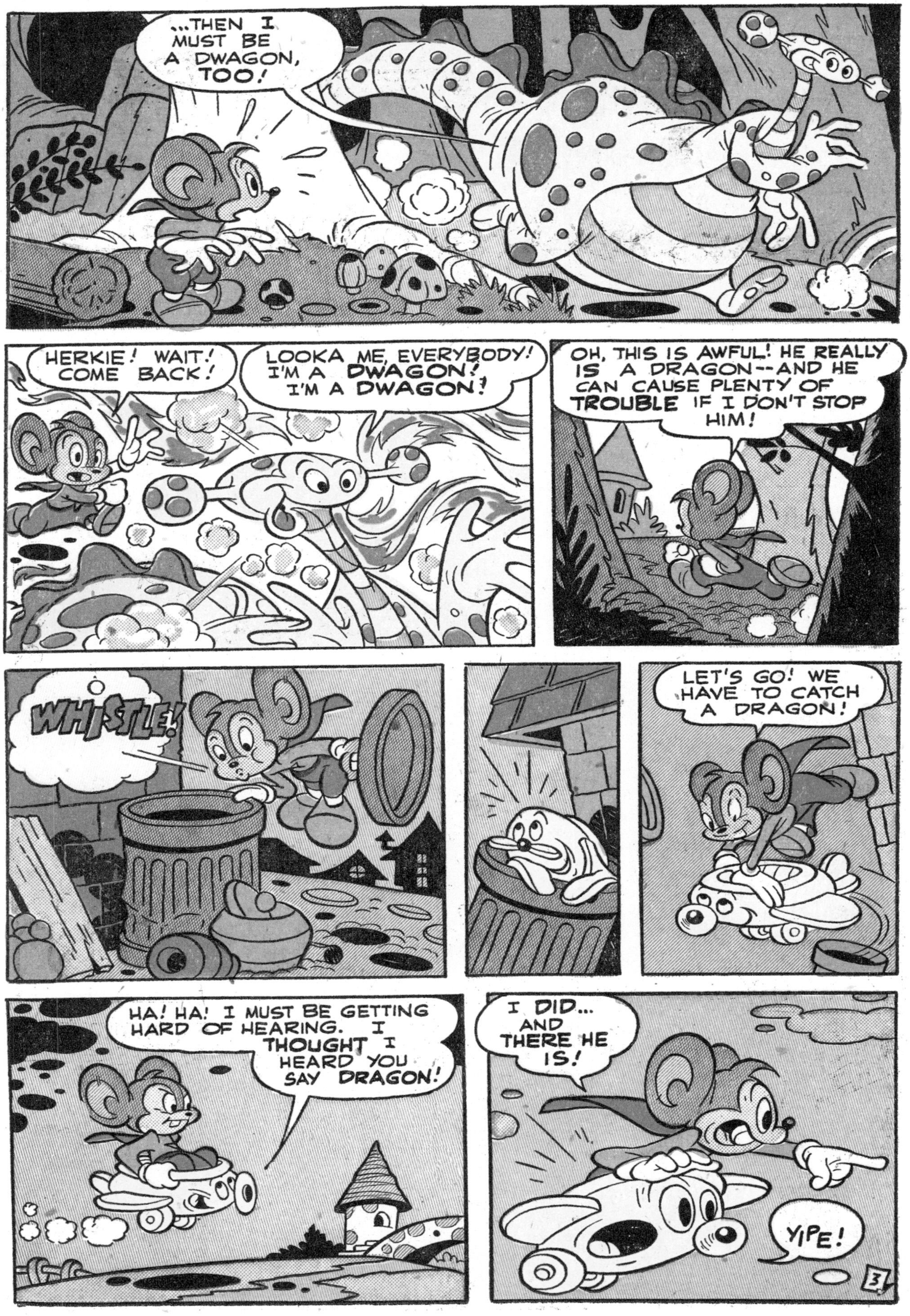
...THEN I MUST BE A DWAGON, TOO!
HERKIE! WAIT! COME BACK!
LOOKA ME, EVERYBODY! I'M A DWAGON! I'M A DWAGON!
OH, THIS IS AWFUL! HE REALLY IS A DRAGON--AND HE CAN CAUSE PLENTY OF TROUBLE IF I DON'T STOP HIM!
WHISTLE!
LET'S GO! WE HAVE TO CATCH A DRAGON!
HA! HA! I MUST BE GETTING HARD OF HEARING. I THOUGHT I HEARD YOU SAY DRAGON!
I DID... AND THERE HE IS!
YIPE!
3

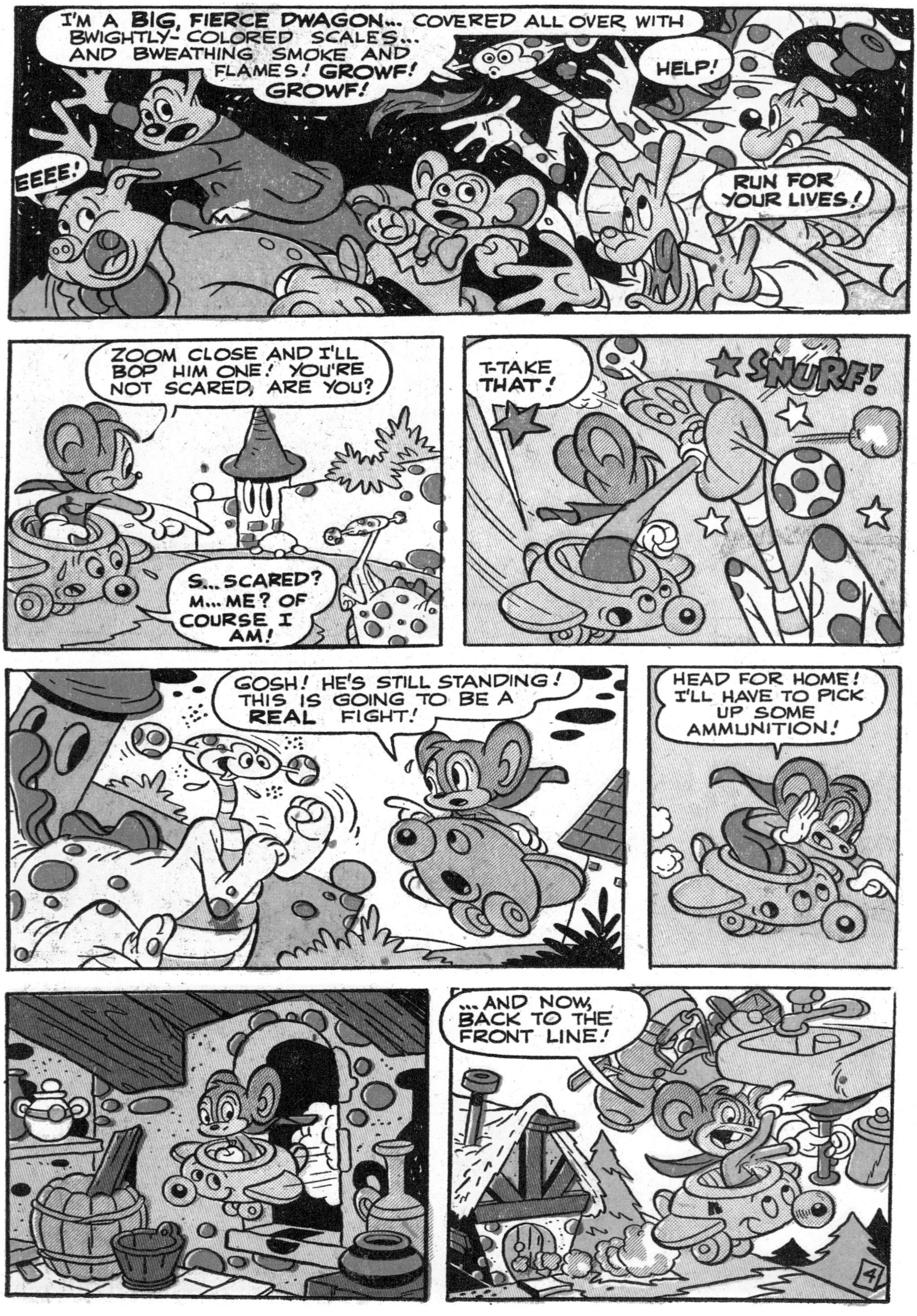
I'M A BIG, FIERCE DWAGON... COVERED ALL OVER WITH BWIGHTLY- COLORED SCALES... AND BWEATHING SMOKE AND FLAMES! GROWF! GROWF!
HELP!
EEEE!
RUN FOR YOUR LIVES!
ZOOM CLOSE AND I'LL BOP HIM ONE! YOU'RE NOT SCARED, ARE YOU?
S... SCARED? M... ME? OF COURSE I AM!
T-TAKE THAT!
SNURF!
GOSH! HE'S STILL STANDING! THIS IS GOING TO BE A REAL FIGHT!
HEAD FOR HOME! I'LL HAVE TO PICK UP SOME AMMUNITION!
...AND NOW, BACK TO THE FRONT LINE!
4

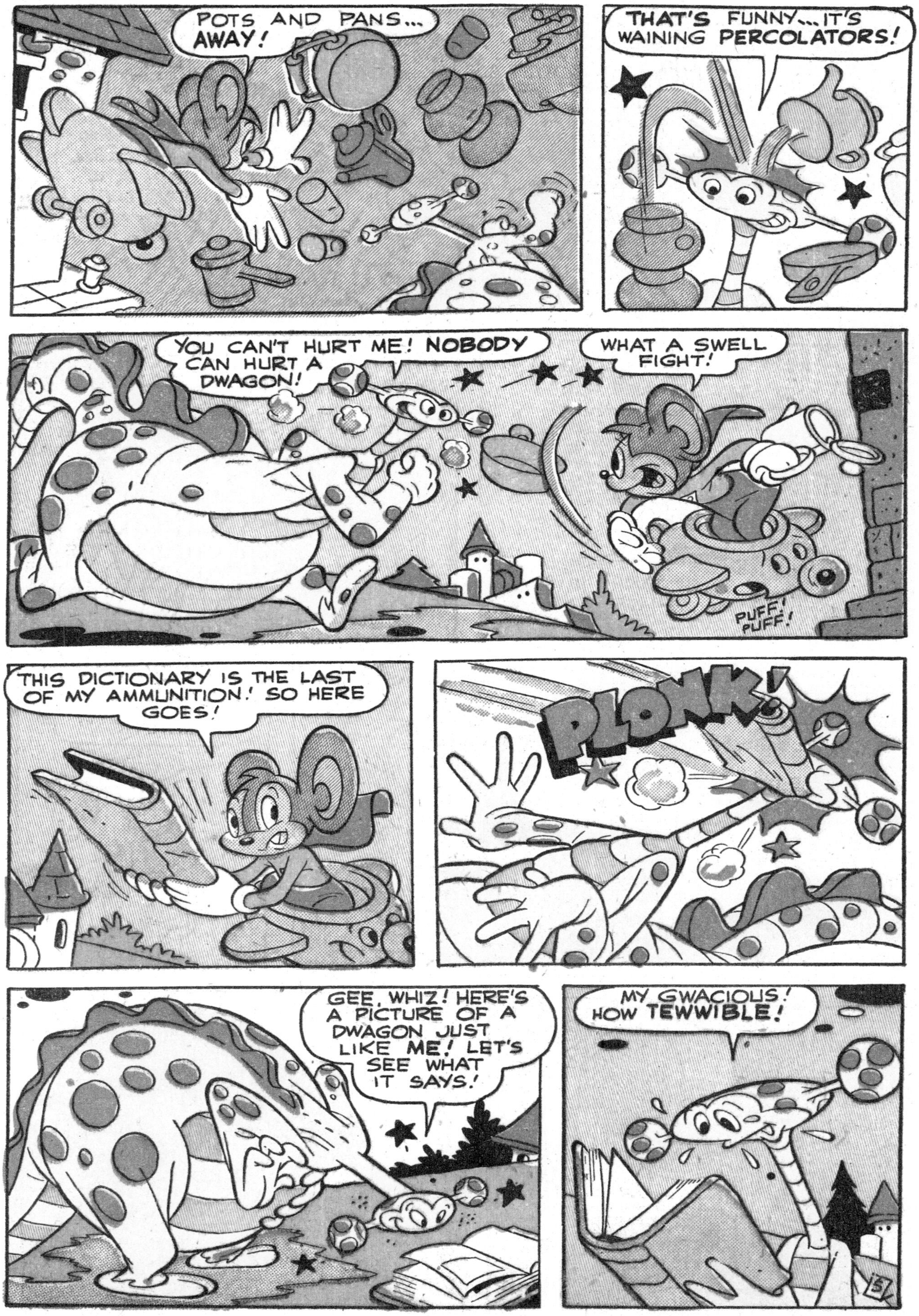
POTS AND PANS... AWAY!
THAT'S FUNNY... IT'S WAINING PERCOLATORS!
YOU CAN'T HURT ME! NOBODY CAN HURT A DWAGON!
WHAT A SWELL FIGHT!
PUFF! PUFF!
THIS DICTIONARY IS THE LAST OF MY AMMUNITION! SO HERE GOES!
PLONK!
GEE, WHIZ! HERE'S A PICTURE OF A DWAGON JUST LIKE ME! LET'S SEE WHAT IT SAYS!
MY GWACIOUS! HOW TEWWIBLE!
5

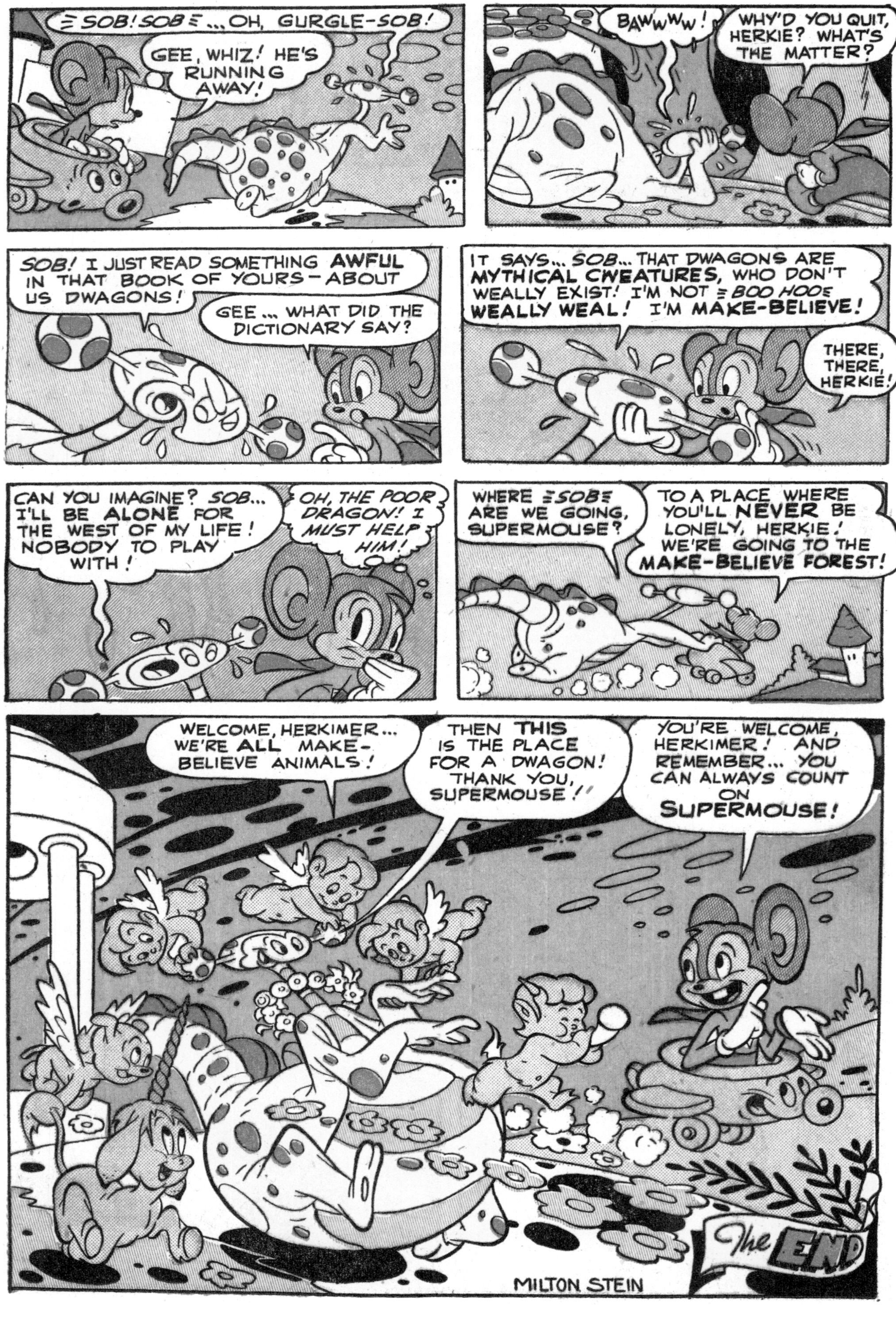
≡SOB! SOB≡ ...OH, GURGLE-SOB!
GEE, WHIZ! HE'S RUNNING AWAY!
BAWWWW!
WHY'D YOU QUIT, HERKIE? WHAT'S THE MATTER?
SOB! I JUST READ SOMETHING AWFUL IN THAT BOOK OF YOURS – ABOUT US DWAGONS!
GEE ... WHAT DID THE DICTIONARY SAY?
IT SAYS... SOB... THAT DWAGONS ARE MYTHICAL CWEATURES, WHO DON'T WEALLY EXIST! I'M NOT ≡BOO HOO≡ WEALLY WEAL! I'M MAKE-BELIEVE!
THERE, THERE, HERKIE!
CAN YOU IMAGINE? SOB... I'LL BE ALONE FOR THE WEST OF MY LIFE! NOBODY TO PLAY WITH!
OH, THE POOR DRAGON! I MUST HELP HIM!
WHERE ≡SOB≡ ARE WE GOING, SUPERMOUSE?
TO A PLACE WHERE YOU'LL NEVER BE LONELY, HERKIE! WE'RE GOING TO THE MAKE-BELIEVE FOREST!
WELCOME, HERKIMER... WE'RE ALL MAKE-BELIEVE ANIMALS!
THEN THIS IS THE PLACE FOR A DWAGON! THANK YOU, SUPERMOUSE!!
YOU'RE WELCOME, HERKIMER! AND REMEMBER... YOU CAN ALWAYS COUNT ON SUPERMOUSE!
The END
MILTON STEIN

The Tweedle Twins vs. The Horrible Groark

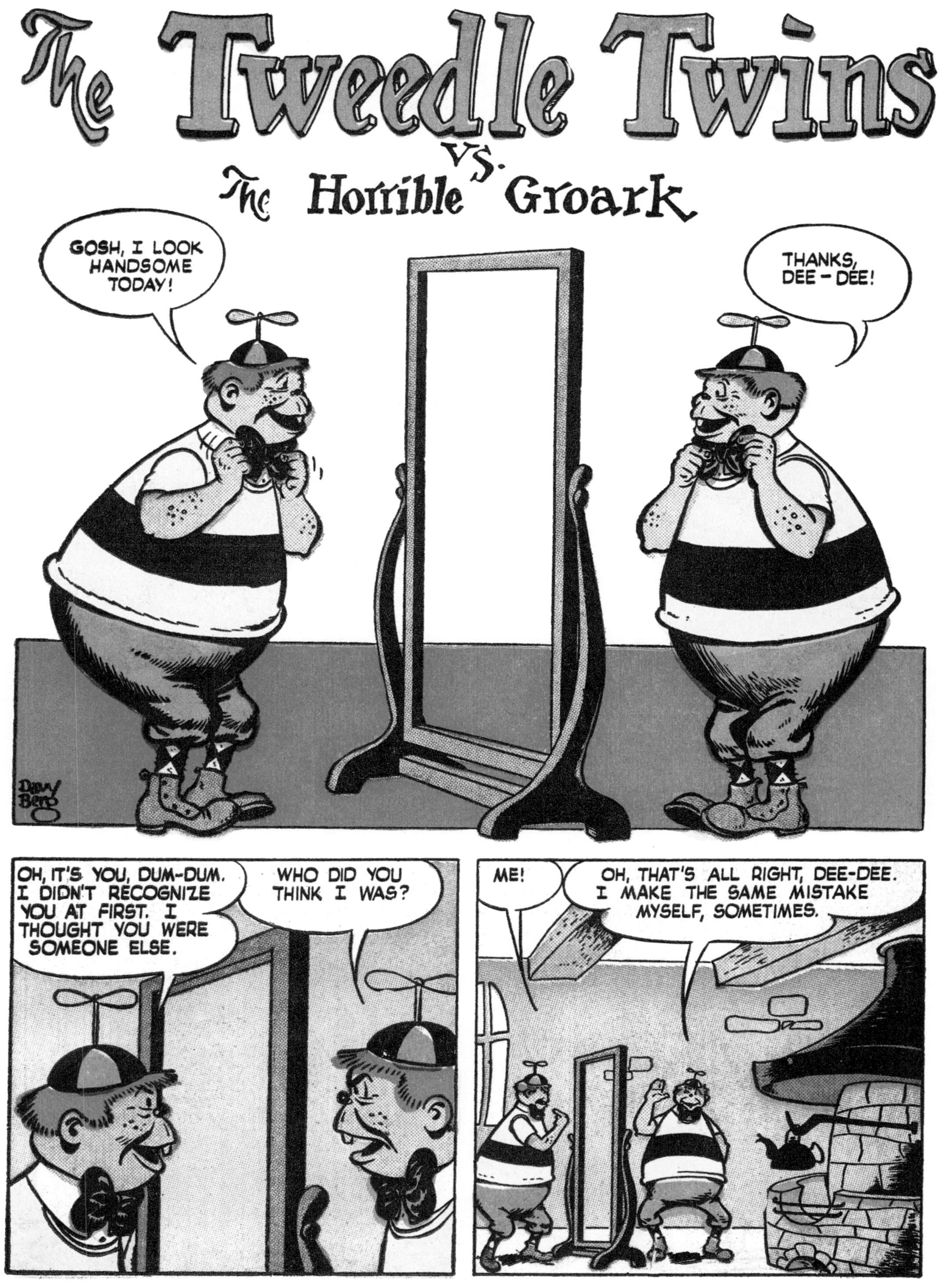
GOSH, I LOOK HANDSOME TODAY!
THANKS, DEE-DEE!
OH, IT'S YOU, DUM-DUM. I DIDN'T RECOGNIZE YOU AT FIRST. I THOUGHT YOU WERE SOMEONE ELSE.
WHO DID YOU THINK I WAS?
ME!
OH, THAT'S ALL RIGHT, DEE-DEE. I MAKE THE SAME MISTAKE MYSELF, SOMETIMES.

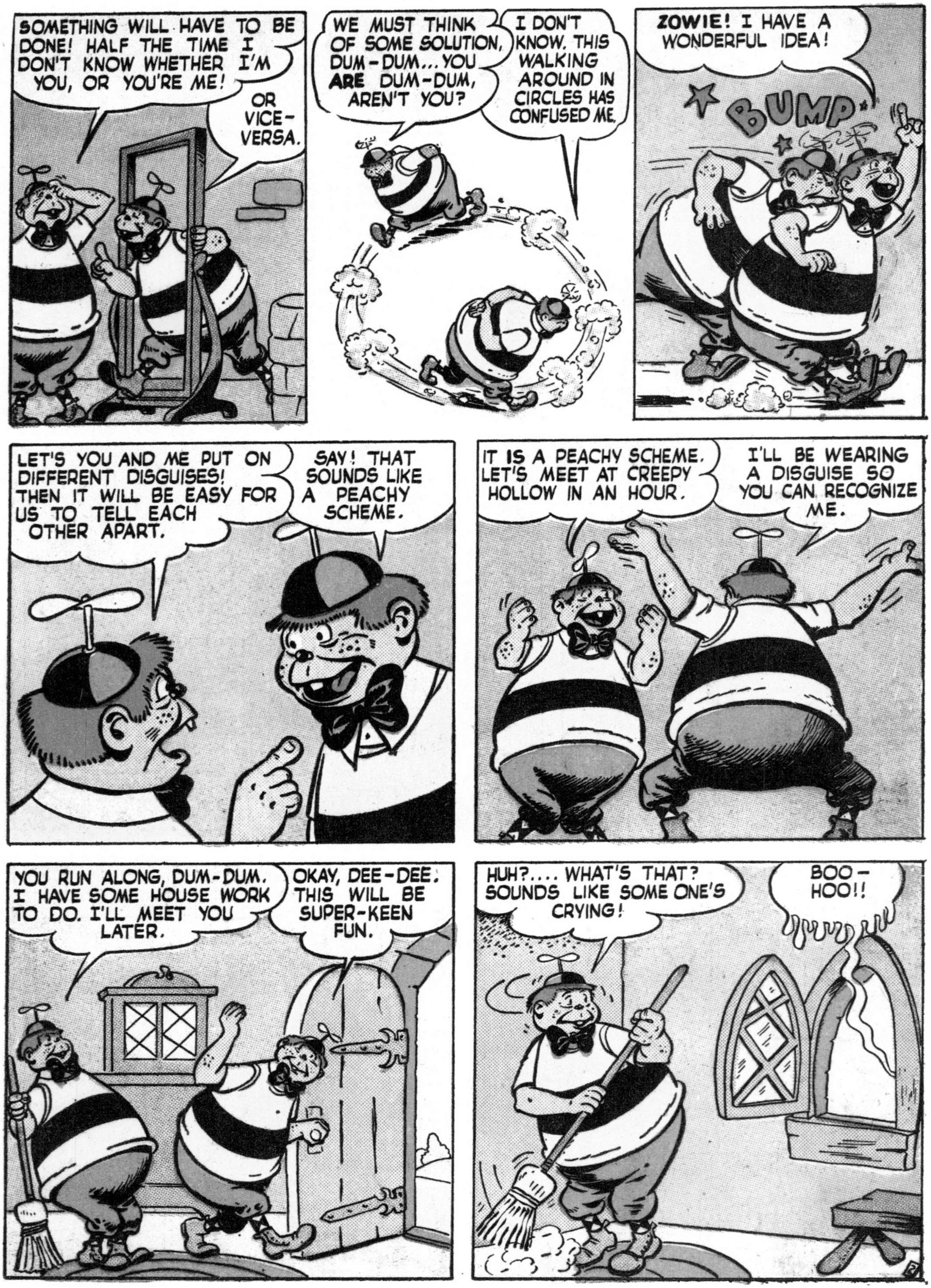
SOMETHING WILL HAVE TO BE DONE! HALF THE TIME I DON'T KNOW WHETHER I'M YOU, OR YOU'RE ME!
OR VICE-VERSA.
WE MUST THINK OF SOME SOLUTION, DUM-DUM... YOU ARE DUM-DUM, AREN'T YOU?
I DON'T KNOW. THIS WALKING AROUND IN CIRCLES HAS CONFUSED ME.
ZOWIE! I HAVE A WONDERFUL IDEA!
BUMP
LET'S YOU AND ME PUT ON DIFFERENT DISGUISES! THEN IT WILL BE EASY FOR US TO TELL EACH OTHER APART.
SAY! THAT SOUNDS LIKE A PEACHY SCHEME.
IT IS A PEACHY SCHEME. LET'S MEET AT CREEPY HOLLOW IN AN HOUR.
I'LL BE WEARING A DISGUISE SO YOU CAN RECOGNIZE ME.
YOU RUN ALONG, DUM-DUM. I HAVE SOME HOUSE WORK TO DO. I'LL MEET YOU LATER.
OKAY, DEE-DEE. THIS WILL BE SUPER-KEEN FUN.
HUH?.... WHAT'S THAT? SOUNDS LIKE SOME ONE'S CRYING!
BOO-HOO!!

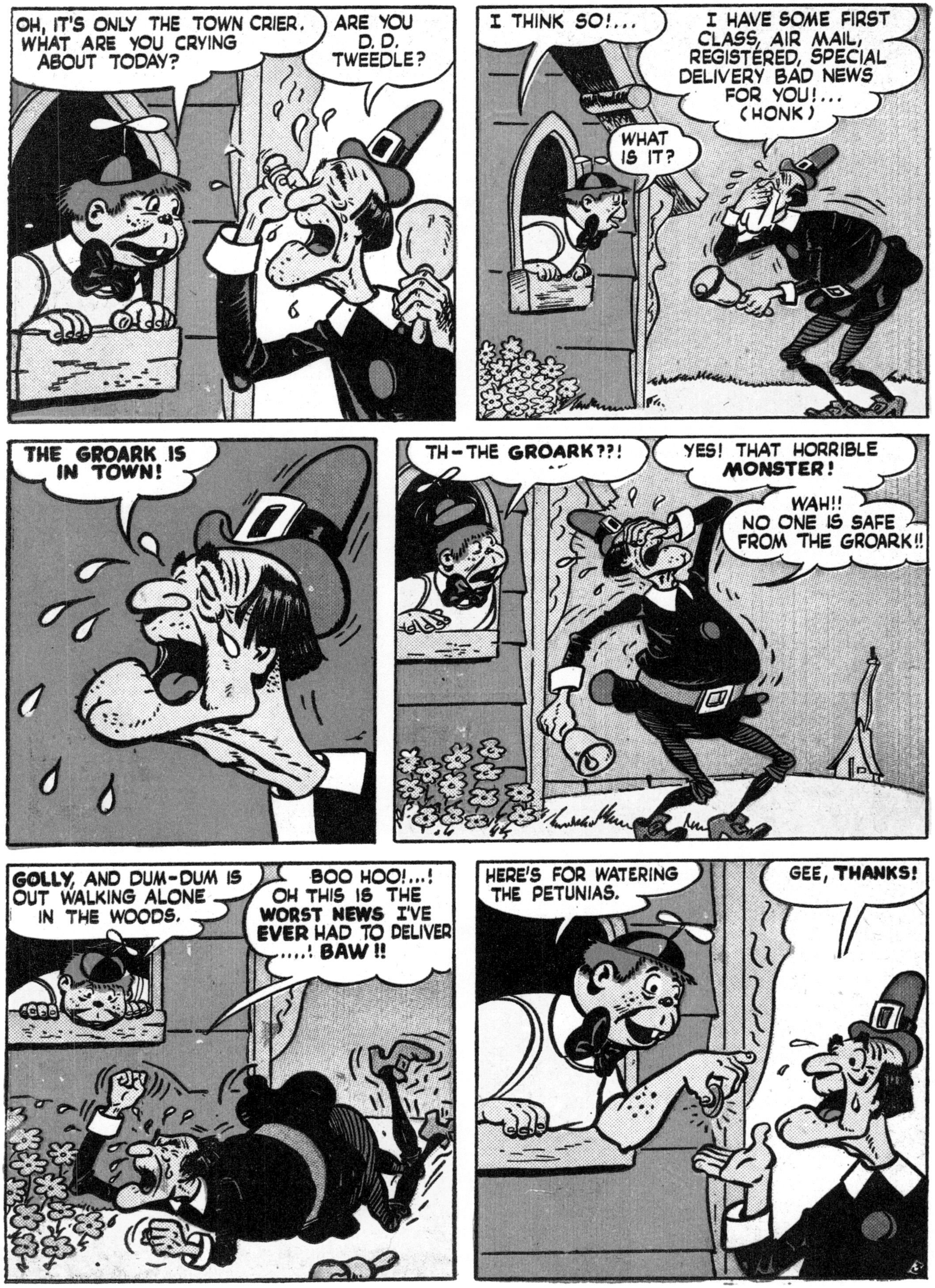
OH, IT'S ONLY THE TOWN CRIER. WHAT ARE YOU CRYING ABOUT TODAY?
ARE YOU D. D. TWEEDLE?
I THINK SO!...
I HAVE SOME FIRST CLASS, AIR MAIL, REGISTERED, SPECIAL DELIVERY BAD NEWS FOR YOU!... (HONK)
WHAT IS IT?
THE GROARK IS IN TOWN!
TH-THE GROARK??!
YES! THAT HORRIBLE MONSTER!
WAH!! NO ONE IS SAFE FROM THE GROARK!!
GOLLY, AND DUM-DUM IS OUT WALKING ALONE IN THE WOODS.
BOO HOO!...! OH THIS IS THE WORST NEWS I'VE EVER HAD TO DELIVER ....! BAW!!
HERE'S FOR WATERING THE PETUNIAS.
GEE, THANKS!

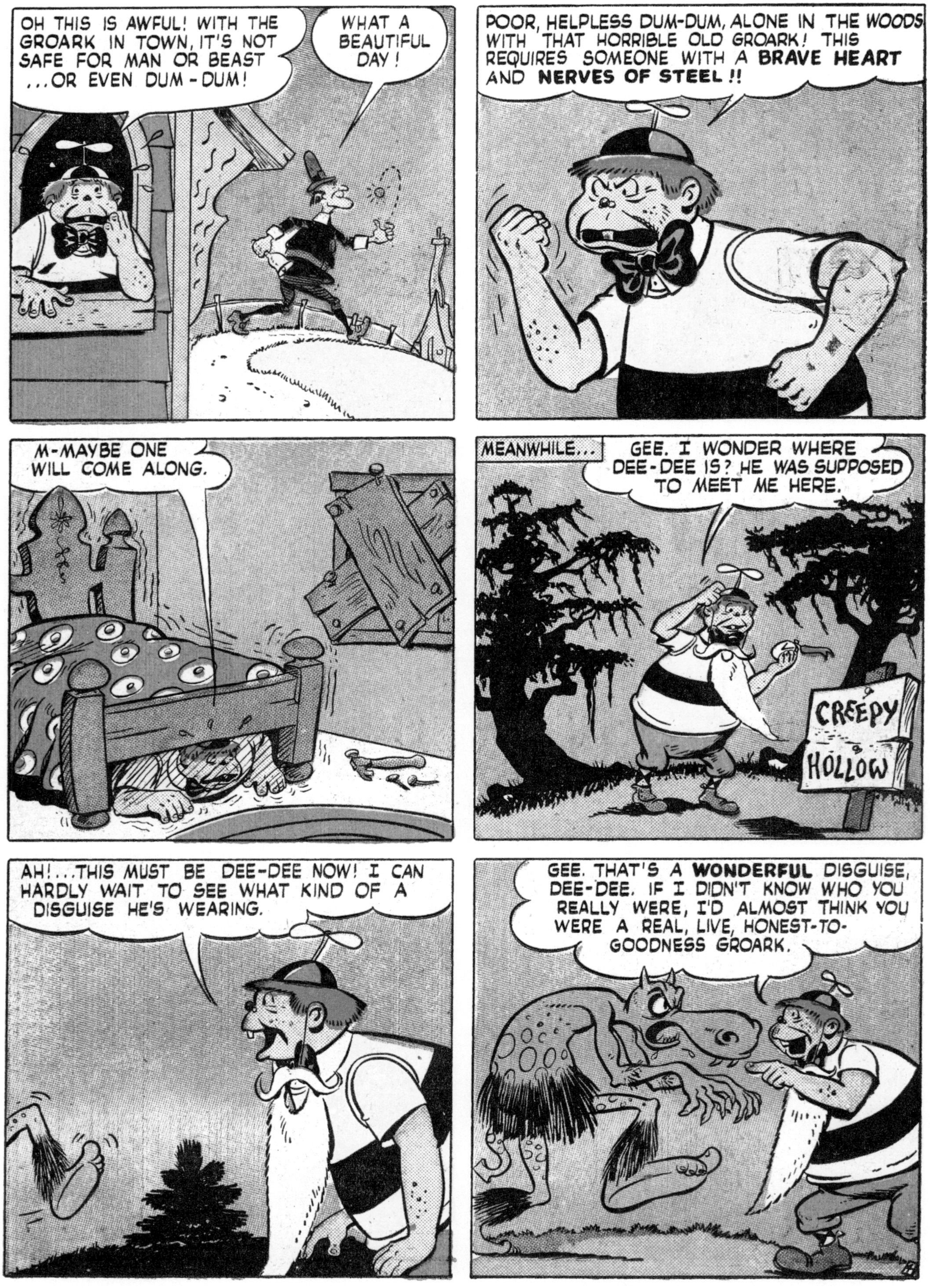
OH THIS IS AWFUL! WITH THE GROARK IN TOWN, IT'S NOT SAFE FOR MAN OR BEAST ...OR EVEN DUM-DUM!
WHAT A BEAUTIFUL DAY!
POOR, HELPLESS DUM-DUM, ALONE IN THE WOODS WITH THAT HORRIBLE OLD GROARK! THIS REQUIRES SOMEONE WITH A BRAVE HEART AND NERVES OF STEEL!!
M-MAYBE ONE WILL COME ALONG.
MEANWHILE...
GEE. I WONDER WHERE DEE-DEE IS? HE WAS SUPPOSED TO MEET ME HERE.
CREEPY
HOLLOW
AH!...THIS MUST BE DEE-DEE NOW! I CAN HARDLY WAIT TO SEE WHAT KIND OF A DISGUISE HE'S WEARING.
GEE. THAT'S A WONDERFUL DISGUISE, DEE-DEE. IF I DIDN'T KNOW WHO YOU REALLY WERE, I'D ALMOST THINK YOU WERE A REAL, LIVE, HONEST-TO-GOODNESS GROARK.

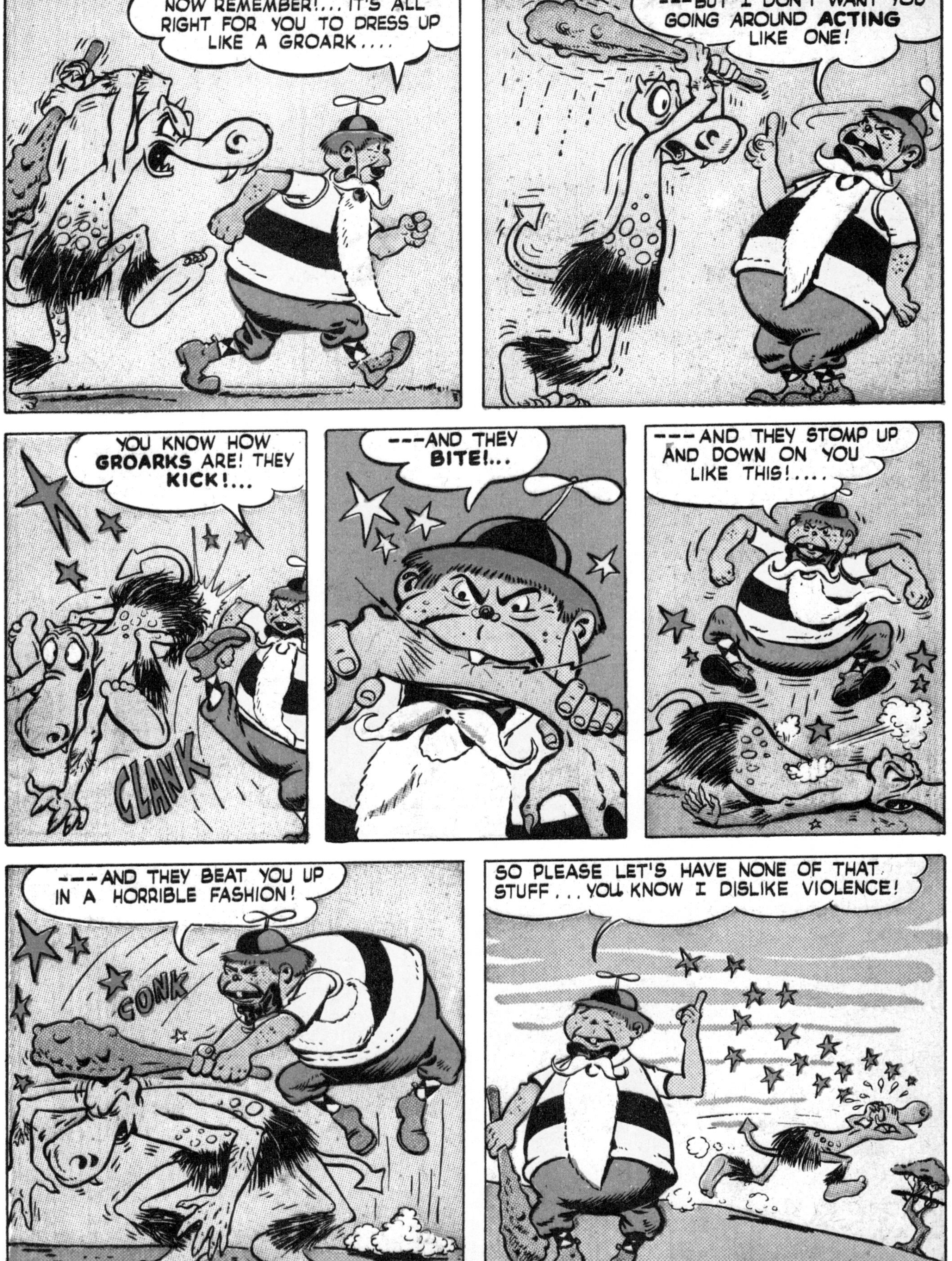
NOW REMEMBER!... IT'S ALL RIGHT FOR YOU TO DRESS UP LIKE A GROARK....
---BUT I DON'T WANT YOU GOING AROUND ACTING LIKE ONE!
YOU KNOW HOW GROARKS ARE! THEY KICK!...
CLANK
---AND THEY BITE!...
---AND THEY STOMP UP AND DOWN ON YOU LIKE THIS!....
---AND THEY BEAT YOU UP IN A HORRIBLE FASHION!
CONK
SO PLEASE LET'S HAVE NONE OF THAT STUFF... YOU KNOW I DISLIKE VIOLENCE!
5

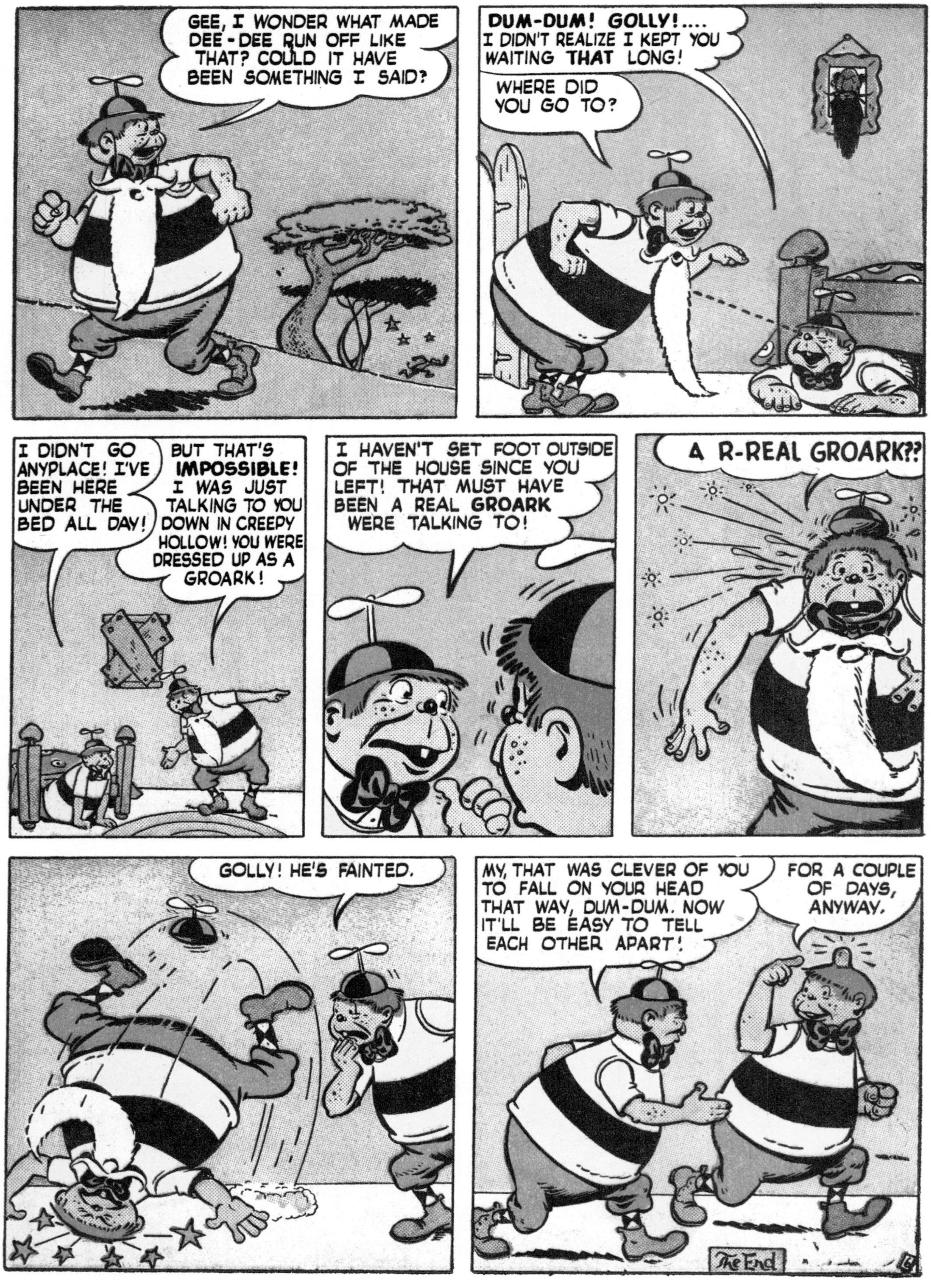
GEE, I WONDER WHAT MADE DEE-DEE RUN OFF LIKE THAT? COULD IT HAVE BEEN SOMETHING I SAID?
DUM-DUM! GOLLY!.... I DIDN'T REALIZE I KEPT YOU WAITING THAT LONG!
WHERE DID YOU GO TO?
I DIDN'T GO ANYPLACE! I'VE BEEN HERE UNDER THE BED ALL DAY!
BUT THAT'S IMPOSSIBLE! I WAS JUST TALKING TO YOU DOWN IN CREEPY HOLLOW! YOU WERE DRESSED UP AS A GROARK!
I HAVEN'T SET FOOT OUTSIDE OF THE HOUSE SINCE YOU LEFT! THAT MUST HAVE BEEN A REAL GROARK WERE TALKING TO!
A R-REAL GROARK??
GOLLY! HE'S FAINTED.
MY, THAT WAS CLEVER OF YOU TO FALL ON YOUR HEAD THAT WAY, DUM-DUM. NOW IT'LL BE EASY TO TELL EACH OTHER APART!
FOR A COUPLE OF DAYS, ANYWAY.
The End
6

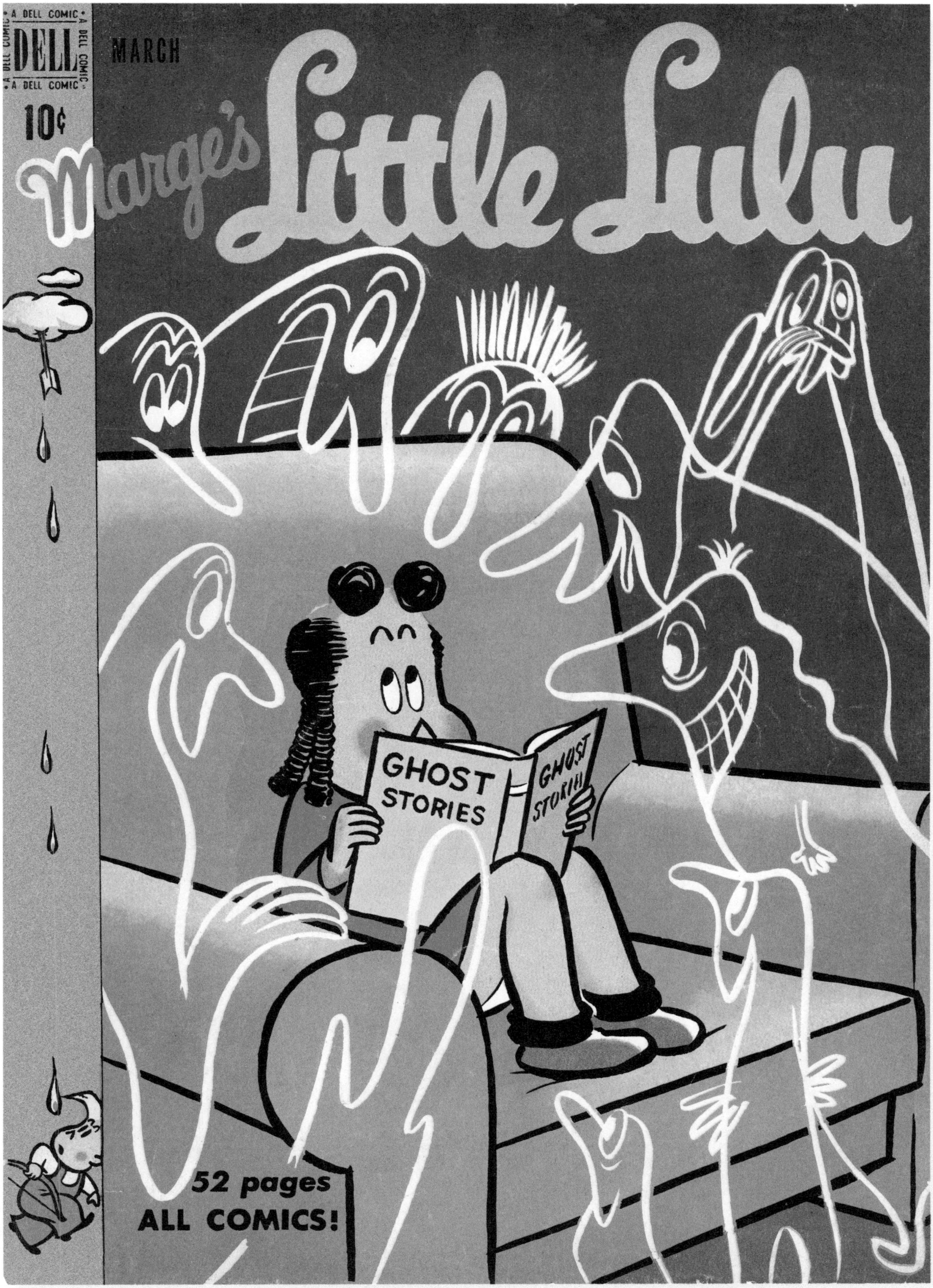
A DELL COMIC
DELL
A DELL COMIC
MARCH
10¢
Marge's Little Lulu
GHOST STORIES
GHOST STORIES
52 pages ALL COMICS!

FANTASYLAND LITTLE LULU COVER by JOHN STANLEY

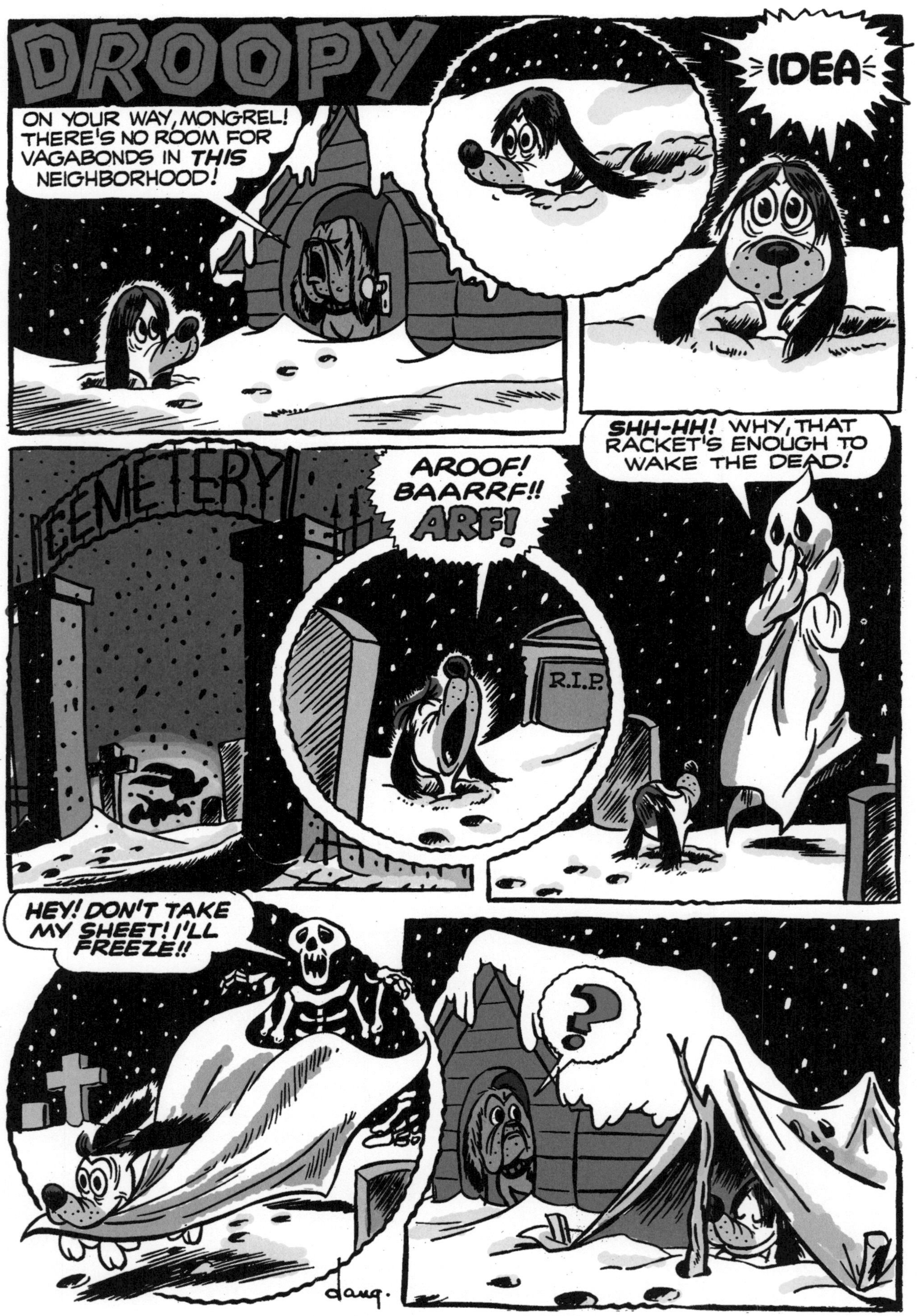
DROOPY
ON YOUR WAY, MONGREL! THERE'S NO ROOM FOR VAGABONDS IN THIS NEIGHBORHOOD!
IDEA
AROOF! BAARRF!! ARF!
SHH-HH! WHY, THAT RACKET'S ENOUGH TO WAKE THE DEAD!
CEMETERY
R.I.P.
HEY! DON'T TAKE MY SHEET! I'LL FREEZE!!
?
dang.

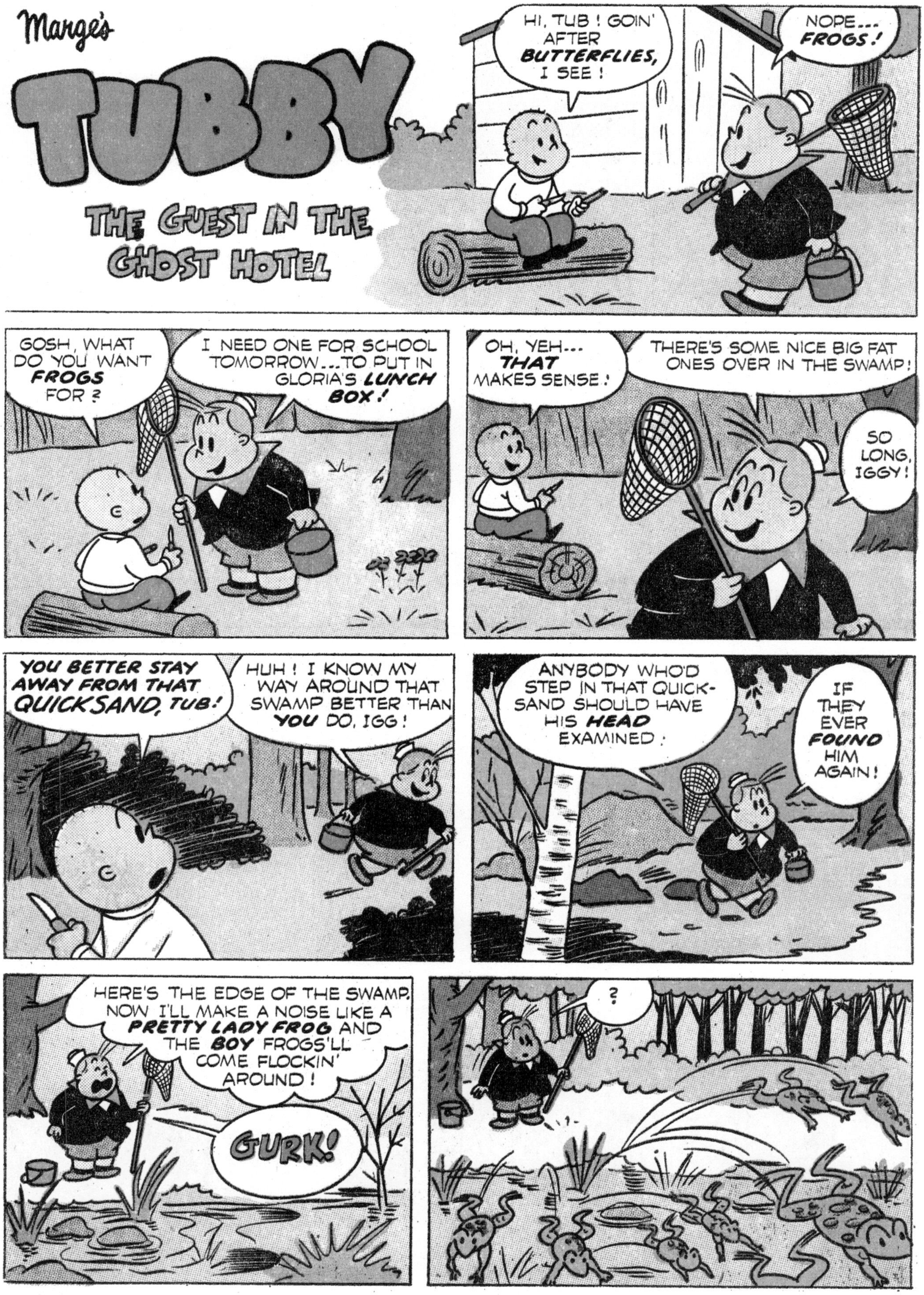
Marge's
TUBBY
THE GUEST IN THE GHOST HOTEL
HI, TUB! GOIN' AFTER BUTTERFLIES, I SEE!
NOPE... FROGS!
GOSH, WHAT DO YOU WANT FROGS FOR?
I NEED ONE FOR SCHOOL TOMORROW... TO PUT IN GLORIA'S LUNCH BOX!
OH, YEH... THAT MAKES SENSE!
THERE'S SOME NICE BIG FAT ONES OVER IN THE SWAMP!
SO LONG, IGGY!
YOU BETTER STAY AWAY FROM THAT QUICKSAND, TUB!
HUH! I KNOW MY WAY AROUND THAT SWAMP BETTER THAN YOU DO, IGG!
ANYBODY WHO'D STEP IN THAT QUICK-SAND SHOULD HAVE HIS HEAD EXAMINED!
IF THEY EVER FOUND HIM AGAIN!
HERE'S THE EDGE OF THE SWAMP. NOW I'LL MAKE A NOISE LIKE A PRETTY LADY FROG AND THE BOY FROGS'LL COME FLOCKIN' AROUND!
GURK!
?

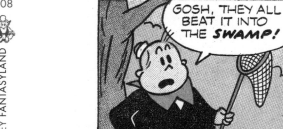

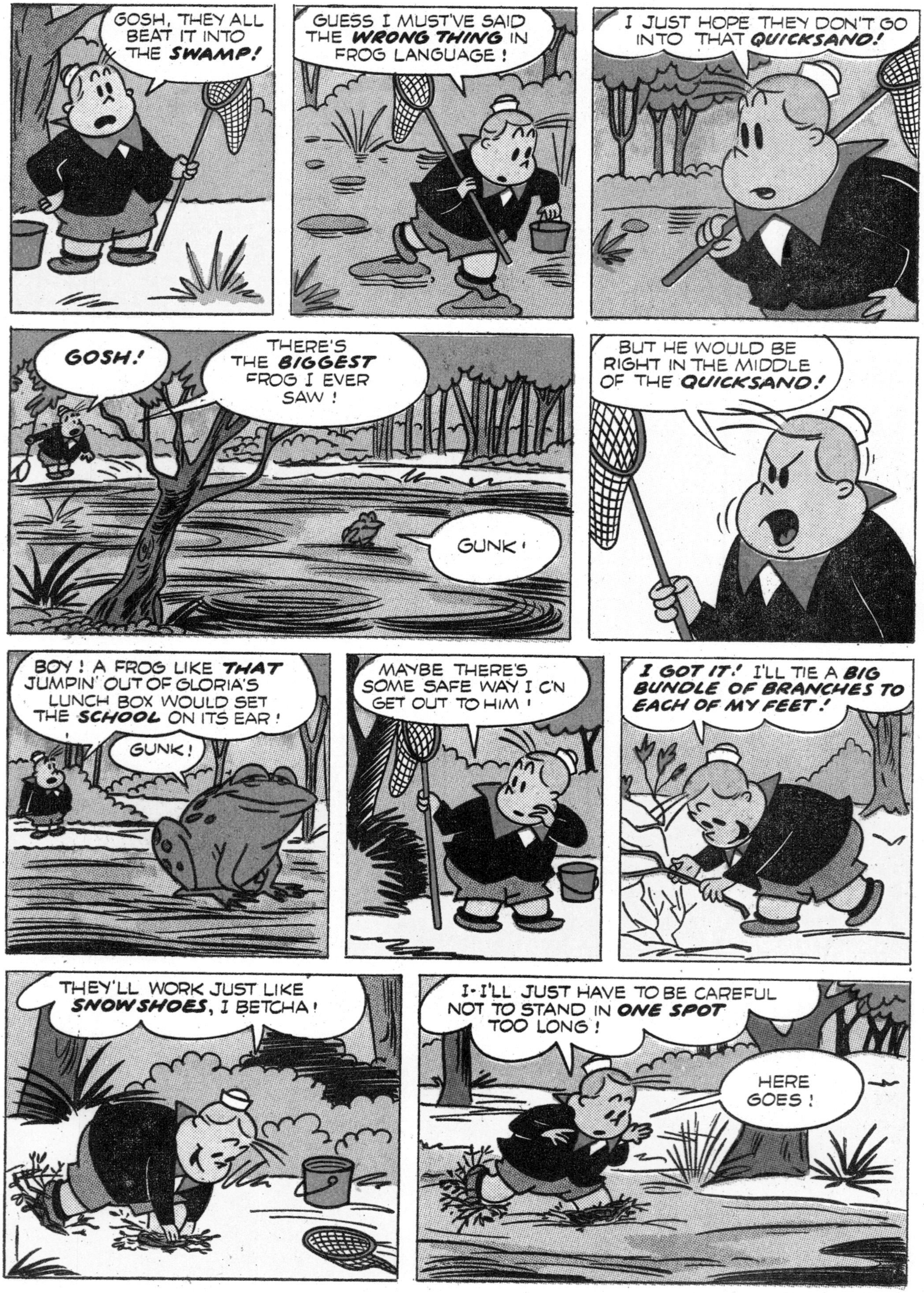
GOSH, THEY ALL BEAT IT INTO THE SWAMP!
GUESS I MUST'VE SAID THE WRONG THING IN FROG LANGUAGE!
I JUST HOPE THEY DON'T GO INTO THAT QUICKSAND!
GOSH!
THERE'S THE BIGGEST FROG I EVER SAW!
GUNK!
BUT HE WOULD BE RIGHT IN THE MIDDLE OF THE QUICKSAND!
BOY! A FROG LIKE THAT JUMPIN' OUT OF GLORIA'S LUNCH BOX WOULD SET THE SCHOOL ON ITS EAR!
GUNK!
MAYBE THERE'S SOME SAFE WAY I C'N GET OUT TO HIM!
I GOT IT! I'LL TIE A BIG BUNDLE OF BRANCHES TO EACH OF MY FEET!
THEY'LL WORK JUST LIKE SNOWSHOES, I BETCHA!
I-I'LL JUST HAVE TO BE CAREFUL NOT TO STAND IN ONE SPOT TOO LONG!
HERE GOES!

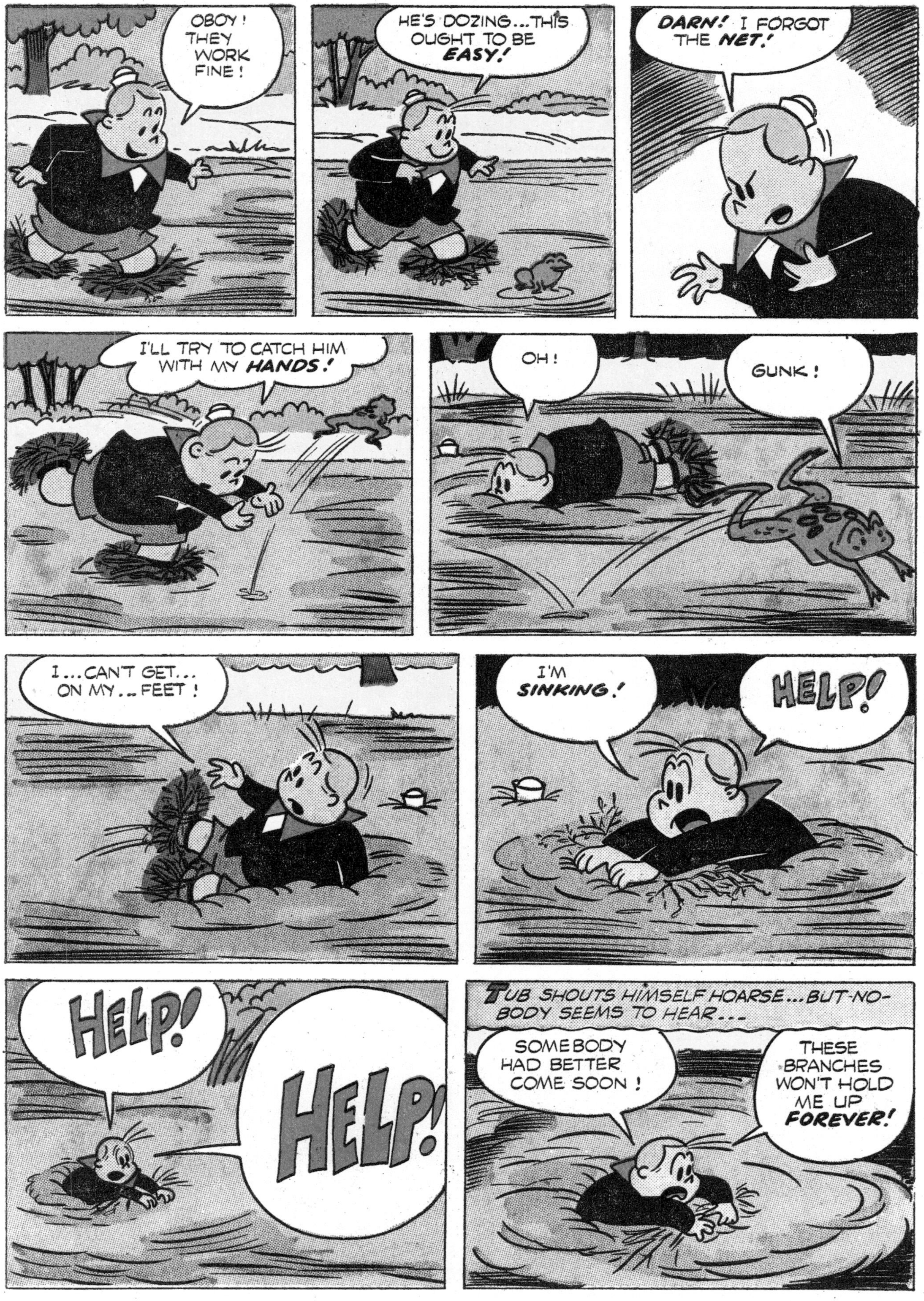
OBOY! THEY WORK FINE!
HE'S DOZING...THIS OUGHT TO BE EASY!
DARN! I FORGOT THE NET!
I'LL TRY TO CATCH HIM WITH MY HANDS!
OH!
GUNK!
I...CAN'T GET... ON MY...FEET!
I'M SINKING!
HELP!
HELP!
HELP!
TUB SHOUTS HIMSELF HOARSE...BUT NOBODY SEEMS TO HEAR...
SOMEBODY HAD BETTER COME SOON!
THESE BRANCHES WON'T HOLD ME UP FOREVER!

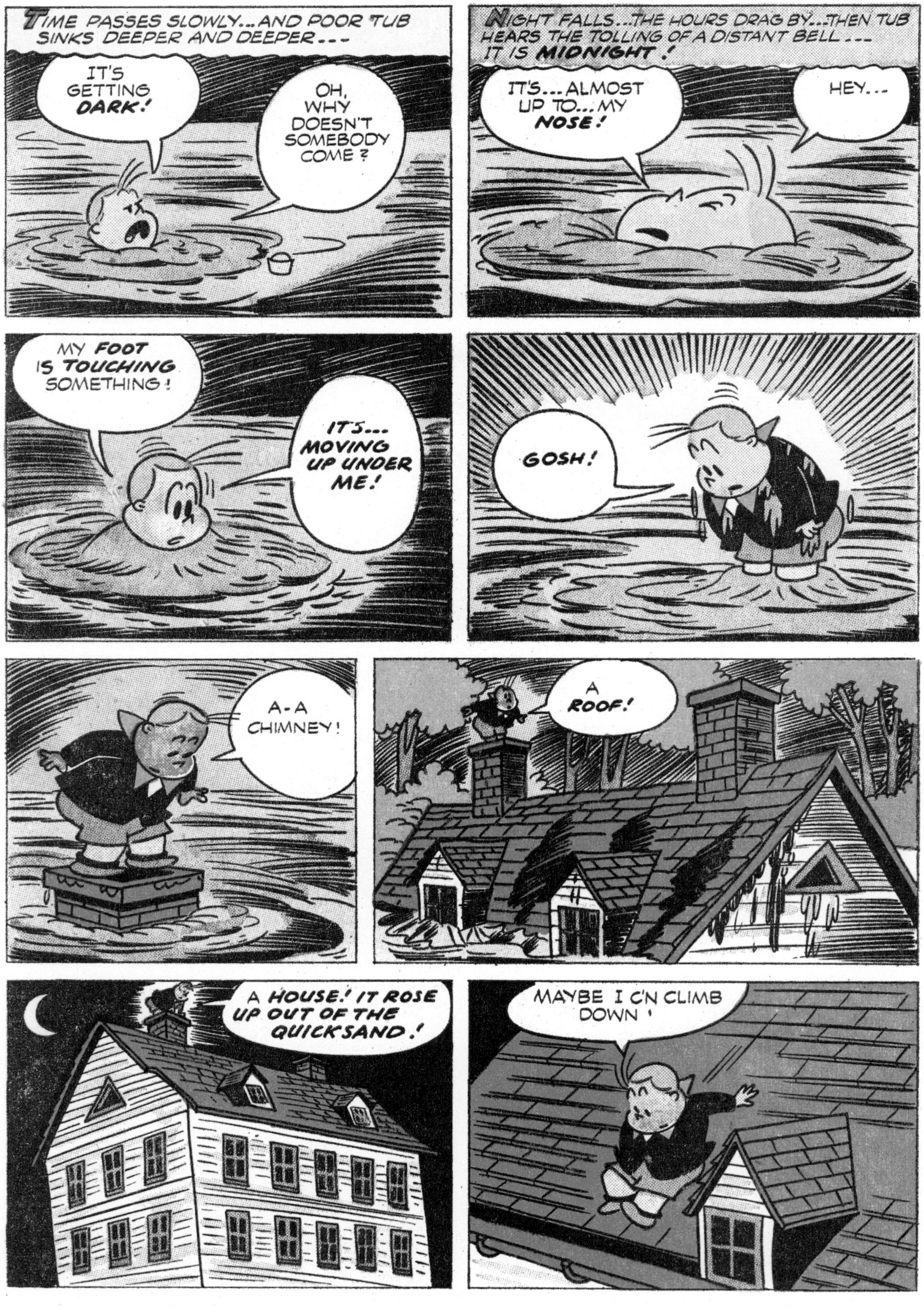
TIME PASSES SLOWLY...AND POOR TUB SINKS DEEPER AND DEEPER---
IT'S GETTING DARK!
OH, WHY DOESN'T SOMEBODY COME?
NIGHT FALLS...THE HOURS DRAG BY...THEN TUB HEARS THE TOLLING OF A DISTANT BELL--- IT IS MIDNIGHT!
IT'S...ALMOST UP TO...MY NOSE!
HEY...
MY FOOT IS TOUCHING SOMETHING!
IT'S... MOVING UP UNDER ME!
GOSH!
A-A CHIMNEY!
A ROOF!
A HOUSE! IT ROSE UP OUT OF THE QUICKSAND!
MAYBE I C'N CLIMB DOWN!

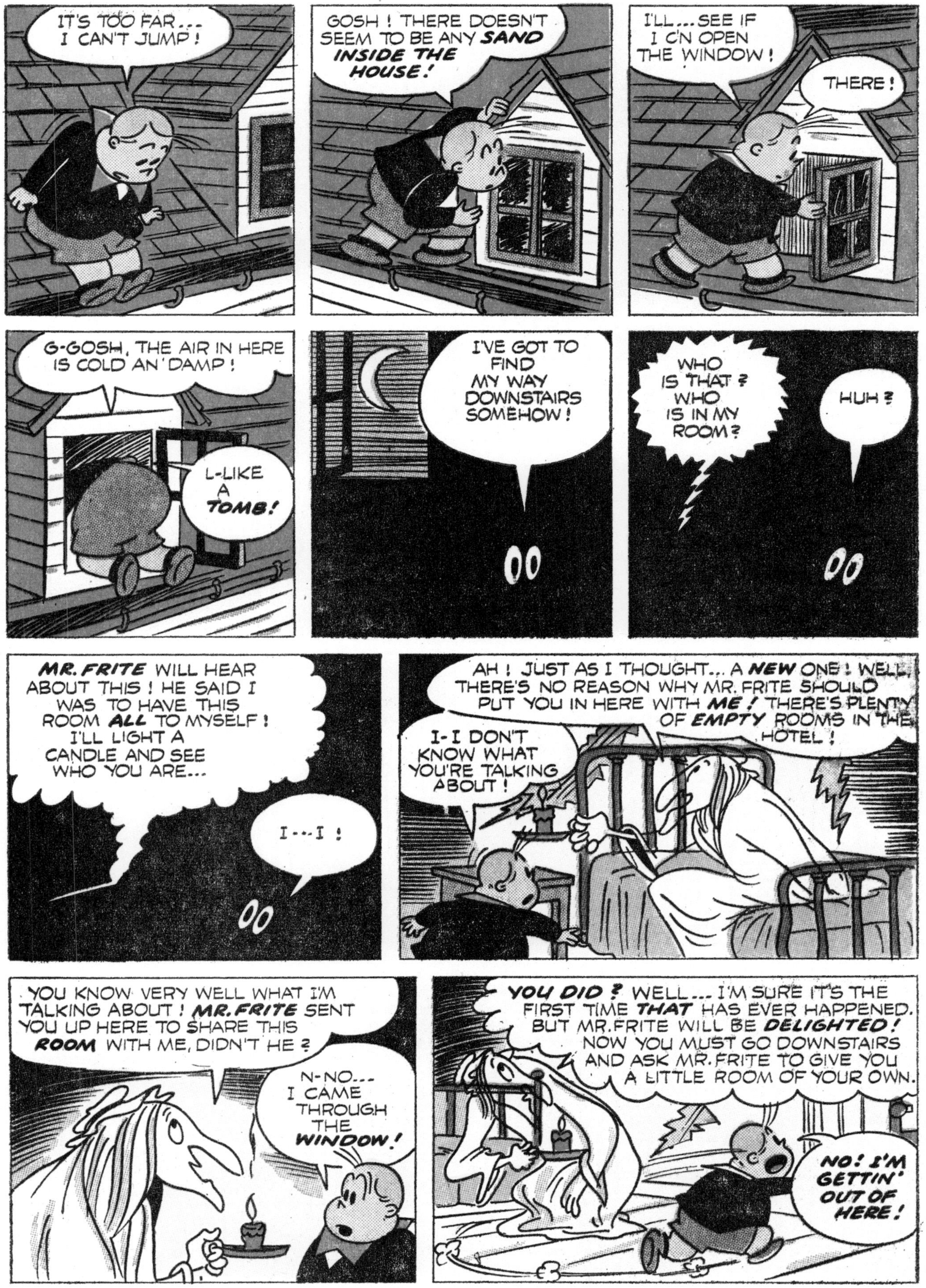
IT'S TOO FAR... I CAN'T JUMP!
GOSH! THERE DOESN'T SEEM TO BE ANY SAND INSIDE THE HOUSE!
I'LL... SEE IF I C'N OPEN THE WINDOW!
THERE!
G-GOSH, THE AIR IN HERE IS COLD AN' DAMP!
L-LIKE A TOMB!
I'VE GOT TO FIND MY WAY DOWNSTAIRS SOMEHOW!
WHO IS THAT? WHO IS IN MY ROOM?
HUH?
MR. FRITE WILL HEAR ABOUT THIS! HE SAID I WAS TO HAVE THIS ROOM ALL TO MYSELF! I'LL LIGHT A CANDLE AND SEE WHO YOU ARE...
I--I!
AH! JUST AS I THOUGHT... A NEW ONE! WELL, THERE'S NO REASON WHY MR. FRITE SHOULD PUT YOU IN HERE WITH ME! THERE'S PLENTY OF EMPTY ROOMS IN THE HOTEL!
I-I DON'T KNOW WHAT YOU'RE TALKING ABOUT!
YOU KNOW VERY WELL WHAT I'M TALKING ABOUT! MR. FRITE SENT YOU UP HERE TO SHARE THIS ROOM WITH ME, DIDN'T HE?
N-NO... I CAME THROUGH THE WINDOW!
YOU DID? WELL... I'M SURE IT'S THE FIRST TIME THAT HAS EVER HAPPENED. BUT MR. FRITE WILL BE DELIGHTED! NOW YOU MUST GO DOWNSTAIRS AND ASK MR. FRITE TO GIVE YOU A LITTLE ROOM OF YOUR OWN.
NO! I'M GETTIN' OUT OF HERE!

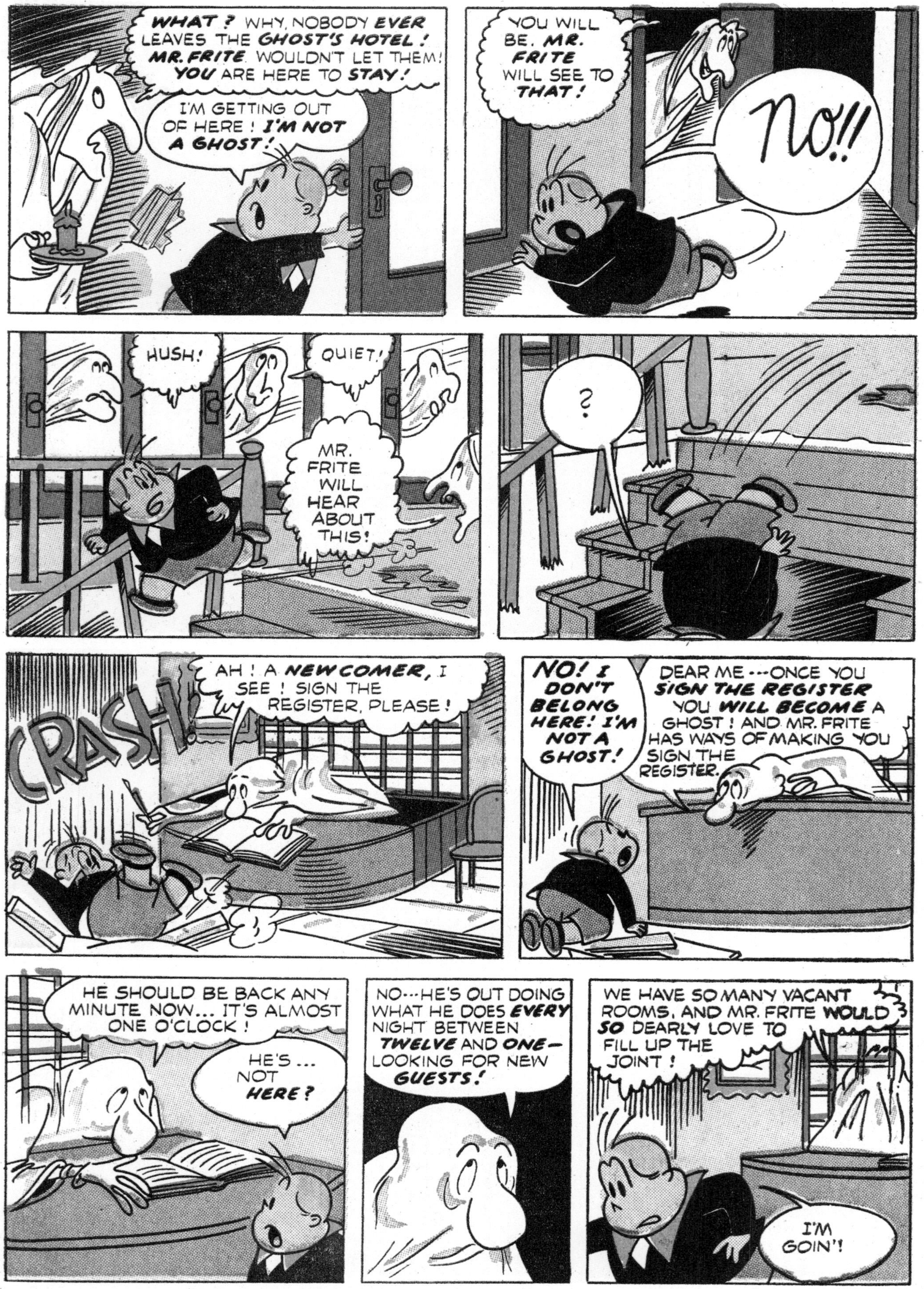
WHAT? WHY, NOBODY EVER LEAVES THE GHOST'S HOTEL! MR. FRITE WOULDN'T LET THEM! YOU ARE HERE TO STAY!
I'M GETTING OUT OF HERE! I'M NOT A GHOST!
YOU WILL BE. MR. FRITE WILL SEE TO THAT!
NO!!
HUSH!
QUIET!
MR. FRITE WILL HEAR ABOUT THIS!
?
CRASH!
AH! A NEWCOMER, I SEE! SIGN THE REGISTER, PLEASE!
NO! I DON'T BELONG HERE! I'M NOT A GHOST!
DEAR ME---ONCE YOU SIGN THE REGISTER YOU WILL BECOME A GHOST! AND MR. FRITE HAS WAYS OF MAKING YOU SIGN THE REGISTER.
HE SHOULD BE BACK ANY MINUTE NOW... IT'S ALMOST ONE O'CLOCK!
HE'S... NOT HERE?
NO---HE'S OUT DOING WHAT HE DOES EVERY NIGHT BETWEEN TWELVE AND ONE—LOOKING FOR NEW GUESTS!
WE HAVE SO MANY VACANT ROOMS, AND MR. FRITE WOULD SO DEARLY LOVE TO FILL UP THE JOINT!
I'M GOIN'!

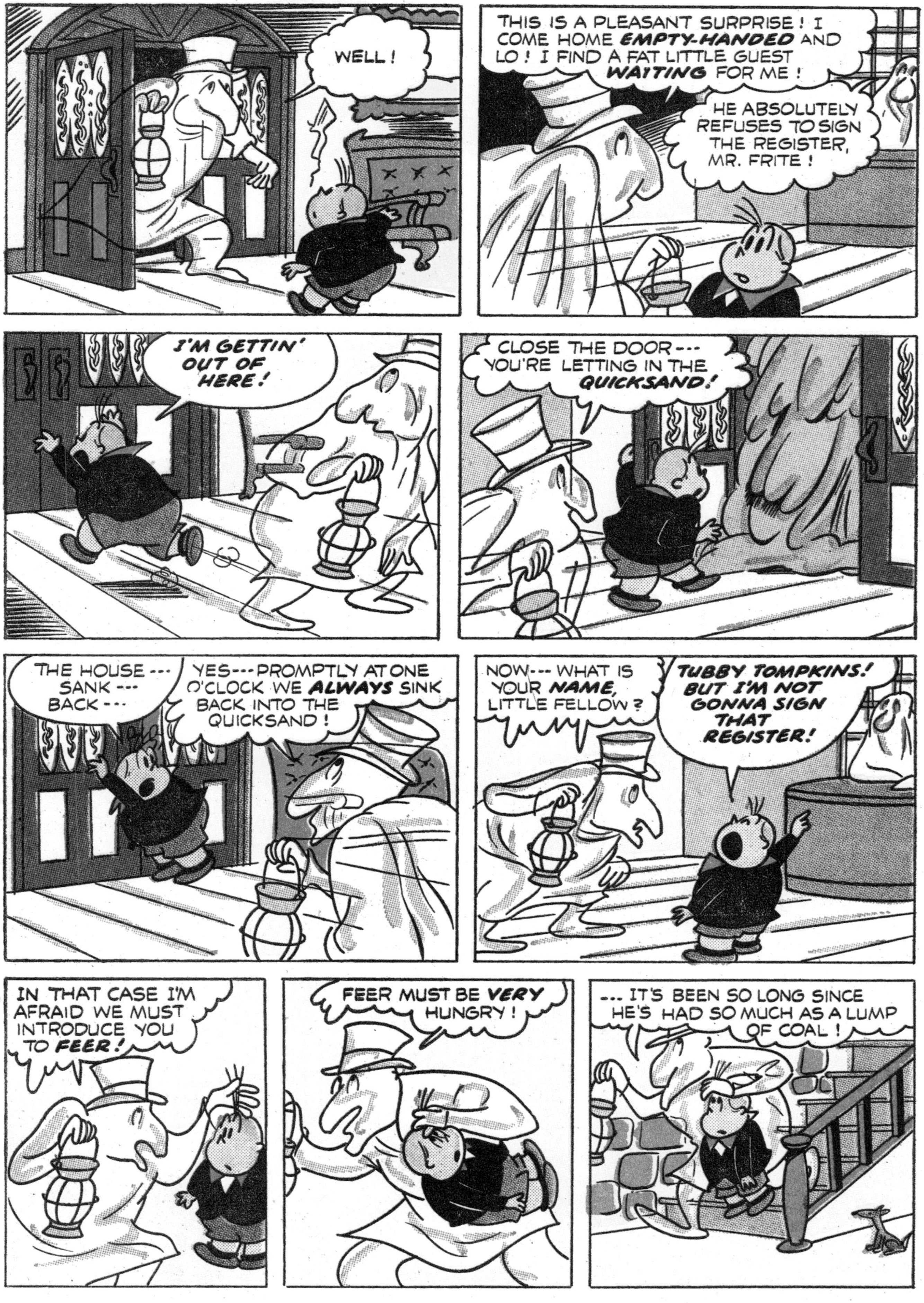
WELL!
THIS IS A PLEASANT SURPRISE! I COME HOME EMPTY-HANDED AND LO! I FIND A FAT LITTLE GUEST WAITING FOR ME!
HE ABSOLUTELY REFUSES TO SIGN THE REGISTER, MR. FRITE!
I'M GETTIN' OUT OF HERE!
CLOSE THE DOOR--- YOU'RE LETTING IN THE QUICKSAND!
THE HOUSE--- SANK--- BACK---
YES---PROMPTLY AT ONE O'CLOCK WE ALWAYS SINK BACK INTO THE QUICKSAND!
NOW--- WHAT IS YOUR NAME, LITTLE FELLOW?
TUBBY TOMPKINS! BUT I'M NOT GONNA SIGN THAT REGISTER!
IN THAT CASE I'M AFRAID WE MUST INTRODUCE YOU TO FEER!
FEER MUST BE VERY HUNGRY!
--- IT'S BEEN SO LONG SINCE HE'S HAD SO MUCH AS A LUMP OF COAL!

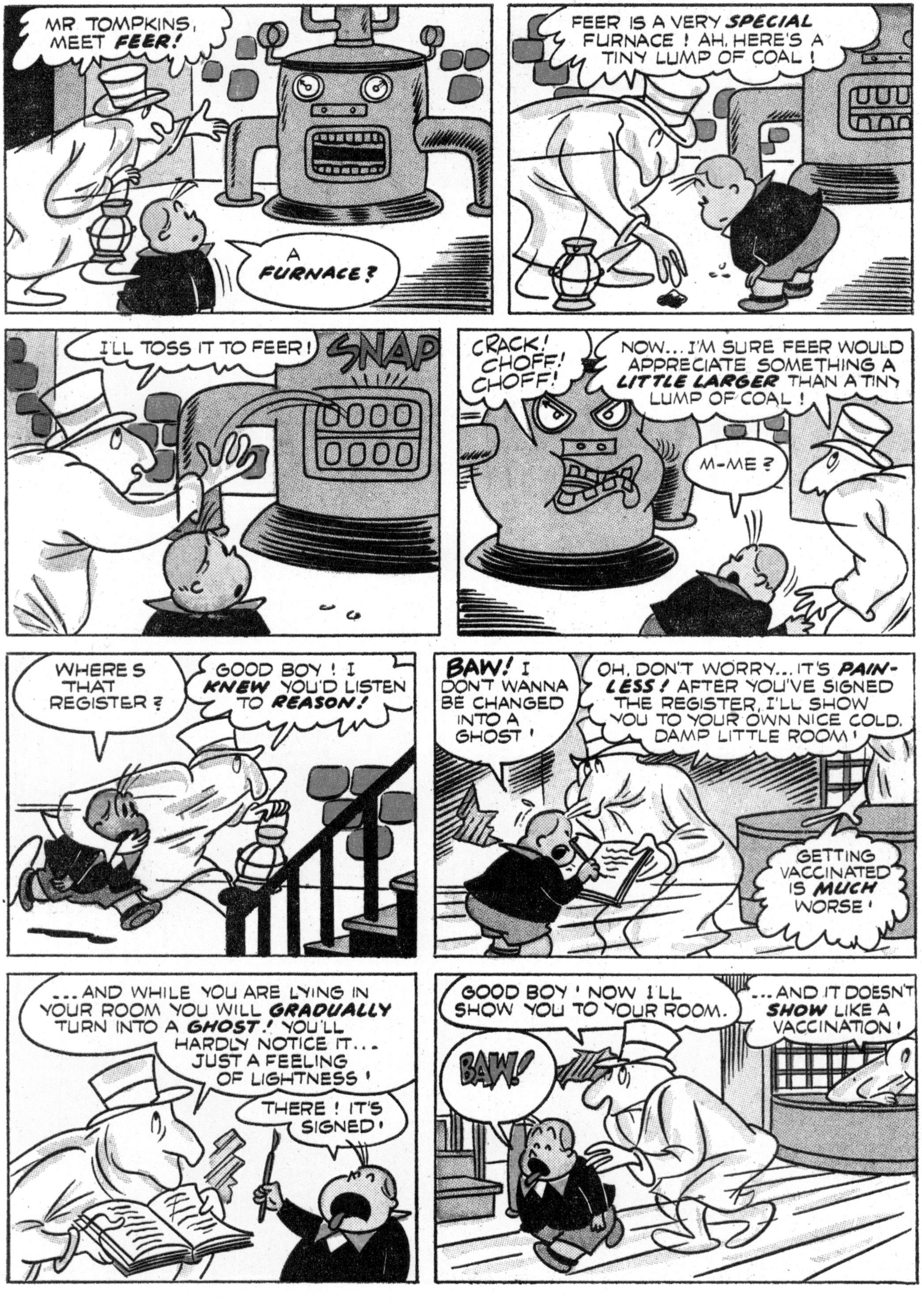
MR TOMPKINS, MEET FEER!
A FURNACE?
FEER IS A VERY SPECIAL FURNACE! AH, HERE'S A TINY LUMP OF COAL!
I'LL TOSS IT TO FEER!
SNAP
CRACK! CHOFF! CHOFF!
NOW... I'M SURE FEER WOULD APPRECIATE SOMETHING A LITTLE LARGER THAN A TINY LUMP OF COAL!
M-ME?
WHERE'S THAT REGISTER?
GOOD BOY! I KNEW YOU'D LISTEN TO REASON!
BAW! I DON'T WANNA BE CHANGED INTO A GHOST!
OH, DON'T WORRY... IT'S PAIN-LESS! AFTER YOU'VE SIGNED THE REGISTER, I'LL SHOW YOU TO YOUR OWN NICE COLD, DAMP LITTLE ROOM!
GETTING VACCINATED IS MUCH WORSE!
...AND WHILE YOU ARE LYING IN YOUR ROOM YOU WILL GRADUALLY TURN INTO A GHOST! YOU'LL HARDLY NOTICE IT... JUST A FEELING OF LIGHTNESS!
THERE! IT'S SIGNED!
GOOD BOY! NOW I'LL SHOW YOU TO YOUR ROOM.
...AND IT DOESN'T SHOW LIKE A VACCINATION!
BAW!

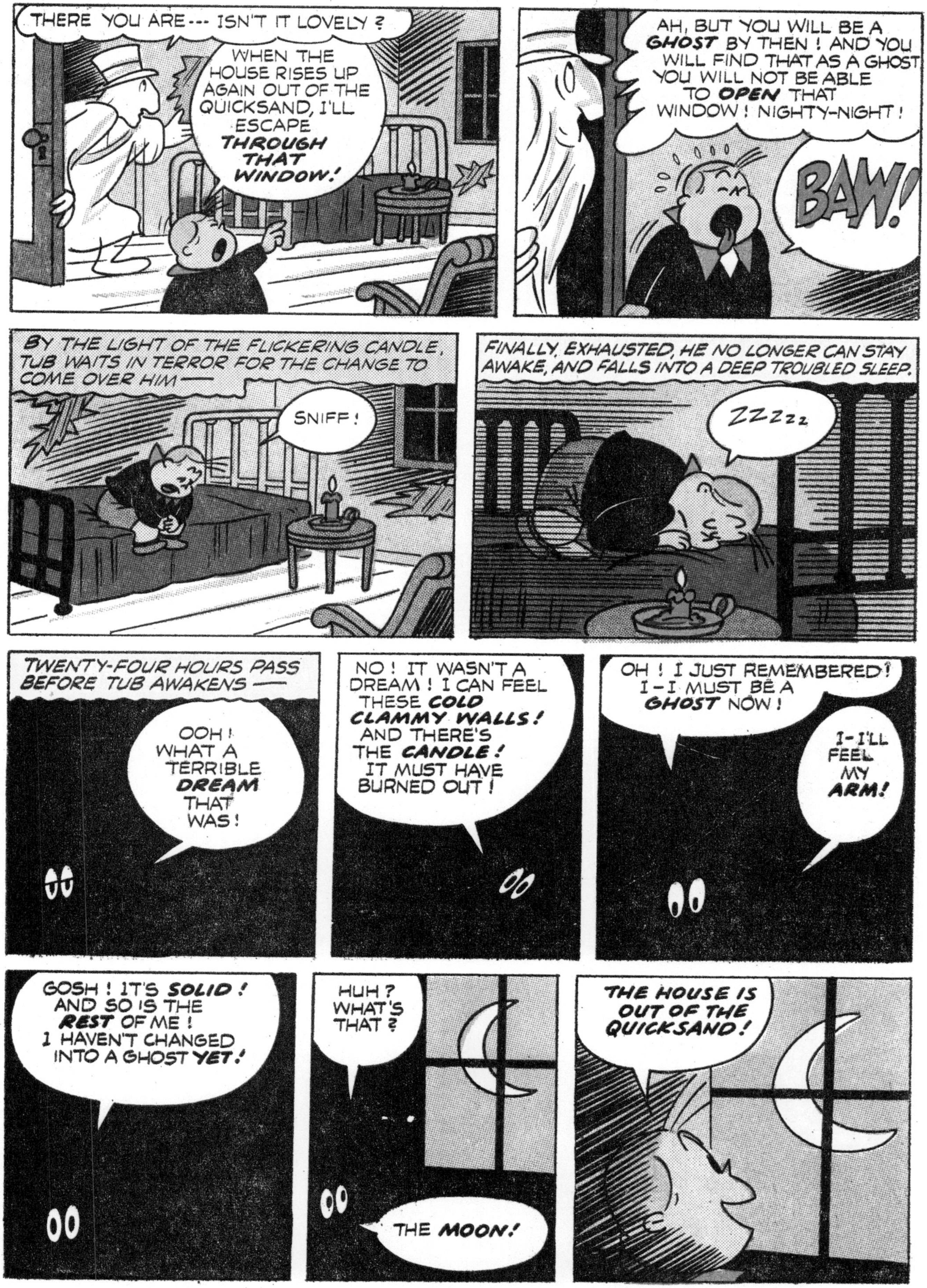
THERE YOU ARE --- ISN'T IT LOVELY ?
WHEN THE HOUSE RISES UP AGAIN OUT OF THE QUICKSAND, I'LL ESCAPE THROUGH THAT WINDOW!
AH, BUT YOU WILL BE A GHOST BY THEN ! AND YOU WILL FIND THAT AS A GHOST YOU WILL NOT BE ABLE TO OPEN THAT WINDOW ! NIGHTY-NIGHT !
BAW!
BY THE LIGHT OF THE FLICKERING CANDLE, TUB WAITS IN TERROR FOR THE CHANGE TO COME OVER HIM —
SNIFF !
FINALLY, EXHAUSTED, HE NO LONGER CAN STAY AWAKE, AND FALLS INTO A DEEP TROUBLED SLEEP.
ZZZzz
TWENTY-FOUR HOURS PASS BEFORE TUB AWAKENS —
OOH ! WHAT A TERRIBLE DREAM THAT WAS !
NO ! IT WASN'T A DREAM ! I CAN FEEL THESE COLD CLAMMY WALLS ! AND THERE'S THE CANDLE ! IT MUST HAVE BURNED OUT !
OH ! I JUST REMEMBERED ! I–I MUST BE A GHOST NOW !
I–I'LL FEEL MY ARM!
GOSH ! IT'S SOLID ! AND SO IS THE REST OF ME ! I HAVEN'T CHANGED INTO A GHOST YET!
HUH ? WHAT'S THAT ?
THE MOON!
THE HOUSE IS OUT OF THE QUICKSAND !

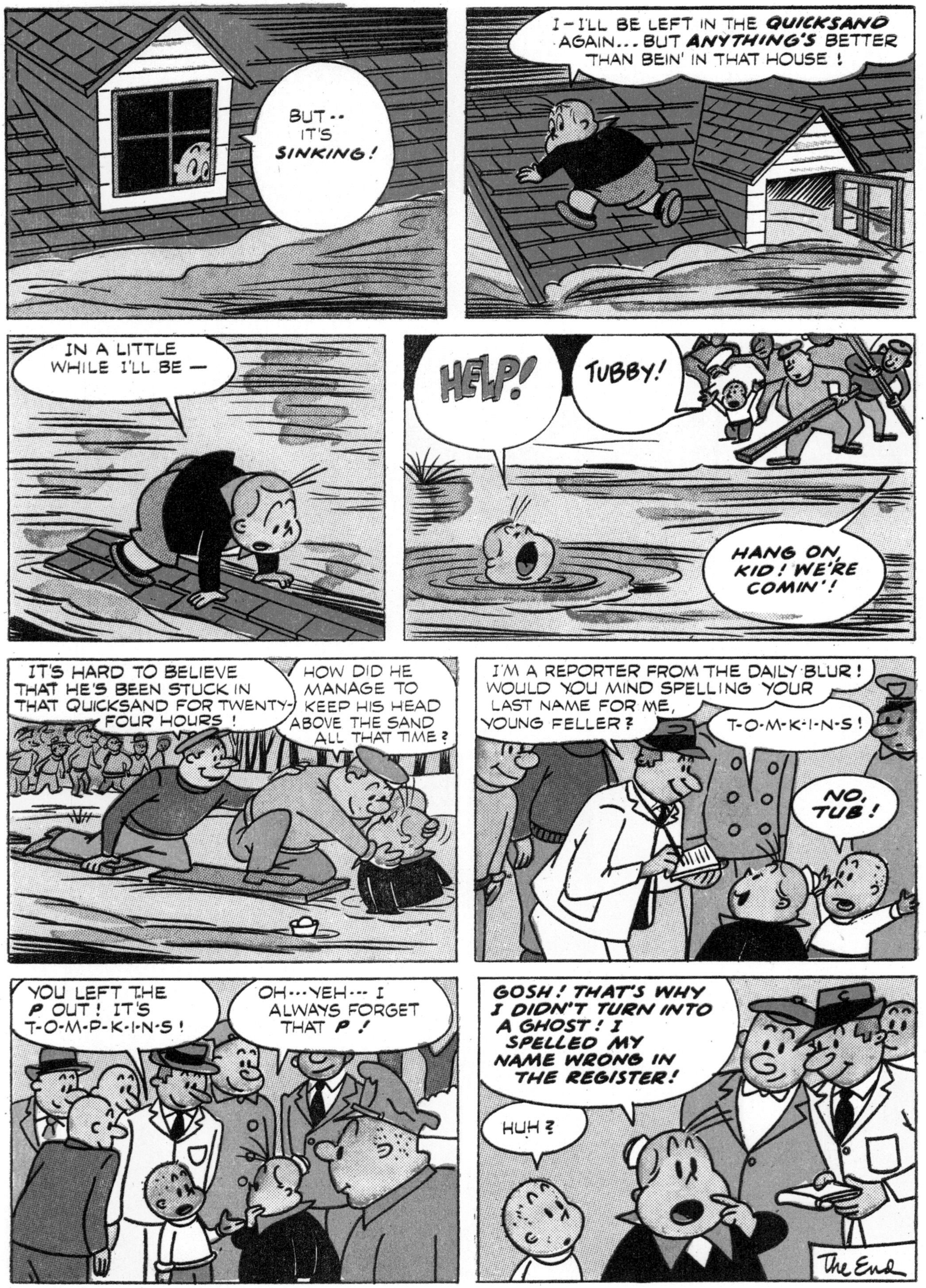
BUT -- IT'S SINKING!
I-I'LL BE LEFT IN THE QUICKSAND AGAIN... BUT ANYTHING'S BETTER THAN BEIN' IN THAT HOUSE!
IN A LITTLE WHILE I'LL BE —
HELP!
TUBBY!
HANG ON, KID! WE'RE COMIN'!
IT'S HARD TO BELIEVE THAT HE'S BEEN STUCK IN THAT QUICKSAND FOR TWENTY-FOUR HOURS!
HOW DID HE MANAGE TO KEEP HIS HEAD ABOVE THE SAND ALL THAT TIME?
I'M A REPORTER FROM THE DAILY BLUR! WOULD YOU MIND SPELLING YOUR LAST NAME FOR ME, YOUNG FELLER?
T-O-M-K-I-N-S!
NO, TUB!
YOU LEFT THE P OUT! IT'S T-O-M-P-K-I-N-S!
OH--- YEH--- I ALWAYS FORGET THAT P!
GOSH! THAT'S WHY I DIDN'T TURN INTO A GHOST! I SPELLED MY NAME WRONG IN THE REGISTER!
HUH?
The End

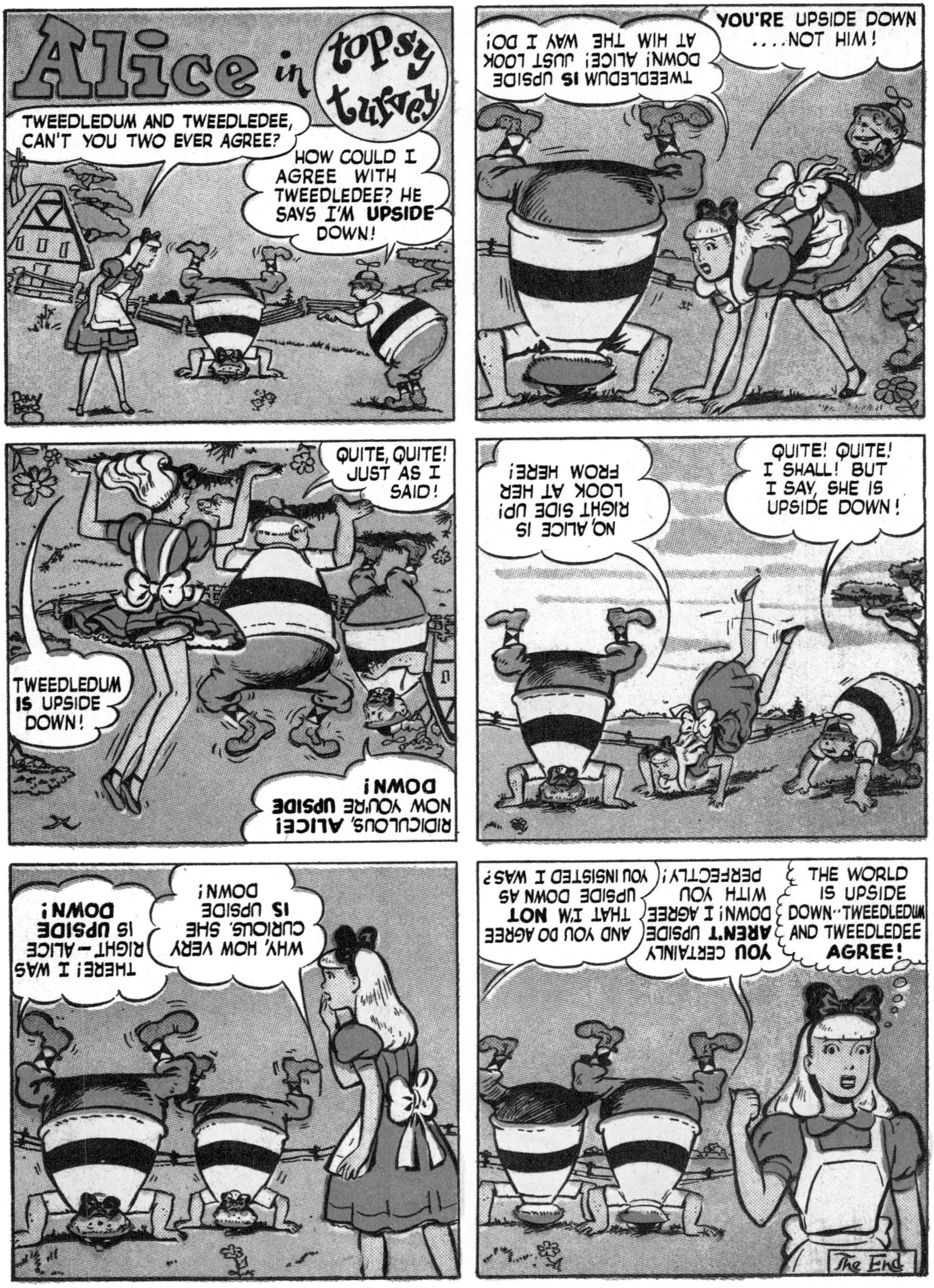
Alice in topsy turvy
TWEEDLEDUM AND TWEEDLEDEE, CAN'T YOU TWO EVER AGREE?
HOW COULD I AGREE WITH TWEEDLEDEE? HE SAYS I'M **UPSIDE** DOWN!
Dave Berg
TWEEDLEDUM **IS** UPSIDE DOWN! ALICE! JUST LOOK AT HIM THE WAY I DO!
YOU'RE UPSIDE DOWN ....NOT HIM!
QUITE, QUITE! JUST AS I SAID!
TWEEDLEDUM **IS** UPSIDE DOWN!
RIDICULOUS, **ALICE!** NOW YOU'RE **UPSIDE DOWN!**
NO, ALICE IS RIGHT SIDE UP! LOOK AT HER FROM HERE!
QUITE! QUITE! I SHALL! BUT I SAY, SHE IS UPSIDE DOWN!
THERE! I WAS RIGHT—ALICE IS **UPSIDE DOWN!**
WHY, HOW VERY CURIOUS. SHE **IS** UPSIDE DOWN!
AND YOU DO AGREE THAT I'M **NOT** UPSIDE DOWN AS YOU INSISTED I WAS?
YOU CERTAINLY **AREN'T** UPSIDE DOWN! I AGREE WITH YOU PERFECTLY!
THE WORLD IS UPSIDE DOWN..TWEEDLEDUM AND TWEEDLEDEE **AGREE!**
The End

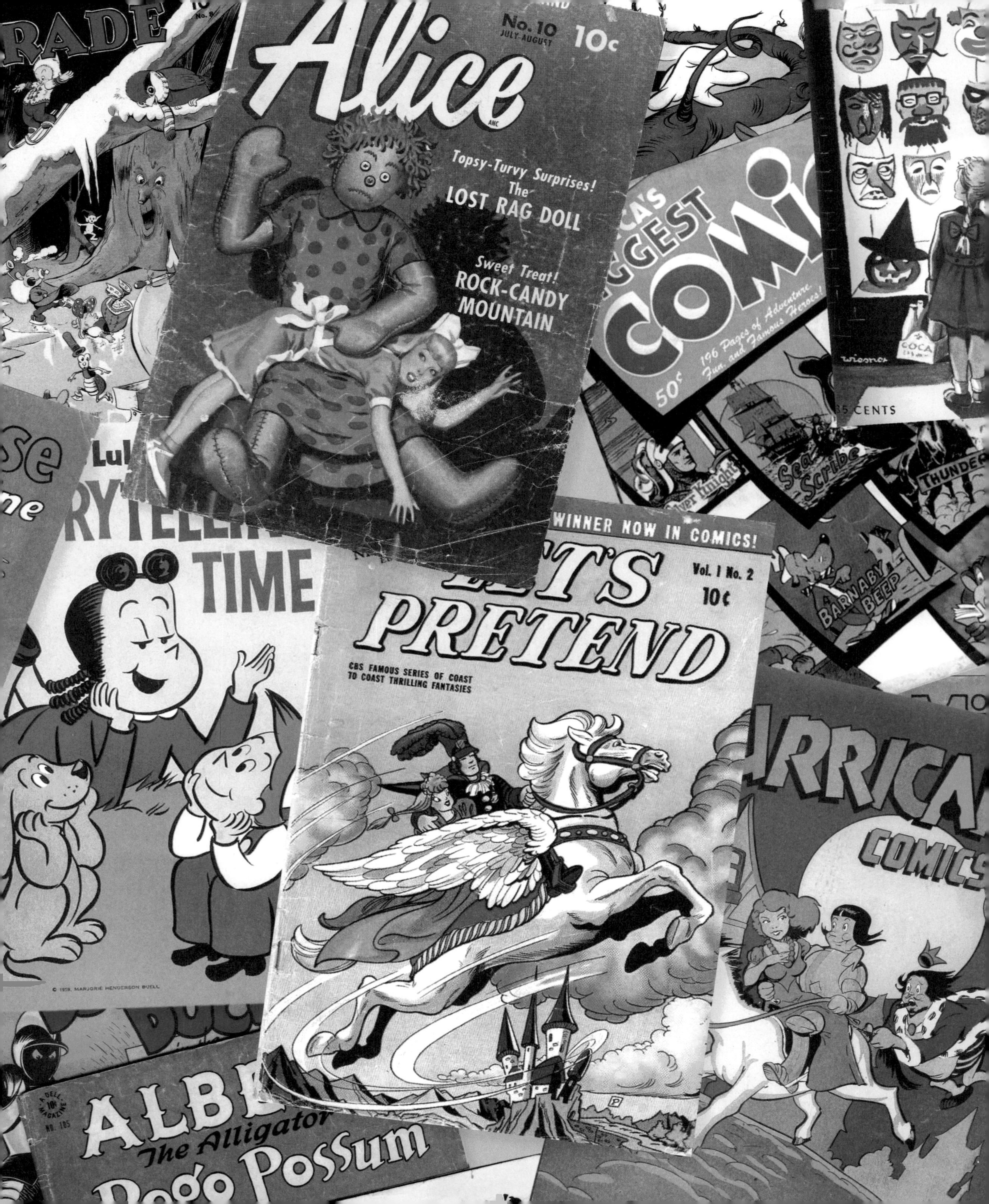
Alice
No. 10
JULY-AUGUST
10c
Topsy-Turvy Surprises!
The
LOST RAG DOLL
Sweet Treat!
ROCK-CANDY
MOUNTAIN
COMIC
196 Pages of Adventure, Fun, and Famous Heroes!
50c
85 CENTS
Sea Scribe
BARNABY BEEP
TIME
© 1959, MARJORIE HENDERSON BUELL
WINNER NOW IN COMICS!
PRETEND
Vol. 1 No. 2
10¢
CBS FAMOUS SERIES OF COAST
TO COAST THRILLING FANTASIES
COMICS
The Alligator
Pogo Possum

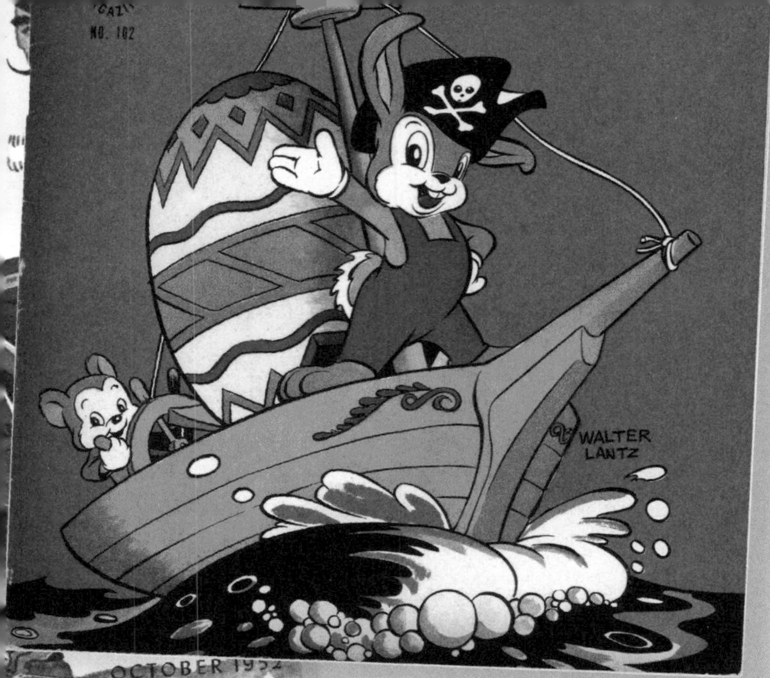
NO. 162
WALTER LANTZ
OCTOBER 1952

Chapter 4

STORYTIME

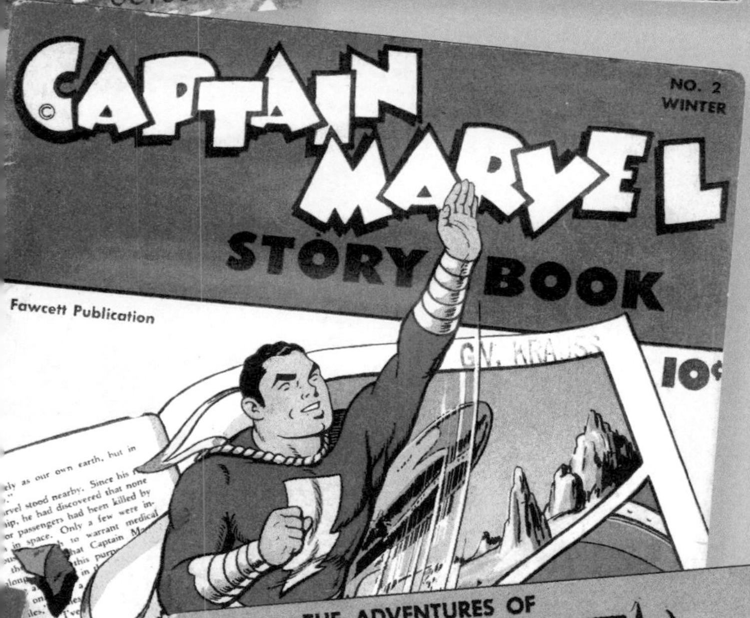
CAPTAIN MARVEL
NO. 2 WINTER
STORY BOOK
Fawcett Publication
10¢

Comics are pictures put together to tell stories.

A few of the stories we have put together here might, um, *bug* you a bit: Intellectual Amos gives you a close-up look at the real world of ants, Billy and Bonnie Bee are threatened by a dragonfly, and Donald Duck is chased by bees. Artist and writer Carl Barks then takes us to the imaginary world of Tralla La, to tell us a lot about how our real world works. Reading a good comic book story is like watching somebody blow up a balloon: You watch it get bigger and bigger until it finally POPS at the end. Another way to think about stories is as a search: Dan Noonan's Egbert and Tuffy go looking for danger, and what they find instead is . . . a new friend. Maybe that's the best way to think about stories: making a surprising new friend you can visit over and over again.

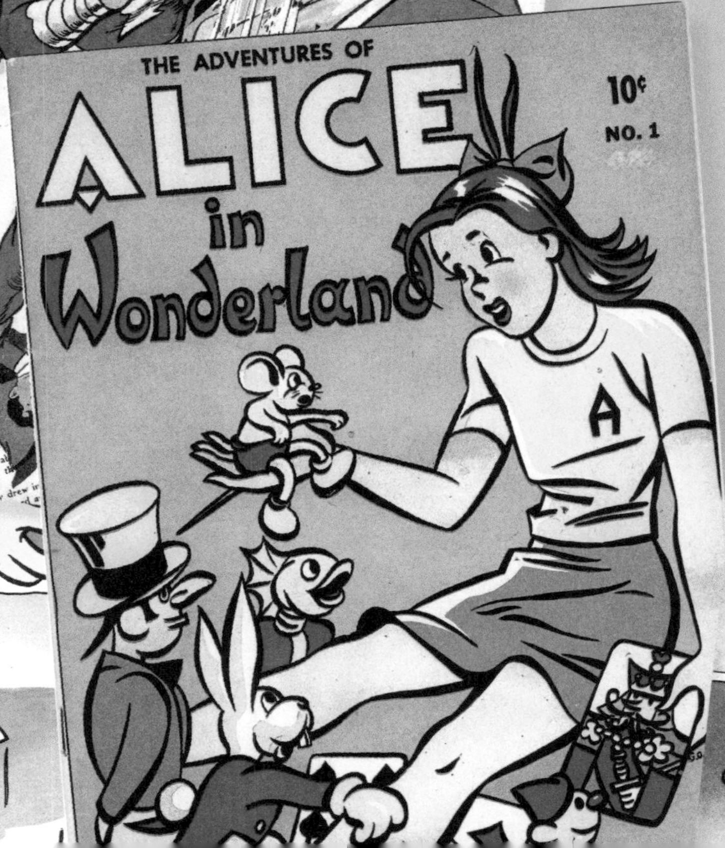
THE ADVENTURES OF
ALICE in Wonderland
10¢
NO. 1

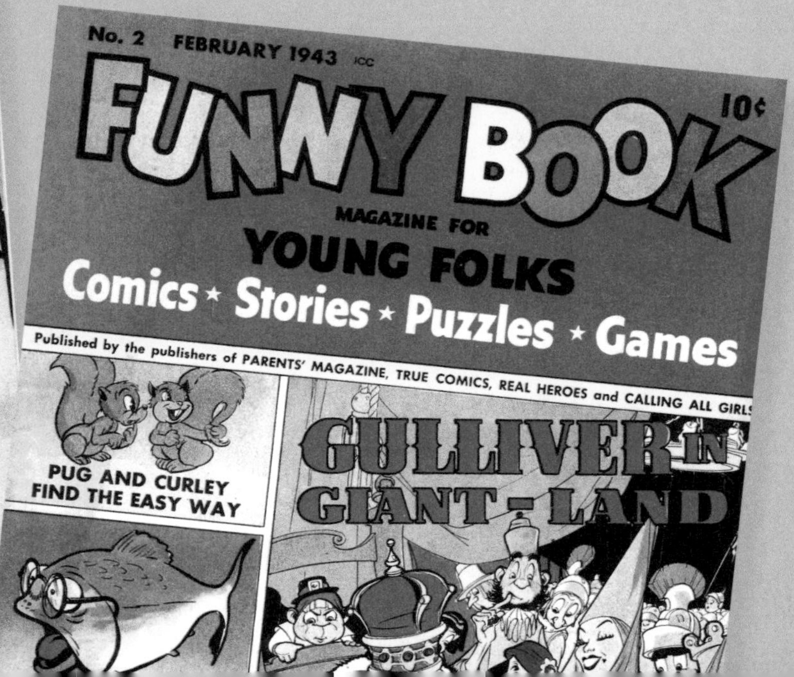
No. 2 FEBRUARY 1943
FUNNY BOOK
10¢
MAGAZINE FOR
YOUNG FOLKS
Comics * Stories * Puzzles * Games
Published by the publishers of PARENTS' MAGAZINE, TRUE COMICS, REAL HEROES and CALLING ALL GIRLS
PUG AND CURLEY FIND THE EASY WAY
GULLIVER IN GIANT-LAND

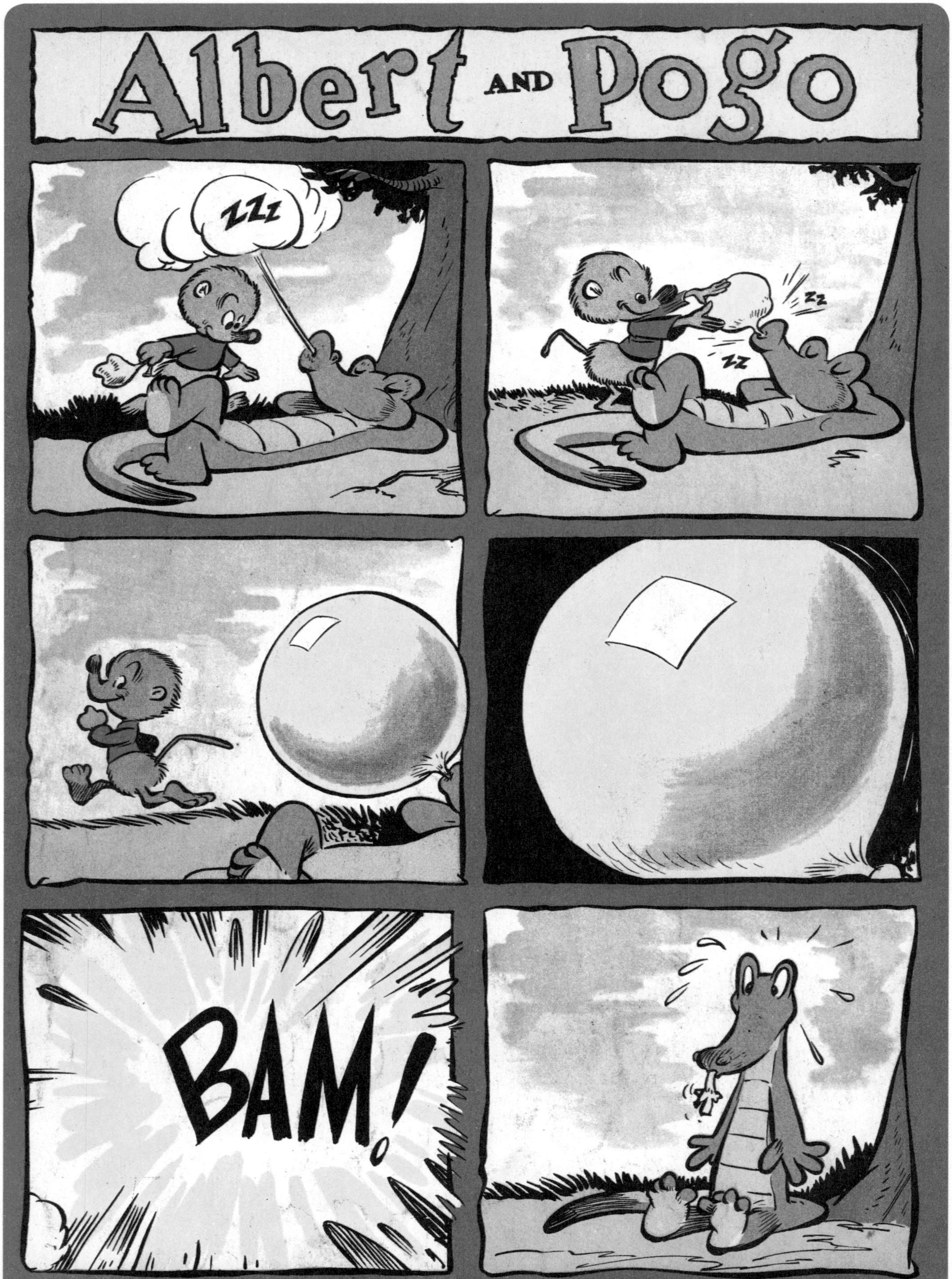
Albert AND Pogo
ZZz
zz
zz
BAM!

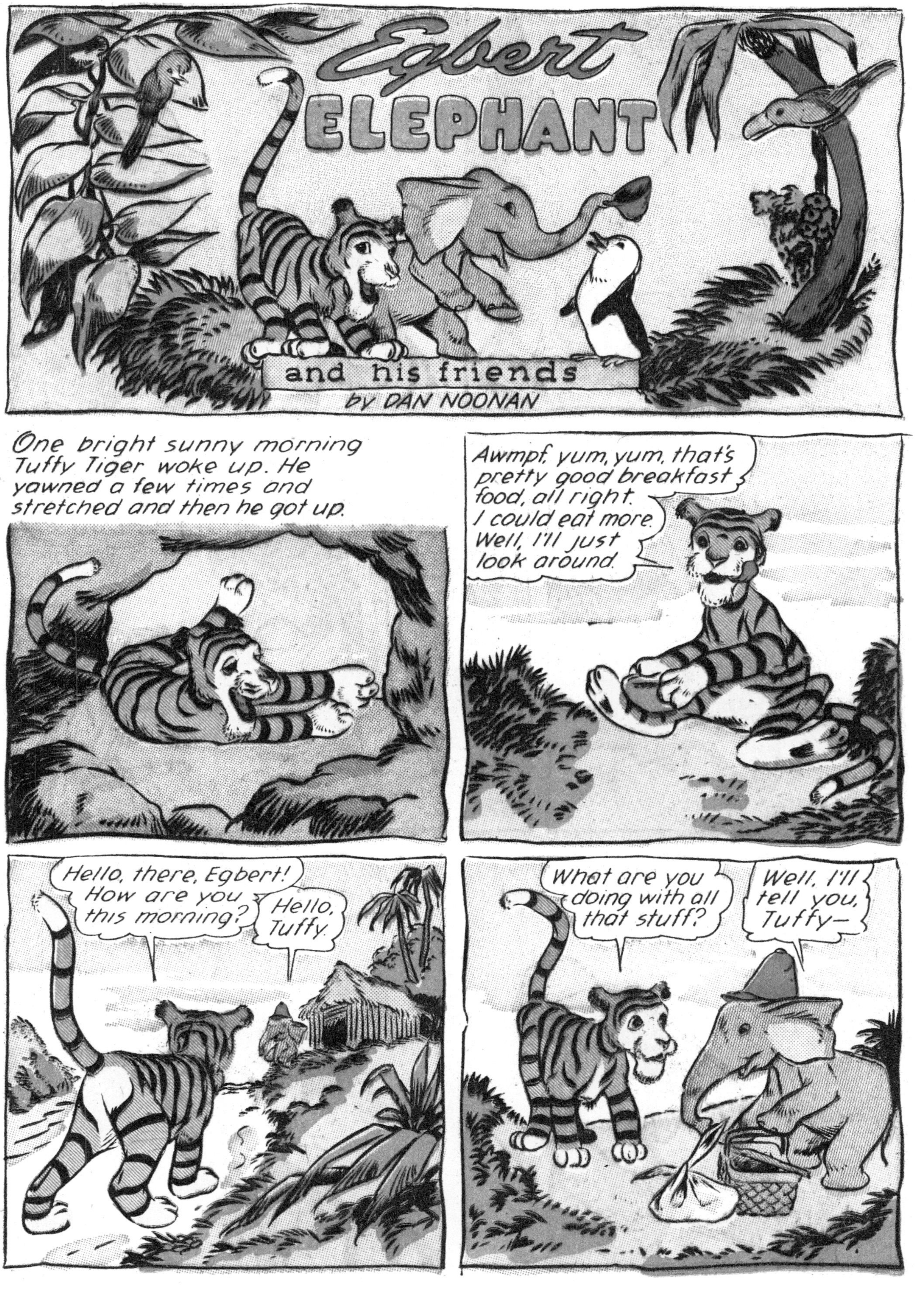
Egbert ELEPHANT
and his friends
by DAN NOONAN
One bright sunny morning Tuffy Tiger woke up. He yawned a few times and stretched and then he got up.
Awmpf, yum, yum, that's pretty good breakfast food, all right. I could eat more. Well, I'll just look around.
Hello, there, Egbert! How are you this morning?
Hello, Tuffy.
What are you doing with all that stuff?
Well, I'll tell you, Tuffy—

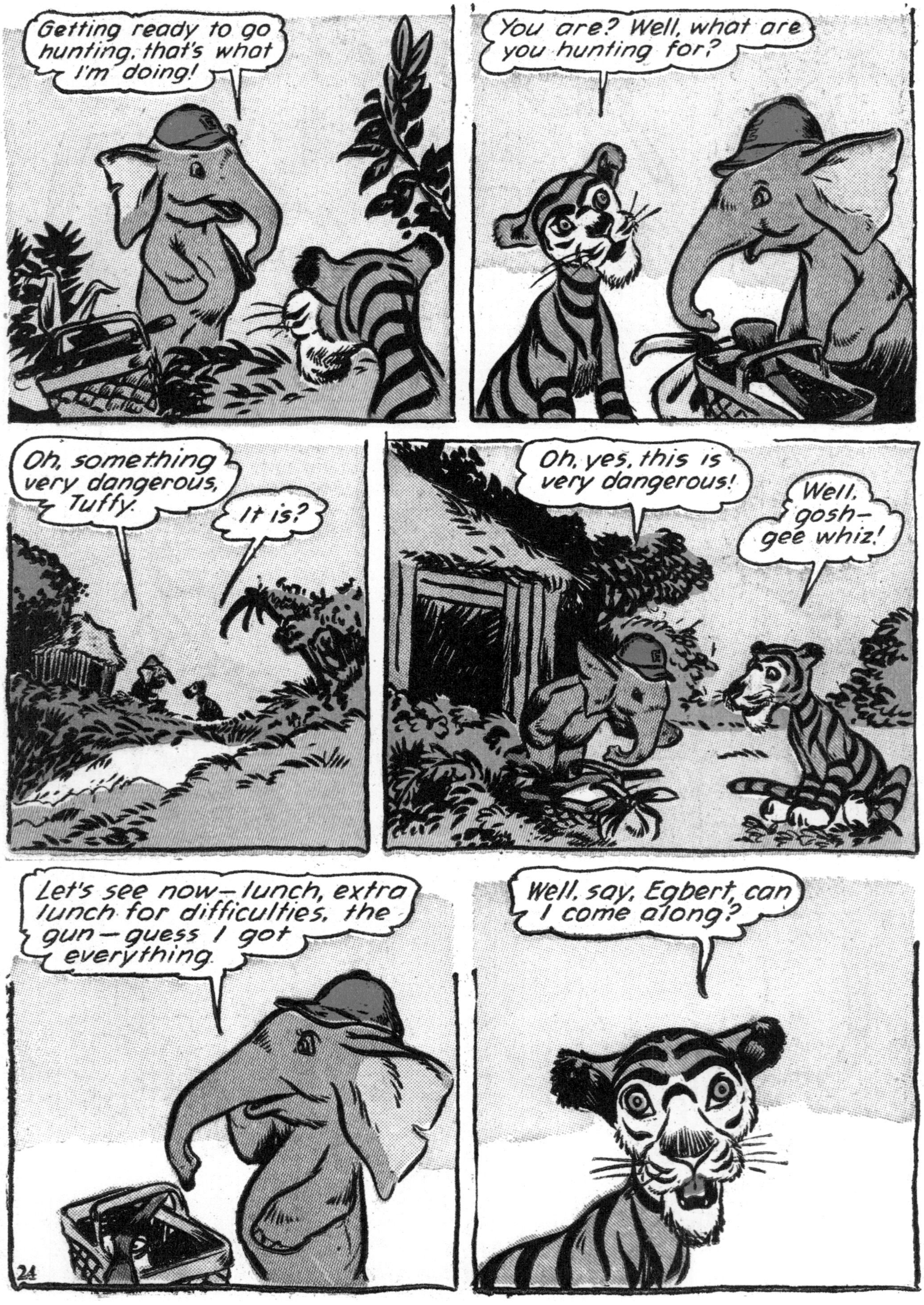
Getting ready to go hunting, that's what I'm doing!
You are? Well, what are you hunting for?
Oh, something very dangerous, Tuffy.
It is?
Oh, yes, this is very dangerous!
Well, gosh-gee whiz!
Let's see now—lunch, extra lunch for difficulties, the gun—guess I got everything.
Well, say, Egbert, can I come along?
24

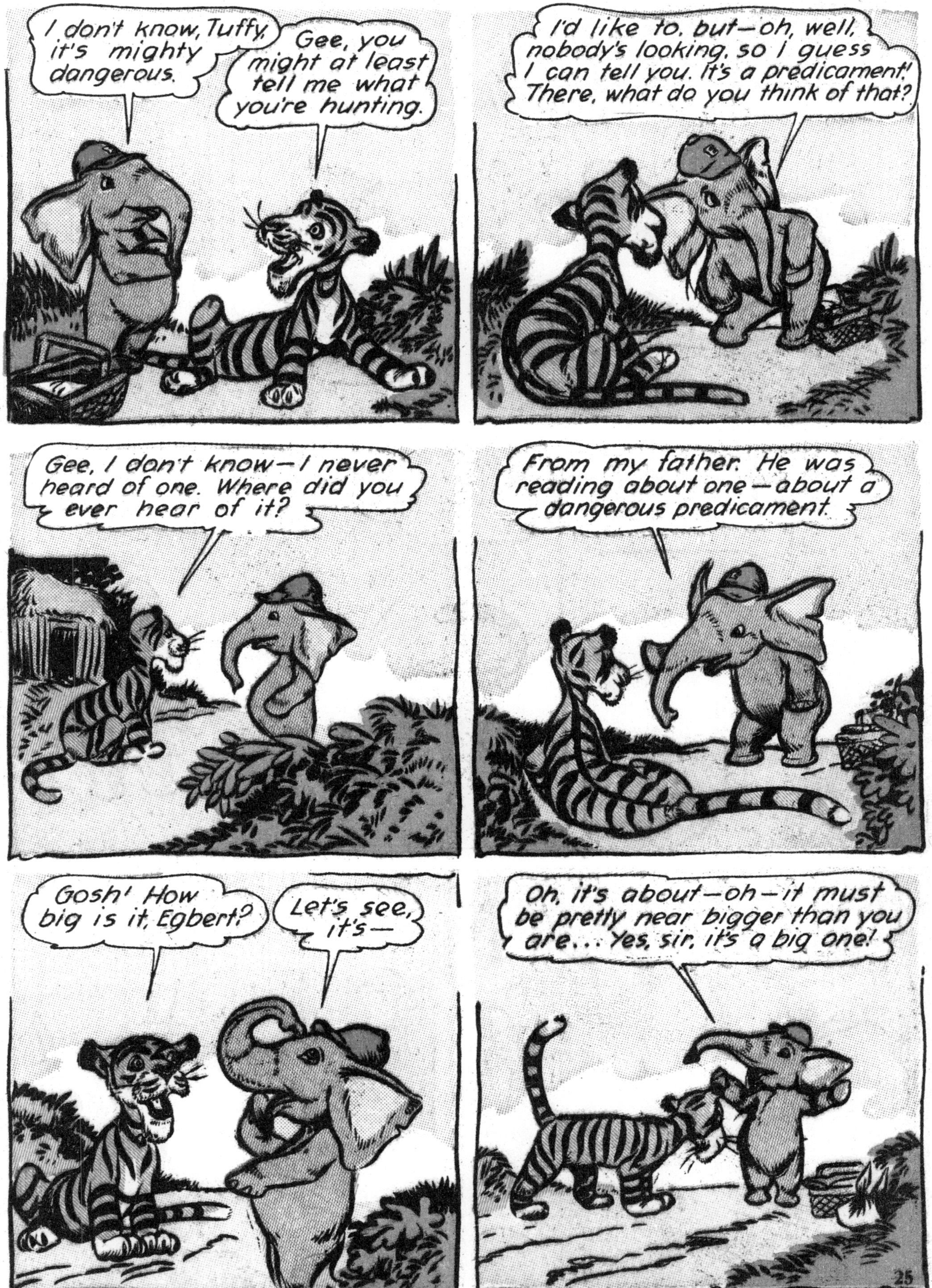
I don't know, Tuffy, it's mighty dangerous.
Gee, you might at least tell me what you're hunting.
I'd like to, but—oh, well, nobody's looking, so I guess I can tell you. It's a predicament! There, what do you think of that?
Gee, I don't know—I never heard of one. Where did you ever hear of it?
From my father. He was reading about one—about a dangerous predicament.
Gosh! How big is it, Egbert?
Let's see, it's—
Oh, it's about—oh—it must be pretty near bigger than you are... Yes, sir, it's a big one!
25

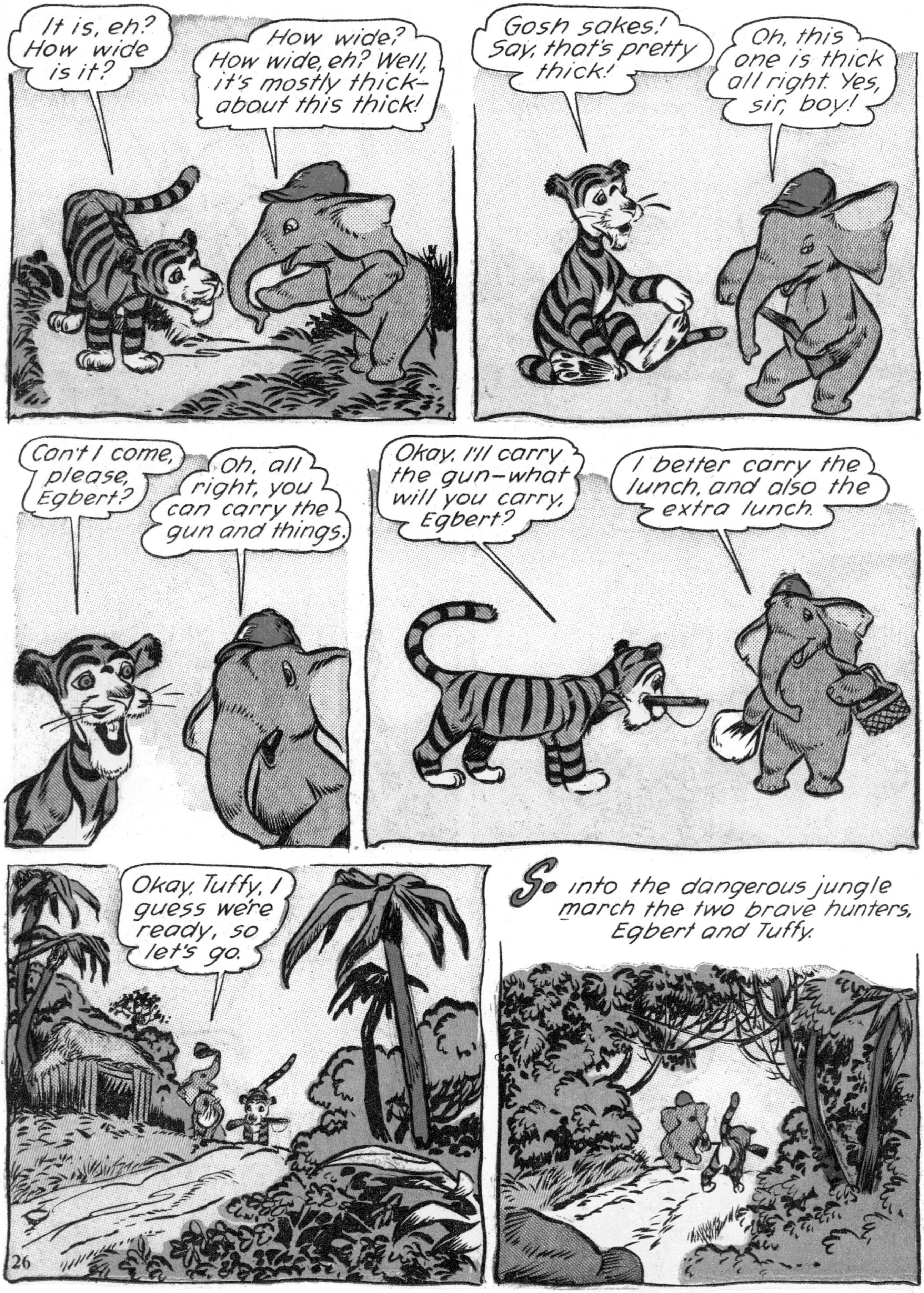
It is, eh? How wide is it?
How wide? How wide, eh? Well, it's mostly thick— about this thick!
Gosh sakes! Say, that's pretty thick!
Oh, this one is thick all right. Yes, sir, boy!
Can't I come, please, Egbert?
Oh, all right, you can carry the gun and things.
Okay, I'll carry the gun—what will you carry, Egbert?
I better carry the lunch, and also the extra lunch.
Okay, Tuffy, I guess we're ready, so let's go.
So into the dangerous jungle march the two brave hunters, Egbert and Tuffy.
26

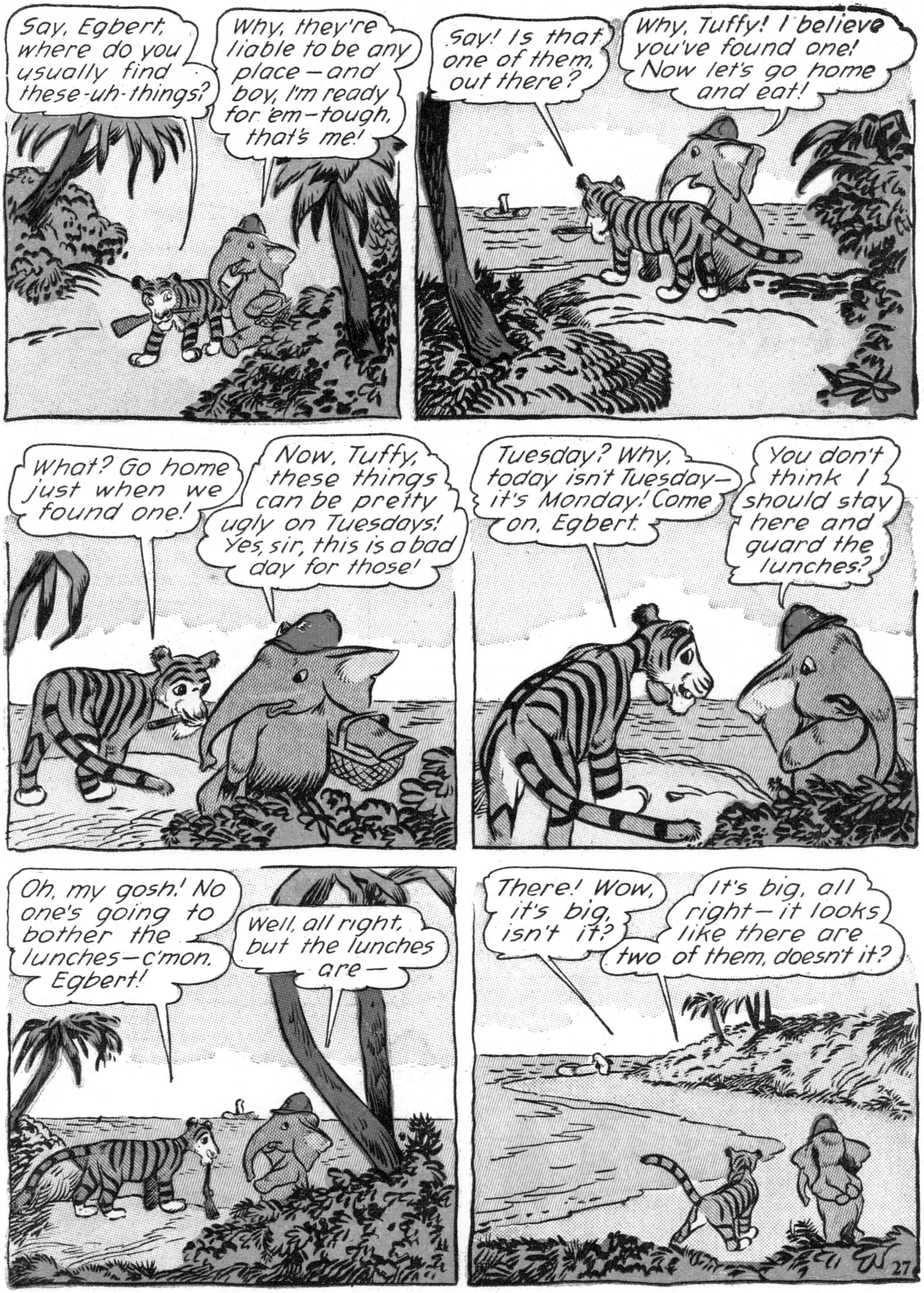
Say, Egbert, where do you usually find these-uh-things?
Why, they're liable to be any place—and boy, I'm ready for 'em—tough, that's me!
Say! Is that one of them, out there?
Why, Tuffy! I believe you've found one! Now let's go home and eat!
What? Go home just when we found one!
Now, Tuffy, these things can be pretty ugly on Tuesdays! Yes, sir, this is a bad day for those!
Tuesday? Why, today isn't Tuesday—it's Monday! Come on, Egbert.
You don't think I should stay here and guard the lunches?
Oh, my gosh! No one's going to bother the lunches—c'mon, Egbert!
Well, all right, but the lunches are—
There! Wow, it's big, isn't it?
It's big, all right—it looks like there are two of them, doesn't it?
27

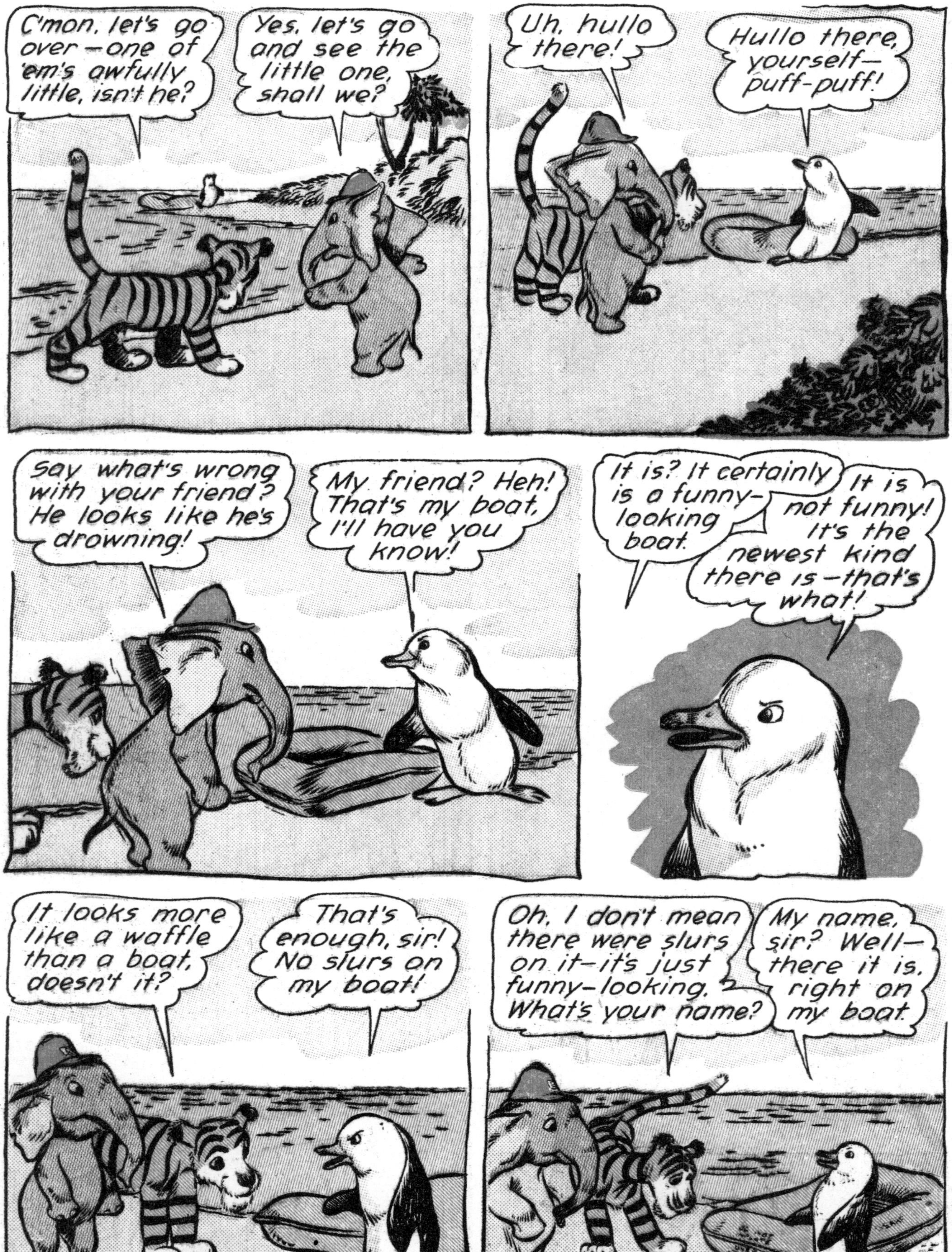
C'mon, let's go over—one of 'em's awfully little, isn't he?
Yes, let's go and see the little one, shall we?
Uh, hullo there!
Hullo there, yourself—puff-puff!
Say what's wrong with your friend? He looks like he's drowning!
My friend? Heh! That's my boat, I'll have you know!
It is? It certainly is a funny-looking boat.
It is not funny! It's the newest kind there is—that's what!
It looks more like a waffle than a boat, doesn't it?
That's enough, sir! No slurs on my boat!
Oh, I don't mean there were slurs on it—it's just funny-looking. What's your name?
My name, sir? Well—there it is, right on my boat.
28

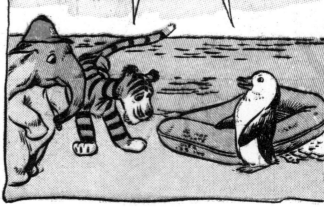

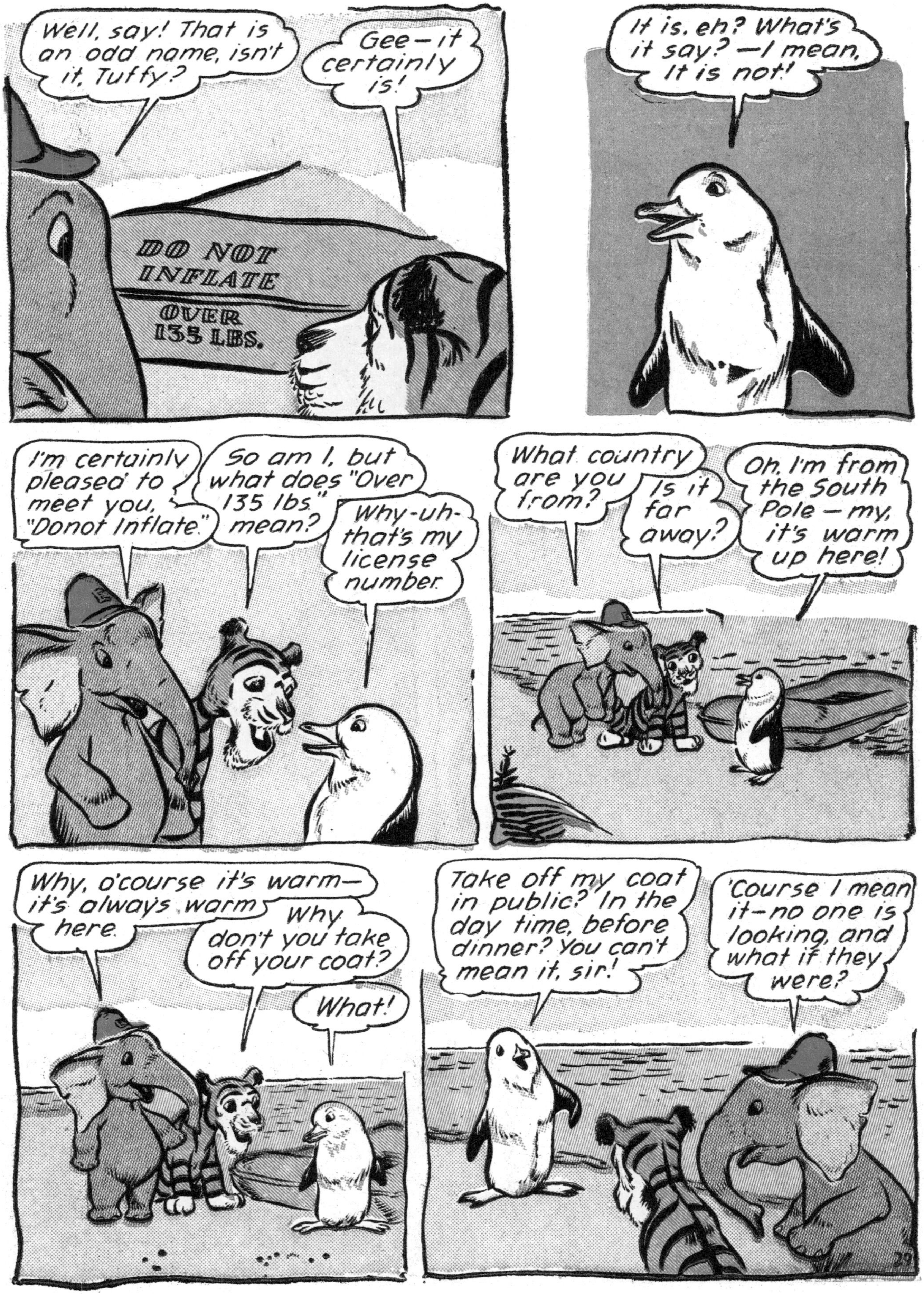
Well, say! That is an odd name, isn't it, Tuffy?
Gee—it certainly is!
DO NOT INFLATE
OVER 135 LBS.
It is, eh? What's it say? —I mean, It is not!
I'm certainly pleased to meet you, "Donot Inflate."
So am I, but what does "Over 135 lbs." mean?
Why-uh-that's my license number.
What country are you from?
Is it far away?
Oh, I'm from the South Pole—my, it's warm up here!
Why, o'course it's warm—it's always warm here.
Why don't you take off your coat?
What!
Take off my coat in public? In the day time, before dinner? You can't mean it, sir!
'Course I mean it—no one is looking, and what if they were?

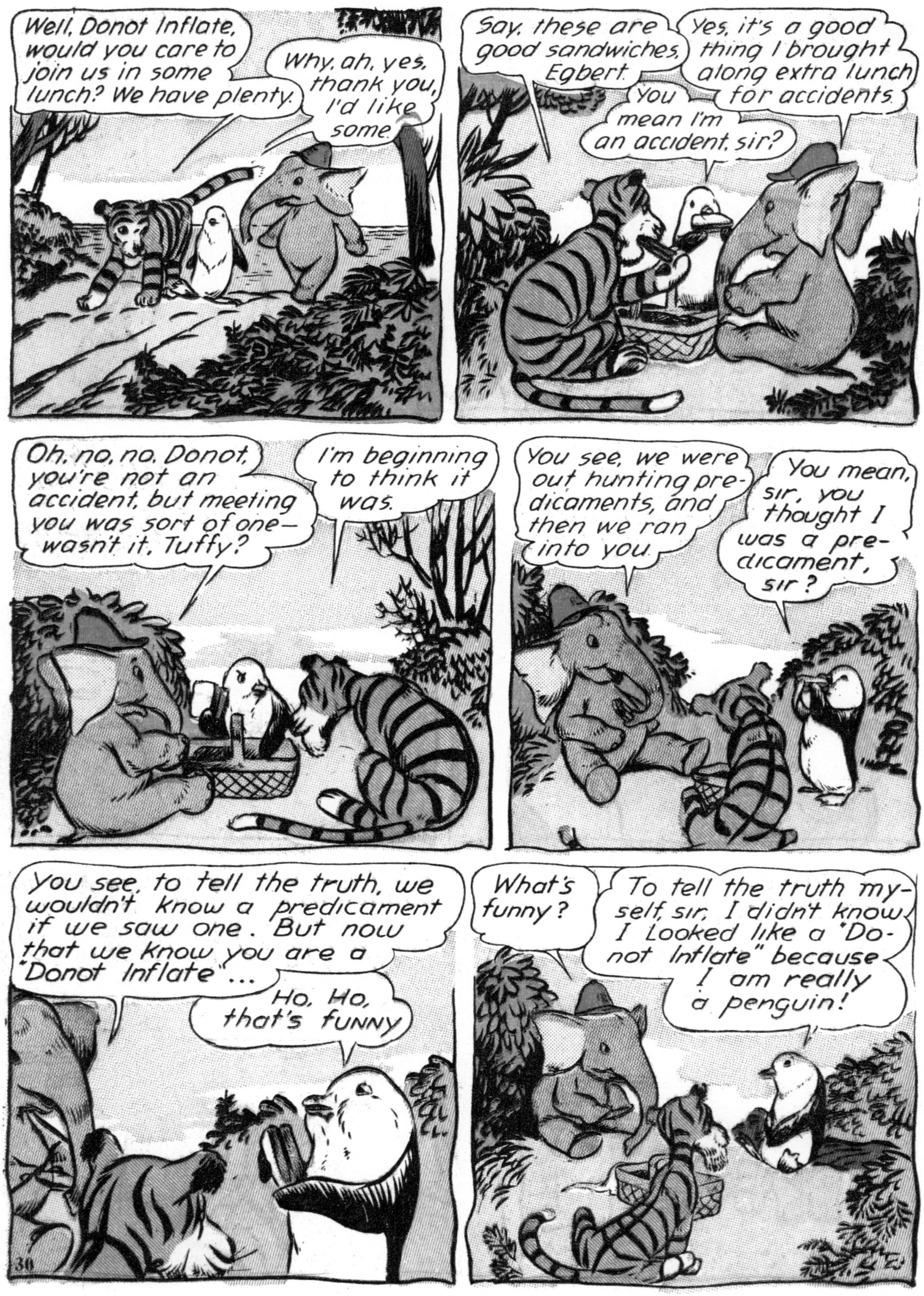
Well, Donot Inflate, would you care to join us in some lunch? We have plenty.
Why, ah, yes, thank you, I'd like some.
Say, these are good sandwiches, Egbert.
Yes, it's a good thing I brought along extra lunch for accidents.
You mean I'm an accident, sir?
Oh, no, no, Donot, you're not an accident, but meeting you was sort of one— wasn't it, Tuffy?
I'm beginning to think it was.
You see, we were out hunting predicaments, and then we ran into you.
You mean, sir, you thought I was a predicament, sir?
You see, to tell the truth, we wouldn't know a predicament if we saw one. But now that we know you are a "Donot Inflate"...
Ho, Ho, that's funny
What's funny?
To tell the truth myself, sir, I didn't know I looked like a "Donot Inflate" because I am really a penguin!

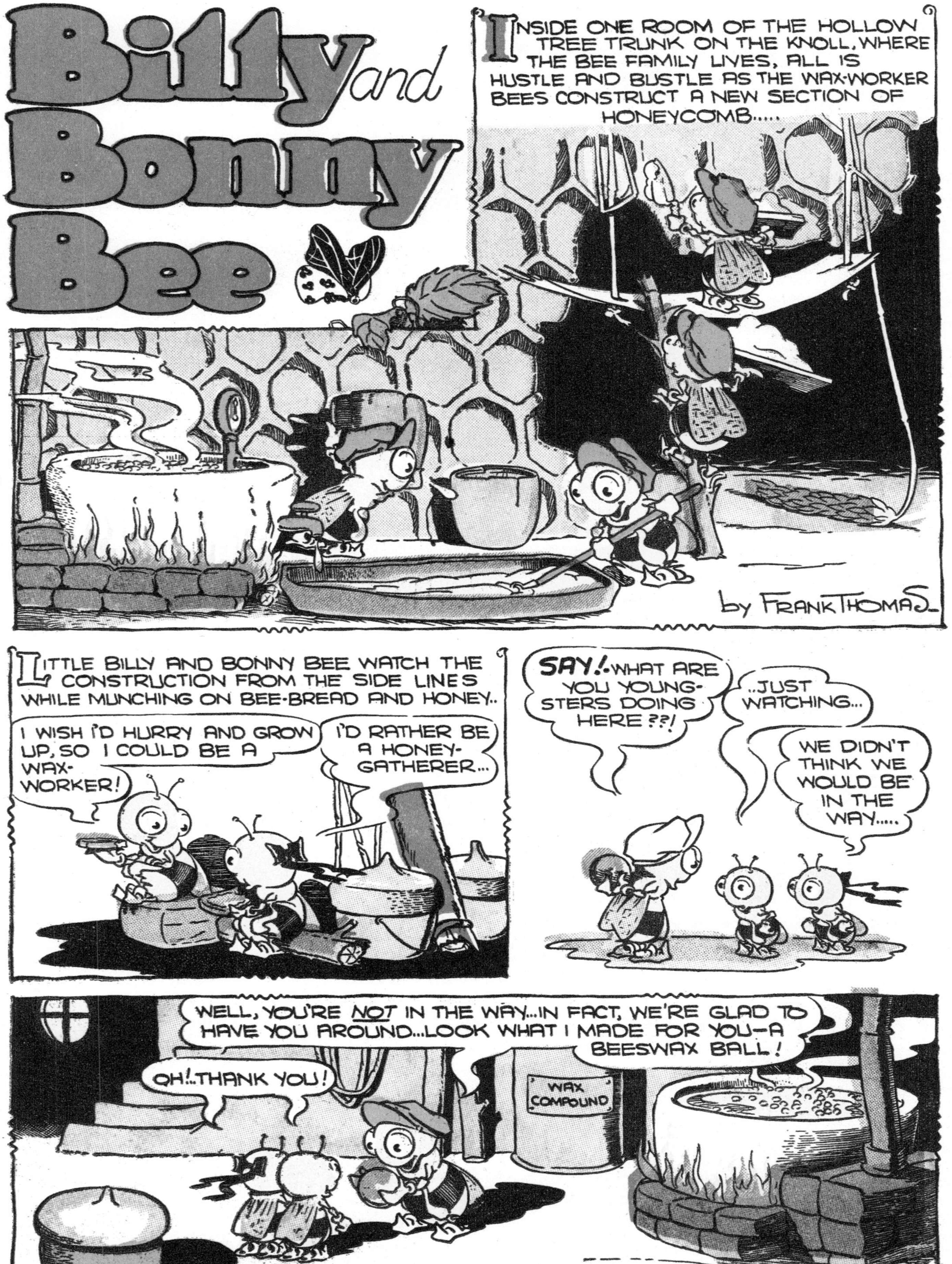
Billy and Bonny Bee
INSIDE ONE ROOM OF THE HOLLOW TREE TRUNK ON THE KNOLL, WHERE THE BEE FAMILY LIVES, ALL IS HUSTLE AND BUSTLE AS THE WAX-WORKER BEES CONSTRUCT A NEW SECTION OF HONEYCOMB.....
by FRANK THOMAS
LITTLE BILLY AND BONNY BEE WATCH THE CONSTRUCTION FROM THE SIDE LINES WHILE MUNCHING ON BEE-BREAD AND HONEY..
I WISH I'D HURRY AND GROW UP, SO I COULD BE A WAX-WORKER!
I'D RATHER BE A HONEY-GATHERER...
SAY!.. WHAT ARE YOU YOUNGSTERS DOING HERE??!
..JUST WATCHING...
WE DIDN'T THINK WE WOULD BE IN THE WAY.....
WELL, YOU'RE NOT IN THE WAY...IN FACT, WE'RE GLAD TO HAVE YOU AROUND...LOOK WHAT I MADE FOR YOU—A BEESWAX BALL!
OH!..THANK YOU!
WAX COMPOUND

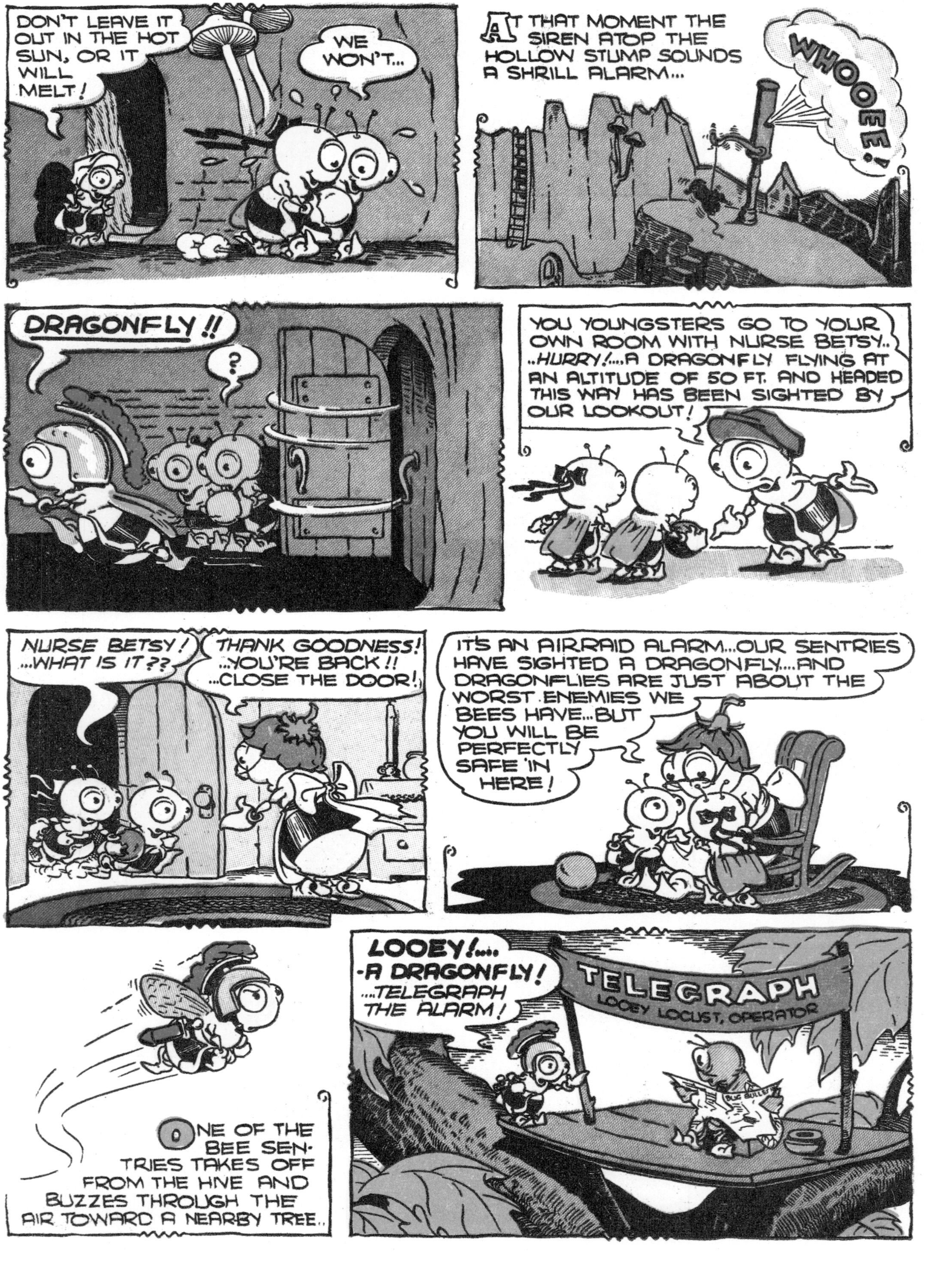
DON'T LEAVE IT OUT IN THE HOT SUN, OR IT WILL MELT!
WE WON'T...
AT THAT MOMENT THE SIREN ATOP THE HOLLOW STUMP SOUNDS A SHRILL ALARM...
WHOOEE!
DRAGONFLY!!
?
YOU YOUNGSTERS GO TO YOUR OWN ROOM WITH NURSE BETSY.. ..HURRY!....A DRAGONFLY FLYING AT AN ALTITUDE OF 50 FT. AND HEADED THIS WAY HAS BEEN SIGHTED BY OUR LOOKOUT!
NURSE BETSY! ...WHAT IS IT??
THANK GOODNESS! ...YOU'RE BACK!! ...CLOSE THE DOOR!
IT'S AN AIRRAID ALARM...OUR SENTRIES HAVE SIGHTED A DRAGONFLY....AND DRAGONFLIES ARE JUST ABOUT THE WORST ENEMIES WE BEES HAVE...BUT YOU WILL BE PERFECTLY SAFE IN HERE!
ONE OF THE BEE SENTRIES TAKES OFF FROM THE HIVE AND BUZZES THROUGH THE AIR TOWARD A NEARBY TREE..
LOOEY!.... -A DRAGONFLY! ...TELEGRAPH THE ALARM!
TELEGRAPH
LOOEY LOCUST, OPERATOR

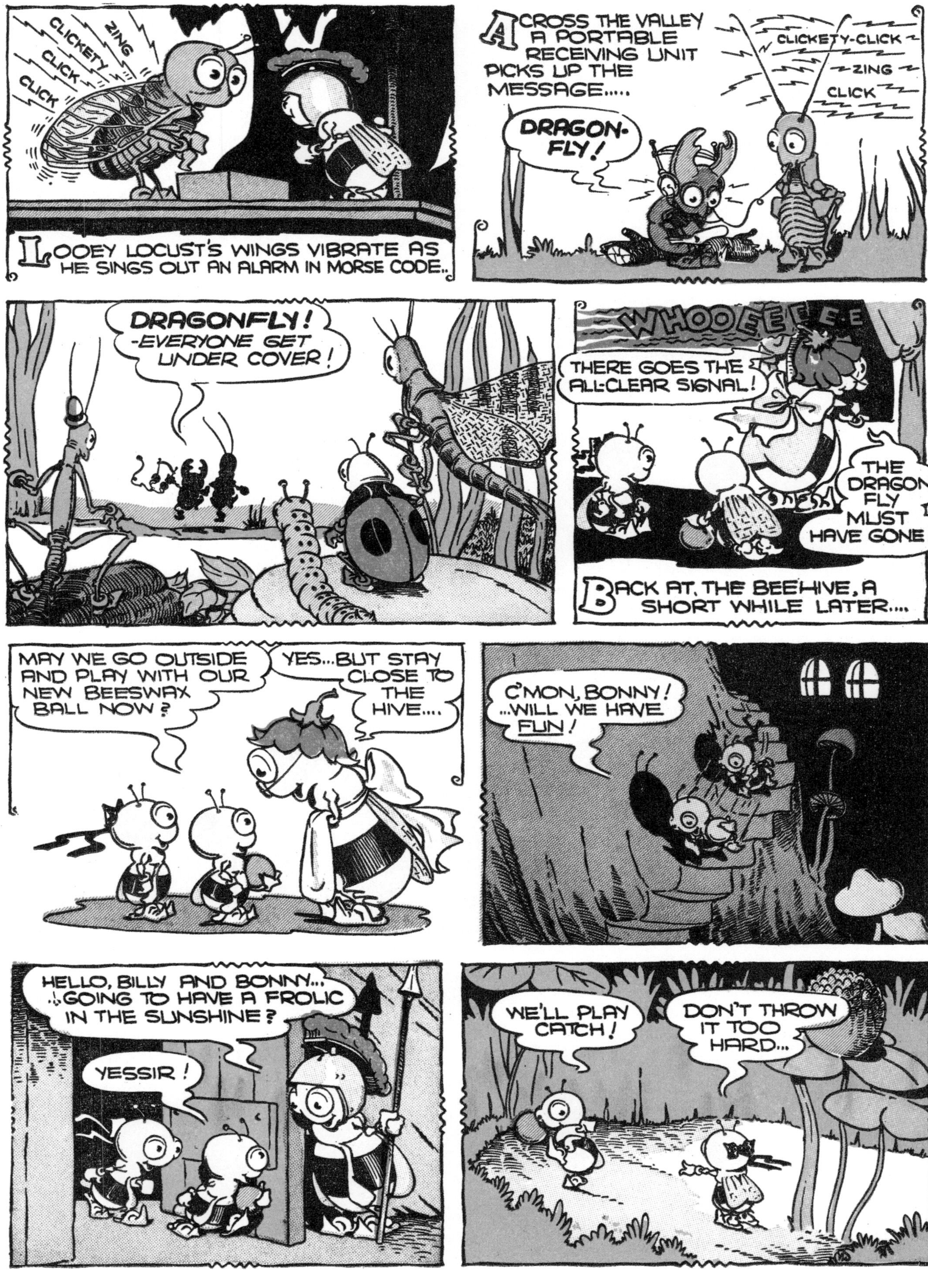
CLICK
CLICK
CLICKETY
ZING
LOOEY LOCUST'S WINGS VIBRATE AS HE SINGS OUT AN ALARM IN MORSE CODE..
ACROSS THE VALLEY A PORTABLE RECEIVING UNIT PICKS UP THE MESSAGE.....
CLICKETY-CLICK
ZING
CLICK
DRAGON-FLY!
DRAGONFLY! -EVERYONE GET UNDER COVER!
WHOOEEEEE
THERE GOES THE ALL-CLEAR SIGNAL!
THE DRAGON-FLY MUST HAVE GONE!
BACK AT THE BEEHIVE, A SHORT WHILE LATER....
MAY WE GO OUTSIDE AND PLAY WITH OUR NEW BEESWAX BALL NOW?
YES...BUT STAY CLOSE TO THE HIVE....
C'MON, BONNY! ...WILL WE HAVE FUN!
HELLO, BILLY AND BONNY... ...GOING TO HAVE A FROLIC IN THE SUNSHINE?
YESSIR!
WE'LL PLAY CATCH!
DON'T THROW IT TOO HARD...

OH!

I DON'T KNOW MY OWN STRENGTH!

WHERE DID IT GO?...COME HELP ME FIND IT....

IT WENT RIGHT DOWN HERE SOMEWHERE...

HERE IT IS!

NOW WE'LL GO BACK AND—

B-BILLY...L-LOOK UP-UP THERE....

WELL WELL!...HELLO, DEAR LITTLE BEE CHILDREN!

H-HELLO...WH-WHO ARE Y-YOU??

I'M A VERY GOOD FRIEND OF YOURS...A VERY GOOD FRIEND... HEH!

YOU HAVE BEAU-TIFUL WINGS!

TWO PAIR OF'EM, TOO! ..I'LL BET YOU'RE SOME FLYER!

AM I?!...JUST WATCH!

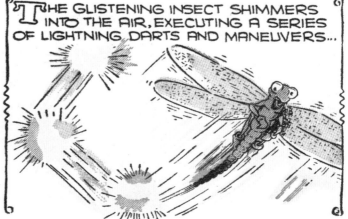

THE GLISTENING INSECT SHIMMERS INTO THE AIR, EXECUTING A SERIES OF LIGHTNING DARTS AND MANEUVERS...

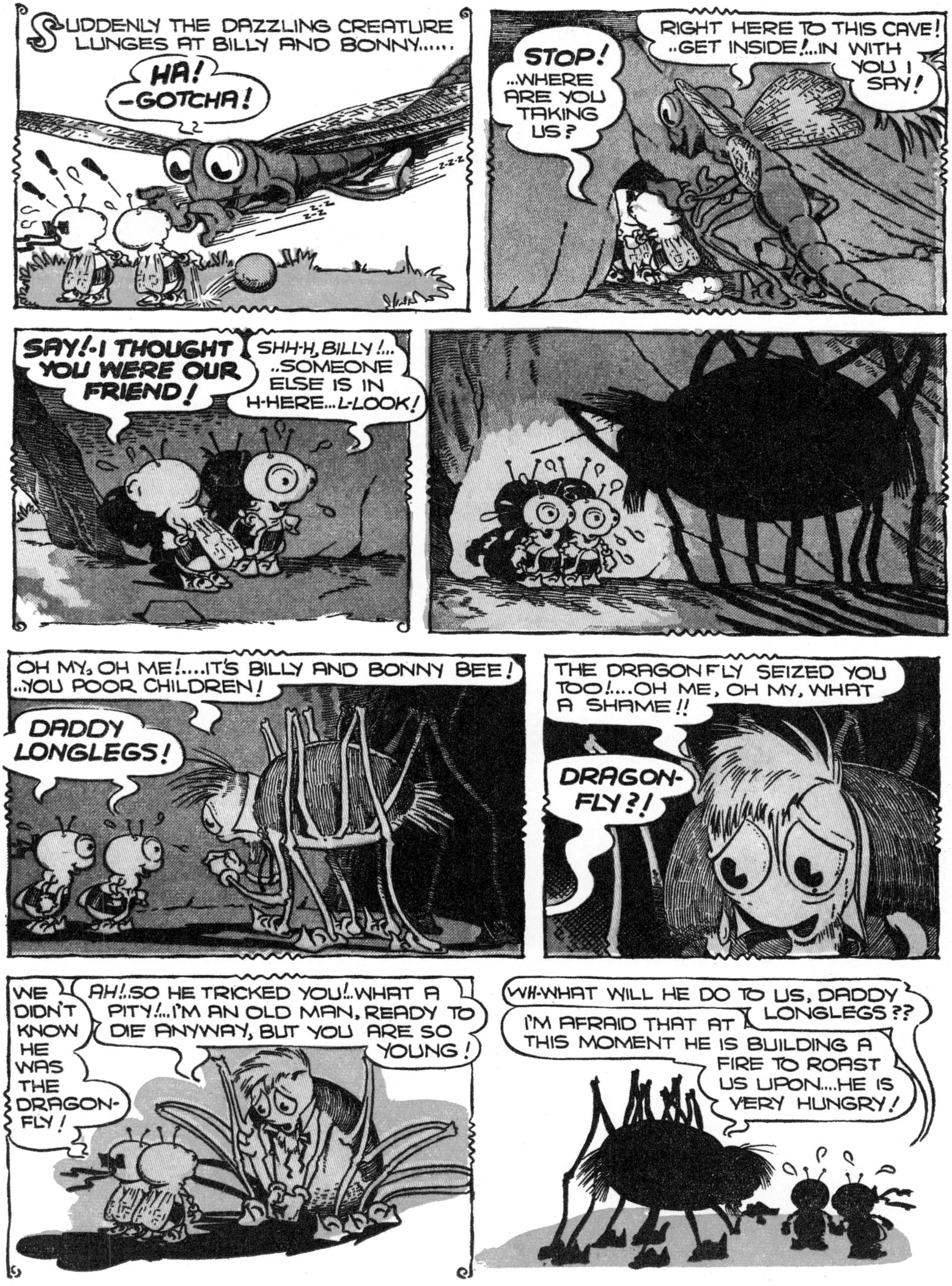
SUDDENLY THE DAZZLING CREATURE LUNGES AT BILLY AND BONNY......
HA! -GOTCHA!
STOP! ..WHERE ARE YOU TAKING US?
RIGHT HERE TO THIS CAVE! ..GET INSIDE!...IN WITH YOU I SAY!
SAY!-I THOUGHT YOU WERE OUR FRIEND!
SHH-H, BILLY!... ..SOMEONE ELSE IS IN H-HERE...L-LOOK!
OH MY, OH ME!....IT'S BILLY AND BONNY BEE! ..YOU POOR CHILDREN!
DADDY LONGLEGS!
THE DRAGONFLY SEIZED YOU TOO!....OH ME, OH MY, WHAT A SHAME!!
DRAGON-FLY?!
WE DIDN'T KNOW HE WAS THE DRAGON-FLY!
AH!..SO HE TRICKED YOU!..WHAT A PITY!...I'M AN OLD MAN, READY TO DIE ANYWAY, BUT YOU ARE SO YOUNG!
WH-WHAT WILL HE DO TO US, DADDY LONGLEGS??
I'M AFRAID THAT AT THIS MOMENT HE IS BUILDING A FIRE TO ROAST US UPON....HE IS VERY HUNGRY!

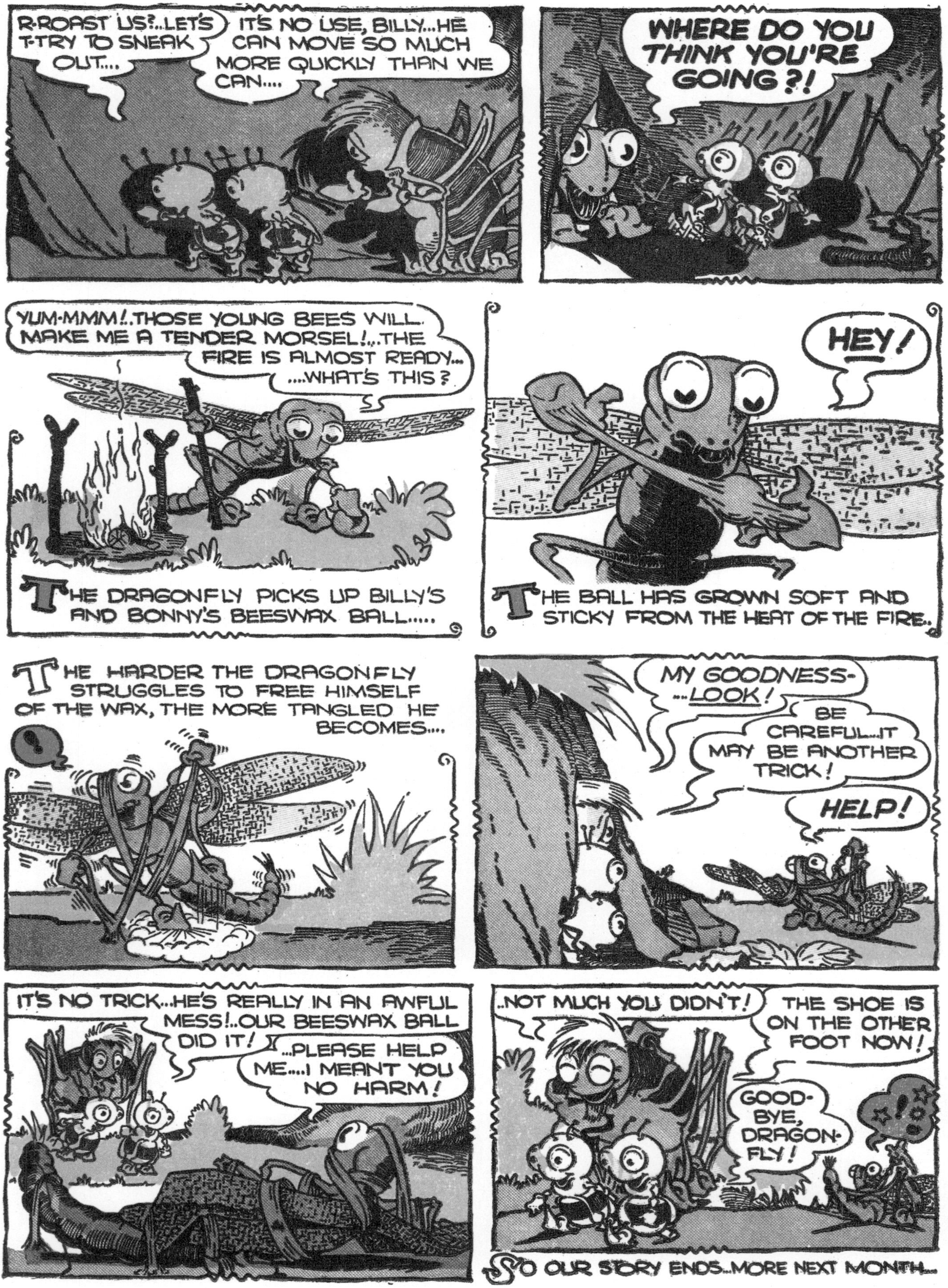
R-ROAST US?..LET'S T-TRY TO SNEAK OUT....
IT'S NO USE, BILLY...HE CAN MOVE SO MUCH MORE QUICKLY THAN WE CAN....
WHERE DO YOU THINK YOU'RE GOING?!
YUM-MMM!..THOSE YOUNG BEES WILL MAKE ME A TENDER MORSEL!...THE FIRE IS ALMOST READY... ...WHAT'S THIS?
THE DRAGONFLY PICKS UP BILLY'S AND BONNY'S BEESWAX BALL.....
HEY!
THE BALL HAS GROWN SOFT AND STICKY FROM THE HEAT OF THE FIRE..
THE HARDER THE DRAGONFLY STRUGGLES TO FREE HIMSELF OF THE WAX, THE MORE TANGLED HE BECOMES....
MY GOODNESS- ...LOOK!
BE CAREFUL...IT MAY BE ANOTHER TRICK!
HELP!
IT'S NO TRICK...HE'S REALLY IN AN AWFUL MESS!..OUR BEESWAX BALL DID IT!
...PLEASE HELP ME....I MEANT YOU NO HARM!
..NOT MUCH YOU DIDN'T!
THE SHOE IS ON THE OTHER FOOT NOW!
GOOD-BYE, DRAGON-FLY!
SO OUR STORY ENDS..MORE NEXT MONTH...

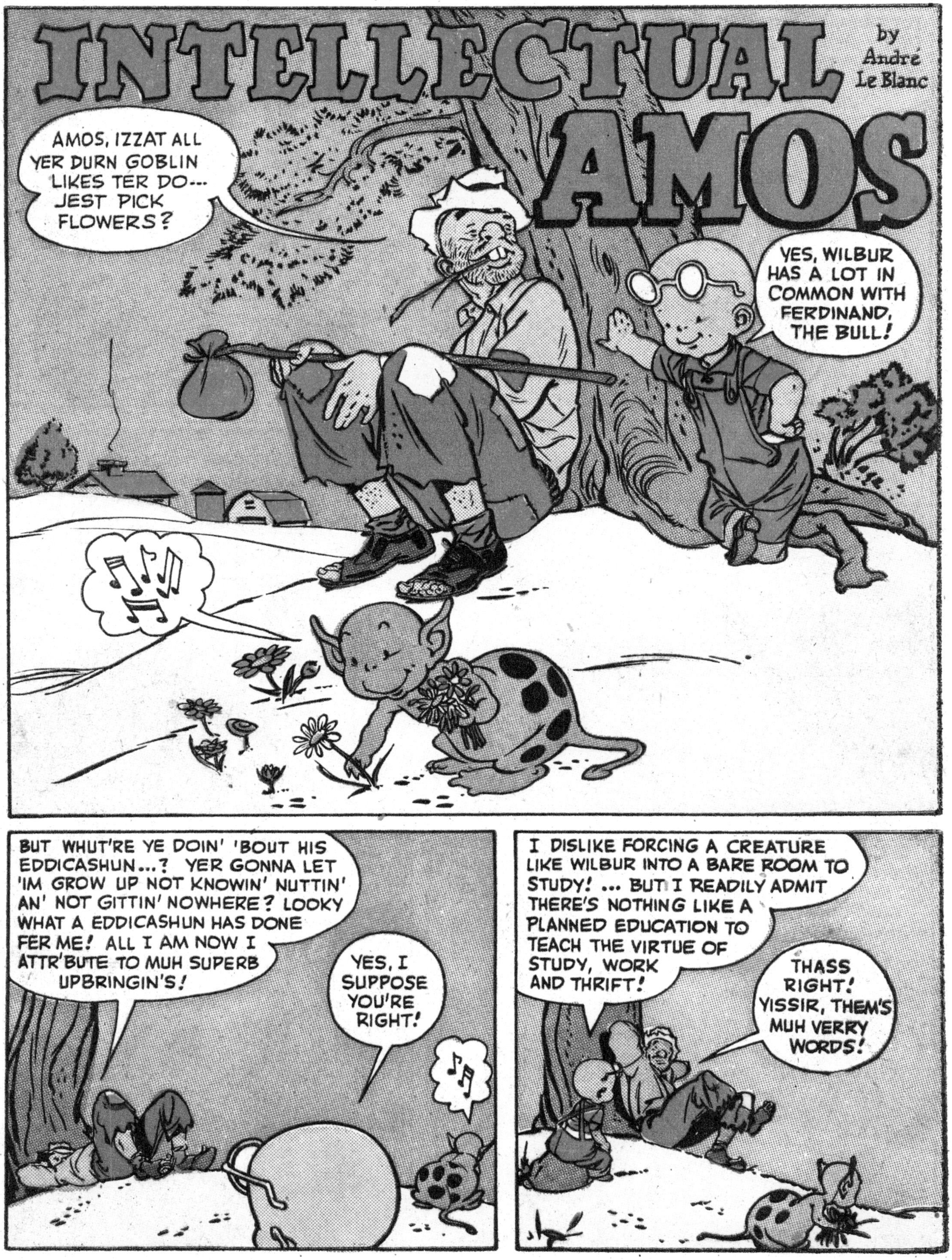
INTELLECTUAL AMOS
by André Le Blanc
AMOS, IZZAT ALL YER DURN GOBLIN LIKES TER DO--- JEST PICK FLOWERS?
YES, WILBUR HAS A LOT IN COMMON WITH FERDINAND, THE BULL!
BUT WHUT'RE YE DOIN' 'BOUT HIS EDDICASHUN...? YER GONNA LET 'IM GROW UP NOT KNOWIN' NUTTIN' AN' NOT GITTIN' NOWHERE? LOOKY WHAT A EDDICASHUN HAS DONE FER ME! ALL I AM NOW I ATTR'BUTE TO MUH SUPERB UPBRINGIN'S!
YES, I SUPPOSE YOU'RE RIGHT!
I DISLIKE FORCING A CREATURE LIKE WILBUR INTO A BARE ROOM TO STUDY! ... BUT I READILY ADMIT THERE'S NOTHING LIKE A PLANNED EDUCATION TO TEACH THE VIRTUE OF STUDY, WORK AND THRIFT!
THASS RIGHT! YISSIR, THEM'S MUH VERRY WORDS!

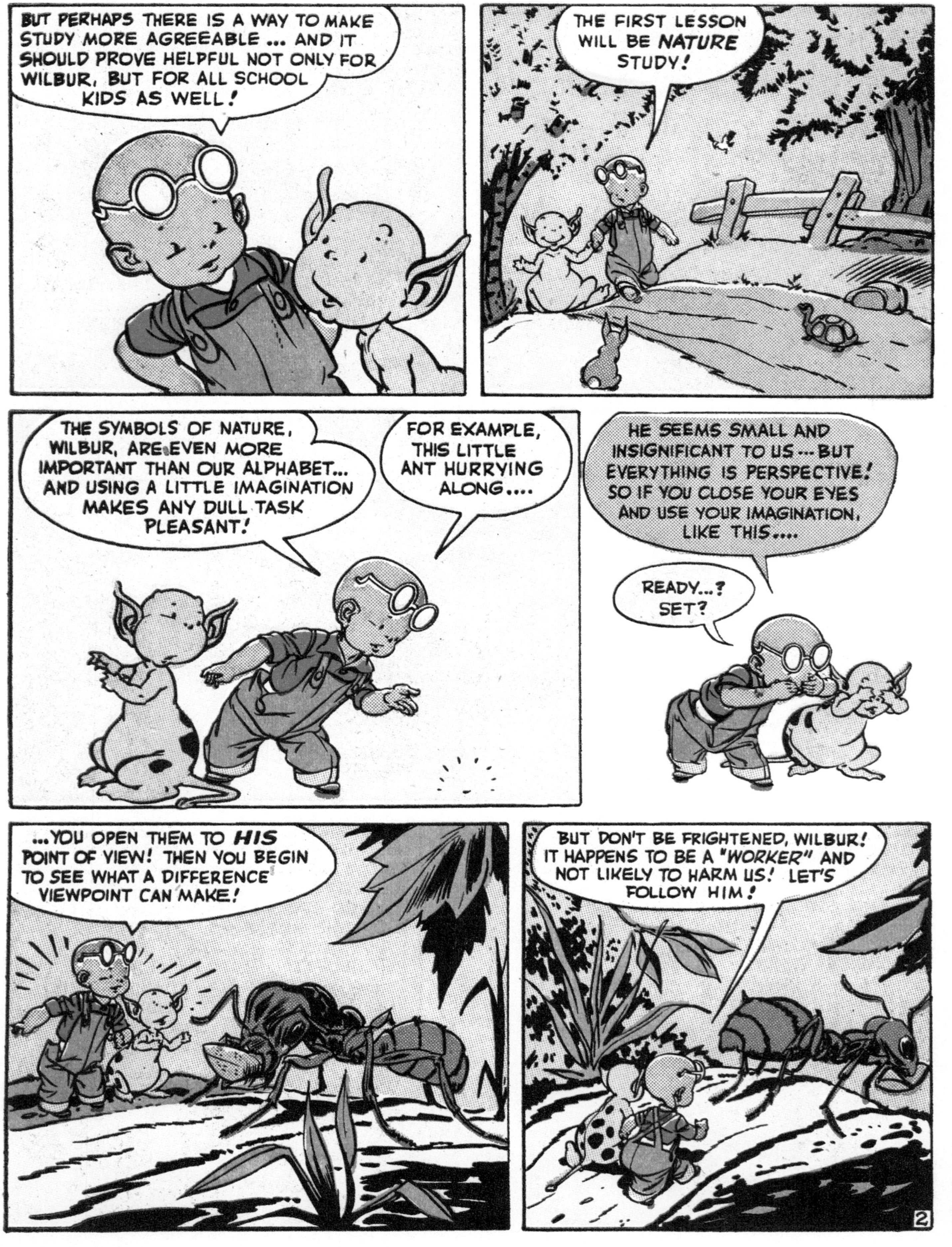
BUT PERHAPS THERE IS A WAY TO MAKE STUDY MORE AGREEABLE ... AND IT SHOULD PROVE HELPFUL NOT ONLY FOR WILBUR, BUT FOR ALL SCHOOL KIDS AS WELL!
THE FIRST LESSON WILL BE NATURE STUDY!
THE SYMBOLS OF NATURE, WILBUR, ARE EVEN MORE IMPORTANT THAN OUR ALPHABET... AND USING A LITTLE IMAGINATION MAKES ANY DULL TASK PLEASANT!
FOR EXAMPLE, THIS LITTLE ANT HURRYING ALONG....
HE SEEMS SMALL AND INSIGNIFICANT TO US ... BUT EVERYTHING IS PERSPECTIVE! SO IF YOU CLOSE YOUR EYES AND USE YOUR IMAGINATION, LIKE THIS....
READY...? SET?
...YOU OPEN THEM TO HIS POINT OF VIEW! THEN YOU BEGIN TO SEE WHAT A DIFFERENCE VIEWPOINT CAN MAKE!
BUT DON'T BE FRIGHTENED, WILBUR! IT HAPPENS TO BE A "WORKER" AND NOT LIKELY TO HARM US! LET'S FOLLOW HIM!
2

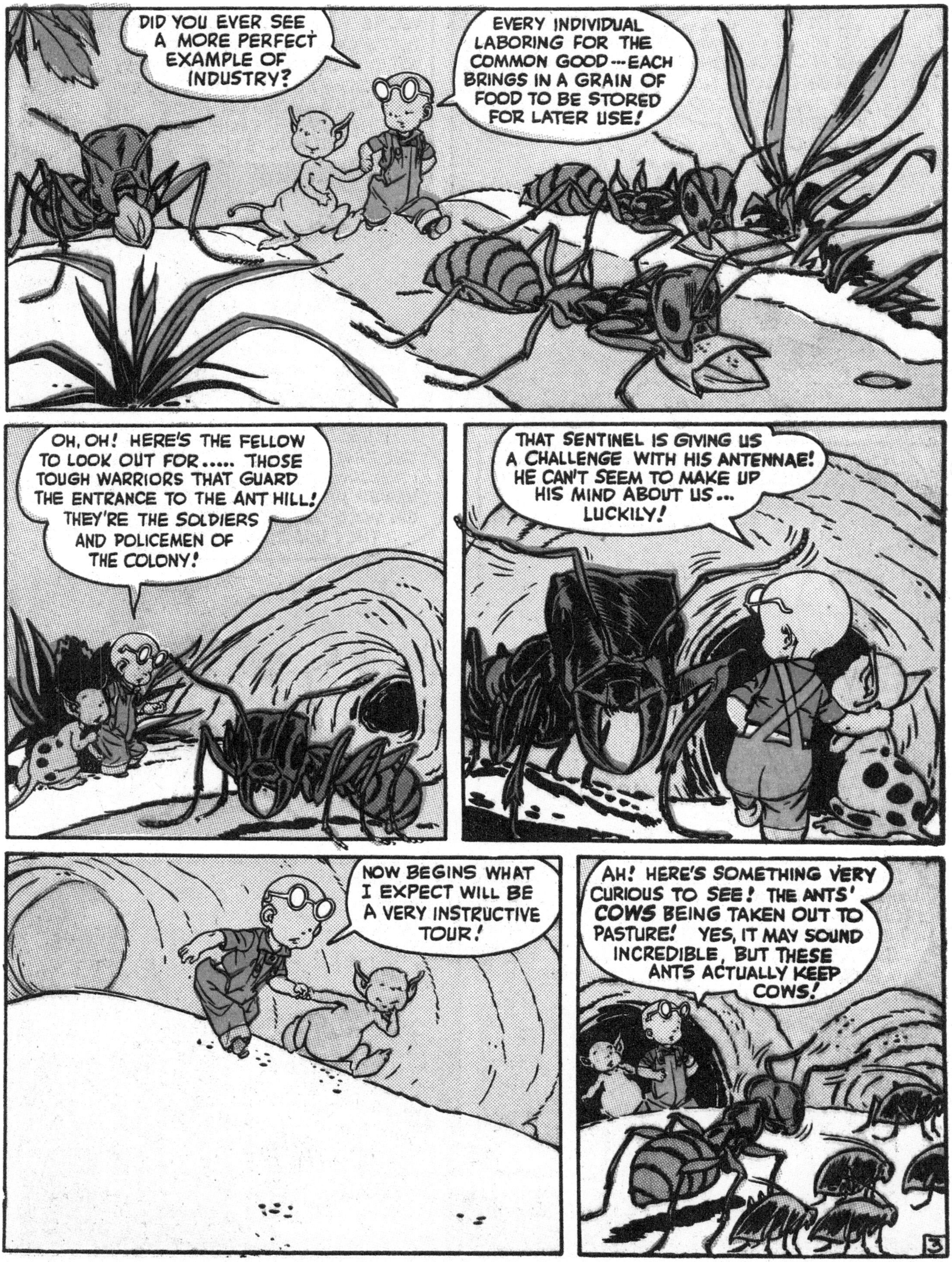
DID YOU EVER SEE A MORE PERFECT EXAMPLE OF INDUSTRY?
EVERY INDIVIDUAL LABORING FOR THE COMMON GOOD---EACH BRINGS IN A GRAIN OF FOOD TO BE STORED FOR LATER USE!
OH, OH! HERE'S THE FELLOW TO LOOK OUT FOR..... THOSE TOUGH WARRIORS THAT GUARD THE ENTRANCE TO THE ANT HILL! THEY'RE THE SOLDIERS AND POLICEMEN OF THE COLONY!
THAT SENTINEL IS GIVING US A CHALLENGE WITH HIS ANTENNAE! HE CAN'T SEEM TO MAKE UP HIS MIND ABOUT US... LUCKILY!
NOW BEGINS WHAT I EXPECT WILL BE A VERY INSTRUCTIVE TOUR!
AH! HERE'S SOMETHING VERY CURIOUS TO SEE! THE ANTS' COWS BEING TAKEN OUT TO PASTURE! YES, IT MAY SOUND INCREDIBLE, BUT THESE ANTS ACTUALLY KEEP COWS!
3

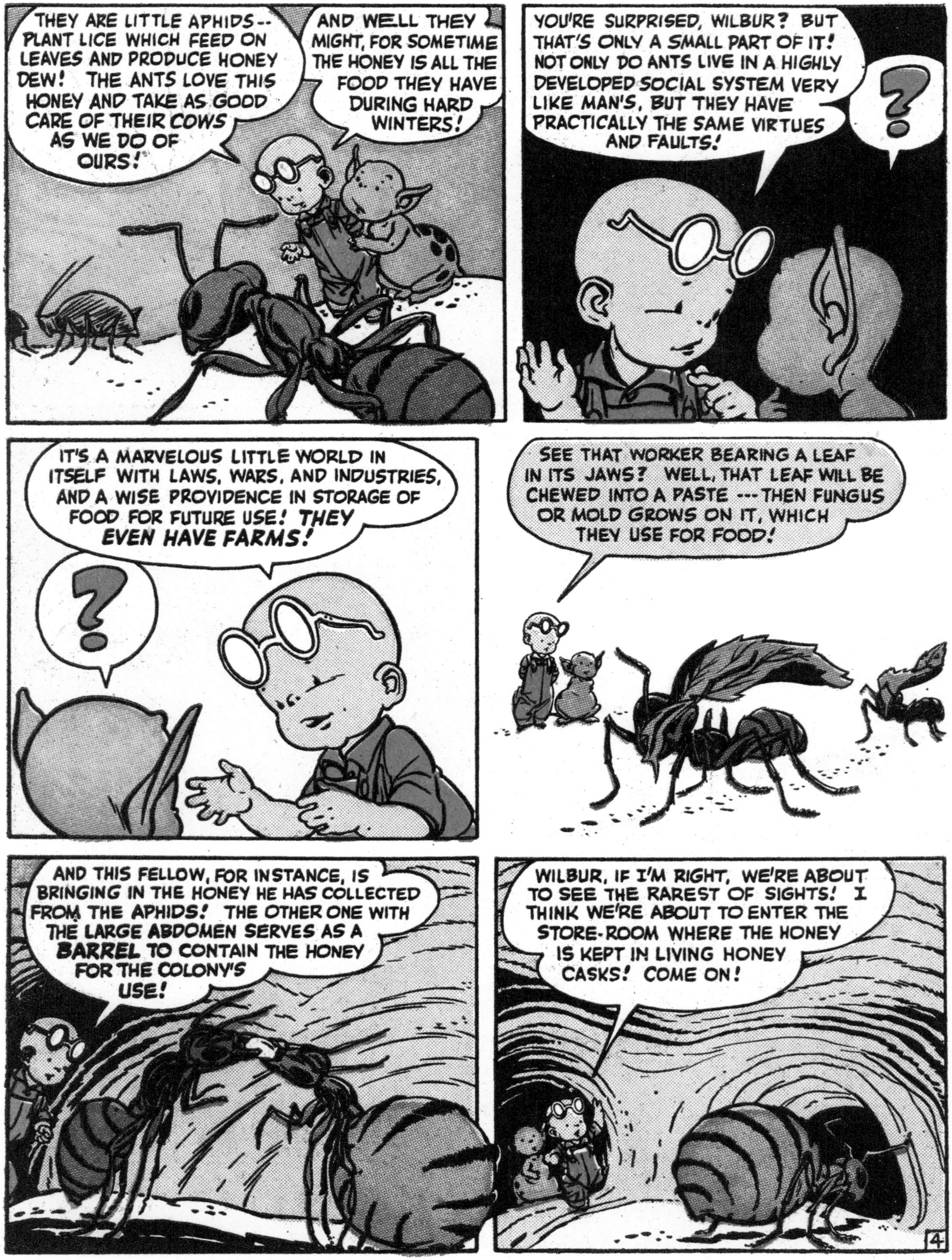
THEY ARE LITTLE APHIDS-- PLANT LICE WHICH FEED ON LEAVES AND PRODUCE HONEY DEW! THE ANTS LOVE THIS HONEY AND TAKE AS GOOD CARE OF THEIR COWS AS WE DO OF OURS!
AND WELL THEY MIGHT, FOR SOMETIME THE HONEY IS ALL THE FOOD THEY HAVE DURING HARD WINTERS!
YOU'RE SURPRISED, WILBUR? BUT THAT'S ONLY A SMALL PART OF IT! NOT ONLY DO ANTS LIVE IN A HIGHLY DEVELOPED SOCIAL SYSTEM VERY LIKE MAN'S, BUT THEY HAVE PRACTICALLY THE SAME VIRTUES AND FAULTS!
?
IT'S A MARVELOUS LITTLE WORLD IN ITSELF WITH LAWS, WARS, AND INDUSTRIES, AND A WISE PROVIDENCE IN STORAGE OF FOOD FOR FUTURE USE! THEY EVEN HAVE FARMS!
?
SEE THAT WORKER BEARING A LEAF IN ITS JAWS? WELL, THAT LEAF WILL BE CHEWED INTO A PASTE ---THEN FUNGUS OR MOLD GROWS ON IT, WHICH THEY USE FOR FOOD!
AND THIS FELLOW, FOR INSTANCE, IS BRINGING IN THE HONEY HE HAS COLLECTED FROM THE APHIDS! THE OTHER ONE WITH THE LARGE ABDOMEN SERVES AS A BARREL TO CONTAIN THE HONEY FOR THE COLONY'S USE!
WILBUR, IF I'M RIGHT, WE'RE ABOUT TO SEE THE RAREST OF SIGHTS! I THINK WE'RE ABOUT TO ENTER THE STORE-ROOM WHERE THE HONEY IS KEPT IN LIVING HONEY CASKS! COME ON!
4

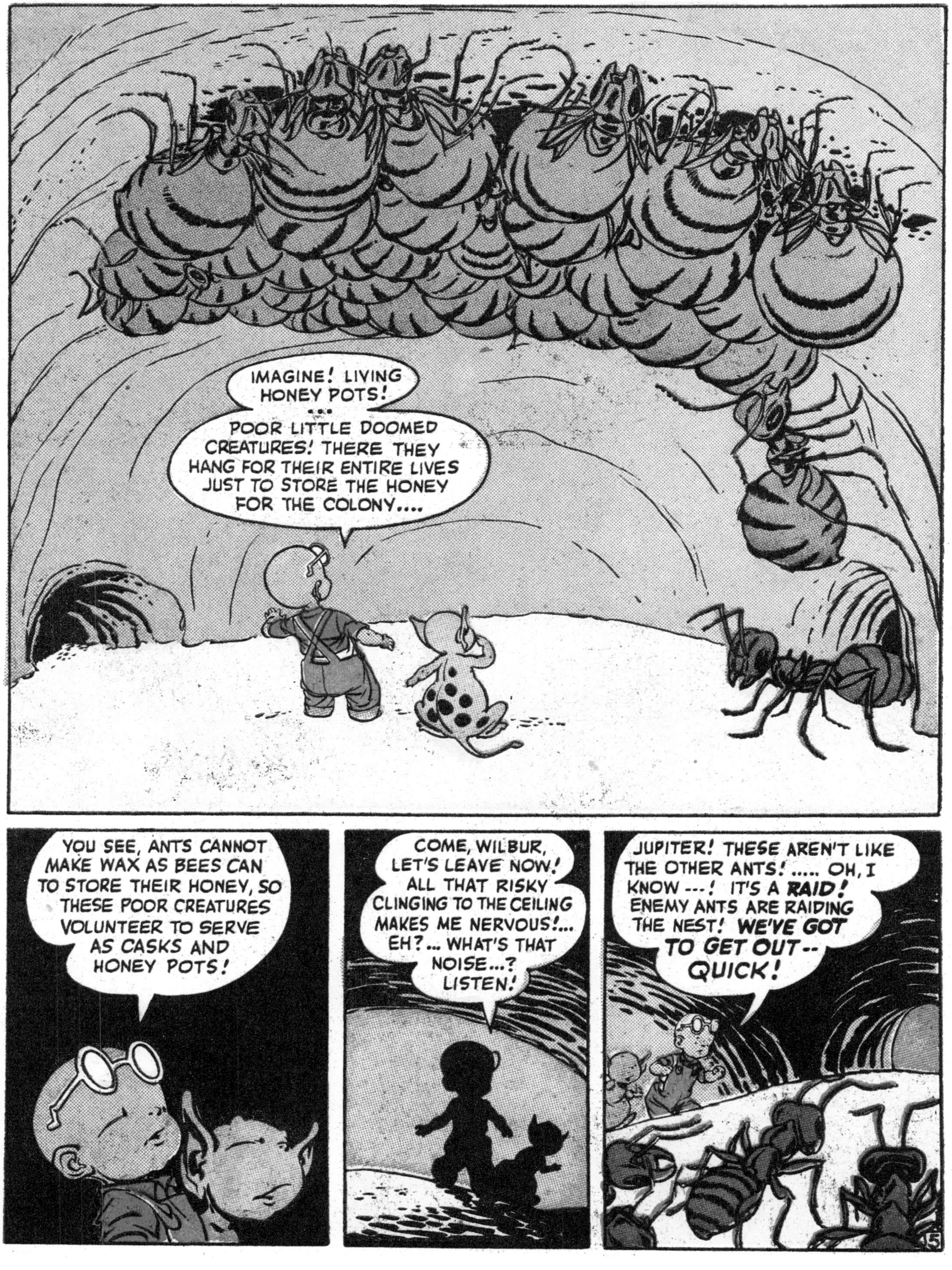
IMAGINE! LIVING HONEY POTS! ... POOR LITTLE DOOMED CREATURES! THERE THEY HANG FOR THEIR ENTIRE LIVES JUST TO STORE THE HONEY FOR THE COLONY....
YOU SEE, ANTS CANNOT MAKE WAX AS BEES CAN TO STORE THEIR HONEY, SO THESE POOR CREATURES VOLUNTEER TO SERVE AS CASKS AND HONEY POTS!
COME, WILBUR, LET'S LEAVE NOW! ALL THAT RISKY CLINGING TO THE CEILING MAKES ME NERVOUS!... EH?... WHAT'S THAT NOISE...? LISTEN!
JUPITER! THESE AREN'T LIKE THE OTHER ANTS! ..... OH, I KNOW ---! IT'S A RAID! ENEMY ANTS ARE RAIDING THE NEST! WE'VE GOT TO GET OUT -- QUICK!

A SWARM OF THEM! AND THEY'RE OVERPOWERING ALL DEFENDERS!

THIS IS NO PLACE FOR US! BUT LET'S HOPE NONE OF THEM TAKES NOTICE OF US BEFORE WE FIND THE WAY OUT!

THE RAIDERS ARE THE FIERCE *RED AMAZONS!* THEY'VE COME TO CAPTURE COCOONS TO HATCH AS THEIR SLAVES!

WELL, AT LAST, HERE WE ARE OUT AGAIN! IT WAS AN INTERESTING JOURNEY AND NOT WITHOUT EXCITEMENT --- BUT THERE'S NO NEED TO CARRY IMAGINATION TOO FAR!

BUT JUST THINK, A COMPLETE WORLD IN ITSELF IS RIGHT UNDER OUR FEET! MAYBE THAT'S WHY WE PAY NO ATTENTION --- BECAUSE IT'S SO CLOSE!

KING SOLOMON WAS VERY WISE AND IT WAS HE WHO INSPIRED THE IMMORTAL ADVICE: "GO TO THE ANT, THOU SLUGGARD, CONSIDER HER WAYS AND BE WISE"!

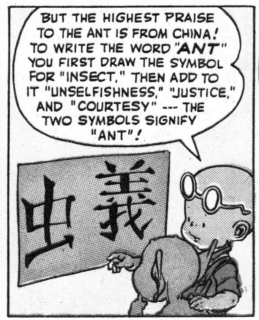

BUT THE HIGHEST PRAISE TO THE ANT IS FROM CHINA! TO WRITE THE WORD "*ANT*" YOU FIRST DRAW THE SYMBOL FOR "INSECT," THEN ADD TO IT "UNSELFISHNESS," "JUSTICE," AND "COURTESY" --- THE TWO SYMBOLS SIGNIFY "ANT"!

I CAN'T THINK OF A MORE PERFECT TRIBUTE, CAN YOU?

蟻

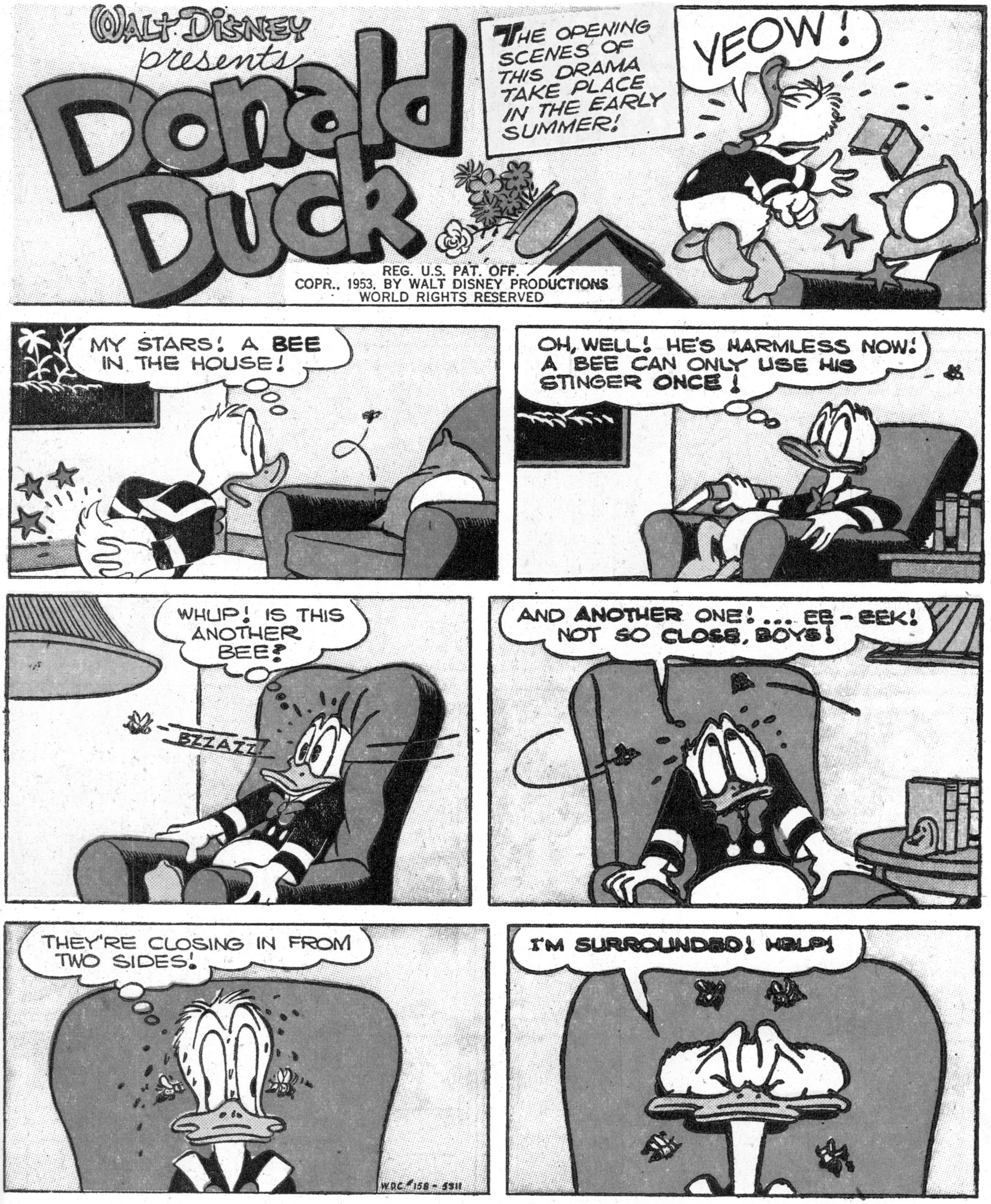
WALT DISNEY
presents
Donald Duck
REG. U.S. PAT. OFF.
COPR., 1953, BY WALT DISNEY PRODUCTIONS
WORLD RIGHTS RESERVED
THE OPENING SCENES OF THIS DRAMA TAKE PLACE IN THE EARLY SUMMER!
YEOW!
MY STARS! A BEE IN THE HOUSE!
OH, WELL! HE'S HARMLESS NOW! A BEE CAN ONLY USE HIS STINGER ONCE!
WHUP! IS THIS ANOTHER BEE?
BZZAZZ
AND ANOTHER ONE! .... EE-EEK! NOT SO CLOSE, BOYS!
THEY'RE CLOSING IN FROM TWO SIDES!
WDC 158 - 5311
I'M SURROUNDED! HELP!

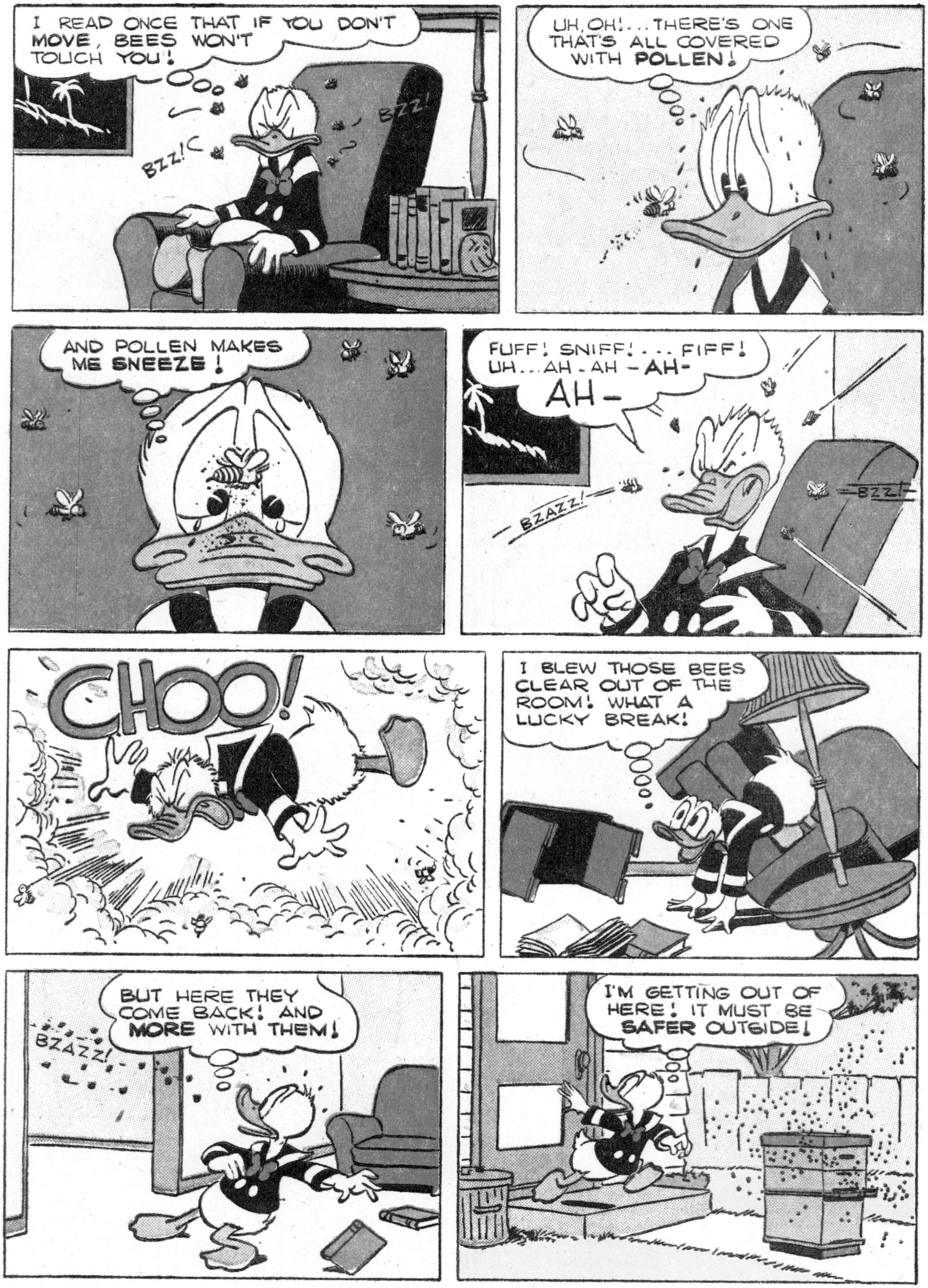
I READ ONCE THAT IF YOU DON'T MOVE, BEES WON'T TOUCH YOU!
BZZ!
BZZ!
UH, OH!... THERE'S ONE THAT'S ALL COVERED WITH POLLEN!
AND POLLEN MAKES ME SNEEZE!
FUFF! SNIFF!... FIFF! UH... AH - AH - AH - AH -
BZAZZ!
BZZ!
CHOO!
I BLEW THOSE BEES CLEAR OUT OF THE ROOM! WHAT A LUCKY BREAK!
BUT HERE THEY COME BACK! AND MORE WITH THEM!
BZAZZ!
I'M GETTING OUT OF HERE! IT MUST BE SAFER OUTSIDE!

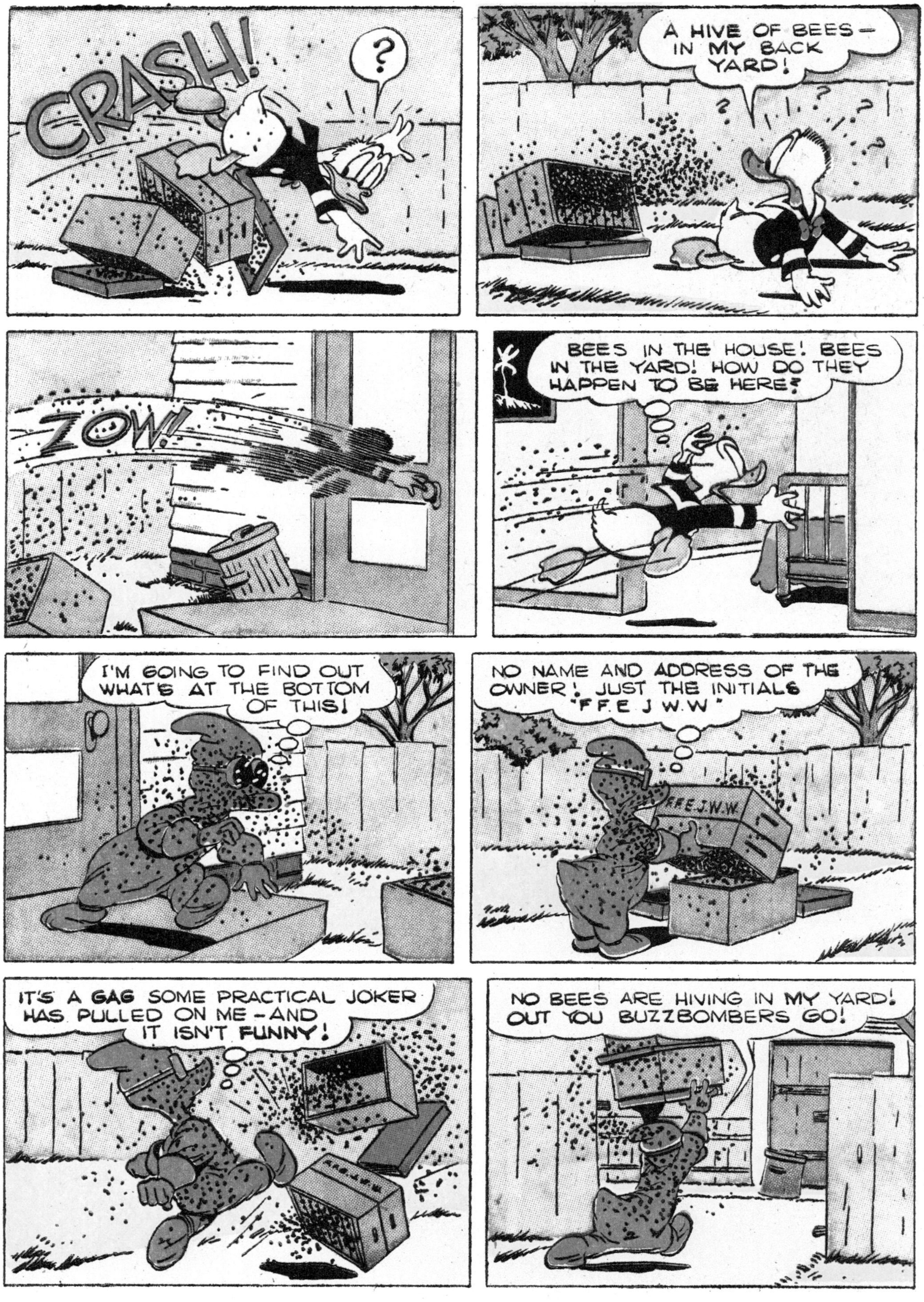
CRASH!
?
A HIVE OF BEES— IN MY BACK YARD!
? ? ? ?
ZOW!
BEES IN THE HOUSE! BEES IN THE YARD! HOW DO THEY HAPPEN TO BE HERE?
I'M GOING TO FIND OUT WHAT'S AT THE BOTTOM OF THIS!
NO NAME AND ADDRESS OF THE OWNER! JUST THE INITIALS "F.F.E.J.W.W."
F.F.E.J.W.W.
IT'S A GAG SOME PRACTICAL JOKER HAS PULLED ON ME—AND IT ISN'T FUNNY!
NO BEES ARE HIVING IN MY YARD! OUT YOU BUZZBOMBERS GO!

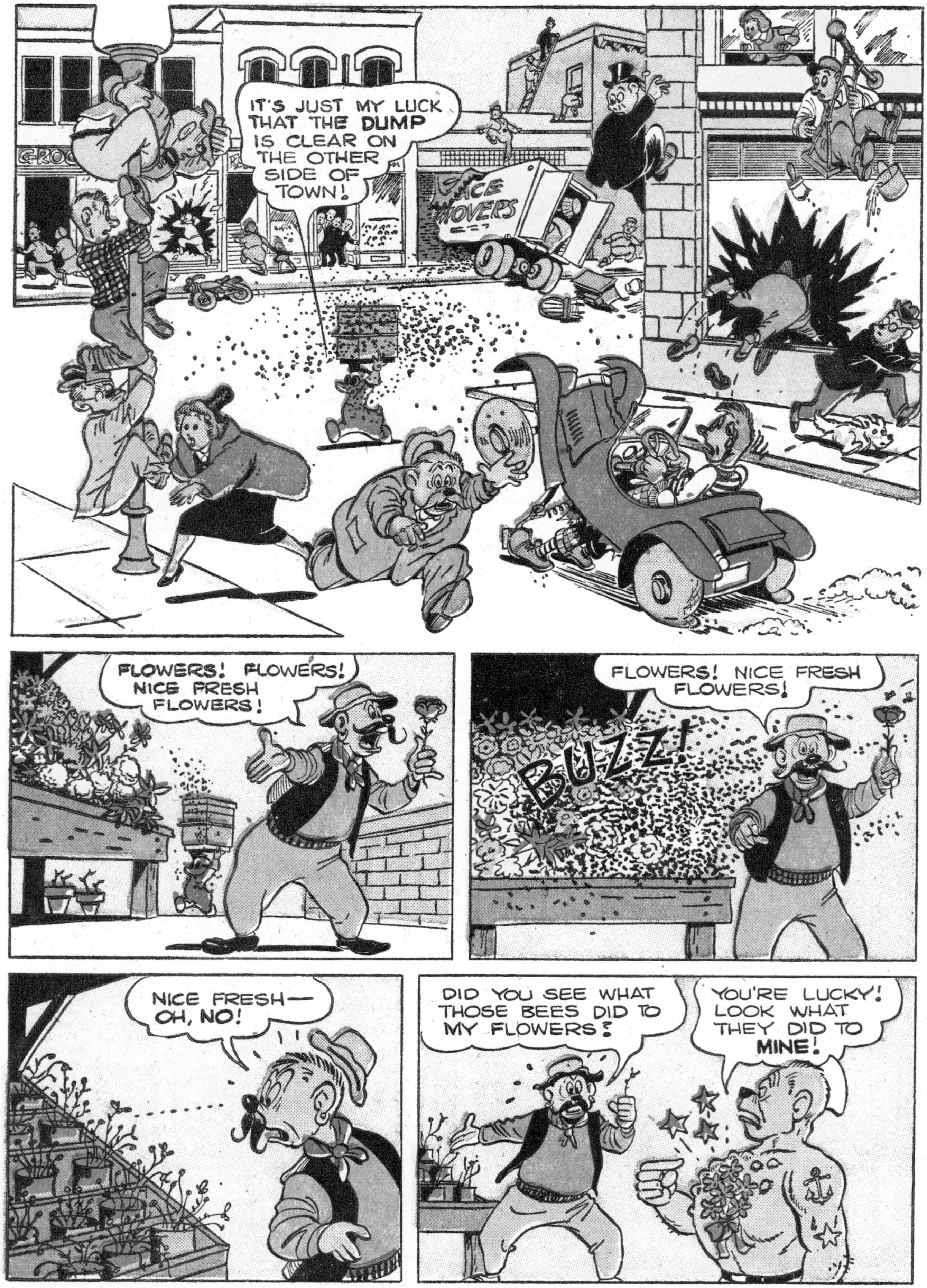
IT'S JUST MY LUCK THAT THE DUMP IS CLEAR ON THE OTHER SIDE OF TOWN!
FLOWERS! FLOWERS! NICE FRESH FLOWERS!
FLOWERS! NICE FRESH FLOWERS!
BUZZ!
NICE FRESH— OH, NO!
DID YOU SEE WHAT THOSE BEES DID TO MY FLOWERS?
YOU'RE LUCKY! LOOK WHAT THEY DID TO MINE!

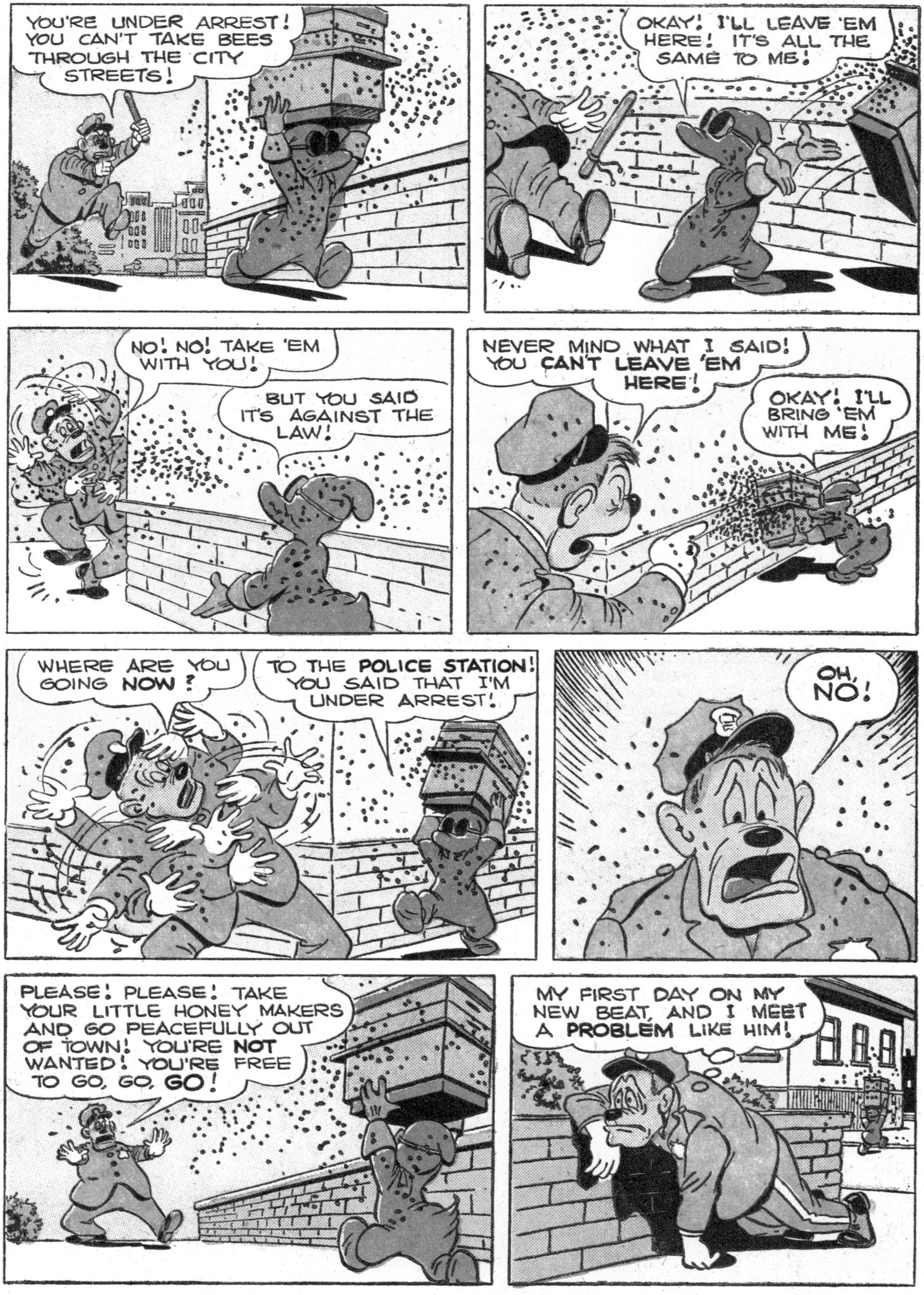
YOU'RE UNDER ARREST! YOU CAN'T TAKE BEES THROUGH THE CITY STREETS!
OKAY! I'LL LEAVE 'EM HERE! IT'S ALL THE SAME TO ME!
NO! NO! TAKE 'EM WITH YOU!
BUT YOU SAID IT'S AGAINST THE LAW!
NEVER MIND WHAT I SAID! YOU CAN'T LEAVE 'EM HERE!
OKAY! I'LL BRING 'EM WITH ME!
WHERE ARE YOU GOING NOW?
TO THE POLICE STATION! YOU SAID THAT I'M UNDER ARREST!
OH, NO!
PLEASE! PLEASE! TAKE YOUR LITTLE HONEY MAKERS AND GO PEACEFULLY OUT OF TOWN! YOU'RE NOT WANTED! YOU'RE FREE TO GO, GO, GO!
MY FIRST DAY ON MY NEW BEAT, AND I MEET A PROBLEM LIKE HIM!

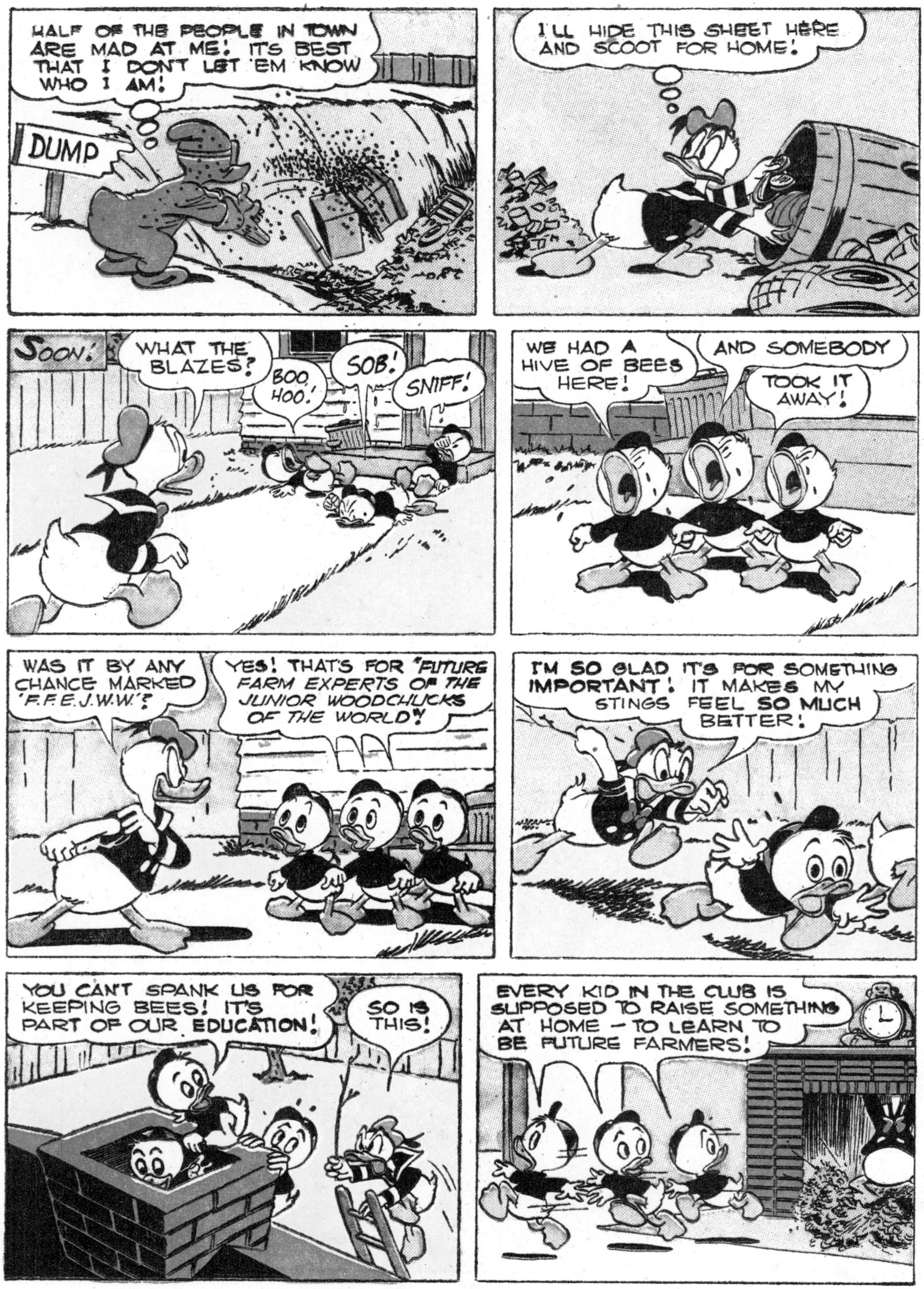
HALF OF THE PEOPLE IN TOWN ARE MAD AT ME! IT'S BEST THAT I DON'T LET 'EM KNOW WHO I AM!
DUMP
I'LL HIDE THIS SHEET HERE AND SCOOT FOR HOME!
SOON!
WHAT THE BLAZES?
BOO HOO!
SOB!
SNIFF!
WE HAD A HIVE OF BEES HERE!
AND SOMEBODY
TOOK IT AWAY!
WAS IT BY ANY CHANCE MARKED 'F.F.E.J.W.W.'?
YES! THAT'S FOR "FUTURE FARM EXPERTS OF THE JUNIOR WOODCHUCKS OF THE WORLD"!
I'M SO GLAD IT'S FOR SOMETHING IMPORTANT! IT MAKES MY STINGS FEEL SO MUCH BETTER!
YOU CAN'T SPANK US FOR KEEPING BEES! IT'S PART OF OUR EDUCATION!
SO IS THIS!
EVERY KID IN THE CLUB IS SUPPOSED TO RAISE SOMETHING AT HOME — TO LEARN TO BE FUTURE FARMERS!

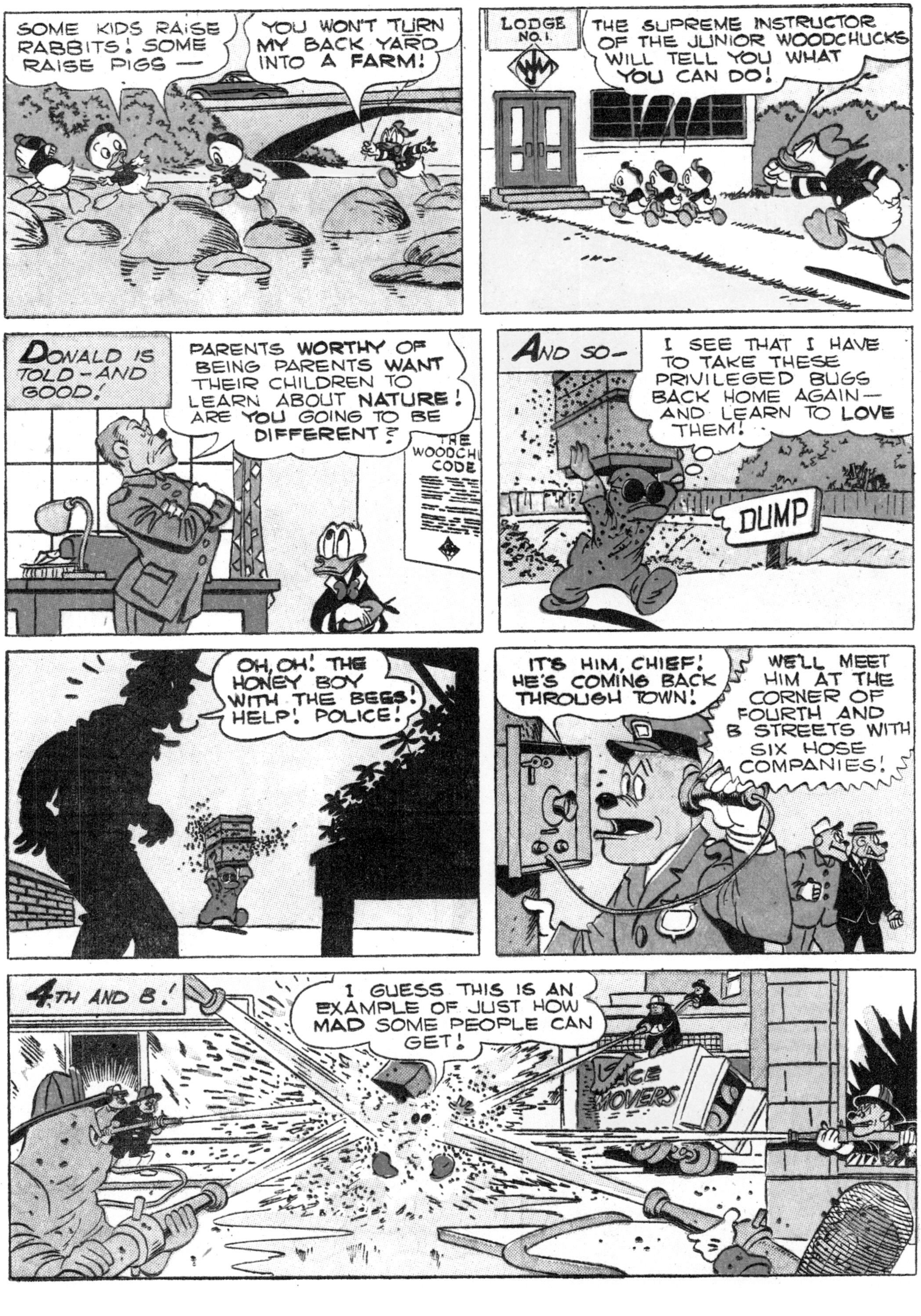
SOME KIDS RAISE RABBITS! SOME RAISE PIGS —
YOU WON'T TURN MY BACK YARD INTO A FARM!
LODGE NO. 1.
THE SUPREME INSTRUCTOR OF THE JUNIOR WOODCHUCKS WILL TELL YOU WHAT YOU CAN DO!
DONALD IS TOLD—AND GOOD!
PARENTS WORTHY OF BEING PARENTS WANT THEIR CHILDREN TO LEARN ABOUT NATURE! ARE YOU GOING TO BE DIFFERENT?
THE WOODCH CODE
AND SO—
I SEE THAT I HAVE TO TAKE THESE PRIVILEGED BUGS BACK HOME AGAIN— AND LEARN TO LOVE THEM!
DUMP
OH, OH! THE HONEY BOY WITH THE BEES! HELP! POLICE!
IT'S HIM, CHIEF! HE'S COMING BACK THROUGH TOWN!
WE'LL MEET HIM AT THE CORNER OF FOURTH AND B STREETS WITH SIX HOSE COMPANIES!
4TH AND B!
I GUESS THIS IS AN EXAMPLE OF JUST HOW MAD SOME PEOPLE CAN GET!
ACE MOVERS

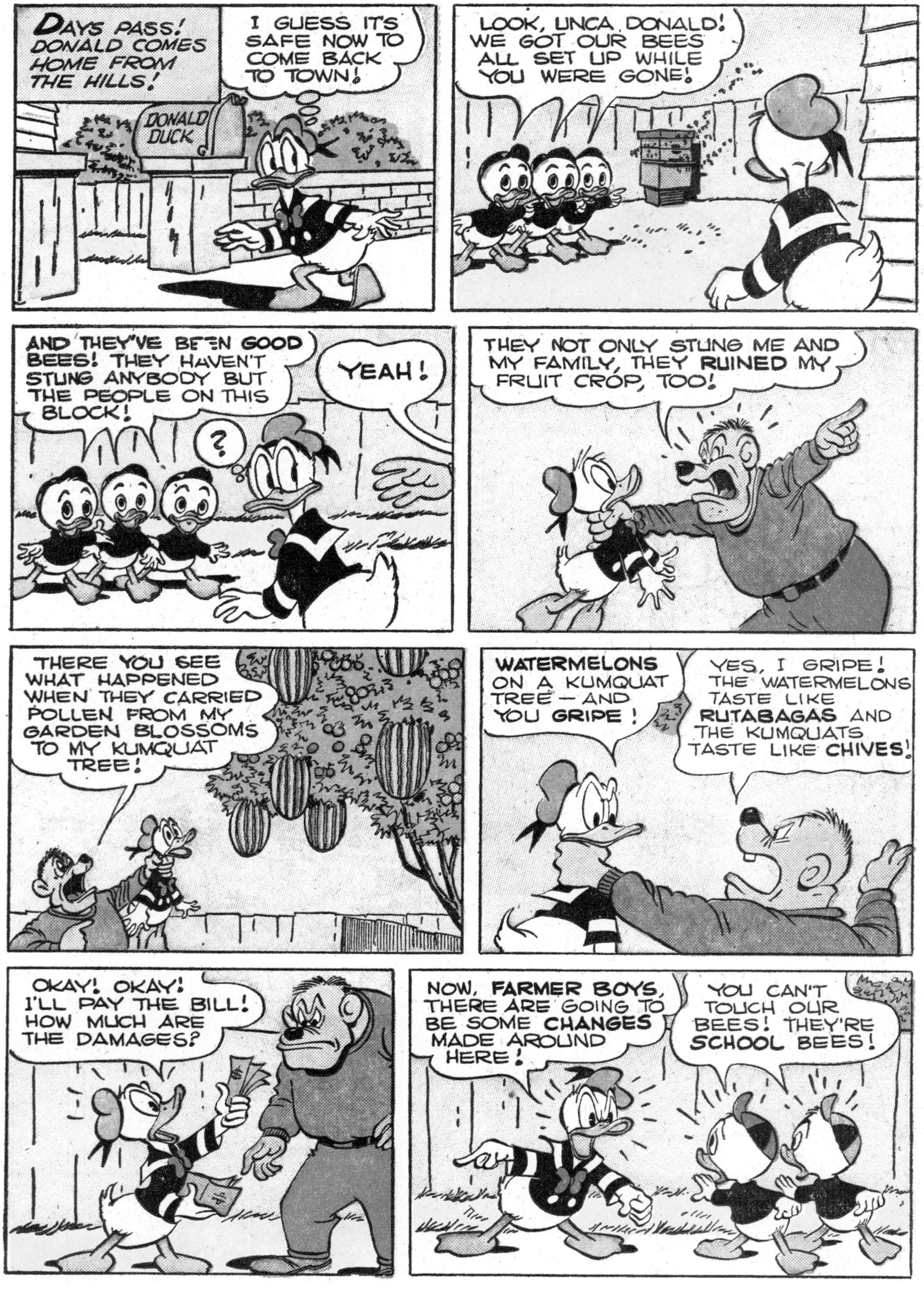
DAYS PASS! DONALD COMES HOME FROM THE HILLS!
I GUESS IT'S SAFE NOW TO COME BACK TO TOWN!
DONALD DUCK
LOOK, UNCA DONALD! WE GOT OUR BEES ALL SET UP WHILE YOU WERE GONE!
AND THEY'VE BEEN GOOD BEES! THEY HAVEN'T STUNG ANYBODY BUT THE PEOPLE ON THIS BLOCK!
YEAH!
?
THEY NOT ONLY STUNG ME AND MY FAMILY, THEY RUINED MY FRUIT CROP, TOO!
THERE YOU SEE WHAT HAPPENED WHEN THEY CARRIED POLLEN FROM MY GARDEN BLOSSOMS TO MY KUMQUAT TREE!
WATERMELONS ON A KUMQUAT TREE — AND YOU GRIPE!
YES, I GRIPE! THE WATERMELONS TASTE LIKE RUTABAGAS AND THE KUMQUATS TASTE LIKE CHIVES!
OKAY! OKAY! I'LL PAY THE BILL! HOW MUCH ARE THE DAMAGES?
NOW, FARMER BOYS, THERE ARE GOING TO BE SOME CHANGES MADE AROUND HERE!
YOU CAN'T TOUCH OUR BEES! THEY'RE SCHOOL BEES!

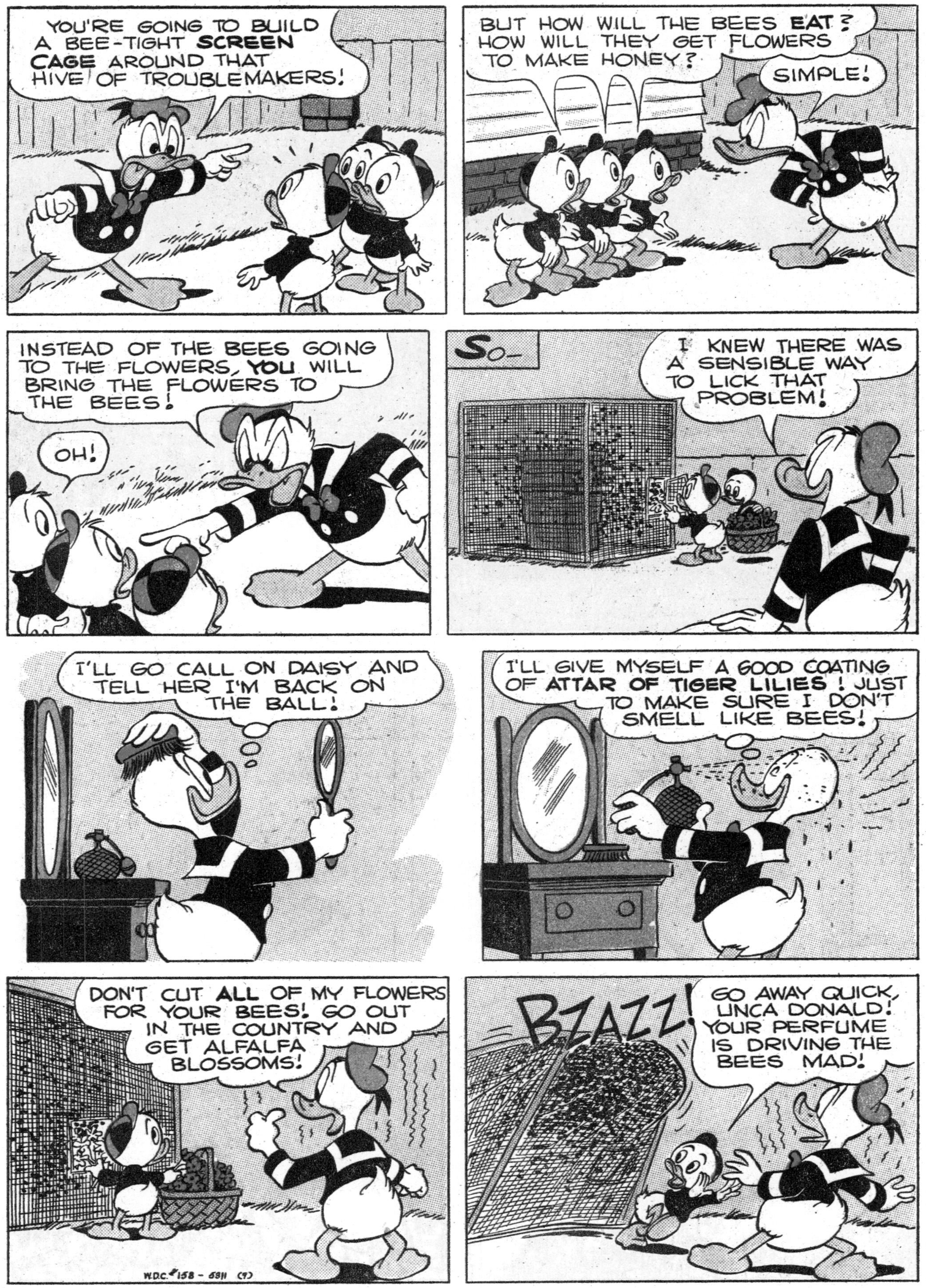
YOU'RE GOING TO BUILD A BEE-TIGHT SCREEN CAGE AROUND THAT HIVE OF TROUBLEMAKERS!
BUT HOW WILL THE BEES EAT? HOW WILL THEY GET FLOWERS TO MAKE HONEY?
SIMPLE!
INSTEAD OF THE BEES GOING TO THE FLOWERS, YOU WILL BRING THE FLOWERS TO THE BEES!
OH!
SO—
I KNEW THERE WAS A SENSIBLE WAY TO LICK THAT PROBLEM!
I'LL GO CALL ON DAISY AND TELL HER I'M BACK ON THE BALL!
I'LL GIVE MYSELF A GOOD COATING OF ATTAR OF TIGER LILIES! JUST TO MAKE SURE I DON'T SMELL LIKE BEES!
DON'T CUT ALL OF MY FLOWERS FOR YOUR BEES! GO OUT IN THE COUNTRY AND GET ALFALFA BLOSSOMS!
W.D.C. #158 - 6811 (9)
BZAZZ!
GO AWAY QUICK, UNCA DONALD! YOUR PERFUME IS DRIVING THE BEES MAD!

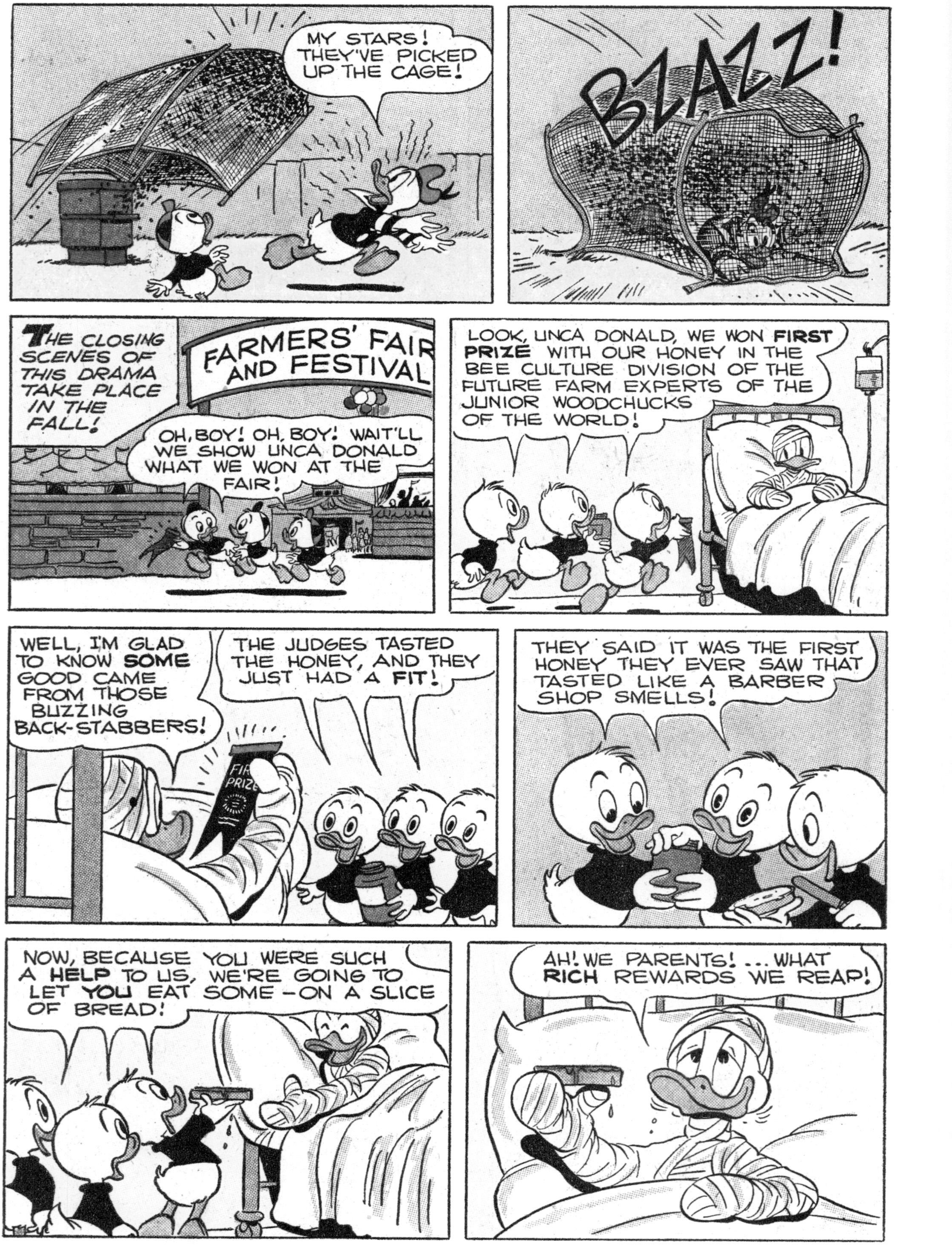
MY STARS! THEY'VE PICKED UP THE CAGE!
BZAZZ!
THE CLOSING SCENES OF THIS DRAMA TAKE PLACE IN THE FALL!
FARMERS' FAIR AND FESTIVAL
OH, BOY! OH, BOY! WAIT'LL WE SHOW UNCA DONALD WHAT WE WON AT THE FAIR!
LOOK, UNCA DONALD, WE WON FIRST PRIZE WITH OUR HONEY IN THE BEE CULTURE DIVISION OF THE FUTURE FARM EXPERTS OF THE JUNIOR WOODCHUCKS OF THE WORLD!
WELL, I'M GLAD TO KNOW SOME GOOD CAME FROM THOSE BUZZING BACK-STABBERS!
THE JUDGES TASTED THE HONEY, AND THEY JUST HAD A FIT!
THEY SAID IT WAS THE FIRST HONEY THEY EVER SAW THAT TASTED LIKE A BARBER SHOP SMELLS!
NOW, BECAUSE YOU WERE SUCH A HELP TO US, WE'RE GOING TO LET YOU EAT SOME—ON A SLICE OF BREAD!
AH! WE PARENTS! ...WHAT RICH REWARDS WE REAP!

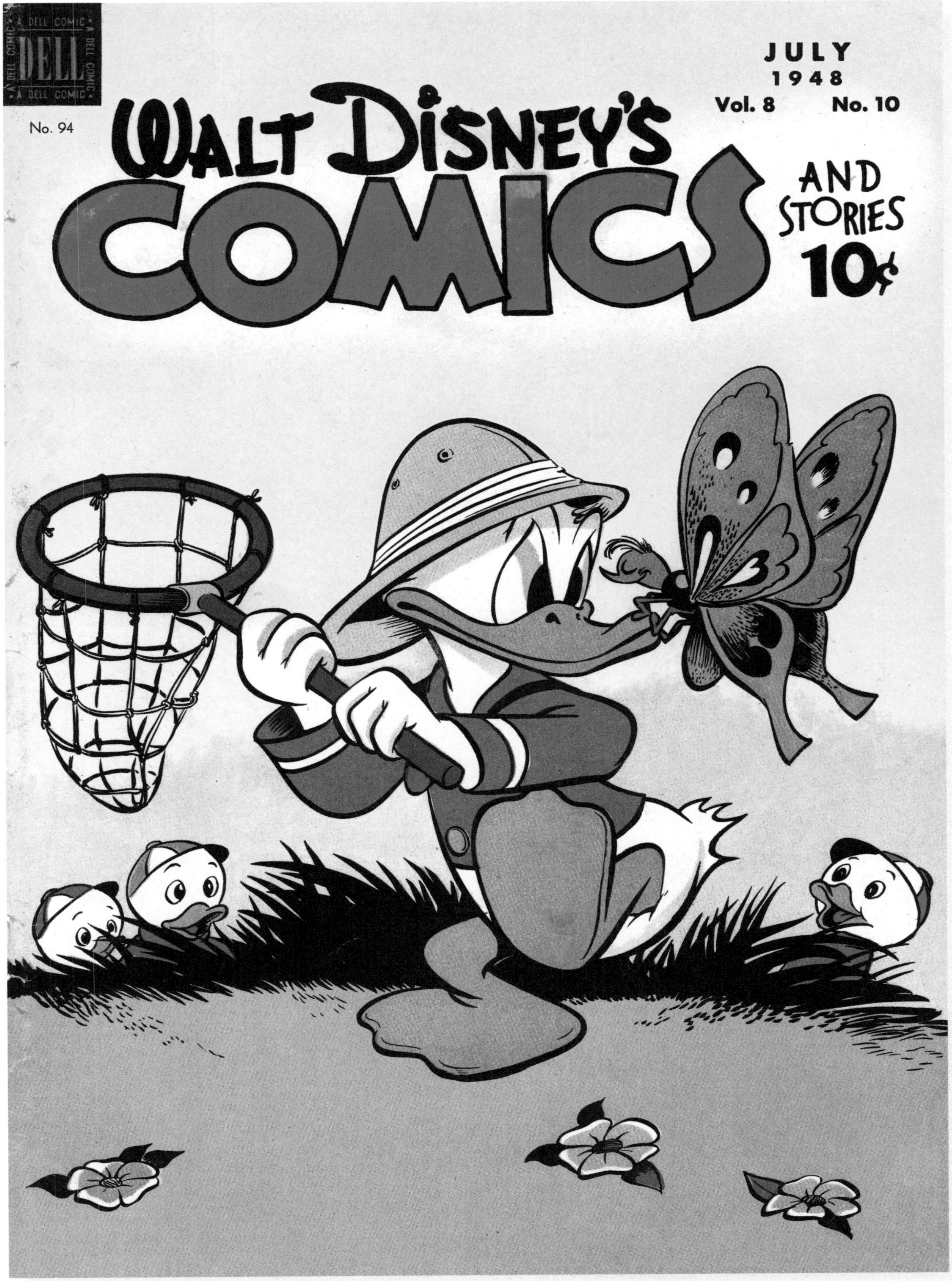
A DELL COMIC
DELL
No. 94
JULY
1948
Vol. 8
No. 10
WALT DISNEY'S
COMICS
AND
STORIES
10¢

STORYTIME WALT DISNEY'S COMICS AND STORIES COVER by WALT KELLY

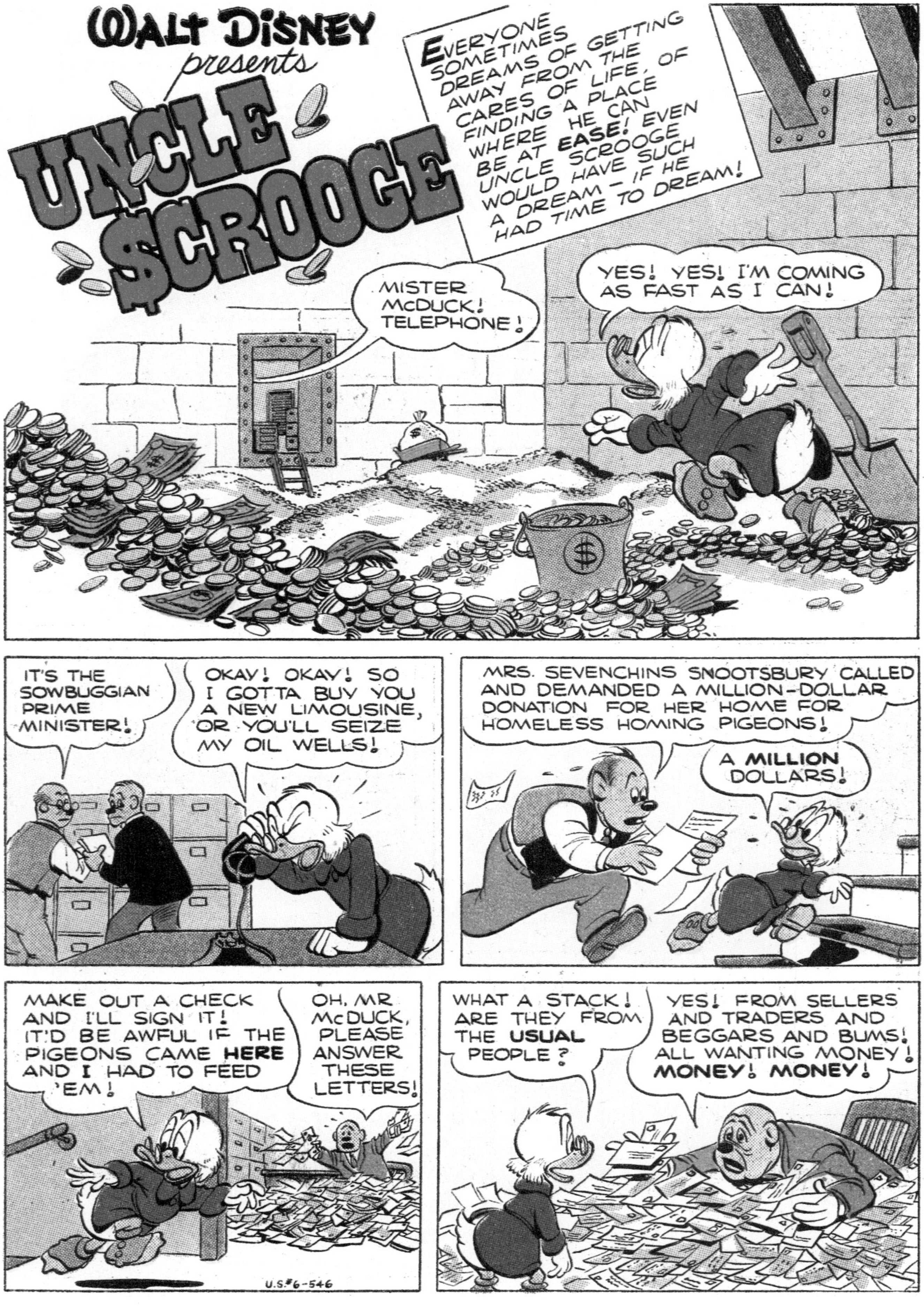
WALT DISNEY presents
UNCLE $CROOGE
EVERYONE SOMETIMES DREAMS OF GETTING AWAY FROM THE CARES OF LIFE, OF FINDING A PLACE WHERE HE CAN BE AT EASE! EVEN UNCLE SCROOGE WOULD HAVE SUCH A DREAM – IF HE HAD TIME TO DREAM!
MISTER McDUCK! TELEPHONE!
YES! YES! I'M COMING AS FAST AS I CAN!
IT'S THE SOWBUGGIAN PRIME MINISTER!
OKAY! OKAY! SO I GOTTA BUY YOU A NEW LIMOUSINE, OR YOU'LL SEIZE MY OIL WELLS!
MRS. SEVENCHINS SNOOTSBURY CALLED AND DEMANDED A MILLION-DOLLAR DONATION FOR HER HOME FOR HOMELESS HOMING PIGEONS!
A MILLION DOLLARS!
MAKE OUT A CHECK AND I'LL SIGN IT! IT'D BE AWFUL IF THE PIGEONS CAME HERE AND I HAD TO FEED 'EM!
OH, MR McDUCK, PLEASE ANSWER THESE LETTERS!
U.S.#6-546
WHAT A STACK! ARE THEY FROM THE USUAL PEOPLE?
YES! FROM SELLERS AND TRADERS AND BEGGARS AND BUMS! ALL WANTING MONEY! MONEY! MONEY!

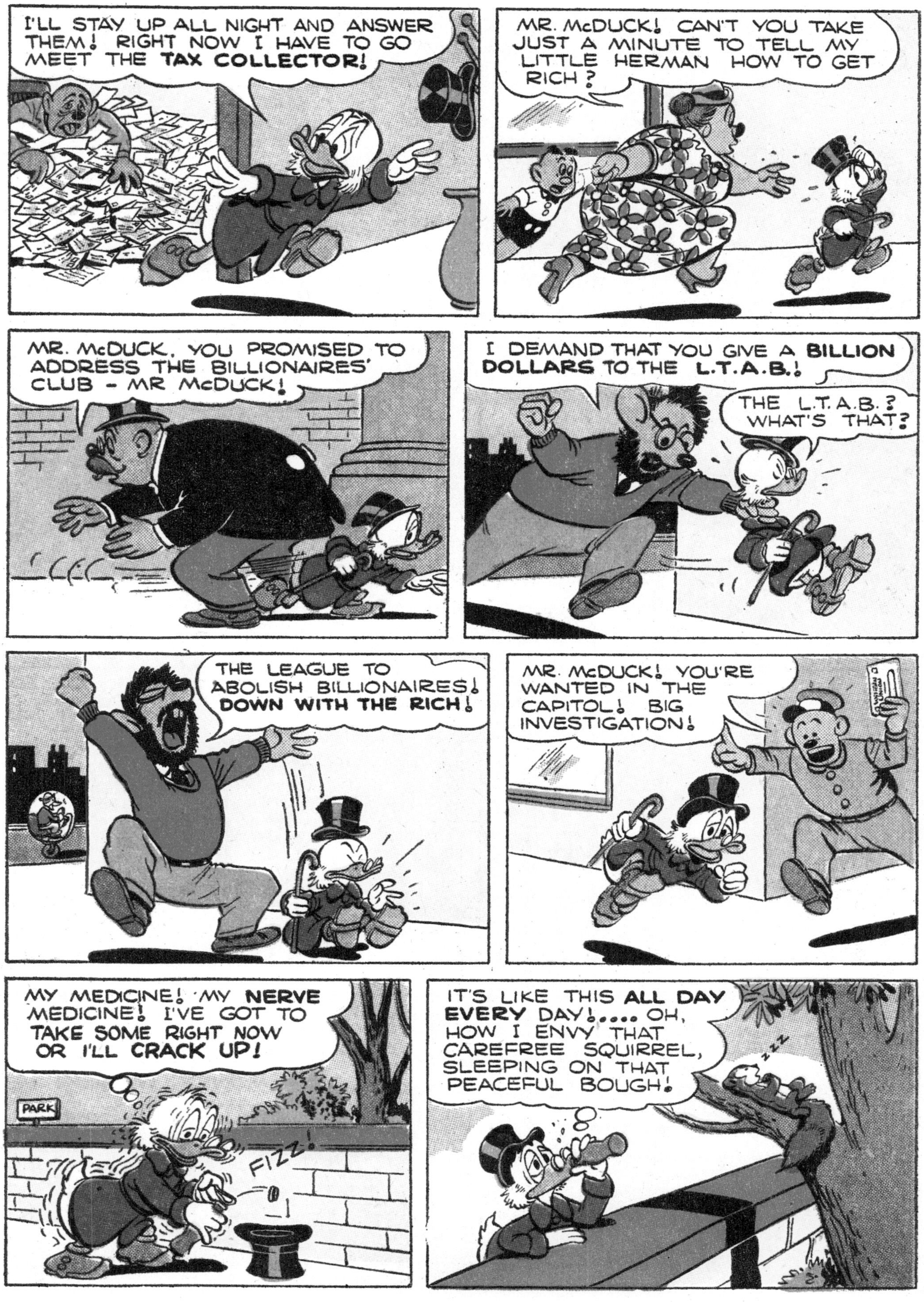
I'LL STAY UP ALL NIGHT AND ANSWER THEM! RIGHT NOW I HAVE TO GO MEET THE **TAX COLLECTOR**!
MR. McDUCK! CAN'T YOU TAKE JUST A MINUTE TO TELL MY LITTLE HERMAN HOW TO GET RICH?
MR. McDUCK, YOU PROMISED TO ADDRESS THE BILLIONAIRES' CLUB - MR McDUCK!
I DEMAND THAT YOU GIVE A **BILLION DOLLARS** TO THE **L.T.A.B.**!
THE L.T.A.B.? WHAT'S THAT?
THE LEAGUE TO ABOLISH BILLIONAIRES! **DOWN WITH THE RICH**!
MR. McDUCK! YOU'RE WANTED IN THE CAPITOL! BIG INVESTIGATION!
MY MEDICINE! MY **NERVE** MEDICINE! I'VE GOT TO **TAKE SOME RIGHT NOW OR I'LL CRACK UP!**
PARK
FIZZ!
IT'S LIKE THIS **ALL DAY EVERY** DAY!.... OH, HOW I ENVY THAT CAREFREE SQUIRREL, SLEEPING ON THAT PEACEFUL BOUGH!

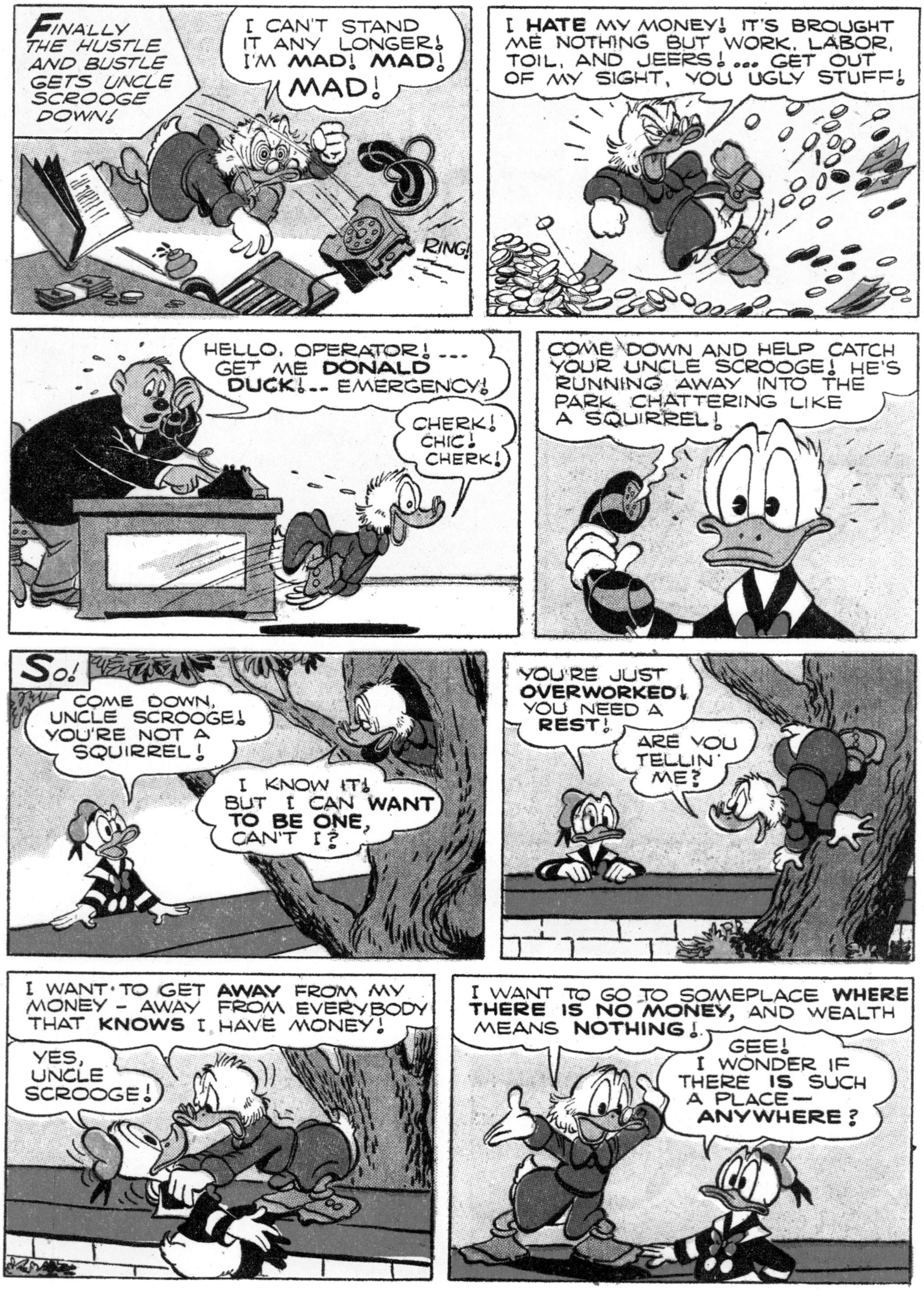
FINALLY THE HUSTLE AND BUSTLE GETS UNCLE SCROOGE DOWN!
I CAN'T STAND IT ANY LONGER! I'M MAD! MAD! MAD!
RING!
I HATE MY MONEY! IT'S BROUGHT ME NOTHING BUT WORK, LABOR, TOIL, AND JEERS!... GET OUT OF MY SIGHT, YOU UGLY STUFF!
HELLO, OPERATOR!... GET ME DONALD DUCK!... EMERGENCY!
CHERK! CHIC! CHERK!
COME DOWN AND HELP CATCH YOUR UNCLE SCROOGE! HE'S RUNNING AWAY INTO THE PARK CHATTERING LIKE A SQUIRREL!
SO!
COME DOWN, UNCLE SCROOGE! YOU'RE NOT A SQUIRREL!
I KNOW IT! BUT I CAN WANT TO BE ONE, CAN'T I?
YOU'RE JUST OVERWORKED! YOU NEED A REST!
ARE YOU TELLIN' ME?
I WANT TO GET AWAY FROM MY MONEY - AWAY FROM EVERYBODY THAT KNOWS I HAVE MONEY!
YES, UNCLE SCROOGE!
I WANT TO GO TO SOMEPLACE WHERE THERE IS NO MONEY, AND WEALTH MEANS NOTHING!
GEE! I WONDER IF THERE IS SUCH A PLACE— ANYWHERE?

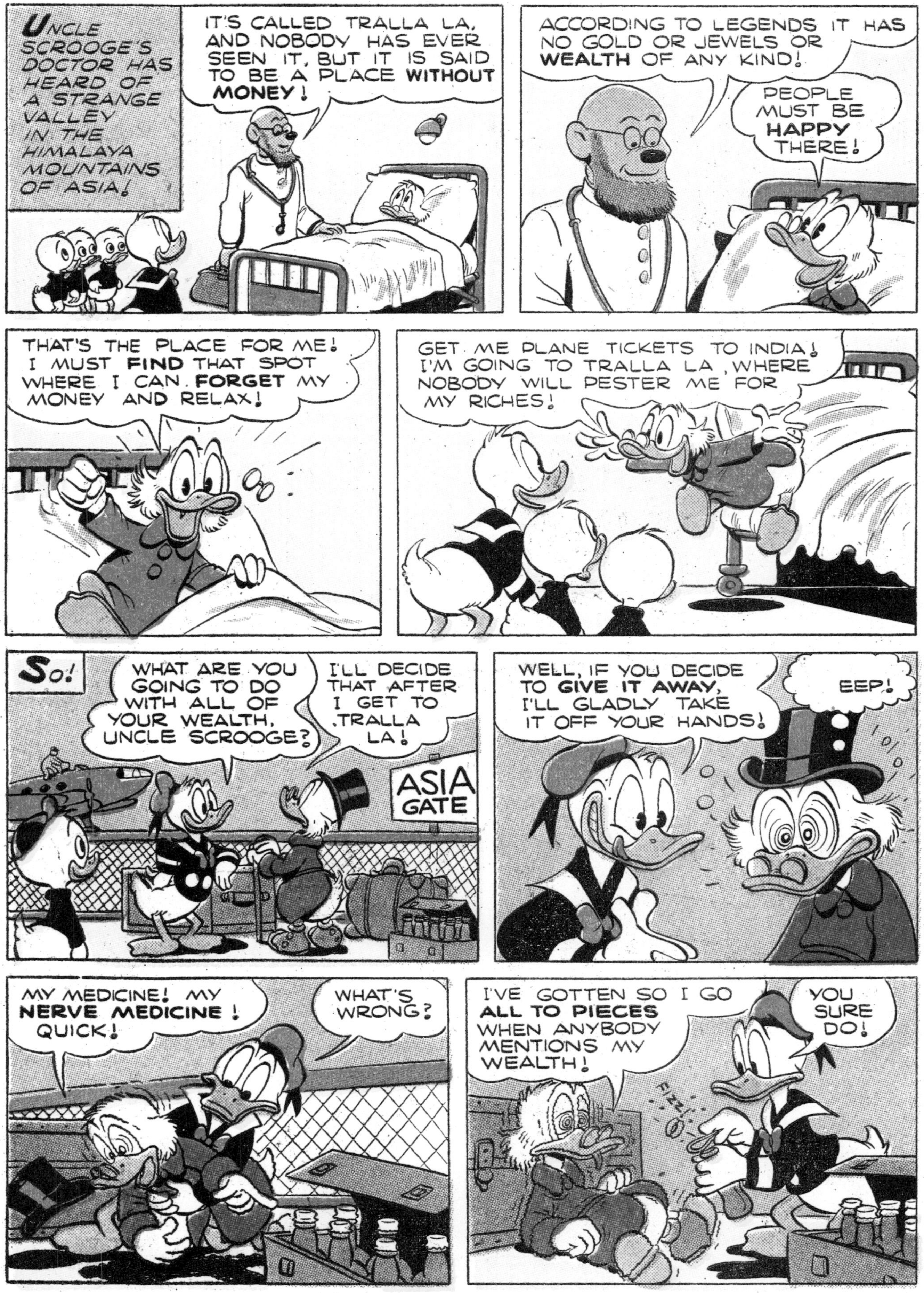
UNCLE SCROOGE'S DOCTOR HAS HEARD OF A STRANGE VALLEY IN THE HIMALAYA MOUNTAINS OF ASIA!
IT'S CALLED TRALLA LA, AND NOBODY HAS EVER SEEN IT, BUT IT IS SAID TO BE A PLACE **WITHOUT MONEY**!
ACCORDING TO LEGENDS IT HAS NO GOLD OR JEWELS OR **WEALTH** OF ANY KIND!
PEOPLE MUST BE **HAPPY** THERE!
THAT'S THE PLACE FOR ME! I MUST **FIND** THAT SPOT WHERE I CAN **FORGET** MY MONEY AND RELAX!
GET ME PLANE TICKETS TO INDIA! I'M GOING TO TRALLA LA, WHERE NOBODY WILL PESTER ME FOR MY RICHES!
SO!
WHAT ARE YOU GOING TO DO WITH ALL OF YOUR WEALTH, UNCLE SCROOGE?
I'LL DECIDE THAT AFTER I GET TO TRALLA LA!
ASIA GATE
WELL, IF YOU DECIDE TO **GIVE IT AWAY**, I'LL GLADLY TAKE IT OFF YOUR HANDS!
EEP!
MY MEDICINE! MY **NERVE MEDICINE**! QUICK!
WHAT'S WRONG?
I'VE GOTTEN SO I GO **ALL TO PIECES** WHEN ANYBODY MENTIONS MY WEALTH!
YOU SURE DO!
FIZZ

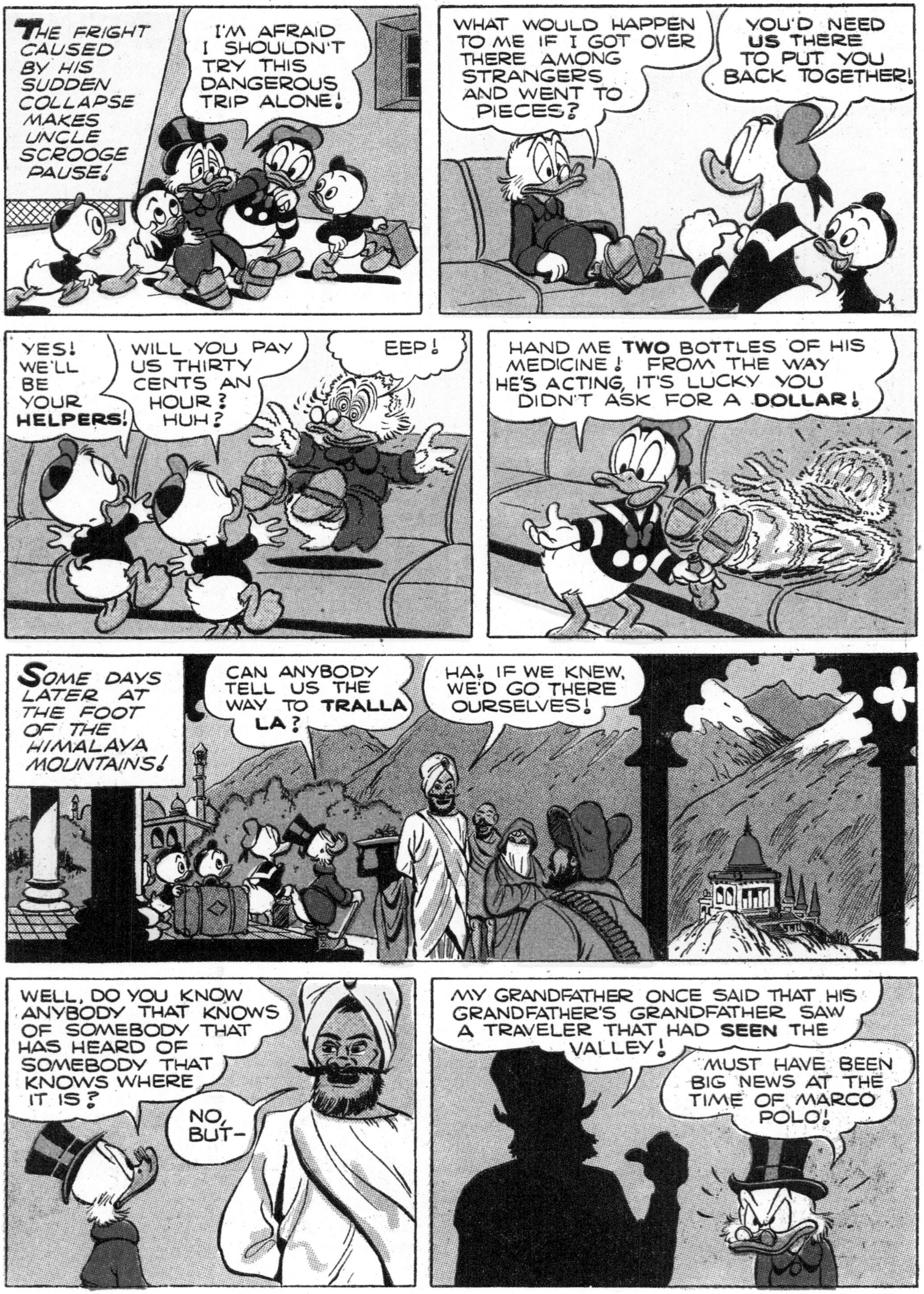
THE FRIGHT CAUSED BY HIS SUDDEN COLLAPSE MAKES UNCLE SCROOGE PAUSE!
I'M AFRAID I SHOULDN'T TRY THIS DANGEROUS TRIP ALONE!
WHAT WOULD HAPPEN TO ME IF I GOT OVER THERE AMONG STRANGERS AND WENT TO PIECES?
YOU'D NEED **US** THERE TO PUT YOU BACK TOGETHER!
YES! WE'LL BE YOUR **HELPERS**!
WILL YOU PAY US THIRTY CENTS AN HOUR? HUH?
EEP!
HAND ME **TWO** BOTTLES OF HIS MEDICINE! FROM THE WAY HE'S ACTING, IT'S LUCKY **YOU** DIDN'T ASK FOR A **DOLLAR**!
SOME DAYS LATER AT THE FOOT OF THE HIMALAYA MOUNTAINS!
CAN ANYBODY TELL US THE WAY TO **TRALLA LA**?
HA! IF WE KNEW, WE'D GO THERE OURSELVES!
WELL, DO YOU KNOW ANYBODY THAT KNOWS OF SOMEBODY THAT HAS HEARD OF SOMEBODY THAT KNOWS WHERE IT IS?
NO, BUT-
MY GRANDFATHER ONCE SAID THAT HIS GRANDFATHER'S GRANDFATHER SAW A TRAVELER THAT HAD **SEEN** THE VALLEY!
MUST HAVE BEEN BIG NEWS AT THE TIME OF MARCO POLO!

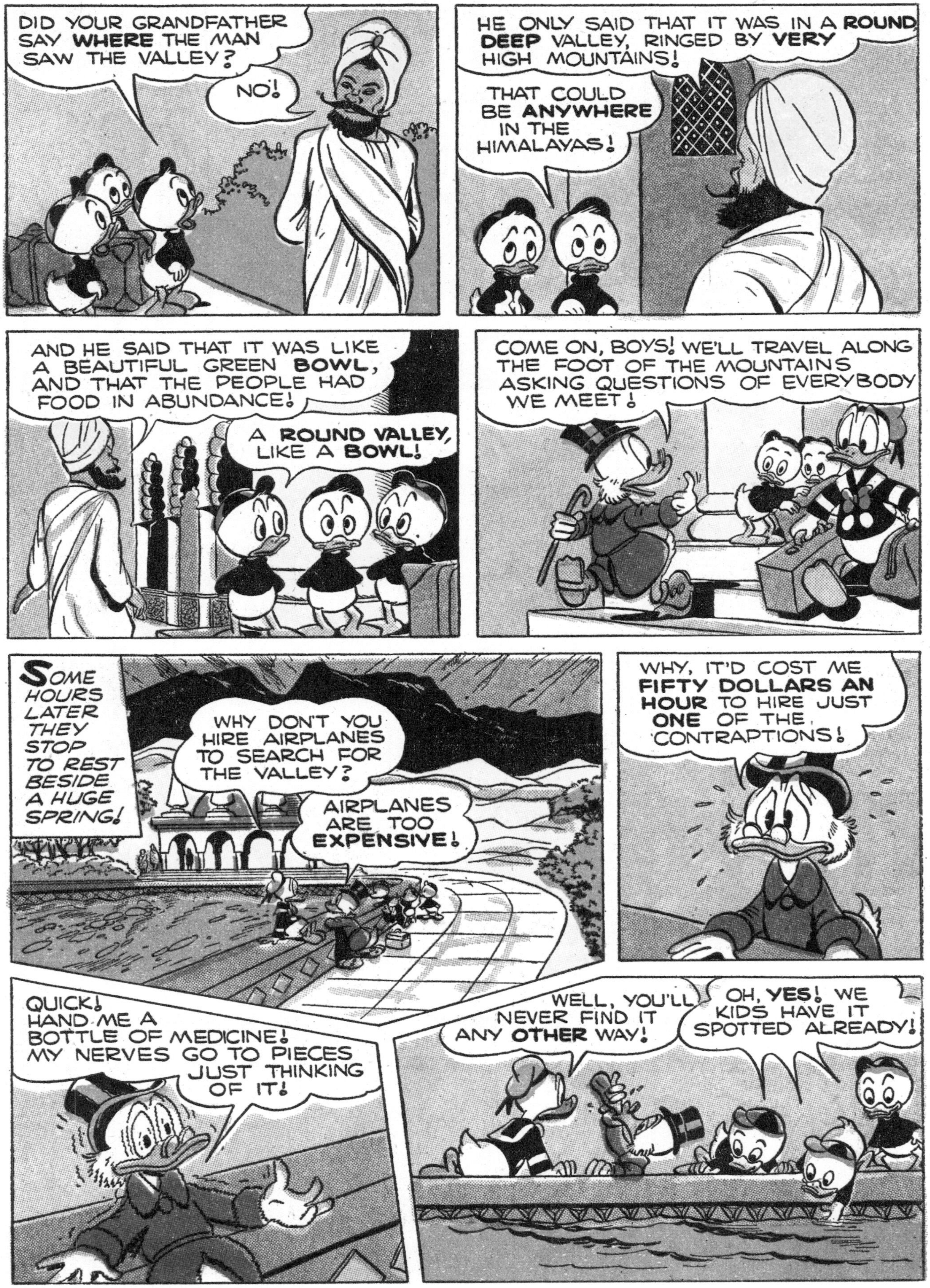
DID YOUR GRANDFATHER SAY **WHERE** THE MAN SAW THE VALLEY?
NO!
HE ONLY SAID THAT IT WAS IN A **ROUND DEEP** VALLEY, RINGED BY **VERY** HIGH MOUNTAINS!
THAT COULD BE **ANYWHERE** IN THE HIMALAYAS!
AND HE SAID THAT IT WAS LIKE A BEAUTIFUL GREEN **BOWL**, AND THAT THE PEOPLE HAD FOOD IN ABUNDANCE!
A **ROUND VALLEY**, LIKE A **BOWL**!
COME ON, BOYS! WE'LL TRAVEL ALONG THE FOOT OF THE MOUNTAINS ASKING QUESTIONS OF EVERYBODY WE MEET!
SOME HOURS LATER THEY STOP TO REST BESIDE A HUGE SPRING!
WHY DON'T YOU HIRE AIRPLANES TO SEARCH FOR THE VALLEY?
AIRPLANES ARE TOO **EXPENSIVE**!
WHY, IT'D COST ME **FIFTY DOLLARS AN HOUR** TO HIRE JUST **ONE** OF THE CONTRAPTIONS!
QUICK! HAND ME A BOTTLE OF MEDICINE! MY NERVES GO TO PIECES JUST THINKING OF IT!
WELL, YOU'LL NEVER FIND IT ANY **OTHER** WAY!
OH, **YES**! WE KIDS HAVE IT SPOTTED ALREADY!

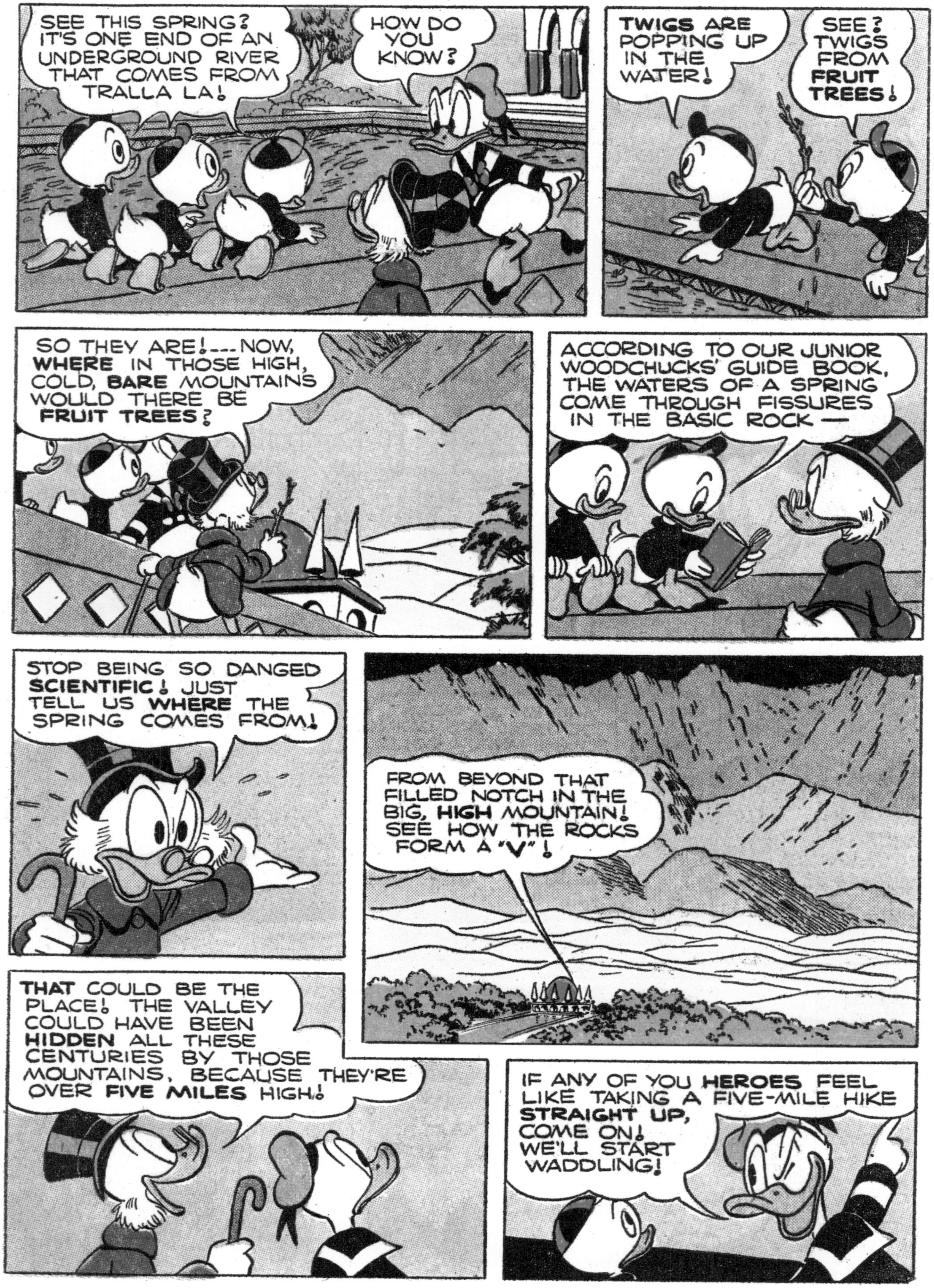
SEE THIS SPRING? IT'S ONE END OF AN UNDERGROUND RIVER THAT COMES FROM TRALLA LA!
HOW DO YOU KNOW?
TWIGS ARE POPPING UP IN THE WATER!
SEE? TWIGS FROM FRUIT TREES!
SO THEY ARE!---NOW, WHERE IN THOSE HIGH, COLD, BARE MOUNTAINS WOULD THERE BE FRUIT TREES?
ACCORDING TO OUR JUNIOR WOODCHUCKS' GUIDE BOOK, THE WATERS OF A SPRING COME THROUGH FISSURES IN THE BASIC ROCK —
STOP BEING SO DANGED SCIENTIFIC! JUST TELL US WHERE THE SPRING COMES FROM!
FROM BEYOND THAT FILLED NOTCH IN THE BIG, HIGH MOUNTAIN! SEE HOW THE ROCKS FORM A "V"!
THAT COULD BE THE PLACE! THE VALLEY COULD HAVE BEEN HIDDEN ALL THESE CENTURIES BY THOSE MOUNTAINS, BECAUSE THEY'RE OVER FIVE MILES HIGH!
IF ANY OF YOU HEROES FEEL LIKE TAKING A FIVE-MILE HIKE STRAIGHT UP, COME ON! WE'LL START WADDLING!

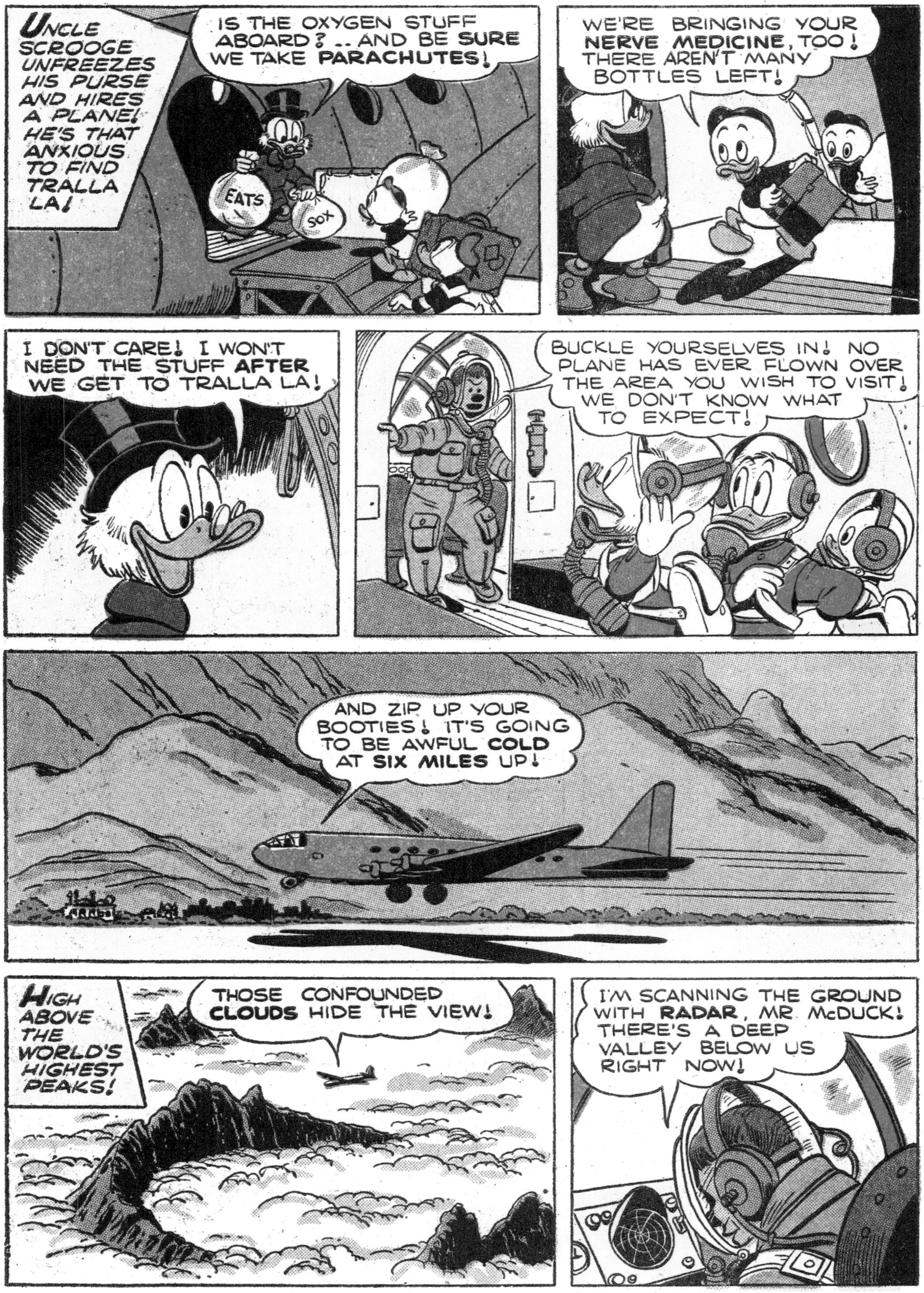
UNCLE SCROOGE UNFREEZES HIS PURSE AND HIRES A PLANE! HE'S THAT ANXIOUS TO FIND TRALLA LA!
IS THE OXYGEN STUFF ABOARD? .. AND BE SURE WE TAKE PARACHUTES!
EATS
SOX
WE'RE BRINGING YOUR NERVE MEDICINE, TOO! THERE AREN'T MANY BOTTLES LEFT!
I DON'T CARE! I WON'T NEED THE STUFF AFTER WE GET TO TRALLA LA!
BUCKLE YOURSELVES IN! NO PLANE HAS EVER FLOWN OVER THE AREA YOU WISH TO VISIT! WE DON'T KNOW WHAT TO EXPECT!
AND ZIP UP YOUR BOOTIES! IT'S GOING TO BE AWFUL COLD AT SIX MILES UP!
HIGH ABOVE THE WORLD'S HIGHEST PEAKS!
THOSE CONFOUNDED CLOUDS HIDE THE VIEW!
I'M SCANNING THE GROUND WITH RADAR, MR. McDUCK! THERE'S A DEEP VALLEY BELOW US RIGHT NOW!

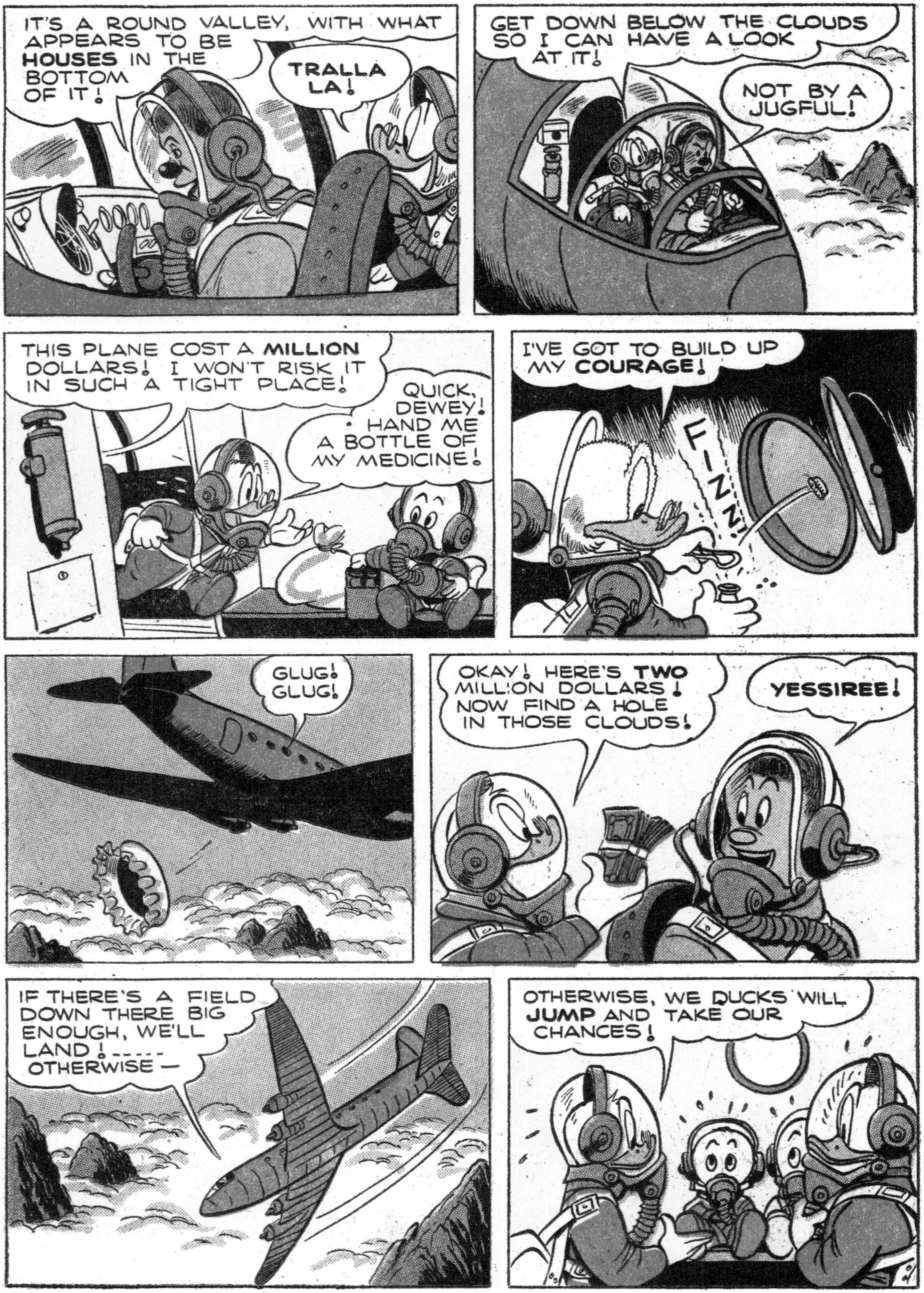
IT'S A ROUND VALLEY, WITH WHAT APPEARS TO BE **HOUSES** IN THE BOTTOM OF IT!
TRALLA LA!
GET DOWN BELOW THE CLOUDS SO I CAN HAVE A LOOK AT IT!
NOT BY A JUGFUL!
THIS PLANE COST A **MILLION** DOLLARS! I WON'T RISK IT IN SUCH A TIGHT PLACE!
QUICK, DEWEY! HAND ME A BOTTLE OF MY MEDICINE!
I'VE GOT TO BUILD UP MY **COURAGE!**
FIZZ
GLUG! GLUG!
OKAY! HERE'S **TWO** MILLION DOLLARS! NOW FIND A HOLE IN THOSE CLOUDS!
YESSIREE!
IF THERE'S A FIELD DOWN THERE BIG ENOUGH, WE'LL LAND! ..... OTHERWISE —
OTHERWISE, WE DUCKS WILL **JUMP** AND TAKE OUR CHANCES!

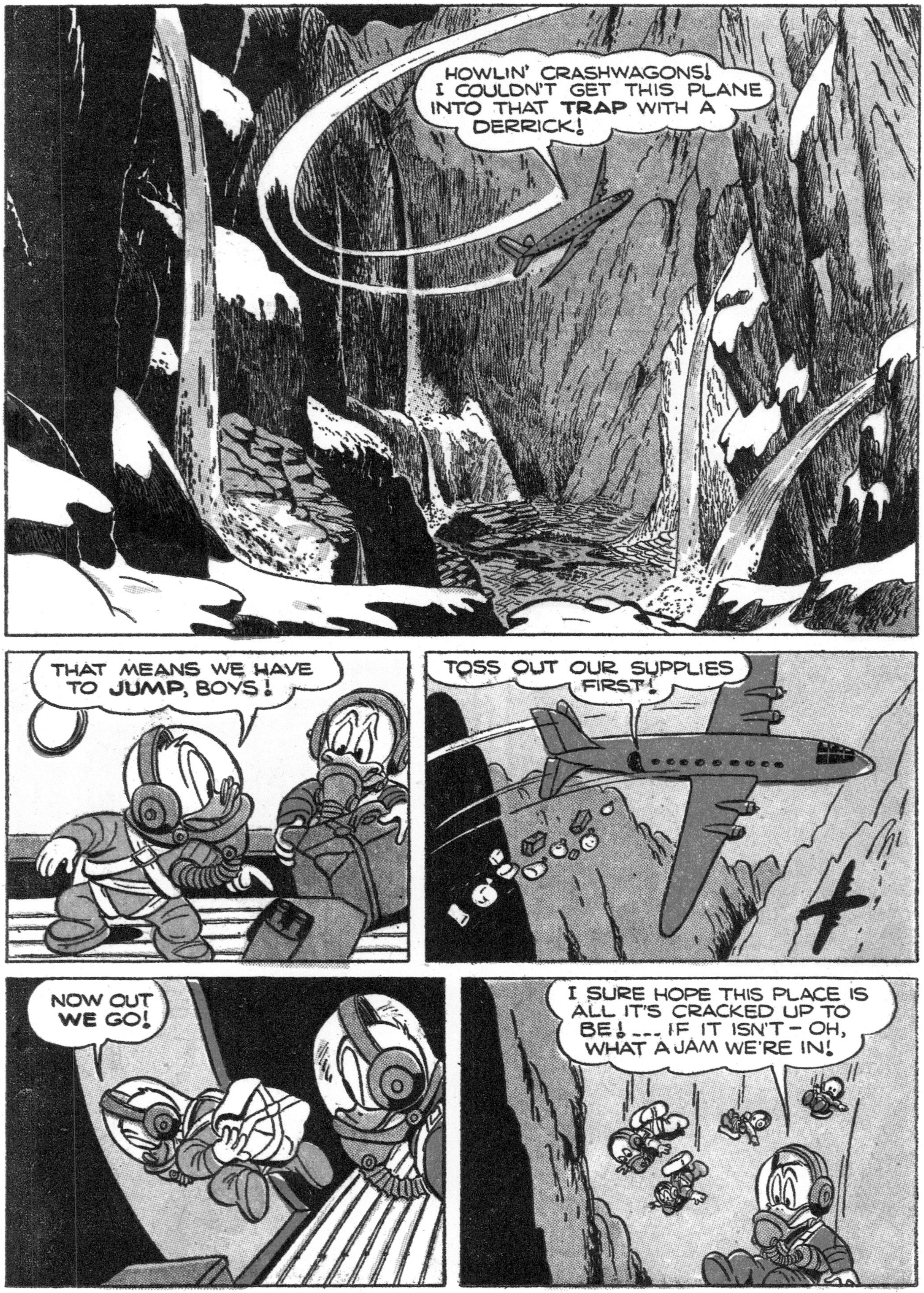
HOWLIN' CRASHWAGONS! I COULDN'T GET THIS PLANE INTO THAT TRAP WITH A DERRICK!
THAT MEANS WE HAVE TO JUMP, BOYS!
TOSS OUT OUR SUPPLIES FIRST!
NOW OUT WE GO!
I SURE HOPE THIS PLACE IS ALL IT'S CRACKED UP TO BE! ... IF IT ISN'T – OH, WHAT A JAM WE'RE IN!

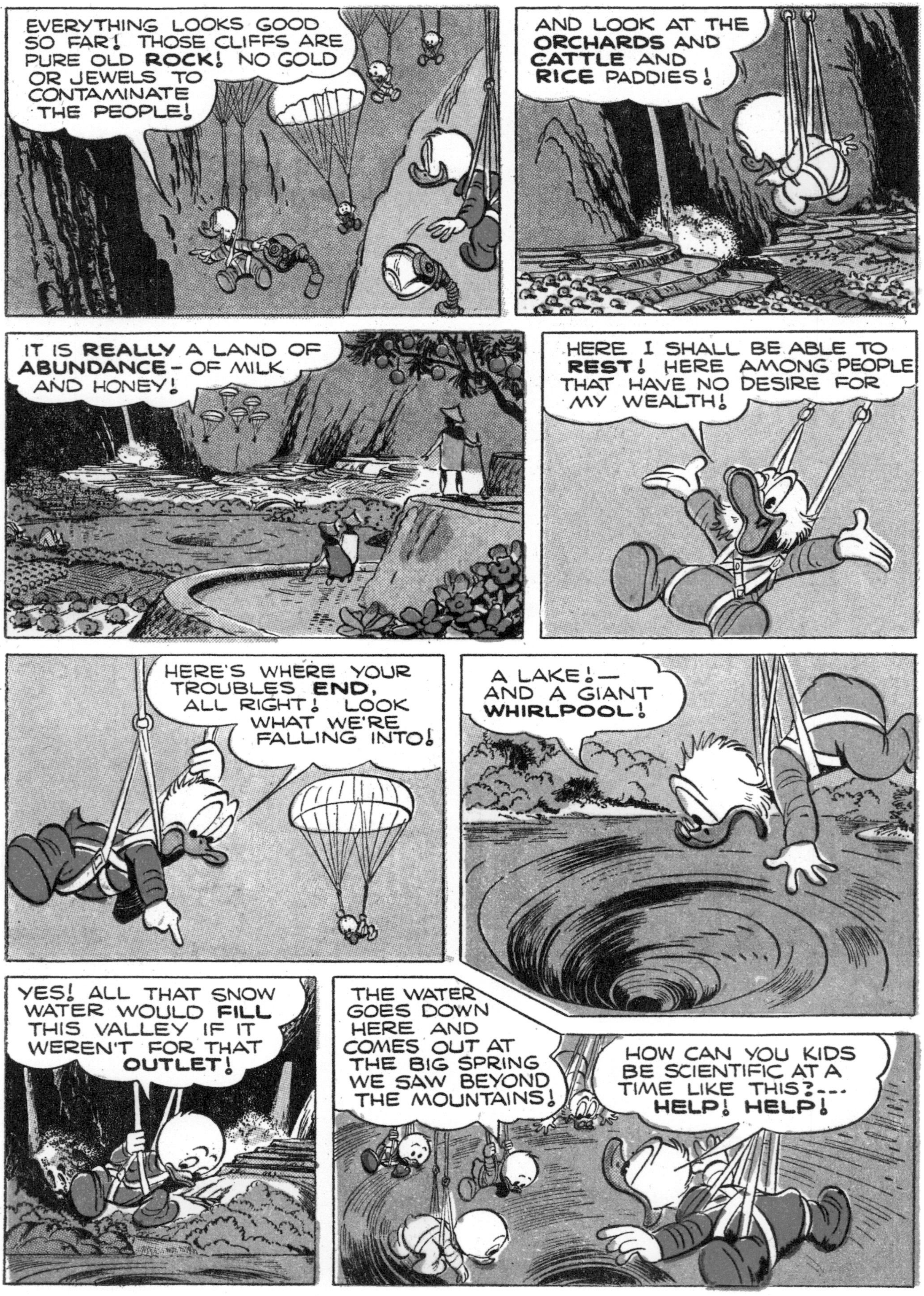
EVERYTHING LOOKS GOOD SO FAR! THOSE CLIFFS ARE PURE OLD ROCK! NO GOLD OR JEWELS TO CONTAMINATE THE PEOPLE!
AND LOOK AT THE ORCHARDS AND CATTLE AND RICE PADDIES!
IT IS REALLY A LAND OF ABUNDANCE – OF MILK AND HONEY!
HERE I SHALL BE ABLE TO REST! HERE AMONG PEOPLE THAT HAVE NO DESIRE FOR MY WEALTH!
HERE'S WHERE YOUR TROUBLES END, ALL RIGHT! LOOK WHAT WE'RE FALLING INTO!
A LAKE! — AND A GIANT WHIRLPOOL!
YES! ALL THAT SNOW WATER WOULD FILL THIS VALLEY IF IT WEREN'T FOR THAT OUTLET!
THE WATER GOES DOWN HERE AND COMES OUT AT THE BIG SPRING WE SAW BEYOND THE MOUNTAINS!
HOW CAN YOU KIDS BE SCIENTIFIC AT A TIME LIKE THIS?--- HELP! HELP!

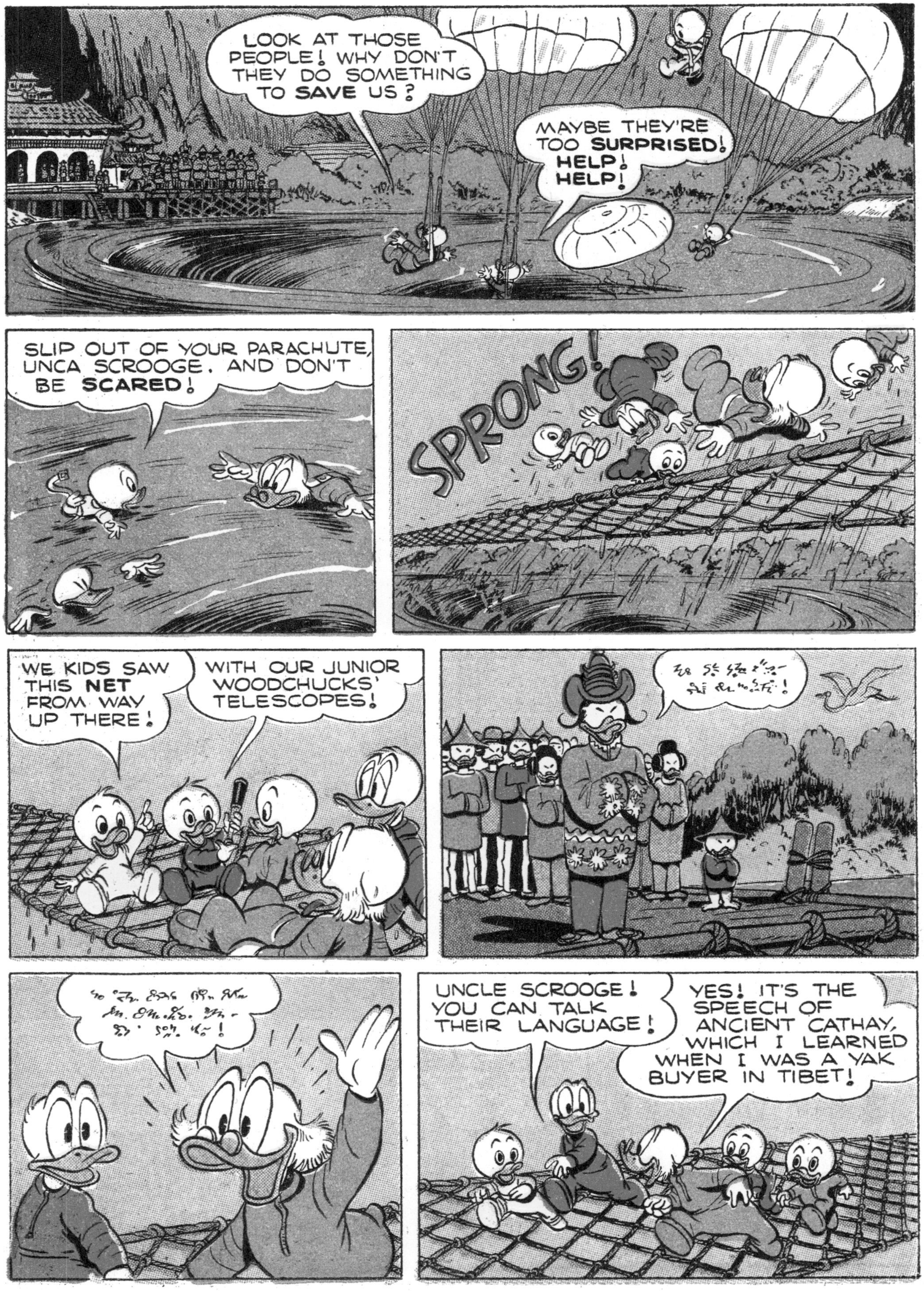
LOOK AT THOSE PEOPLE! WHY DON'T THEY DO SOMETHING TO SAVE US?
MAYBE THEY'RE TOO SURPRISED! HELP! HELP!
SLIP OUT OF YOUR PARACHUTE, UNCA SCROOGE, AND DON'T BE SCARED!
SPRONG!
WE KIDS SAW THIS NET FROM WAY UP THERE!
WITH OUR JUNIOR WOODCHUCKS' TELESCOPES!
UNCLE SCROOGE! YOU CAN TALK THEIR LANGUAGE!
YES! IT'S THE SPEECH OF ANCIENT CATHAY, WHICH I LEARNED WHEN I WAS A YAK BUYER IN TIBET!

TRALLA LA PROVES TO BE EVERYTHING THAT UNCLE SCROOGE EXPECTED OF IT!

WE TRALLA LALLIANS HAVE NEVER KNOWN GREED! **FRIENDSHIP** IS THE THING WE VALUE MOST!

IT **IS** WONDERFUL HERE! NOBODY **WANTS** ANYTHING THAT BELONGS TO ANYBODY ELSE!

THE PEOPLE ROUNDED UP ALL OF OUR SUPPLIES AND RETURNED THEM TO US!

AND NOBODY ASKED FOR A SINGLE FAVOR!

YESSIR! ALL WE HAVE TO DO IS BEAR OUR SHARE OF THE WORK, AND THE PEOPLE WILL LEAVE US STRICTLY ALONE!

AT LAST I CAN RELAX WITHOUT HAVING A BUNCH OF PESTS TRYING TO CHISEL ME OUT OF MY MONEY!

LIFE IN TRALLA LA IS INDEED *IDEAL* — UNTIL ONE DAY—

HMM! WHAT IS THIS **OBJECT?**

IT IS THE SHINY STUFF CALLED **METAL!**... MUST BELONG TO THE OLD DUCK NAMED SCROOGE! I TAKE IT TO HIM!

I BRING YOU SOMETHING THAT YOU LOST!

HUH? WHY, THAT'S ONLY AN OLD **BOTTLE CAP!**

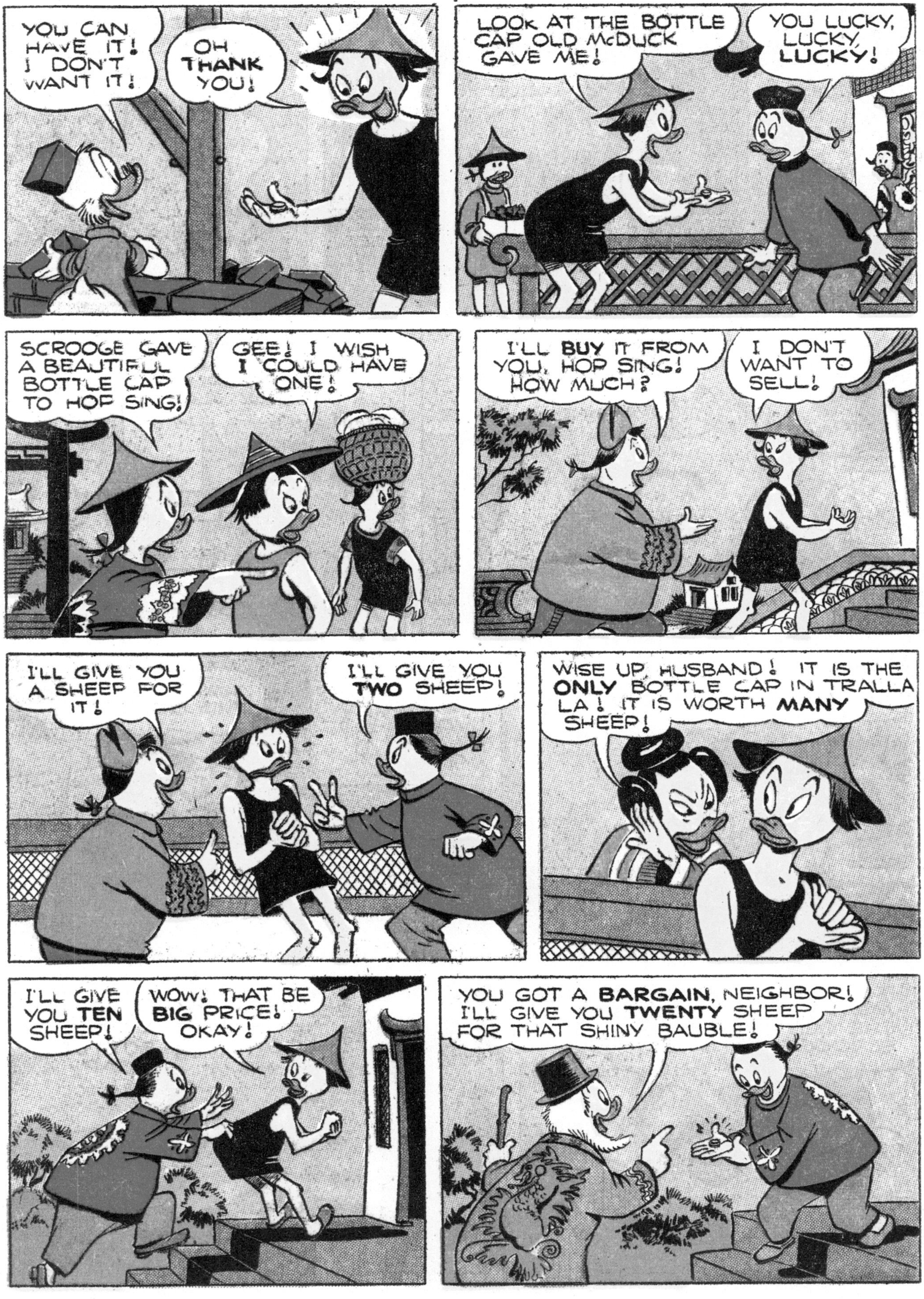
YOU CAN HAVE IT! I DON'T WANT IT!
OH THANK YOU!
LOOK AT THE BOTTLE CAP OLD McDUCK GAVE ME!
YOU LUCKY, LUCKY, LUCKY!
SCROOGE GAVE A BEAUTIFUL BOTTLE CAP TO HOP SING!
GEE! I WISH I COULD HAVE ONE!
I'LL BUY IT FROM YOU, HOP SING! HOW MUCH?
I DON'T WANT TO SELL!
I'LL GIVE YOU A SHEEP FOR IT!
I'LL GIVE YOU TWO SHEEP!
WISE UP, HUSBAND! IT IS THE ONLY BOTTLE CAP IN TRALLA LA! IT IS WORTH MANY SHEEP!
I'LL GIVE YOU TEN SHEEP!
WOW! THAT BE BIG PRICE! OKAY!
YOU GOT A BARGAIN, NEIGHBOR! I'LL GIVE YOU TWENTY SHEEP FOR THAT SHINY BAUBLE!

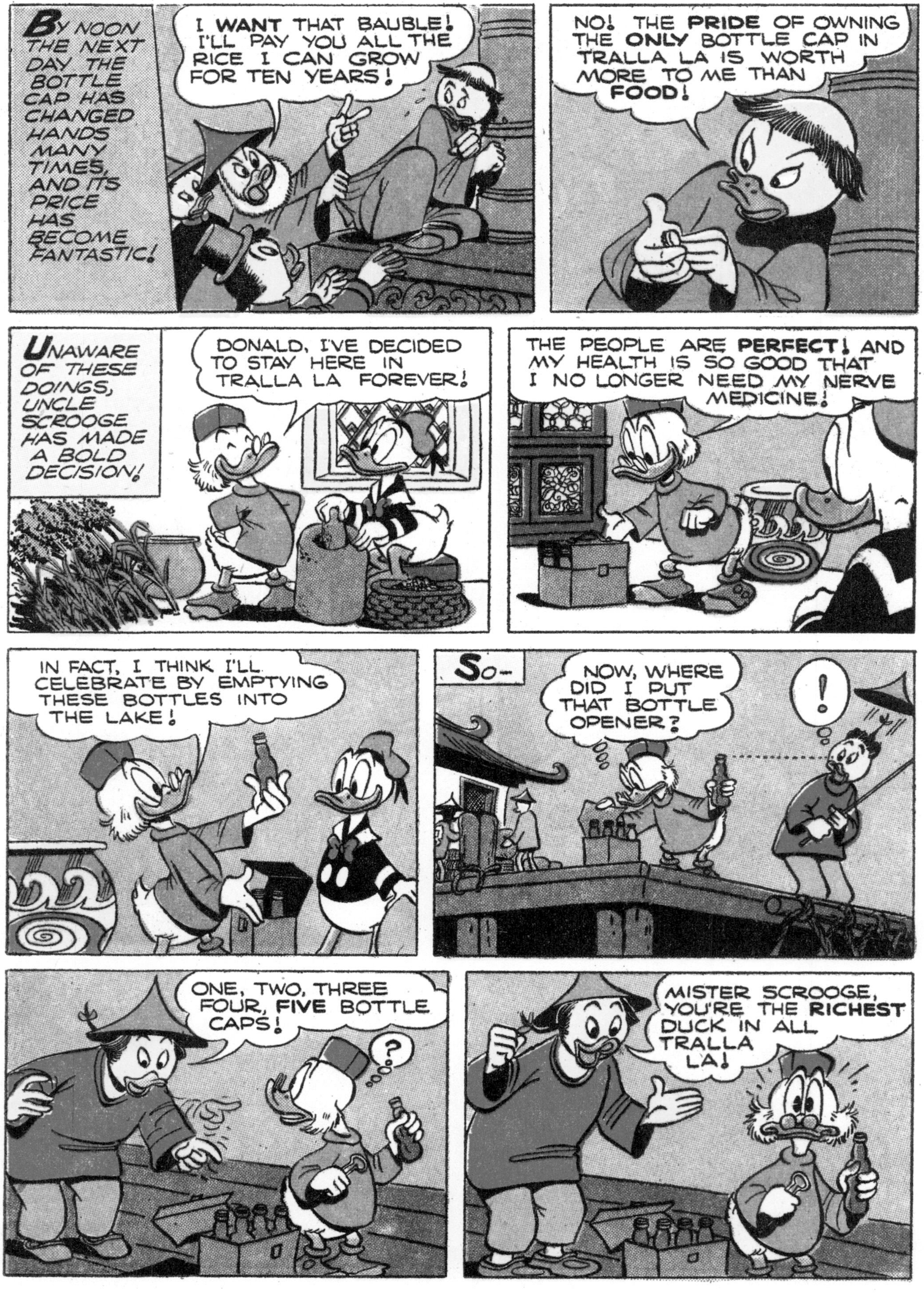
BY NOON THE NEXT DAY THE BOTTLE CAP HAS CHANGED HANDS MANY TIMES, AND ITS PRICE HAS BECOME FANTASTIC!
I WANT THAT BAUBLE! I'LL PAY YOU ALL THE RICE I CAN GROW FOR TEN YEARS!
NO! THE PRIDE OF OWNING THE ONLY BOTTLE CAP IN TRALLA LA IS WORTH MORE TO ME THAN FOOD!
UNAWARE OF THESE DOINGS, UNCLE SCROOGE HAS MADE A BOLD DECISION!
DONALD, I'VE DECIDED TO STAY HERE IN TRALLA LA FOREVER!
THE PEOPLE ARE PERFECT! AND MY HEALTH IS SO GOOD THAT I NO LONGER NEED MY NERVE MEDICINE!
IN FACT, I THINK I'LL CELEBRATE BY EMPTYING THESE BOTTLES INTO THE LAKE!
SO–
NOW, WHERE DID I PUT THAT BOTTLE OPENER?
!
ONE, TWO, THREE FOUR, FIVE BOTTLE CAPS!
?
MISTER SCROOGE, YOU'RE THE RICHEST DUCK IN ALL TRALLA LA!

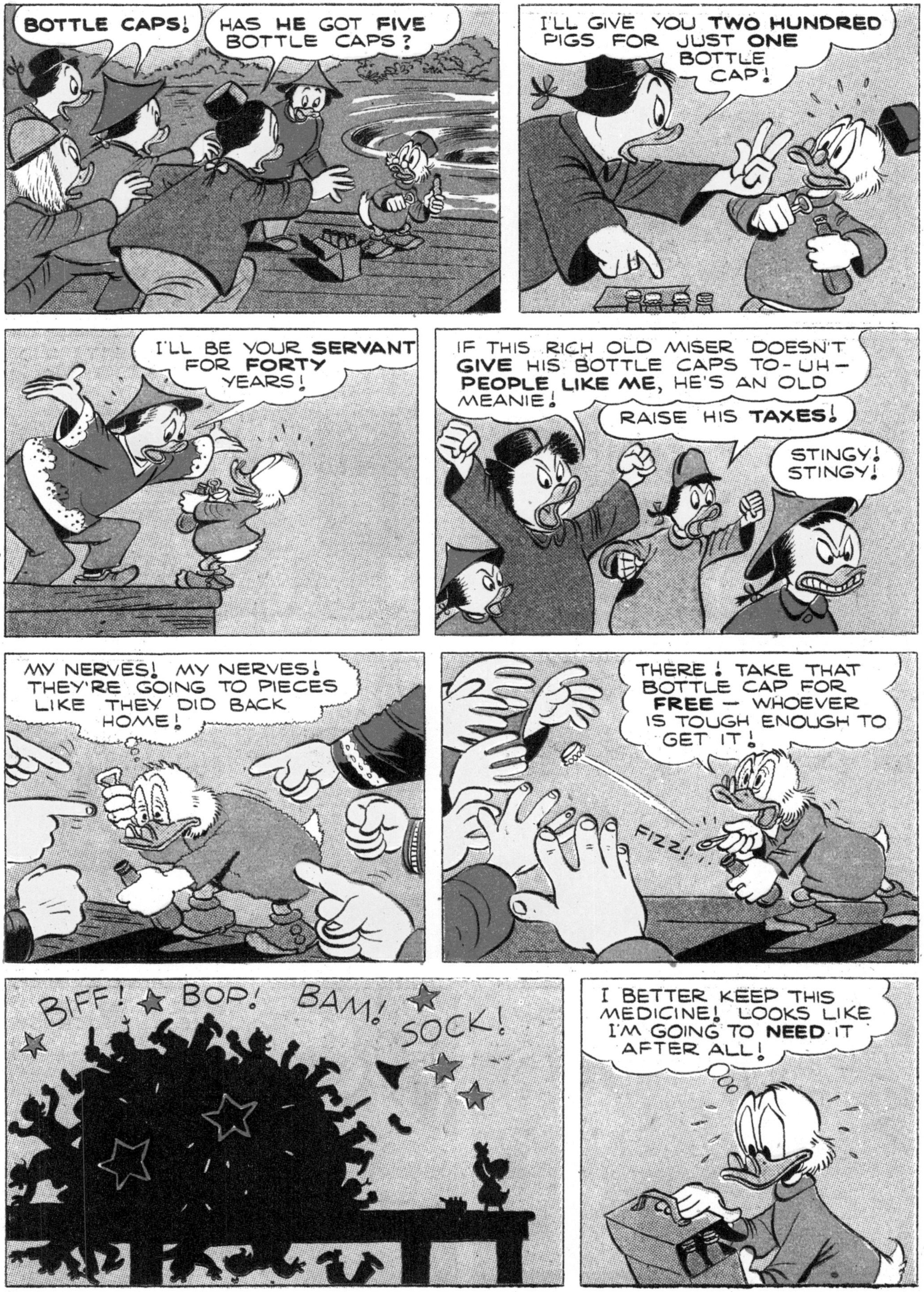
BOTTLE CAPS!
HAS HE GOT FIVE BOTTLE CAPS?
I'LL GIVE YOU TWO HUNDRED PIGS FOR JUST ONE BOTTLE CAP!
I'LL BE YOUR SERVANT FOR FORTY YEARS!
IF THIS RICH OLD MISER DOESN'T GIVE HIS BOTTLE CAPS TO-UH- PEOPLE LIKE ME, HE'S AN OLD MEANIE!
RAISE HIS TAXES!
STINGY! STINGY!
MY NERVES! MY NERVES! THEY'RE GOING TO PIECES LIKE THEY DID BACK HOME!
THERE! TAKE THAT BOTTLE CAP FOR FREE — WHOEVER IS TOUGH ENOUGH TO GET IT!
FIZZ!
BIFF! BOP! BAM! SOCK!
I BETTER KEEP THIS MEDICINE! LOOKS LIKE I'M GOING TO NEED IT AFTER ALL!

FROM THIS DAY ON THE TRALLA LALLIANS GIVE UNCLE SCROOGE NO REST!

MISTER SCROOGE! I'LL SELL YOU MY BRICK FACTORY FOR **ONE** OF YOUR BOTTLE CAPS!

WAM! BAM!

YE CATS! WHY ARE YOU PEOPLE SO **GREEDY** FOR BOTTLE CAPS? WHY AREN'T YOU GREEDY FOR **GOOD** THINGS — LIKE **SHEEP**?

PHOOEY! SHEEP ARE **COMMON**!

ANYBODY CAN OWN SHEEP!

BOTTLE CAPS ARE **RARE**!

IF UNCA DONALD COULD GET OVER THE MOUNTAINS AND SEND BACK ENOUGH CAPS FOR EVERYONE —

THAT'S THE ANSWER! DONALD, I'LL SEND YOU OUT TO BUY A MILLION BOTTLE CAPS — NO, BY GOLLY! I'LL MAKE IT A **BILLION**!

A FREIGHT PLANE COULD DUMP THE CAPS INTO THE VALLEY!

THEN EVERYBODY WOULD BE HAPPY!

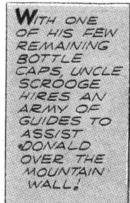

WITH ONE OF HIS FEW REMAINING BOTTLE CAPS, UNCLE SCROOGE HIRES AN ARMY OF GUIDES TO ASSIST DONALD OVER THE MOUNTAIN WALL!

'BYE, UNCLE SCROOGE! SEE YOU LATER!

NOW, IN A FEW DAYS THIS PLACE WILL BE **PERFECT** AGAIN!

AS TIME PASSES, THE TRALLA LALLIANS BECOME **VERY** IMPATIENT!

SCROOGE PROMISED A RAIN OF BOTTLE CAPS FROM THE SKY! **WHEN** DOES IT START RAINING?

THEY'RE NEGLECTING THEIR CROPS!

THEIR COWS ARE UNMILKED!

THEY JUST SIT AND **WAIT!**

PURSUING **FALSE** WEALTH! MEN HAVE DONE THAT STUPID THING SINCE THE BEGINNING OF TIME!

YOU SHOULD TALK!

YOU'VE PURSUED A LITTLE WEALTH IN **YOUR** TIME, **TOO!**

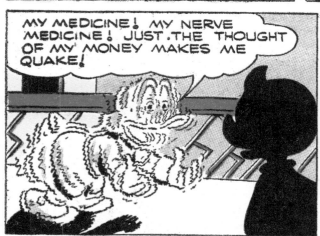

MY MEDICINE! MY NERVE MEDICINE! JUST THE THOUGHT OF MY MONEY MAKES ME QUAKE!

TWO BOTTLES OF MEDICINE LEFT! IF THOSE BOTTLE CAPS DON'T SHOW UP **SOON**, WE'LL HAVE TO HOLD UNCA SCROOGE TOGETHER WITH HOOPS!

AND THEN IT HAPPENS!

BOTTLE CAPS!

IT'S **RAINING** BOTTLE CAPS!

RICHES! MILLIONS OF SHEEP'S WORTH OF BEAUTIFUL, SHINY BOTTLE CAPS!

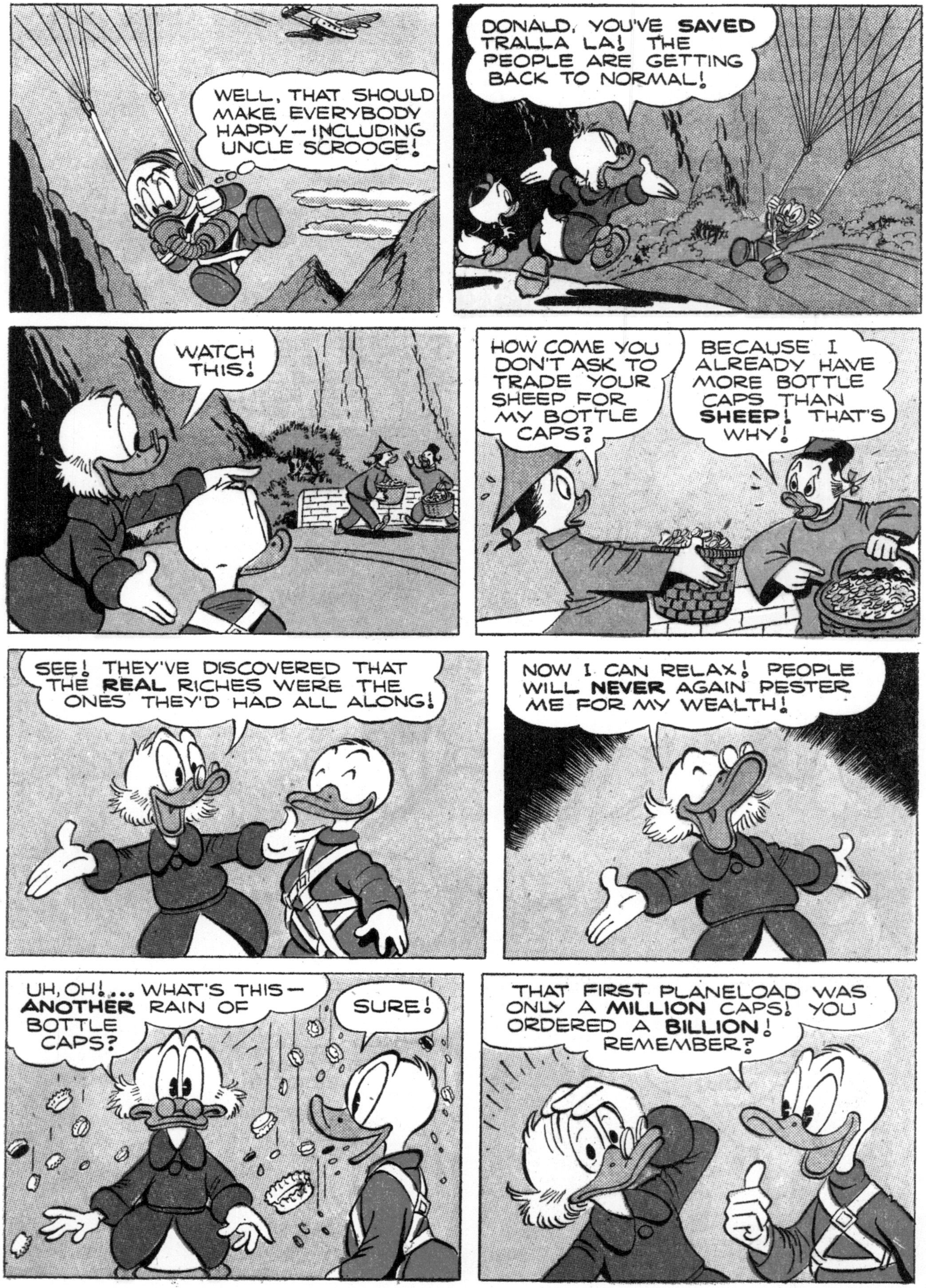
WELL, THAT SHOULD MAKE EVERYBODY HAPPY—INCLUDING UNCLE SCROOGE!
DONALD, YOU'VE SAVED TRALLA LA! THE PEOPLE ARE GETTING BACK TO NORMAL!
WATCH THIS!
HOW COME YOU DON'T ASK TO TRADE YOUR SHEEP FOR MY BOTTLE CAPS?
BECAUSE I ALREADY HAVE MORE BOTTLE CAPS THAN SHEEP! THAT'S WHY!
SEE! THEY'VE DISCOVERED THAT THE REAL RICHES WERE THE ONES THEY'D HAD ALL ALONG!
NOW I CAN RELAX! PEOPLE WILL NEVER AGAIN PESTER ME FOR MY WEALTH!
UH, OH!... WHAT'S THIS—ANOTHER RAIN OF BOTTLE CAPS?
SURE!
THAT FIRST PLANELOAD WAS ONLY A MILLION CAPS! YOU ORDERED A BILLION! REMEMBER?

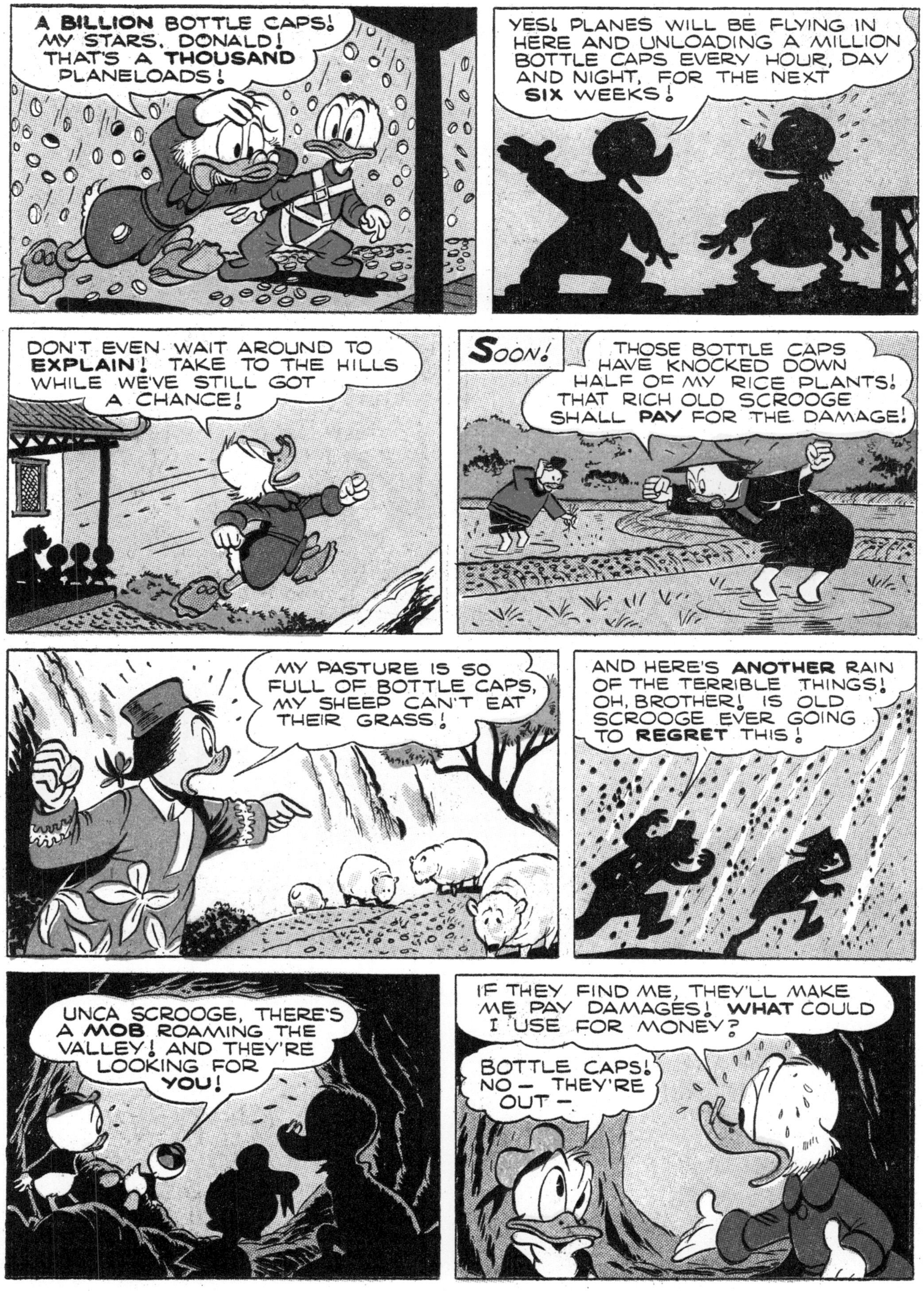
A BILLION BOTTLE CAPS! MY STARS, DONALD! THAT'S A THOUSAND PLANELOADS!
YES! PLANES WILL BE FLYING IN HERE AND UNLOADING A MILLION BOTTLE CAPS EVERY HOUR, DAY AND NIGHT, FOR THE NEXT SIX WEEKS!
DON'T EVEN WAIT AROUND TO EXPLAIN! TAKE TO THE HILLS WHILE WE'VE STILL GOT A CHANCE!
SOON!
THOSE BOTTLE CAPS HAVE KNOCKED DOWN HALF OF MY RICE PLANTS! THAT RICH OLD SCROOGE SHALL PAY FOR THE DAMAGE!
MY PASTURE IS SO FULL OF BOTTLE CAPS, MY SHEEP CAN'T EAT THEIR GRASS!
AND HERE'S ANOTHER RAIN OF THE TERRIBLE THINGS! OH, BROTHER! IS OLD SCROOGE EVER GOING TO REGRET THIS!
UNCA SCROOGE, THERE'S A MOB ROAMING THE VALLEY! AND THEY'RE LOOKING FOR YOU!
IF THEY FIND ME, THEY'LL MAKE ME PAY DAMAGES! WHAT COULD I USE FOR MONEY?
BOTTLE CAPS! NO — THEY'RE OUT —

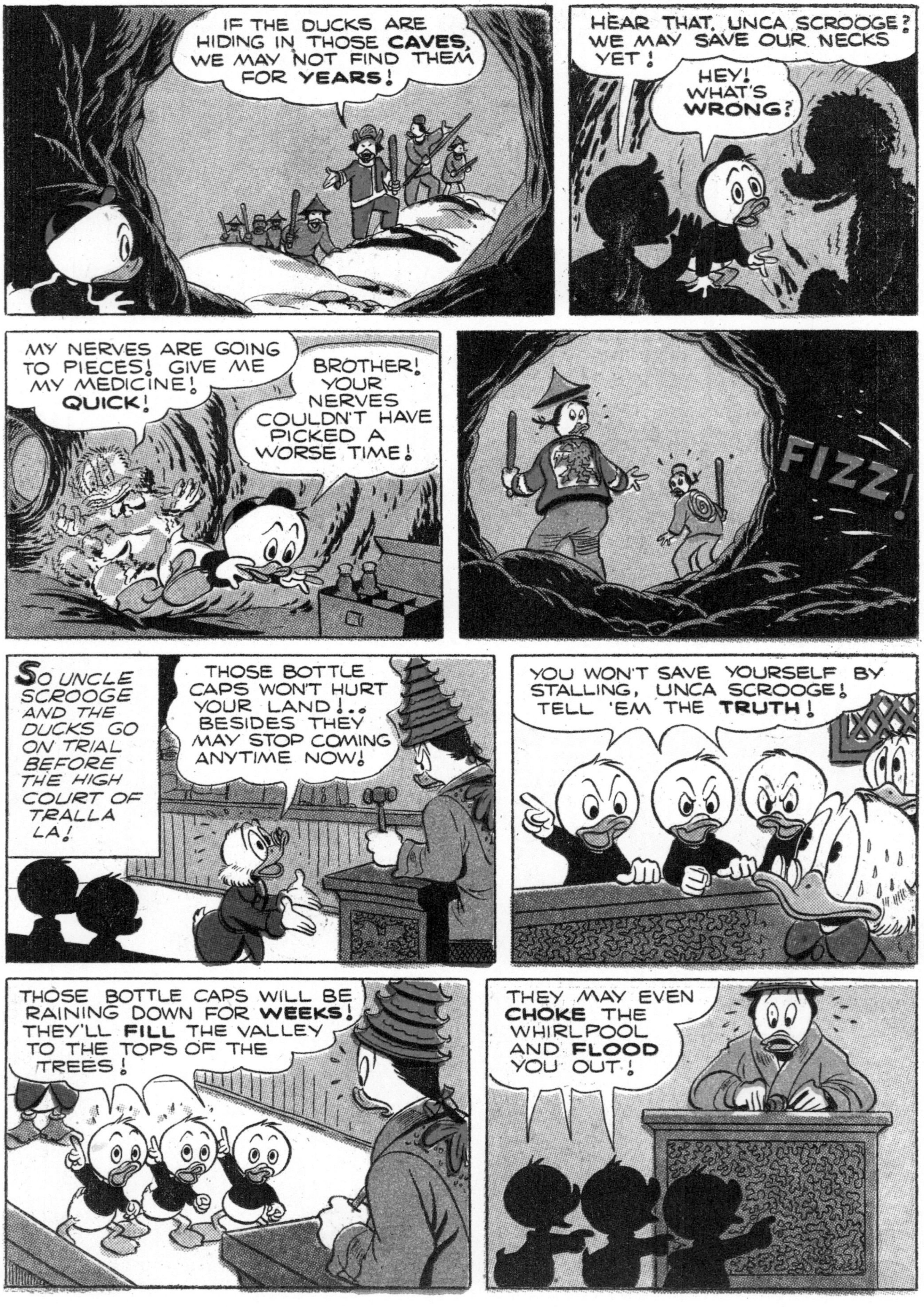
IF THE DUCKS ARE HIDING IN THOSE CAVES, WE MAY NOT FIND THEM FOR YEARS!
HEAR THAT, UNCA SCROOGE? WE MAY SAVE OUR NECKS YET!
HEY! WHAT'S WRONG?
MY NERVES ARE GOING TO PIECES! GIVE ME MY MEDICINE! QUICK!
BROTHER! YOUR NERVES COULDN'T HAVE PICKED A WORSE TIME!
FIZZ!
SO UNCLE SCROOGE AND THE DUCKS GO ON TRIAL BEFORE THE HIGH COURT OF TRALLA LA!
THOSE BOTTLE CAPS WON'T HURT YOUR LAND!.. BESIDES THEY MAY STOP COMING ANYTIME NOW!
YOU WON'T SAVE YOURSELF BY STALLING, UNCA SCROOGE! TELL 'EM THE TRUTH!
THOSE BOTTLE CAPS WILL BE RAINING DOWN FOR WEEKS! THEY'LL FILL THE VALLEY TO THE TOPS OF THE TREES!
THEY MAY EVEN CHOKE THE WHIRLPOOL AND FLOOD YOU OUT!

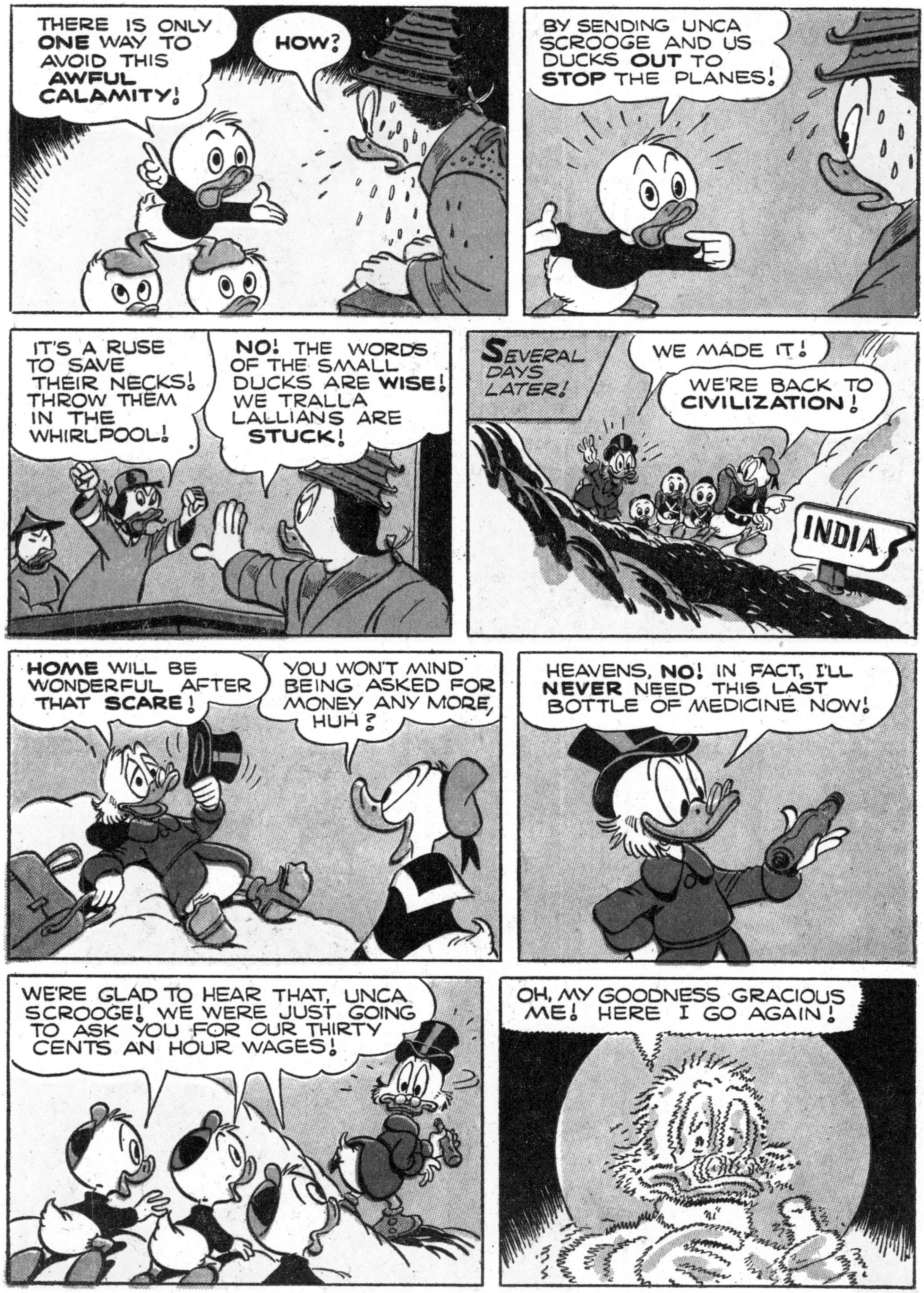
THERE IS ONLY ONE WAY TO AVOID THIS AWFUL CALAMITY!
HOW?
BY SENDING UNCA SCROOGE AND US DUCKS OUT TO STOP THE PLANES!
IT'S A RUSE TO SAVE THEIR NECKS! THROW THEM IN THE WHIRLPOOL!
NO! THE WORDS OF THE SMALL DUCKS ARE WISE! WE TRALLA LALLIANS ARE STUCK!
SEVERAL DAYS LATER!
WE MADE IT!
WE'RE BACK TO CIVILIZATION!
INDIA
HOME WILL BE WONDERFUL AFTER THAT SCARE!
YOU WON'T MIND BEING ASKED FOR MONEY ANY MORE, HUH?
HEAVENS, NO! IN FACT, I'LL NEVER NEED THIS LAST BOTTLE OF MEDICINE NOW!
WE'RE GLAD TO HEAR THAT, UNCA SCROOGE! WE WERE JUST GOING TO ASK YOU FOR OUR THIRTY CENTS AN HOUR WAGES!
OH, MY GOODNESS GRACIOUS ME! HERE I GO AGAIN!

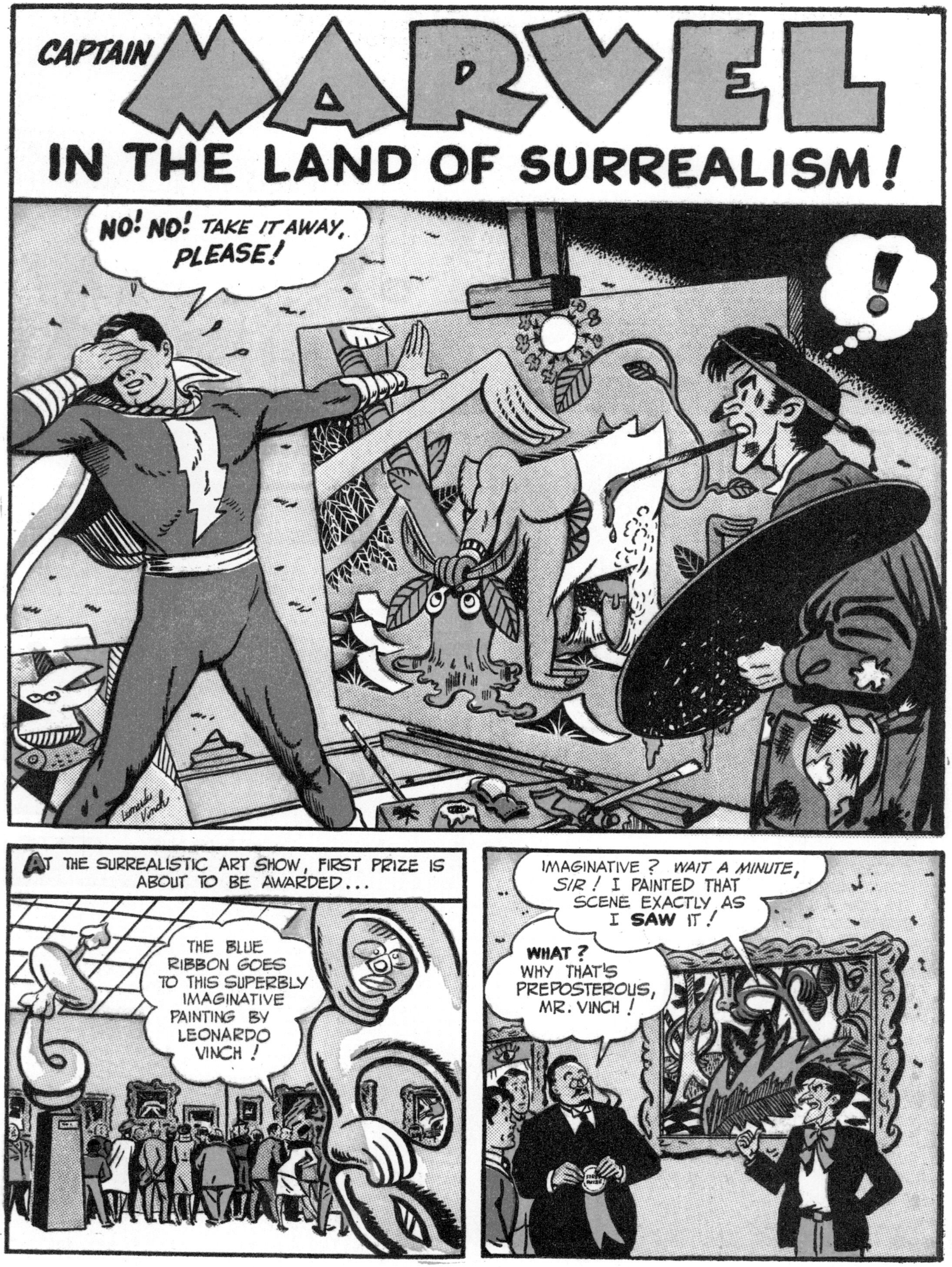
CAPTAIN MARVEL
IN THE LAND OF SURREALISM!
NO! NO! TAKE IT AWAY, PLEASE!
!
Leonardo Vinch
AT THE SURREALISTIC ART SHOW, FIRST PRIZE IS ABOUT TO BE AWARDED...
THE BLUE RIBBON GOES TO THIS SUPERBLY IMAGINATIVE PAINTING BY LEONARDO VINCH!
IMAGINATIVE? WAIT A MINUTE, SIR! I PAINTED THAT SCENE EXACTLY AS I SAW IT!
WHAT? WHY THAT'S PREPOSTEROUS, MR. VINCH!

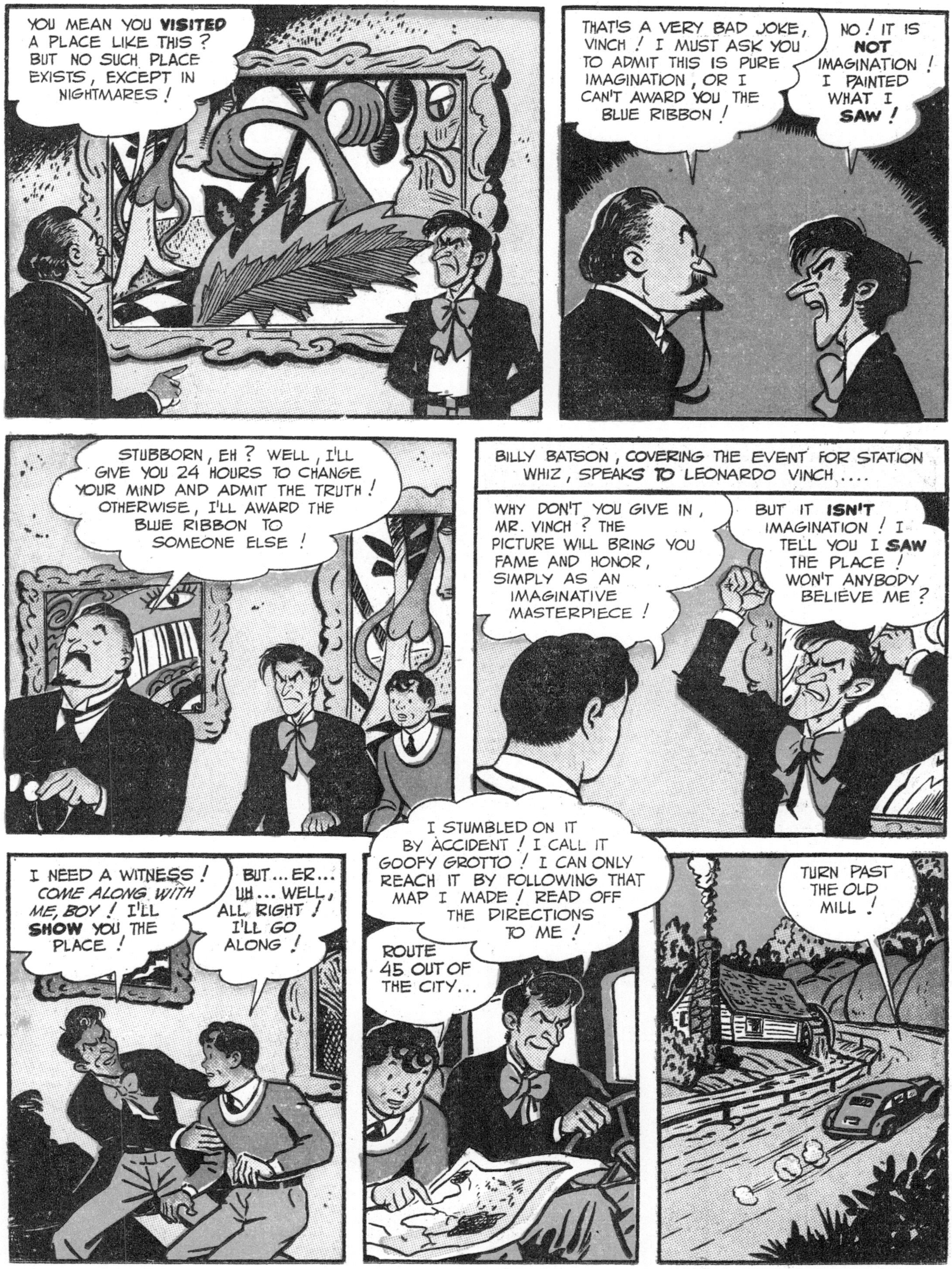
YOU MEAN YOU VISITED A PLACE LIKE THIS ? BUT NO SUCH PLACE EXISTS, EXCEPT IN NIGHTMARES !
THAT'S A VERY BAD JOKE, VINCH ! I MUST ASK YOU TO ADMIT THIS IS PURE IMAGINATION, OR I CAN'T AWARD YOU THE BLUE RIBBON !
NO ! IT IS NOT IMAGINATION ! I PAINTED WHAT I SAW !
STUBBORN, EH ? WELL, I'LL GIVE YOU 24 HOURS TO CHANGE YOUR MIND AND ADMIT THE TRUTH ! OTHERWISE, I'LL AWARD THE BLUE RIBBON TO SOMEONE ELSE !
BILLY BATSON, COVERING THE EVENT FOR STATION WHIZ, SPEAKS TO LEONARDO VINCH ....
WHY DON'T YOU GIVE IN, MR. VINCH ? THE PICTURE WILL BRING YOU FAME AND HONOR, SIMPLY AS AN IMAGINATIVE MASTERPIECE !
BUT IT ISN'T IMAGINATION ! I TELL YOU I SAW THE PLACE ! WON'T ANYBODY BELIEVE ME ?
I NEED A WITNESS ! COME ALONG WITH ME, BOY ! I'LL SHOW YOU THE PLACE !
BUT ... ER ... UH ... WELL, ALL RIGHT ! I'LL GO ALONG !
I STUMBLED ON IT BY ACCIDENT ! I CALL IT GOOFY GROTTO ! I CAN ONLY REACH IT BY FOLLOWING THAT MAP I MADE ! READ OFF THE DIRECTIONS TO ME !
ROUTE 45 OUT OF THE CITY...
TURN PAST THE OLD MILL !

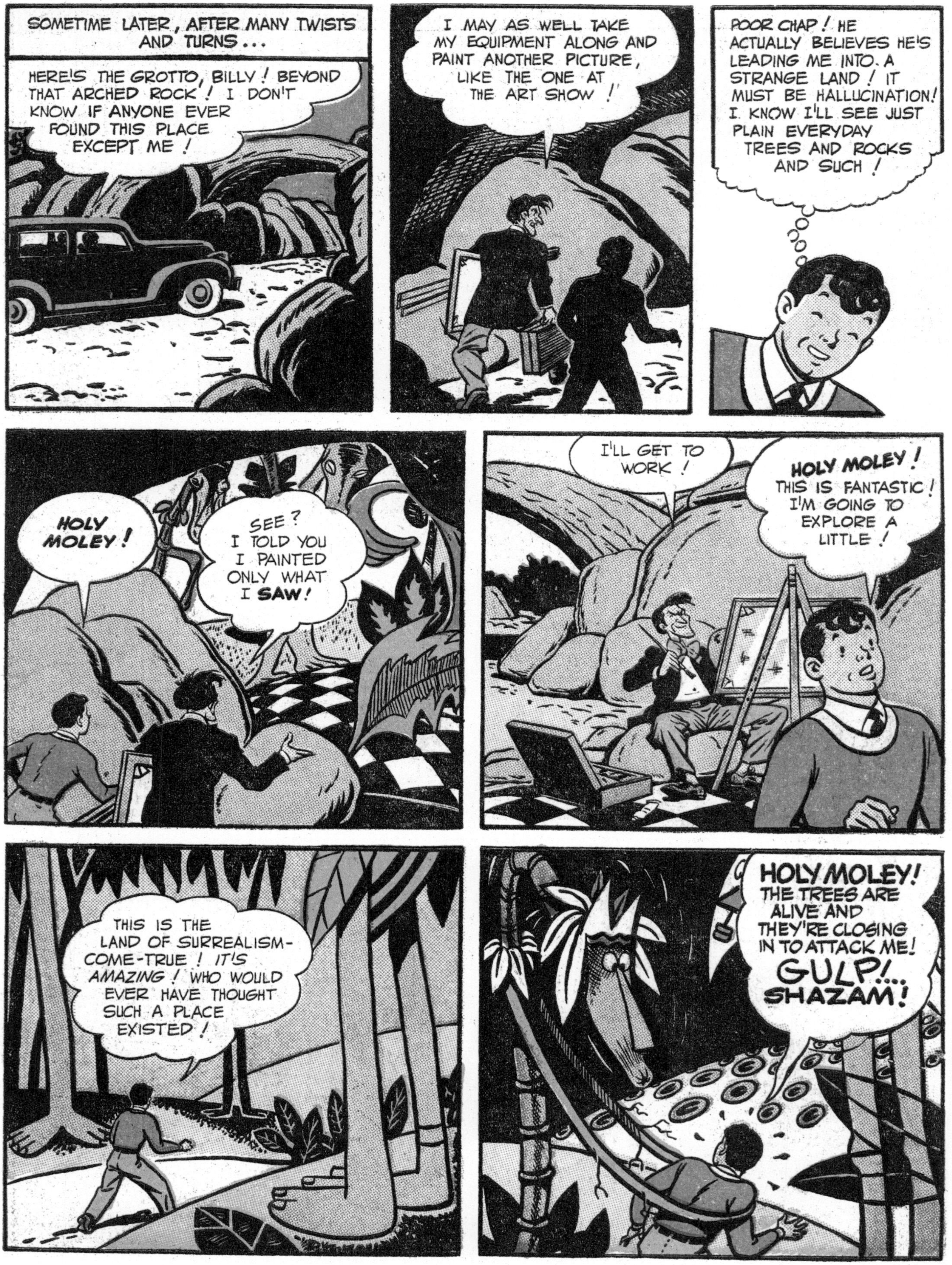
SOMETIME LATER, AFTER MANY TWISTS AND TURNS...
HERE'S THE GROTTO, BILLY! BEYOND THAT ARCHED ROCK! I DON'T KNOW IF ANYONE EVER FOUND THIS PLACE EXCEPT ME!
I MAY AS WELL TAKE MY EQUIPMENT ALONG AND PAINT ANOTHER PICTURE, LIKE THE ONE AT THE ART SHOW!
POOR CHAP! HE ACTUALLY BELIEVES HE'S LEADING ME INTO A STRANGE LAND! IT MUST BE HALLUCINATION! I KNOW I'LL SEE JUST PLAIN EVERYDAY TREES AND ROCKS AND SUCH!
HOLY MOLEY!
SEE? I TOLD YOU I PAINTED ONLY WHAT I SAW!
I'LL GET TO WORK!
HOLY MOLEY! THIS IS FANTASTIC! I'M GOING TO EXPLORE A LITTLE!
THIS IS THE LAND OF SURREALISM-COME-TRUE! IT'S AMAZING! WHO WOULD EVER HAVE THOUGHT SUCH A PLACE EXISTED!
HOLY MOLEY! THE TREES ARE ALIVE AND THEY'RE CLOSING IN TO ATTACK ME! GULP!... SHAZAM!

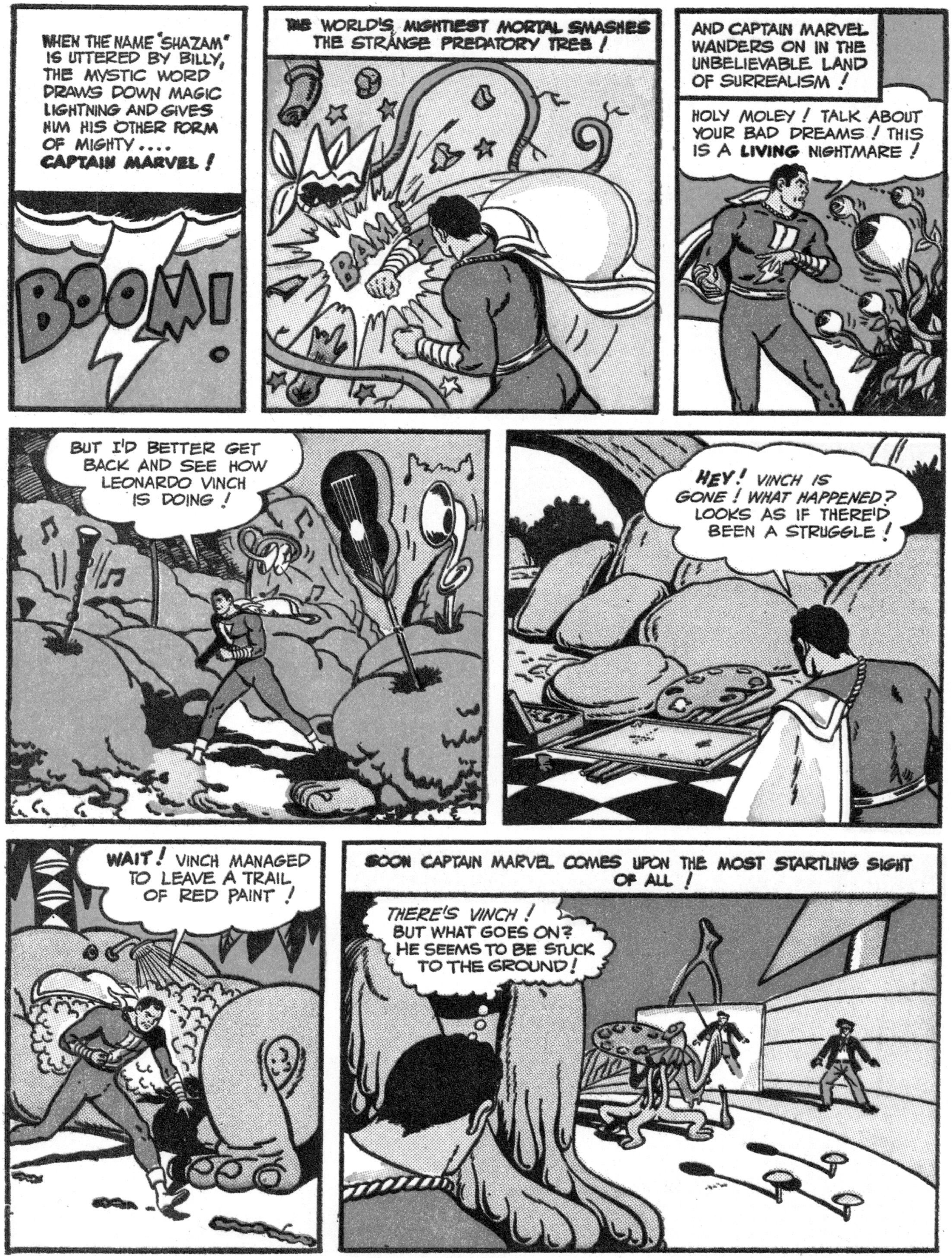
WHEN THE NAME "SHAZAM" IS UTTERED BY BILLY, THE MYSTIC WORD DRAWS DOWN MAGIC LIGHTNING AND GIVES HIM HIS OTHER FORM OF MIGHTY.... CAPTAIN MARVEL!
BOOM!
THE WORLD'S MIGHTIEST MORTAL SMASHES THE STRANGE PREDATORY TREE!
BAM!
AND CAPTAIN MARVEL WANDERS ON IN THE UNBELIEVABLE LAND OF SURREALISM!
HOLY MOLEY! TALK ABOUT YOUR BAD DREAMS! THIS IS A LIVING NIGHTMARE!
BUT I'D BETTER GET BACK AND SEE HOW LEONARDO VINCH IS DOING!
HEY! VINCH IS GONE! WHAT HAPPENED? LOOKS AS IF THERE'D BEEN A STRUGGLE!
WAIT! VINCH MANAGED TO LEAVE A TRAIL OF RED PAINT!
SOON CAPTAIN MARVEL COMES UPON THE MOST STARTLING SIGHT OF ALL!
THERE'S VINCH! BUT WHAT GOES ON? HE SEEMS TO BE STUCK TO THE GROUND!

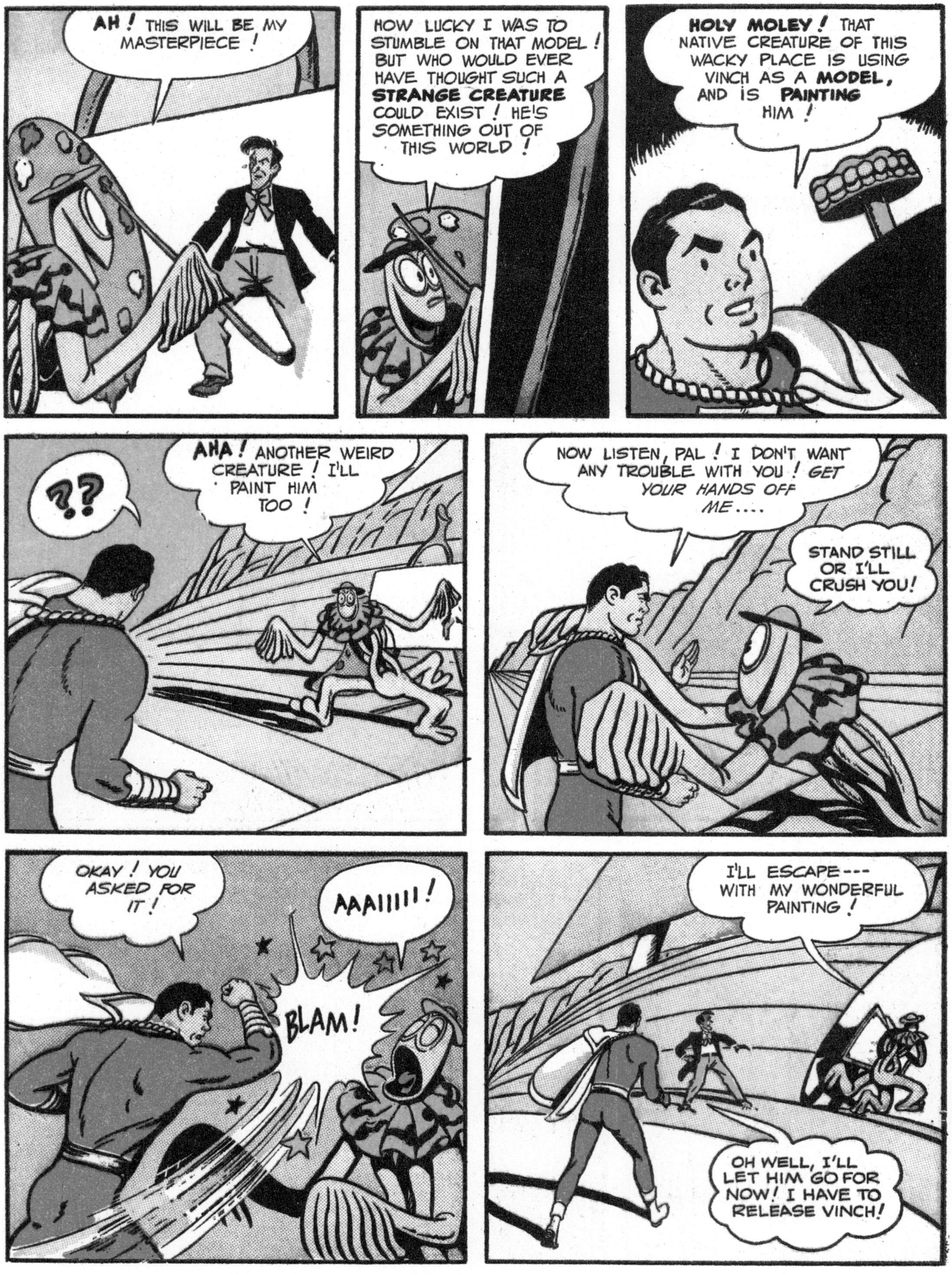
AH! THIS WILL BE MY MASTERPIECE!
HOW LUCKY I WAS TO STUMBLE ON THAT MODEL! BUT WHO WOULD EVER HAVE THOUGHT SUCH A STRANGE CREATURE COULD EXIST! HE'S SOMETHING OUT OF THIS WORLD!
HOLY MOLEY! THAT NATIVE CREATURE OF THIS WACKY PLACE IS USING VINCH AS A MODEL, AND IS PAINTING HIM!
??
AHA! ANOTHER WEIRD CREATURE! I'LL PAINT HIM TOO!
NOW LISTEN, PAL! I DON'T WANT ANY TROUBLE WITH YOU! GET YOUR HANDS OFF ME....
STAND STILL OR I'LL CRUSH YOU!
OKAY! YOU ASKED FOR IT!
AAAIIIII!
BLAM!
I'LL ESCAPE--- WITH MY WONDERFUL PAINTING!
OH WELL, I'LL LET HIM GO FOR NOW! I HAVE TO RELEASE VINCH!

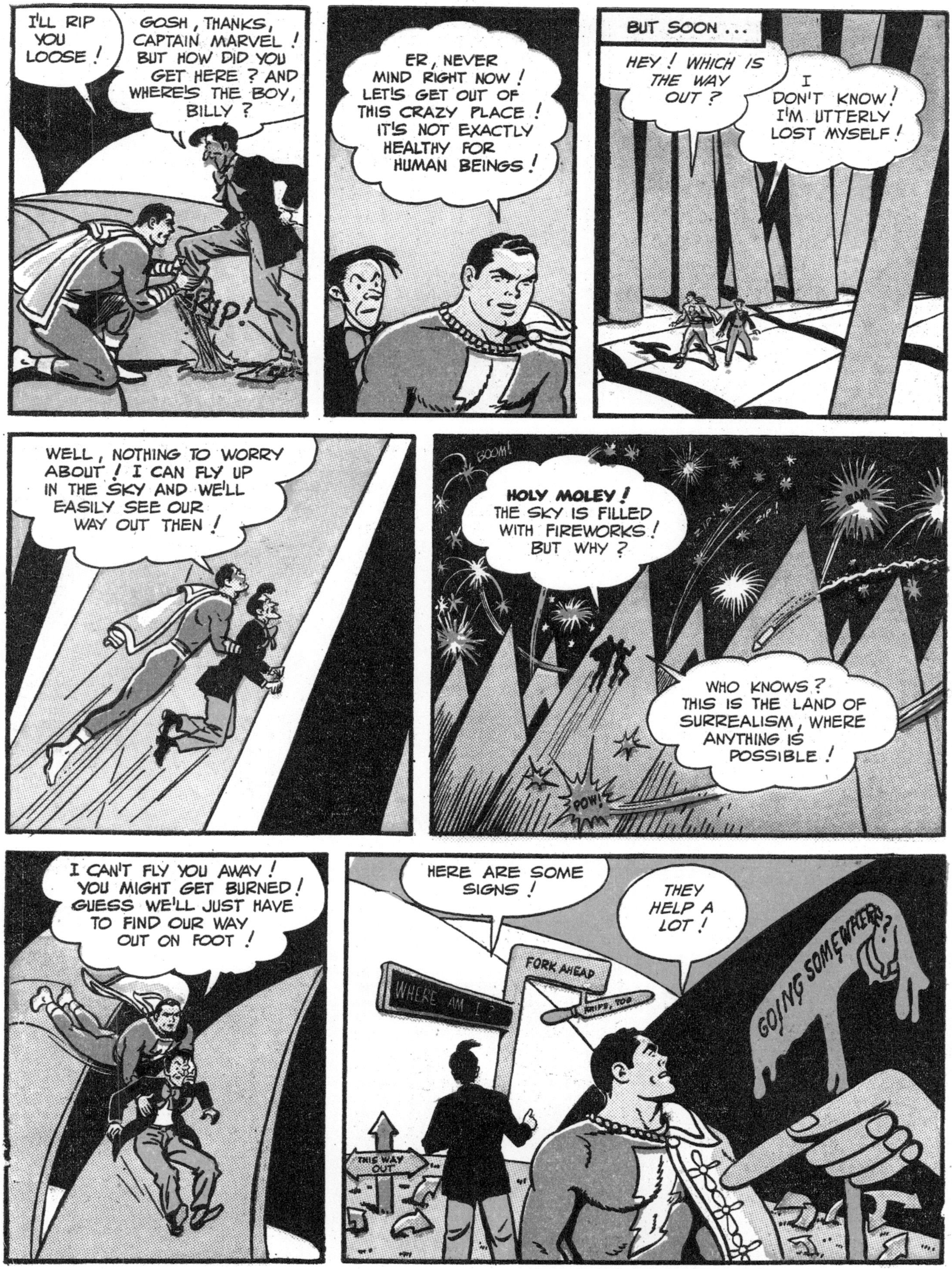
I'LL RIP YOU LOOSE!
GOSH, THANKS, CAPTAIN MARVEL! BUT HOW DID YOU GET HERE? AND WHERE'S THE BOY, BILLY?
RIP!
ER, NEVER MIND RIGHT NOW! LET'S GET OUT OF THIS CRAZY PLACE! IT'S NOT EXACTLY HEALTHY FOR HUMAN BEINGS!
BUT SOON...
HEY! WHICH IS THE WAY OUT?
I DON'T KNOW! I'M UTTERLY LOST MYSELF!
WELL, NOTHING TO WORRY ABOUT! I CAN FLY UP IN THE SKY AND WE'LL EASILY SEE OUR WAY OUT THEN!
BOOM!
HOLY MOLEY! THE SKY IS FILLED WITH FIREWORKS! BUT WHY?
BAM
ZIP!
ZIP!
WHO KNOWS? THIS IS THE LAND OF SURREALISM, WHERE ANYTHING IS POSSIBLE!
POW!
I CAN'T FLY YOU AWAY! YOU MIGHT GET BURNED! GUESS WE'LL JUST HAVE TO FIND OUR WAY OUT ON FOOT!
HERE ARE SOME SIGNS!
THEY HELP A LOT!
FORK AHEAD
WHERE AM I?
KNIFE, TOO
GOING SOMEWHERE?
THIS WAY OUT

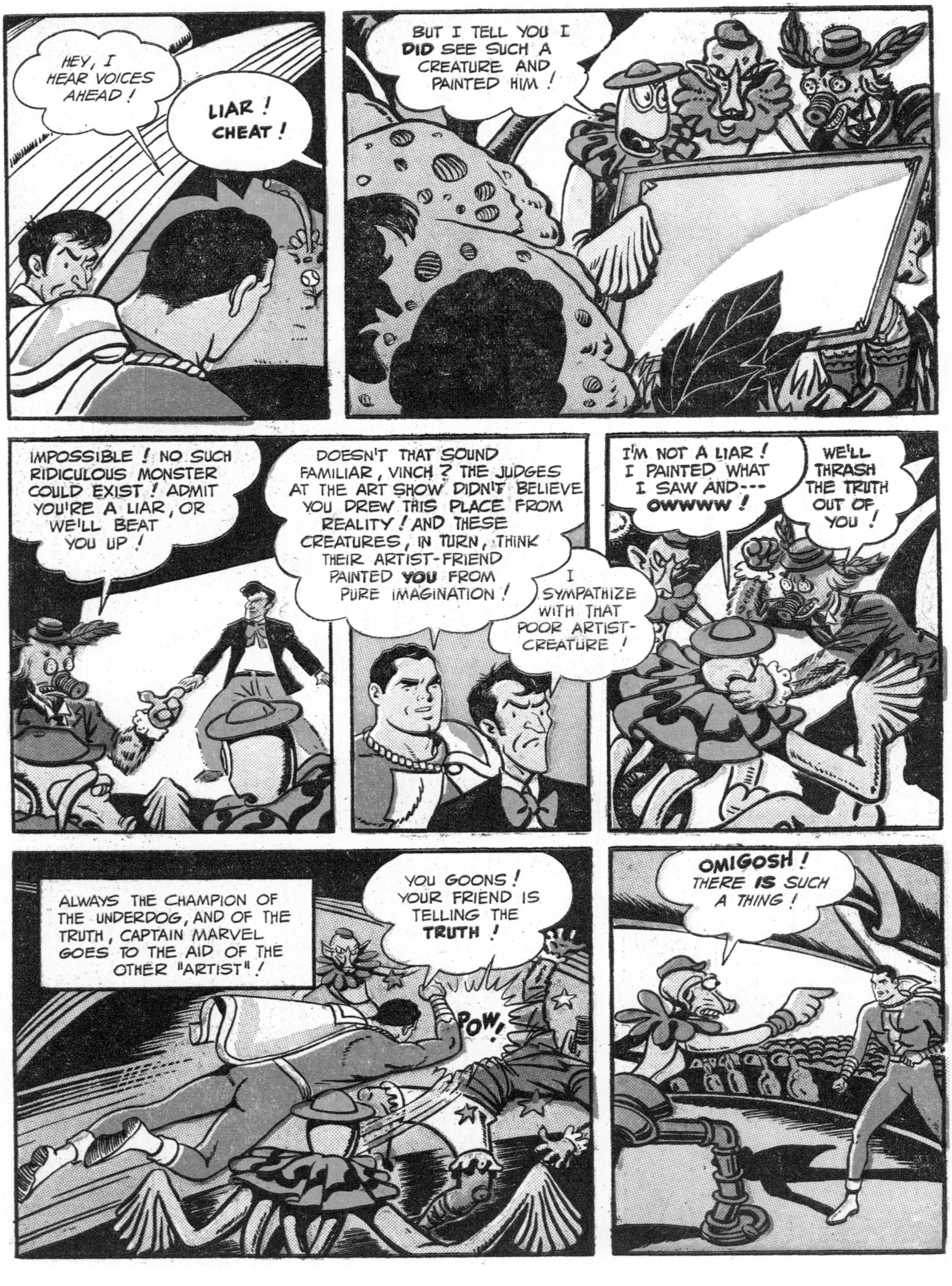
HEY, I HEAR VOICES AHEAD!
LIAR! CHEAT!
BUT I TELL YOU I DID SEE SUCH A CREATURE AND PAINTED HIM!
IMPOSSIBLE! NO SUCH RIDICULOUS MONSTER COULD EXIST! ADMIT YOU'RE A LIAR, OR WE'LL BEAT YOU UP!
DOESN'T THAT SOUND FAMILIAR, VINCH? THE JUDGES AT THE ART SHOW DIDN'T BELIEVE YOU DREW THIS PLACE FROM REALITY! AND THESE CREATURES, IN TURN, THINK THEIR ARTIST-FRIEND PAINTED YOU FROM PURE IMAGINATION!
I SYMPATHIZE WITH THAT POOR ARTIST-CREATURE!
I'M NOT A LIAR! I PAINTED WHAT I SAW AND--- OWWWW!
WE'LL THRASH THE TRUTH OUT OF YOU!
ALWAYS THE CHAMPION OF THE UNDERDOG, AND OF THE TRUTH, CAPTAIN MARVEL GOES TO THE AID OF THE OTHER "ARTIST"!
YOU GOONS! YOUR FRIEND IS TELLING THE TRUTH!
POW!
OMIGOSH! THERE IS SUCH A THING!

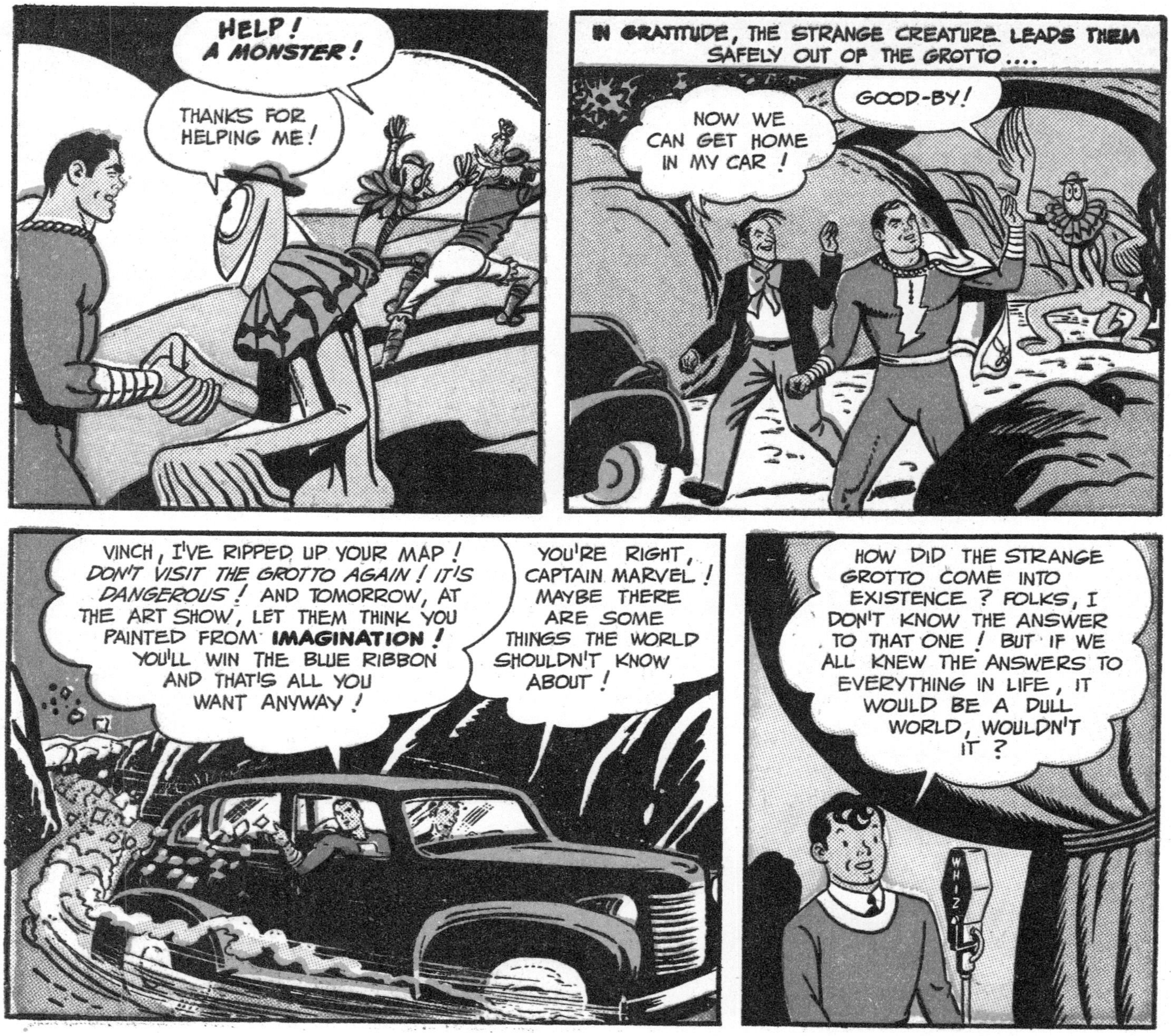
HELP! A MONSTER!
THANKS FOR HELPING ME!
IN GRATITUDE, THE STRANGE CREATURE LEADS THEM SAFELY OUT OF THE GROTTO....
NOW WE CAN GET HOME IN MY CAR!
GOOD-BY!
VINCH, I'VE RIPPED UP YOUR MAP! DON'T VISIT THE GROTTO AGAIN! IT'S DANGEROUS! AND TOMORROW, AT THE ART SHOW, LET THEM THINK YOU PAINTED FROM IMAGINATION! YOU'LL WIN THE BLUE RIBBON AND THAT'S ALL YOU WANT ANYWAY!
YOU'RE RIGHT, CAPTAIN MARVEL! MAYBE THERE ARE SOME THINGS THE WORLD SHOULDN'T KNOW ABOUT!
HOW DID THE STRANGE GROTTO COME INTO EXISTENCE? FOLKS, I DON'T KNOW THE ANSWER TO THAT ONE! BUT IF WE ALL KNEW THE ANSWERS TO EVERYTHING IN LIFE, IT WOULD BE A DULL WORLD, WOULDN'T IT?
WHIZ

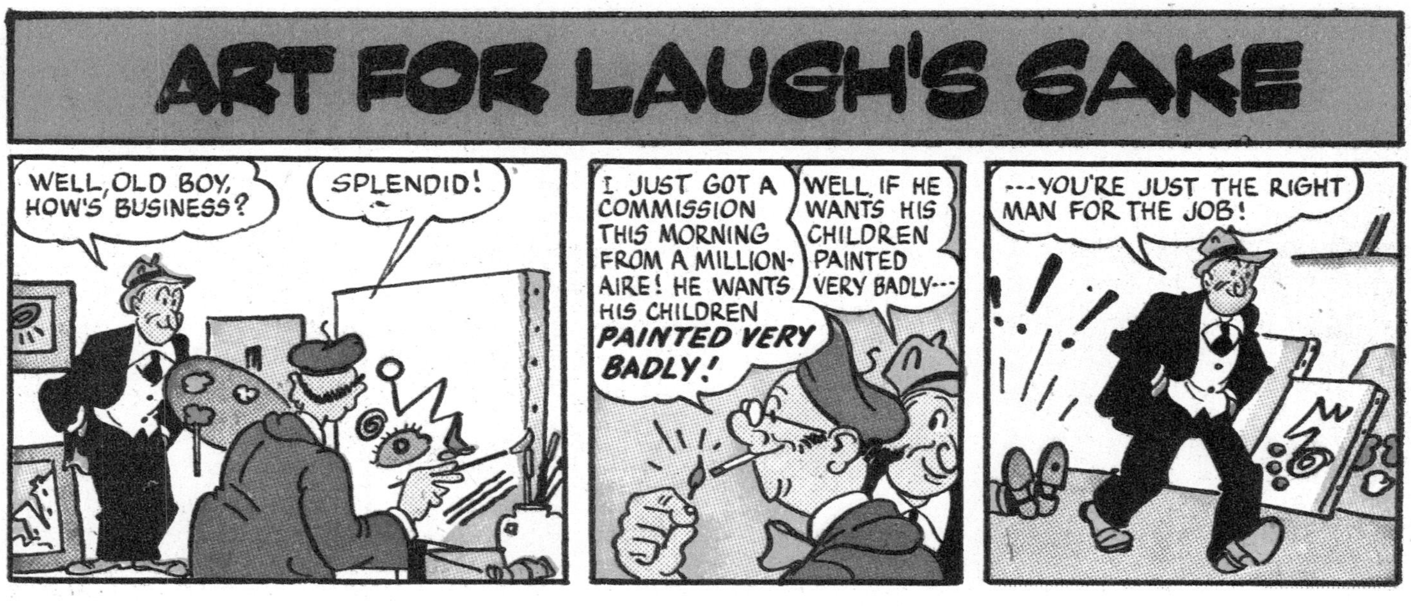
ART FOR LAUGH'S SAKE
WELL, OLD BOY, HOW'S BUSINESS?
SPLENDID!
I JUST GOT A COMMISSION THIS MORNING FROM A MILLIONAIRE! HE WANTS HIS CHILDREN PAINTED VERY BADLY!
WELL, IF HE WANTS HIS CHILDREN PAINTED VERY BADLY---
---YOU'RE JUST THE RIGHT MAN FOR THE JOB!

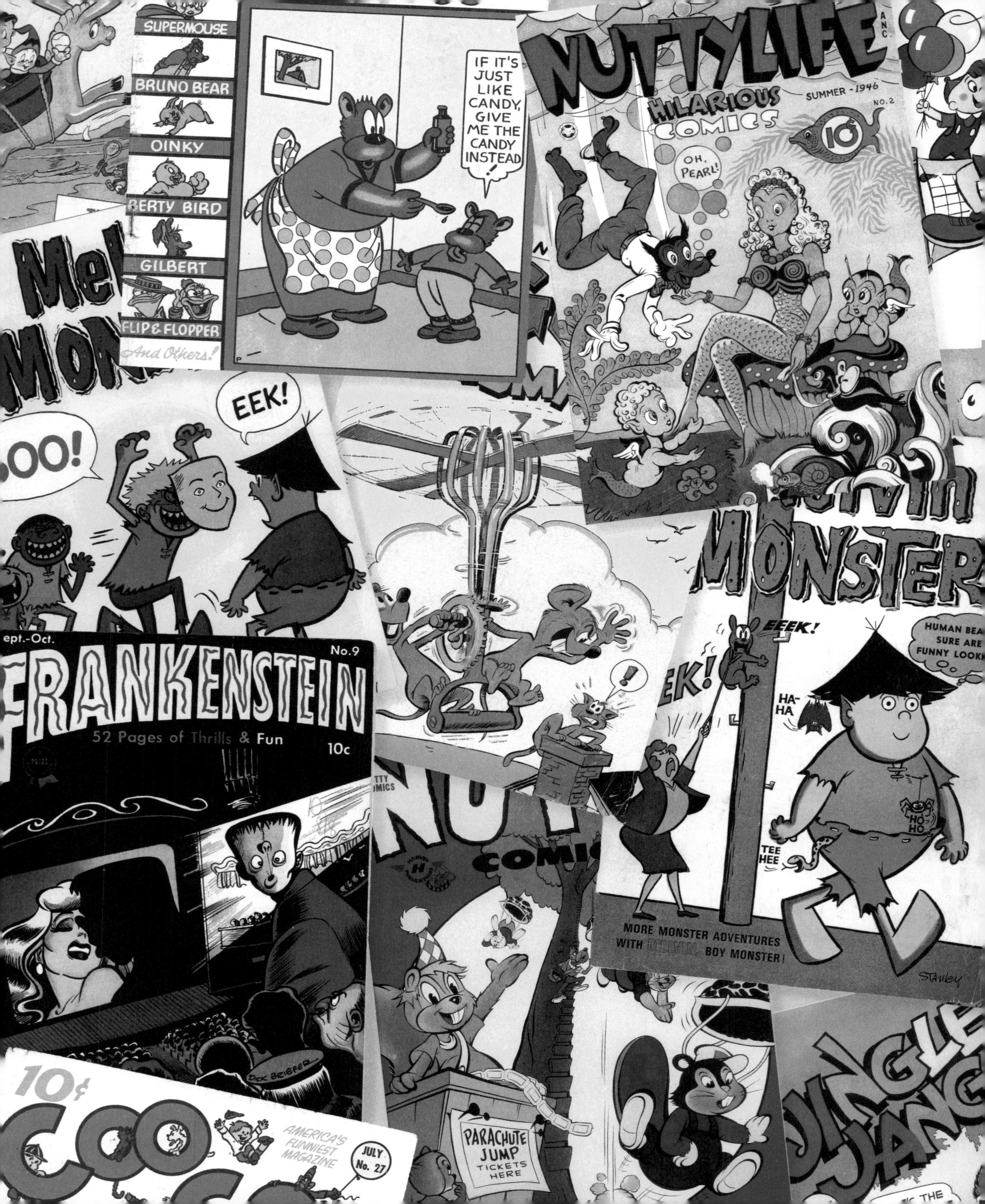
SUPERMOUSE
BRUNO BEAR
OINKY
BERTY BIRD
GILBERT
FLIP & FLOPPER
And Others!
IF IT'S JUST LIKE CANDY, GIVE ME THE CANDY INSTEAD!
NUTTYLIFE
HILARIOUS COMICS
SUMMER - 1946
NO. 2
10¢
OH, PEARL!
EEK!
FRANKENSTEIN
No.9
52 Pages of Thrills & Fun
10c
DICK BRIEFER
EEEK!
HA-HA
HO HO
TEE HEE
MORE MONSTER ADVENTURES WITH MELVIN, BOY MONSTER!
STANLEY
PARACHUTE JUMP TICKETS HERE
10¢
AMERICA'S FUNNIEST MAGAZINE
JULY No. 27

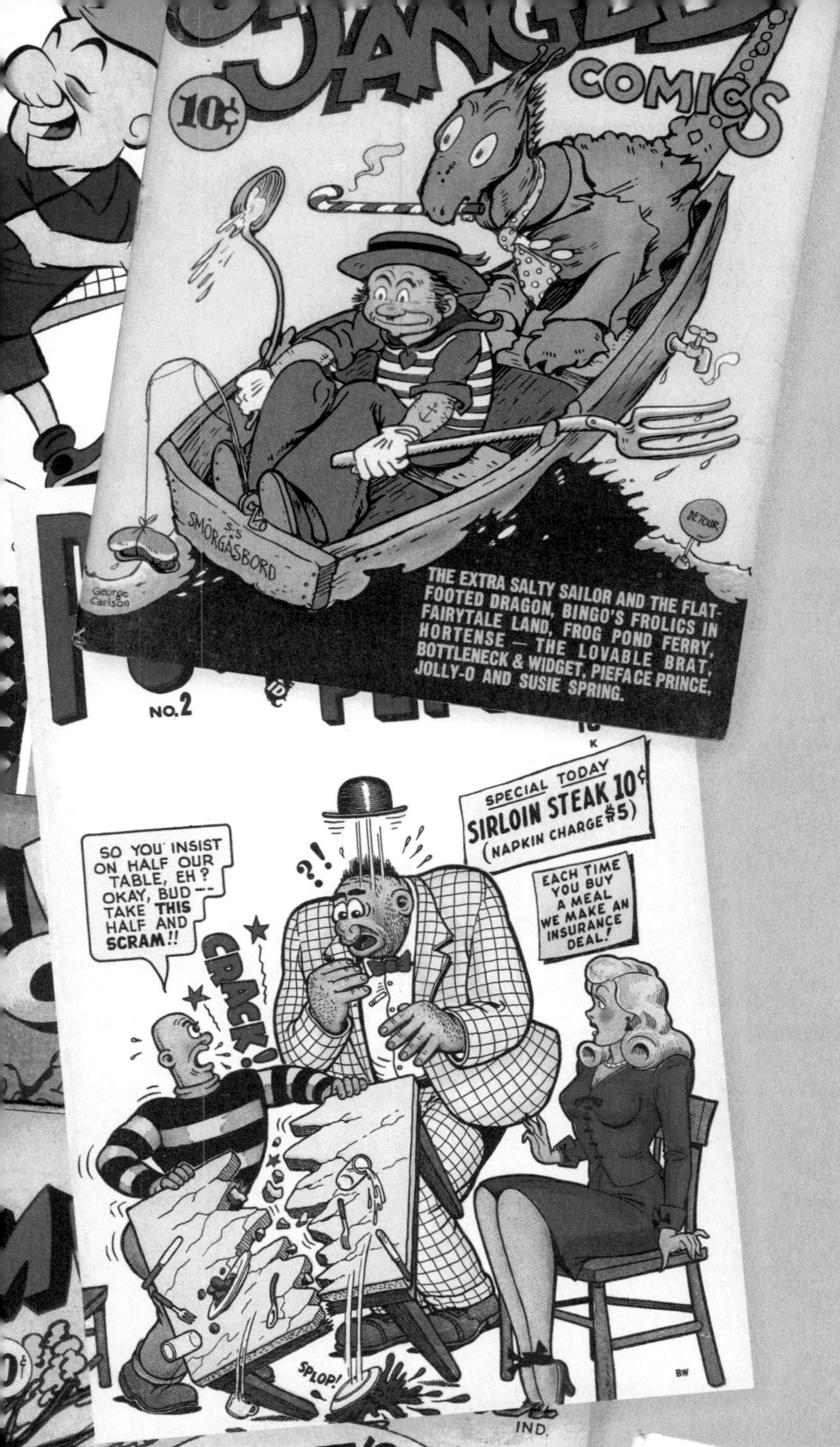
JANGLE
COMICS
10¢
S.S. SMÖRGÅSBORD
DETOUR
George Carlson
THE EXTRA SALTY SAILOR AND THE FLAT-FOOTED DRAGON, BINGO'S FROLICS IN FAIRYTALE LAND, FROG POND FERRY, HORTENSE — THE LOVABLE BRAT, BOTTLENECK & WIDGET, PIEFACE PRINCE, JOLLY-O AND SUSIE SPRING.
NO.2
SPECIAL TODAY SIRLOIN STEAK 10¢ (NAPKIN CHARGE $5)
SO YOU INSIST ON HALF OUR TABLE, EH? OKAY, BUD — TAKE THIS HALF AND SCRAM!!
EACH TIME YOU BUY A MEAL WE MAKE AN INSURANCE DEAL!
CRACK!
SPLOP!
BW

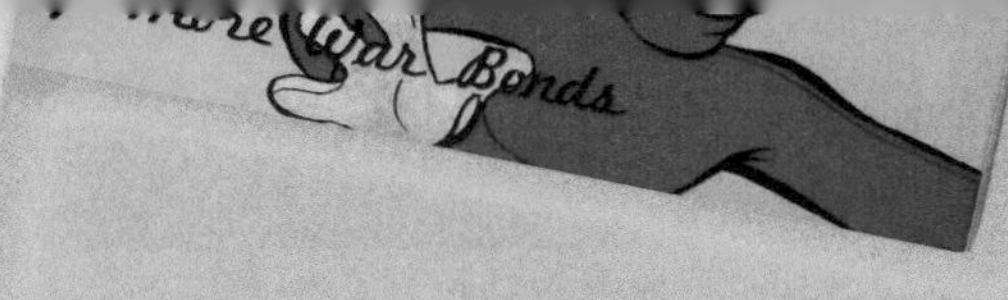
War Bonds

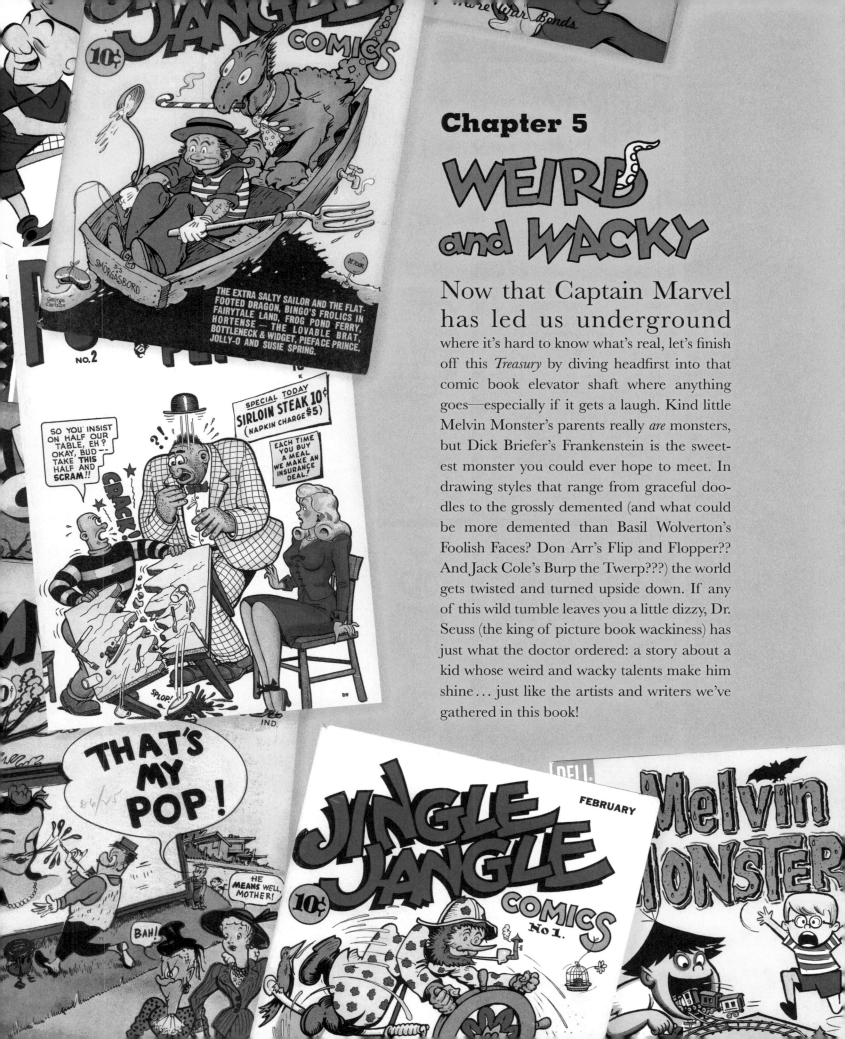

Chapter 5

WEIRD and WACKY

Now that Captain Marvel has led us underground where it's hard to know what's real, let's finish off this *Treasury* by diving headfirst into that comic book elevator shaft where anything goes—especially if it gets a laugh. Kind little Melvin Monster's parents really *are* monsters, but Dick Briefer's Frankenstein is the sweetest monster you could ever hope to meet. In drawing styles that range from graceful doodles to the grossly demented (and what could be more demented than Basil Wolverton's Foolish Faces? Don Arr's Flip and Flopper?? And Jack Cole's Burp the Twerp???) the world gets twisted and turned upside down. If any of this wild tumble leaves you a little dizzy, Dr. Seuss (the king of picture book wackiness) has just what the doctor ordered: a story about a kid whose weird and wacky talents make him shine... just like the artists and writers we've gathered in this book!

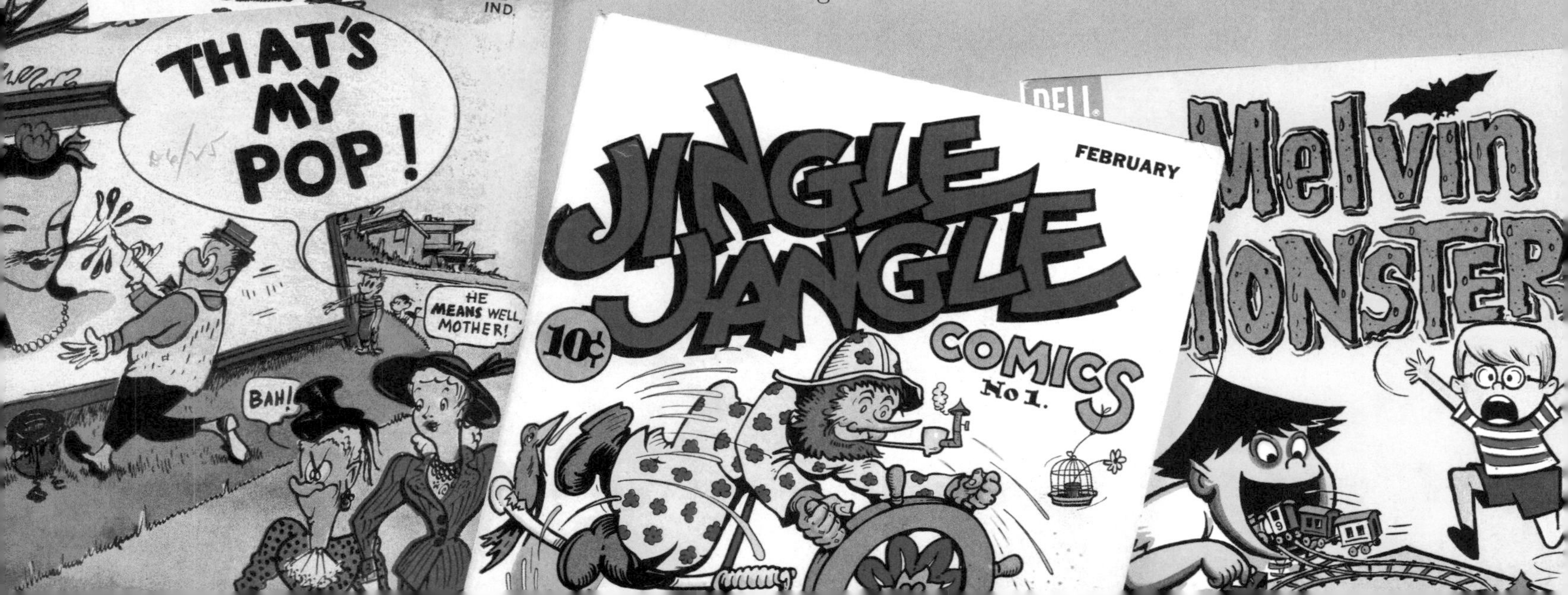
THAT'S MY POP!
HE MEANS WELL, MOTHER!
BAH!
JINGLE JANGLE COMICS
FEBRUARY
10¢
No 1.
DELL
Melvin MONSTER

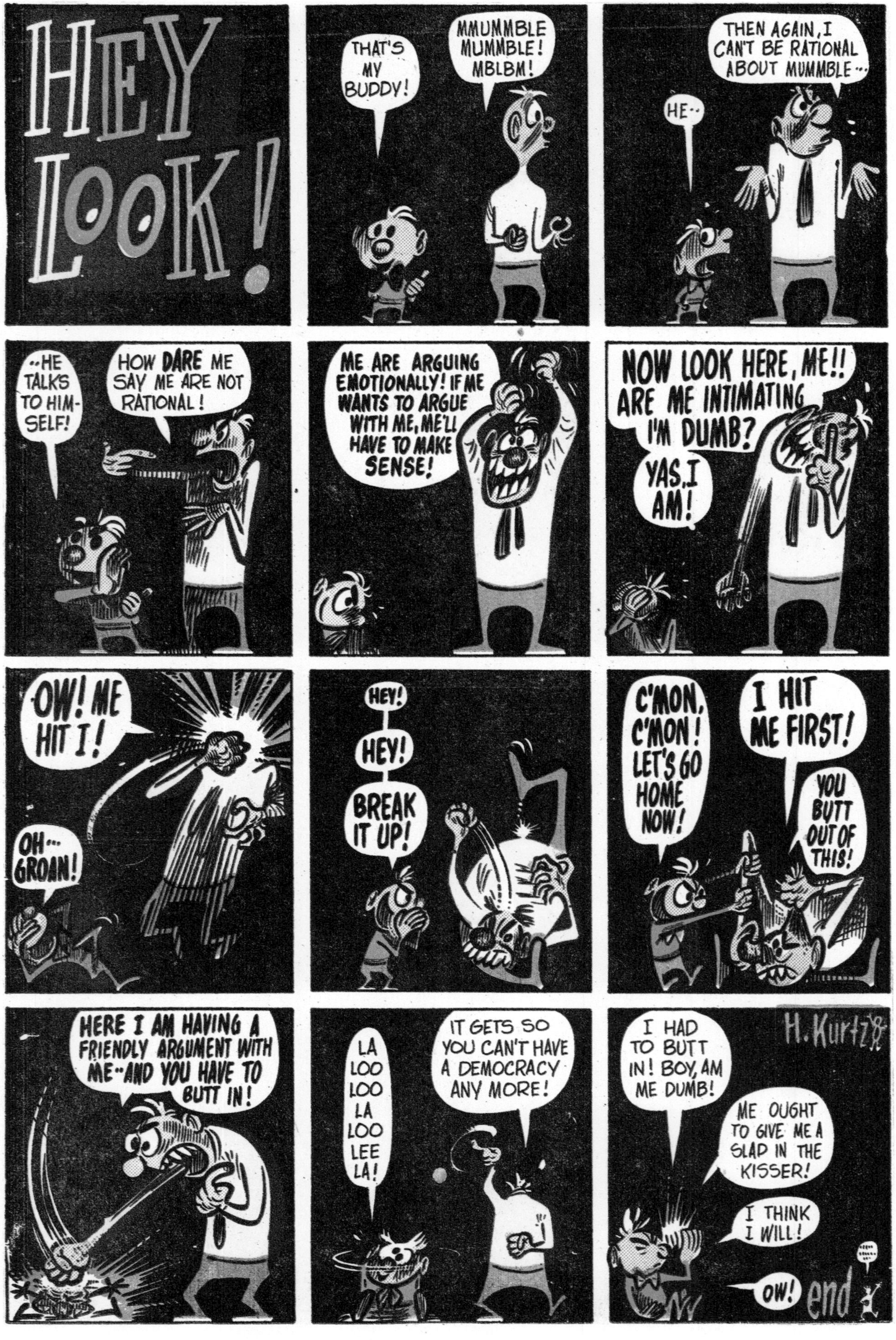
HEY LOOK!
THAT'S MY BUDDY!
MMUMMBLE MUMMBLE! MBLBM!
THEN AGAIN, I CAN'T BE RATIONAL ABOUT MUMMBLE...
HE..
..HE TALKS TO HIM-SELF!
HOW DARE ME SAY ME ARE NOT RATIONAL!
ME ARE ARGUING EMOTIONALLY! IF ME WANTS TO ARGUE WITH ME, ME'LL HAVE TO MAKE SENSE!
NOW LOOK HERE, ME!! ARE ME INTIMATING I'M DUMB?
YAS, I AM!
OW! ME HIT I!
OH... GROAN!
HEY!
HEY!
BREAK IT UP!
C'MON, C'MON! LET'S GO HOME NOW!
I HIT ME FIRST!
YOU BUTT OUT OF THIS!
HERE I AM HAVING A FRIENDLY ARGUMENT WITH ME..AND YOU HAVE TO BUTT IN!
LA LOO LOO LA LOO LEE LA!
IT GETS SO YOU CAN'T HAVE A DEMOCRACY ANY MORE!
H. Kurtz
I HAD TO BUTT IN! BOY, AM ME DUMB!
ME OUGHT TO GIVE ME A SLAP IN THE KISSER!
I THINK I WILL!
OW!
end

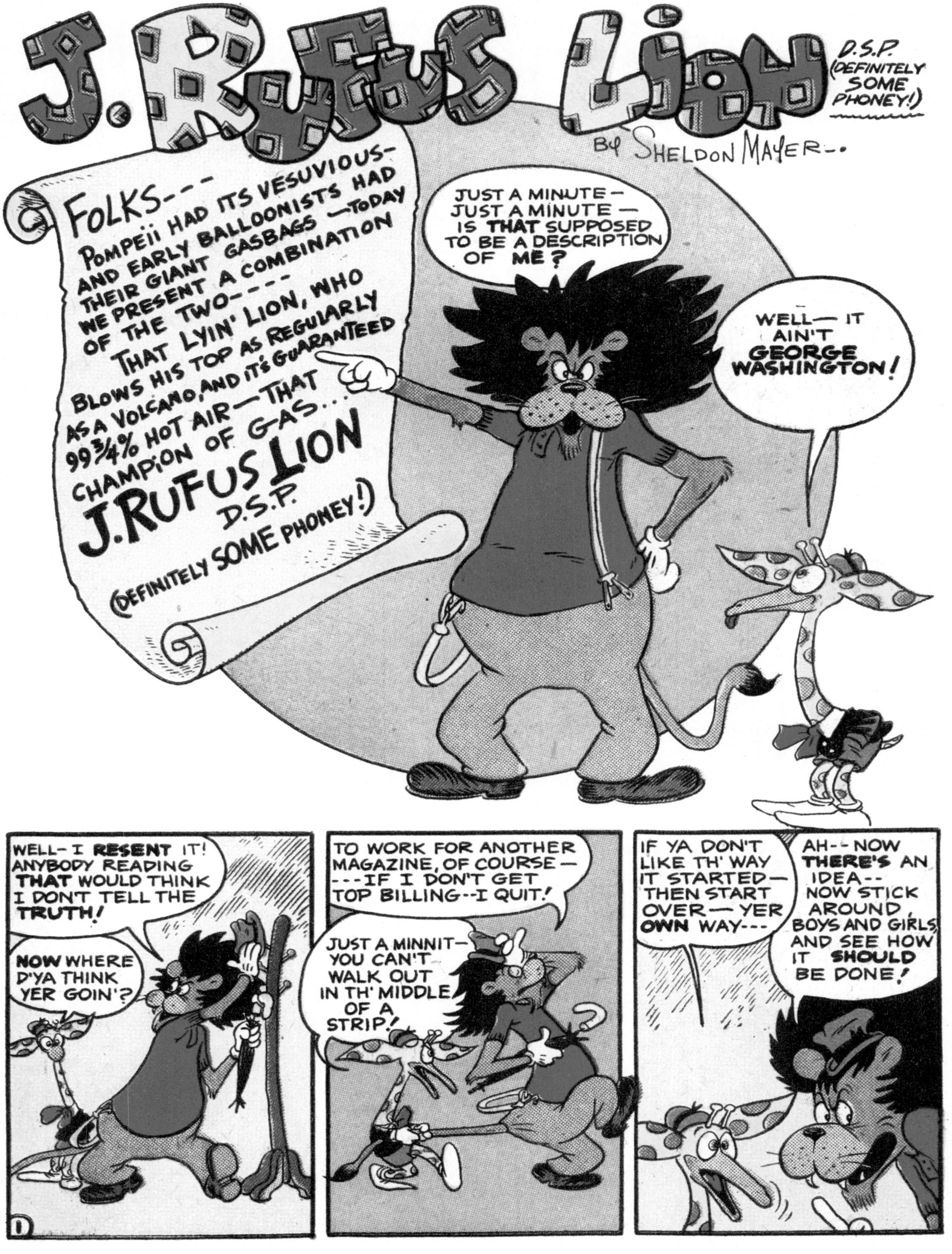
J. RUFUS LION
D.S.P. (DEFINITELY SOME PHONEY!)
BY SHELDON MAYER--.
FOLKS--- POMPEII HAD ITS VESUVIOUS- AND EARLY BALLOONISTS HAD THEIR GIANT GASBAGS —TODAY WE PRESENT A COMBINATION OF THE TWO--- THAT LYIN' LION, WHO BLOWS HIS TOP AS REGULARLY AS A VOLCANO, AND IT'S GUARANTEED 99 3/4% HOT AIR—THAT CHAMPION OF G-A-S... J. RUFUS LION D.S.P. (DEFINITELY SOME PHONEY!)
JUST A MINUTE— JUST A MINUTE — IS THAT SUPPOSED TO BE A DESCRIPTION OF ME?
WELL— IT AIN'T GEORGE WASHINGTON!
WELL- I RESENT IT! ANYBODY READING THAT WOULD THINK I DON'T TELL THE TRUTH!
NOW WHERE D'YA THINK YER GOIN'?
TO WORK FOR ANOTHER MAGAZINE, OF COURSE— ---IF I DON'T GET TOP BILLING--I QUIT!
JUST A MINNIT— YOU CAN'T WALK OUT IN TH' MIDDLE OF A STRIP!
IF YA DON'T LIKE TH' WAY IT STARTED— THEN START OVER— YER OWN WAY---
AH--NOW THERE'S AN IDEA-- NOW STICK AROUND, BOYS AND GIRLS, AND SEE HOW IT SHOULD BE DONE!
1

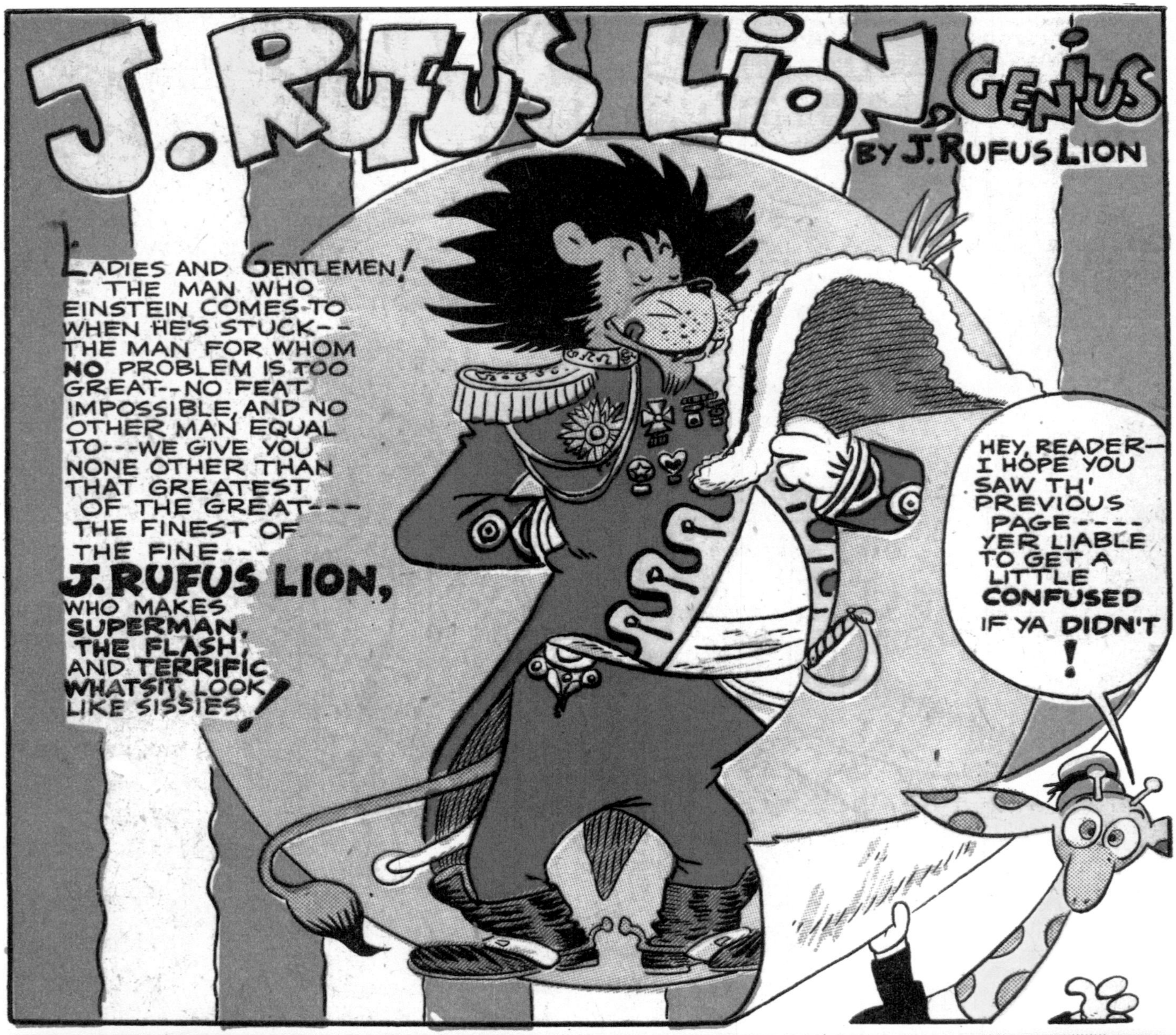
J. RUFUS LION, GENIUS
BY J. RUFUS LION
LADIES AND GENTLEMEN! THE MAN WHO EINSTEIN COMES TO WHEN HE'S STUCK-- THE MAN FOR WHOM NO PROBLEM IS TOO GREAT--NO FEAT IMPOSSIBLE, AND NO OTHER MAN EQUAL TO---WE GIVE YOU NONE OTHER THAN THAT GREATEST OF THE GREAT--- THE FINEST OF THE FINE--- J. RUFUS LION, WHO MAKES SUPERMAN, THE FLASH, AND TERRIFIC WHATSIT, LOOK LIKE SISSIES!
HEY, READER-- I HOPE YOU SAW TH' PREVIOUS PAGE---- YER LIABLE TO GET A LITTLE CONFUSED IF YA DIDN'T!

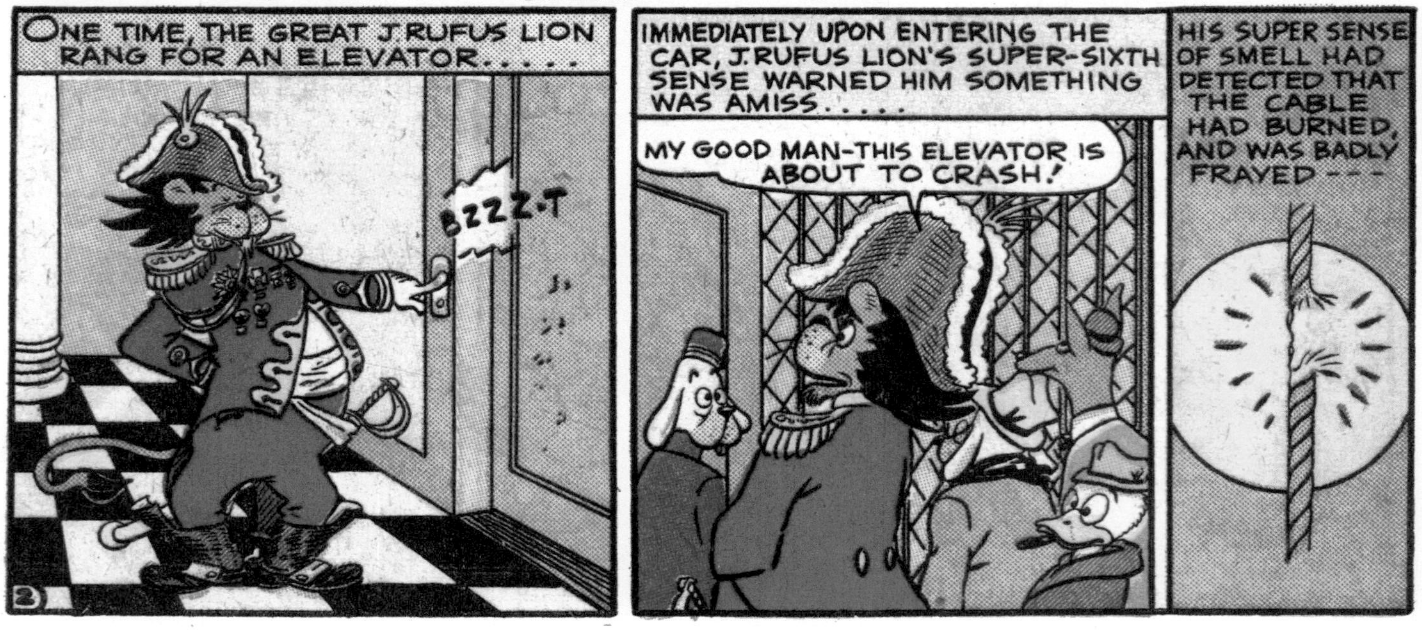
ONE TIME, THE GREAT J. RUFUS LION RANG FOR AN ELEVATOR....
BZZZ-T
IMMEDIATELY UPON ENTERING THE CAR, J. RUFUS LION'S SUPER-SIXTH SENSE WARNED HIM SOMETHING WAS AMISS....
MY GOOD MAN-THIS ELEVATOR IS ABOUT TO CRASH!
HIS SUPER SENSE OF SMELL HAD DETECTED THAT THE CABLE HAD BURNED, AND WAS BADLY FRAYED---

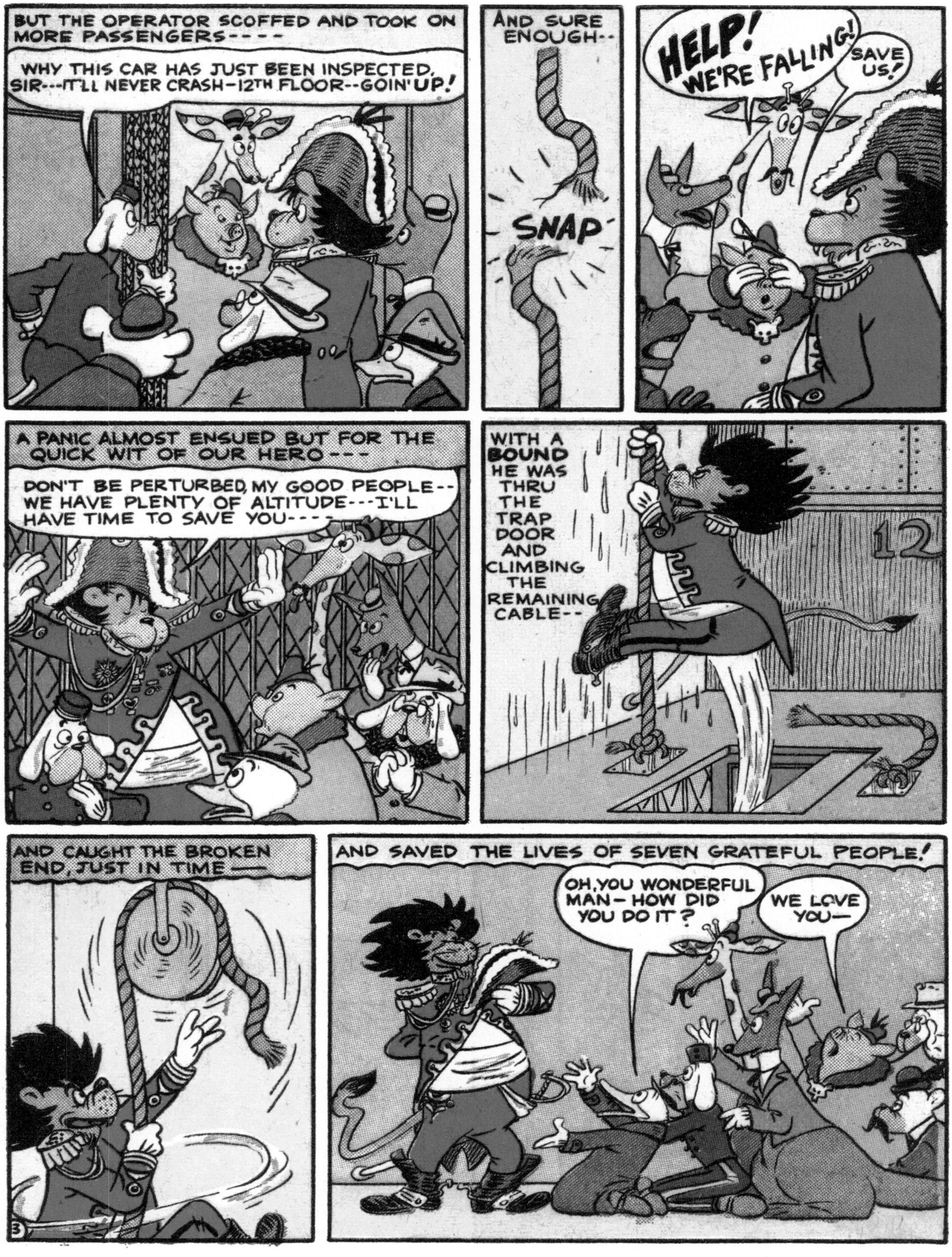
BUT THE OPERATOR SCOFFED AND TOOK ON MORE PASSENGERS----
WHY THIS CAR HAS JUST BEEN INSPECTED, SIR---IT'LL NEVER CRASH-12TH FLOOR--GOIN' UP!
AND SURE ENOUGH--
SNAP
HELP! WE'RE FALLING!
SAVE US!
A PANIC ALMOST ENSUED BUT FOR THE QUICK WIT OF OUR HERO---
DON'T BE PERTURBED, MY GOOD PEOPLE--WE HAVE PLENTY OF ALTITUDE---I'LL HAVE TIME TO SAVE YOU----
WITH A BOUND HE WAS THRU THE TRAP DOOR AND CLIMBING THE REMAINING CABLE--
12
AND CAUGHT THE BROKEN END, JUST IN TIME—
AND SAVED THE LIVES OF SEVEN GRATEFUL PEOPLE!
OH, YOU WONDERFUL MAN—HOW DID YOU DO IT?
WE LOVE YOU—

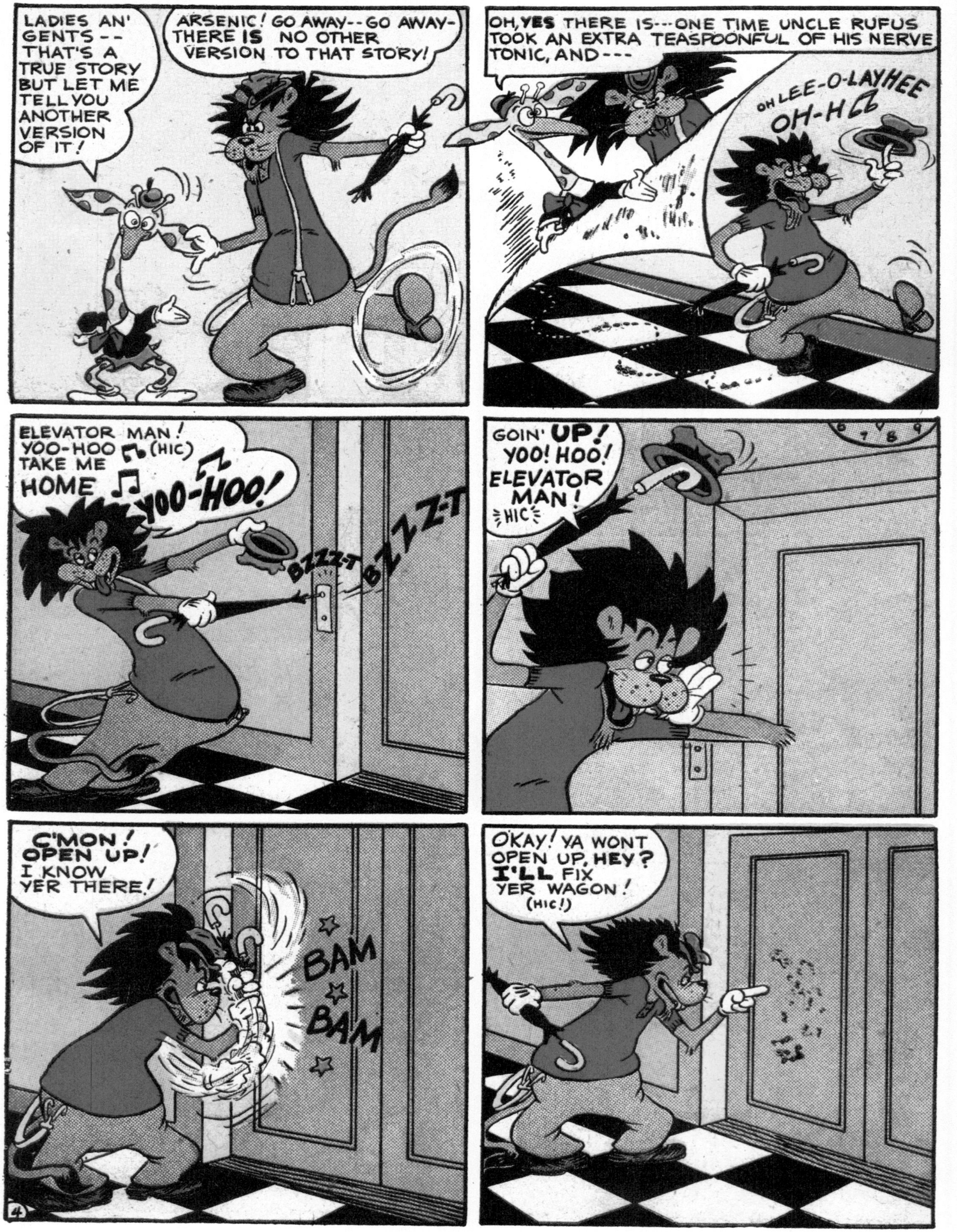
LADIES AN' GENTS -- THAT'S A TRUE STORY BUT LET ME TELL YOU ANOTHER VERSION OF IT!
ARSENIC! GO AWAY-- GO AWAY- THERE IS NO OTHER VERSION TO THAT STORY!
OH, YES THERE IS--- ONE TIME UNCLE RUFUS TOOK AN EXTRA TEASPOONFUL OF HIS NERVE TONIC, AND---
OH LEE-O-LAYHEE OH-HEE
ELEVATOR MAN! YOO-HOO (HIC) TAKE ME HOME YOO-HOO!
BZZZ-T BZZZ-T
GOIN' UP! YOO! HOO! ELEVATOR MAN!
HIC
C'MON! OPEN UP! I KNOW YER THERE!
BAM
BAM
O'KAY! YA WONT OPEN UP, HEY? I'LL FIX YER WAGON! (HIC!)
4

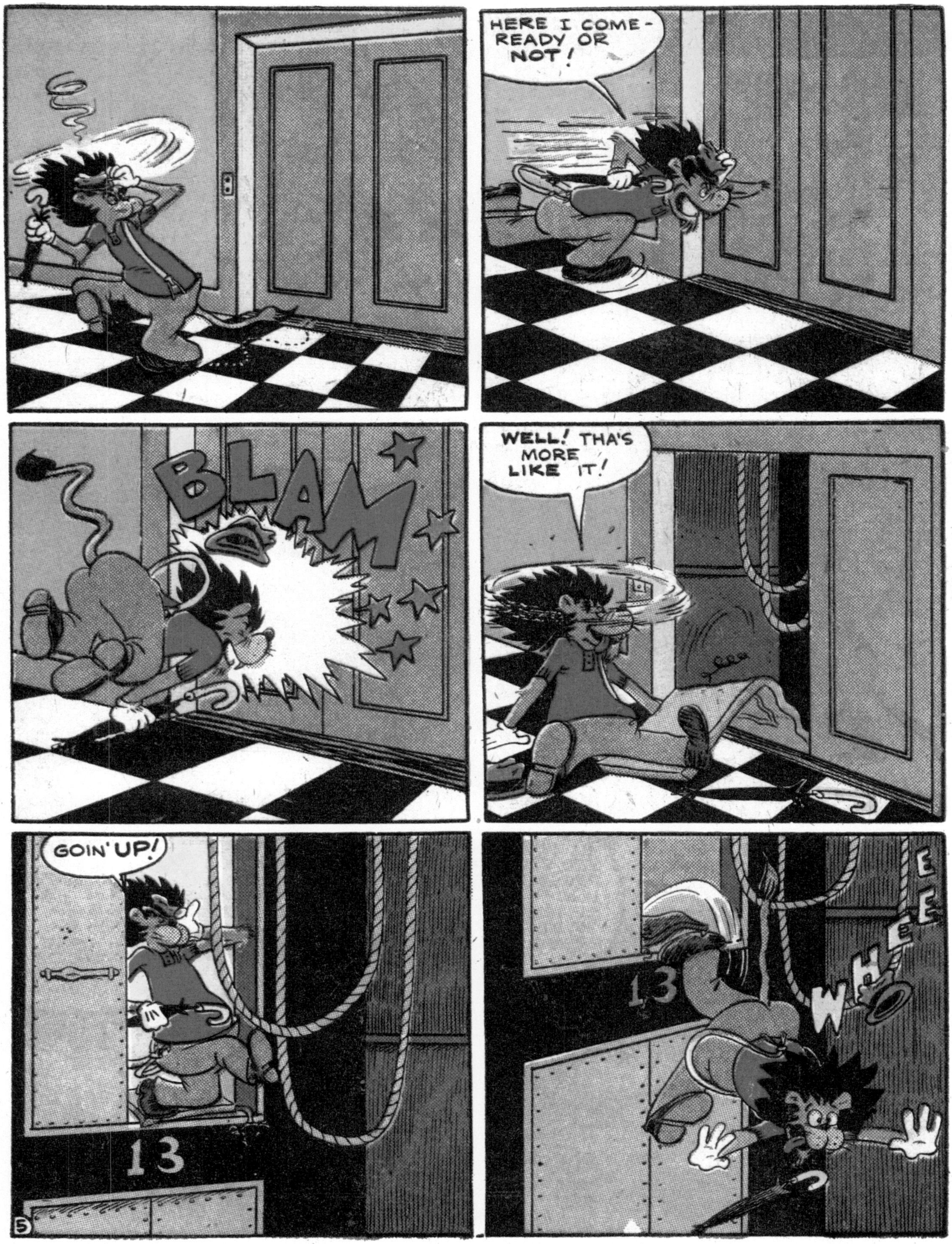
HERE I COME - READY OR NOT!
BLAM
WELL! THA'S MORE LIKE IT!
GOIN' UP!
13
5
13
WHEEE

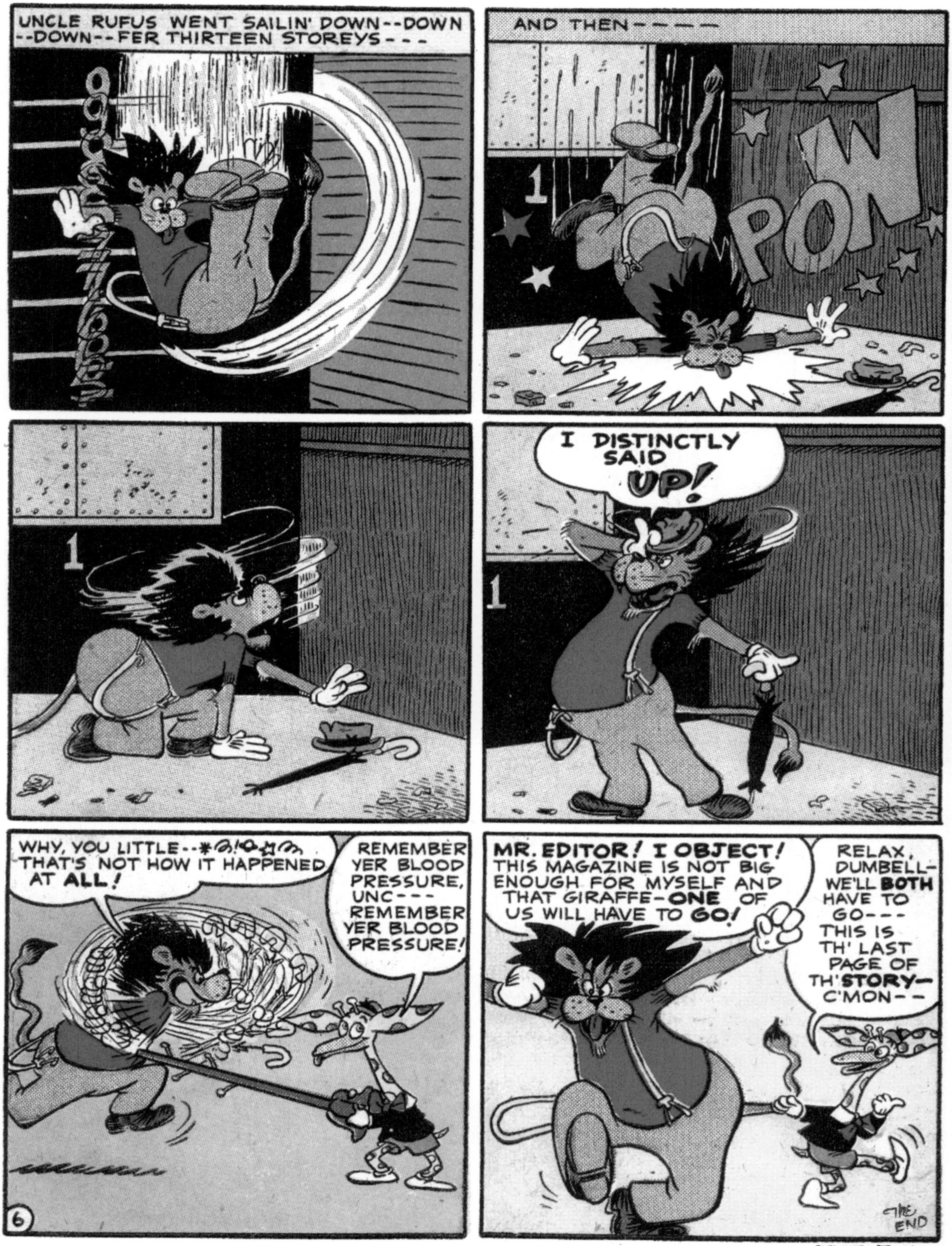
UNCLE RUFUS WENT SAILIN' DOWN--DOWN --DOWN--FER THIRTEEN STOREYS---
AND THEN----
POW
I DISTINCTLY SAID UP!
WHY, YOU LITTLE-- THAT'S NOT HOW IT HAPPENED AT ALL!
REMEMBER YER BLOOD PRESSURE, UNC--- REMEMBER YER BLOOD PRESSURE!
MR. EDITOR! I OBJECT! THIS MAGAZINE IS NOT BIG ENOUGH FOR MYSELF AND THAT GIRAFFE-ONE OF US WILL HAVE TO GO!
RELAX, DUMBELL- WE'LL BOTH HAVE TO GO--- THIS IS TH' LAST PAGE OF TH' STORY- C'MON--
6
THE END

THE END

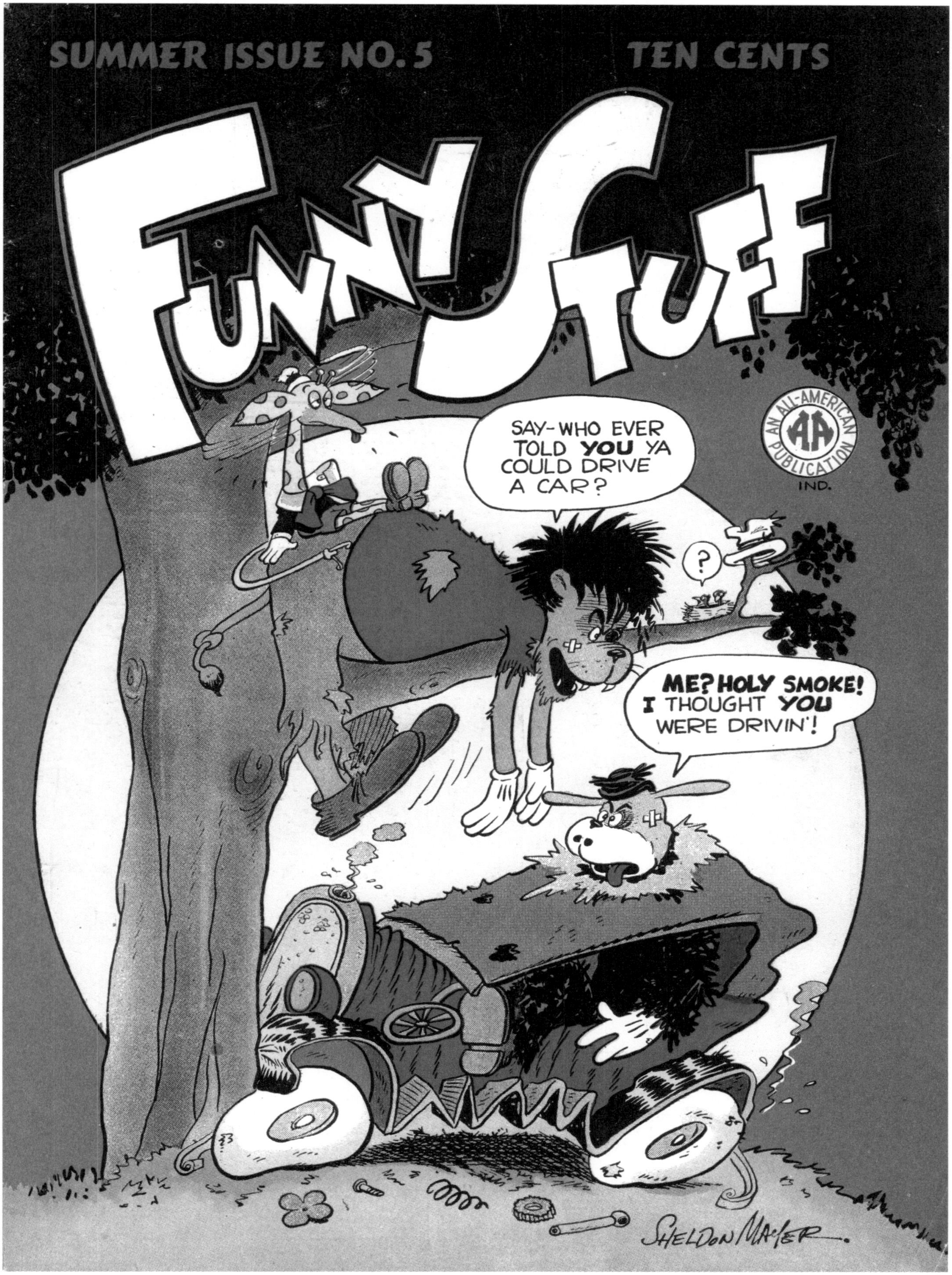
SUMMER ISSUE NO. 5
TEN CENTS
FUNNY STUFF
AN ALL-AMERICAN PUBLICATION IND.
SAY-WHO EVER TOLD YOU YA COULD DRIVE A CAR?
?
ME? HOLY SMOKE! I THOUGHT YOU WERE DRIVIN'!
SHELDON MAYER

WEIRD AND WACKY FUNNY STUFF COVER by SHELDON MAYER

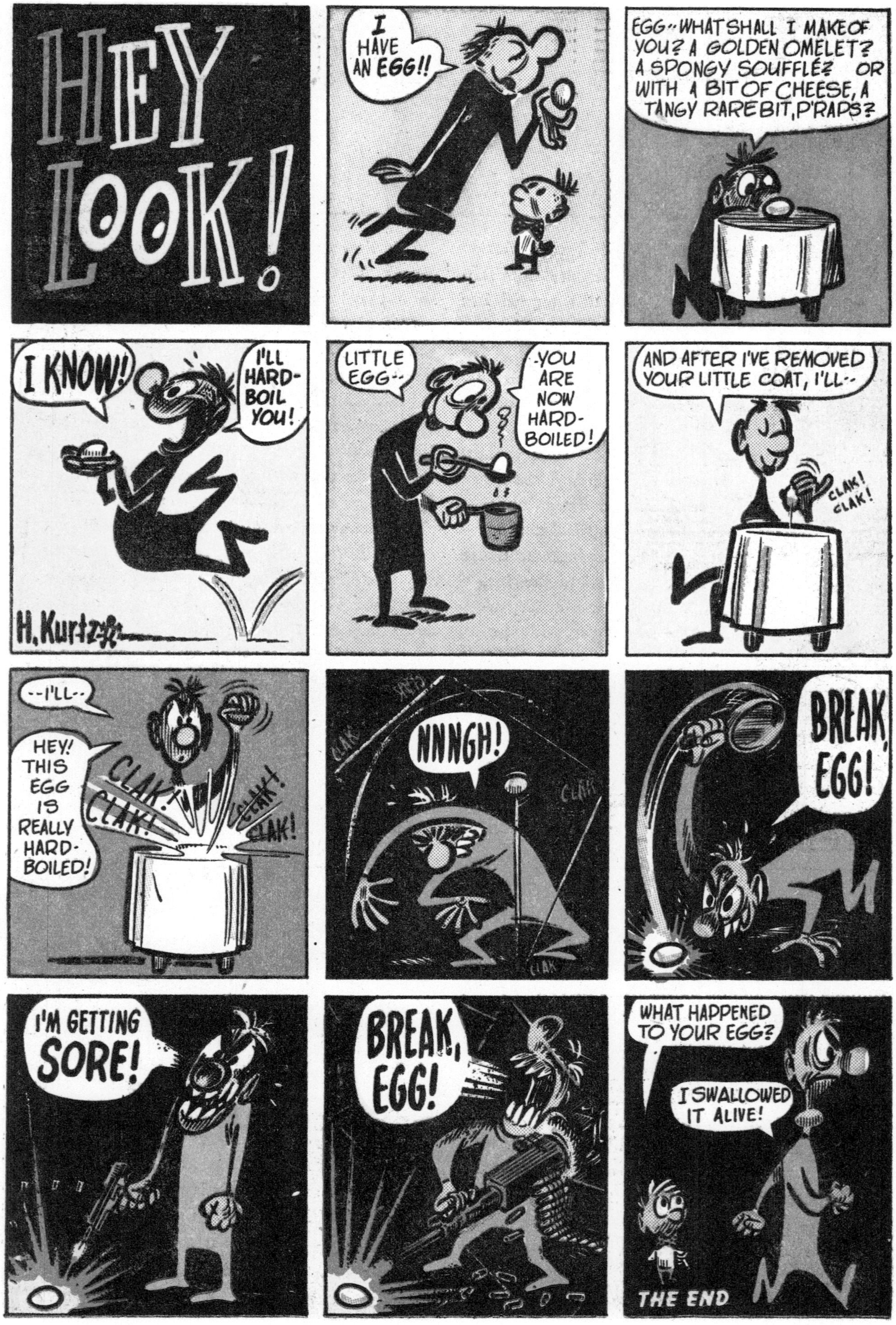
HEY LOOK!
I HAVE AN EGG!!
EGG-- WHAT SHALL I MAKE OF YOU? A GOLDEN OMELET? A SPONGY SOUFFLÉ? OR WITH A BIT OF CHEESE, A TANGY RAREBIT, P'RAPS?
I KNOW!
I'LL HARD-BOIL YOU!
H. Kurtzman
LITTLE EGG--
YOU ARE NOW HARD-BOILED!
AND AFTER I'VE REMOVED YOUR LITTLE COAT, I'LL--
CLAK! CLAK!
--I'LL--
HEY! THIS EGG IS REALLY HARD-BOILED!
CLAK! CLAK! CLAK! CLAK!
NNNGH!
BREAK, EGG!
I'M GETTING SORE!
BREAK, EGG!
WHAT HAPPENED TO YOUR EGG?
I SWALLOWED IT ALIVE!
THE END

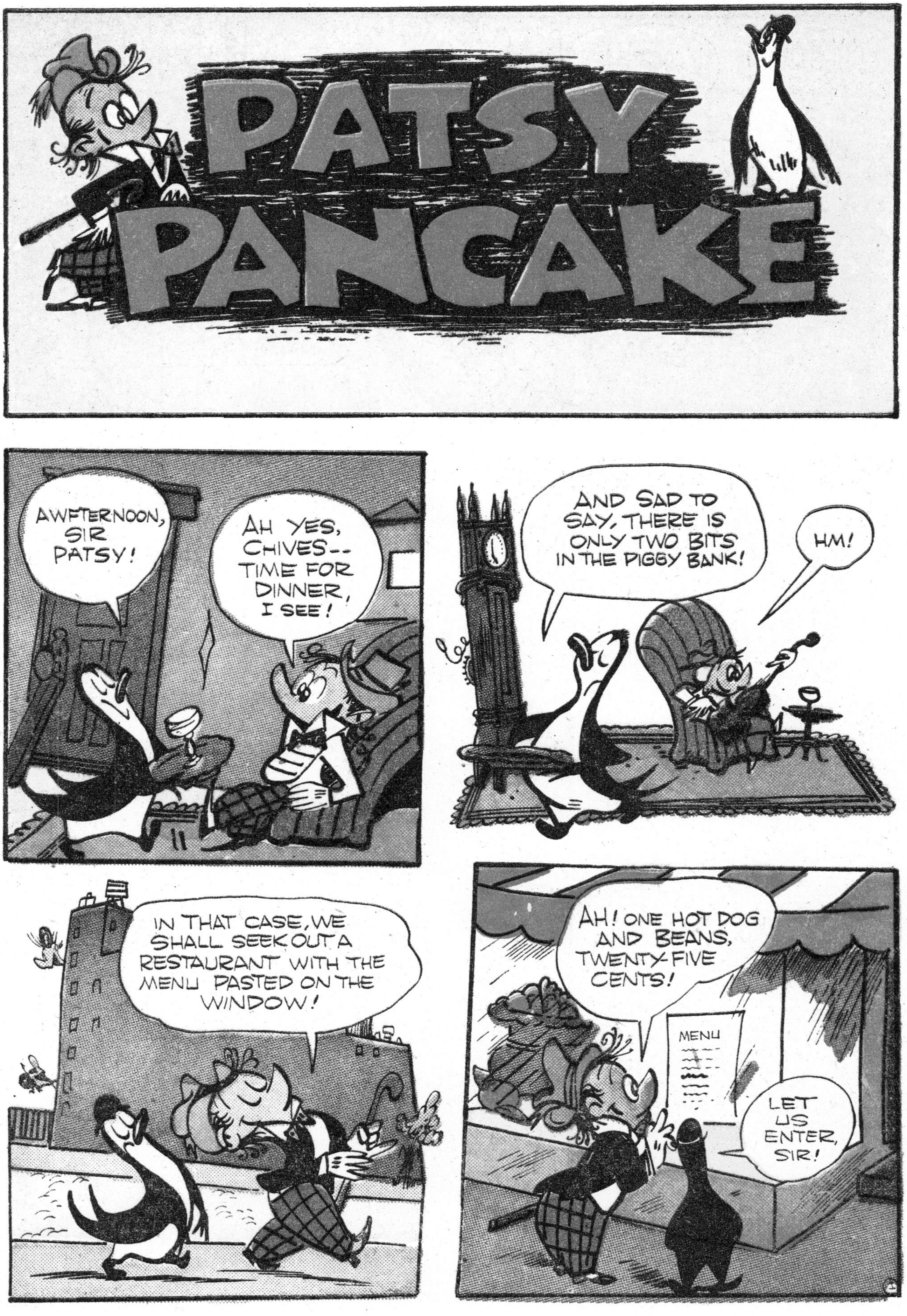
PATSY PANCAKE
AWFTERNOON, SIR PATSY!
AH YES, CHIVES-- TIME FOR DINNER, I SEE!
AND SAD TO SAY, THERE IS ONLY TWO BITS IN THE PIGGY BANK!
HM!
IN THAT CASE, WE SHALL SEEK OUT A RESTAURANT WITH THE MENU PASTED ON THE WINDOW!
AH! ONE HOT DOG AND BEANS, TWENTY-FIVE CENTS!
MENU
LET US ENTER, SIR!

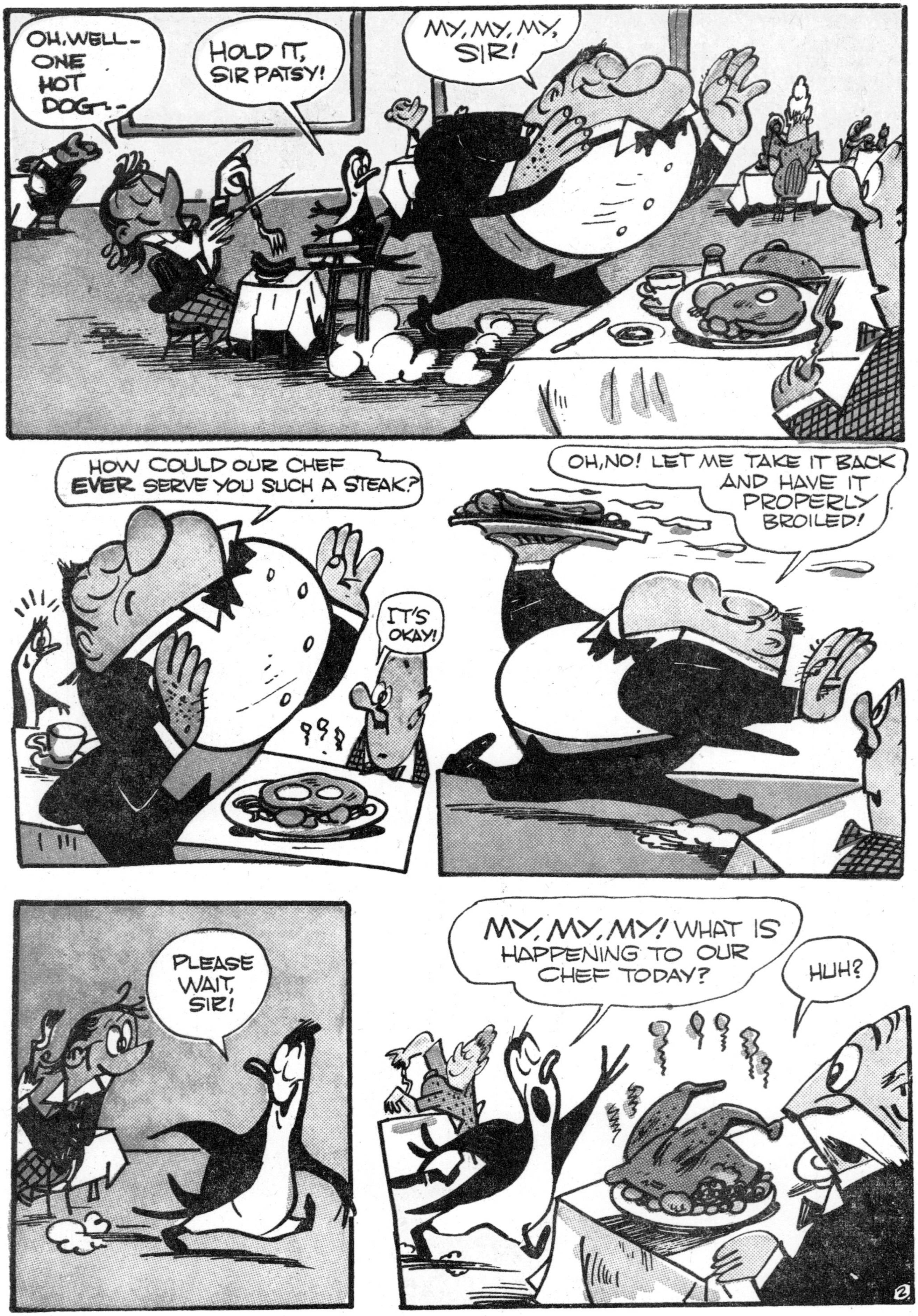
OH, WELL - ONE HOT DOG - -
HOLD IT, SIR PATSY!
MY, MY, MY, SIR!
HOW COULD OUR CHEF EVER SERVE YOU SUCH A STEAK?
IT'S OKAY!
OH, NO! LET ME TAKE IT BACK AND HAVE IT PROPERLY BROILED!
PLEASE WAIT, SIR!
MY, MY, MY! WHAT IS HAPPENING TO OUR CHEF TODAY?
HUH?
2

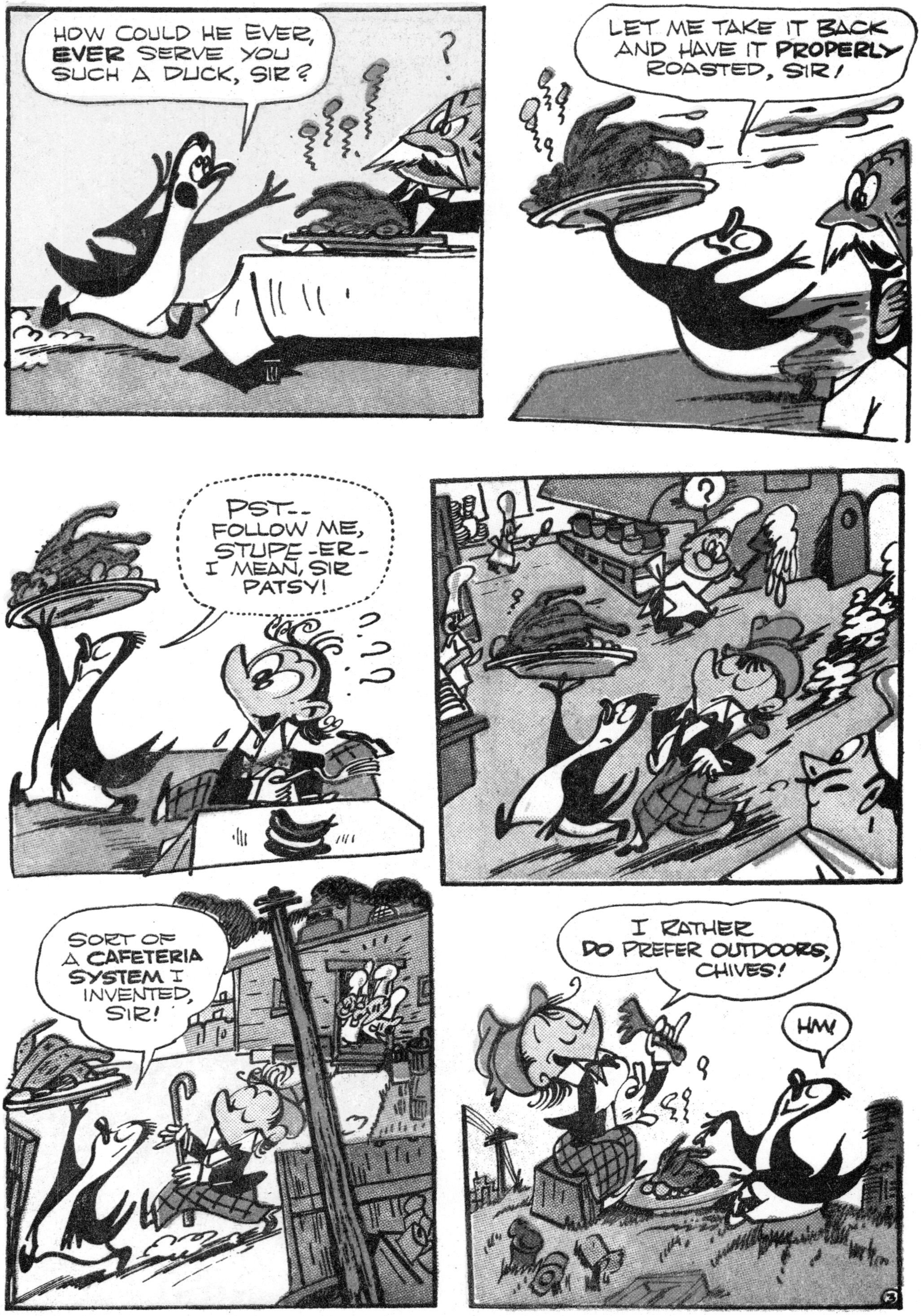
HOW COULD HE EVER, **EVER** SERVE YOU SUCH A DUCK, SIR?
?
LET ME TAKE IT BACK AND HAVE IT **PROPERLY** ROASTED, SIR!
PST-- FOLLOW ME, STUPE-ER- I MEAN, SIR PATSY!
SORT OF A **CAFETERIA SYSTEM** I INVENTED, SIR!
I RATHER **DO** PREFER OUTDOORS, CHIVES!
HM!

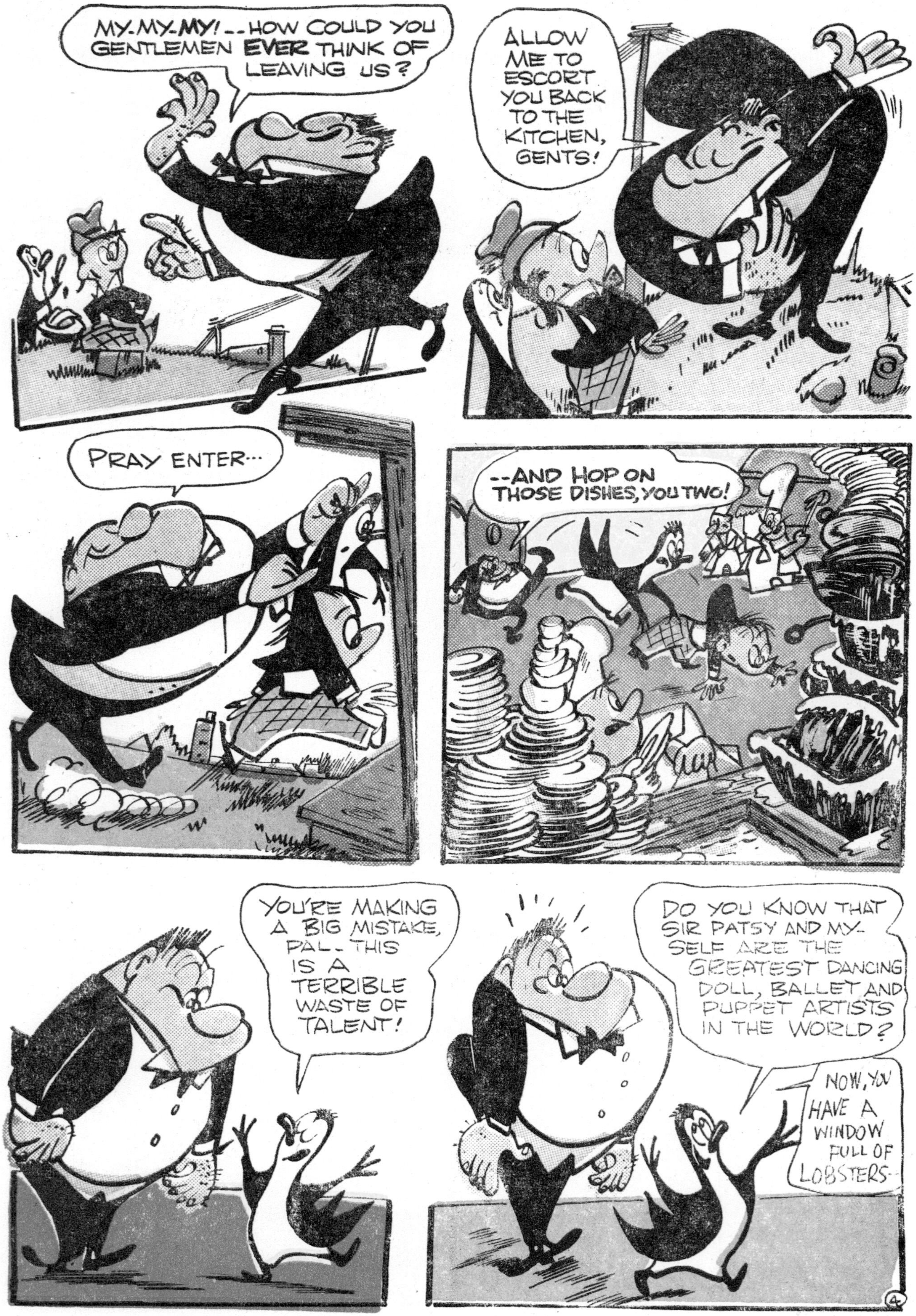
MY-MY-MY! -- HOW COULD YOU GENTLEMEN EVER THINK OF LEAVING US?
ALLOW ME TO ESCORT YOU BACK TO THE KITCHEN, GENTS!
PRAY ENTER...
--AND HOP ON THOSE DISHES, YOU TWO!
YOU'RE MAKING A BIG MISTAKE, PAL-- THIS IS A TERRIBLE WASTE OF TALENT!
DO YOU KNOW THAT SIR PATSY AND MY-SELF ARE THE GREATEST DANCING DOLL, BALLET AND PUPPET ARTISTS IN THE WORLD?
NOW, YOU HAVE A WINDOW FULL OF LOBSTERS-
4

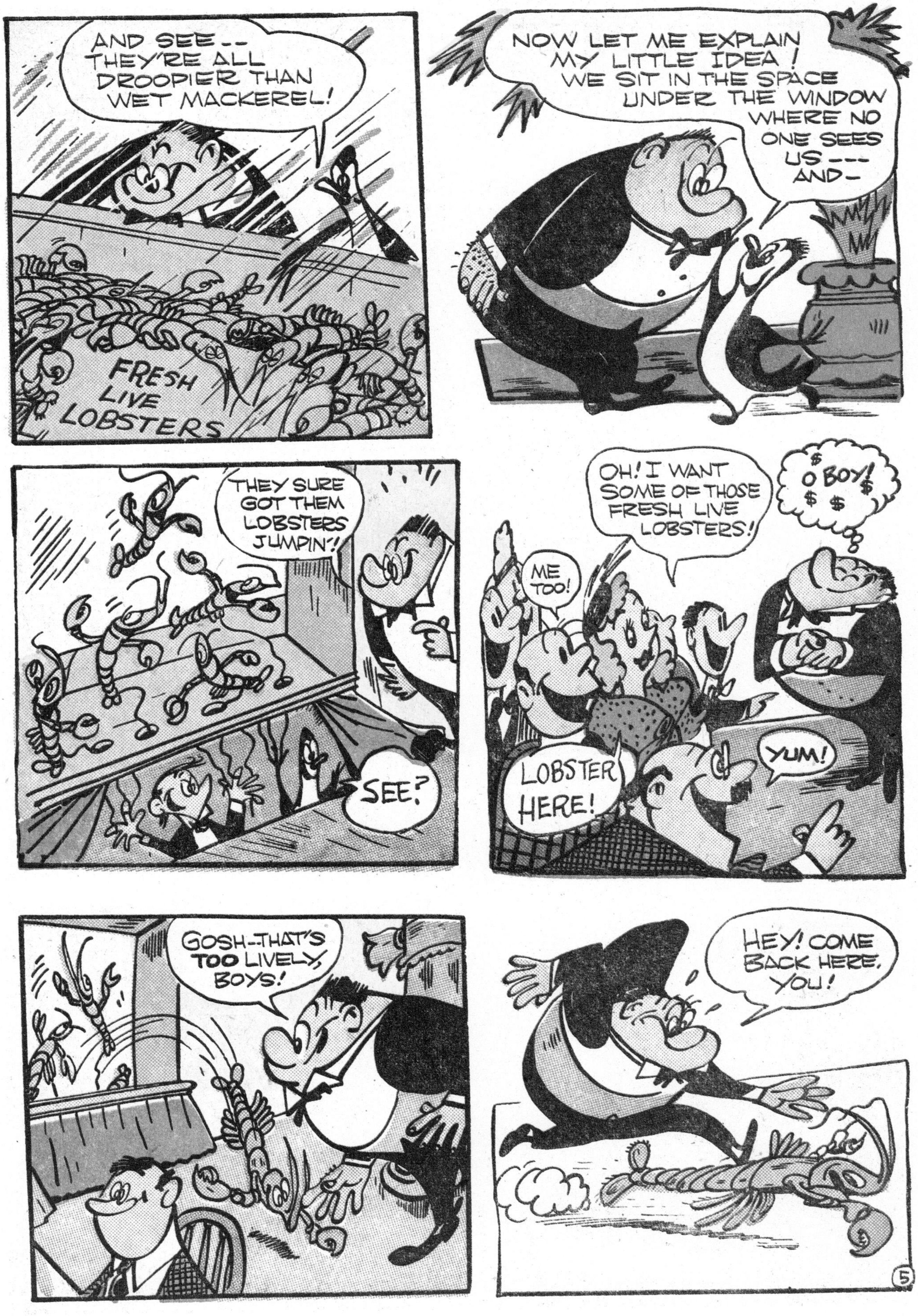
AND SEE -- THEY'RE ALL DROOPIER THAN WET MACKEREL!
FRESH LIVE LOBSTERS
NOW LET ME EXPLAIN MY LITTLE IDEA! WE SIT IN THE SPACE UNDER THE WINDOW WHERE NO ONE SEES US --- AND-
THEY SURE GOT THEM LOBSTERS JUMPIN'!
SEE?
OH! I WANT SOME OF THOSE FRESH LIVE LOBSTERS!
$ O BOY! $ $ $
ME TOO!
LOBSTER HERE!
YUM!
GOSH--THAT'S TOO LIVELY, BOYS!
HEY! COME BACK HERE, YOU!
5

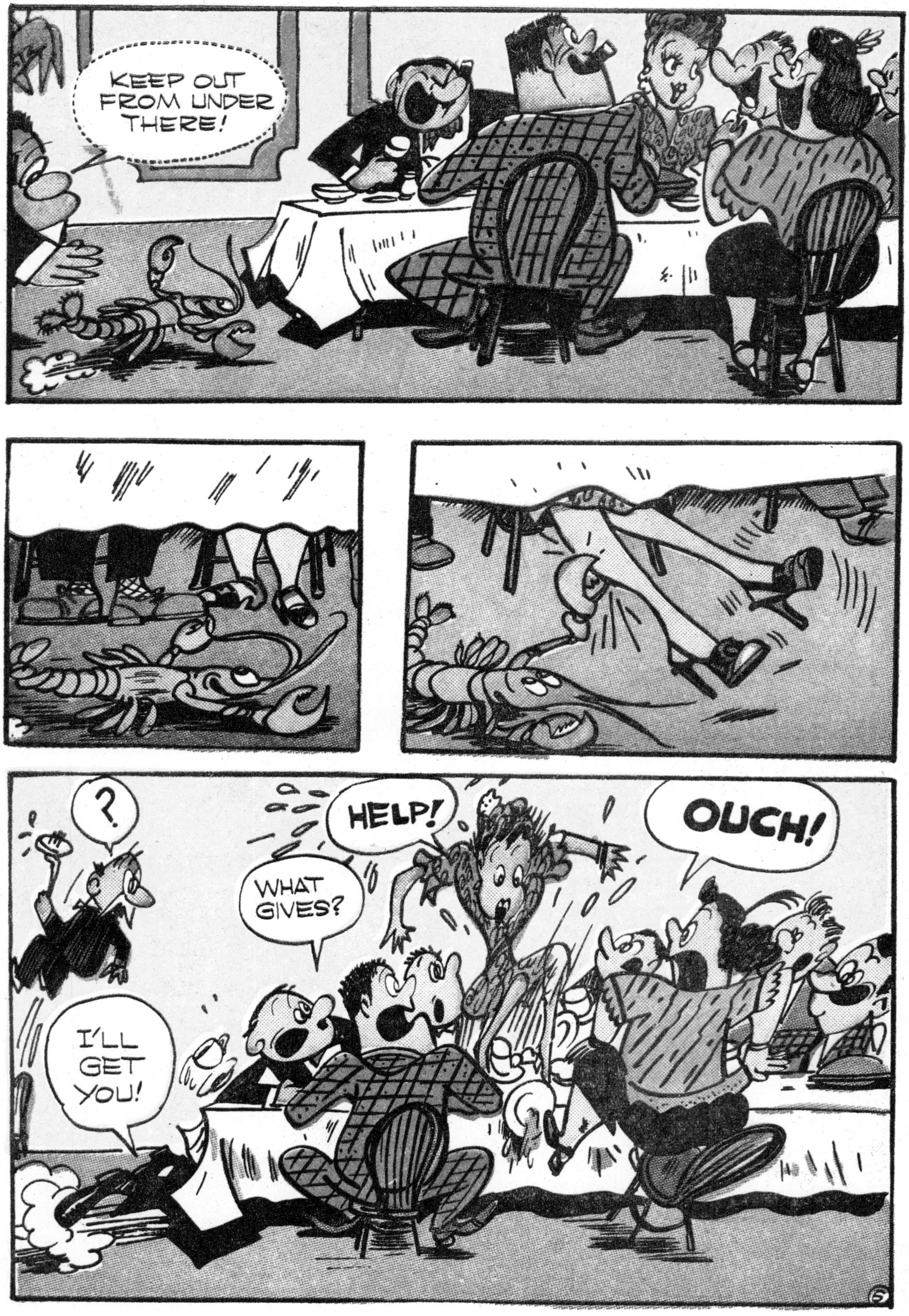
KEEP OUT FROM UNDER THERE!
?
HELP!
OUCH!
WHAT GIVES?
I'LL GET YOU!

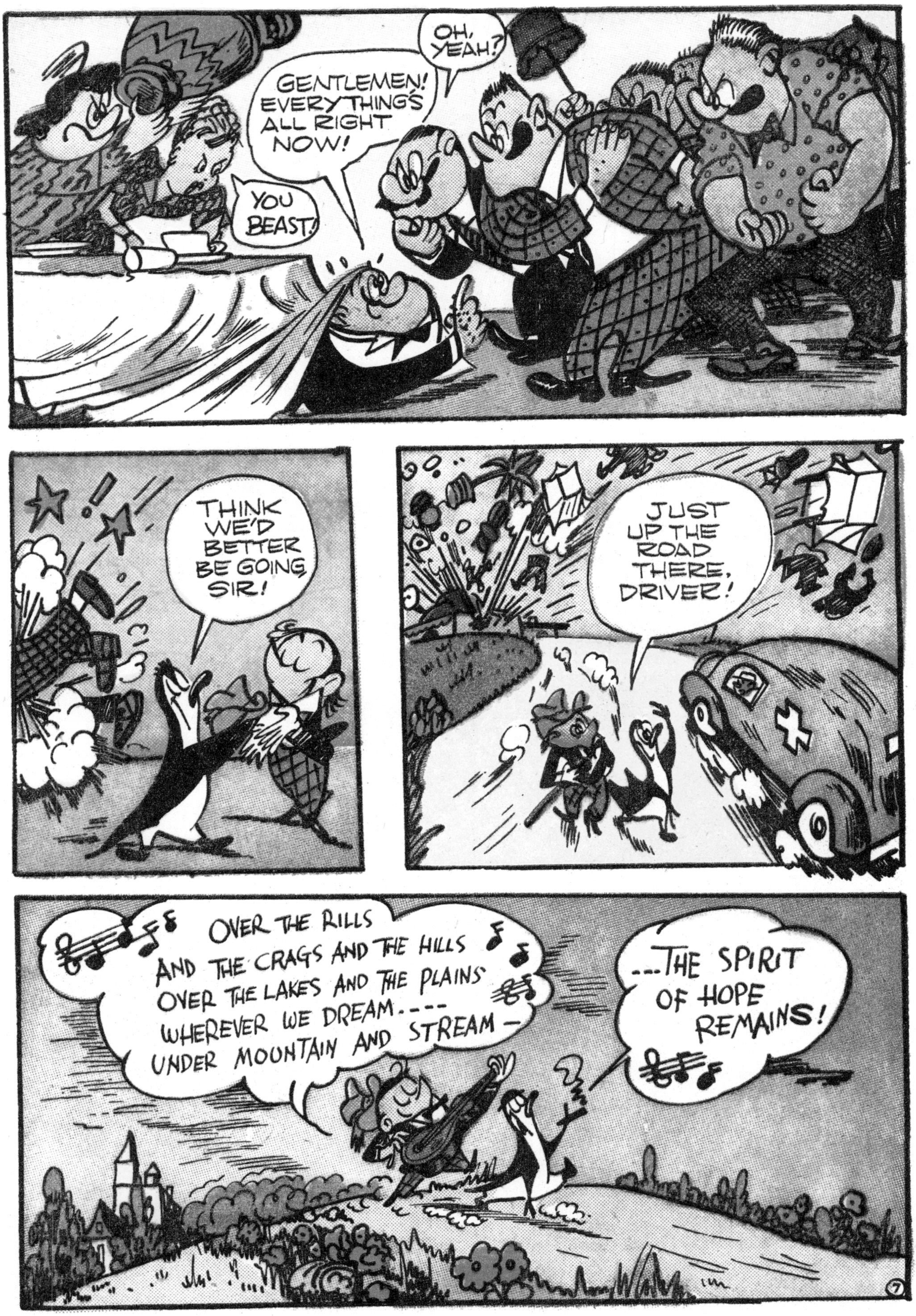
GENTLEMEN! EVERYTHING'S ALL RIGHT NOW!
OH, YEAH?
YOU BEAST!
THINK WE'D BETTER BE GOING SIR!
JUST UP THE ROAD THERE, DRIVER!
OVER THE RILLS AND THE CRAGS AND THE HILLS OVER THE LAKES AND THE PLAINS WHEREVER WE DREAM.--- WHEREVER WE DREAM AND STREAM — UNDER MOUNTAIN AND STREAM —
---THE SPIRIT OF HOPE REMAINS!

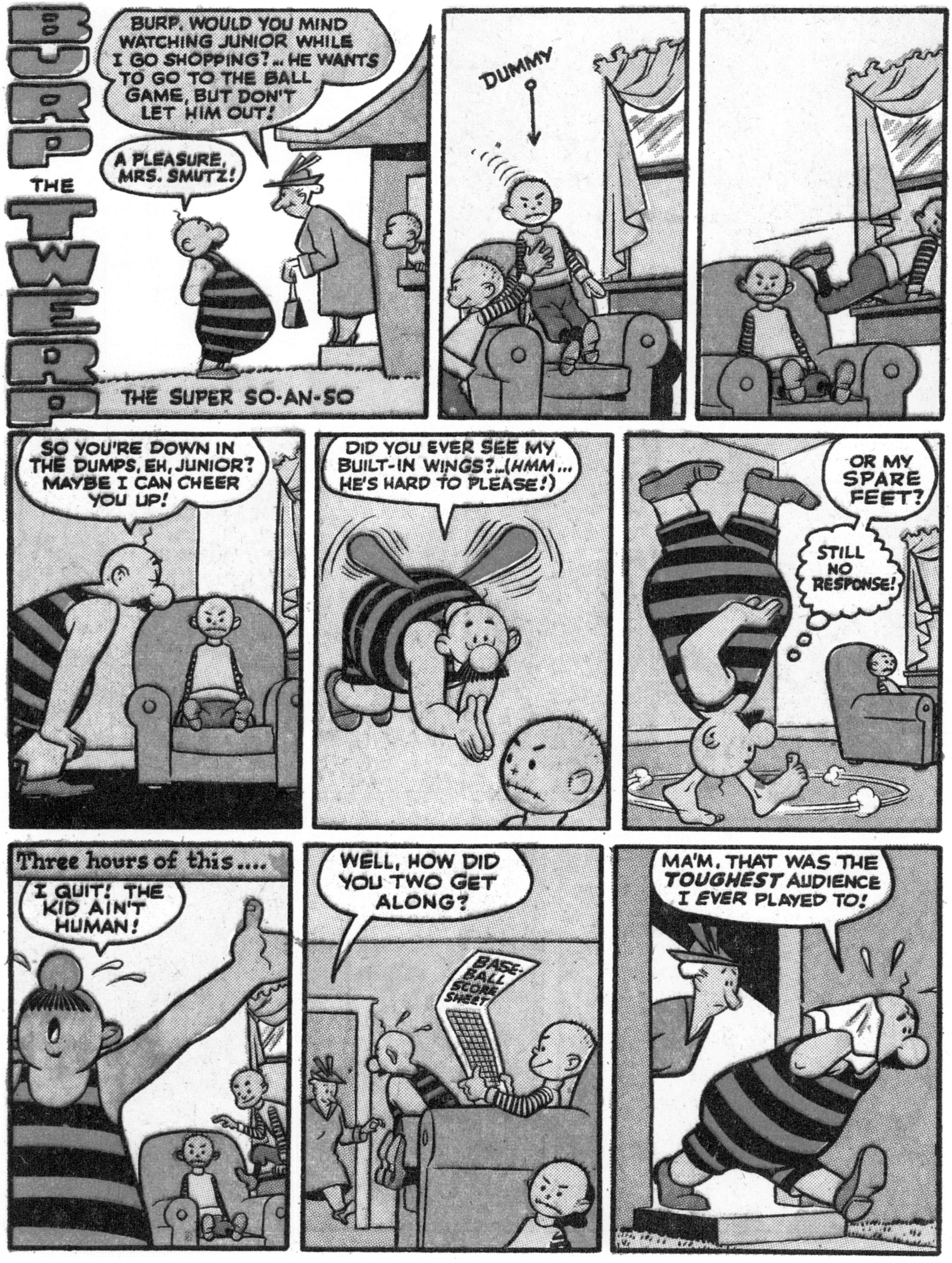
BURP THE TWERP
THE SUPER SO-AN-SO
BURP, WOULD YOU MIND WATCHING JUNIOR WHILE I GO SHOPPING?... HE WANTS TO GO TO THE BALL GAME, BUT DON'T LET HIM OUT!
A PLEASURE, MRS. SMUTZ!
DUMMY
SO YOU'RE DOWN IN THE DUMPS, EH, JUNIOR? MAYBE I CAN CHEER YOU UP!
DID YOU EVER SEE MY BUILT-IN WINGS?...(HMM... HE'S HARD TO PLEASE!)
OR MY SPARE FEET?
STILL NO RESPONSE!
Three hours of this....
I QUIT! THE KID AIN'T HUMAN!
WELL, HOW DID YOU TWO GET ALONG?
BASE-BALL SCORE SHEET
MA'M, THAT WAS THE TOUGHEST AUDIENCE I EVER PLAYED TO!

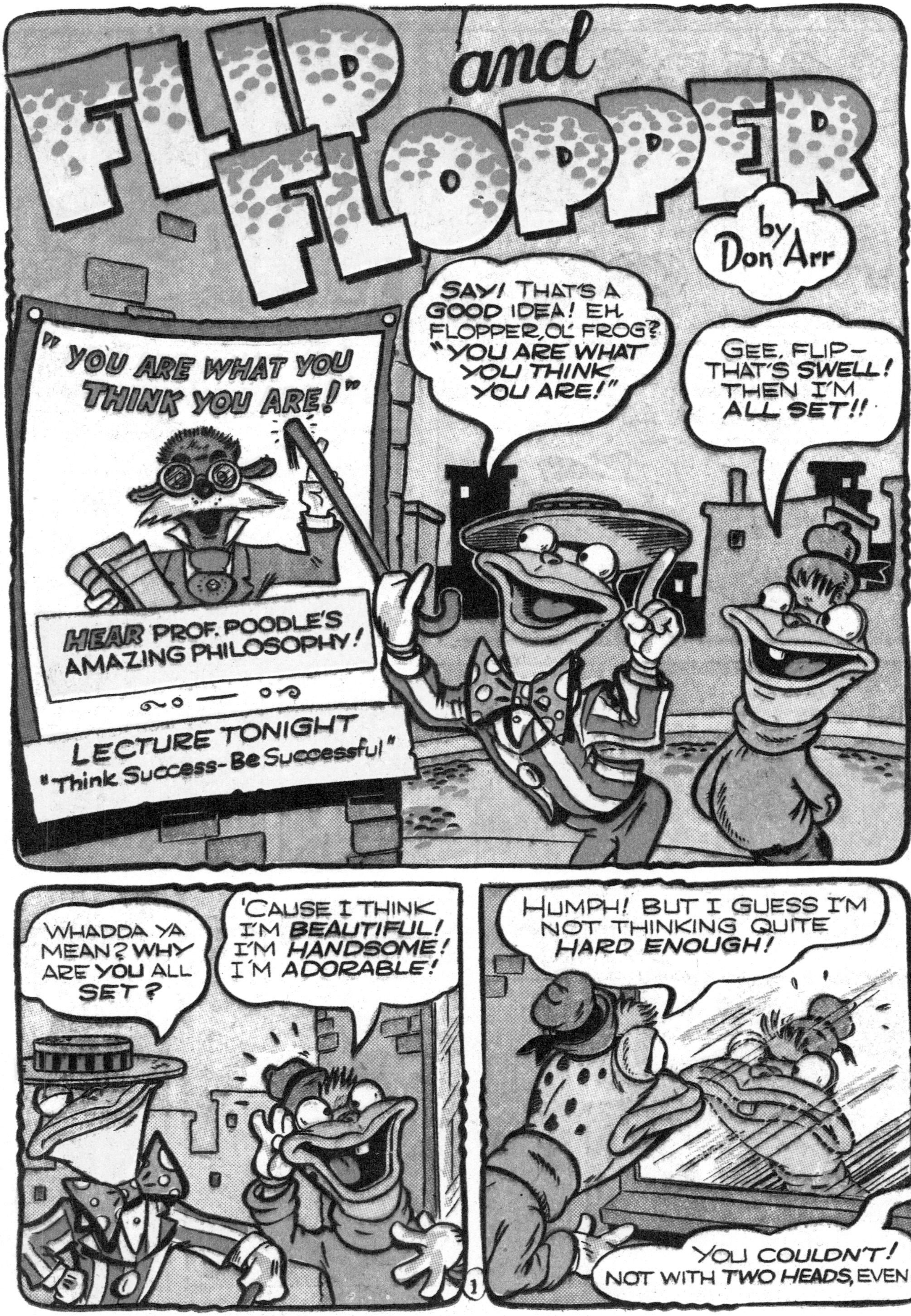
FLIP and FLOPPER
by Don Arr
"YOU ARE WHAT YOU THINK YOU ARE!"
HEAR PROF. POODLE'S AMAZING PHILOSOPHY!
LECTURE TONIGHT "Think Success-Be Successful"
SAY! THAT'S A GOOD IDEA! EH, FLOPPER, OL' FROG? "YOU ARE WHAT YOU THINK YOU ARE!"
GEE, FLIP-THAT'S SWELL! THEN I'M ALL SET!!
WHADDA YA MEAN? WHY ARE YOU ALL SET?
'CAUSE I THINK I'M BEAUTIFUL! I'M HANDSOME! I'M ADORABLE!
HUMPH! BUT I GUESS I'M NOT THINKING QUITE HARD ENOUGH!
YOU COULDN'T! NOT WITH TWO HEADS, EVEN!
1

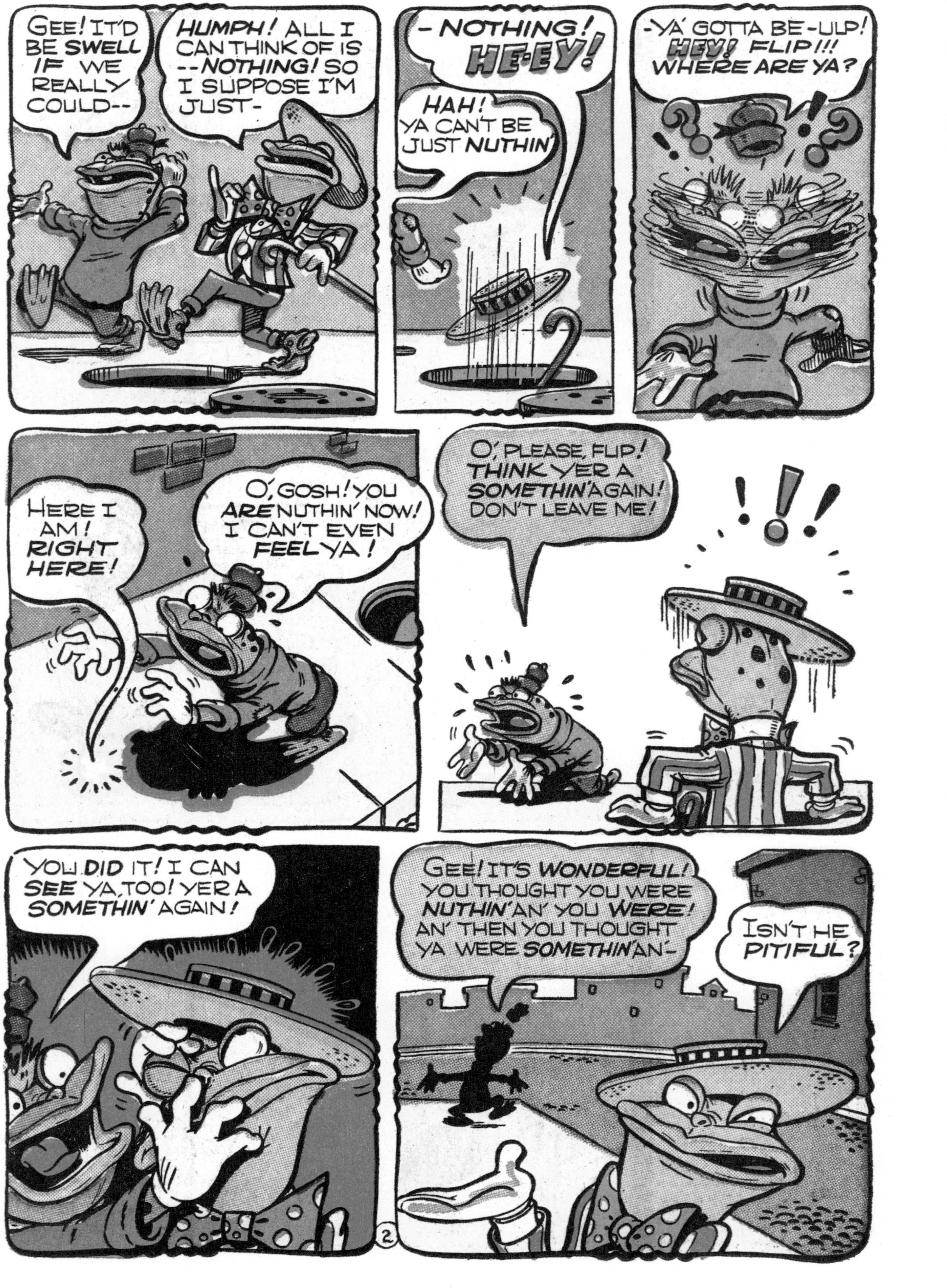
GEE! IT'D BE SWELL IF WE REALLY COULD--
HUMPH! ALL I CAN THINK OF IS --NOTHING! SO I SUPPOSE I'M JUST-
- NOTHING! HE-EY!
HAH! YA CAN'T BE JUST NUTHIN'
-YA' GOTTA BE -ULP! HEY! FLIP!!! WHERE ARE YA?
HERE I AM! RIGHT HERE!
O', GOSH! YOU ARE NUTHIN' NOW! I CAN'T EVEN FEEL YA!
O', PLEASE, FLIP! THINK YER A SOMETHIN' AGAIN! DON'T LEAVE ME!
YOU DID IT! I CAN SEE YA, TOO! YER A SOMETHIN' AGAIN!
2
GEE! IT'S WONDERFUL! YOU THOUGHT YOU WERE NUTHIN' AN' YOU WERE! AN' THEN YOU THOUGHT YA WERE SOMETHIN' AN'-
ISN'T HE PITIFUL?

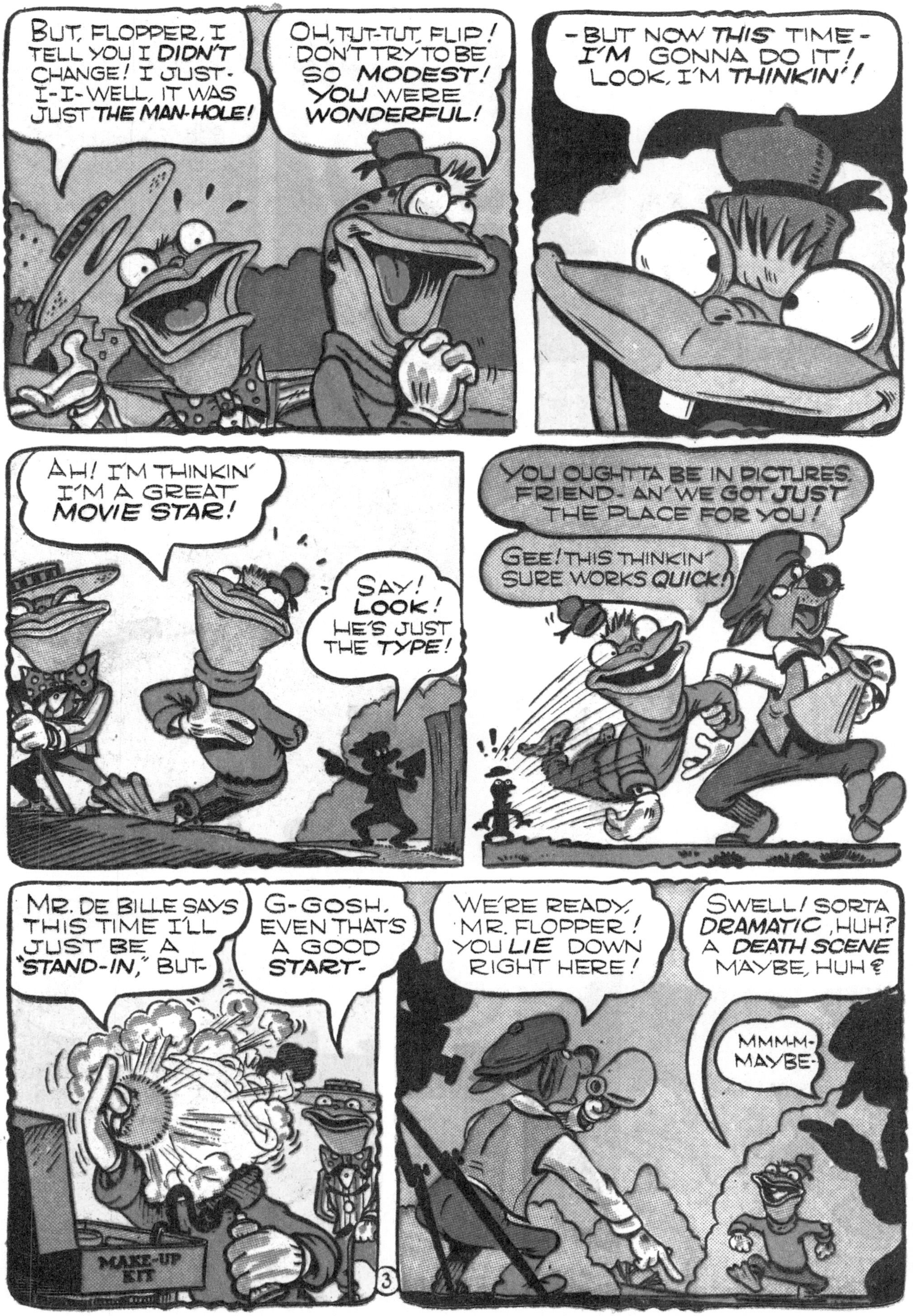
BUT, FLOPPER, I TELL YOU I DIDN'T CHANGE! I JUST- I-I-WELL, IT WAS JUST THE MAN-HOLE!
OH, TUT-TUT, FLIP! DON'T TRY TO BE SO MODEST! YOU WERE WONDERFUL!
-BUT NOW THIS TIME - I'M GONNA DO IT! LOOK, I'M THINKIN'!
AH! I'M THINKIN' I'M A GREAT MOVIE STAR!
SAY! LOOK! HE'S JUST THE TYPE!
YOU OUGHTTA BE IN PICTURES, FRIEND- AN' WE GOT JUST THE PLACE FOR YOU!
GEE! THIS THINKIN' SURE WORKS QUICK!
MR. DE BILLE SAYS THIS TIME I'LL JUST BE A "STAND-IN," BUT-
G-GOSH, EVEN THAT'S A GOOD START-
MAKE-UP KIT
WE'RE READY, MR. FLOPPER! YOU LIE DOWN RIGHT HERE!
SWELL! SORTA DRAMATIC, HUH? A DEATH SCENE MAYBE, HUH?
MMM-M-MAYBE-

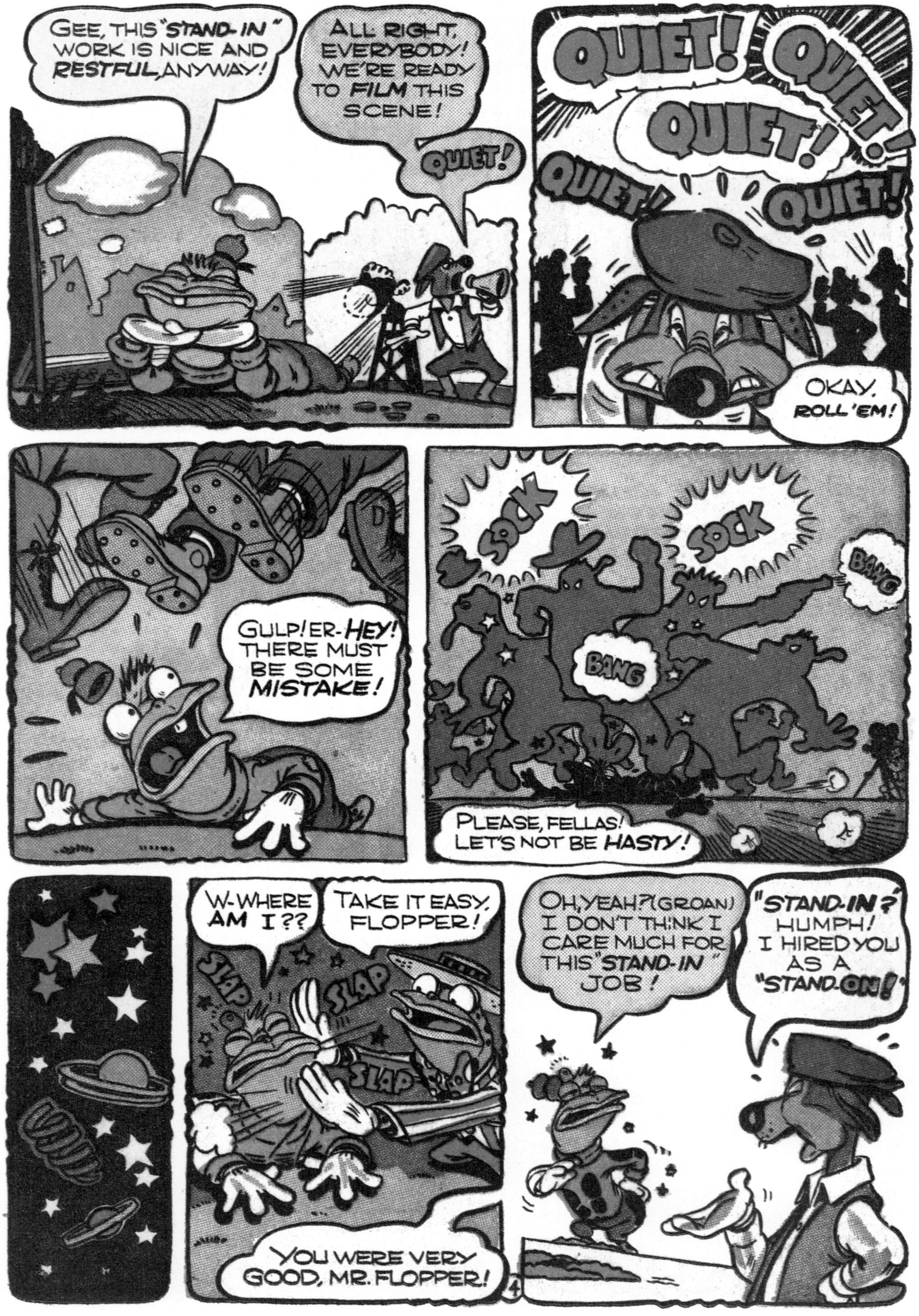
GEE, THIS "STAND-IN" WORK IS NICE AND RESTFUL, ANYWAY!
ALL RIGHT, EVERYBODY! WE'RE READY TO FILM THIS SCENE!
QUIET!
QUIET! QUIET! QUIET! QUIET! QUIET!
OKAY. ROLL 'EM!
GULP! ER-HEY! THERE MUST BE SOME MISTAKE!
SOCK
SOCK
BANG
BANG
PLEASE, FELLAS! LET'S NOT BE HASTY!
W-WHERE AM I??
TAKE IT EASY, FLOPPER!
SLAP
SLAP
SLAP
YOU WERE VERY GOOD, MR. FLOPPER!
4
OH, YEAH? (GROAN) I DON'T THINK I CARE MUCH FOR THIS "STAND-IN" JOB!
"STAND-IN?" HUMPH! I HIRED YOU AS A "STAND-ON!"

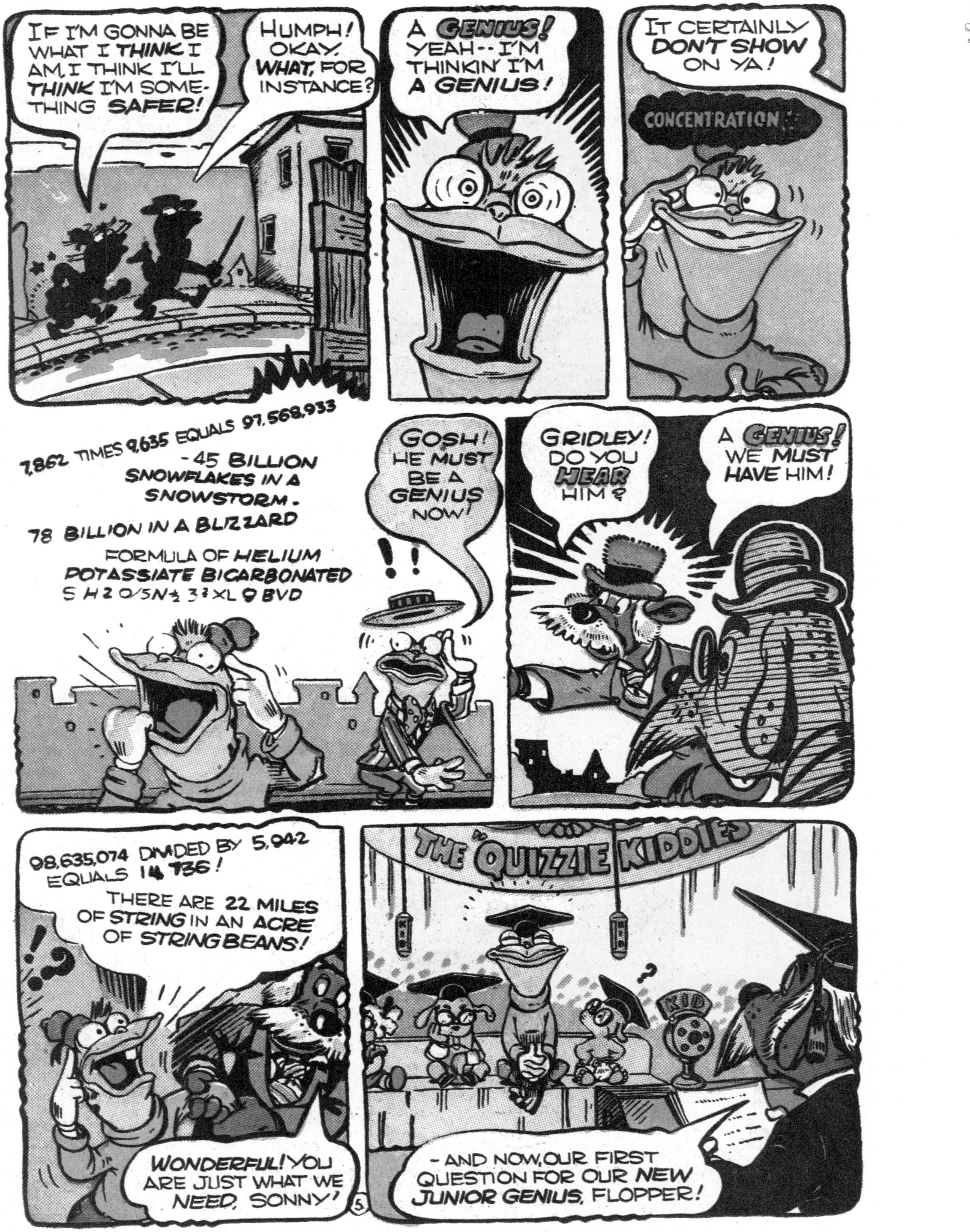
IF I'M GONNA BE WHAT I THINK I AM, I THINK I'LL THINK I'M SOMETHING SAFER!
HUMPH! OKAY. WHAT, FOR INSTANCE?
A GENIUS! YEAH-- I'M THINKIN' I'M A GENIUS!
IT CERTAINLY DON'T SHOW ON YA!
CONCENTRATION
7,862 TIMES 9,635 EQUALS 97,568,933
-45 BILLION SNOWFLAKES IN A SNOWSTORM.
78 BILLION IN A BLIZZARD
FORMULA OF HELIUM POTASSIATE BICARBONATED
GOSH! HE MUST BE A GENIUS NOW!
GRIDLEY! DO YOU HEAR HIM?
A GENIUS! WE MUST HAVE HIM!
98,635,074 DIVIDED BY 5,942 EQUALS 14 736!
THERE ARE 22 MILES OF STRING IN AN ACRE OF STRING BEANS!
WONDERFUL! YOU ARE JUST WHAT WE NEED, SONNY!
5
THE QUIZZIE KIDDIES
KID
-AND NOW, OUR FIRST QUESTION FOR OUR NEW JUNIOR GENIUS, FLOPPER!

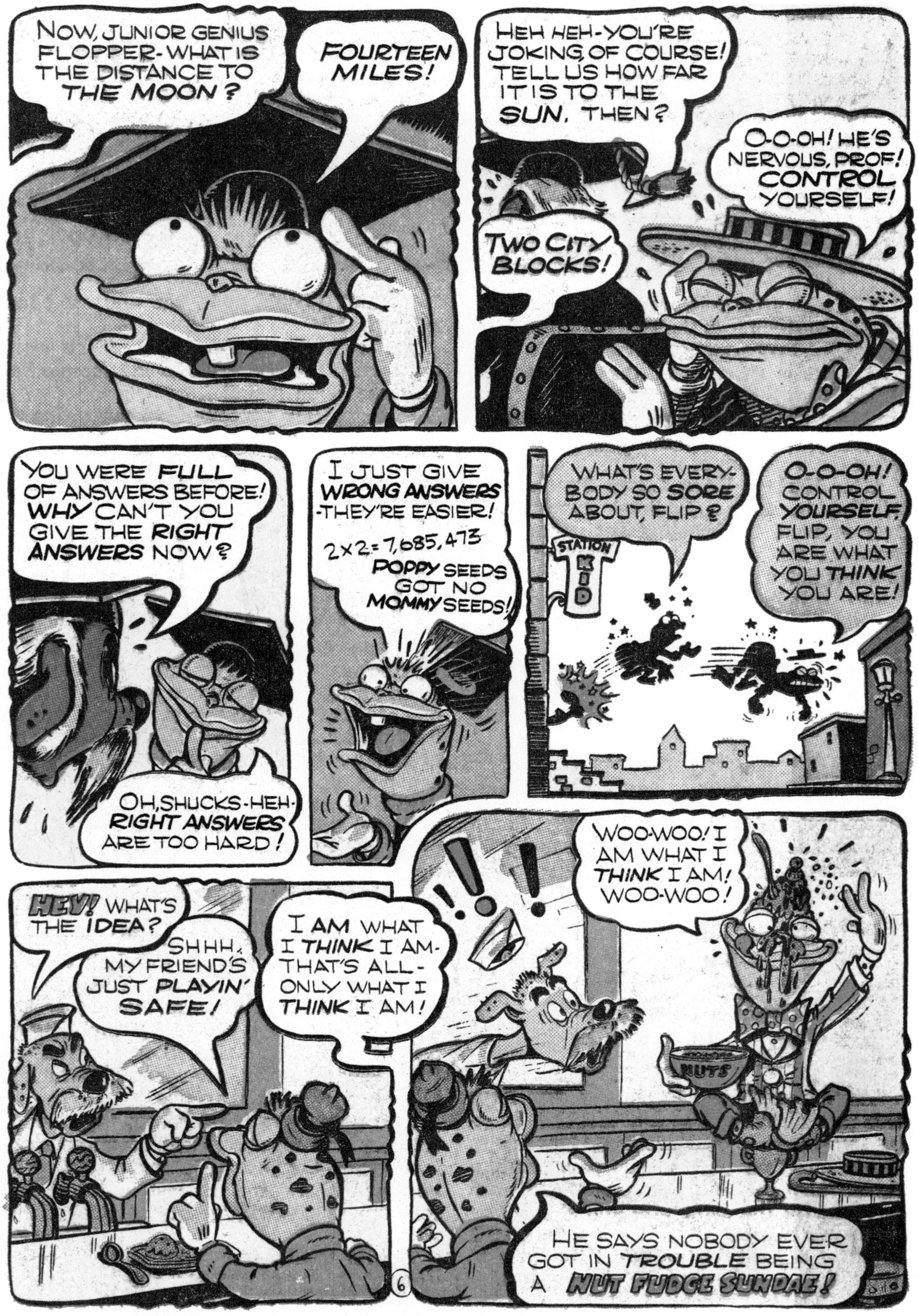
NOW, JUNIOR GENIUS FLOPPER-WHAT IS THE DISTANCE TO THE MOON?
FOURTEEN MILES!
HEH HEH-YOU'RE JOKING, OF COURSE! TELL US HOW FAR IT IS TO THE SUN, THEN?
TWO CITY BLOCKS!
O-O-OH! HE'S NERVOUS, PROF! CONTROL YOURSELF!
YOU WERE FULL OF ANSWERS BEFORE! WHY CAN'T YOU GIVE THE RIGHT ANSWERS NOW?
OH, SHUCKS-HEH-RIGHT ANSWERS ARE TOO HARD!
I JUST GIVE WRONG ANSWERS-THEY'RE EASIER!
2×2=7,685,473
POPPY SEEDS GOT NO MOMMY SEEDS!
WHAT'S EVERY-BODY SO SORE ABOUT, FLIP?
STATION KID
O-O-OH! CONTROL YOURSELF, FLIP, YOU ARE WHAT YOU THINK YOU ARE!
HEY! WHAT'S THE IDEA?
SHHH, MY FRIEND'S JUST PLAYIN' SAFE!
I AM WHAT I THINK I AM-THAT'S ALL-ONLY WHAT I THINK I AM!
WOO-WOO! I AM WHAT I THINK I AM! WOO-WOO!
NUTS
HE SAYS NOBODY EVER GOT IN TROUBLE BEING A NUT FUDGE SUNDAE!
6

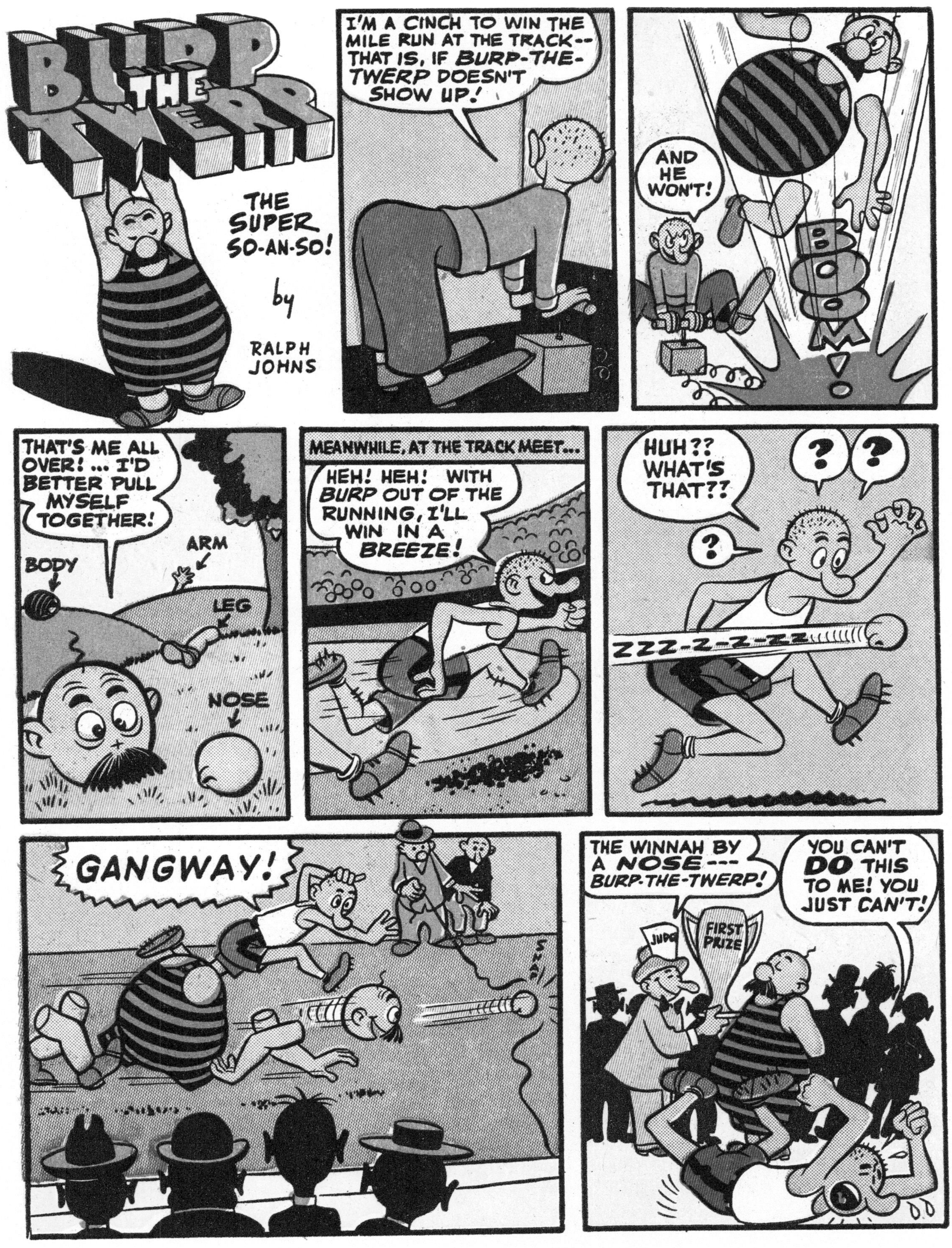
BURP THE TWERP
THE SUPER SO-AN-SO!
by
RALPH JOHNS
I'M A CINCH TO WIN THE MILE RUN AT THE TRACK-- THAT IS, IF BURP-THE-TWERP DOESN'T SHOW UP!
AND HE WON'T!
BOOM!
THAT'S ME ALL OVER! ... I'D BETTER PULL MYSELF TOGETHER!
BODY
ARM
LEG
NOSE
MEANWHILE, AT THE TRACK MEET...
HEH! HEH! WITH BURP OUT OF THE RUNNING, I'LL WIN IN A BREEZE!
HUH?? WHAT'S THAT??
?
??
ZZZ-Z-Z-Z-ZZ
GANGWAY!
THE WINNAH BY A NOSE--- BURP-THE-TWERP!
YOU CAN'T DO THIS TO ME! YOU JUST CAN'T!
FIRST PRIZE
JUDG

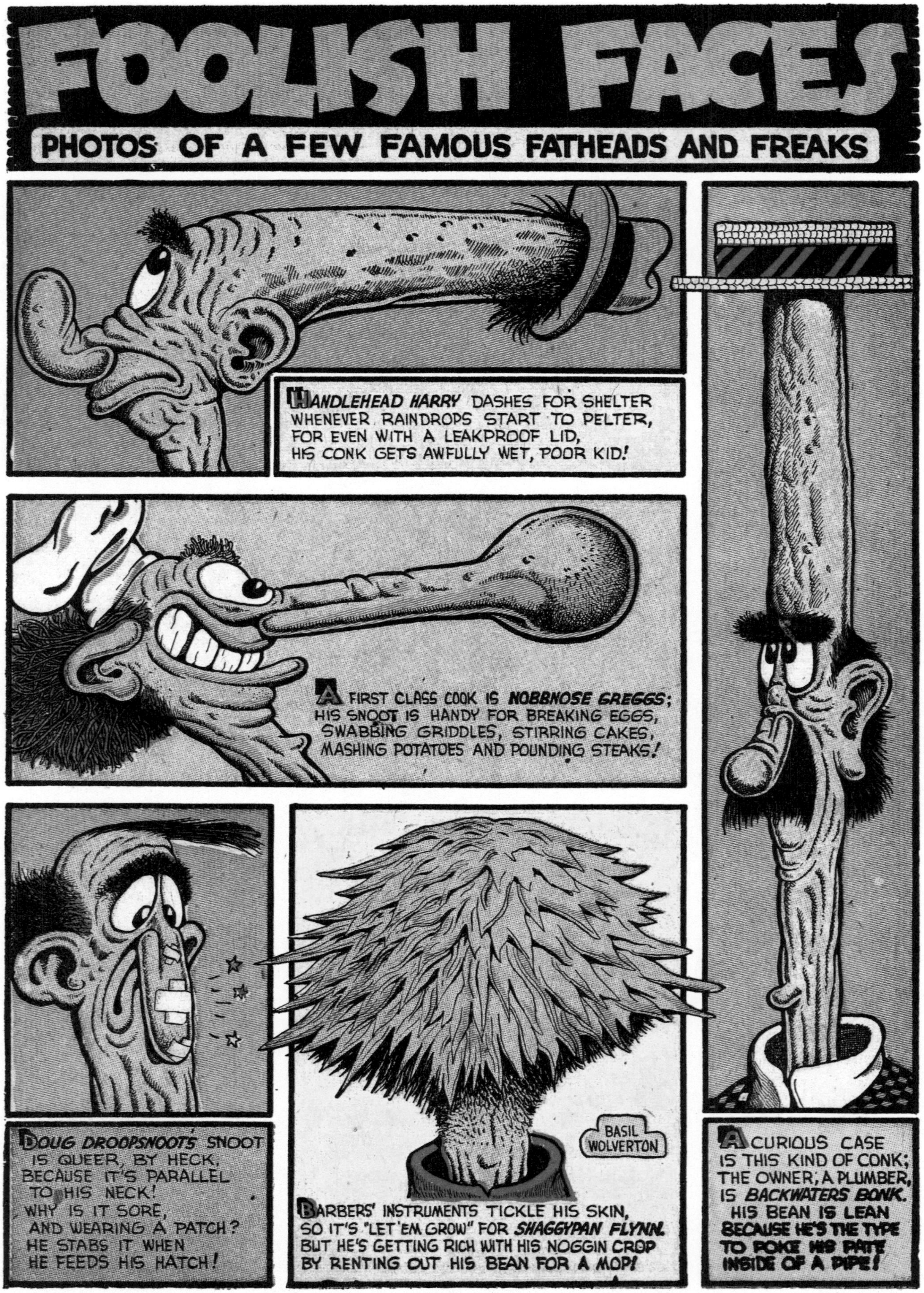
FOOLISH FACES
PHOTOS OF A FEW FAMOUS FATHEADS AND FREAKS
HANDLEHEAD HARRY DASHES FOR SHELTER
WHENEVER RAINDROPS START TO PELTER,
FOR EVEN WITH A LEAKPROOF LID,
HIS CONK GETS AWFULLY WET, POOR KID!
A FIRST CLASS COOK IS NOBBNOSE GREGGS;
HIS SNOOT IS HANDY FOR BREAKING EGGS,
SWABBING GRIDDLES, STIRRING CAKES,
MASHING POTATOES AND POUNDING STEAKS!
DOUG DROOPSNOOT'S SNOOT
IS QUEER, BY HECK,
BECAUSE IT'S PARALLEL
TO HIS NECK!
WHY IS IT SORE,
AND WEARING A PATCH?
HE STABS IT WHEN
HE FEEDS HIS HATCH!
BASIL WOLVERTON
BARBERS' INSTRUMENTS TICKLE HIS SKIN,
SO IT'S "LET 'EM GROW" FOR SHAGGYPAN FLYNN.
BUT HE'S GETTING RICH WITH HIS NOGGIN CROP
BY RENTING OUT HIS BEAN FOR A MOP!
A CURIOUS CASE
IS THIS KIND OF CONK;
THE OWNER, A PLUMBER,
IS BACKWATERS BONK.
HIS BEAN IS LEAN
BECAUSE HE'S THE TYPE
TO POKE HIS PATE
INSIDE OF A PIPE!

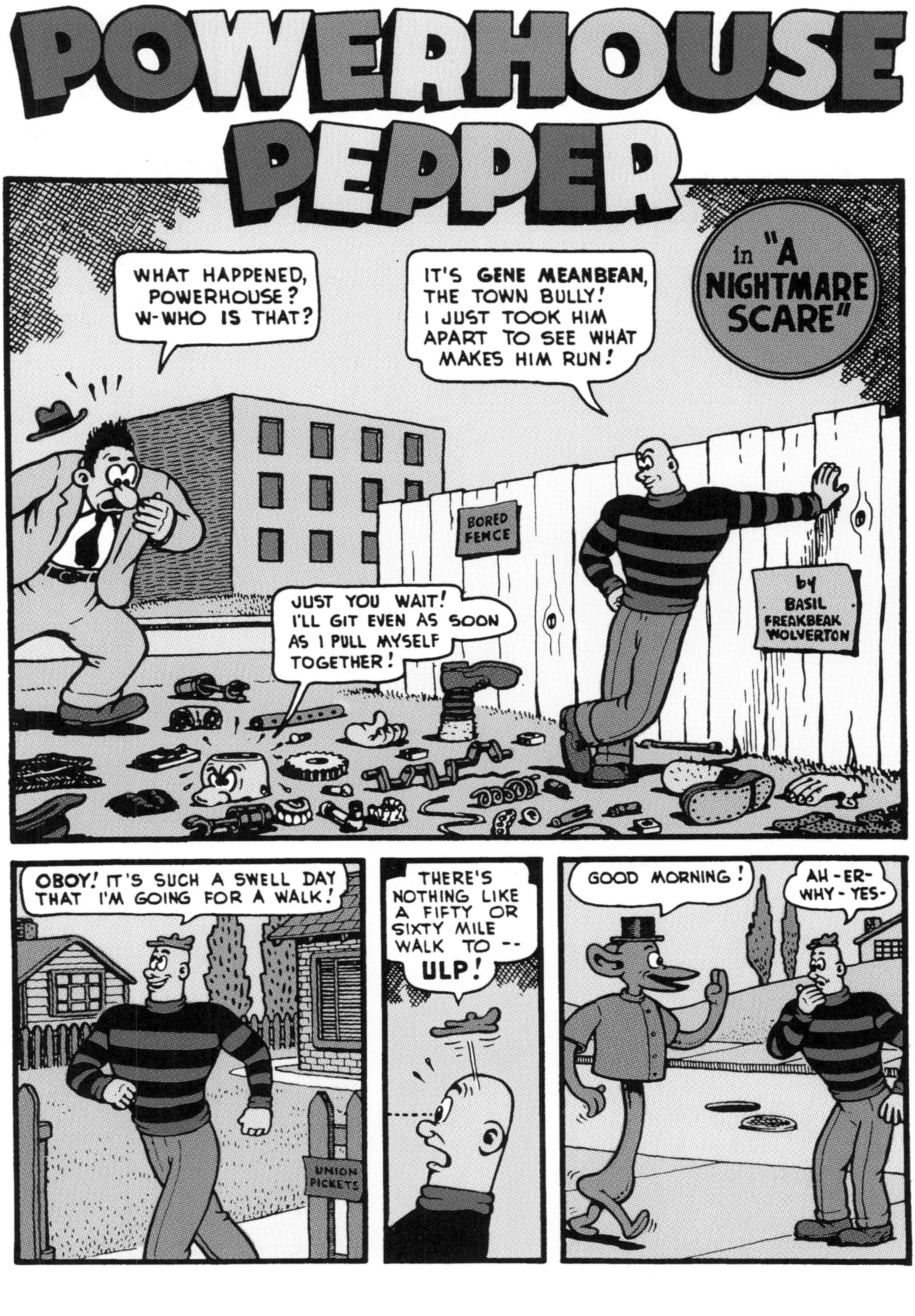
POWERHOUSE PEPPER
in "A NIGHTMARE SCARE"
WHAT HAPPENED, POWERHOUSE? W-WHO IS THAT?
IT'S GENE MEANBEAN, THE TOWN BULLY! I JUST TOOK HIM APART TO SEE WHAT MAKES HIM RUN!
BORED FENCE
by BASIL FREAKBEAK WOLVERTON
JUST YOU WAIT! I'LL GIT EVEN AS SOON AS I PULL MYSELF TOGETHER!
OBOY! IT'S SUCH A SWELL DAY THAT I'M GOING FOR A WALK!
UNION PICKETS
THERE'S NOTHING LIKE A FIFTY OR SIXTY MILE WALK TO -- ULP!
GOOD MORNING!
AH-ER-WHY-YES-

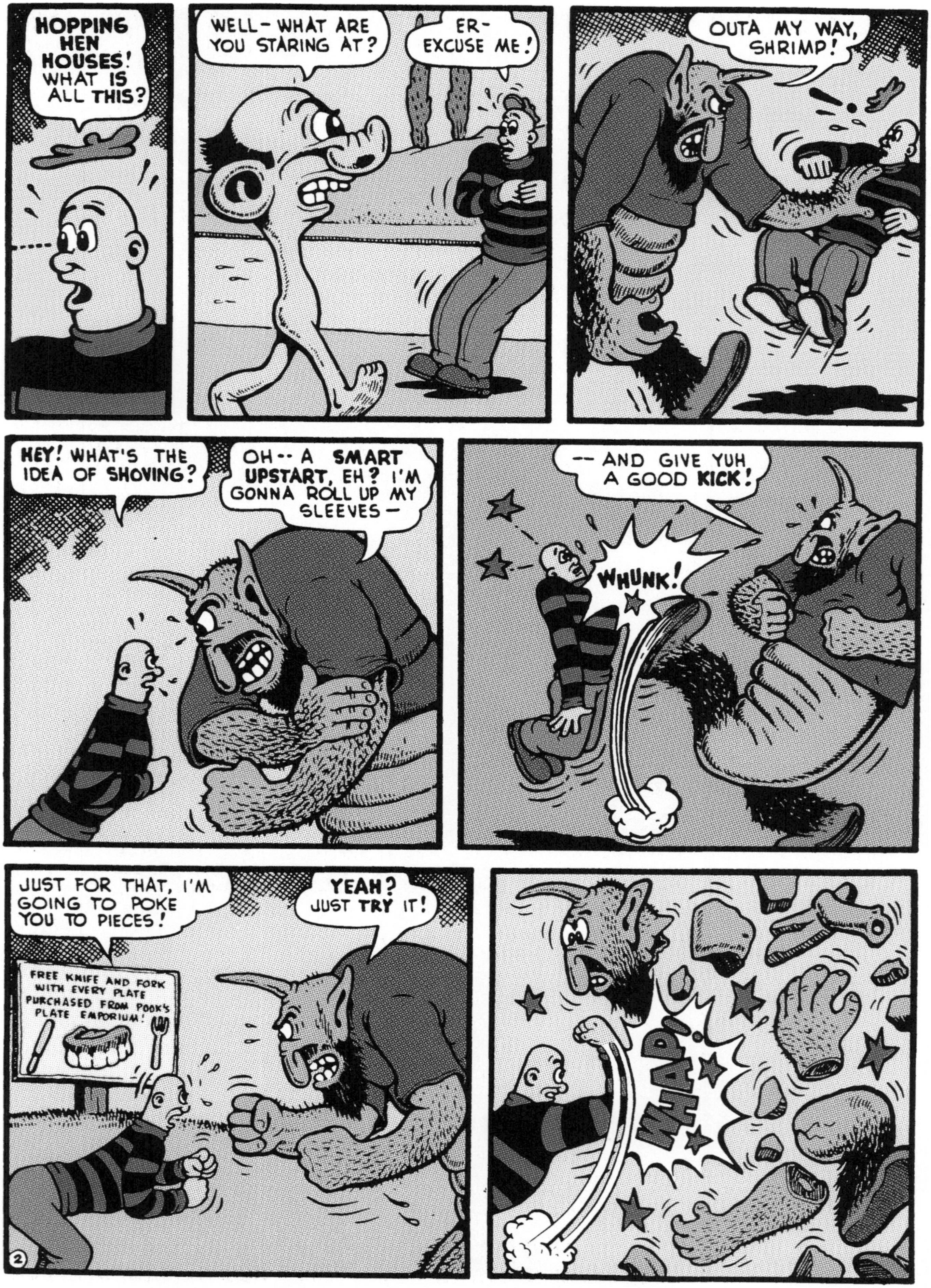
HOPPING HEN HOUSES! WHAT IS ALL THIS?
WELL- WHAT ARE YOU STARING AT?
ER- EXCUSE ME!
OUTA MY WAY, SHRIMP!
HEY! WHAT'S THE IDEA OF SHOVING?
OH-- A SMART UPSTART, EH? I'M GONNA ROLL UP MY SLEEVES -
-- AND GIVE YUH A GOOD KICK!
WHUNK!
JUST FOR THAT, I'M GOING TO POKE YOU TO PIECES!
YEAH? JUST TRY IT!
FREE KNIFE AND FORK WITH EVERY PLATE PURCHASED FROM POOK'S PLATE EMPORIUM!
2
WHAP!

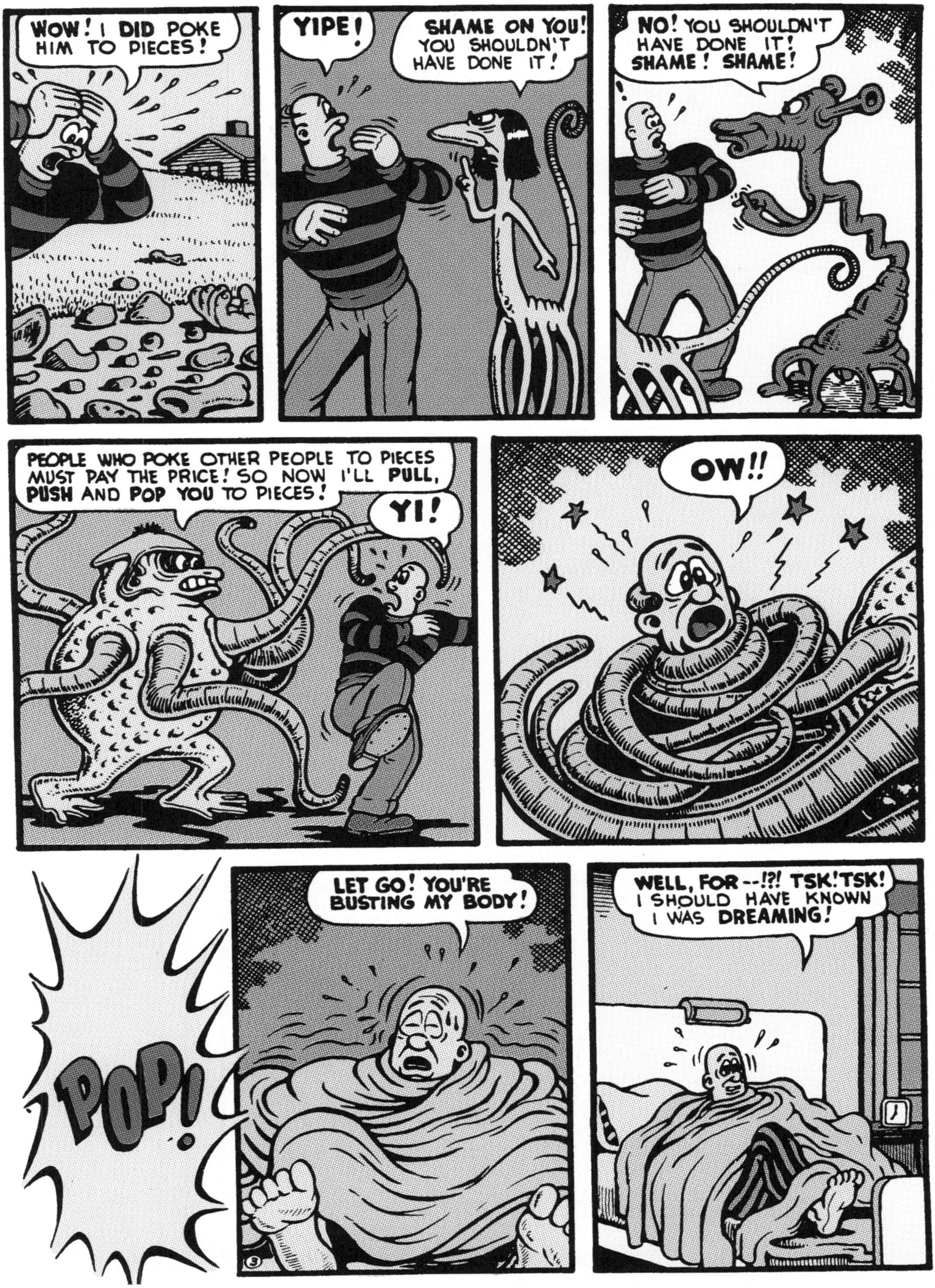
WOW! I DID POKE HIM TO PIECES!
YIPE!
SHAME ON YOU! YOU SHOULDN'T HAVE DONE IT!
NO! YOU SHOULDN'T HAVE DONE IT! SHAME! SHAME!
PEOPLE WHO POKE OTHER PEOPLE TO PIECES MUST PAY THE PRICE! SO NOW I'LL PULL, PUSH AND POP YOU TO PIECES!
YI!
OW!!
POP!
LET GO! YOU'RE BUSTING MY BODY!
WELL, FOR --!?! TSK! TSK! I SHOULD HAVE KNOWN I WAS DREAMING!

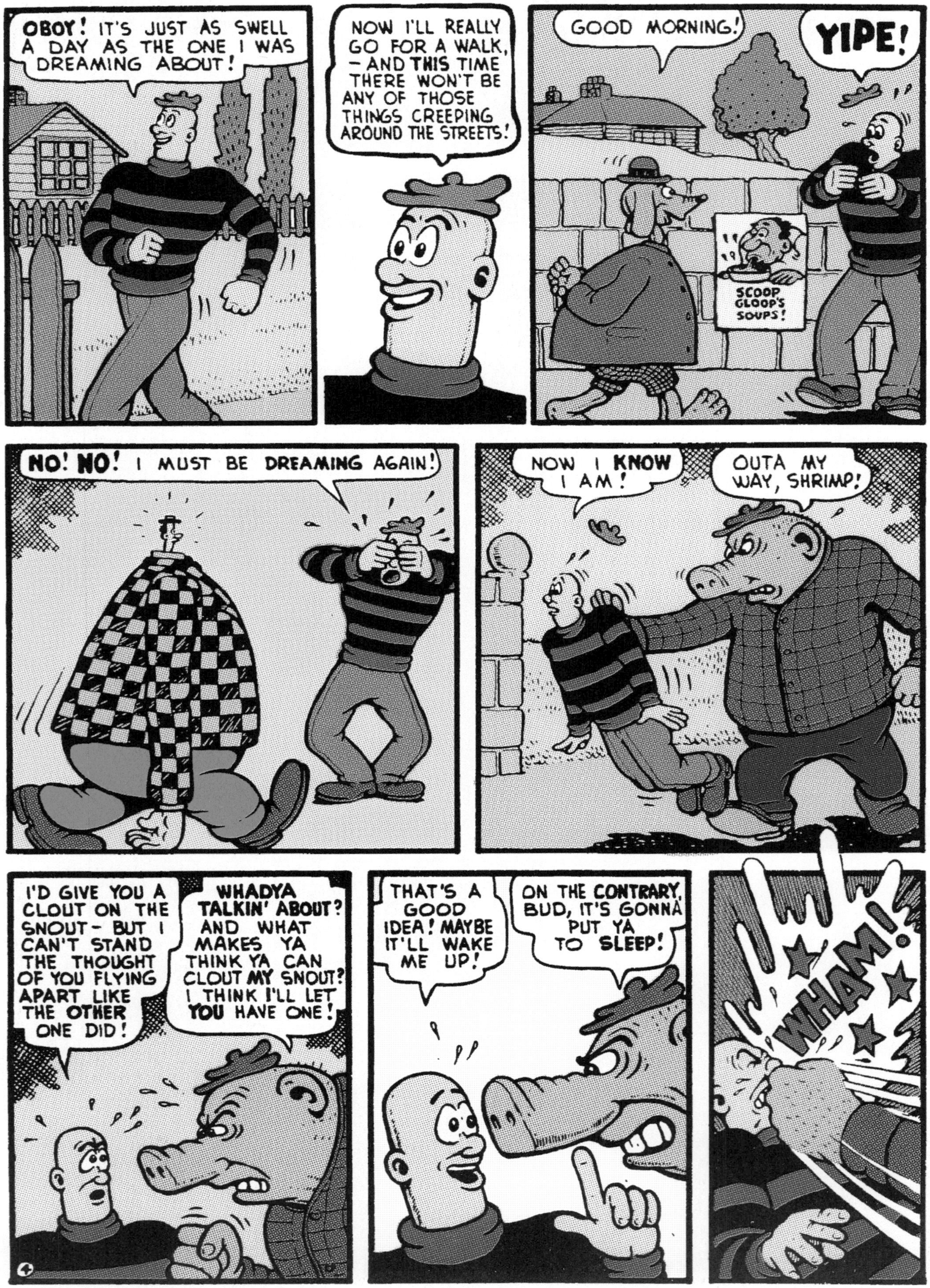
OBOY! IT'S JUST AS SWELL A DAY AS THE ONE I WAS DREAMING ABOUT!
NOW I'LL REALLY GO FOR A WALK, — AND THIS TIME THERE WON'T BE ANY OF THOSE THINGS CREEPING AROUND THE STREETS!
GOOD MORNING!
YIPE!
SCOOP GLOOP'S SOUPS!
NO! NO! I MUST BE DREAMING AGAIN!
NOW I KNOW I AM!
OUTA MY WAY, SHRIMP!
I'D GIVE YOU A CLOUT ON THE SNOUT - BUT I CAN'T STAND THE THOUGHT OF YOU FLYING APART LIKE THE OTHER ONE DID!
WHADYA TALKIN' ABOUT? AND WHAT MAKES YA THINK YA CAN CLOUT MY SNOUT? I THINK I'LL LET YOU HAVE ONE!
THAT'S A GOOD IDEA! MAYBE IT'LL WAKE ME UP!
ON THE CONTRARY, BUD, IT'S GONNA PUT YA TO SLEEP!
WHAM!

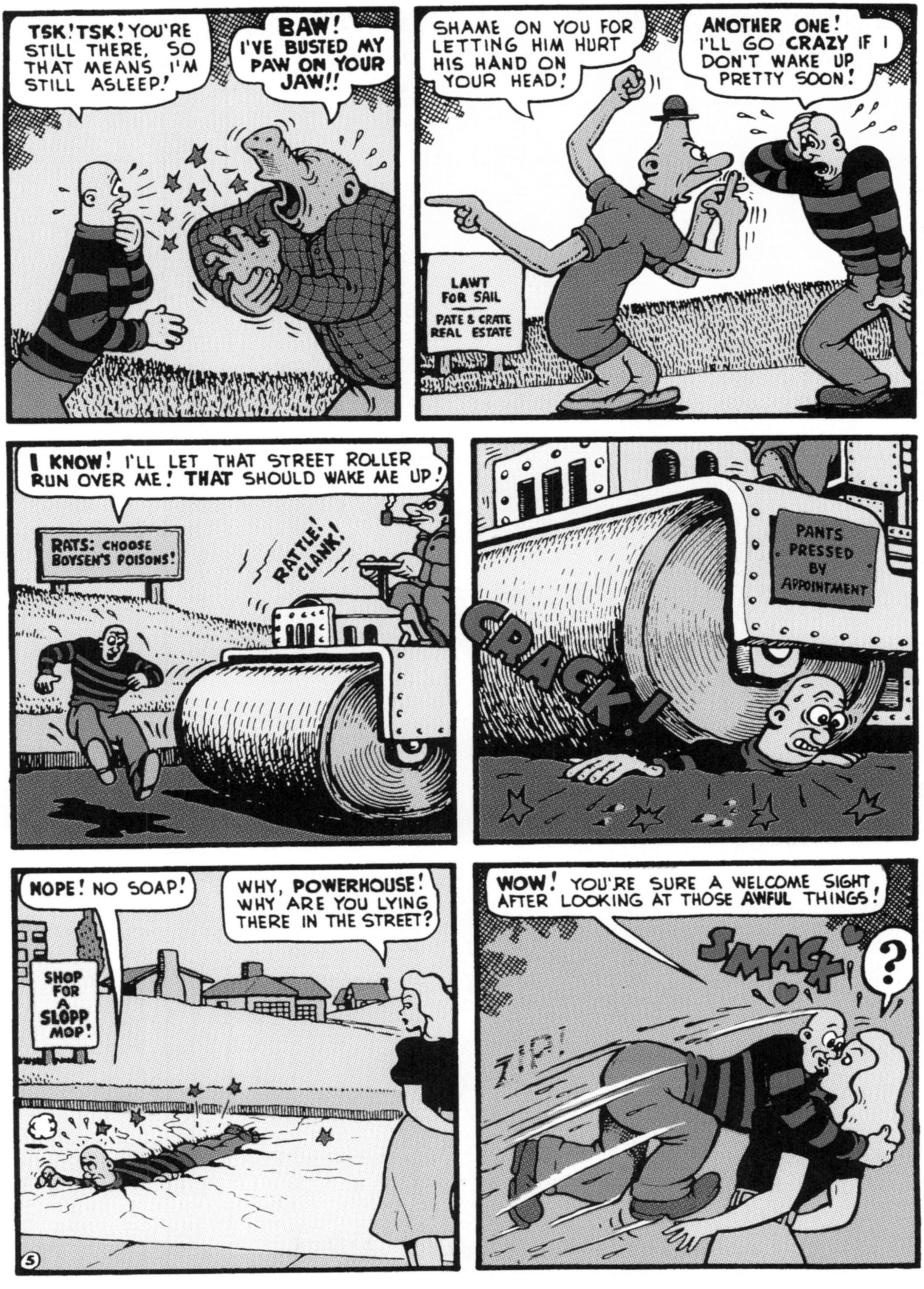
TSK! TSK! YOU'RE STILL THERE, SO THAT MEANS I'M STILL ASLEEP!
BAW! I'VE BUSTED MY PAW ON YOUR JAW!!
SHAME ON YOU FOR LETTING HIM HURT HIS HAND ON YOUR HEAD!
ANOTHER ONE! I'LL GO CRAZY IF I DON'T WAKE UP PRETTY SOON!
LAWT FOR SAIL
PATE & CRATE REAL ESTATE
I KNOW! I'LL LET THAT STREET ROLLER RUN OVER ME! THAT SHOULD WAKE ME UP!
RATS: CHOOSE BOYSEN'S POISONS!
RATTLE! CLANK!
PANTS PRESSED BY APPOINTMENT
CRACK!
NOPE! NO SOAP!
WHY, POWERHOUSE! WHY ARE YOU LYING THERE IN THE STREET?
SHOP FOR A SLOPP MOP!
5
WOW! YOU'RE SURE A WELCOME SIGHT AFTER LOOKING AT THOSE AWFUL THINGS!
SMACK
?
ZIP!

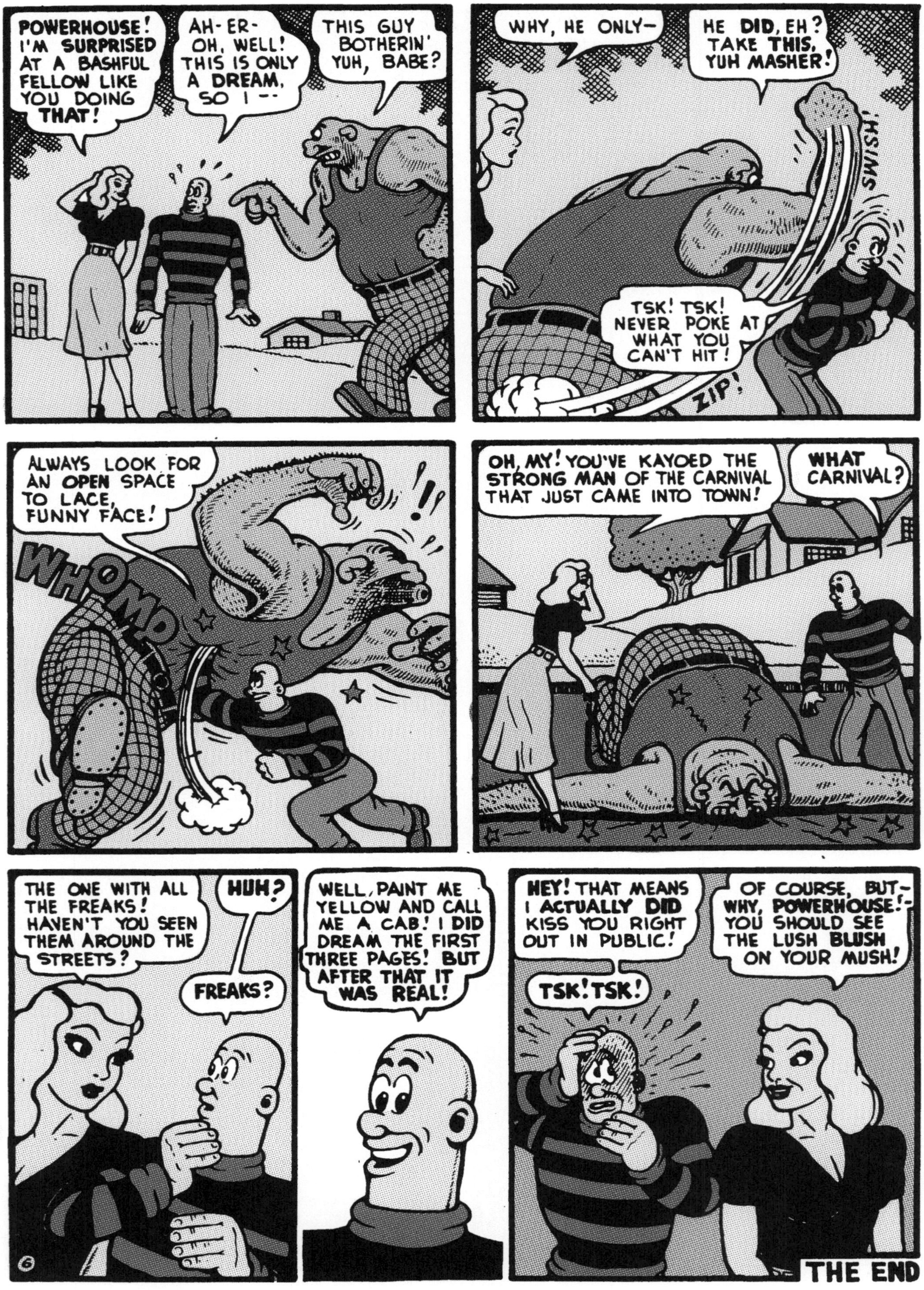
POWERHOUSE! I'M SURPRISED AT A BASHFUL FELLOW LIKE YOU DOING THAT!
AH-ER-OH, WELL! THIS IS ONLY A DREAM, SO I --
THIS GUY BOTHERIN' YUH, BABE?
WHY, HE ONLY—
HE DID, EH? TAKE THIS, YUH MASHER!
SWISH!
TSK! TSK! NEVER POKE AT WHAT YOU CAN'T HIT!
ZIP!
ALWAYS LOOK FOR AN OPEN SPACE TO LACE, FUNNY FACE!
WHOMP
OH, MY! YOU'VE KAYOED THE STRONG MAN OF THE CARNIVAL THAT JUST CAME INTO TOWN!
WHAT CARNIVAL?
THE ONE WITH ALL THE FREAKS! HAVEN'T YOU SEEN THEM AROUND THE STREETS?
HUH?
FREAKS?
WELL, PAINT ME YELLOW AND CALL ME A CAB! I DID DREAM THE FIRST THREE PAGES! BUT AFTER THAT IT WAS REAL!
HEY! THAT MEANS I ACTUALLY DID KISS YOU RIGHT OUT IN PUBLIC!
OF COURSE, BUT—WHY, POWERHOUSE!—YOU SHOULD SEE THE LUSH BLUSH ON YOUR MUSH!
TSK! TSK!
6
THE END

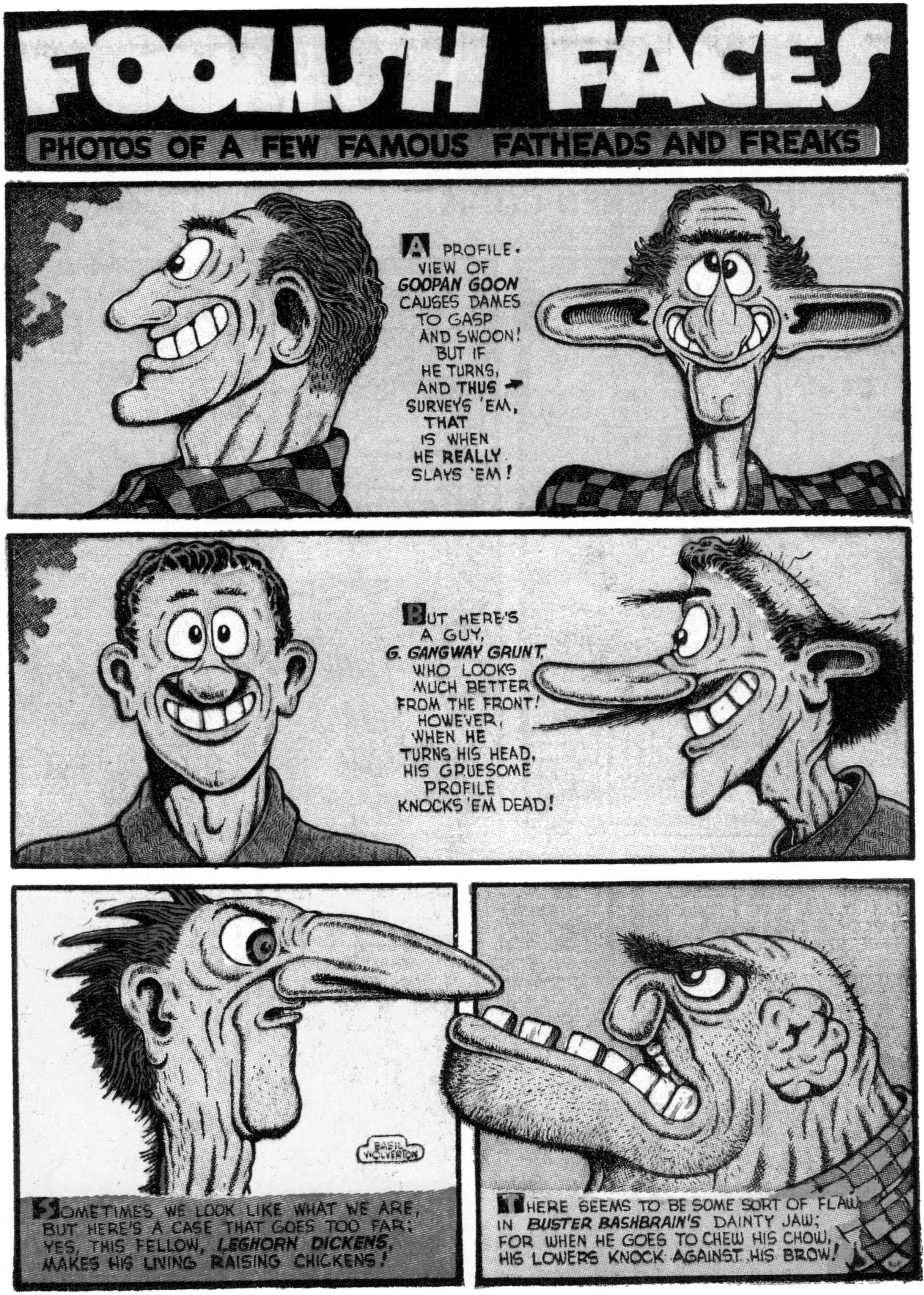
FOOLISH FACES
PHOTOS OF A FEW FAMOUS FATHEADS AND FREAKS
A PROFILE VIEW OF GOOPAN GOON CAUSES DAMES TO GASP AND SWOON! BUT IF HE TURNS, AND THUS SURVEYS 'EM, THAT IS WHEN HE REALLY SLAYS 'EM!
BUT HERE'S A GUY, G. GANGWAY GRUNT, WHO LOOKS MUCH BETTER FROM THE FRONT! HOWEVER, WHEN HE TURNS HIS HEAD, HIS GRUESOME PROFILE KNOCKS 'EM DEAD!
BASIL WOLVERTON
SOMETIMES WE LOOK LIKE WHAT WE ARE, BUT HERE'S A CASE THAT GOES TOO FAR; YES, THIS FELLOW, LEGHORN DICKENS, MAKES HIS LIVING RAISING CHICKENS!
THERE SEEMS TO BE SOME SORT OF FLAW IN BUSTER BASHBRAIN'S DAINTY JAW; FOR WHEN HE GOES TO CHEW HIS CHOW, HIS LOWERS KNOCK AGAINST HIS BROW!

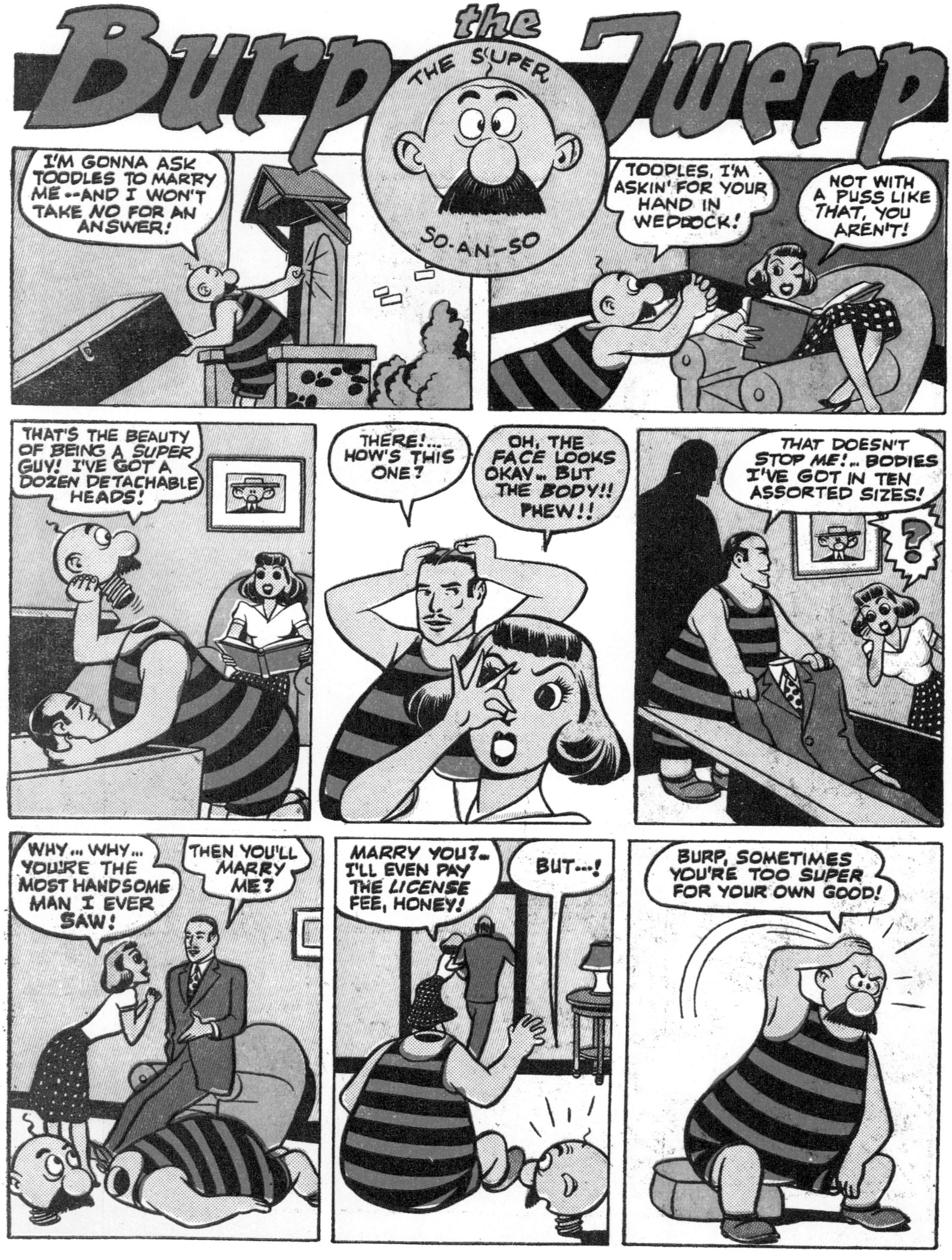
Burp the Twerp
THE SUPER SO-AN-SO
I'M GONNA ASK TOODLES TO MARRY ME --AND I WON'T TAKE NO FOR AN ANSWER!
TOODLES, I'M ASKIN' FOR YOUR HAND IN WEDLOCK!
NOT WITH A PUSS LIKE THAT, YOU AREN'T!
THAT'S THE BEAUTY OF BEING A SUPER GUY! I'VE GOT A DOZEN DETACHABLE HEADS!
THERE!... HOW'S THIS ONE?
OH, THE FACE LOOKS OKAY.. BUT THE BODY!! PHEW!!
THAT DOESN'T STOP ME!.. BODIES I'VE GOT IN TEN ASSORTED SIZES!
?
WHY... WHY... YOU'RE THE MOST HANDSOME MAN I EVER SAW!
THEN YOU'LL MARRY ME?
MARRY YOU?.. I'LL EVEN PAY THE LICENSE FEE, HONEY!
BUT...!
BURP, SOMETIMES YOU'RE TOO SUPER FOR YOUR OWN GOOD!

Melvin MONSTER

MICE BUSINESS

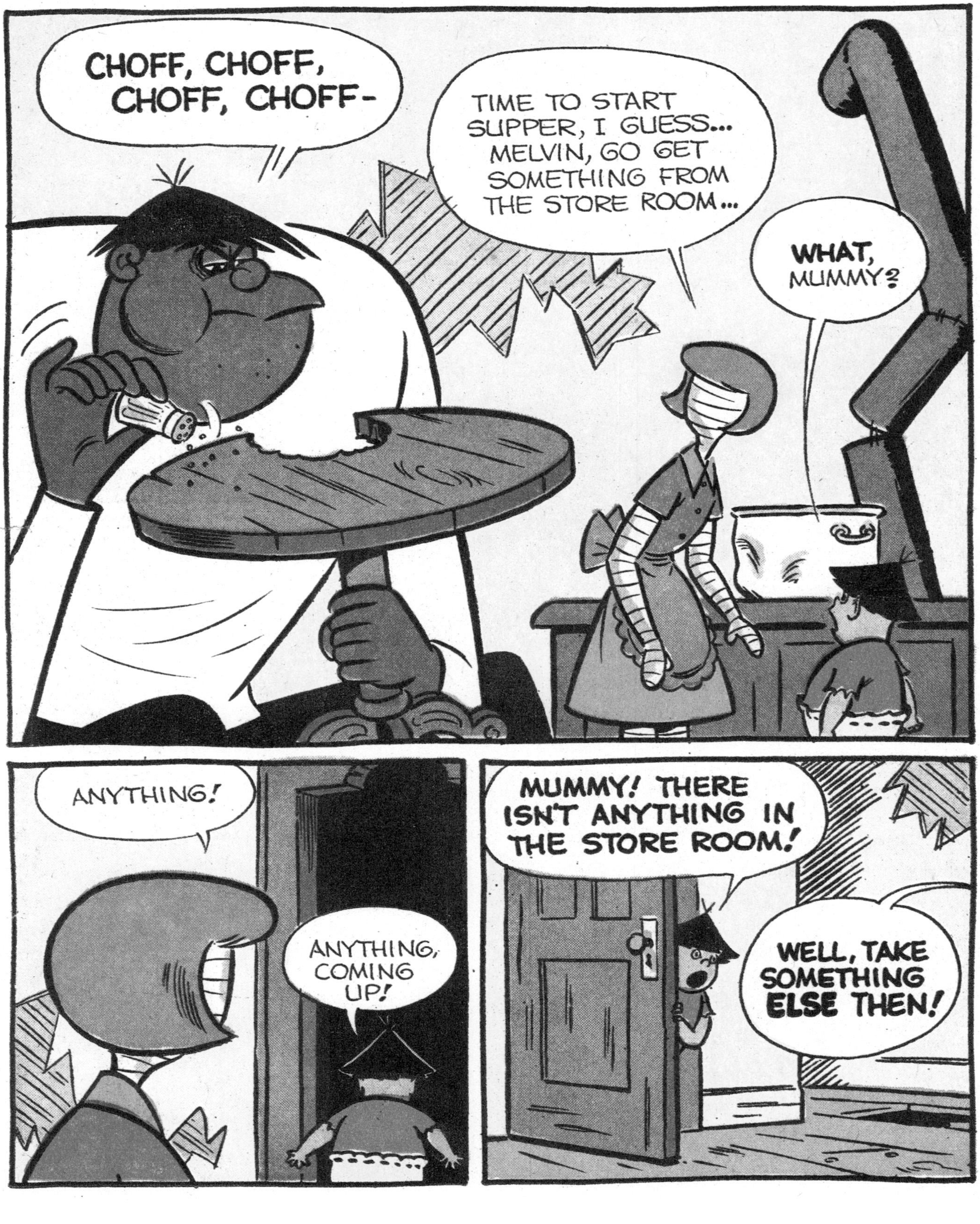
CHOFF, CHOFF, CHOFF, CHOFF-
TIME TO START SUPPER, I GUESS... MELVIN, GO GET SOMETHING FROM THE STORE ROOM...
WHAT, MUMMY?
ANYTHING!
ANYTHING, COMING UP!
MUMMY! THERE ISN'T ANYTHING IN THE STORE ROOM!
WELL, TAKE SOMETHING ELSE THEN!

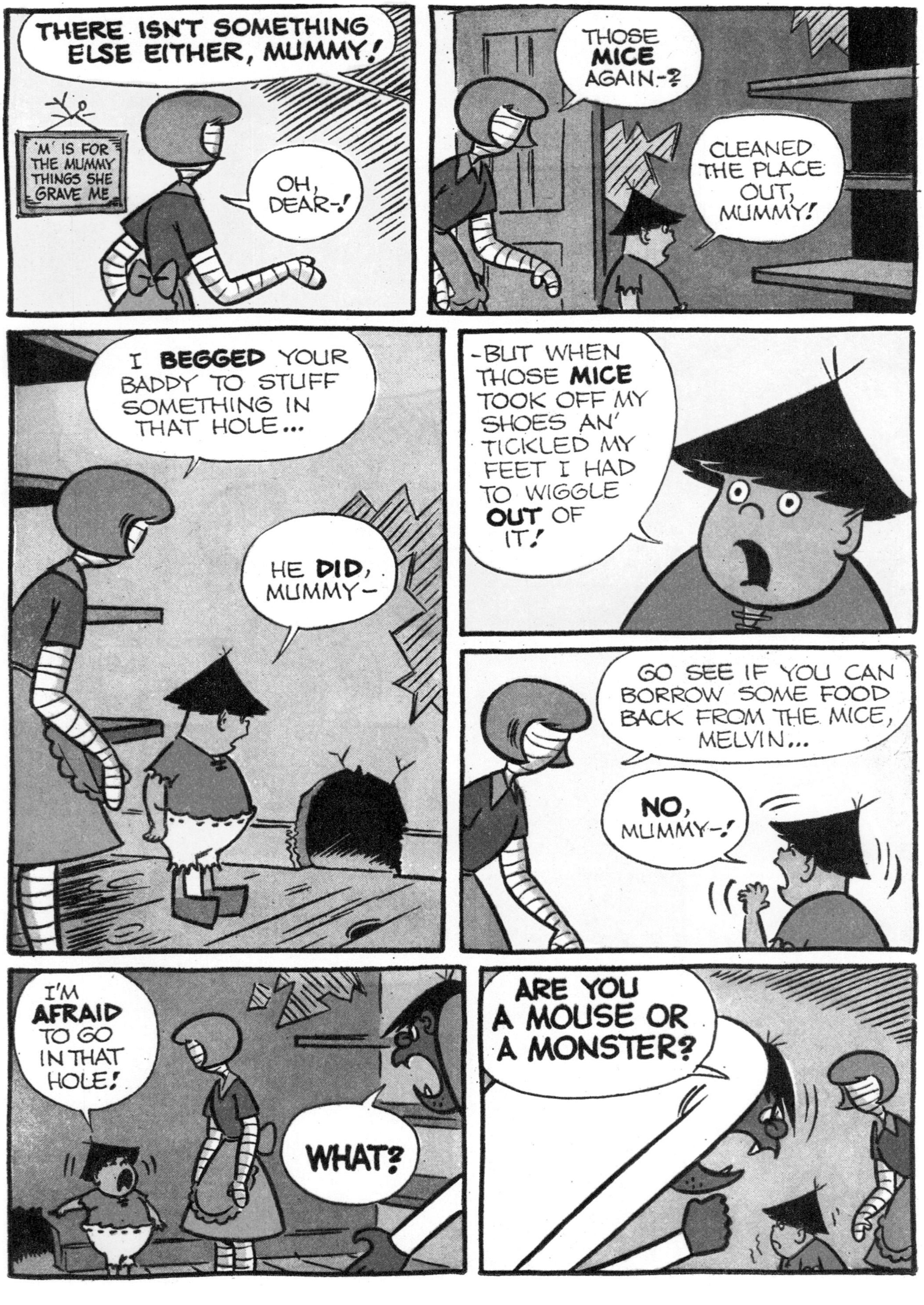
THERE ISN'T SOMETHING ELSE EITHER, MUMMY!
'M' IS FOR THE MUMMY THINGS SHE GRAVE ME
OH, DEAR-!
THOSE MICE AGAIN-?
CLEANED THE PLACE OUT, MUMMY!
I BEGGED YOUR BADDY TO STUFF SOMETHING IN THAT HOLE...
HE DID, MUMMY-
-BUT WHEN THOSE MICE TOOK OFF MY SHOES AN' TICKLED MY FEET I HAD TO WIGGLE OUT OF IT!
GO SEE IF YOU CAN BORROW SOME FOOD BACK FROM THE MICE, MELVIN...
NO, MUMMY-!
I'M AFRAID TO GO IN THAT HOLE!
WHAT?
ARE YOU A MOUSE OR A MONSTER?

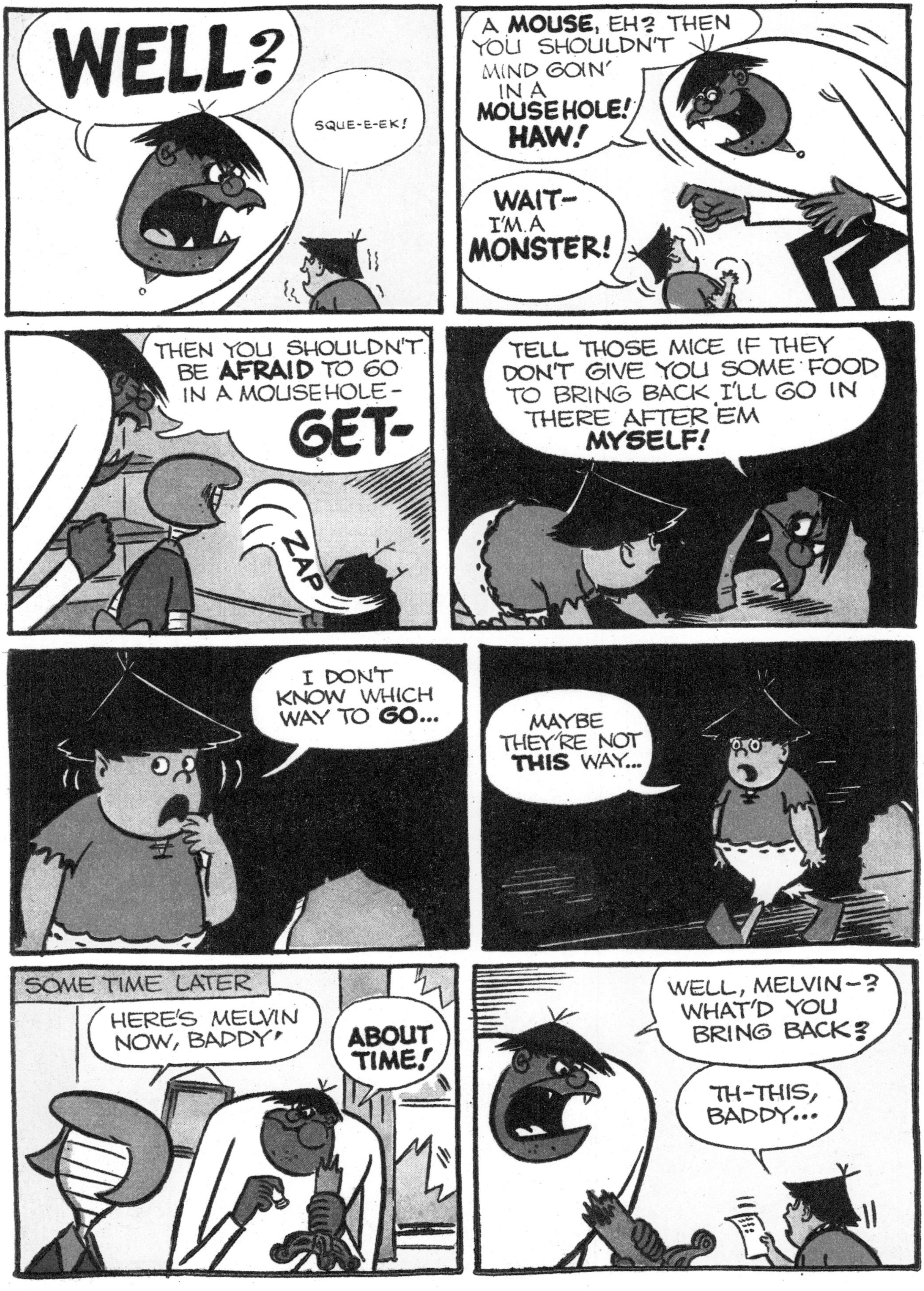
WELL?
SQUE-E-EK!
A MOUSE, EH? THEN YOU SHOULDN'T MIND GOIN' IN A MOUSEHOLE! HAW!
WAIT- I'M A MONSTER!
THEN YOU SHOULDN'T BE AFRAID TO GO IN A MOUSEHOLE- GET-
ZAP
TELL THOSE MICE IF THEY DON'T GIVE YOU SOME FOOD TO BRING BACK I'LL GO IN THERE AFTER 'EM MYSELF!
I DON'T KNOW WHICH WAY TO GO...
MAYBE THEY'RE NOT THIS WAY...
SOME TIME LATER
HERE'S MELVIN NOW, BADDY!
ABOUT TIME!
WELL, MELVIN-? WHAT'D YOU BRING BACK?
TH-THIS, BADDY...

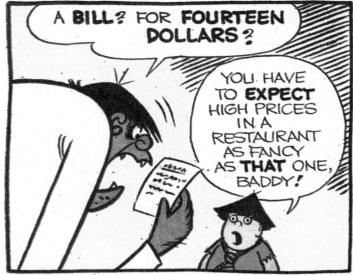

A **BILL?** FOR **FOURTEEN** DOLLARS?

YOU HAVE TO **EXPECT** HIGH PRICES IN A RESTAURANT AS FANCY AS **THAT** ONE, BADDY!

THE **CHEF** IS A **FRENCH** MOUSE!

ROAR!

THOSE MISERABLE MICE STEAL ALL OUR FOOD, OPEN A RESTAURANT WITH IT—

—AND THEN CHARGE YOU FOURTEEN BUCKS FOR EATING THERE

IT WOULD'VE COST A **LOT MORE** IF I **ATE** THERE, BADDY!

I ONLY STUCK MY HEAD IN THE DOOR AND TOOK A **DEEP BREATH.!..**

FOURTEEN DOLLARS FOR **THAT**?

ROAR!

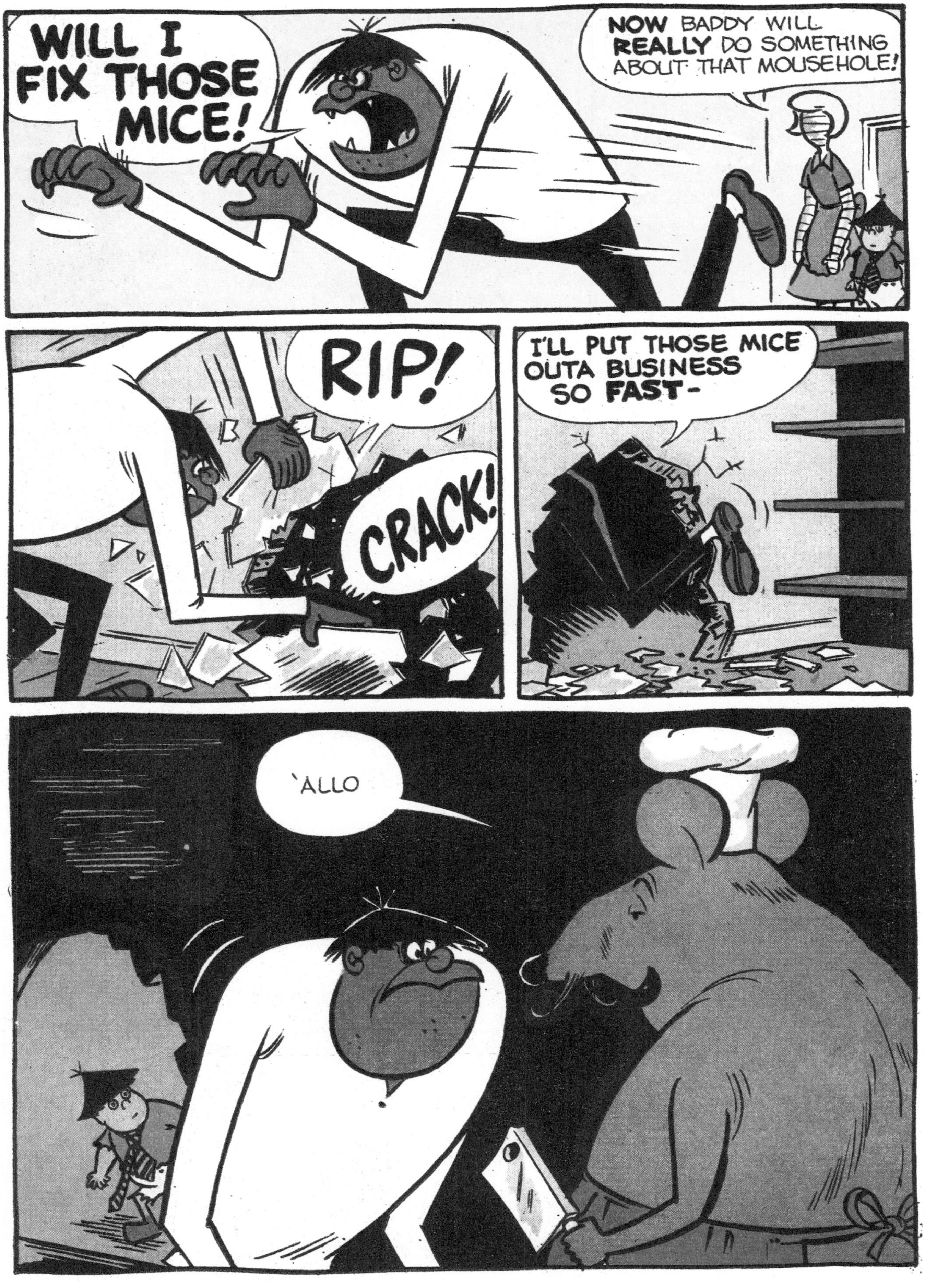
WILL I FIX THOSE MICE!
NOW BADDY WILL REALLY DO SOMETHING ABOUT THAT MOUSEHOLE!
RIP!
CRACK!
I'LL PUT THOSE MICE OUTA BUSINESS SO FAST-
`ALLO

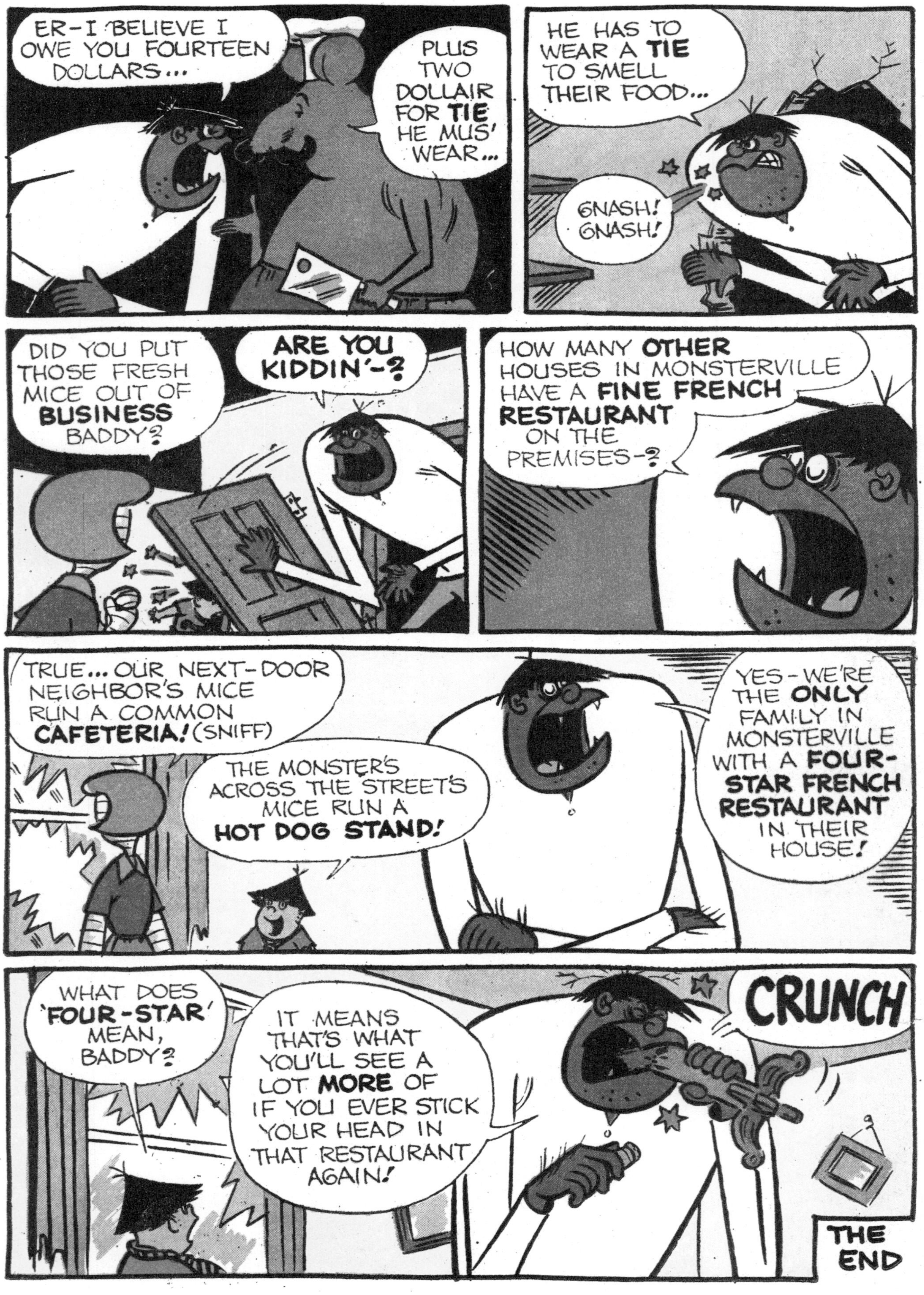
ER–I BELIEVE I OWE YOU FOURTEEN DOLLARS...
PLUS TWO DOLLAIR FOR TIE HE MUS' WEAR...
HE HAS TO WEAR A TIE TO SMELL THEIR FOOD...
GNASH! GNASH!
DID YOU PUT THOSE FRESH MICE OUT OF BUSINESS BADDY?
ARE YOU KIDDIN'–?
HOW MANY OTHER HOUSES IN MONSTERVILLE HAVE A FINE FRENCH RESTAURANT ON THE PREMISES–?
TRUE... OUR NEXT-DOOR NEIGHBOR'S MICE RUN A COMMON CAFETERIA! (SNIFF)
THE MONSTER'S ACROSS THE STREET'S MICE RUN A HOT DOG STAND!
YES–WE'RE THE ONLY FAMILY IN MONSTERVILLE WITH A FOUR-STAR FRENCH RESTAURANT IN THEIR HOUSE!
WHAT DOES 'FOUR-STAR' MEAN, BADDY?
IT MEANS THAT'S WHAT YOU'LL SEE A LOT MORE OF IF YOU EVER STICK YOUR HEAD IN THAT RESTAURANT AGAIN!
CRUNCH
THE END

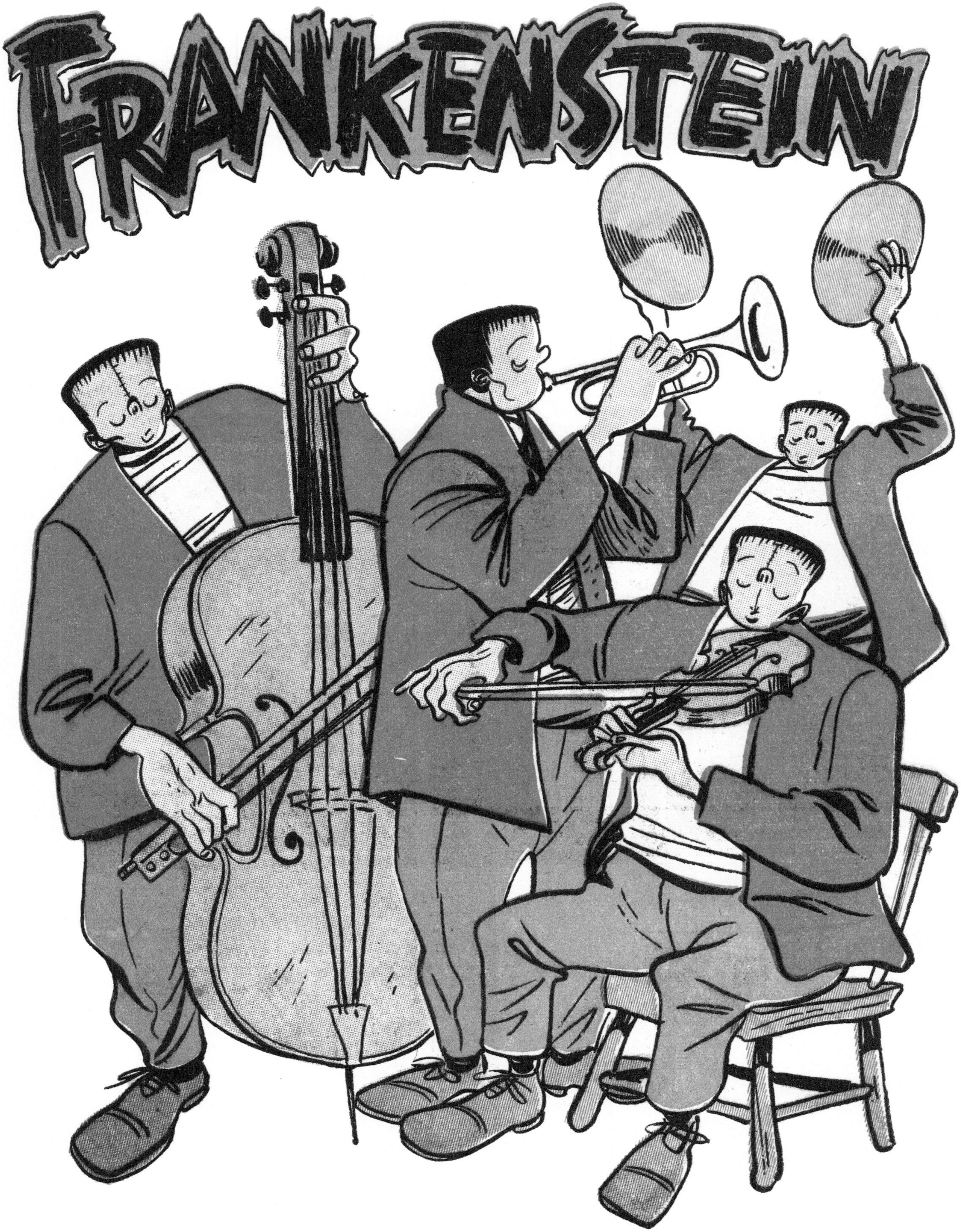
FRANKENSTEIN

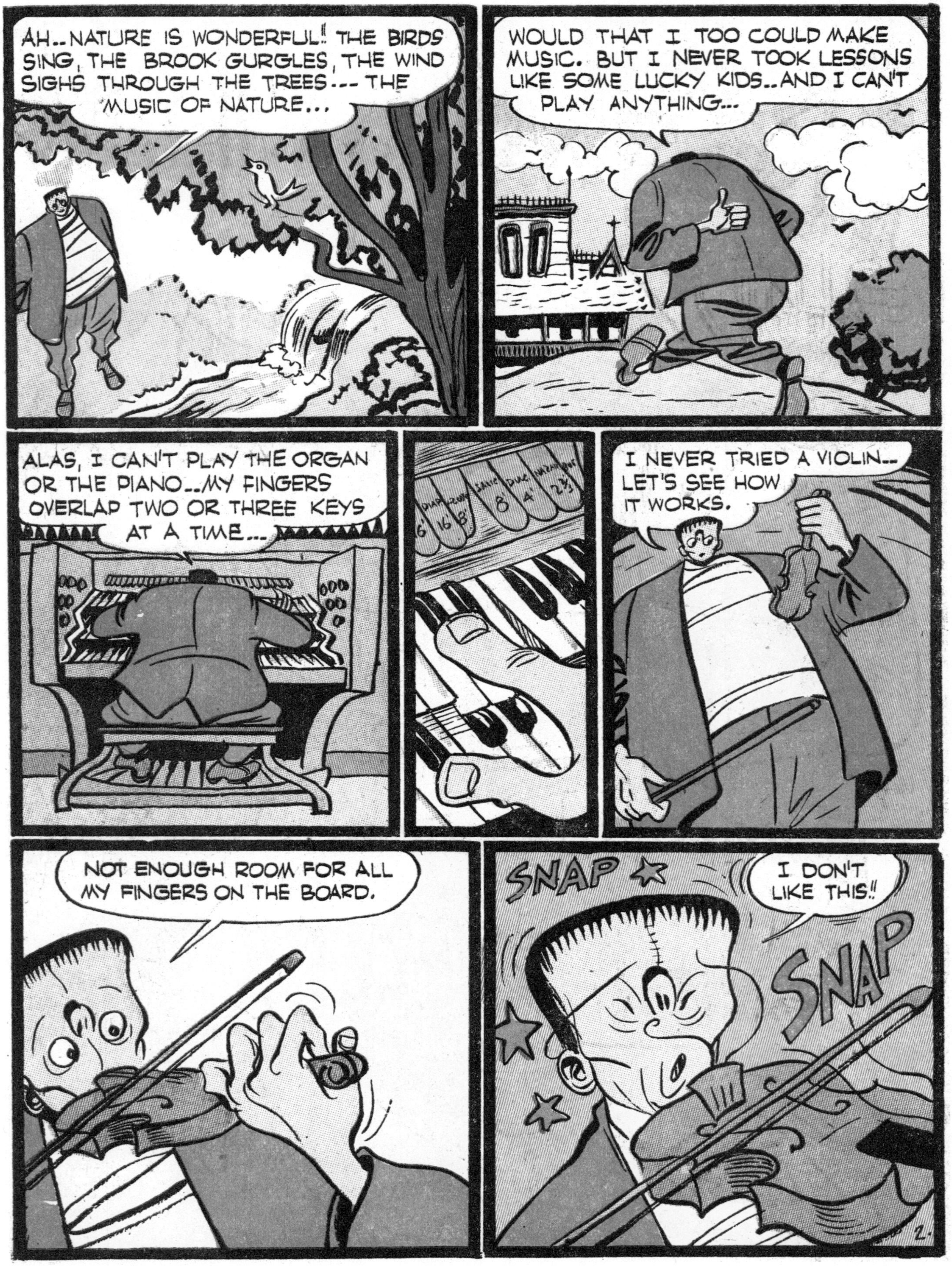
AH..NATURE IS WONDERFUL!! THE BIRDS SING, THE BROOK GURGLES, THE WIND SIGHS THROUGH THE TREES--- THE MUSIC OF NATURE...
WOULD THAT I TOO COULD MAKE MUSIC. BUT I NEVER TOOK LESSONS LIKE SOME LUCKY KIDS..AND I CAN'T PLAY ANYTHING...
ALAS, I CAN'T PLAY THE ORGAN OR THE PIANO...MY FINGERS OVERLAP TWO OR THREE KEYS AT A TIME...
I NEVER TRIED A VIOLIN.. LET'S SEE HOW IT WORKS.
NOT ENOUGH ROOM FOR ALL MY FINGERS ON THE BOARD.
SNAP
I DON'T LIKE THIS!!
SNAP

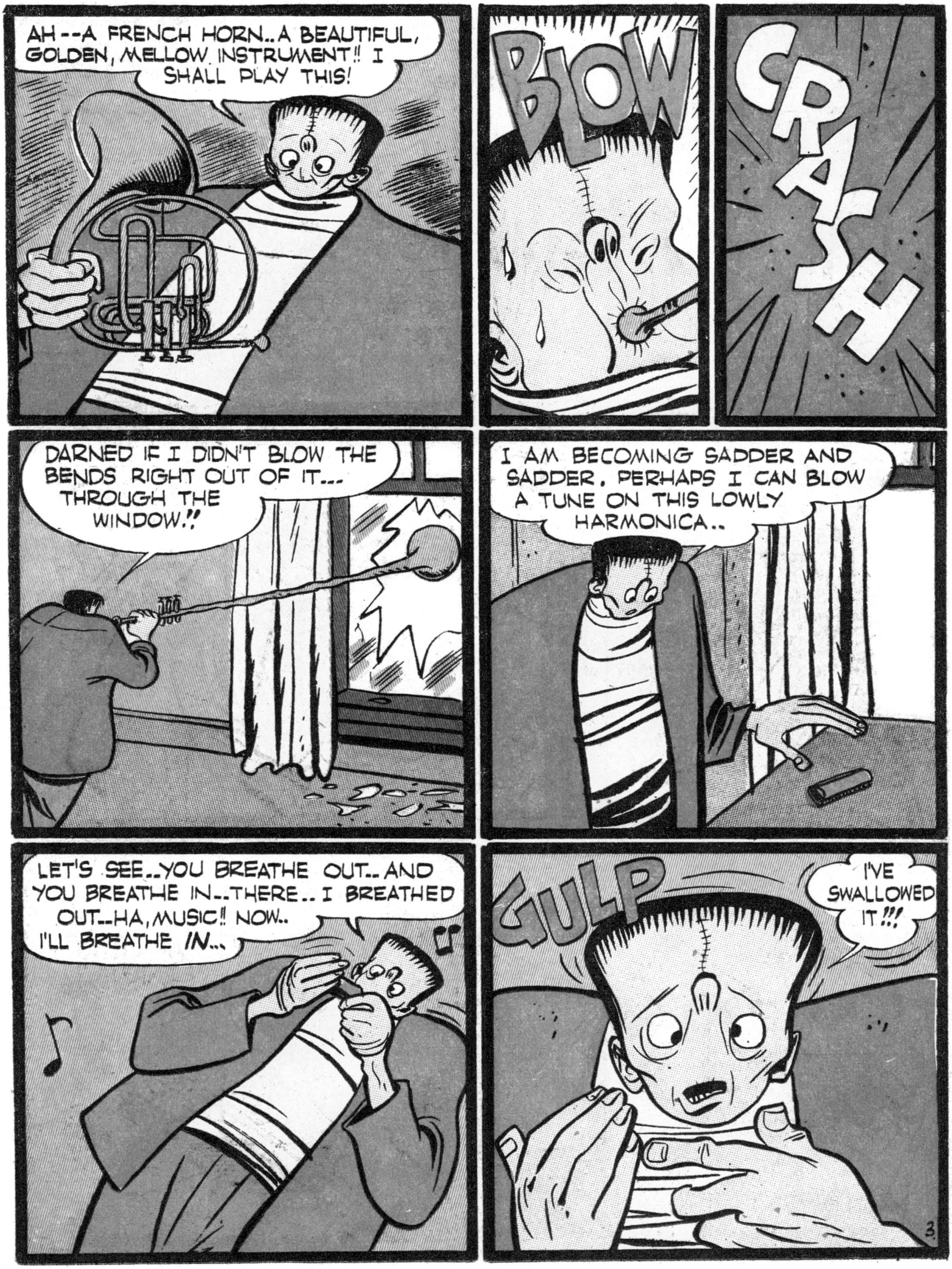
AH--A FRENCH HORN..A BEAUTIFUL, GOLDEN, MELLOW INSTRUMENT!! I SHALL PLAY THIS!
BLOW
CRASH
DARNED IF I DIDN'T BLOW THE BENDS RIGHT OUT OF IT... THROUGH THE WINDOW.!!
I AM BECOMING SADDER AND SADDER. PERHAPS I CAN BLOW A TUNE ON THIS LOWLY HARMONICA..
LET'S SEE..YOU BREATHE OUT..AND YOU BREATHE IN..THERE..I BREATHED OUT..HA, MUSIC!! NOW.. I'LL BREATHE IN...
GULP
I'VE SWALLOWED IT!!!
3.

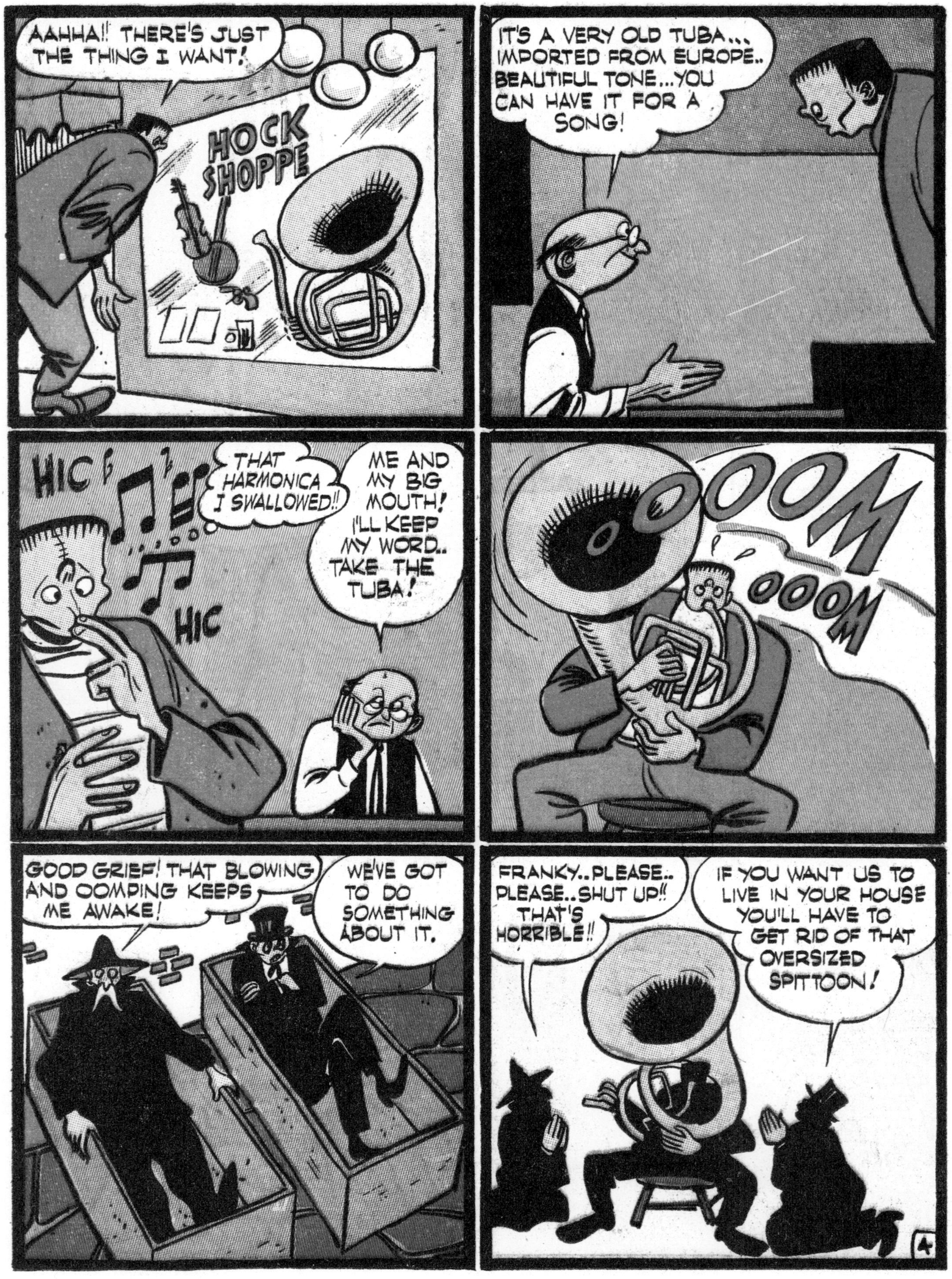
AAHHA!! THERE'S JUST THE THING I WANT!
HOCK SHOPPE
IT'S A VERY OLD TUBA... IMPORTED FROM EUROPE.. BEAUTIFUL TONE...YOU CAN HAVE IT FOR A SONG!
HIC
HIC
THAT HARMONICA I SWALLOWED!!
ME AND MY BIG MOUTH! I'LL KEEP MY WORD.. TAKE THE TUBA!
OOOOM
OOOM
GOOD GRIEF! THAT BLOWING AND OOMPING KEEPS ME AWAKE!
WE'VE GOT TO DO SOMETHING ABOUT IT.
FRANKY..PLEASE.. PLEASE..SHUT UP!! THAT'S HORRIBLE!!
IF YOU WANT US TO LIVE IN YOUR HOUSE YOU'LL HAVE TO GET RID OF THAT OVERSIZED SPITTOON!
4

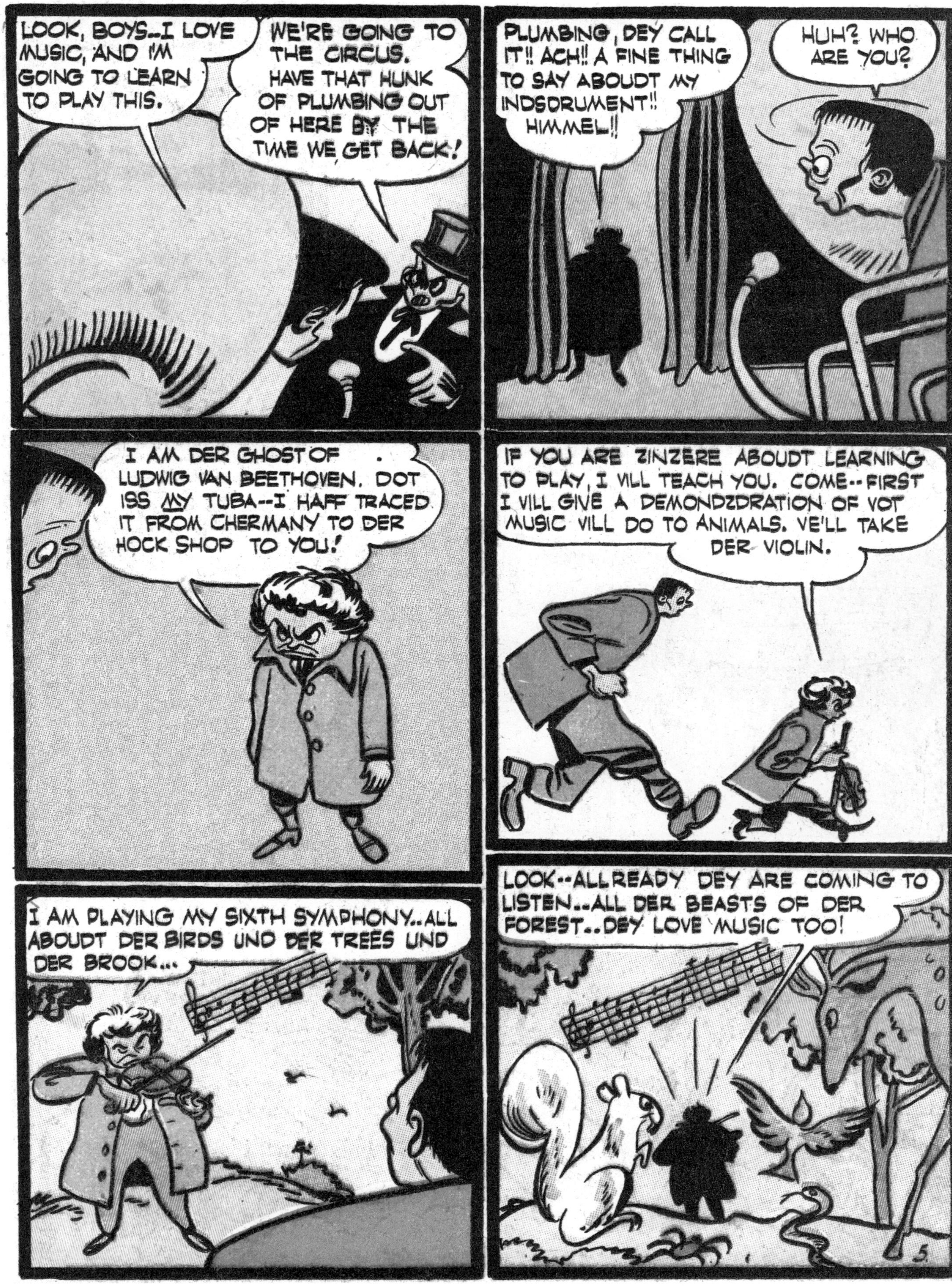
LOOK, BOYS..I LOVE MUSIC, AND I'M GOING TO LEARN TO PLAY THIS.
WE'RE GOING TO THE CIRCUS. HAVE THAT HUNK OF PLUMBING OUT OF HERE BY THE TIME WE GET BACK!
PLUMBING, DEY CALL IT!! ACH!! A FINE THING TO SAY ABOUDT MY INDSDRUMENT!! HIMMEL!!
HUH? WHO ARE YOU?
I AM DER GHOST OF LUDWIG VAN BEETHOVEN. DOT ISS MY TUBA--I HAFF TRACED IT FROM CHERMANY TO DER HOCK SHOP TO YOU!
IF YOU ARE ZINZERE ABOUDT LEARNING TO PLAY, I VILL TEACH YOU. COME--FIRST I VILL GIVE A DEMONDZDRATION OF VOT MUSIC VILL DO TO ANIMALS. VE'LL TAKE DER VIOLIN.
I AM PLAYING MY SIXTH SYMPHONY..ALL ABOUDT DER BIRDS UND DER TREES UND DER BROOK...
LOOK--ALLREADY DEY ARE COMING TO LISTEN..ALL DER BEASTS OF DER FOREST..DEY LOVE MUSIC TOO!
5

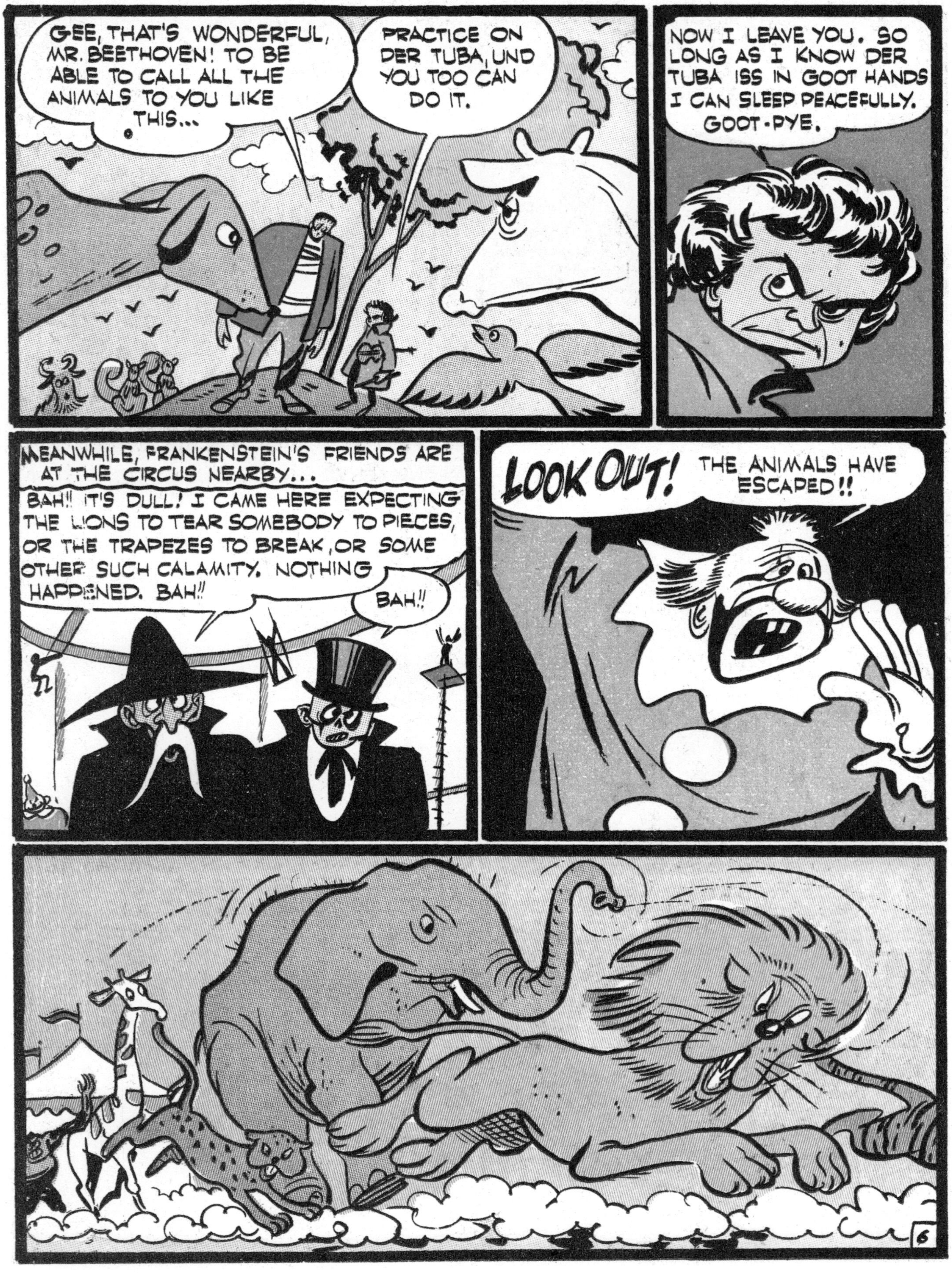
GEE, THAT'S WONDERFUL, MR. BEETHOVEN! TO BE ABLE TO CALL ALL THE ANIMALS TO YOU LIKE THIS...
PRACTICE ON DER TUBA, UND YOU TOO CAN DO IT.
NOW I LEAVE YOU. SO LONG AS I KNOW DER TUBA ISS IN GOOT HANDS I CAN SLEEP PEACEFULLY. GOOT-PYE.
MEANWHILE, FRANKENSTEIN'S FRIENDS ARE AT THE CIRCUS NEARBY...
BAH!! IT'S DULL! I CAME HERE EXPECTING THE LIONS TO TEAR SOMEBODY TO PIECES, OR THE TRAPEZES TO BREAK, OR SOME OTHER SUCH CALAMITY. NOTHING HAPPENED. BAH!!
BAH!!
LOOK OUT!
THE ANIMALS HAVE ESCAPED!!
6

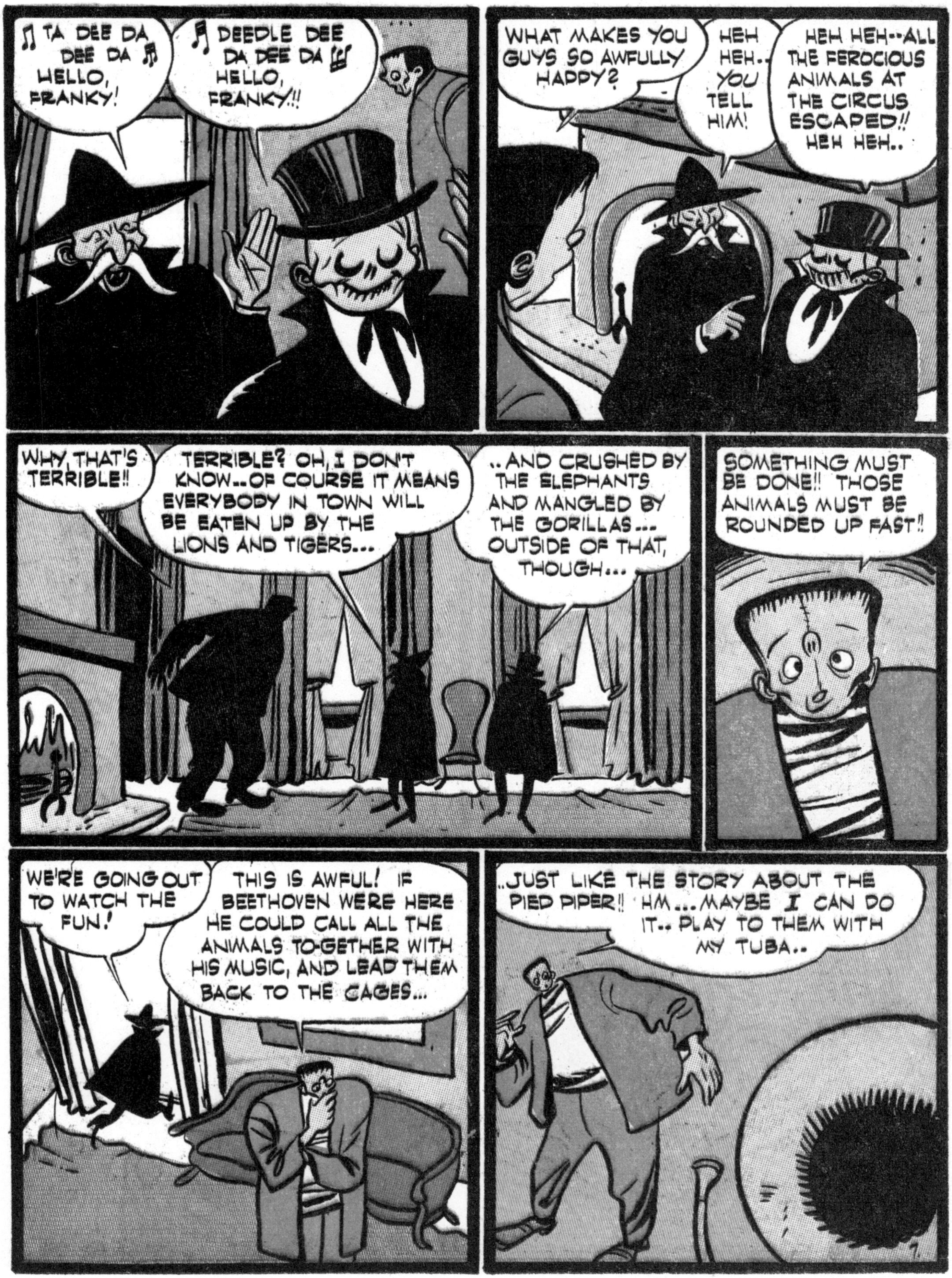
♫ TA DEE DA DEE DA ♬ HELLO, FRANKY!
♪ DEEDLE DEE DA DEE DA HELLO, FRANKY!!
WHAT MAKES YOU GUYS SO AWFULLY HAPPY?
HEH HEH.. YOU TELL HIM!
HEH HEH--ALL THE FEROCIOUS ANIMALS AT THE CIRCUS ESCAPED!! HEH HEH..
WHY, THAT'S TERRIBLE!!
TERRIBLE? OH, I DON'T KNOW..OF COURSE IT MEANS EVERYBODY IN TOWN WILL BE EATEN UP BY THE LIONS AND TIGERS...
..AND CRUSHED BY THE ELEPHANTS AND MANGLED BY THE GORILLAS... OUTSIDE OF THAT, THOUGH...
SOMETHING MUST BE DONE!! THOSE ANIMALS MUST BE ROUNDED UP FAST!!
WE'RE GOING OUT TO WATCH THE FUN!
THIS IS AWFUL! IF BEETHOVEN WERE HERE HE COULD CALL ALL THE ANIMALS TO-GETHER WITH HIS MUSIC, AND LEAD THEM BACK TO THE CAGES...
..JUST LIKE THE STORY ABOUT THE PIED PIPER!! HM...MAYBE I CAN DO IT.. PLAY TO THEM WITH MY TUBA..

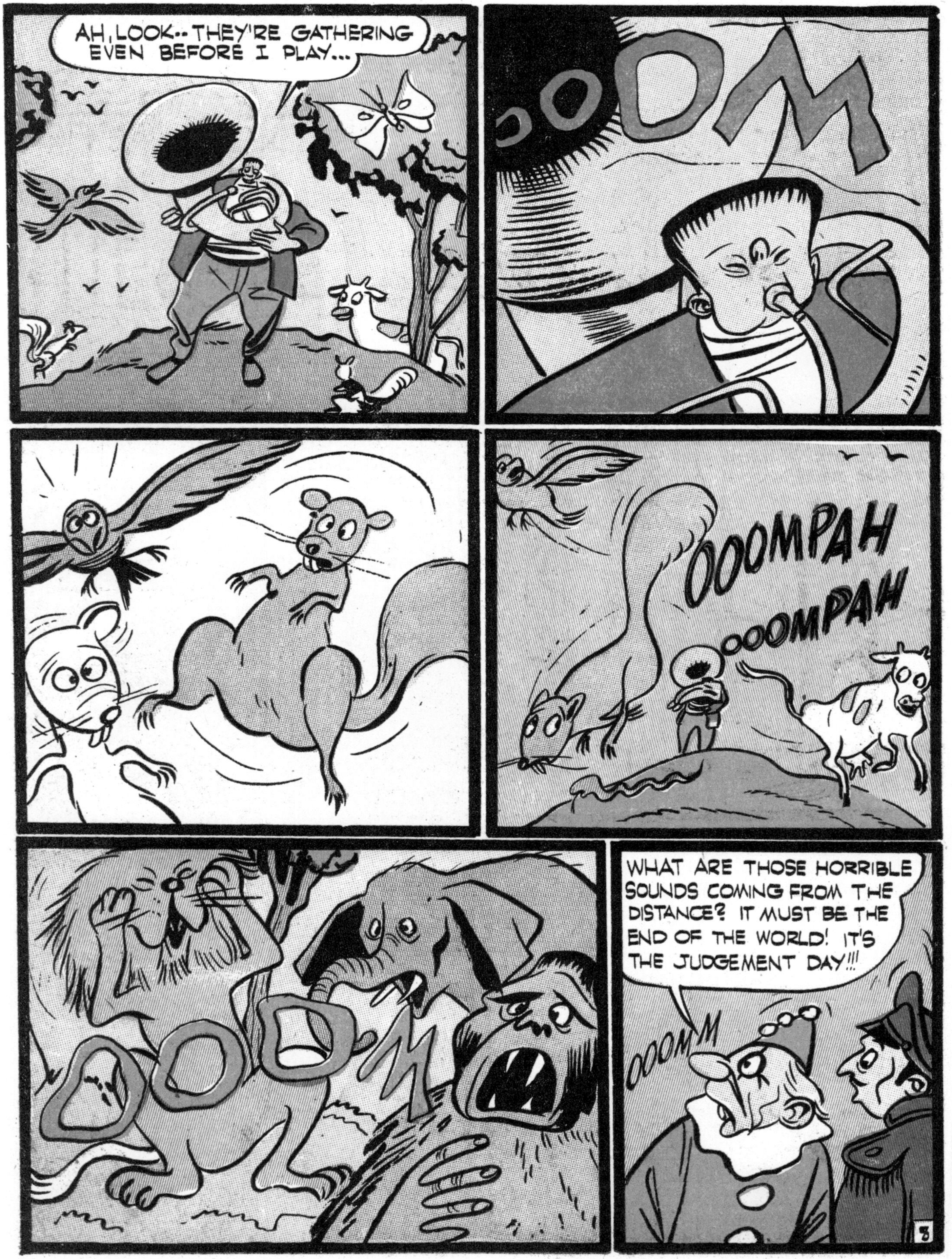
AH, LOOK.. THEY'RE GATHERING EVEN BEFORE I PLAY...
OOOMPAH
OOOMPAH
WHAT ARE THOSE HORRIBLE SOUNDS COMING FROM THE DISTANCE? IT MUST BE THE END OF THE WORLD! IT'S THE JUDGEMENT DAY!!!
OOOMM
3

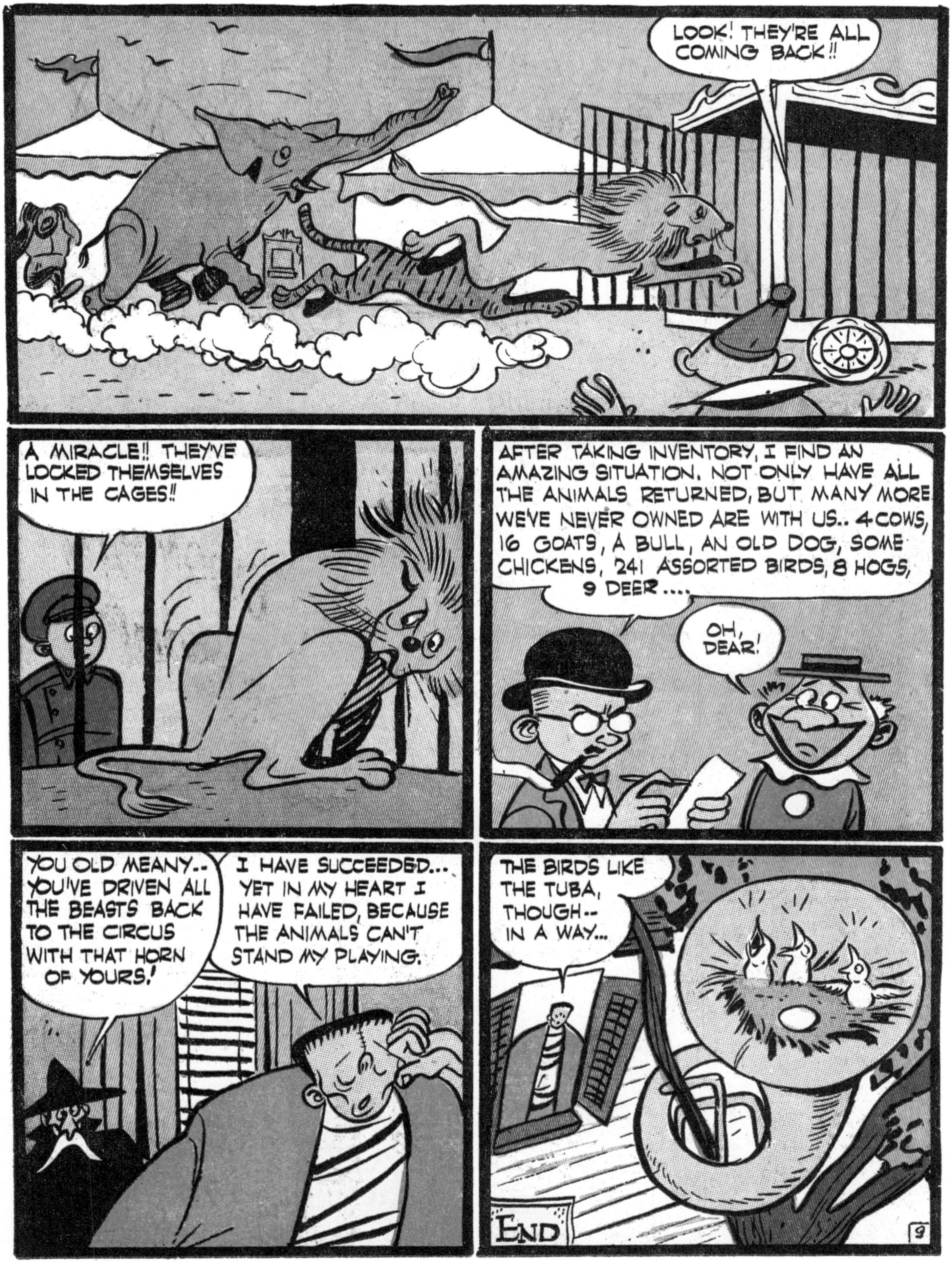
LOOK! THEY'RE ALL COMING BACK!!
A MIRACLE!! THEY'VE LOCKED THEMSELVES IN THE CAGES!!
AFTER TAKING INVENTORY, I FIND AN AMAZING SITUATION. NOT ONLY HAVE ALL THE ANIMALS RETURNED, BUT MANY MORE WE'VE NEVER OWNED ARE WITH US.. 4 COWS, 16 GOATS, A BULL, AN OLD DOG, SOME CHICKENS, 241 ASSORTED BIRDS, 8 HOGS, 9 DEER....
OH, DEAR!
YOU OLD MEANY.. YOU'VE DRIVEN ALL THE BEASTS BACK TO THE CIRCUS WITH THAT HORN OF YOURS!
I HAVE SUCCEEDED... YET IN MY HEART I HAVE FAILED, BECAUSE THE ANIMALS CAN'T STAND MY PLAYING.
THE BIRDS LIKE THE TUBA, THOUGH-- IN A WAY...
END
9

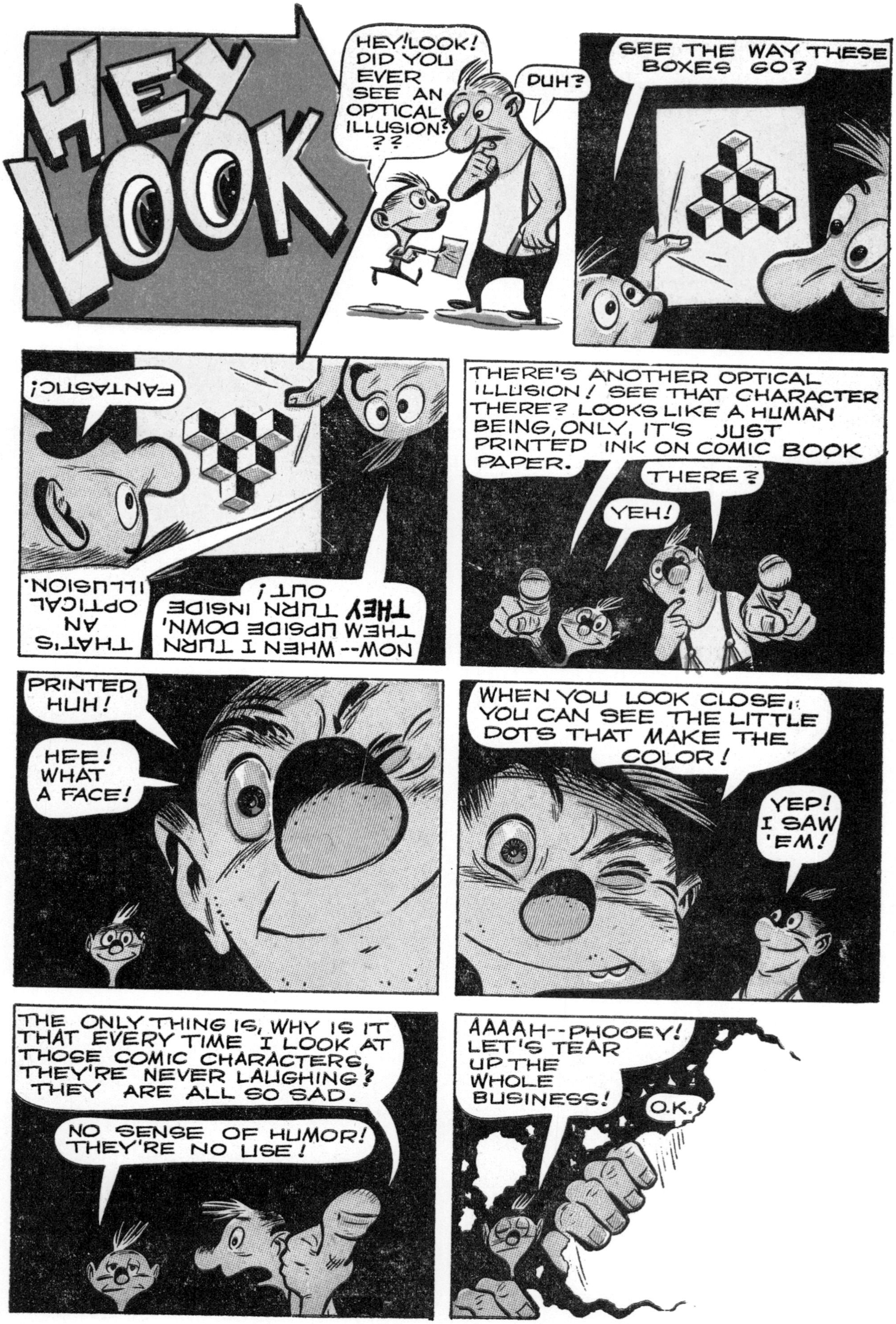
HEY LOOK
HEY! LOOK! DID YOU EVER SEE AN OPTICAL ILLUSION? ??
DUH?
SEE THE WAY THESE BOXES GO?
NOW--WHEN I TURN THEM UPSIDE DOWN, THEY TURN INSIDE OUT!
THAT'S AN OPTICAL ILLUSION.
FANTASTIC!
THERE'S ANOTHER OPTICAL ILLUSION! SEE THAT CHARACTER THERE? LOOKS LIKE A HUMAN BEING, ONLY, IT'S JUST PRINTED INK ON COMIC BOOK PAPER.
THERE?
YEH!
PRINTED, HUH!
HEE! WHAT A FACE!
WHEN YOU LOOK CLOSE, YOU CAN SEE THE LITTLE DOTS THAT MAKE THE COLOR!
YEP! I SAW 'EM!
THE ONLY THING IS, WHY IS IT THAT EVERY TIME I LOOK AT THOSE COMIC CHARACTERS, THEY'RE NEVER LAUGHING? THEY ARE ALL SO SAD.
NO SENSE OF HUMOR! THEY'RE NO USE!
AAAAH--PHOOEY! LET'S TEAR UP THE WHOLE BUSINESS!
O.K.

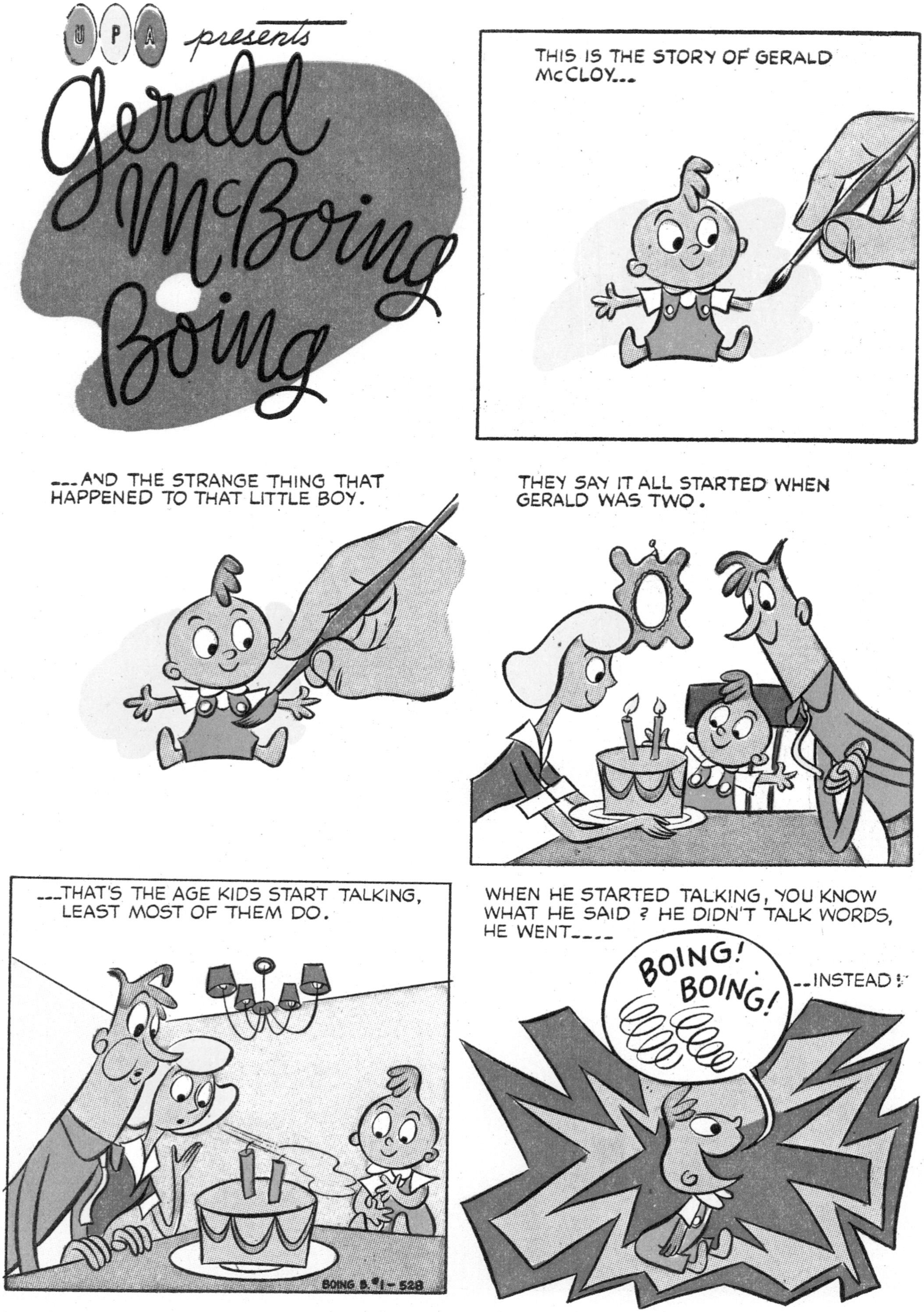
UPA presents
Gerald McBoing Boing
THIS IS THE STORY OF GERALD McCLOY...
...AND THE STRANGE THING THAT HAPPENED TO THAT LITTLE BOY.
THEY SAY IT ALL STARTED WHEN GERALD WAS TWO.
...THAT'S THE AGE KIDS START TALKING, LEAST MOST OF THEM DO.
BOING B. #1 - 528
WHEN HE STARTED TALKING, YOU KNOW WHAT HE SAID? HE DIDN'T TALK WORDS, HE WENT....
BOING! BOING!
--INSTEAD!

"WHAT'S THAT?" CRIED HIS FATHER, HIS FACE TURNING GREY---

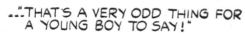

..."THAT'S A VERY ODD THING FOR A YOUNG BOY TO SAY!"

BOING! BOING!

AND POOR GERALD'S FATHER RUSHED TO THE PHONE---

---AND QUICK DIALED THE NUMBER OF DOCTOR MALONE.

"COME OVER FAST!" THE POOR FATHER PLED---

..."OUR BOY CAN'T SPEAK WORDS--- HE GOES---

BOING BOING ---INSTEAD!"

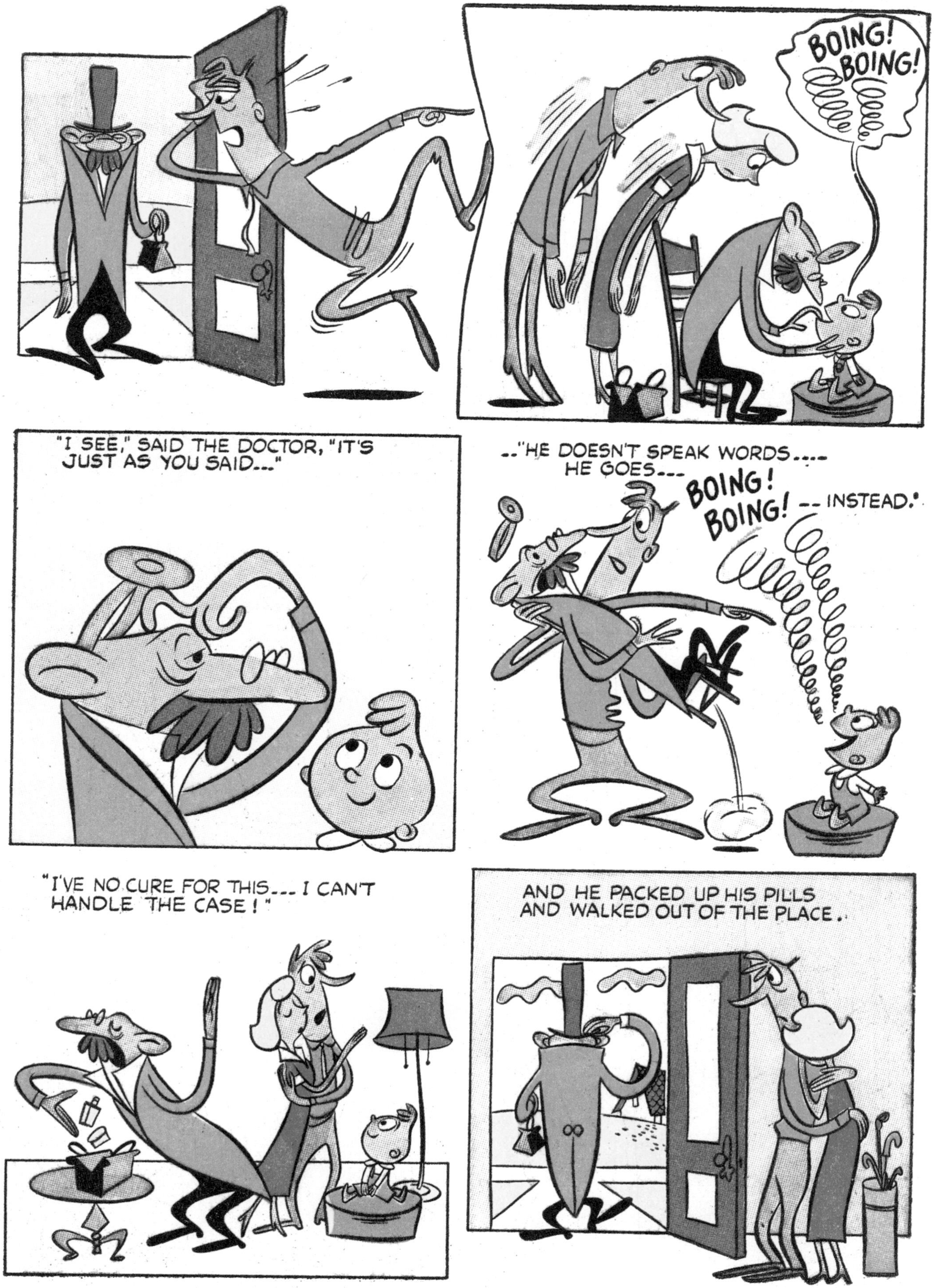
BOING! BOING!
"I SEE," SAID THE DOCTOR, "IT'S JUST AS YOU SAID..."
.."HE DOESN'T SPEAK WORDS.... HE GOES...
BOING! BOING!
-- INSTEAD."
"I'VE NO CURE FOR THIS... I CAN'T HANDLE THE CASE!"
AND HE PACKED UP HIS PILLS AND WALKED OUT OF THE PLACE..

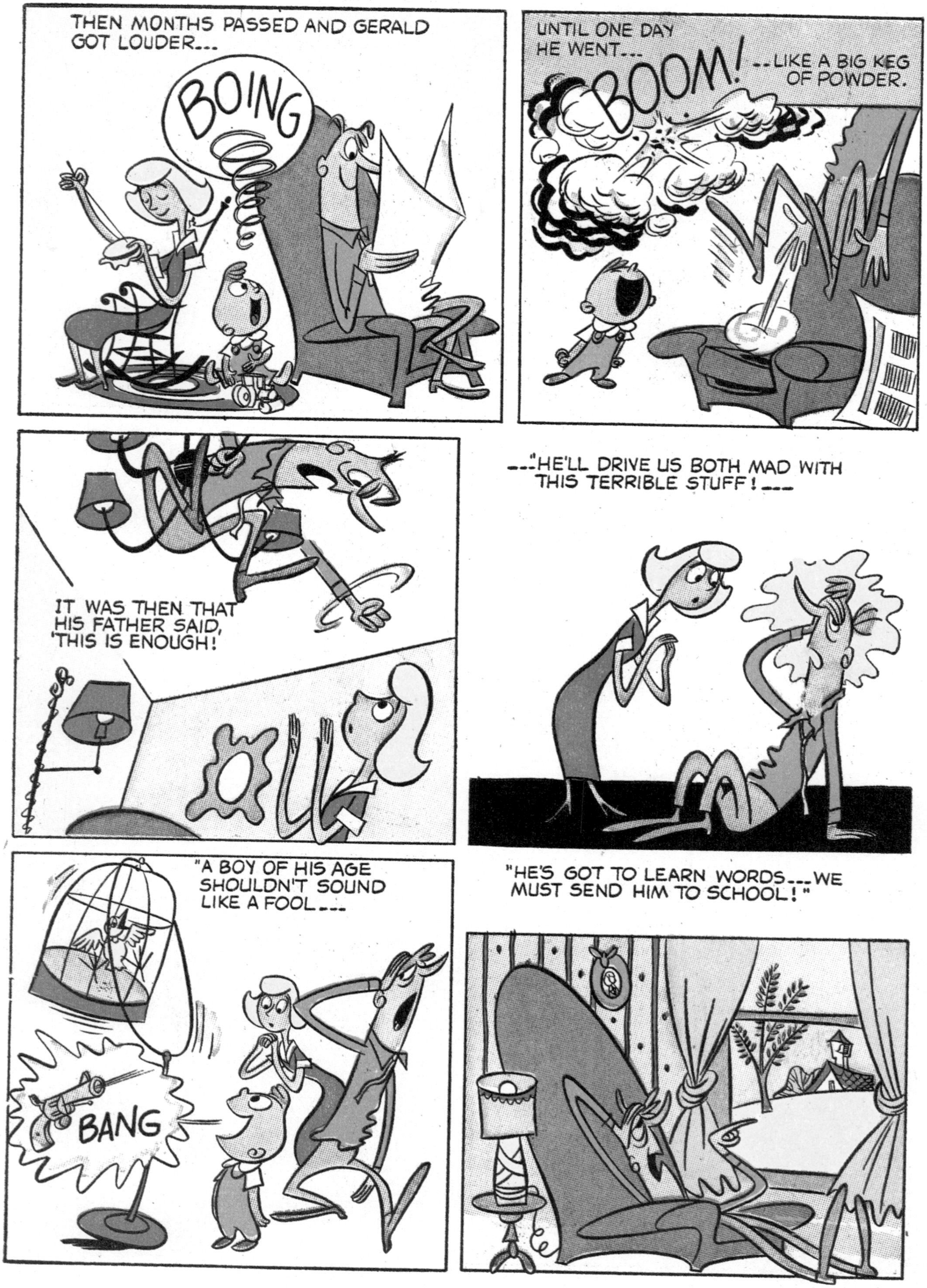
THEN MONTHS PASSED AND GERALD GOT LOUDER...
BOING
UNTIL ONE DAY HE WENT...
BOOM!
..LIKE A BIG KEG OF POWDER.
IT WAS THEN THAT HIS FATHER SAID, 'THIS IS ENOUGH!
--"HE'LL DRIVE US BOTH MAD WITH THIS TERRIBLE STUFF! ---
"A BOY OF HIS AGE SHOULDN'T SOUND LIKE A FOOL---
BANG
"HE'S GOT TO LEARN WORDS---WE MUST SEND HIM TO SCHOOL!"

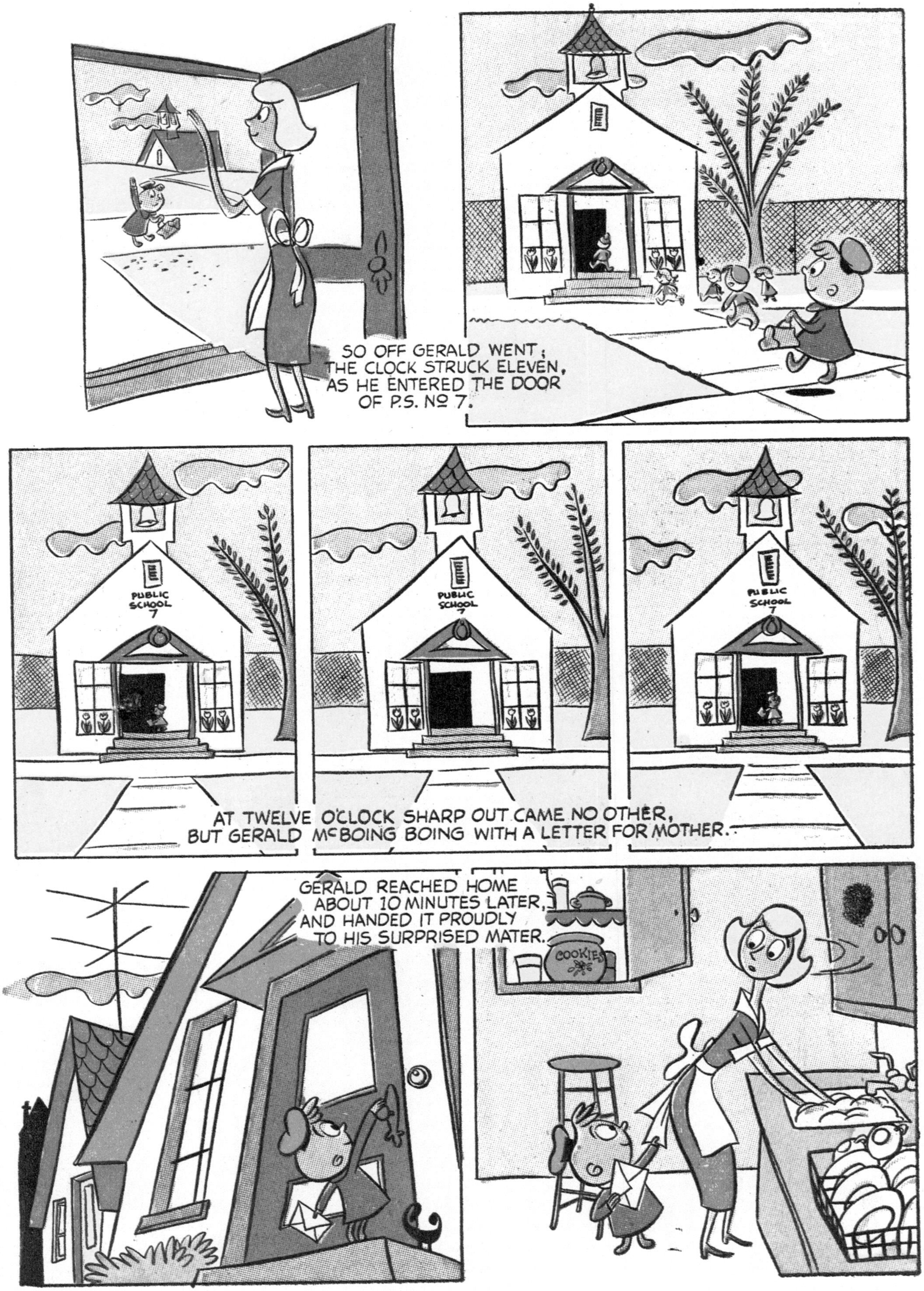
SO OFF GERALD WENT; THE CLOCK STRUCK ELEVEN, AS HE ENTERED THE DOOR OF P.S. Nº 7.
PUBLIC SCHOOL 7
PUBLIC SCHOOL 7
PUBLIC SCHOOL 7
AT TWELVE O'CLOCK SHARP OUT CAME NO OTHER, BUT GERALD McBOING BOING WITH A LETTER FOR MOTHER.
GERALD REACHED HOME ABOUT 10 MINUTES LATER, AND HANDED IT PROUDLY TO HIS SURPRISED MATER.
COOKIES

From Public School Seven to Mrs. McCloy:

Your little son Gerald's a most hopeless boy....

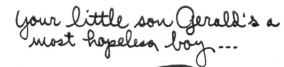

"We cannot accept him for we have a rule...

"That pupils must not go....

CUCKOO in our school.

"Your boy will go HONK!—all his life, I'm afraid.

"Sincerely yours, Fanny Schultz, Teacher, First Grade."

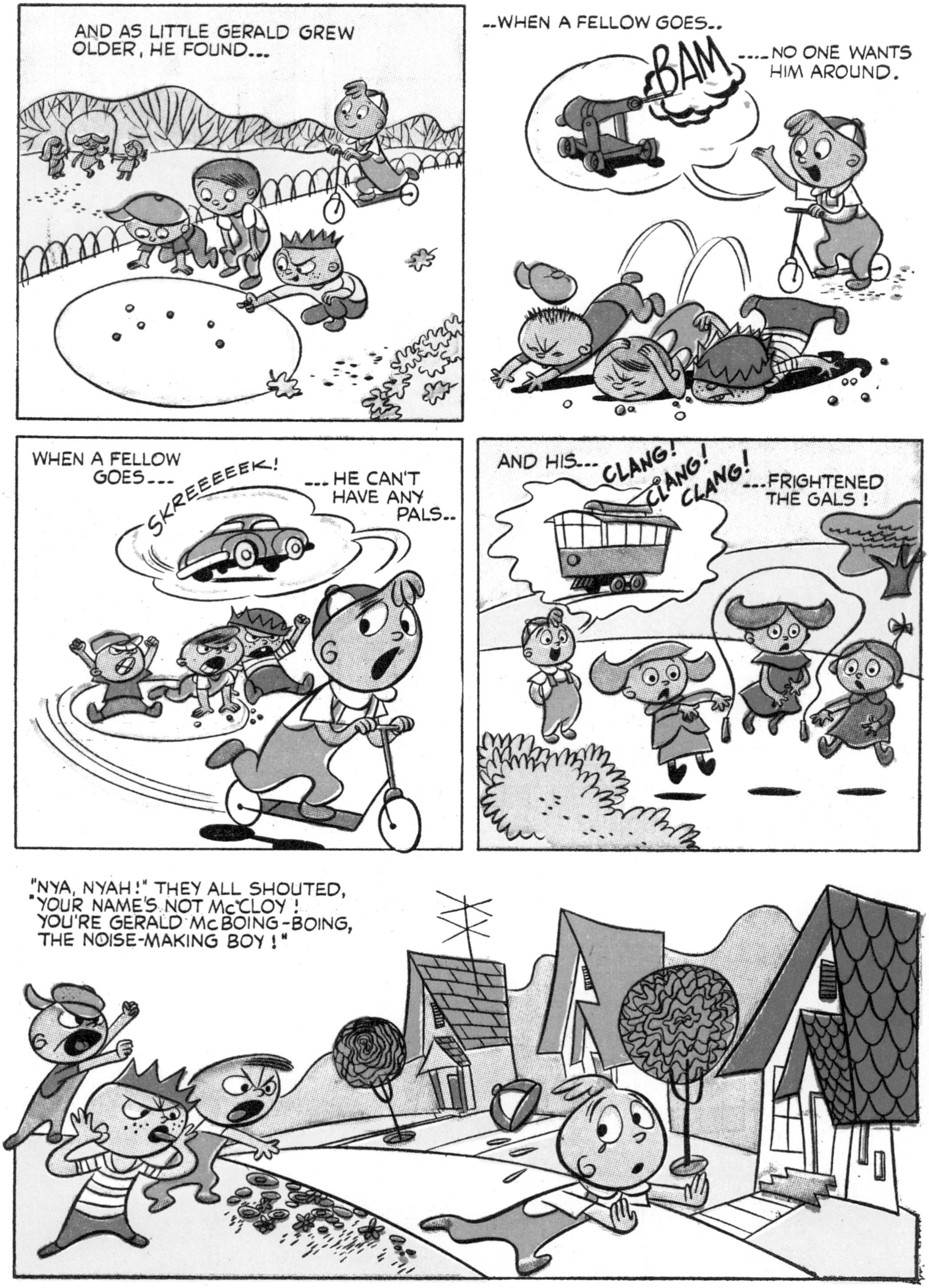
AND AS LITTLE GERALD GREW OLDER, HE FOUND...
..WHEN A FELLOW GOES..
BAM
....NO ONE WANTS HIM AROUND.
WHEN A FELLOW GOES---
SKREEEEEEK!
---HE CAN'T HAVE ANY PALS..
AND HIS---
CLANG!
CLANG!
CLANG!
---FRIGHTENED THE GALS!
"NYA, NYAH!" THEY ALL SHOUTED, "YOUR NAME'S NOT McCLOY! YOU'RE GERALD McBOING-BOING, THE NOISE-MAKING BOY!"

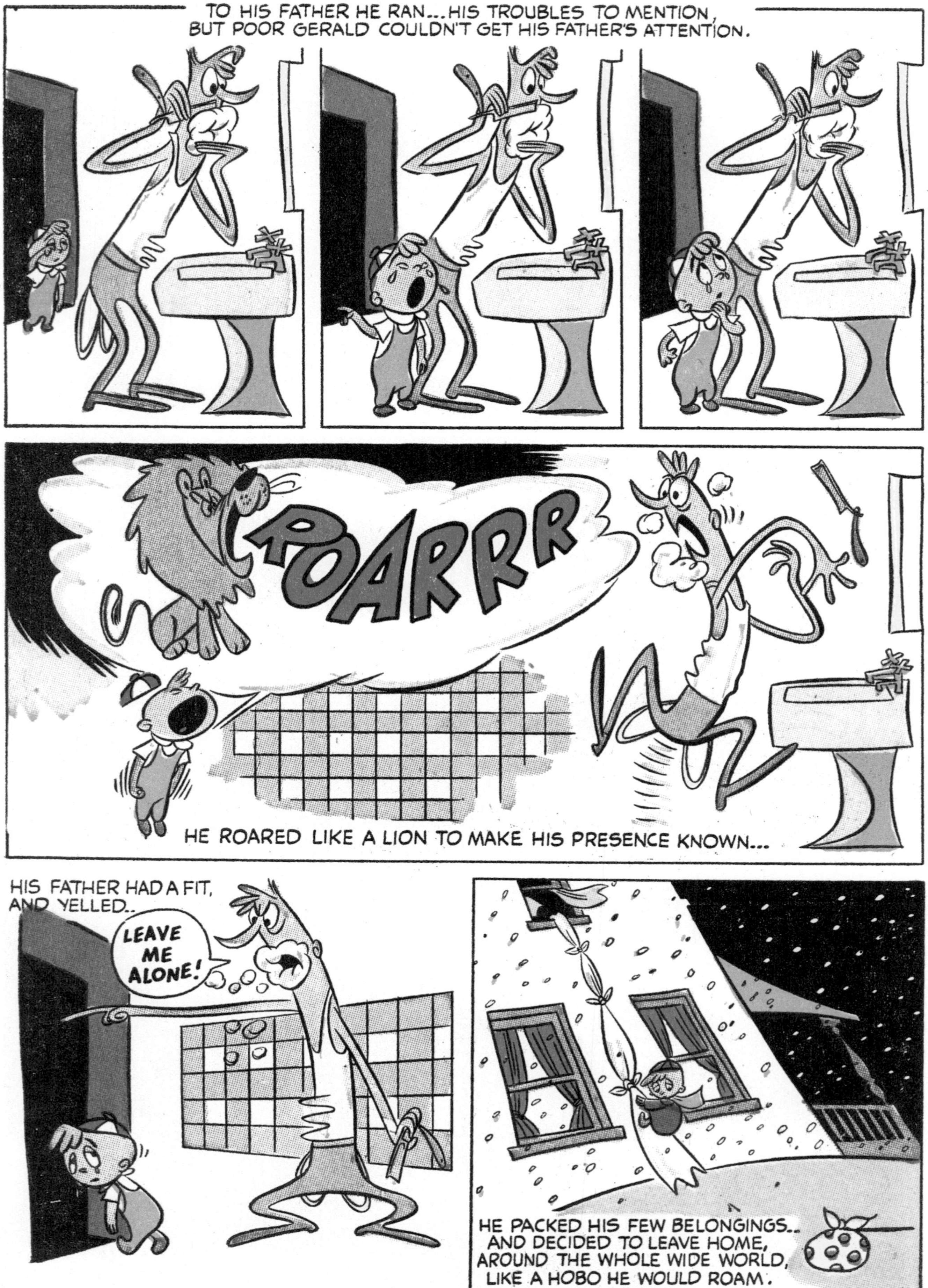
TO HIS FATHER HE RAN... HIS TROUBLES TO MENTION, BUT POOR GERALD COULDN'T GET HIS FATHER'S ATTENTION.
ROARRR
HE ROARED LIKE A LION TO MAKE HIS PRESENCE KNOWN...
HIS FATHER HAD A FIT, AND YELLED..
LEAVE ME ALONE!
HE PACKED HIS FEW BELONGINGS.. AND DECIDED TO LEAVE HOME, AROUND THE WHOLE WIDE WORLD, LIKE A HOBO HE WOULD ROAM.

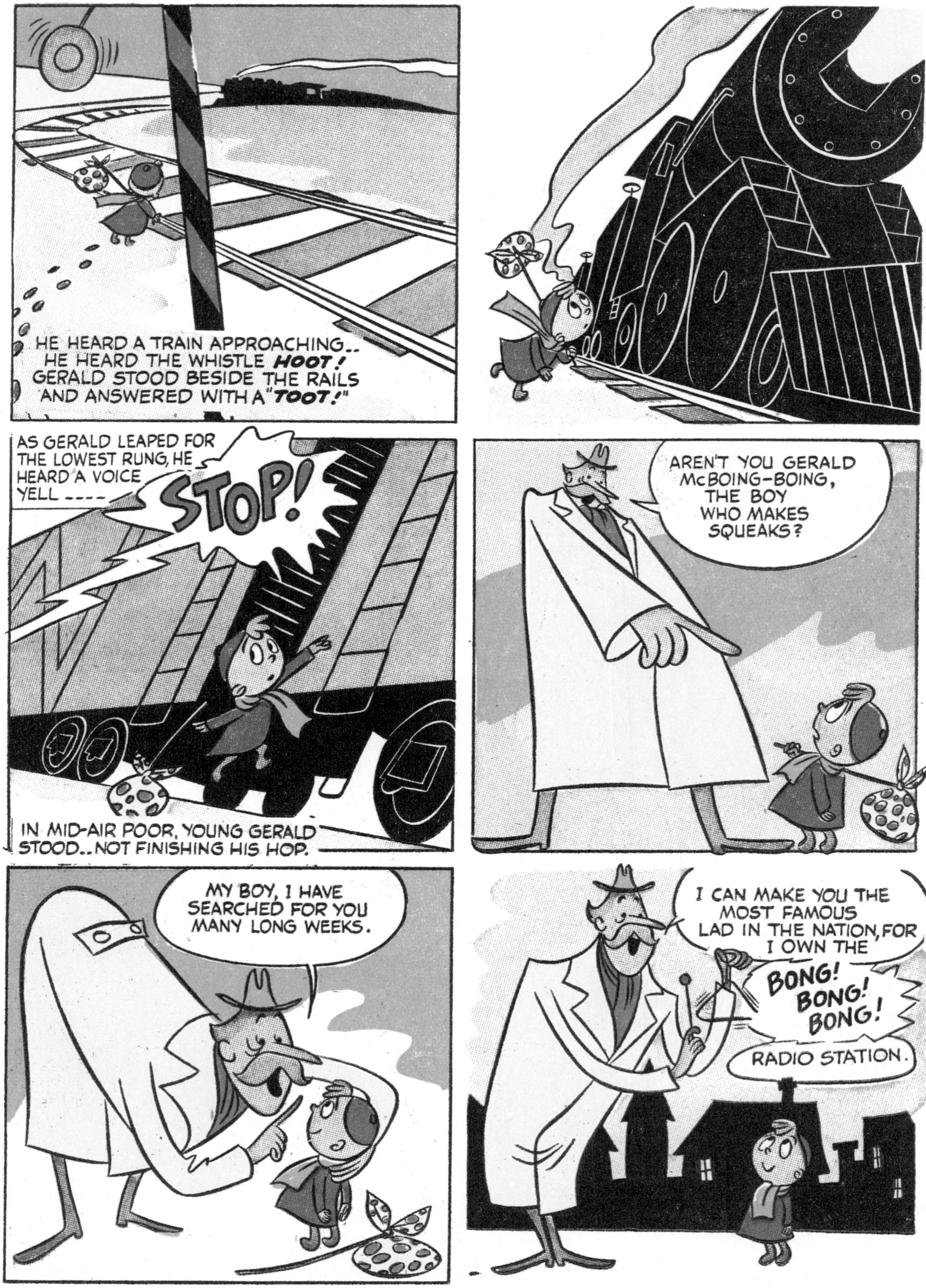
HE HEARD A TRAIN APPROACHING.. HE HEARD THE WHISTLE HOOT! GERALD STOOD BESIDE THE RAILS AND ANSWERED WITH A "TOOT!"
AS GERALD LEAPED FOR THE LOWEST RUNG, HE HEARD A VOICE YELL ----
STOP!
IN MID-AIR POOR, YOUNG GERALD STOOD.. NOT FINISHING HIS HOP.
AREN'T YOU GERALD McBOING-BOING, THE BOY WHO MAKES SQUEAKS?
MY BOY, I HAVE SEARCHED FOR YOU MANY LONG WEEKS.
I CAN MAKE YOU THE MOST FAMOUS LAD IN THE NATION, FOR I OWN THE
BONG! BONG! BONG!
RADIO STATION.

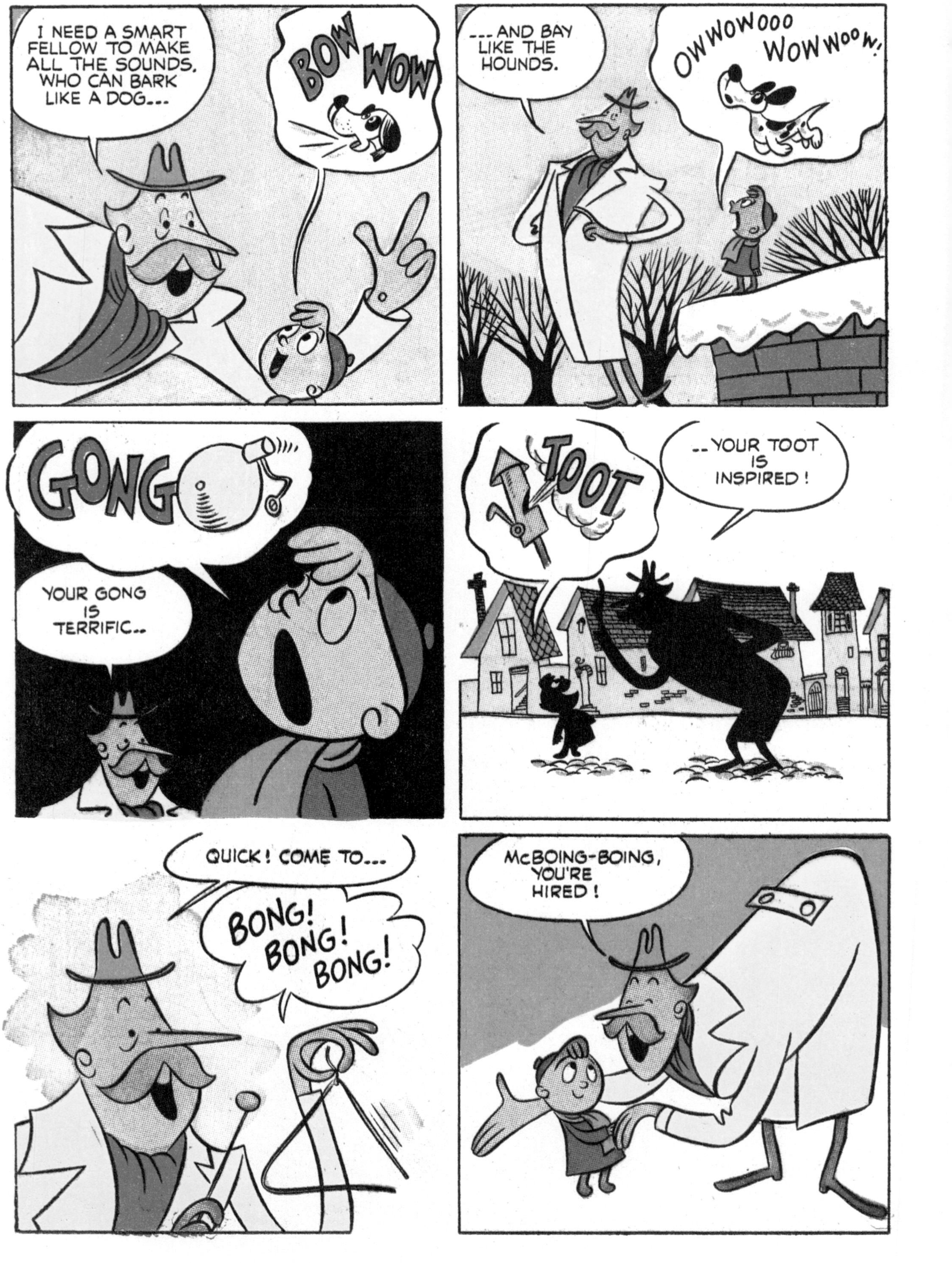
I NEED A SMART FELLOW TO MAKE ALL THE SOUNDS, WHO CAN BARK LIKE A DOG...
BOW WOW
...AND BAY LIKE THE HOUNDS.
OWWOWOOO WOWWOOW!
GONG
YOUR GONG IS TERRIFIC..
TOOT
..YOUR TOOT IS INSPIRED!
QUICK! COME TO...
BONG! BONG! BONG!
McBOING-BOING, YOU'RE HIRED!

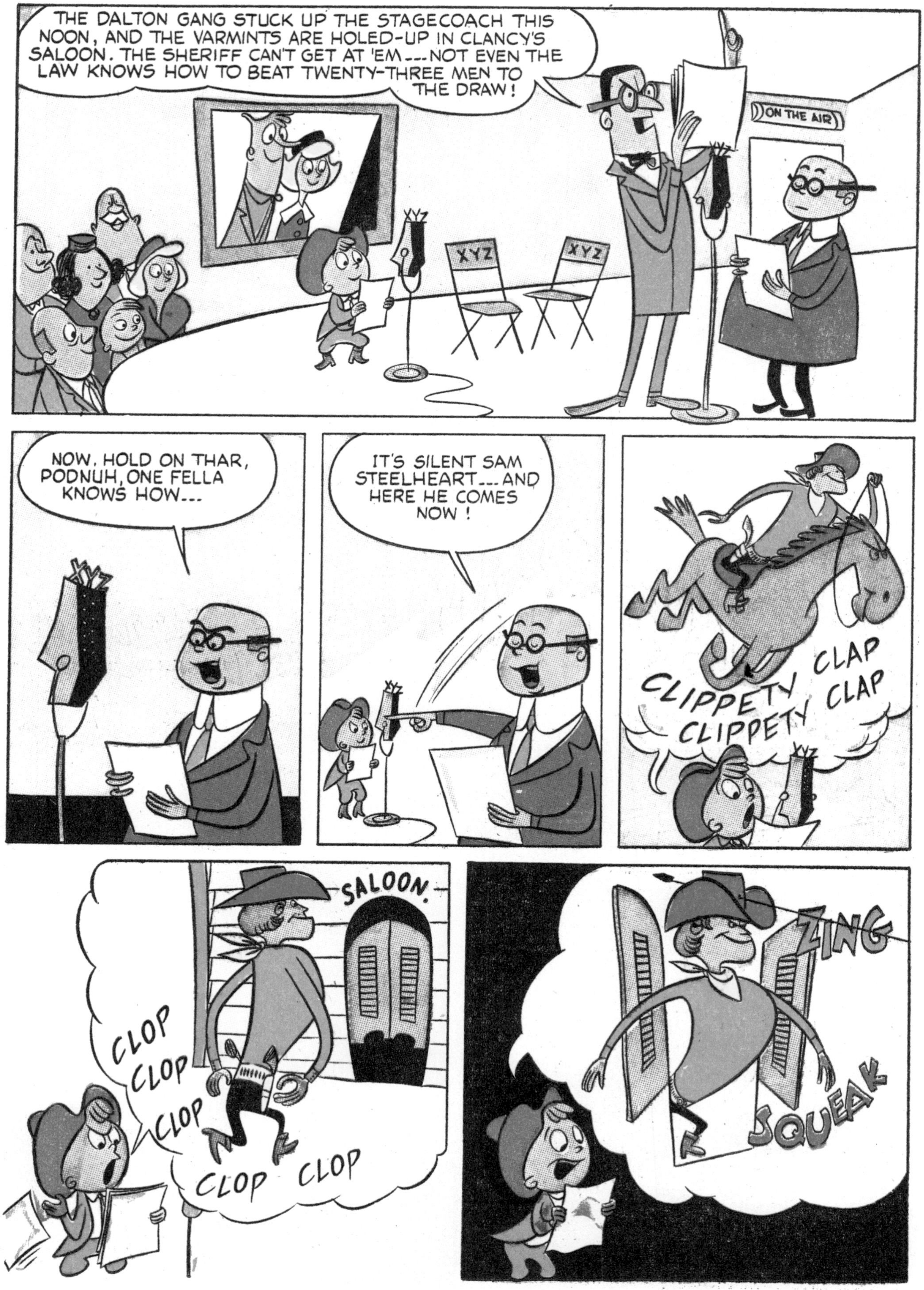
THE DALTON GANG STUCK UP THE STAGECOACH THIS NOON, AND THE VARMINTS ARE HOLED-UP IN CLANCY'S SALOON. THE SHERIFF CAN'T GET AT 'EM --- NOT EVEN THE LAW KNOWS HOW TO BEAT TWENTY-THREE MEN TO THE DRAW!
ON THE AIR
XYZ
NOW, HOLD ON THAR, PODNUH, ONE FELLA KNOWS HOW---
IT'S SILENT SAM STEELHEART --- AND HERE HE COMES NOW!
CLIPPETY CLAP CLIPPETY CLAP
SALOON.
CLOP CLOP CLOP CLOP CLOP
ZING
SQUEAK

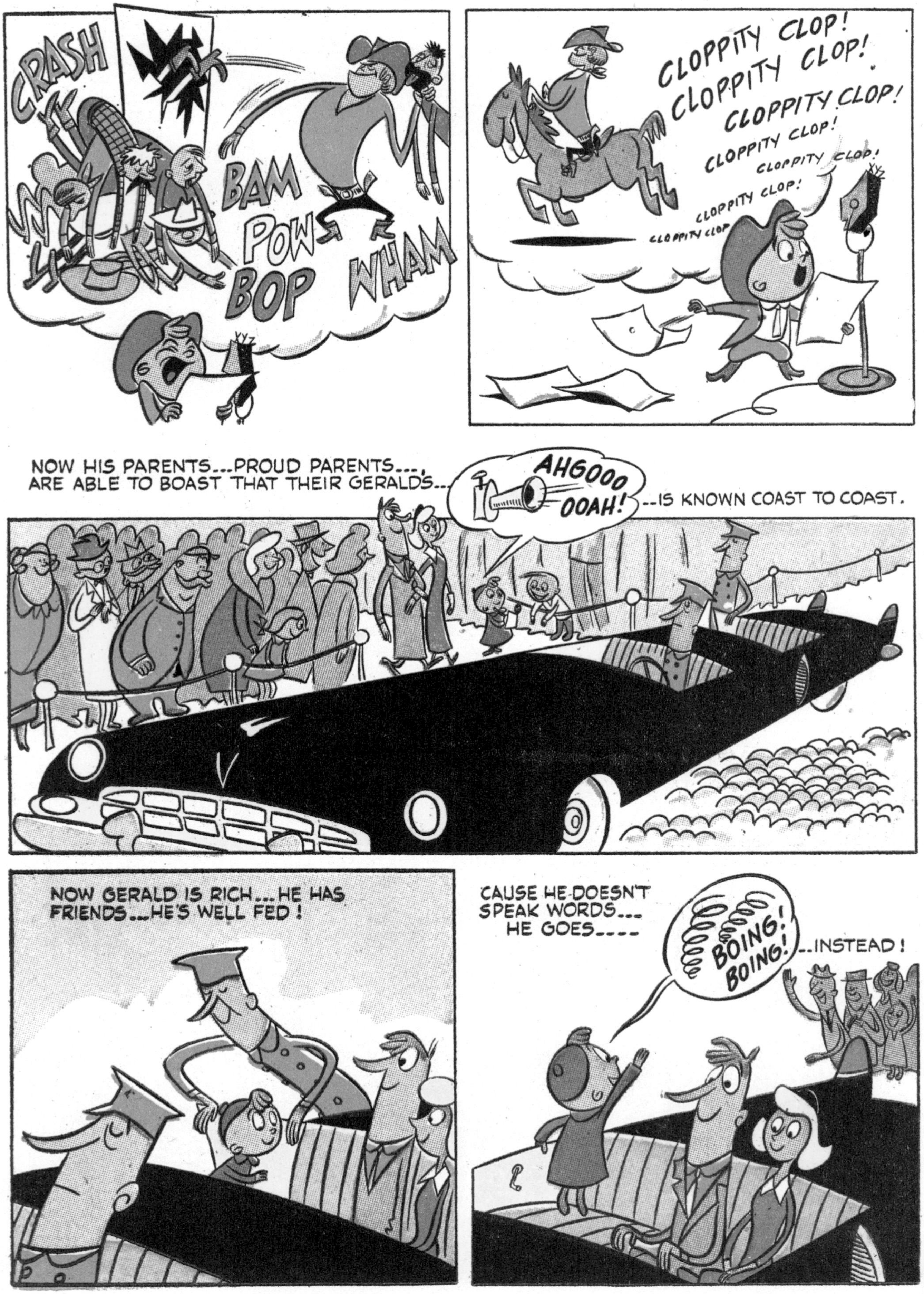
CRASH
BAM
POW
BOP
WHAM
CLOPPITY CLOP!
CLOPPITY CLOP!
CLOPPITY CLOP!
CLOPPITY CLOP!
CLOPPITY CLOP!
CLOPPITY CLOP!
CLOPPITY CLOP
NOW HIS PARENTS---PROUD PARENTS---, ARE ABLE TO BOAST THAT THEIR GERALD'S--
AHGOOO OOAH!
--IS KNOWN COAST TO COAST.
NOW GERALD IS RICH...HE HAS FRIENDS...HE'S WELL FED!
CAUSE HE DOESN'T SPEAK WORDS... HE GOES----
BOING! BOING!
..INSTEAD!

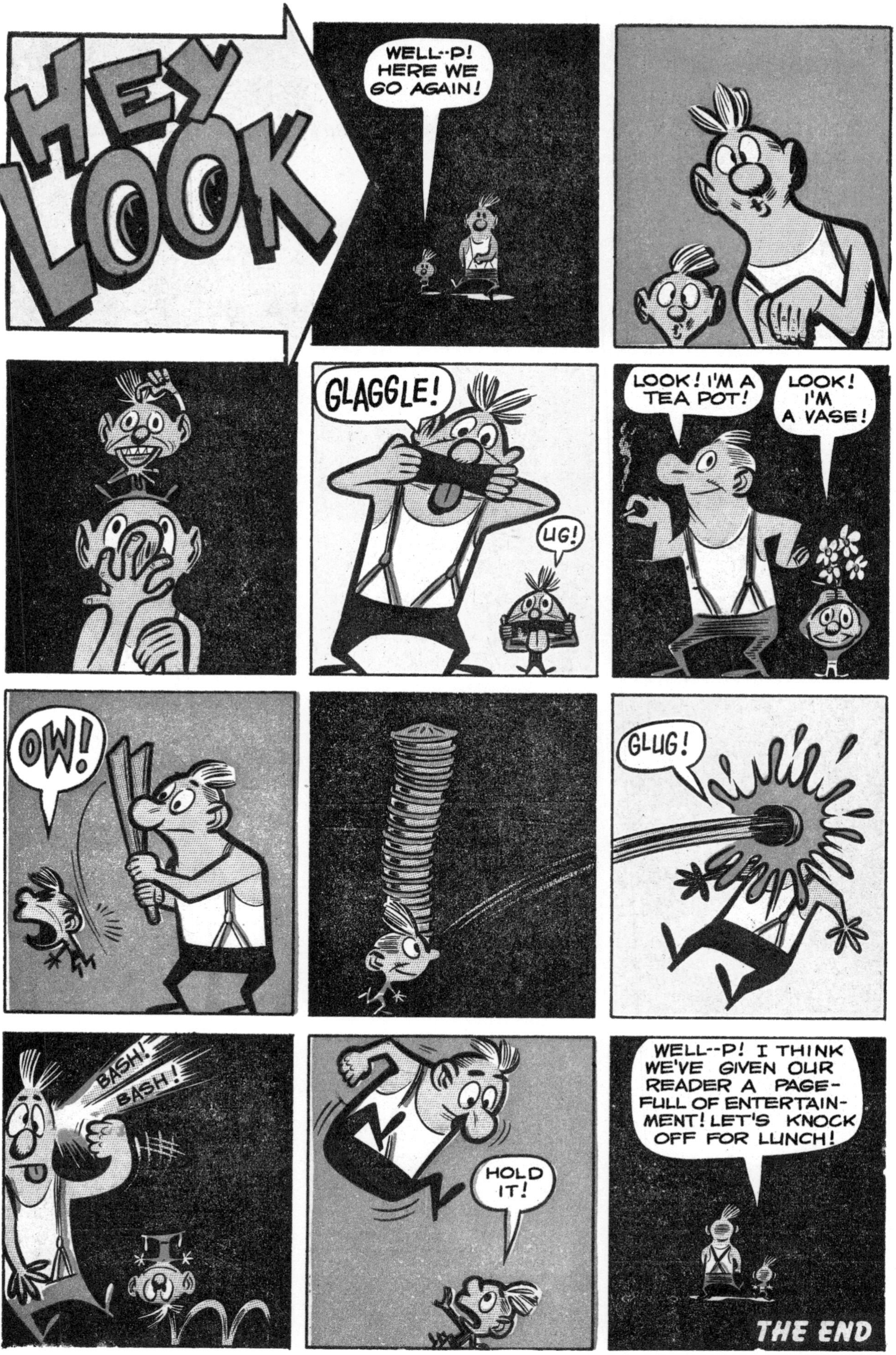
HEY LOOK
WELL--P! HERE WE GO AGAIN!
GLAGGLE!
UG!
LOOK! I'M A TEA POT!
LOOK! I'M A VASE!
OW!
GLUG!
BASH! BASH!
HOLD IT!
WELL--P! I THINK WE'VE GIVEN OUR READER A PAGE-FULL OF ENTERTAIN-MENT! LET'S KNOCK OFF FOR LUNCH!
THE END

About the Artists

ARR, DON (1916–2006) was born Donald R. Christensen in Minneapolis, Minnesota, and studied at the Minnesota School of Art. He worked for the Walt Disney Studio for four years (1937–41) before moving to Warner Bros., where he briefly worked as a storybook artist, primarily for director Bob Clampett. Moving over to comic books, Arr helped write and illustrate such wide-ranging titles as *Flip and Flopper, Uncle Scrooge*, and *Magnus, Robot Fighter*. In the 1960s Arr was the art director for Saturday morning cartoon programs including *The Marvel Superheroes* and *Star Trek*. Arr was also president of the Comic Art Professional Society.

BARKS, CARL (1901–2000) is legendary as a master story teller, prolific artist/writer (over 650 stories), and creator of the denizens of Duckburg, including Scrooge McDuck, Gladstone Gander, Gyro Gearloose, and the Beagle Boys, as well as endowing the Donald Duck family with a range of believable characteristics. Born in Merrill, Oregon, Barks left school early, and as a young man held a variety of jobs, including woodcutter, mule driver, prospector, and cowboy. He was hired by Walt Disney Studios in 1935 as a storyboard artist and writer for Donald Duck cartoons. In 1942 Barks left Disney to freelance at Western Printing and Lithographing Co., where over the next thirty years he created and populated Duckburg in a number of comic books under the Walt Disney banner, but was never allowed to sign his own name to his work. In the years following his retirement in 1966, Barks's anonymity ceased. Fans commissioned Barks to paint fanciful scenes of Donald Duck and friends, even re-creating many of his tableaux from the comics. Barks was inducted into the Eisner Hall of Fame in 1987, and received a Disney Legends Award in 1991.

BECK, C. C. (1910–89) joined Fawcett Publications in 1933. When the publisher began to print comic books in 1939, Beck was there to draw series like *Spy Smasher* and *Ibis the Invincible*. Beck helped to create the flagship Fawcett character Captain Marvel, whose whimsical, cartoony style remained an anomaly through the heyday of the super hero genre. Beck was inducted into the Eisner Hall of Fame in 1993. **PETE COSTANZA** often assisted Beck on his Captain Marvel stories. The scriptwriter most associated with these stories is science fiction writer **OTTO BINDER**.

BERG, DAVE (1920–2002) was born in Brooklyn, New York, and attended Pratt Institute and Cooper Union. He joined Will Eisner's studio in 1940, producing work primarily for Quality Comics. "The Tweedle Twins" is an example of the humorous touch that Berg brought to a variety of short-lived backup features for publishers such as Dell and Fawcett. The versatile stylist even drew a couple of war stories for Harvey Kurtzman's E.C. war comics. Berg was not associated with a single ongoing feature until he started at *MAD*, where he worked for nearly fifty years writing and illustrating the perennial "The Lighter Side of . . ." feature.

BOLLING, BOB (b. 1928) was born in Brockton, Massachusetts. He worked on such comics as *Marlin Keel* and *Wally the Wizard*, before creating in the mid-1950s the character that he is most associated with: *Little Archie*, which he both wrote and drew. Unlike many of the other Archie artists, Bolling began to sign his name to his work with the second issue of *Little Archie*. He writes and draws for Archie Publications to this day.

BRIEFER, DICK (1915–80) was born in New York City and studied at the Art Students League. His first comic book work was published in *Wow, What a Magazine!*, Will Eisner and Jerry Iger's short-lived early comic book from 1936. Briefer continued to freelance for Eisner and Iger in the 1930s. A versatile draftsman and writer, Briefer took the Frankenstein monster character through the 1940s and 1950s, restyling the monster's adventures to suit the tastes of the fickle public. His loopy, humorous version of the monster is virtually the opposite of the dramatic psychological portrait of the monster he would create years later.

CARLSON, GEORGE (1887–1962) started his career as a children's book illustrator for Gene Stone's *Jane and the Owl* and *Adventures of Jane*. In 1936, Carlson drew the dust jacket for the first edition of *Gone with the Wind*, which today is a collector's item. He went on to illustrate *Uncle Wiggily*, and often produced two full-length stories in each issue of *Jingle Jangle Tales*. These tales are marked for their playful layouts, wacky inner logic, and incessant punning . . . plus they are exquisitely lettered. Carlson also wrote and illustrated a series of how-to books, including *Draw Comics Here's How* and *Points on Cartooning*, as well as comics-themed puzzle books.

COLE, JACK (1914–58) was born Ralph Johns in New Castle, Pennsylvania. In 1936 he began drawing for Centaur Publications. Cole went on to work at Lev Gleason Publications but found his comic book home at Quality Comics, where he created a series of characters as writer/artist (including Burp the Twerp, under the name Ralph Johns) before relinquishing the chores to other hands. Cole's long run on *Plastic Man* shows off his abilities as an auteur: writing, penciling, and inking a long string of stories that deftly combined super hero, crime, science fiction, and horror, which, unbelievably, were also funny. In addition, Cole drew some of the grimmest crime comics of all time without a trace of humor. As the comic book waned in the 1950s, Cole began a long association with *Playboy*, where his lusciously executed watercolor gags set the bar high for the color gag cartoon. Cole had begun to produce a daily comic strip, "Betsy and Me," which appeared in over fifty newspapers, when he committed suicide on August 13, 1958. Although there is plenty of speculation, the reason for Cole's death remains a mystery. Cole was inducted into the Jack Kirby Hall of Fame of 1991 and the Eisner Hall of Fame in 1999.

DAVIS, JIM (1915–96) had a long career as an animator for Disney, Fleischer Studios, Warner Bros., and others. His work can be detected in *Snow White and the Seven Dwarfs*, *The Pink Panther*, and *Fritz the Cat*. While continuing to animate during the day, Davis also drew comics for the B. W. Sangor Shop, later called the American Comics Group. As an artist and an agent for fellow animators he helped to supply such titles as *Giggle* and *Ha Ha Comics* with funny animal stories that reflected an animator's deep understanding of structure, gesture, and figure drawing . . . albeit with pigs, squirrels, and rabbits. Davis helped create the comic book series *The Fox and the Crow*, based on the animated cartoons of Frank Tashlin.

DRESSLER, IRVING (d. 2003) worked for Fleischer Studios and later for Famous–Paramount. He drew the first model designs of the character Nutsy Squirrel (created by writer Woody Gelman), at first a minor character in the DC Comics funny animal pantheon, until he moved up through the ranks and finally got his name on the cover of his own comic book. Dressler is best known for his writing and animation work at Famous Studios, where he worked on *Popeye*, *Casper*, and *Little Lulu* cartoons.

EASTMAN, PHILIP DEY (P. D.) (1909–86) was born in Amherst, Massachusetts. He worked in the story departments of Walt Disney Productions and Warner Bros. before beginning his career at United Productions of America. While at UPA, Eastman collaborated on the original screenplay and storyboard for Dr. Seuss's Oscar-winning short "Gerald McBoing Boing." Eastman went on to illustrate Seuss's work in a Dell comic book adaptation of the "Gerald McBoing Boing" story. Under the name P. D. Eastman, he wrote and illustrated many children's books, including *Are You My Mother?*, *Sam and the Firefly*, and *Go, Dog. Go!*

FEIFFER, JULES (b. 1929) was born in the Bronx, New York, and studied at the Art Students League and Pratt Institute. He started work as an assistant for Will Eisner in the 1940s. "Clifford," Feiffer's earliest comic strip, was published in the back of Eisner's *The Spirit* comic newspaper insert in 1949. Feiffer went on to work for Terrytoons and the Signal Corps before beginning "Feiffer," a political comic serialized first in the *Village Voice*. In addition to his work in comics, Feiffer has written screenplays (*Carnal Knowledge*, *Popeye*), written and illustrated children's books (*The Man in the Ceiling*, *Meanwhile . . .*), and won an Academy Award in 1961 for his animated short *Munro*. In 1986 Feiffer was awarded the Pulitzer Prize for political cartooning, and in 2004 he received the Milton Caniff Lifetime Achievement Award from the National Cartoonists Society.

GEISEL, THEODOR SEUSS (1904–91) is one of the most beloved children's book authors in the world. He was born in Springfield, Massachusetts, and attended Dartmouth College. After graduating, he began submitting humorous drawings and articles to magazines such as the *Saturday Evening Post*, *Vanity Fair*, and *Life* under the pen name Dr. Seuss. During the Depression, he drew advertising campaigns for products such as Flit. In 1937, he wrote his first children's book, *And to Think That I Saw It on Mulberry Street*, and over the next fifty years created such classics as *The Cat in the Hat*, *How the Grinch Stole Christmas!* and *Oh, the Places You'll Go!* He has won many awards, including the Pulitzer and the Peabody. Three of his books were given Caldecott Honors, and two movies inspired by his work, including *Gerald McBoing Boing*, won Academy Awards.

GELMAN, WOODY (1915–78) attended Cooper Union and Pratt Institute before becoming an animator for Fleischer Studios in 1939. During his time there and at Famous Studios, he created such characters as Nutsy Squirrel. In 1953 Gelman began working at the Topps Company, where he supervised the production of the Mars Attacks and Wacky Packages trading card series. He was also the publisher of Nostalgia Press.

GORDON, DAN (1918–69) In 1936 Gordon began his career as an animator at Van Beuren Studios. When Van Beuren closed, Gordon moved to Fleischer Studios, where he wrote and directed many of the 1940s *Superman* and *Popeye* animated shorts. A freelance comic book artist, Gordon regularly contributed to American Comic Book titles *Giggle* and *Ha Ha Comics*, where he exercised his animator's solid drawing skills regularly working on *Superkatt* as well as various one-shot tales such as "Anthony the Rogue." During the 1960s, Gordon drew storyboards at Hanna-Barbera for *Huckleberry Hound* and *The Flintstones*.

GROSS, MILT (1895–1953) was born in the Bronx, New York, and published his first comic strip, "Phool Phan Phables," at age twenty. In 1930 he created what many call his masterpiece, the wordless graphic novel *He Done Her Wrong*. Gross produced a string of humorous illustrated prose books (including *Nize Baby* and *Dunt Esk*), often written in his uniquely famous Yiddish/English patois. A prolific cartoonist, Gross deployed a banana-peel-and-custard-pie strategy to topple hypocrites and poseurs in *Count Screwloose of Tooloose*, *Nize Baby*, *That's My Pop*, and *Dave's Delicatessen*. In addition to his newspaper comics and novels, Gross irregularly contributed to the American Comics Group, which also published two issues of *Milt Gross Funnies* in the late 1940s in which "Patsy Pancake" appeared.

KELLY, WALT (1913–73) One of the most popular and enduring American cartoonists, Walt Kelly was born in Philadelphia, Pennsylvania. After graduating from high school, Kelly started work at the *Bridgeport Post*, where he began cartooning. In 1935 he joined Walt Disney Studios and helped animate *Pinocchio* and *Dumbo*. In 1941 his work began to appear in Dell comic books, where he created whimsical stories specifically for younger children, such as "Prince Robin and the Dwarfs," in titles like *Walt Disney's Comics and Stories*, *Santa Claus Funnies*, and *Uncle Wiggily*. In 1943 Kelly published his first story featuring Pogo Possum in *Animal Comics*. Pogo became his most popular character and starred in his own comic book, *Pogo*, before becoming syndicated in newspapers throughout America. The beloved character even sparked a Pogo for President campaign in 1952. In 1954 Kelly became president of the National Cartoonists Society.

KURTZMAN, HARVEY (1924–93) was born in Brooklyn, New York, and as a young man became a freelance comics writer and artist. For Timely Comics he drew a series of one-page gags called "Hey Look!" and "Egghead Doodle." In 1949 Kurtzman joined E.C. Comics, where he wrote, edited, and drew stories for *Two-Fisted Tales* and *Frontline Combat*, demonstrating a masterly, innovative approach toward comic book storytelling. Most significantly, Kurtzman founded *MAD*, in which he wrote every word and sketched every story for the first twenty-three issues, establishing his role as one of the most important humorists of the twentieth century. After his run at *MAD*, Kurtzman went on to launch several magazines, including *Trump*, *Humbug*, and *Help!*, and created the strip "Little Annie Fanny" for *Playboy*, which ran for almost twenty-five years.

LeBLANC, ANDRÉ (1921–98) was born in Haiti and moved to America as a child. LeBlanc was a key member of the team that Will Eisner assembled to produce the weekly Spirit adventures. Although much of his work was uncredited as an assistant or main artist for comics and comic strips such as "Apartment 3-G" and "The Phantom," under his own name LeBlanc created the original comics "Intellectual Amos" and "Morena Flor." LeBlanc taught at the School of Visual Arts in New York. Later, he moved to Brazil, where he received the prestigious Southern Cross Award for his classical literature illustrations, including those for *The Picture Bible*.

MAYER, SHELDON (1917–91) was born in New York City. In 1938, while working for the McClure Syndicate under the direction of comics pioneer M. C. Gaines, Mayer advocated the inclusion in their *Action Comics* of a strip that had been rejected everywhere else—a strip that changed the nature of comic book publishing: "Superman." In 1939, Mayer began work at National (later DC Comics), where he was the first editor of *All-American Comics*. In addition to editing, Mayer was a prolific writer/artist on features including *Scribbly*, *The Three Mouseketeers*, and *Sugar and Spike*. Mayer continued to work for DC for the rest of his life. Into the 1970s he was still writing stories for *Black Orchid* and *House of Mystery*.

McNAMARA, TOM (1886–1964) Long before his comic book work, McNamara had a career in film as early as 1917 writing title cards. By the early 1920s he was writing and co-directing Our Gang comedies for Hal Roach. In film or comics his work generally centered around children. His comic strip "Teddy and Jack" ran in several newspapers. In the 1930s he was an animator for Ub Iwerks, and became a writer for Walt Disney in the 1940s. McNamara worked for Major Malcolm Wheeler-Nicholson as an editor and contributor for one of the first comic books, *New Fun*, published by National Comics (later DC), where he also drew *Buzzy* and illustrated stories such as "After School" and "Alix in Folly-land." McNamara also created the artwork for a series of humorous pins that were given away with packs of cigarettes from 1910 to 1940. His work was published by Fawcett and Centaur Publications through the 1940s.

NOONAN, DAN (1911–82) Noonan was an inker/cel painter at Terrytoons in 1934. He began to work at Disney in 1935 as an inbetweener, but eventually graduated to animator. Noonan worked for Dell Comics in the 1940s. There he illustrated such titles as *Animal Comics*, *Fairytale Parade*, and *Raggedy Ann and Andy*, and assisted Walt Kelly on his Pogo strip and Disney comics. Noonan later worked as an animator and layout artist for Filmation and Hanna-Barbera.

STANLEY, JOHN (1914–93) is best known for his work at Dell Comics, imprinting his particular point of view, timing, and staging in his comic book adaptations of the strips "Little Lulu" and "Nancy." Stanley studied at the Art Students League in New York before briefly working at Fleischer Studios in the 1930s. Later in that decade he started at Western Publishing, where he created stories for Bugs Bunny, Woody Woodpecker, and Andy Panda. Stanley drew *Little Lulu* from its inception as a regular comic book series in 1948, and expanded her universe to include Tubby and Witch Hazel. In 1959 Stanley started writing *Nancy and Sluggo*. He also scripted and drew many other comics for Dell, including *Choo Choo Charlie* and *Melvin Monster*. John Stanley received the Inkpot Award in 1980, and was inducted into the Eisner Hall of Fame in 2004. **IRVING TRIPP** collaborated on most of Stanley's Little Lulu stories.

STEIN, MILTON (MILT) (1921–77) was an animator at Terrytoons and Fleischer Famous Studios during the 1940s. Later, as a member of Al Fago's studio, Stein drew several features for Better Publications, including *Bonny Bunny*, *Coo Coo*, and *Supermouse*, and others for Quality Comics. Stein returned to his animating roots in the 1960s, working on such cartoons as *Batfink*, *Return to Oz*, and the cult classic *Cosmic Raymond*. Stein committed suicide in 1977.

THOMAS, FRANK (b. 1914) illustrated the 1938 syndicated strip "All-American Football." In the 1940s he worked for Centaur Publications, where he created such characters as Dr. Hypno and Solarman. Thomas later joined Dell Comics, where he created the Owl, Billy and Bonnie Bee, and contributed scripts for *Little Lulu* and *Woody Woodpecker*.

WISEMAN, AL (1918–88) worked in advertising before he began drawing the classic comic *Dennis the Menace*. Along with writer Fred Toole, Wiseman worked on the comic book for almost two decades. He also contributed work to the "Belvedere" and "Yogi Bear" newspaper strips. **FRED TOOLE** worked in advertising before he began writing for *Dennis the Menace* as Al Wiseman's partner.

WOLVERTON, BASIL (1909–78) was born in Central Point, Oregon, and as a young man worked as a vaudeville performer and cartoonist. In 1946 he won a contest sponsored by Li'l Abner creator Al Capp to draw Lena Hyena, "the world's ugliest woman." Most of Wolverton's stories were published by Timely Comics. Wolverton's widely varied line allowed a home for both his humorous work (such as "Powerhouse Pepper") and his science fiction and horror work. Wolverton was also a contributor to *Life*, *Pageant*, and *MAD*.

Index

L

M

N

O

P

Q

R

S

T

U

V

W

X

Y

More comics for your reading pleasure!

AGES 5–8

The Adventures of Polo
series by Regis Faller
(Roaring Brook Press, 2006–09)

Big Fat Little Lit
edited by Art Spiegelman
& Françoise Mouly
(Puffin Picture Books, 2006)

Elephant and Piggie
series by Mo Willems
(Hyperion, 2007–09)

**Little Lit: Folklore & Fairy
Tale Funnies; Little Lit:
Strange Stories for Strange
Kids; Little Lit: "It Was a
Dark and Silly Night..."**
edited by Art Spiegelman
& Françoise Mouly
(Joanna Cotler Books, 2000–03)

AGES 8–12

Amelia Rules!
series by Jimmy Gownley
(Renaissance Press, 2006–07)

Amulet
series by Kazu Kibuishi
(Graphix, 2008-09)

Babymouse
series by Jennifer Holm
and Matthew Holm
(Random House, 2005–09)

Bone
series by Jeff Smith
(Scholastic, 2005–09)

Diary of a Wimpy Kid
series by Jeff Kinney
(Amulet Books, 2007–09)

Knights of the Lunch Table
series by Frank Cammuso
(Graphix, 2008–09)

Owly
series by Andy Runton
(Top Shelf Productions, 2004–08)

Sardine in Outer Space
series by Emmanuel Guibert
& Joann Sfar
(First Second, 2006–09)

**Satchel Paige: Striking Out
Jim Crow** by James Sturm and
Rich Tommaso
(Hyperion Books for Children, 2007)

Simpsons Comics
by Matt Groening
(Harper Paperbacks, various)

REPRINTS

The Adventures of Tintin
series by Hergé
(Little, Brown, 1994–97)

**Carl Barks' Greatest Disney's
DuckTales Stories, Vols. 1–2**
by Carl Barks
(Gemstone, 2006)

The Complete Peanuts
series by Charles M. Schulz
(Fantagraphics, 2004–09)

The Groo Treasury
by Mark Evanier
and Sergio Aragonés
(Dark Horse, 2009)

**The Indispensable
Calvin and Hobbes**
by Bill Watterson
(Andrews McMeel Publishing, 1992)

Little Lulu
series by John Stanley
and Irving Tripp
(Dark Horse, 2005–09)

Melvin Monster
series by John Stanley
(Drawn and Quarterly, 2009)

**Moomin: The Complete
Tove Jansson Comic Strip**
series by Tove Jansson
(Drawn and Quarterly, 2006–09)

Nancy
series by John Stanley
(Drawn and Quarterly, 2009)

**Walt Kelly's Our Gang,
Vol. 3**
by Walt Kelly
(Fantagraphics, 2008)

A word on TOON Books

**Benny and Penny
in Just Pretend**
by Geoffrey Hayes

**Benny and Penny
in The Big No-No!**
by Geoffrey Hayes

Jack and the Box
by Art Spiegelman

**Little Mouse
Gets Ready**
by Jeff Smith

Luke on the Loose
by Harry Bliss

**Mo and Jo
Fighting Together Forever**
by Dean Haspiel & Jay Lynch

Otto's Orange Day
by Frank Cammuso & Jay Lynch

**Silly Lilly
and the Four Seasons**
by Agnes Rosenstiehl

Stinky
by Eleanor Davis
A Theodor Seuss Geisel Honor Book

TOON BOOKS, a new line of comics for early readers launched in
spring 2008 by RAW Junior, represents a whole new approach to books
for emerging readers. Edited by Françoise Mouly with series advisor Art
Spiegelman, the TOON Books are written and illustrated by outstanding
talent from across the comics and children's book worlds.

For more information, please visit www.TOON-Books.com

TOON
BOOKS
make reading
FUN!

Cover: Background by Walt Kelly from *Fairy Tale Parade* no. 2 (1942), copyright © Okefenokee Glee & Perloo, Inc., used by permission of the Walt Kelly estate; Supermouse by Milt Stein from *Supermouse* no. 12 (April 1951), copyright © 1951 Animated Cartoons, Inc.; hand lettering by Gary Hallgren. | Page 15: "Parents and children (3–7) looking at comic book (B&W)," image #AB06260, used by permission of FPG/Getty Images. | "Reading Comics" from *The Spirit*, October 29, 1950, used by permission of Jules Feiffer. | "First Meeting" from *Sugar and Spike* no. 1 (April–May 1956), copyright © 1956 National Comics Publications, Inc., used by permission. | "Pint-Size Love Story" from *Sugar and Spike* no. 21 (February–March 1959), copyright © 1958 National Comics Publications, Inc., used by permission. | "We Want a Clubhouse!" from *Dennis the Menace* no. 24 (September 1957), copyright © 1957 Hall-Den Comics, Inc., used by permission of Hank Ketcham Enterprises, 2009. | "Crossing the Street" from *The Spirit*, July 17, 1949, used by permission of Jules Feiffer. | "It's Friendship" from *Little Archie* no. 4 (Fall 1957), copyright © 1957 Archie Comic Publications, Inc., used by permission of Archie Comic Publications, Inc. | "Five Little Babies" from *Marge's Little Lulu* no. 38 (August 1951), copyright © 1951 by Marjorie H. Buell, used by permission of Dell Publishing, a division of Random House, Inc., Little Lulu is a trademark of Classic Media. All rights reserved. | "The Cartoonist" from *All-American Comics* no. 8 (November 1939) and *All-American Comics* no. 9 (December 1939), copyright © 1939 National Comics Publications, Inc., used by permission. | "Quiet" from *Patsy Walker* no. 30 (September 1950), used by permission of the Harvey Kurtzman estate. | "In the Library" from *The Spirit*, April 29,1945, section of *The Spirit* in *The Philadelphia Record*. | "Grown-Up Game" from *Sugar and Spike* no. 20 (December 1958), copyright © 1958 National Comics Publications, Inc., used by permission. | "Double Talk" from *Dennis the Menace* no. 24 (September 1957), copyright © 1957 Hall-Den Comics, Inc., used by permission of Hank Ketcham Enterprises, 2009. | "Two Foots Is Feet" from *Marge's Little Lulu* no. 94 (April 1956), copyright © 1956 Marjorie H. Buell, used by permission of Dell Publishing, a division of Random House, Inc. Little Lulu is a trademark of Classic Media. All rights reserved. | "Watering Lilies" from *Animal Comics* no. 23 (October–November 1946), copyright © Okefenokee Glee & Perloo, Inc., used by permission of the Walt Kelly estate. | "Hickory and Dickory Help the Easter Bunny" from *Four Color Comics* no. 220 (March 1949), copyright © 1949 Western Printing & Lithographing Co. and Okefenokee Glee & Perloo, Inc., used by permission of the Walt Kelly estate. | "Flying Squirrel" from *Funny Folks* no. 7 (April–May 1947), copyright © 1947 National Comics Publications, Inc., used by permission. | "Never Give a Diving Board an Even Break" from *Pogo Possum* no. 2 (April–June 1950), copyright © 1950 Western Printing & Lithographing Co. and Okefenokee Glee & Perloo, Inc., used by permission of the Walt Kelly estate. | "Night Life" from *Giggle Comics* no. 91 (October 1953), copyright © 1953 Creston Publications Corp. | "Mouseketeering" from *The Three Mouseketeers* no. 1 (March–April 1956), copyright © 1956 National Comics Publications, Inc., used by permission. | "Digging for Treasure" from *Real Screen Comics* no. 36 (March 1951), copyright © Columbia Pictures Industries Inc., used by permission. | "Cold Cuts" from *Real Screen Comics* no. 33 (December 1950) and *Real Screen Comics* no. 36 (March 1951), copyright © Columbia Pictures Industries Inc., used by permission. | "The Great Chiseler" from *Real Screen Comics* no. 42 (September 1951), copyright © Columbia Pictures Industries Inc., used by permission. | "Hypno-Gun" from *Walt Disney's Comics and Stories* no. 1 (October 1952), Copyright © 1952 by Disney Enterprises, Inc., used by permission of Disney. | "A Queer Bird" from *National Comics* no. 58 (February 1947), copyright © 1946 Comic Magazines, used by permission. | Cover from *Animal Comics* no. 27 (June–July 1947), copyright © Okefenokee Glee & Perloo, Inc., used by permission of the Walt Kelly estate. | "Gone Fishing" from *Animal Comics* no. 19 (February–March 1946), copyright © Okefenokee Glee & Perloo, Inc., used by permission of the Walt Kelly estate. | "Wolf Attack" from *Animal Comics* no. 21 (June–July 1946), copyright © 1946 Oskar Lebeck. | "A Day in the Country" from *Animal Comics* no. 28 (August–September 1947) copyright © 1947 Oskar Lebeck. | "The Moon in the Lake" from *Fairy Tale Parade* no. 87 (November–December 1945), copyright © Okefenokee Glee & Perloo, Inc., used by permission of the Walt Kelly estate. | "One Little Match" from *Buzzy* no. 9 (September–October 1946), copyright © 1946 Detective Comics, Inc., used by permission. | "Gooseberry Jam" from *Jingle Jangle Comics* no. 6 (December 1943), copyright © 1943 Famous Funnies, Inc. | Cover from *Fairy Tale Parade* no. 7 (August–September 1943), copyright © Okefenokee Glee & Perloo, Inc., used by permission of the Walt Kelly estate. | "Map of the Fairy Tale Lands" from *Fairy Tale Parade* no. 6 (May–July 1943), copyright © Okefenokee Glee & Perloo, Inc., used by permission of the Walt Kelly estate. | "Prince Robin and the Dwarfs" from *Fairy Tale Parade* no. 9 (November–December 1943), copyright © Okefenokee Glee & Perloo, Inc., used by permission of the Walt Kelly estate. | Cover from *Puzzle Fun Comics* no. 1 (Spring 1946), copyright © 1946 George W. Dougherty. | "Tom Thumb Is Lost!" from *Puzzle Fun Comics* no. 1 (Spring 1946), copyright © 1946 George W. Dougherty. | "Daze of Yore" from *Supermouse* no. 4 (August 1950), copyright © 1950 Animated Cartoons, Inc. | "The Horrible Groark" from *Alice* no. 10 (July–August 1951), copyright © 1951 Approved Comics, Inc. | Cover from *Marge's Little Lulu* no. 21 (March 1950), copyright © 1950 Marjorie H. Buell, used by permission of Dell Publishing, a division of Random House, Inc. Little Lulu is a trademark of Classic Media. All rights reserved. | "Snow Day" from *Laffy-Daffy Comics* no. 1 (February 1945), copyright © 1944 Rural Home Publishing Co. | "The Guest in the Ghost Hotel" from *Marge's Tubby* no. 7 (January–March 1954), copyright © 1953 Marjorie H. Buell. Little Lulu and Tubby are trademarks of Classic Media. All rights reserved. | "Topsy Turvy" from *Alice* no. 10 (July–August 1951), copyright © 1951 Approved Comics, Inc. | "Bam!" from *Animal Comics* no. 22 (August–September 1946), copyright © Okefenokee Glee & Perloo, Inc., used by permission of the Walt Kelly estate. | "The Hunters" from *Raggedy Ann and Andy* no. 5 (October 1946). | "The Dragonfly" from *New Funnies* no. 72 (February 1943), copyright © 1943 Dell Publishing Co., Inc. | "Ants" from *National Comics* no. 55 (August 1946), copyright © 1946 Comic Magazines, used by permission. | "Bee Bumbler" from *Walt Disney's Comics and Stories* no. 2 (November 1953), Copyright © 1953 by Disney Enterprises, Inc., used by permission of Disney. | Cover from *Walt Disney's Comics and Stories* no. 94 (July 1948), Copyright © 1948 by Disney Enterprises, Inc., used by permission of Disney. | "Tralla La" from *Walt Disney's Uncle Scrooge* no. 6 (June 1954), Copyright © 1954 by Disney Enterprises, Inc., used by permission of Disney. | "In the Land of Surrealism" from *Captain Marvel Adventures* no. 80 (January 1948), copyright © 1947 Fawcett Publications, Inc., used by permission. | "Hey Look! Me Hit I!" from *Hedy De Vine Comics* no. 29 (October 1948), used by permission of the Harvey Kurtzman estate. | "Lyin' Lion" from *Funny Stuff* no. 5 (June 1945), copyright © 1945 All American Comics Inc., used by permission. | Cover from *Funny Stuff* no. 5 (Summer 1945), copyright © 1945 All American Comics Inc. | "Hey Look! Hard-Boiled Egg" from *Gay Comics* no. 34 (October 1948), used by permission of the Harvey Kurtzman estate. | "Dinner Is Served" from *Milt Gross Funnies* no. 2 (September 1947), copyright © 1947 Gross Publications, Inc. | "Babysitting" from *Police Comics* no. 46 (September 1945), copyright © 1945 Comic Magazines, used by permission. | "You Are What You Think You Are" from *Coo Coo Comics* no. 27 (July 1946), copyright © 1946 Animated Cartoons, Inc. | "By a Nose" from *Police Comics* no. 38 (January 1945), copyright © 1944 Comic Magazines, used by permission. | "Foolish Faces: Five Curious Cases" from *Powerhouse Pepper Comics* no. 1 (January 1943), copyright © 1943 Marvel Comics, used by permission of the Basil Wolverton estate. | "A Nightmare Scare" from *Powerhouse Pepper Comics* no. 1 (January 1943), copyright © 1943 Marvel Comics, used by permission of the Basil Wolverton estate. | "Foolish Faces: Profiles" from *Powerhouse Pepper Comics* no. 1 (January 1943), copyright © 1943 Marvel Comics, used by permission of the Basil Wolverton estate. | "The Proposal" from *Police Comics* no. 35 (October 1944), copyright © 1944 by Comic Magazines, used by permission. | "Mice Business" from *Melvin Monster* no. 3 (December 1965), copyright © 1965 by Dell Publishing Co., Inc. | "Musical Monster" from *Prize Comics* no. 61 (September–October 1946), copyright © 1946 Feature Publications, Inc. | "Hey Look! Optical Illusions" from *Hedy De Vine Comics* no. 25 (February 1948), used by permission of the Harvey Kurtzman estate. | "Boing Boing" from *Gerald McBoing Boing and the Nearsighted Mr. Magoo* no. 1 (August–October 1952), copyright © 1952 based on the Columbia Pictures Corporation animation *Gerald McBoing Boing*. "Gerald McBoing Boing" and associated character names, images, and other indicia are trademarks of Classic Media, Inc., all rights reserved. | "Hey Look! I'm a Teapot!" from *Gay Comics* no. 31 (Spring 1948), used by permission of the Harvey Kurtzman estate.

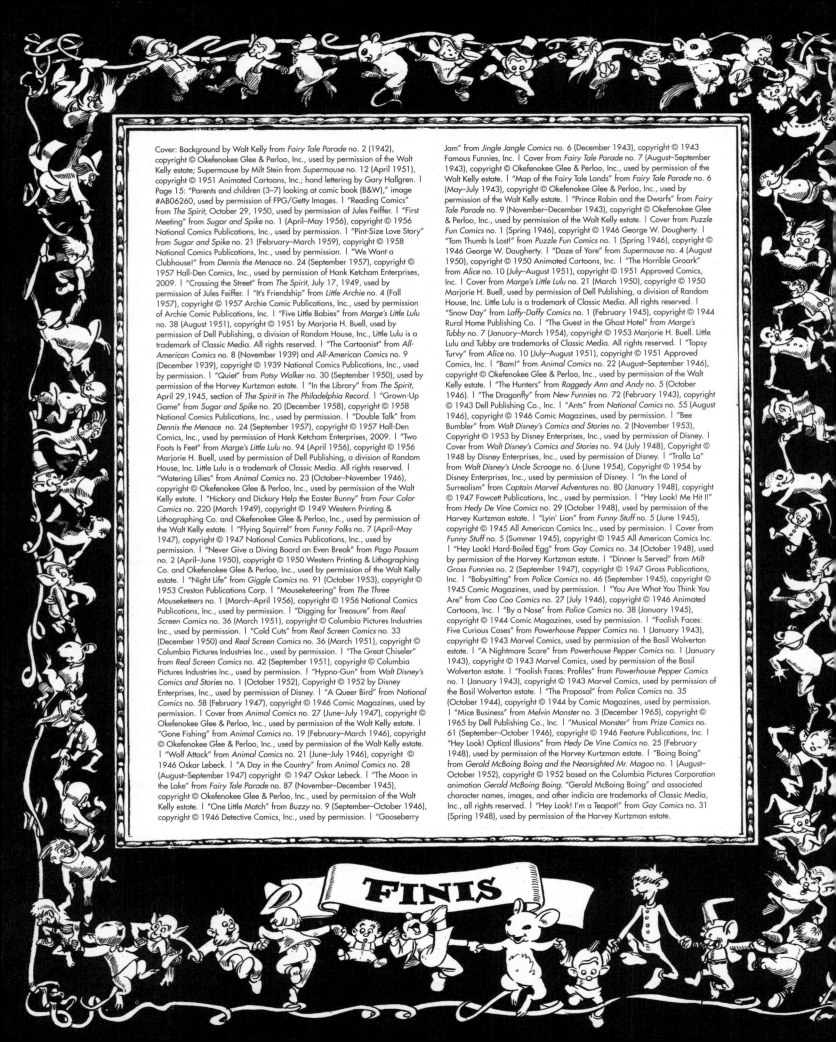

FINIS

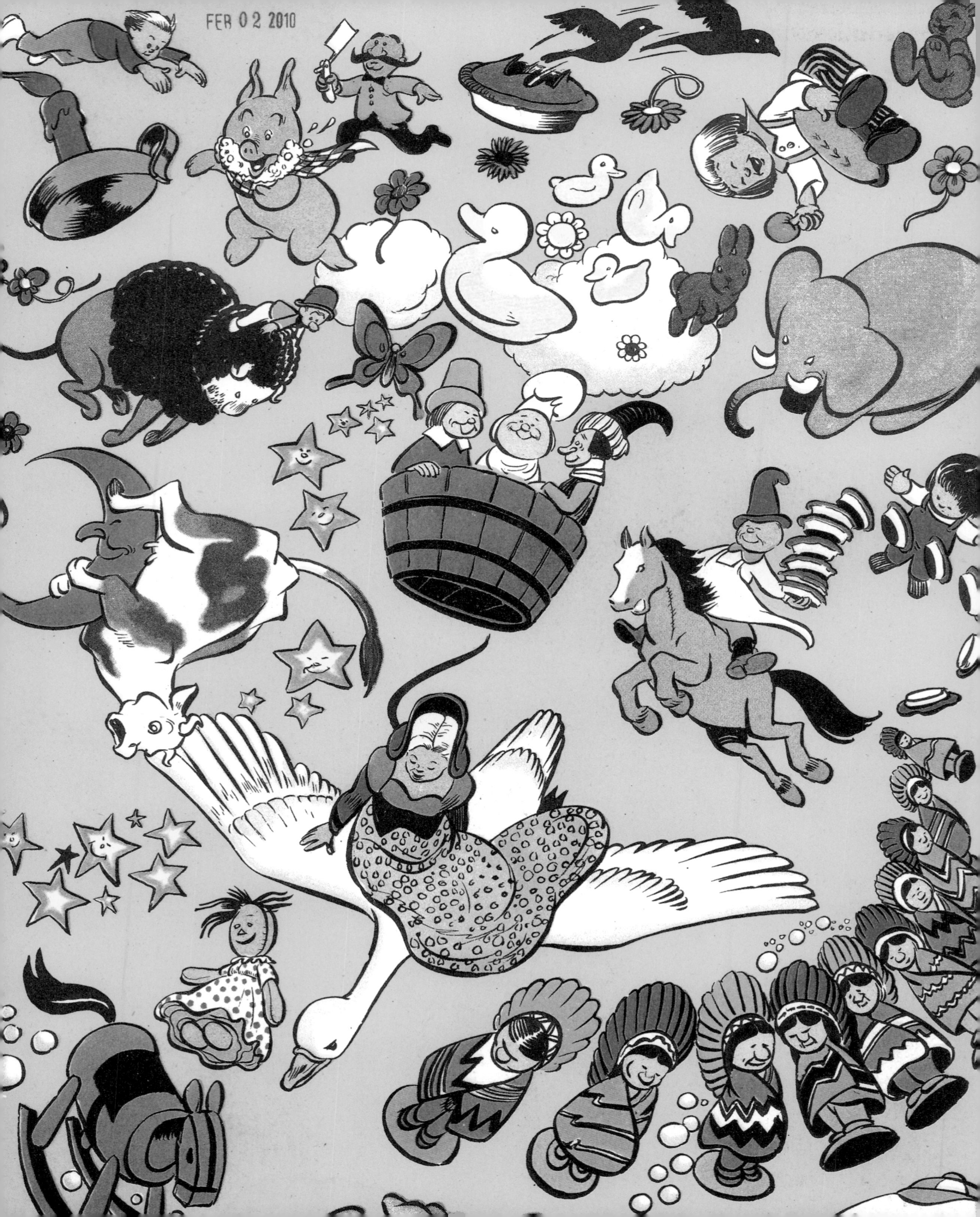